PENGUIN

THE RING OF THE NIBELUNG

RICHARD WAGNER was a nineteenth-century German writer
and composer who had a great influence on opera and European
culture. His ideal of the *Gesamtkunstwerk*, or Total Work of Art,
affected musicians, painters, literary figures and other artists up
to the First World War. His legacy has continued to be a palpable
and often provocative presence in the twentieth and twenty-first
centuries.

He was born in 1813, into a Leipzig family with strong con-
nections to the theatre and the publishing trade. His father, Carl
Friedrich, was an amateur actor, and his oldest brother Albert
and sister Rosalie became well-known theatre professionals. He
came relatively late to music, first realizing that he was destined
for it when he wrote an ambitious five-act play in his teens called
Leubald and tried to write the incidental music himself.

Wagner quickly became a composer and conductor of instru-
mental music and opera, though not until his fourth complete
opera, *The Flying Dutchman*, premièred in Dresden in 1843 did
he find his true creative voice. He was a prodigious writer of his
own libretti in addition to books and journalism covering thou-
sands of printed pages. His colourful biography, including his
active participation in the 1849 Dresden Revolution and polem-
ics against the Jews and the French, has itself been researched to
within an inch of its life.

The most important thing about Wagner is that he finished
nine more stage works after the *Dutchman*, culminating in *Par-
sifal*, which premièred six months before his death in February
1883. They set new standards for writing words for opera as well
as revolutionizing its formal conventions; and their symphonic
continuities at one with their characters' interior worlds were
soon an influence on music in cinema.

The four dramas of *The Ring of the Nibelung* are at the centre
of Wagner's legacy. First performed as a cycle in 1876 in a spe-
cially built festival theatre in Bayreuth, they were invitations to
their first audiences to enter unforgettable worlds of sheer
beauty, heartbreak and redemption that can still touch human
feeling with rare intensity and insight.

JOHN DEATHRIDGE is Emeritus King Edward Professor of Music, King's College London, and one of the world's most respected experts on the life and work of Richard Wagner. Before his appointment to King's London in 1996, he was, for ten years, full-time choirmaster and organist of the Catholic church of St Wolfgang in Munich and, for another fourteen, after returning to the United Kingdom, a Fellow of King's College Cambridge and Lecturer (then Reader) at the University. He has taught at Princeton, Chicago and Vienna, served as President of the Royal Musical Association, and contributed to innumerable radio and television discussions about music. His books on Wagner include *Wagner's Rienzi*, *The New Grove Wagner* (with Carl Dahlhaus), the *Wagner-Werk-Verzeichnis* (with Martin Geck and Egon Voss) and *Wagner Beyond Good and Evil*. He has also contributed an essay to the composer's 200th anniversary, *Waiting for Wagner*.

RICHARD WAGNER

The Ring of the Nibelung

Translated and Edited with an Introduction by
JOHN DEATHRIDGE

PENGUIN CLASSICS
an imprint of
PENGUIN BOOKS

PENGUIN CLASSICS

UK | USA | Canada | Ireland | Australia
India | New Zealand | South Africa

Penguin Books is part of the Penguin Random House group of companies
whose addresses can be found at global.penguinrandomhouse.com.

Penguin
Random House
UK

First published in Penguin Classics 2018
This edition published 2019
002

Translation and editorial material © John Deathridge, 2018

The moral right of the editor and translator has been asserted

Cover design: Coralie Bickford-Smith
Illustration: Despotica

Set in 10.25/12.25 pt Adobe Sabon
Typeset by Dinah Drazin
Printed and bound in Great Britain by Clays Ltd, Elcograf S.p.A.

ISBN: 978-0-241-42228-1

Contents

Translator's Dedication:

To Vicki

Chronology

1813 Born in Leipzig, Saxony, on 22 May, the last of nine children, to Johanna Rosina and police actuary Carl Friedrich Wagner

1813 Napoleon defeated in Battle of Nations near Leipzig, 16–19 October

1813–14 Carl Friedrich dies of typhoid fever and soon after Johanna Rosina marries Ludwig Geyer, a painter and actor; the family moves to Dresden

1814–15 Congress of Vienna, September to June

1821 Ludwig Geyer dies of tuberculosis

1822 Enters Dresden Kreuzschule as Richard 'Geyer'

1827 Death of Ludwig van Beethoven

1828 Enters Leipzig Nicolaischule as Richard Wagner and starts lessons with first composition teacher Christian Müller

1829 First (instrumental) compositions

1830 Offers publisher Schott piano arrangement of Beethoven's Ninth Symphony; witnesses October Leipzig demonstrations in the wake of the Paris 'July Revolution'

1831 Giacomo Meyerbeer becomes a celebrity overnight after the sensational Paris première of his opera *Robert the Devil*

1831 Studies with Leipzig Thomaskantor Theodor Weinlig

1832 Composes a symphony in C major and has it performed in Prague in November

1832 Death of Johann Wolfgang von Goethe; posthumous publication of *Faust: The Second Part of the Tragedy*

1833–4 Libretto and music of first complete opera *The Fairies* (first performed posthumously in 1888) after Carlo Gozzi's fairy tale *The Serpent Woman*; through Heinrich Laube comes under the influence of the literary Young Germany movement

1835–6 Libretto and music of second opera *The Ban on Love* after Shakespeare's *Measure for Measure*, performed only once complete in Magdeburg in March 1836

1837 Settles in Königsberg and marries the actress Minna Planer

1838 After accepting a conducting post in Riga, begins libretto and music of third opera *Rienzi, the Last of the Tribunes* after Bulwer-Lytton's novel *Rienzi, the Last of the Roman Tribunes*

1839 Flees creditors in Riga by sea via London to Paris and on the way meets Meyerbeer for the first time

1839–40 Plans a *Grand Faust Symphony* after Goethe; completes only the first movement

1840 Finishes *Rienzi* and writes for a Paris music journal

1840–41 Conceives and finishes fourth opera *The Flying Dutchman* after a story by Heinrich Heine; Meyerbeer recommends *Rienzi* to the Royal Court Theatre in Dresden

1842 Returns to Dresden from Paris and rehearses *Rienzi* for its first performance on 20 October to great public acclaim

1843 Conducts première of *The Flying Dutchman* on 2 January (with moderate success) and commissioned by Laube publishes his first autobiographical essay; appointed Royal Saxon Kapellmeister

1843–4 Reads Jacob Grimm's *German Mythology*

1843–5 Composes fifth opera *Tannhäuser and the Song Contest at Wartburg* and conducts first performance on 19 October 1845

1844–6 Publishes scores of *Rienzi*, *The Flying Dutchman* and *Tannhäuser*

1846 Conducts Beethoven's Ninth Symphony for the first time on 5 April; essay on it with citations from Goethe's *Faust* published

1846–8 Composes sixth opera *Lohengrin*; presents revised German version of Gluck's opera *Iphigenia in Aulis* in Dresden and engages in a detailed study of Greek drama

1848 February insurrections in Paris; writes libretto of a new opera, *Siegfried's Death*

1849 Participation in Dresden May uprising; flees to Zurich into twelve-year exile and warrant issued for his arrest

1850 Première of *Lohengrin* in Weimar (in Wagner's absence) conducted by Franz Liszt on 28 August, 101st anniversary of Goethe's birth

1850–51 Publishes radical writings including *The Artwork of the Future* and (under a pseudonym) *Judaism in Music* aimed at Meyerbeer among others; aborts composition of *Siegfried's Death* and completes libretto of a prequel called *The Young Siegfried*

1851–2 Decides to expand *Siegfried's Death* into a cycle of four works, to cease calling his stage works 'operas', and to complete texts of *The Valkyrie* and *The Rhinegold*; the *Lohengrin* score is published

1852 Second French Empire under Napoleon III established; publishes treatise *Opera and Drama*

1853 Private printing of *The Ring* text (fifty copies) and public reading in Zurich 16–19 February; begins composition of *The Rhinegold* in November

1854 Completes the composition of *The Rhinegold* and the first musical draft of *The Valkyrie*; reads Schopenhauer's *The World as Will and Representation*

1855 Orchestrates *The Valkyrie* and conducts London concerts

1856 Finishes *The Valkyrie* and begins composing *Siegfried*; first sketches for *Tristan und Isolde*

1857 Moves with his wife Minna into a villa on the estate of Otto and Mathilde Wesendonck; abandons composition of *Siegfried* at end of Act II to complete the *Tristan* text and to compose Act I

1858 Begins composition of *Tristan* Act II; tensions on Wesendonck estate prompt departure for Venice

1859 Completes *Tristan* Act II in Venice and moves to Lucerne to compose Act III; moves to Paris in September and sells publishing rights of *The Ring* to Otto Wesendonck

1860 *Tristan* orchestral score published on 13 January;

conducts three concerts in Paris with the *Tristan* prelude
and begins revisions of *Tannhäuser* for new production at
the Opéra commissioned by Napoleon III

1861 Vocal score of *The Rhinegold* published

1861 Paris *Tannhäuser* withdrawn after three scandalous per-
formances in March (although sold out for the rest of the
run)

1861 After partial amnesty Wagner hears *Lohengrin* for the
first time in Vienna, where *Tristan* rehearsals begin (aban-
doned two years later)

1862 Text and overture of *The Mastersingers of Nuremberg*
composed

1862–3 Excerpts from *The Ring*, including The Ride of the
Valkyries, heard publicly for the first time in three concerts
in Vienna

1863 *The Ring* poem published for the book trade with an
appeal to a German prince to finance it

1864 Ludwig II ascends to the Bavarian throne on 10 March

1864 Summoned to Munich by Ludwig II on 3 May; affair
with Cosima von Bülow, daughter of Franz Liszt, begins in
earnest

1864 Signs contract on 18 October for completion of *The
Ring* transferring all property and performance rights to
Ludwig II

1865 Vocal score of *The Valkyrie* published; première of
Tristan in Munich on 10 June conducted by Hans von Bülow

1866 Death of Minna Wagner in Dresden

1866 Having been forced to leave Munich, rents Villa Trib-
schen on Lake Lucerne and lives with Cosima; continues
composing *The Mastersingers*

1867 Cosima with daughters returns to her husband Hans in
Munich; composition of *The Mastersingers* completed in
October

1868 Publishes brochure *German Art and German Politics*
and second edition of *Opera and Drama*

1868 Publication of the score of *The Mastersingers* and pub-
lic success of its première on 21 June conducted by Hans
von Bülow; Cosima decides to divorce Hans and return to
Tribschen

1869 Cosima begins her diaries on 1 January and Friedrich Nietzsche visits Tribschen for the first time in May

1869 Reissues *Judaism in Music* as a brochure under real name with an explanatory essay, composes *Siegfried* Act III and begins work on the music of *Twilight of the Gods*; première of *The Rhinegold* in September in Munich against Wagner's wishes (and in his absence)

1870 Reads about Bayreuth in Brockhaus's *Conversations-Lexicon* on 5 March (later declared the 'day of Bayreuth') and thinks seriously about a festival there

1870 Première of *The Valkyrie* in Munich in June again without Wagner's co-operation; Cosima's divorce from Hans is ratified and she marries Wagner on 25 August in a Protestant church

1870 Publishes extended essay *Beethoven* for the centenary of the composer's birth and composes the *Siegfried Idyll* for Cosima's birthday (24 December)

1871 18 January German Empire declared after Prussian victory over France; meets Bismarck on 3 May

1871 Publishes vocal score of *Siegfried* and initiates plans with Bayreuth city council for theatre and festival in November and December

1872 Nietzsche's last visit to Tribschen; Cosima and family join Wagner in Bayreuth where he lays the foundation stone of the festival theatre on his birthday and conducts Beethoven's Ninth in celebration

1874 Preparations for performance of *The Ring* begin in May and June; publishes orchestral score of *The Valkyrie* in June and completes that of *Twilight of the Gods* on 21 November

1875 July–August preliminary rehearsals with piano and orchestra of *The Ring* in the Bayreuth festival theatre; publishes *Siegfried* (orchestral score) and *Twilight of the Gods* (vocal score)

1876 Publishes orchestral score of *Twilight of the Gods* in June

1876 1 June–4 August piano and orchestral rehearsals of *The Ring* followed by open dress rehearsals 6–9 August; official world première on 13, 14 and – a day later than scheduled

due to indisposition of Franz Betz (Wotan/Wanderer) – 16
and 17 August conducted by Hans Richter

1877 Writes text of his final stage work *Parsifal*, calling it a
'Festival Play for the Consecration of the Stage', and begins
composing the music in September

1877 30 April–4 June travels to London to conduct eight con-
certs in the Albert Hall (with Hans Richter) to raise money
to pay off festival debts

1878 Helps to establish the 'house' journal *Bayreuther Blätter*
(continues publication until 1938) for which he writes art-
icles on vegetarianism, vivisection, race and the supposedly
parlous state of the German Empire

1881–3 Impresario Angelo Neumann buys the Bayreuth scen-
ery of *The Ring* and the rights to tour the cycle throughout
Europe with full cast and orchestra, including four cycles in
London beginning in May 1882 at Her Majesty's Theatre

1882 Orchestral score of *Parsifal* completed on 13 January;
première on 26 July 1882 in the Bayreuth festival theatre
conducted by Hermann Levi

1883 Death on 13 February; posthumous publication of the
orchestral score of *Parsifal* in December

1885 Cosima agrees to take charge of the 1886 Bayreuth
festival, a role she retained until 1907

Introduction

Richard Wagner's *The Ring of the Nibelung* is an epic cycle of four musical dramas in the spirit of Greek tragedy about the nature and future of human existence seen through the lens of the mid-nineteenth century. Already in its first two scenes it presents a world beset by abuse, primal crime and grandiose narcissism, the terrifying consequences of which can only be – and are – overcome by the power of human love.

It also happens to be one of the greatest texts ever written for the lyric stage. This is a translation of it for reading, not singing, though any thought that it could be translated independently from the marvellous score to which it is now attached – the rhythms, pitches and lengths of its musical notes – is probably utopian, a bit like *The Ring* itself. The thought has at least helped me to read, and above all to hear, the pungency and vitality of Wagner's words on their own, even on occasion their raw violence. Indeed, the more I translated them, the greater was my admiration. I always used to think that the following passage about Wagner's texts for his mature operas from Nietzsche's essay *Richard Wagner in Bayreuth*, a contribution to the first Bayreuth festival in 1876 and the world première of *The Ring*, was flattery expressed through gritted teeth. Nietzsche's private notes at the time, after all, show unmistakable signs of his later falling out with Wagner. His comments now strike me as entirely genuine:

> Wagner's poetry is all about revelling in the German language, the warmth and candour in his communion with it, something that as such cannot be felt in any other German writer except

Goethe. Earthiness of expression, reckless terseness, control
and rhythmic diversity, an extraordinary richness of powerful
and significant words, the simplification of syntactical construc-
tions, an almost unique inventiveness in the language of surg-
ing feeling and presentiment, and every now and then a totally
pure bubbling forth of colloquialisms and proverbs – we ought
to make a list of such characteristics, and even then we would
forget the most powerful and admirable of them . . . the forging
of a distinctive new language for each work and the giving of a
new body and a new sound to each new interior world.[1]

TOWARDS BAYREUTH

Writing and personally directing *The Ring* for the stage was
by far the longest artistic journey Wagner ever undertook.
The first concrete signs in the historical record are in the dia-
ries of two of his colleagues in Dresden, where in the 1840s he
was, for the only time in his life, in the sustained employment
of a state authority as Kapellmeister to Frederick Augustus II
of Saxony. 'Wagner tells me about a new plan for an opera
on the Siegfried saga,' the theatre director Eduard Devrient
reported on 1 April 1848.[2] Two months later the composer
Robert Schumann wrote on 2 June: 'Evening stroll with Wag-
ner – his Nibelung text.'[3]

Twenty-eight years later, the journey was effectively at an
end. By that time Wagner had passed through dangerous
front-line action in the 1849 Dresden revolution, a warrant
for his urgent arrest issued by the police of Saxony that led to
over a decade of political exile in Switzerland, a twelve-year
gap in work on *The Ring* devoted to other projects, partial
and full amnesty, near-bankruptcy, the lavish royal protection
of Ludwig II, a second marriage, three children, overseeing
the construction of his own home in Bayreuth after years of
moving from place to place in rented accommodation, and
the founding of a major international festival. To cap it all, he
had also supervised the design of a new building in Bayreuth
specifically for the four evenings of *The Ring*, a theatre where

he imagined that performances of the cycle could be realized and celebrated as in no other.

In 1872 the foundation stone of the new theatre was laid in pouring rain – an occasion marked by a (dry, indoor) gala performance of Beethoven's Ninth Symphony – and three years later, in the summer of 1875, enough of the building was ready for rehearsals. After a further intensive two-and-a-half-month period of rehearsal from June into August in the following year, the world première of *The Ring* in its entirety took place with three cycles in all, each programmed on consecutive evenings with three 'recovery' days in between each cycle.

At the end of the final set of performances on 30 August 1876, during wild applause, the curtain opened again to reveal the entire orchestra and cast on stage, including those from previous evenings, who had donned their costumes again especially for the occasion. Standing in an enormous half-circle with their conductor Hans Richter in the middle, they included some of the most distinguished musicians of the day. Together, they had helped to turn the motley collection of characters from gods to dwarfs to seeresses, not to mention the animals of the entire drama into the realities of earth-bound theatre. And by offering his warm thanks, Wagner acknowledged everyone who had made it possible: the set designers, costume makers, make-up artists, assistant stage directors and music staff, stage hands, lighting technicians, operators of a specially adapted steam locomotive to create fog and smoke effects, and last but by no means least the English firm of Richard Keene. They had provided props for a big snake with horrible rolling eyes required for the first evening, yoked rams for a goddess's chariot for the one after that, a bear plus a huge dragon plus a magpie and an ouzel (a bird resembling a blackbird) for the third evening, and for the last a medley of sacrificial beasts and two ravens.[4]

One animal was not a prop. This was Brünnhilde's horse Grane, which she famously rides into a burning pyre at the end of *The Ring*. Presumably it was standing on the stage as well, a black nine-year-old stallion called Cocotte loaned

from King Ludwig II, who was himself sitting in the audi-
ence, and to whom the published score of *The Ring* was form-
ally dedicated 'with faith in the German spirit' (*im Vertrauen
auf den deutschen Geist*). Wagner wished everyone a heartfelt
farewell, after which, according to his first biographer and
firsthand witness Carl Glasenapp, they left the theatre with
feelings that 'cannot be described in words'.[5]

BEYOND READING, BEETHOVEN'S
NINTH AND THE END OF OPERA

Wagner issued a notice for audiences during the first Bayreuth
festival warning them that he would be taking the unusual
step of dimming the lights to achieve 'the correct effect of
the scenic image'.[6] Contrary to expectations of what normally
happened in opera theatres up until then, it would be impos-
sible for them to read the libretto during the performance. He
therefore suggested that either the complete text be studied
beforehand, or parts of it during the intervals between the
acts. Libretti were usually issued in the opera world as part of
immediate pre-performance publicity. They could be bought
shortly before a performance and read at home in advance,
or failing that obtained at the box office and scrutinized in
the theatre as the singers were singing. But this was different.
Wagner's new-found 'revelling in the German language' (Nie-
tzsche) since leaving his early Romantic operas behind meant
that its unusual literary ambitions were preparing the way
for a markedly different kind of theatrical event. The clear
implication of Wagner's notice was that the printed words
were not as in previous opera a mere adjunct to the music that
one could consume as the action unfolded, but an important
step towards a transformative experience *beyond reading* – an
entrance ticket to a utopia of pure human feeling, an immer-
sion in vision and sound in a darkened space without the dis-
traction of 'literature', the price of which, paradoxically, was
literature of no mean order.

The paradox had consequences. During the years leading up to the laying of the foundation stone of the Bayreuth festival theatre in 1872, the advance availability of the text of *The Ring* led to an unusual situation. The first two parts of the cycle – *The Rhinegold* and *The Valkyrie* – had been produced in Munich in 1869 and 1870 at the request of Ludwig II against Wagner's wishes. A few concerts under Wagner's direction in Vienna and Budapest in 1862 and 1863 had also seen the first performances of some excerpts from the first three parts of the cycle. In the absence of radio, television and the internet, these were isolated events heard by relatively few people; in any case they gave only a fragmentary impression of *The Ring* as a whole. But since the first private publication of the complete text in 1853 before the musical score had even been started, and its first trade appearance ten years later in 1863 when Wagner was still only two-thirds of the way through writing the music, *The Ring* continued to have the attention of the German-speaking reading public. Since working on its early stages Wagner also called it a poem (*Dichtung*) to distinguish it from an opera libretto and to give it literary status. Even an entire book about it, the first of many, had long since been on the market.[7] The problem was how best to celebrate the laying of the foundation stone musically and prepare people for a new theatre and the première of *The Ring*, many of whom were likely to be more familiar with the poem and the overall vision of the cycle it offered than the music.

Wagner's solution was to perform Beethoven's Ninth Symphony. Why? His idea that with the Ninth 'the *last* symphony had *already been written*',[8] or in other words that it was the final work of any real historical consequence in a supposedly now exhausted genre, was a grandiose message already well known at the time. And from the moment he publicly announced it in 1850 it had had to do with the idea of a symphony destined to be superseded by a new artwork of the future – one by Wagner of course that eventually turned out to be *The Ring*. The poem of *The Ring* from the beginning, in other words, was destined to take over from the point when Beethoven, with his decision to bring voices singing Schiller's

'Ode to Joy' into the Ninth's last movement, felt the necessity *as Musician* to throw himself into the arms of the Poet'.[9]

Wagner also saw the symphony as a premonition of *The Ring*, if not the yet-to-be-built theatre itself. 'R. prepares for his performance of the 9th,' his second wife Cosima wrote in her diaries more than once, as usual not offering much detail.[10] But she does report how he remembered conducting it in three carefully prepared performances in his Dresden years (1846, 1847, 1849) with elaborate programme notes littered with quotations from Goethe's *Faust*. What he 'discovered' then, she reports, a time when he was starting to research and write *The Ring*, was that this music was 'not just to be listened to; the true sense of it is gained only by those who are swept along inside it'.[11]

The involvement of musicians, singers and audience being swept up in performance was part of Wagner's vision from the start. So was his view of the actual content of the Ninth. Take, for instance, the uncanny bare musical interval of the fifth at the start, as if emerging from a faraway archaic world. As Wagner interprets it, it tumbles into a utopian battle against 'hostile forces that rear up between us and earthly happiness'.[12] The interval of the open fifth emerging out of the depths of the Rhine at the start of *The Ring* is surely similar in intent, gradually filling the theatrical space and spilling forwards into a scene where the earth's happily slumbering gold is unceremoniously ripped from its bed by a hostile force. The idea of silence gradually infiltrated by distant sounds that Beethoven exploits in his opening bars to evoke dreamlike memories was influential too. Wagner promised at the foundation-stone ceremony that something very similar would happen in his theatre-to-be once the audience had accepted the idea that the new proportions of the building and its seating would place them in a relationship to the stage which they had never experienced anywhere else: 'the mysterious entry of the music will prepare you for the unveiling and distinct portrayal of scenic pictures that seem to appear from an ideal world of dreams'.[13]

For Wagner, reading the poem of *The Ring* was a journey

towards a completely new kind of theatrical experience that signified the end of opera itself. 'I shall write no more operas,' he declared at an early stage of writing it.[14] Schematic sequences of arias, choruses and ensembles were gone. Instead, the continuous dialogue of the poem was to be heightened with a more fluid musical setting and a halo of thematically intricate orchestral commentary to lend it dramatic force and coherence. Wagner thought that this would discourage the naive wallowing in vocal pleasures without dramatic purpose that had plagued the opera of old. Or to put it another way: he intended to stand firm and refuse to dilute the tragedy of *The Ring* and its violence by anaesthetizing audiences with opera's seductive accoutrements. He was not exactly deaf to diva A's divine stratospheric soprano or the gorgeous sonorities of Herr B's bass and their ability to liquefy the ardent hearts of opera lovers. But in *The Ring* he was ready to cast them in a new role as a way of seriously exploring the inspiring, but also the shocking, aspects of what it means to be human.

The effects of this new sensibility, considerably enhanced by the advanced musical language Wagner invented for *The Ring*, were similar for many to the effects of a drug, a dangerous feeling of disorientation compared by Nietzsche to the sense of losing one's depth in a large ocean. The drug metaphor was cleverly modified by Igor Stravinsky to make his peace with Wagner. The wonderful web-like blending of the orchestra with the stage in *Parsifal* (Wagner's final work) was a 'headache with aspirin'.[15] It was a witty way of admitting that even someone light years from Bayreuth in taste and imagination could appreciate Wagner's medicine that aided music's entrance into the twentieth century. But the drugs inside the dramas were always stronger. The two potions leading to the death of the hero in *Twilight of the Gods*, the finale of *The Ring*, for example, are in fact powerful triggers, via the hero's murder, to the potential opening of humanity's path to divine happiness. Here Wagner's analogy with the Ninth Symphony is most potent. The sentiments in the first three lines of Schiller's 'Ode to Joy' alone – the giddy search for the divine (*Götterfunken* / 'spark of the gods'), the Greek idea of Elysium where the happiness of the blessed will find its home (*Tochter aus Elysium* / 'Daughter from Elysium'), intoxication through fire (*feuertrunken* / 'drunk with fire') – are at the heart of the apotheosis of *The Ring* when the audience gets swept up with the help of the now blessed daughter of the gods in the symphonic vortex of its concluding moments.

ANCIENT TRAGEDY AND
THE FESTIVAL IDEA

The ending of *The Ring* is overwhelmingly triumphant, a magnificent vision of human sacrifice and loving compassion so awe-inspiring that in any good performance it leaves the audience speechless. There is no specific message about the future: only a thrilling monologue from the heroine about human love and the downfall of the gods followed by a concluding stretch of orchestral music, a stunning combination of vision and sound not just beyond reading, but words as well. Wagner described it, appealing frankly to the visceral reactions of his audience, as 'saying everything'. Chunks of the score extracted from significant moments in the epic gone by are loosely spliced together in one last grand revival of ancient memory to build – as Wagner himself is reported to have said – a 'symphonic conclusion of this world drama where the spirit of ancient tragedy and that of Shakespeare appear to have joined hands . . . the themes and melodies must pile themselves up before us like Cyclopean walls'.[16]

Wagner let it be known time and again that ancient tragedy was a key inspiration behind *The Ring*. Already heroes like Oedipus, or barbarian witches like Medea, as Simon Goldhill reminds us, were for the Athenian public in the fifth century BC 'others' in different cities and far in the past.[17] The violent actions of remote beings were already for the Greeks deliberately unreal, yet – as Wagner himself said – 'overpowering' in their 'truthfulness'.[18] *The Ring*'s vast landscape and dark visions are no different, conditioned as they are by primal envy

(*Neid*), a pitiless and relentless search for glory by all power-seeking parties: giants, gods, goddesses, heroes and dwarfs alike. Ancient family bonds and fealties go spectacularly awry, and immense faith and trust can shatter at a moment's notice. Brother kills brother; a father murders his son by proxy and selfishly punishes his daughter; a foster son peremptorily slays his guardian; a blood oath is brutally betrayed. Futile antagonisms between individuals, and conflicts between opposed groups, even whole tribes, pale before a cosmic confrontation with nature itself. In the end, all reason and its expression in law, which audiences know underpins their modern lives, is destroyed by a fire outrageously impervious to it as well as animal and human life. What *The Ring* definitely is not is a rational sermon about 'truth'. Wagner was perfectly serious when he remarked to Franz Liszt after sending him the first private edition of the poem in 1853 that it contained 'the world's beginning and downfall (*Untergang*)!'.[19]

But the scorched post-Enlightenment landscape of *The Ring* with the critical betrayal of reason by its gods and their subsequent self-effacement through fire would not have made sense to the Greeks. At a more basic level, too, it points to another, more formal difference. Wagner called the dramas collectively 'a stage festival play', but conceived their four evenings – with seeming perversity – as a trilogy over three days preceded by a preliminary evening. In fact it was an allusion to the four-day Athenian festival of the Great Dionysia in the fifth century BC when the custom was to commission from three reputable playwrights a trilogy of serious tragedies and one shorter satyr-play, each group of plays to be performed on consecutive days followed by a fourth day of comedies. As was the custom, the satyr-play courted absurdity by inverting the tragic narrative of each trilogy. But modern scholars are still unclear about where exactly it was introduced. In Wagner's day the accepted opinion was that it came at the end, an assumption that gave rise to the mistaken notion that he had merely inverted the Greek sequence in *The Ring* by putting his own satyr-play at the beginning.

The preliminary evening, *The Rhinegold*, is something else entirely: a bracingly austere tale about crime and deception that unfolds principally within the world of the gods. What is really unusual about it when compared with the Greek example is the exclusion of the human element, announcing right at the start of the cycle that the actions of the gods and the apocalyptic prospect of their demise are going to be just as central to the story as the fate of the mortals under their control. Putting the gods at the centre of a cycle of plays to show their foibles and brute power was familiar to the Greeks, as in the play *Prometheus Bound*, which is supposed to be by Aeschylus (doubts have arisen about his authorship). Placing the prospect of the spectacular destruction of the gods right at the start of the story definitely was not.

The Ring does have in common with Greek tragedy the idea of the festival. But just how the Athenian festival of the Great Dionysia celebrated the god Dionysus has been a topic of lively debate. Was it just entertainment or religious instruction? Did the plays question civic discourse, dramatizing the unpredictable space between conforming to it and challenging its authority? Goldhill cogently argues on the basis of good evidence that they did, and is not tempted like some scholars simply to assume that all the vast numbers of spectators did was to cram into the open-air theatre at the foot of the Acropolis and take advantage of a city-approved chance in the spirit of Dionysus to get drunk.[20]

There is no easy answer to what these festivals, including Wagner's, were actually celebrating. It could possibly be said that the pattern of norm and transgression Goldhill sees in the Great Dionysia events only became part of their supposed Bayreuth equivalent after the Second World War. This was the age of modernity with a vengeance. The norms of behavior supposedly according to the wishes of the master that for years had kept the Bayreuth audiences in thrall to ritual and conformity under the aegis of the master's second wife Cosima, and then his son Siegfried and daughter-in-law Winifred, had led to Hitler's dominant presence at the Bayreuth festival in the 1930s – a stigma that needed to be overcome. Indeed it was largely the critical success of Wieland Wagner's first post-war 1951 production of *The Ring* with its sleekly clear and visually beautiful lines that banished the clunky bear-skinned heroes of Bayreuth's yesteryear for good, though the Wagner faithful were far from happy. With the stage now set for an endless fight between the enemies of modernity wanting their old *Ring* back and friends of the new ready to challenge the very idea, Bayreuth looked as if it had become 'Greek' at last.

Or had it? Audiences loved the 1876 performances, despite their technical imperfections. But critical reaction in newspapers was already deeply divided, and at times almost perversely contradictory. There were musical conservatives like Max Kalbeck, the future biographer of Johannes Brahms, who actually thought the music sublime, but objected to the poem's 'ethical anarchy' as 'outrageous and provocative, a slap in the face for all religious feeling'. There were nationalists like Gustav Engel, a singing teacher and writer on music from Berlin, who demanded that Germany reject a work written in its name that identifies with 'raw egotism, animalistic sensuality, cynical loutishness, brutal guile and perfidy'. And there were representatives of the Protestant Church like Hermann Messner who tied themselves in knots decrying a text supposedly littered with 'chilling acerbities' rooted in paganism, while also noticing at length that its admirers were flocking to Bayreuth for spiritual refreshment in order to fill the aching void caused by a 'lack of respect' in the modern state for 'living Christianity'. Messner noticed correctly that Wagner's disciples, who were beginning to regard Bayreuth as a cult, were symptomatic of an ever-widening gap between modernity and religion in an age of growing secularism. But he refused to ask why, consoling himself instead with the lordly observation that the 'words and sounds' of what he had heard were incapable of elevating 'the soul of the German people above its current level'.[21]

A THEATRE FOR *THE RING*

If Wagner's festival was meant to be a religious event after the manner of the Greeks, the intention clearly fell on stony ground. There is little convincing evidence to support the idea anyway. But as nearly always with Wagner, who despite his reputation as a philosophizing artist of the future was always better as a pragmatist in the present, his contradictions are best seen at a hard materialist level. We know for example that in 1876 Wagner's audience in Bayreuth filled 1,395 seats of his theatre. (Over time the number has increased to 1,965). The large chasm between the numbers of spectators in the Acropolis theatre – 14,000 to 16,000 at a rough estimate – and Wagner's underscores an enormous difference of scale and intent. The geometric fan-shaped arrangement of unbroken rows of seating spreading from left to right in front of the Bayreuth stage inspired by the Greek *theatron*, on the other hand, illustrates more vividly than anything else Wagner's productive straddling of the very old and the very new in *The Ring* that riled his Bayreuth critics. The magisterial surveyor of theatre design history, George C. Izenour, put it starkly like this: 'the Wagnerian Festspielhaus . . . broke finally and irrevocably the hold of 2½ centuries on theater design by the baroque ring-balconied horseshoe-shaped auditorium.'[22] Not only did *The Ring* poem abolish the old hierarchies of operatic forms at the outset, the representation of sharp social differences in the tiered seating structures of the old baroque-style theatres had vanished by the end of the project as well.

Together with the architect Otto Brückwald and the theatre consultant Carl Brandt (with the architect Gottfried Semper hovering in the background), Wagner masterminded an avant-garde theatre building with the help of the Greeks like no other in the nineteenth century. Good, Brandt's stagecraft and stage illumination were still mired in the old baroque two-dimensional scenery and flammable light sources, though the gaslight Wagner mostly used was more controllable and brighter, if really only marginally less dangerous than the

candlelight of the old baroque stage. A good deal of the sup-
posedly impractical scenic directions that take up significant
portions of *The Ring* poem – swelling waters, mountain
vistas, gathering clouds, a dragon, a forest bird, two ravens
and Valkyries on horses flying through air – were actually
not far from seventeenth-century French theatre. Oceans even
then could transform into spectacular landscapes with the
help of machines and there was nothing that could not be put
on the end of big sticks raised up at the back of the stage and
moved up and down or side to side by invisible assistants.
Brandt improved things with modern camshafts, trolleys,
gears or winches and flew people through the air without the
wires showing. But in the end all he was really doing, albeit
with the assistance of up-to-date mechanisms and great skill,
was streamlining the old baroque illusionist tricks.

In stark contrast Wagner's new auditorium was a revolution,
heralding a new kind of seeing and hearing, a total immersion
in the stage picture. In essence it was all about hiding the
wires. The theatres built by the Greeks were so huge according
to Wagner that he felt moved to ask about a comedy by
Aristophanes, only a year after the foundation stone of his
own theatre had been laid:

> 'How could the audience follow it at that distance? I can only
> conclude that the Greeks saw and heard things in quite a differ-
> ent way from us stay-at-homes (*Stubenhocker*) with our glasses
> on.'[23]

Stubenhocker can be translated anachronistically now as
'couch potatoes'. Had Wagner known the phrase he would –
well, just might – have approved of it. In his new theatre, ver-
tical and horizontal sightlines for the modern spectator were
to be so redefined that he or she could enter into an environ-
ment that felt more real than the world they were actually
in. The *theatron* model led to rational limits. Seats outside
lateral and vertical viewing angles of about 30 degrees were
to be eliminated, automatically ridding the space of stacked
ring-balconies in favour of a fan-shaped concentric seating

arrangement in unbroken rows that was steeply raked. Five pairs of ever-widening wings engaged with the side-walls on both sides of the auditorium were to be added to help make the acoustics so clear that every word from the singers could be understood. What had been read in advance would, contrary to what usually happens in opera auditoria, actually *be heard*.

In near darkness, the view of the entire stage from each sitting position also had to have high definition. Not even the orchestra should be in the way. It must affect the ear, Wagner decreed, but remain invisible. Otherwise the eye would perceive something real, real people playing instruments, the conductor conducting. In turn that would mean the audience measuring the actors on stage according to their 'true' size and not submitting to the virtual reality of the stage image. Wagner wanted the effect for which he and the architect Gottfried Semper assumed 'the Greek tragedians were striving', namely that 'the persons to which they entrusted their heroic roles should exceed human proportion (*das menschliche Maß*) through the use of masks, laced high boots [to make them look taller], and other means'.[24] The means for that Wagner and Semper wanted to use for the new festival theatre for *The Ring* – first intended for Munich but never built and then transferred to Bayreuth, by which time Semper had withdrawn from the project – were quite different, basically amounting to a narrowing of the audience's sightlines without the distraction of visible human beings playing in the orchestra straight into the stage area via a series of three increasingly smaller frames or proscenium arches. But the principle was the same: the actors had to look larger than life. The allure of cinema, of television, of smartphones and modern media in general was already on the horizon.

JACOB GRIMM AND THE
NEW MYTHOLOGY

Significant tensions in negotiating *The Ring*, whether trans-
lating or producing it, interpreting it or building a space for it,
arise from Wagner's love affair with the archaic. This was not
just a fascination with medieval German literature and ancient
culture, but a belief that the farther one goes back in time
to the origins of language and myth, the closer one gets to
an uncorrupted ideal of life that should be, but supposedly is
not, manifest in the present. From the time of their supposed
pristine original form on the way into the modern age, so the
narrative goes, the words and deeds of conscious living beings
have been utterly despoiled. Even if it can never be proven
conclusively that such a state of life ever existed, it feels right,
and is right, to infer that it once did.

'Now if such inferences as to what is non-extant are valid in
language, if its present condition carries us far back to an older
and oldest; a like proceeding must be justifiable in mythology
too.'[25] This sentiment expressed in Jacob Grimm's vast trea-
tise *Deutsche Mythologie* (*German Mythology*) in its second,
1844, edition, which we know Wagner had in his Dresden lib-
rary, was in all likelihood the key that unlocked the door to
The Ring. Wagner himself confesses in a little-discussed pas-
sage in his autobiography *My Life* that Grimm's researches
changed his whole way of thinking as an artist:

> Formed from the scanty fragments of a vanished world . . . I
> found here the outline of a chaotic building . . . Nothing in it
> was complete, nor was there anything resembling an architec-
> tural line, and I was often tempted to abandon the bleak task of
> building something from it all. And yet I was firmly in the pow-
> er of its marvellous magic . . . There rose up in my soul a whole
> world of shapes, which proved to be unexpectedly graphic and
> related to one another in some fundamental way . . . The effect
> they produced on my innermost being I can only describe as a
> complete rebirth.[26]

Except for the famous fairy tales he collected with his brother Wilhelm, Jacob Grimm rarely appears on anyone's radar screen now. Which is why Wagner's reading of various philosophers and political thinkers in the years leading up to the 1848–9 revolutions in Europe when he started planning *The Ring* usually takes precedence in the minds of commentators. No doubt the political instability of the times contributed to the forging of *The Ring*. But the New Mythology of the 1830s – Tom Shippey's twenty-first-century re-christening of the antiquarian activities of Grimm and his colleagues – obviously seized Wagner's imagination from the start. Not only did Jacob Grimm establish 'Grimm's Law', the proof that Germanic and Proto-Indo-European languages have common ancestors in ancient languages like Greek and Latin, he also did more than most to collect massive amounts of data about German mythology to propose, albeit on less secure grounds than in his work on language, that one can logically trace its disparate strands back to pure archaic origins. It was in effect a revolution in the study of ancient myth. Shippey refers implicitly to the phenomenally popular work of J.R.R. Tolkien, J.K. Rowling and not a few others in modern times when he reminds us that it was 'the New Mythology, not ancient folk-tradition', that gave us 'the orcs and trolls, the elves and dwarfs and dragons and werewolves which now crowd the shelves of every bookstore' – 'the shadow-walkers' and 'shapes from the cover of darkness ... which now haunt the imagination'.[27]

What was it about Jacob Grimm's *German Mythology* that appealed to Wagner? The first thing was its sheer range. Grimm was a Protestant who in his mythological universe not surprisingly wanted to keep Christianity in pole position as the logical outcome of the pagan worship of the gods. Even so, he was willing to include so many different gods, languages and diverse forms of life that ironically by the end of it all no attentive reader could still be a completely convinced Christian, assuming that they had been that in the first place. Grimm was – and Wagner suggests as much – comprehensive, but disorganized. He left it to others to join the dots, and ironically provided so much tantalizingly incomplete data about intertwined dialects, dwarfs, dragons, let alone various gods and half-gods, that to any devout Christian Noah's Ark and the Tower of Babel by the end must seem barely adequate as explanations of humanity's origins.

The lead chapter is devoted to God ('the supreme being'). Another soon comes tumbling by on Wodan/Odin ('the supreme divinity'), followed by erudite sections on other pagan gods, goddesses, heroes, dwarfs and elves, giants, ghosts, magic, superstition, animals, the devil, and for the purposes of understanding *The Ring* an extremely important one on the four elements water, fire, air and earth. 'In their silent greatness,' Grimm writes, '[they] wield an immediate power over the human mind.'[28] After the collapse of the gods, these naked substances to which the 'essence' of the gods were mysteriously wedded come to the fore again.

With this idea we probably have the first seed of the ending of *The Ring*. Brünnhilde rides on her horse through air into a burning pyre, water bursts the banks of the Rhine to flood the earth, and the whole spectacle ends with a vision of the gods completely engulfed by fire. Moreover the four parts of *The Ring* poem were already held together by striking images of the elements in the order that Grimm describes them: the underwater beginning of *The Rhinegold,* the unforgettable magic fire at the end of *The Valkyrie*, the open air spaces of *Siegfried*, and the earthly feudal community and its rituals in *Twilight of the Gods*. The sequence is also underpinned by a series of journeys through the same elements in reverse order, a magnificent palindrome that locks the mythic structure of the whole in place: Siegfried's journey down the Rhine in *Twilight of the Gods*, his passing through fire up the mountain to find Brünnhilde in *Siegfried*, the ride of the Valkyries through air in *The Valkyrie*, and the journey through earth down to Nibelheim in *The Rhinegold*. In its 'silent greatness', the framework is massive, and certainly intentional.

One of Grimm's main ideas was that the rich stories of the gods to be found in the thirteenth-century Icelandic sources were in fact the leftover traces of a crucial missing

piece in the jigsaw of early Germanic peoples caused by the
'arrogant notion' that they were 'pervaded by a soulless
cheerless barbarism'.[29] It all boiled down to the utterly fan-
tastical proposition of early German culture as a black hole
– the notion that the universe of the gods in the form of
'pure' early versions of the Norse sagas had been there all
the time despite their lack of appearance to the naked literary
and historical eye. Not surprisingly Grimm's fantasy caused
friction with Scandinavian scholars in the course of time,
who understandably suspected that their literature had been
hijacked for inappropriate nationalistic and religious reasons.
Even a conservative German scholar later in the nineteenth
century like Wolfgang Golther, who had inherited from senior
colleagues the idea that the world of Odin, the Valkyries
and the fairy-tale and mythical parts of the Siegfried legend
that saturate Norse myth were *urdeutsch* – proto-German –
admitted in his account of the sources for *The Ring* that 'in
Germany there was no trace of any of this, not because its
features are extinct, but because they never existed in the first
place'.[30]

But for Wagner it was literally a godsend. It allowed him
to indulge in the idea of spear-carrying gods and horse-riding
Valkyries as essentially German. (That they are not may have
something to do with the fact that an epic dedicated 'with
trust in the German spirit' turned out to have such enduring
universal appeal.) And reading Grimm and other inventors
of the New Mythology also encouraged him to desert history
for myth, to abandon concrete figures of the past, whose pol-
itical intrigues were continuing to provide endless theatrical
fodder for French grand opera. He had already tried his hand
at the genre with his five-act opera *Rienzi, the Last of the
Tribunes*, an early work and a huge success with the public
at its first performances in Dresden in 1842, indeed one of
the most spectacular of his entire career. And during the late
1830s and 1840s he had three other five-act operas based on
historical subjects in the pipeline as well, for all of which he
left behind ideas in draft form.[31] The last of these, *Friedrich*

I, based on the life of the legendary Holy Roman Emperor Frederick Barbarossa, who in the twelfth century had tried to unite the 1,600 or so German states large and small, is particularly interesting because Wagner was working seriously on it from 1846 to just before the Dresden uprising in 1849 while he was also researching *The Ring*.

During his studies of Barbarossa, Wagner came to see Frederick fancifully as 'a historical rebirth of the old-pagan Siegfried'. Connecting the dots backwards in this imaginative way was in the spirit of Grimm. But what really took courage – as Wagner openly confesses in his autobiographical writings – was eventually to abandon Frederick and to see Siegfried in his earliest and 'purest human form' free of all later historical trappings.[32] In any case Siegfried was never going to be the 'gallant knight' from the *Nibelungenlied* ('Song of the Nibelungs'), a Middle High German epic poem of anonymous authorship based on events from the fifth century, written down at the turn of the thirteenth, and regarded since its discovery in the eighteenth as a German *Iliad*. Heaven forbid that he should have the same character as in that poem, the son of the king and queen Siegmund and Sieglind, who commanded that he be 'dressed in elegant clothes' and well trained 'in matters of honour'.[33] This figure rooted in the likely historical context of the *Nibelungenlied* in the fifth century had to be superseded without further ado by the rougher fairy-tale hero of the thirteenth-century Icelandic sagas.

The main advantage, again in the spirit of Grimm, was that an imaginative re-invention of Siegfried's pedigree could make him a direct descendant of the gods, the grandson of Wotan. And the same was true of Brünnhilde, whom Wagner created as a Valkyrie and daughter of a powerful god and goddess, Wotan and Erda, quite unlike the formidable queen of Iceland Brunhild in the *Nibelungenlied*, whose forebears and fate remain unclear, and who in any case disappears halfway through the story to cede pride of place in the narrative to her antagonist Kriemhild, the powerful Burgundian queen of Worms. The wild, kaleidoscopic fairy tales and brutal stories

xxxiiINTRODUCTION

of turbulent gods and unstable tribal warfare of Norse mythology had entered the sturdy cathedral-like structure of the *Nibelungenlied*, so to speak, through the front door.

TOWARDS THE POEM
AND A TRANSLATION

The writing of *The Ring* poem began in 1848 with the libretto of a single 'grand heroic opera', *Siegfried's Death*, an early version of the final drama *Twilight of the Gods* based on the *Nibelungenlied*. The idea of turning the medieval epic into an opera had already been considered by several people, among them Fanny and Felix Mendelssohn and Robert Schumann, as well as a minor philosopher F. T. Vischer from Tübingen, who suggested it as early as 1844 as a possible opera for potential German supremacy in the genre. We do not know if Wagner knew of the proposal. If he did, Vischer's diagnosis that 'German music has yet to acquire its Schiller and Shakespeare'[34] could not have fallen on deaf ears. But the plan invented by Vischer for the envisioned opera lacked artistry; it was too long – a grand opera in five acts over two evenings – and provided (ironically) with a health warning about the perils of adding stories from the Icelandic sagas that would make it even longer.

Wagner ignored any such warning. *Siegfried's Death* was to be a heroic opera with a dark halo about the past chicanery of the gods culled mainly from the thirteenth-century Eddic poems and particularly the Icelandic prose rendition *Saga of the Volsungs* containing most of the detail he wanted. But colleagues and friends were confused. This was not the lord Siegfried of the *Nibelungenlied* they were expecting. And the central idea of the opera that, in order 'to reach [the] high goal of erasing their own guilt, the gods now educate human beings, and their goal would be reached if they extinguished themselves in this creation of humanity, namely that they forego their direct influence in favor of the freedom of human consciousness',[35] looked abstrusely political. While the gods were an obvious symbol of the ruling feudal class, their crimes were reported only in onstage narrations. And in the end they survived anyway. The opera finished with a great choral scene in which Wotan is addressed as 'Father of the Universe' and Siegfried's sacrifice as 'guarantor' of the god's eternal power.

It was hardly the stuff of revolution. Wagner tried to set *Siegfried's Death* to music two years later, after participating in the 1849 Dresden Revolution and going into exile, but abandoned the attempt. Not long after, in May 1851, he made the momentous decision to give *Siegfried's Death* a more radical ending to encompass the destruction of the gods, and to write three more dramas to explain it. Once the material from Scandinavian sources about gods and heroes embedded obscurely inside *Siegfried's Death* was unfurled as drama beforehand over three extra evenings, audiences would at last understand what the story was about. Moreover the working titles of the new dramas reflected an emerging grand scheme worthy of the great novels of the nineteenth century. In the order they were written they were: *The Young Siegfried*, *The Theft of the Rhinegold* and *Siegmund and Sieglinde: The Punishment of the Valkyrie*. The implied sense of these titles, and the one already in existence (*Siegfried's Death*), was innocence, crime, punishment and sacrifice. The big subjects were at last coming to the fore.

Without mention of Wagner's name (perhaps because Germany's warrant for his arrest was still in force), the libretti of the four dramas were published privately in 1853 as *The Rhinegold*, *The Valkyrie*, *The Young Siegfried* and *Siegfried's Death*, with the collective title and description *The Ring of the Nibelung. A Stage Festival Play for Three Days and a Preliminary Evening.* From here on the whole text led a double existence: one destined for music, and another as poetry in its own right. Some who managed to get hold of a copy were baffled. But others were enthusiastic, including Franz Liszt and the Swiss writer Gottfried Keller, a fastidious man of letters, who recommended it to a friend as 'powerful poetry, pure German, purified by the classical tragic spirit'.[36] Further title changes were considered in 1856 and subsequently introduced. The third drama became simply *Siegfried* and the fourth *Twilight of the Gods*, a title aligning it accurately with the idea in Norse mythology of *Ragnarök* (twilight of the gods) that was now the work's principal focus.

When the first Bayreuth festival took place in 1876, the complete poem of *The Ring* had appeared three times under Wagner's supervision over a period of twenty years. Given the changes he had constantly been making while setting it to music, no edition was identical with another. And he continued changing things and inventing new ideas during the Bayreuth rehearsals as well. Indeed, the whole idea of an ironclad authentic final version of *The Ring* is moot. Wagner's idiosyncratic handling of punctuation underwent startling transformation from source to source. Alterations of words or word order in his more ambitious alliterative schemes were not uncommon. And puzzling disappearances or amplifications and additions of scenic descriptions and directions, often without apparent reason, were not infrequent. Even in the full version of the poem included in his collected writings as late as 1872, the crucial final image of the gods sitting in Valhalla and being consumed by fire is missing – though this did have an explicable and highly interesting reason (see Notes).

The first problem confronting the translator is therefore which version of the German text to choose. There can never be one that is truly authentic in every detail, if only because Wagner's whole approach to his texts was contradictory. He liked to have them enshrined in print, spending a great deal of time fussing about how they were to be fixed on the page. On the other hand, myriad details of text and music were not always sacrosanct when it came to performance. Witnesses reporting Wagner's remarks from the rich sources of his 1876 rehearsals of *The Ring* relating to scene and word that are included in this translation (see Sources of the German Text) show that his attitude towards gesture and expression in particular was continuously inventive – and surprising.

At Brünnhilde's *Ewig war ich, / ewig bin ich* ('For ever I

was, / for ever I am') in *Siegfried* Act 3 (lines 2602–3), for ex-
ample, where the existing stage direction describes her face as
showing 'an image of grace', Wagner recited the immediately
preceding passage to his singers with 'an upsetting power of
expression', calling it a 'terrible moment'. Here Brünnhilde is
not so much in love with Siegfried as teetering on an exis-
tential precipice on her mountainous journey from immortal
goddess to human being. The gorgeous lyrical outpouring that
follows is a famous set piece for singers. But in light of Wag-
ner's personal demonstration of the utter despair leading into
it, the singing in context must surely feel highly vulnerable,
as if walking on thin ice. Wagner obviously felt that he had
to make this clear to his performers. Even now the dramatic
point does not always come across.

In assembling the German text, I have kept strictly to the
Wagner also carried on adding new scenic ideas. Towards
the end of *The Rhinegold* (after line 1828), Wotan picks up
a shabby sword left lying around by Fafner to illustrate his
grand idea as he points it towards the fortress. In the opening
scene of *Twilight of the Gods*, the Norns read the fate of the
world directly off their rope as if it were cosmic ticker tape.
Neither example (nor the others I have included in the text)
was meant to be temporary, as far as I can see. If Wagner had
lived long enough to publish another 'definitive' version of
the poem after staging *The Ring*, we can only guess what it
might have looked like. It would surely have again included
further modifications and additions.

In assembling the German text, I have kept strictly to the
wording and punctuation of the dialogue in the full orches-
tral scores of the new Schott critical edition (1980–2014) and
the vocal scores based on it (2010–14). With the stage dir-
ections I have chosen more randomly from either the new
critical edition or the full version of the text in Wagner's col-
lected writings, whichever was most detailed. (No systematic
concordance of these two sources, by the way, as yet exists.)
With Wagner's remarks during the arduous *Ring* rehearsals in
1876 in vocal scores annotated by his assistants Julius Kniese
and Heinrich Porges, and the conductors Hermann Levi and
Felix Mottl, I have selected only what I feel are Wagner's most

telling comments about scenic action, gesture and expression. In the same spirit I have also drawn on Heinrich Porges' long-since published essay on the 1876 rehearsals written specifically at Wagner's request (see n.16).

As for my translation, I decided to resist, in most but not all cases, Wagner's penchant for the archaic. For me there is absolutely no point in trying to find Old Anglo-Saxon equivalents, say, for words like *Wag, Harst, queck, freislich* or *glau* that few German speakers understood in the nineteenth century and still don't, unless they were, or are, professional linguists. On the other hand, Wagner often uses familiar words in the sense of their older meanings that need to be expressed. Two prominent cases are *Neid* (envy) and *Not* (need). In its older usage *Neid* is not merely passive or passive aggressive (the way it is mostly used now) but a signal for drastic action, for damage to the enemy in battle. In *Siegfried* (line 985) as an adjective in *Neidliches Schwert!*, for instance, I have translated it as 'pitiless sword' rather than the inaccurate 'sword of my need' (Andrew Porter), or even the more accurate 'fearsome sword' (Stewart Spencer). I also use the modern spelling of *Not*, but leave an older one (*Noth*) inside the name of the sword, a reminder of the word's feudal resonance. *Not* is never simply 'need' in *The Ring*; invariably it denotes a bitter, warlike state of emergency, again one signalling action: extreme peril demanding a way out.

The language of *The Ring* is a language of extremes. Its guttural violence and over-the-top ecstasy, plus everything in between, are so vivid and vital that a good deal of thought is needed about how to bring them uncompromised into another language. Particularly difficult are Wagner's alliterative language games. Alfred Forman, the first-ever English translator of *The Ring*, happened to be the London go-between for Wagner's big order of animal props for the Bayreuth première in 1876. While that was truly helpful, his *Ring* translation, which prides itself on being 'in the alliterative verse of the original', was a disaster. Wagner thought highly of it at first – perhaps because even with his limited English he could see that it was a near replica of his text – and his publisher Schott duly added it to their first imprints of *The Ring*. But it soon caused controversy. The diaries of Wagner's second wife Cosima report on 5 March 1882 that Forman's *Ring* translation 'is being very severely criticized', adding somewhat sourly: 'we have to admit that all these things seem to us of very little account'.

But they are of account to any translator of *The Ring* because Forman made a classic error that has been repeated, albeit less egregiously, a number of times since: overzealous fealty to the original. Forman's translation is an early example, a bad case of miscalculation and a tin ear for language. 'Better beset / the slumberer's bed, / or grief will bring us your game!' near the opening of *The Rhinegold* (lines 17–19) not only replicates Wagner's alliteration and the German word order far too exactly. The clumsy choice of words also dooms them to virtual meaninglessness from the start.

The really big mistake Forman made was not to strive independently for a translation that could reflect the literary power of Wagner's text without straying from its sense and dramatic energy. I hope I am not guilty of that too. I would be the last to claim that I have come close enough in English to the 'extraordinary richness of powerful and significant words', the zest for language and the daring syntactical concision that Nietzsche admired in *The Ring*. But I have tried to make it as close as I could for the reader to grasp the sheer verve of this magnificent epic tale of crime, punishment, gods trapped by their own hypocrisies, fated, short-lived freedoms, and a heroine who avenges the death of the hero by expiating the crimes of the gods in a moment of spectacular self-sacrifice. Since its first staging in Bayreuth all those years ago, it still feels strangely disquieting and uplifting, both at once – perhaps even more so now than it did then.

NOTES

1   Friedrich Nietzsche, 'Richard Wagner in Bayreuth', in *Nietzsche Werke*, ed. Giorgio Colli and Mazzino Montinari, IV/1 (Berlin, 1967), p. 59 (all translations from German sources JD). For the whole essay in English, see Nietzsche, *Untimely*

Meditations, ed. Daniel Breazeale, trans. R. J. Hollingdale (Cambridge, 1997), pp. 195–254 (this passage differently translated pp. 237–8).

2 Eduard Devrient, *Aus seinen Tagebüchern*, ed. Rolf Kabel, 2 vols (Weimar, 1964), i, p. 427.

3 Robert Schumann, *Tagebücher*, ed. Gerd Nauhaus, 3 vols (Leipzig, 1982), iii/2, p. 462.

4 See Ernest Newman, *The Life of Richard Wagner*, 4 vols (Cambridge, 1976), iv, p. 475.

5 Carl Friedrich Glasenapp, *Das Leben Richard Wagners*, 6 vols, 3–5th ed. (Leipzig, 1908–23), v, p. 307.

6 Richard Wagner, 'Über den Gebrauch des Textbuches' [On the Use of the Libretto], in *Sämtliche Schriften und Dichtungen*, 16 vols (Leipzig, 1911–14), xvi, p. 160.

7 Franz Carl Friedrich Müller, *Der Ring des Nibelungen: eine Studie zur Einführung in die gleichnamige Dichtung Richard Wagners* (Leipzig, 1862).

8 Richard Wagner, 'The Art-Work of the Future', in *Richard Wagner's Prose Works*, trans. William Ashton Ellis, 8 vols (London, 1892–9; repr. Lincoln and London, 1993–5), i, p. 127. Wagner's emphasis.

9 Richard Wagner, 'Opera and Drama', in *Prose Works*, ii, p. 107. Wagner's emphasis.

10 *Cosima Wagner's Diaries*, ed. Martin Gregor-Dellin and Dietrich Mack, trans. with an Introduction by Geoffrey Skelton, vol. 1: 1869–1877 (London, 1978), pp. 475, 476 (10 and 12 April 1872).

11 *Cosima Wagner's Diaries*, p. 447 (6 January 1872). Trans. modified.

12 Richard Wagner, 'Beethoven's Choral Symphony at Dresden, 1846', in *Prose Works*, vii, p. 247. Trans. modified.

13 Richard Wagner, 'The Festival Theatre and Stage in Bayreuth', in *Prose Works*, v, p. 325. Trans. modified.

14 Richard Wagner, 'A Communication to My Friends', in *Prose Works*, i, p. 391. Trans. modified.

15 Igor Stravinsky and Robert Craft, *Themes and Episodes* (New York, 1966), p. 189.

16 Heinrich Porges, *Wagner Rehearsing the 'Ring': An Eye-Witness Account of the Stage Rehearsals of the First Bayreuth Festival*, trans. Robert L. Jacobs (Cambridge, 1983), p. 145. Trans. modified.

17 Simon Goldhill, Introduction to *Greek Tragedy* (Penguin Classics), ed. Shomit Dutta (London, 2004), p. xx.

18 *Cosima Wagner's Diaries*, p. 992 (1 November 1877).

19 *Selected Letters of Richard Wagner*, trans. and ed. Stewart Spencer and Barry Millington (London and Melbourne, 1987), p. 281 (letter of 11 February 1853). Trans. modified.

20 Simon Goldhill, 'The Great Dionysia and Civic Ideology', *The Journal of Hellenic Studies*, vol. 107 (1987), pp. 58–76.

21 All citations in this paragraph from the collection of press reports in Susanna Großmann-Vendrey, *Bayreuth in der deutschen Presse*, Dokumentenband 1: '*Die Grundsteinlegung und die ersten Festspiele*' (Regensburg, 1977), pp. 193 (Kalbeck), 164 (Engel), 77, 80 (Messner).

22 George C. Izenour, *Theater Design*, 2nd ed. (New Haven and London, 1996), p. 76. I am also indebted in the discussion below to the same author's *Theater Technology*, 2nd ed. (New Haven and London, 1996), pp. 54–7.

23 *Cosima Wagner's Diaries*, p. 630 (5 May 1873). Trans. modified.

24 See the 'Explanatory Report for the Principal Plans for the Monumental Festival Theatre [in Munich]' submitted by Wagner and Semper to the Munich authorities and Ludwig II in Appendix I of Manfred Semper, *Das Münchner Festspielhaus, Gottfried Semper und Richard Wagner* (Hamburg, 1906), pp. 107 and 110.

25 Jacob Grimm, *Teutonic Mythology*, trans. James Steven Stallybrass from the fourth edition, 4 vols (London 1880–88; repr. Cambridge, 2012), iii, p. vi. Stallybrass's use of the more general word 'Teutonic' in the title was in all likelihood a tactical manoeuvre to deflect attention from Grimm's late-nineteenth-century critics, who among other things balked at his claim that Norse mythology was purely German in origin. In the text I use the more accurate *German Mythology*.

26 Richard Wagner, *My Life*, trans. Andrew Gray and ed. Mary Whittall (Cambridge, 1983), p. 260. Trans. modified.

27 Tom Shippey, 'A Revolution Reconsidered: Mythography and Mythology in the Nineteenth Century', in *The Shadow-Walkers: Jacob Grimm's Mythology of the Monstrous*, ed. Tom Shippey (Tempe, Ariz., 2005), pp. 1–2.

28 Grimm, *Teutonic Mythology*, ii, p. 582.

29 Grimm, *Teutonic Mythology*, iii, p. vii. See also Shippey, 'A Revolution Reconsidered', pp. 11–12.

30 Wolfgang Golther, *Die sagengeschichtlichen Grundlagen der Ringdichtung Richard Wagners* [The Foundations of Richard Wagner's Ring Poem in the History of Myth] (Berlin, 1902),

p. 9. Golther himself had already published a major study ref-
uting the thesis that the roots of the Nibelung myth in Norse
legend lay in a remote Germanic past. 'An unprejudiced ex-
amination of the northern sources', he wrote, 'has shown that
not only the writing down of them, but also their content are
from a much later period'. Wolfgang Golther, *Studien zur ger-
manischen sagengeschichte. I der valkyrjenmythus. II über das
verhältniss der nordischen und deutschen form der Nibelungen-
sage* (Munich, 1888), p. 3.

31   In fact there were four potential five-act works, if we include
Wagner's realignment of the New Testament in an opera to
be called *Jesus of Nazareth*, for which he wrote a thirty-page
scenario in early 1849 and did not give it up until early 1850.
The other projected scenarios were *The High-Born Bride*
(1836–42), *The Saracen Woman* (1841–3) and *Friedrich I*
(1846–9). Whether the last was to be a spoken play or an opera
is not clear from available evidence.

32   Wagner, 'A Communication to My Friends', *Prose Works*, i,
pp. 358–9. Trans. modified.

33   *The Nibelungenlied* (Penguin Classics), trans. A. T. Hatto (Lon-
don, 1965), p. 20. This may be one aspect Hatto is referring to
on the first page of his Foreword when he somewhat crustily
accuses Wagner of 'intruding reckless distortions' in *The Ring*
'between us and an ancient masterpiece'.

34   Friedrich Theodor Vischer, 'Vorschlag zu einer Oper' [Proposal
for an Opera], in *Kritische Gänge*, vol. 2 (Tübingen, 1844), p.
400.

35   Richard Wagner, 'The Nibelungen Myth', in *Wagner's* Ring *in
1848: New Translations of* The Nibelung Myth *and* Siegfried's
Death, trans. and with an introduction by Edward. R. Haymes
(Rochester, NY, 2010), p. 47.

36   Cited in Arthur Groos, 'Appropriation in Wagner's *Tristan*
Libretto', in *Reading Opera*, eds Arthur Groos and Roger
Parker (Princeton, 1988), p. 13, n. 3.

SYNOPSES

THE RHINEGOLD / *DAS RHEINGOLD*

Preliminary Evening / *Vorabend*
In four scenes

CAST

Gods: Wotan *high bass*, Donner *high bass*, Froh *tenor*, Loge
tenor
Goddesses: Fricka *low soprano*, Freia *high soprano*, Erda
low soprano
Nibelungs: Alberich *high bass*, Mime *tenor*
Giants: Fasolt *high bass*, Fafner *low bass*
Rhinedaughters: Woglinde *high soprano*, Wellgunde *high
soprano*, Flosshilde *low soprano*
Nibelungs

SCENE ONE
In the depths of the Rhine

In greenish twilight steep rocks are visible. Water swirls
around them at the top while the waves dissolve into a damp
mist lower down. The Rhinedaughters circle round the central
reef which points upward to the brighter light above. Alberich
comes out of a cleft in the rocks and makes advances to the
Rhinedaughters who cruelly lead him on. Alberich eventually
realizes that he is being ridiculed. Silenced by anger, he catches
sight of the gleaming Rhinegold high on the central reef.

Wellgunde imprudently reveals that whoever can fashion an all-powerful ring from the gold will inherit the world. Woglinde adds that the required magic can be attained by whoever denies the power of love. Alberich curses love with hideous passion and snatches the gold before vanishing into the depths.

SCENE TWO
An open mountaintop area, situated near the Rhine

The light of dawn reflects off the battlements of a magnificent castle. Wotan dreams of eternal power and a fortress for the gods. His wife Fricka rudely awakens him. While Wotan gazes enraptured at the magnificent edifice he has just been dreaming about, Fricka bluntly reminds him of its price. Built by the giant brothers Fasolt and Fafner, the fortress is to be paid for by giving them Freia, keeper of the golden apples of eternal youth.

Freia rushes in, complaining that she has been threatened by Fasolt. The giants enter and Fasolt proceeds to lecture Wotan on the significance of contracts. The more pragmatic Fafner, however, knowing that Freia is indispensable to the gods, proposes to abduct her by force. Donner and Froh, Freia's brothers, hurry in to protect their sister, but the giants invoke their contract. The long-awaited god of fire, Loge, on whom Wotan is relying to find a way out of the dilemma, joins the gods at last and tells of many things, including Alberich's theft of the gold and the mighty ring he has fashioned from it.

The giants agree to take Freia away as a provisional hostage until evening, and then to hand her over in exchange for the gold. A pallid mist fills the stage. As Loge taunts the gods, calling them 'a wilting travesty to the entire world' and predicting their demise, they begin to age, fearfully looking to Wotan for a way out of their plight. Wotan decides to travel with Loge to Nibelheim to take possession of the gold.

SCENE THREE
Nibelheim's underground chasms

Tormented in the first scene, Alberich is now the tormenter. With great skill and at his brother Alberich's behest, Mime has created the Tarnhelm, a magic helmet that enables its wearer to assume any form at will. Alberich takes it from him by force and uses its power to make himself invisible, vanishing in a column of mist. Mime writhes in agony from Alberich's whiplashes without being able to see the whip. Alberich takes off the Tarnhelm and drives a pack of Nibelung dwarfs laden with treasure before him.

Eventually he notices Wotan and Loge. Unable to resist a demonstration of his power, he kisses the ring on his finger, causing the screaming Nibelungs to scatter. He then dons the Tarnhelm again to turn himself into a monstrous dragon. Loge cunningly suggests to Alberich that a small creature would better escape danger, but that the transformation would probably be too hard to accomplish. Alberich rises to the challenge and turns himself into a toad. Loge and Wotan easily capture him and drag him back to the earth's surface.

SCENE FOUR
An open mountaintop area, situated near the Rhine

Alberich is forced to give up the hoard, which is dragged up through a chasm by the Nibelungs. Already humiliated in front of his own slaves, Alberich is completely ruined when Wotan violently takes the ring from him. Driven to confront Wotan, among other things with the telling argument that his own theft of the gold was a peccadillo compared with Wotan's present betrayal of the laws he supposedly upholds, Alberich curses the ring to destroy its owners. Henceforth no one who possesses the ring will escape death.

The giants enter with Freia and plant two stakes in the ground on either side of her. They demand that the hoard be piled up until her shape is concealed. Now it is Wotan's turn to be humiliated: to fill the final crack the giants demand the ring. Wotan refuses until Erda, the goddess of earth, intervenes to deliver a sphinx-like warning about the destruction of the gods, advising him to discard the prize.

With sudden resolve he throws the ring on to the pile. Freia is free and the gods return to their immortal state, at least for the moment. But to their horror they witness the first effects of the curse as Fafner kills Fasolt in the ensuing struggle for the ring. Donner conjures up a storm to clear the sultry air. Valhalla lies gleaming in the evening sun at the end of a rainbow bridge, which the gods begin to cross in triumph.

Diffidently joining the procession, Loge remarks that the gods are really hastening towards their destruction. Their refurbished glory is also dimmed momentarily by the Rhinedaughters, who lament from the depths that their demand that the gold be returned to its original purity has gone unheeded. 'Up there' in the realm of the gods, they complain, it may thrill; but it remains 'false and accursed'.

THE VALKYRIE / DIE WALKÜRE

First Day / Erster Tag

In three acts

CAST
Siegmund *tenor*, Hunding *bass*, Wotan *high bass*, Sieglinde *soprano*, Brünnhilde *soprano*, Fricka *soprano*
Valkyries: Gerhilde, Ortlinde, Waltraute, Schwertleite, Helmwige, Siegrune, Grimgerde, Rossweisse, *soprano and contralto*

ACT ONE
Inside Hunding's house

SCENE ONE

A man is being pursued. He enters the house and staggers towards the hearth. The wife of Hunding, the absent master of the house, gives him water. The stranger explains that a storm has driven him there and prepares to leave. But the woman begs him to stay. A secret bond begins to grow between them.

SCENE TWO

Hunding returns from combat. He is instinctively distrustful of the stranger, but reluctantly grants him hospitality for the night. Hunding insists on knowing his guest's name. The stranger says he calls himself 'Ruled by Sorrow' (Wehwalt) and explains by telling the story of his childhood. He and his father Wolf returned one day from the hunt to find his mother murdered and his twin sister abducted. He eventually lost track of his father and has been cursed with bad luck ever since, hence his name. A woman forced to marry someone she did not love had asked him for help, whereupon he killed her brothers whose kinsmen are now hunting him.

Hunding realizes that 'Ruled by Sorrow' is the killer. He reveals that he is one of the hunters and challenges the stranger to combat the next day. Only the laws of hospitality protect him for the moment. Hunding's wife has tried to intervene, but Hunding orders her to leave to prepare his nightly drink.

SCENE THREE

Alone, the stranger recalls his father's promise to provide him with a sword when in the direst circumstances. The woman returns. She has put a sleeping draught in Hunding's drink and proceeds to show the stranger a sword thrust into the tree. It was put there by a one-eyed man during her wedding to Hunding. None of the guests, nor anyone since, has had the strength to draw it out. She believes that the hero who can will more than make up for the shame she has had to endure since robbers forced her to marry Hunding.

She embraces the stranger passionately as the great door opens to let in a beautiful spring night. The stranger sings in praise of spring, which, like a brother, has freed love, its sister, from the storms of winter.

The image soon turns into reality. The woman knew from the single eye of the old man who planted the sword that she was his daughter. Seeing the same look in the stranger's eyes, she suspects that she is related to him too. The stranger asks her to give him a name she loves. When he tells her that his father's name was not Wolf, but Wälse, she knows for certain that he is the Wälsung for whom the sword is intended. She calls him Siegmund, Protector of Victory. In turn, Siegmund grips the sword and calls it Nothung, a weapon that can save him from peril. Revelling in his new name, Siegmund pulls the sword from the tree with a mighty wrench. Rapt with wonder and delight, the woman tells him that she is his twin sister Sieglinde. They embrace in ecstasy as Siegmund calls for the blossoming of the Wälsung race.

ACT TWO
Wild rocky mountains

SCENE ONE

Wotan knows that Siegmund and Sieglinde (a son and daughter borne to him by an unnamed mortal woman since the end of *Das Rheingold*) are fleeing from Hunding, and that Hunding will eventually overtake them. He charges his favourite daughter Brünnhilde (also borne to him since the end of *Das Rheingold*, this time by the earth goddess Erda) with the task of ensuring Siegmund's victory in his forthcoming duel with

Hunding. Brünnhilde warns Wotan of the 'violent storm' in store for him from his wife Fricka, the guardian of marriage, who is approaching in a chariot drawn by a pair of rams.

Fricka insists that Hunding has a right to vengeance. She upholds the law in the face of Wotan's advocacy of nature. The power of spring may have brought the twins together, but their incestuous union is a monstrous affront to reason. As for Wotan's grand idea of a free hero who would allow the gods to escape their guilty complicity in the theft of the Rhinegold, this is just false: Siegmund is not free, but merely a pawn in a game invented by Wotan, who is himself severely compromised by his promiscuity.

Humbled by the sheer force of Fricka's reasoning, Wotan agrees to forbid Brünnhilde to let Siegmund win the battle against Hunding. The hero must be sacrificed to preserve the divine law.

SCENE TWO

Alone with Brünnhilde, Wotan confesses that all along he has been deceiving himself. Master of the laws of the universe, he is also their victim. Only the destruction of everything he has built will cleanse the guilt of the gods. And to that end Alberich is working. He has created a son whom Wotan now blesses: may the hate of Alberich's child feed on the empty glory of the gods' divinity. Brünnhilde cannot accept Wotan's bleak nihilism and argues to protect Siegmund. Wotan threatens her with the direst consequences if she rebels.

SCENE THREE

Siegmund and Sieglinde enter. Sieglinde is haunted by nightmarish visions of Hunding and his dogs in pursuit of them. She faints in Siegmund's arms.

xlviii   SYNOPSES

SCENE FOUR

Brünnhilde appears to Siegmund and announces his impend-
ing death. But he refuses to go to Valhalla if Sieglinde cannot
join him. Rather than put her and their unborn child at the
mercy of a hostile world, he threatens to kill them with his
sword Nothung. Brünnhilde is overcome by this display of
human emotion and promises to defy her father's command.
Sounds of Hunding's approach are heard summoning Sieg-
mund to battle. Brünnhilde tells Siegmund to put his faith in
the sword.

SCENE FIVE

Sieglinde's nightmare is now becoming a reality. Siegmund
places her carefully on a stone seat and bids her farewell with
a kiss. He goes to confront Hunding as they hurl insults at
each other in the dark storm clouds. Sieglinde has awoken
from her dreams and calls out to the men to stop fighting,
pleading to them to murder her instead. But already a light-
ning flash has revealed the men engaged in a vicious battle.
Brünnhilde protects Siegmund with her shield. But just as
Siegmund is about to deal Hunding a deadly blow, Wotan
intervenes, forcing Siegmund's sword to shatter on his spear.
Hunding drives his spear into the breast of the unarmed Sieg-
mund. Wotan looks in anguish at Siegmund's body and with
a dismissive wave of the hand causes Hunding to fall down
dead.
    Meanwhile Brünnhilde has fled with Sieglinde on horse-
back after gathering up the sword Nothung's shattered frag-
ments. In a thunderous rage Wotan storms off in pursuit of
them.

ACT THREE
On the summit of a rocky mountain ('Brünnhilde's rock')

SCENE ONE

The Valkyries gather together with warlike exuberance, each with a slain hero destined for Valhalla on the saddle of her horse. To their astonishment Brünnhilde arrives with a woman. The Valkyrie sisters, fearful of Wotan's wrath, refuse to protect them. Brünnhilde tells Sieglinde to flee to a forest in the east where she will be safe. There she will give birth to 'the noblest hero of the world'. Brünnhilde gives her the shattered pieces of the sword and names him Siegfried, Joyous in Victory, predicting that he will one day forge the fragments anew. Brünnhilde asks her sisters for protection and they surround her to conceal her.

SCENE TWO

Wotan enters in extreme rage looking for Brünnhilde. The Valkyrie sisters do their best to protect her. But Wotan's condemnation of his daughter is so powerful that she is compelled to step out of the Valkyrie throng and face him. To their horror he condemns her to lie defenceless in a magic sleep, vulnerable to the first man who finds her. The Valkyries storm off wildly in tight formation.

SCENE THREE

Left alone with Wotan, Brünnhilde justifies her actions. Although she is not wise, she knew in her heart that Wotan loved Siegmund, which is why she disobeyed his order.

Wotan is moved against his better judgement by her courage. Reluctantly he grants her only request. She is to be surrounded by a magic fire, which only the freest hero who knows no fear can penetrate. With great emotion, Wotan bids farewell to his daughter and summons Loge to encircle her with fire: only one freer than himself will be able to win her.

SIEGFRIED

Second Day / *Zweiter Tag*

In three acts

CAST
Siegfried *tenor*, Mime *tenor*, the Wanderer (Wotan) *bass*, Fafner *bass*, Erda *contralto*, Brünnhilde *soprano*, Forest Bird *boy soprano*

ACT ONE
A rock cave in the forest

SCENE ONE

Mime is frustrated that he can neither forge a sword strong enough for Siegfried, his ward, nor piece together the shattered fragments of Nothung. Nothung is the only weapon adequate for the task Mime has in mind for his powerful charge: the killing of the dragon Fafner in order to win back the ring. Siegfried enters boisterously from the forest. He has no respect for the puny dwarf who pretends to be his father. Siegfried forces him to confess the truth. A dying woman emerged from the forest, Mimi relates, to give birth in the cave. She entrusted the child to him insisting that he should be called Siegfried, and gave him the fragments of Nothung, which had been shattered when the child's father was slain.

Siegfried is thrilled by the story and, before racing back into the forest from which he senses freedom at last, orders Mime to repair the sword.

SCENE TWO

The Wanderer, dressed in a long dark blue cloak, appears un-invited at Mime's hearth. Mime can be rid of him only by agreeing to a game of riddles. The Wanderer stakes his head on three questions from his unwilling host who, over-confident in his own cunning, agrees to ask them.

The unwanted guest answers correctly and insists that Mime stake his own head on three questions in turn. But Mime, panic-stricken, cannot solve the third riddle: who will weld Nothung together again? The Wanderer solves it for him: 'Only he who's never felt fear' and the one to whom, he adds casually, Mime's head is now forfeit. Mime slumps down on his stool in front of the anvil looking devastated.

SCENE THREE

Mime promises to take Siegfried to Fafner's lair to teach him fear. Disconcertingly for Mime, Siegfried is only too willing to co-operate.

Siegfried starts to forge Nothung himself, deliberately ig-noring Mime's expertise. Dimly aware of Siegfried's destiny, Mime brews a poison to kill him once he has slain the dragon. Siegfried sings lustily of Nothung as he forges and Mime skips around the cave in delight at the secret plan he has concocted to save his head. With the finished sword, Siegfried cuts the anvil in two and exultantly lifts Nothung high in the air as Mime jumps onto a stool in heady rapture, only to fall off it to the ground in fright.

ACT TWO
Deep in the forest

SCENE ONE

Alberich is on watch outside Fafner's cave. The Wanderer enters and stops to face Alberich who, as a shaft of moonlight illuminates the scene, quickly recognizes his adversary. Alberich, suspicious of the Wanderer's nonchalance, confronts him with his main weakness: his inability to steal the hoard yet again – an act that would shatter the rule of law once and for all.

As if to prove his indifference, the Wanderer generously tells Alberich of Mime's plans to get the hoard for himself, and suggests warning Fafner who, to avoid being murdered, might relinquish the ring to Alberich before Mime arrives. The Wanderer even offers to waken the dragon himself. Predictably the dragon refuses to listen and goes back to sleep. The Wanderer knows full well that everything is set on a course that no one, not even Alberich, can alter. He vanishes quickly into the forest.

SCENE TWO

Siegfried and Mime arrive as day breaks. Mime conjures up threatening images of Fafner. But Siegfried is more intent on ridding himself of his guardian, whom he finds increasingly repulsive. Mime leaves Siegfried beneath a linden tree to muse on his origins.

Siegfried cuts a reed pipe and tries to play it in order to converse with the birds. He loses patience and instead uses his silver horn. As the sounds of the horn grow faster and louder Fafner begins to stir. Spewing venom out of its nostrils, the dragon heaves itself up to crush the interloper, only to expose its heart into which Siegfried swiftly plunges his sword. Realizing that his killer is only a naïve boy being used

by someone more sinister, the dying Fafner warns Siegfried
of Mime's true plans. Some of the dragon's blood spills on to
Siegfried's hand. After involuntarily licking it, Siegfried can
at last understand the song of one of the birds, who tells him
that the hoard is now his. Siegfried climbs down into the cave
to look for it and quickly disappears.

SCENE THREE

Mime and Alberich sidle back into sight, quarrelling about
their right to the hoard. Siegfried emerges from the cave
looking thoughtfully at the ring and the Tarnhelm. Alberich
withdraws as Mime persuades Siegfried to take the poisonous
drink. But the dragon's blood also enables Siegfried to hear
the murderous intent beneath Mime's ingratiating phrases.

Instead of taking the drink, Siegfried kills Mime in a mo-
ment of disgust with a single stroke of his sword. Alberich's
mocking laughter echoes in the background, but Siegfried,
oblivious, simply asks the Forest Bird for a new and pref-
erably more congenial companion. The Forest Bird obliges
by telling him of Brünnhilde who, asleep on a high rock and
imprisoned by a magic fire, awaits a fearless hero to set her
free. The Forest Bird flies off to show Siegfried the way.

ACT THREE
A wild region at the foot of a rocky mountain

SCENE ONE

The Wanderer awakens Erda from a deep sleep. Bleakly ob-
serving that nothing can change the destiny of the world, he
still wants to ask her: 'how can a rolling wheel be stopped?'
She replies that the 'deeds of men darken my spirit'. She was
raped by Wotan and bore him Brünnhilde. She is confused
and not even clear who her rude awakener is.

Irritated but not surprised, the Wanderer announces that

their child 'will carry out the deed that redeems the world'. He tells Erda to go down to 'eternal sleep'.

SCENE TWO

The Wanderer awaits Siegfried who enters in high spirits. Their banter is good-humoured until the old man asks the young hero who it was who first created Nothung. The Wanderer laughs at Siegfried's ignorance. Siegfried, hurt by the condescension, pours scorn on the Wanderer in turn.

With a single blow Siegfried cuts the Wanderer's spear in two. The Wanderer picks up the pieces and disappears in total darkness. Siegfried puts his horn to his lips and plunges into the billowing fire spreading down from the mountain.

SCENE THREE
On the summit of 'Brünnhilde's rock'

Siegfried has reached the sleeping Brünnhilde, whom he mistakes at first for a male warrior. He cuts away the armour to discover a feminine form that fills him with a strange emotion, asking himself whether he is learning fear at last. He sinks down, as if about to die, and with closed eyes places a kiss on Brünnhilde's lips.

She awakens slowly from the darkness of sleep, sitting up gradually to praise the sun and the earth. Siegfried and Brünnhilde are lost in delight, she praising the gods and the divine hero who woke her, and both giving thanks to the mother who bore Siegfried and made their situation possible. As Siegfried tries passionately to embrace her, she violently pushes him away. 'Even gods never neared me', she protests, bemoaning her newly found 'inglorious' condition. 'I am Brünnhilde no more.'

Miraculously regaining his fearlessness, Siegfried manages to calm Brünnhilde's emotional turmoil. Together they become ecstatically blind to the world. Siegfried rejoices that he is

'gloriously lit by Brünnhilde's star'. Brünnhilde, more pres-
ciently, welcomes the coming of the 'twilight of the gods' and
the 'night of annihilation' when 'darkness will arise' and 'fog
will be let in'. They both end their duet with the words: 'radi-
ant love, laughing death'.

TWILIGHT OF THE GODS /
GÖTTERDÄMMERUNG

Third Day / *Dritter Tag*
Prologue and three acts

CAST

Siegfried *tenor*, Gunther *high bass*, Alberich *high bass*,
Hagen *low bass*, Brünnhilde *soprano*, Gutrune *soprano*,
Waltraute *low soprano*, First Norn *contralto*, Second Norn
soprano, Third Norn *soprano*, vassals *tenor, bass*, women
soprano
Rhinedaughters: Woglinde *soprano*, Wellgunde *soprano*,
Flosshilde *contralto*

PROLOGUE
On the Valkyries' rock

The three Norns, daughters of Erda, spin the golden rope of
world knowledge and read from it the world's future and past.
The rope was once tied to the World Ash Tree until Wotan
desecrated the Tree to create his spear and establish his rule
of order over the universe. Wanting to know when the fate of
the world they are predicting will come to pass, the Norns try
to keep the rope taut. But its threads tangle and it breaks. The
Norns' primeval wisdom is at an end.

Brünnhilde and Siegfried emerge from a cave with the rising
of the sun, he in full armour, she leading her horse Grane.

Brünnhilde sings that her love for Siegfried would not be true
if she refused to let him go forth into the world to perform
new deeds. Siegfried leaves Brünnhilde the ring as a token, and
she in turn gives him Grane. Carrying his sword, he begins his
descent from the rock and vanishes with the horse. His horn is
heard from below as Brünnhilde bids him farewell.

ACT ONE
Gunther's royal hall near the Rhine

SCENE ONE

Hagen, the illegitimate son of Alberich and Grimhild, is
plotting to regain the ring for his father. His legitimate half-
siblings Gunther and Gutrune, who have inherited their king-
dom from their dead parents Gibich and Grimhild, sit on a
throne to one side.

Hagen gives them some (seemingly) sensible advice. If they
are to retain the respect of their subjects, they must marry
without delay. Hagen suggests Siegfried for Gutrune and
Brünnhilde for Gunther. The lacklustre Gibichungs are over-
whelmed with the thought, but sceptical until Hagen suggests
a way of attracting their powerful partners-to-be.

Gutrune is to give Siegfried a potion that will erase his mem-
ory of all other women. Once Gutrune has captured his heart,
it will be easy for her brother to persuade him to woo Brünn-
hilde. Siegfried's horn sounds from his boat on the Rhine.

SCENE TWO

Hagen calls out to Siegfried to come ashore. Siegfried steps
on to land with his sword and Grane. He tells Gunther of the
Tarnhelm and the ring. As planned, Gutrune offers him the
potion of forgetfulness, which he unwittingly accepts, ded-
icating his first drink before drinking it to Brünnhilde and
faithful love.

The effect of the drink is immediate: spellbound by Gutrune, he hears Gunther talk of the woman Gunther desires, but cannot win because she lives on a high mountain surrounded by fire. Siegfried shows no sign of recognition. Knowing that he can penetrate the fire, he offers to woo the woman, using the Tarnhelm to disguise himself as his host.

After sealing his promise with an oath of blood brotherhood, Siegfried sets off with Gunther for Brünnhilde's rock, leaving Hagen to guard the hall. Sitting without moving and leaning against a pillar, Hagen savours the plot he has set in motion.

SCENE THREE
The Valkyries' rock

Brünnhilde sits at the entrance of her cave gazing rapturously at the ring. Dark storm clouds appear as Waltraute, one of the Valkyries, arrives to tell her of Wotan seated morosely in Valhalla, waiting passively for the destruction of the gods.
Despite Waltraute's pleading, Brünnhilde refuses Wotan's only remaining wish: to free the gods from the curse by returning the ring to the Rhinedaughters. Brünnhilde vows never to renounce the ring, or the love it supposedly symbolizes. Waltraute hastens away distraught.

The brightening flames and the sound of a horn herald the arrival of Siegfried. But to Brünnhilde's horror a different figure steps out of the fire. In Gunther's shape, Siegfried wrestles with her and wrenches the ring from her finger. He forces her into the cave and lays his sword between them as witness that his wooing of Gunther's bride is chaste.

ACT TWO
In front of Gunther's hall

SCENE ONE

Hagen is asleep. As the moon suddenly appears, Alberich can be seen in front of him, resting his arms on his son's knees. He exhorts Hagen to keep faith with their plan to ruin Siegfried and win back the ring.

SCENE TWO

With the help of the Tarnhelm, Siegfried arrives at the Gibichungs' court ahead of Gunther and Brünnhilde. In a detailed dialogue with Hagen and Gutrune, he describes his successsful wooing of Brünnhilde for Gunther and announces their imminent arrival.

SCENE THREE

As if calling the Gibichung vassals to battle, Hagen summons them to greet Gunther and his bride. The vassals do not understand Hagen's warlike tone, or the need for the sharp weapons and bellowing horns. Hagen explains by proposing a barbaric feast, including the slaughter of animals for the gods, and uninhibited drunkenness.

SCENE FOUR

Solemnly, the vassals greet Gunther and Brünnhilde as they disembark. Brünnhilde appears crushed and humiliated until she sees the ring on Siegfried's finger. Roused to furious anger, she declares that Siegfried is her husband and flings desperate charges at him. To clear his name Siegfried swears an oath on Hagen's spear that its point may pierce his body if he is lying about who he is. Brünnhilde dedicates the sharp point of Hagen's spear to Siegfried's downfall.

SCENE FIVE

After Siegfried has left to prepare for his marriage, Brünnhilde tells Hagen that she did not protect Siegfried's back with her magic as he would never have turned it towards an enemy. Now his enemy, she reveals that his back is the only place where he can be mortally wounded.

Gunther, the deceived deceiver, is convinced of Siegfried's treachery by Hagen, but worried about the effect Siegfried's death will have on Gutrune. Hagen decides to make it look like a hunting accident. All are now dedicated to Siegfried's death.

Calling on Wotan, guardian of vows, Brünnhilde and Gunther swear an oath of vengeance. Hagen in turn invokes the spirit of his father, Alberich, lord of the ring. Siegfried returns with Gutrune and the bridal procession, while Hagen forces Brünnhilde to join Gunther to prepare for a double wedding.

ACT THREE
A forest region near the Rhine

SCENE ONE

A dwarf has lured Siegfried away from his hunting companions to the riverbank where the Rhinedaughters are playing. They tell him he will die later that day if he keeps the ring. Laughing, he ignores them. They lament his blindness and swim away to 'a proud woman', who will soon inherit his treasure and give them a better hearing.

SCENE TWO

Siegfried has rejoined his hunting companions, who sit down
to rest and drink. At Hagen's prompting he regales them with
stories of Mime and Nothung, of Fafner and the Forest Bird.
But Hagen slips an antidote into Siegfried's drink that enables
him to tell the true story of Brünnhilde. Siegfried gives a rap-
turous account of how he learned about her from the Forest
Bird and how passionately she embraced him after his bold
kiss. Gunther is horrified at what he hears.

Wotan's two ravens fly up out of a bush. Hagen asks
Siegfried if he can understand them too. Siegfried turns, and
immediately Hagen thrusts his spear into Siegfried's back.
Hagen gloats to the horrified onlookers that Siegfried's perjury
is avenged.

The vassals take up Siegfried's body to form a solemn
cortège as the magnificent funeral march recollects and reflects
on the hero's life.

SCENE THREE

In the hall of Gunther's court, Gutrune has been plagued by
disturbing dreams and the sight of Brünnhilde walking to
the banks of the Rhine. When she discovers Siegfried's body,
brought back by the hunters, she nearly faints with shock.
Hagen freely admits the murder and kills Gunther in a fight
over the ring. But when Hagen reaches for the ring, the dead
Siegfried's hand rises menacingly to prevent him from taking
it.

Brünnhilde comes forward to silence Gutrune's lament
and to contemplate the dead Siegfried. She orders his body
to be placed on a funeral pyre. Now, after talking to the
Rhinedaughters, she understands Wotan's will to destroy the
gods, to rid them of the curse that also ensnared her innocent
lover. She takes the ring, puts it on her finger and casts a torch
on the pyre. To cleanse the ring from the curse with fire before

it is returned to the Rhinedaughters, she leaps with her horse into the burning pyre, united with Siegfried in love and death.

The Rhine overflows its banks and pours over the flames. As the Rhinedaughters appear on the waves, Hagen rushes headlong into the flood to demand the return of the ring. Woglinde and Wellgunde draw him into the depths, while Flosshilde holds up the ring in triumph. In the ruins of Gunther's hall the men and women watch apprehensively as an increasingly bright glow appears in the sky.

Gradually the hall of Valhalla becomes visible, filled with gods and heroes just as Waltraute described it in Act I. Bright flames appear to blaze up in the hall. When the gods are completely engulfed by them, the curtain falls.

THE RING OF
THE NIBELUNG

*DER RING
DES NIBELUNGEN*

A Stage Festival Play for Three Days
and a Preliminary Evening

*Ein Bühnenfestspiel für drei Tage
und einen Vorabend*

Author's dedication:

Conceived with faith in the German spirit and brought to
completion for the glory of his noble benefactor
King Ludwig II of Bavaria by
Richard Wagner.

*Im Vertrauen auf den deutschen Geist entworfen und zum
Ruhme seines erhabenen Wohltäters des Königs Ludwig II
von Bayern vollendet von
Richard Wagner.*

DAS RHEINGOLD

(VORABEND)

VORSPIEL UND ERSTE SZENE

In der Tiefe des Rheines

Grünliche Dämmerung, nach oben zu lichter, nach unten zu dunkler. Die Höhe ist von wogendem Gewässer erfüllt, das rastlos von rechts nach links zu strömt. Nach der Tiefe zu lösen die Fluten sich in einen immer feineren feuchten Nebel auf, so daß der Raum der Manneshöhe vom Boden auf gänzlich frei vom Wasser zu sein scheint, welches wie in Wolkenzügen über den nächtlichen Grund dahinfließt. Überall ragen schroffe Felsenriffe aus der Tiefe auf und grenzen den Raum der Bühne ab; der ganze Boden ist in ein wildes Zackengewirr zerspalten, so daß er nirgends vollkommen eben ist und nach allen Seiten hin in dichtester Finsternis tiefere Schlüfte annehmen läßt. – Das Orchester beginnt bei noch niedergezogenem Vorhange.

Hier wird der Vorhang aufgezogen [Takt 126].

Volles Wogen der Wassertiefe

Um ein Riff in der Mitte der Bühne, welches mit seiner schlanken Spitze bis in die dichtere, heller dämmernde Wasserflut hinaufragt, kreist in anmutig schwimmender Bewegung eine der Rheintöchter.

WOGLINDE
Weia! Waga!
Woge, du Welle,
walle zur Wiege!

THE RHINEGOLD

(PRELIMINARY EVENING)

PRELUDE AND SCENE ONE

In the depths of the Rhine

Greenish twilight, getting lighter towards the top, darker towards the bottom. Surging waters fill the upper space, flowing restlessly from right to left. Deeper down, the floods evaporate into a damp mist, constantly thinning out so that a space the height of a man, from the floor up, seems to be entirely free of the water that floats instead over the nocturnal river bed like moving slivers of cloud. Everywhere steep rocky reefs rear up out of the depths, bordering the stage and defining its space; the entire bottom of the river is fractured by a maze of jagged edges, making it nowhere completely flat and suggesting deeper ravines on all sides stretching out into a chain of darkness. – The curtain remains closed when the orchestra starts playing.

The curtain is raised here [bar 126].

Deep water currents at full force

With graceful swimming movements at the centre of the stage picture, one of the Rhinedaughters circles a reef, its slender pinnacle towering upwards into a denser flood of water and brighter dawning light.

WOGLINDE
    Weia! Waga!
    Swell up, you waters,
    in waves to our cradle!

Wagalaweia!
Wallala weiala weia!
Wellgundes Stimme von oben

WELLGUNDE
Woglinde, wachst du allein?
Sie taucht aus der Flut zum Riff herab.

WOGLINDE
Mit Wellgunde wär' ich zu zwei.

WELLGUNDE
Laß sehn, wie du wachst!
Sie sucht Woglinde zu erhaschen.

WOGLINDE *entweicht ihr schwimmend*
Sicher vor dir!
Sie necken sich und suchen sich spielend zu fangen.
Floßhildes Stimme von oben

FLOSSHILDE
10 Heiala weia!
Wildes Geschwister!

WELLGUNDE
Floßhilde, schwimm!
Woglinde flieht:
hilf mir, die Fließende fangen!
Floßhilde taucht herab und fährt zwischen die Spielenden.

FLOSSHILDE
Des Goldes Schlaf
hütet ihr schlecht!
Besser bewacht
des Schlummernden Bett,
sonst büßt ihr beide das Spiel!
Mit muntrem Gekreisch fahren die beiden auseinander:
Floßhilde sucht, bald die eine, bald die andere zu erha-
schen; sie entschlüpfen ihr und vereinigen sich endlich, um
gemeinsam auf Floßhilde Jagd zu machen. So schnellen sie
gleich Fischen von Riff zu Riff, scherzend und lachend. –
Aus einer finstren Schlucht ist währenddem Alberich, an
einem Riffe klimmend, dem Abgrunde entstiegen. Er hält,
noch vom Dunkel umgeben, an und schaut dem Spiele der
Rheintöchter mit steigendem Wohlgefallen zu.

Wagalaweia!

Wallala weiala weia!

Wellgunde's voice from above

WELLGUNDE

Woglinde, you're on watch alone?

She dives down out of the water onto the reef.

WOGLINDE

With Wellgunde there'd be two of us.

WELLGUNDE

Let's see how awake you are!

She tries to catch Woglinde.

WOGLINDE *swimming out of her reach*

Safe from you!

They tease and playfully try to lure each other into a trap.

Flosshilde's voice from above

FLOSSHILDE

Heiala weia!

You sisters are wild!

WELLGUNDE

Flosshilde, swim!

Woglinde's getting away:

help me catch the slippery thing!

Flosshilde dives down and intervenes in her sisters' games.

FLOSSHILDE

You're careless with

the gold's slumber!

Better to watch

the bed where it rests,

or you'll both rue the fun and games!

Screaming with laughter, the two separate: Flosshilde tries to snatch first one, then the other; they elude her and eventually unite to chase Flosshilde together. In this formation they dive like fish quickly from reef to reef, joking and laughing. – Meanwhile, Alberich, clambering on one of the reefs, has emerged from a murky chasm in the abyss. Still surrounded by darkness, he stops to look at the Rhinedaughters' games, liking what he sees more and more.

ALBERICH *mit rauher Trockenheit im Ton**

20   Hehe! Ihr Nicker!
     Die Mädchen halten, sobald sie Alberichs Stimme hören,
     mit dem Spiele ein.
     Wie seid ihr niedlich,
     neidliches Volk!
     Aus Nibelheims Nacht
     naht' ich mich gern,
     neigtet ihr euch zu mir!

WOGLINDE
     Hei! Wer ist dort?

WELLGUNDE
     Es dämmert und ruft!

FLOSSHILDE
     Lugt, wer uns belauscht!
     Sie tauchen tiefer herab und erkennen den Nibelung.

WOGLINDE *und* WELLGUNDE
     Pfui! Der Garstige!

FLOSSHILDE *schnell auftauchend*

30   Hütet das Gold!
     Die beiden andern folgen ihr, und alle drei versammeln
     sich schnell um das mittlere Riff.
     Vater warnte
     vor solchem Feind.

ALBERICH
     Ihr da oben!

WOGLINDE, WELLGUNDE, FLOSSHILDE
     Was willst du dort unten?

ALBERICH
     Stör' ich eu'r Spiel,
     wenn staunend ich still hier steh'?
     Tauchtet ihr nieder,
     mit euch tollte
     und neckte der Niblung sich gern.

WOGLINDE

40   Mit uns will er spielen?

ALBERICH *with a raw dryness of tone**

Hey! You sprites there! 20

    The girls stop playing their games as soon as they hear
    Alberich's voice.

How lovable you look,

you quarrelsome people!

Out of Nibelheim's night

I'll gladly approach,

if you'll get closer to me!

WOGLINDE

Hey! Who's there?

WELLGUNDE

It's dim and it's calling!

FLOSSHILDE

Well, look who's eavesdropping on us!

    They dive deeper down and see the Nibelung.

WOGLINDE *and* WELLGUNDE

Ugh! What filth!

FLOSSHILDE *quickly diving upwards*

Protect the gold! 30

    The other two follow her, and all three fall into line
    quickly around the reef in the middle.

Father warned

of an enemy like this.

ALBERICH

You up there!

WOGLINDE, WELLGUNDE, FLOSSHILDE

You down there, what's up?

ALBERICH

Am I a spoilsport

just standing here, quietly marvelling?

If you dive down here,

the Nibelung will be glad to play

and raise hell with you.

WOGLINDE

He wants to play with us? 40

---

* Asterisks indicate Wagner's directions from the 1876 Bayreuth rehearsals.
See Sources of the German Text, p. 723

WELLGUNDE
Ist ihm das Spott?

ALBERICH
Wie scheint im Schimmer
ihr hell und schön!
Wie gern umschlänge
der Schlanken eine mein Arm,
schlüpfte hold sie herab!

FLOSSHILDE
Nun lach' ich der Furcht:
der Feind ist verliebt!

WELLGUNDE
Der lüsterne Kauz!

WOGLINDE
50 Laßt ihn uns kennen!
*Sie läßt sich auf die Spitze des Riffes hinab, an dessen
Fuße Alberich angelangt ist.*

ALBERICH
Die neigt sich herab!

WOGLINDE
Nun nahe dich mir!
*Alberich klettert mit koboldartiger Behendigkeit, doch
wiederholt aufgehalten, der Spitze des Riffes zu.*

ALBERICH *hastig*
Garstig glatter
glitschriger Glimmer!
Wie gleit' ich aus!
Mit Händen und Füßen
nicht fasse noch halt' ich
das schlecke Geschlüpfer!
Er prustet.
Feuchtes Naß
60 füllt mir die Nase –
verfluchtes Niesen!
Er ist in Woglindes Nähe angelangt.

WOGLINDE *lachend*
Prustend naht
meines Freiers Pracht!

WELLGUNDE
  Is he serious?
ALBERICH
  In the gleaming light you look
  so fair and lovely!
  How my arms would love
  to embrace one of those slim shapes,
  should she obligingly slip down here!
FLOSSHILDE
  Now I laugh at my fear:
  our enemy's in love!
WELLGUNDE
  Horny freak!
WOGLINDE
  Let's teach him who we are!   50
    She lowers herself onto the pinnacle of the reef, the foot
    of which Alberich has reached.
ALBERICH
  Down she comes!
WOGLINDE
  Get closer to me!
    With imp-like alacrity, Alberich clambers up towards the
    pinnacle of the reef, but repeatedly gets stuck.
ALBERICH *rushed*
  Filthy, slithery,
  slimy surface!
  I'm sliding off!
  With hands and feet
  I can't catch or hold
  the slippery lovelies!
    He sneezes violently.
  My nose's stuffed up
  with soggy slime –   60
  sneezing be damned!
    He has arrived close to Woglinde.
WOGLINDE *laughing*
  The wheezing splendour
  of my suitor is nigh!

ALBERICH
  Mein Friedel sei,
  du fräuliches Kind!
    Er sucht, sie zu umfassen.
WOGLINDE *sich ihm entwindend*
  Willst du mich frein,
  so freie mich
    Sie taucht zu einem andern Riff auf.
                hier!
    Die Schwestern lachen.
ALBERICH *kratzt sich den Kopf*
  O weh! Du entweichst?
  Komm doch wieder!
70 Schwer ward mir,
    *[Woglinde] schwingt sich auf ein drittes Riff in grösserer
    Tiefe.*
  was so leicht du erschwingst.
WOGLINDE
  Steig nur zu Grund,
  da greifst du mich sicher!
ALBERICH *hastig hinabkletternd*
  Wohl besser da unten!
WOGLINDE *schnellt sich rasch aufwärts nach einem höheren
    Riff zur Seite.*
  Nun aber nach oben!
WELLGUNDE, FLOSSHILDE *lachend*
  Hahahahahaha!
ALBERICH
  Wie fang' ich im Sprung
  den spröden Fisch?
  Warte, du Falsche!
    Er will ihr eilig nachklettern.
WELLGUNDE *hat sich auf ein tieferes Riff auf der andern Seite
    gesenkt.*
80 Heia, du Holder!
  Hörst du mich nicht?
ALBERICH *sehr heftig und gierig**
    sich umwendend
  Rufst du nach mir?

ALBERICH
  Be my beloved,
  you womanly child!
    He tries to embrace her.
WOGLINDE *twisting out of his grasp*
  If win me you will,
  then win me
    She dives up to another reef.
        here!
    The sisters laugh.
ALBERICH *scratches his head*
  Oh no! You're escaping?
  Please come back!
  It's hard for me   70
    *[Woglinde] swings herself over to a third reef deeper
    down.*
  to move as easily as you.
WOGLINDE
  Just climb to the bottom,
  there you'll get me for sure!
ALBERICH *hurriedly clambering downwards*
  Down there's much better!
WOGLINDE *dives upwards quickly to a higher reef at the
    side.*
  Now up to the top!
WELLGUNDE, FLOSSHILDE *laughing*
  Hahahahahaha!
ALBERICH
  How do I jump and catch
  the tiresome fish?
  Wait, you cheat!
    He wants to clamber after her fast.
WELLGUNDE *has settled down on a lower reef on the other
    side.*
  Hey, my darling!   80
  Can't you hear me?
ALBERICH *very fiercely and covetously* *
    swivelling around
  Are you talking to me?

WELLGUNDE
  Ich rate dir wohl:
  zu mir wende dich,
  Woglinde meide!
ALBERICH *indem er hastig über den Bodengrund zu Well-*
    gunde hin klettert
  Viel schöner bist du
  als jene Scheue,
  die minder gleißend
  und gar zu glatt.
90 Nur tiefer tauche,
  willst du mir taugen.
WELLGUNDE *noch etwas mehr sich herabsenkend*
  Bin nun ich dir nah?
ALBERICH
  Noch nicht genug!
  Die schlanken Arme
  schlinge um mich,
  daß ich den Nacken
  dir neckend betaste,
  mit schmeichelnder Brunst
  an die schwellende Brust mich dir schmiege!
WELLGUNDE
100 Bist du verliebt
  und lüstern nach Minne,
  laß sehn, du Schöner,
  wie bist du zu schaun?
  Pfui! Du haariger,
  höckriger Geck!
  Schwarzes, schwieliges
  Schwefelgezwerg!
  Such dir ein Friedel,
  dem du gefällst!
ALBERICH *sucht, sie mit Gewalt zu halten.*
110 Gefall' ich dir nicht,
  dich faß' ich doch fest!
WELLGUNDE *schnell zum mittleren Riff auftauchend*
  Nur fest, sonst fließ' ich dir fort!

WELLGUNDE
   Here's good advice:
   start turning to me,
   avoid Woglinde!
ALBERICH *while he's clambering hurriedly over the river bed*
    to Wellgunde
   You're much prettier
   than your bashful sister;
   she's less sparky,
   and much too slippery.
   But dive deeper   90
   if you want to please me.
WELLGUNDE *sinking herself down a bit more*
   Am I now close to you?
ALBERICH
   Not enough yet!
   Put those slender arms
   right around me,
   that I may teasingly
   touch that neck,
   and with lusting flattery
   snuggle myself into your swelling bosom!
WELLGUNDE
   As you're smitten   100
   and lusting for love,
   let's see, you handsome creature,
   what you're like to look at?
   Ugh! You hairy
   humpback of a fool!
   Black, bumpy
   sulphurous dwarf!
   Seek out a lover
   who'll like you!
ALBERICH *tries with force to hang onto her.*
   You don't like me,   110
   but I'll hold you tight!
WELLGUNDE *diving up quickly to the central reef*
   Tightly then, or I'll slither away!

WOGLINDE, FLOSSHILDE *lachend*
> Hahahahahaha!

ALBERICH *Wellgunden erbost nachzankend*
> Falsches Kind!
> Kalter, grätiger Fisch!
> Schein' ich nicht schön dir,
> niedlich und neckisch,
> glatt und glau –
> hei! So buhle mit Aalen,
120 > ist dir eklig mein Balg!

FLOSSHILDE
> Was zankst du, Alb?
> Schon so verzagt?
> Du freitest um zwei:
> frügst du die dritte,
> süßen Trost
> schüfe die Traute dir!

ALBERICH
> Holder Sang
> singt zu mir her!
> Wie gut, daß ihr
130 > eine nicht seid:
> von vielen gefall' ich wohl einer,
> bei einer kieste mich keine!
> Soll ich dir glauben,
> so gleite herab!
>> *[Floßhilde] taucht zu Alberich herab.*

FLOSSHILDE
> Wie törig seid ihr,
> dumme Schwestern,
> dünkt euch dieser nicht schön!

ALBERICH *hastig ihr nahend*
> Für dumm und häßlich
> darf ich sie halten,
140 > seit ich dich Holdeste seh'!

FLOSSHILDE *schmeichelnd*
> O singe fort
> so süß und fein,

WOGLINDE, FLOSSHILDE *laughing*
　Hahahahahaha!
ALBERICH *bawling furiously in Wellgunde's wake*
　Treacherous brat!
　Cold, bony, grump of a fish!
　To you I'm not handsome,
　sweet or sparkling,
　smooth or sharp –
　hey! So hang out with eels,
　if my body disgusts you!   120
FLOSSHILDE
　What's the fuss, dwarf?
　Already losing heart?
　Two you've pursued:
　if you ask the third,
　your life's love will bring
　sweet consolation!
ALBERICH
　Lovely singing
　sounds in my ear!
　It's good there's more
　than one of you: 130
　with many I can please at least one,
　with only one, nobody would have me!
　So if I'm to believe you,
　glide down here!
　　[Flosshilde] dives down to Alberich.
FLOSSHILDE
　How foolish you are,
　stupid sisters,
　to think him not handsome!
ALBERICH *hurriedly getting close to her*
　I'm minded to think
　them vapid and vile
　now I see you, fairest of all!   140
FLOSSHILDE *flatteringly*
　O sing more
　that's sweet and fine,

wie hehr verführt es mein Ohr!

ALBERICH *zutraulich sie berührend*
Mir zagt, zuckt
und zehrt sich das Herz,
lacht mir so zierliches Lob.

FLOSSHILDE *ihn sanft abwehrend*
Wie deine Anmut
mein Aug' erfreut,
deines Lächelns Milde
150 den Mut mir labt!
      Sie zieht ihn zärtlich an sich.
Seligster Mann!

ALBERICH
Süßeste Maid!

FLOSSHILDE
Wärst du mir hold!

ALBERICH
Hielt' ich dich immer.

FLOSSHILDE *ihn ganz in ihren Armen haltend*
Deinen stechenden Blick,
deinen struppigen Bart,
o säh ich ihn, faßt' ich ihn stets!
Deines stachligen Haares
strammes Gelock,
160 umflöss' es Floßhilde ewig!
Deine Krötengestalt,
deiner Stimme Gekrächz,
o dürft' ich staunend und stumm
sie nur hören und sehn!
      Woglinde und Wellgunde sind nahe herabgetaucht.

WOGLINDE, WELLGUNDE *lachend*
Hahahahahaha!

ALBERICH *erschreckt aus Floßhildes Armen auffahrend*
Lacht ihr Bösen mich aus?

FLOSSHILDE *sich plötzlich ihm entreißend*
      lustig
Wie billig am Ende vom Lied!

how nobly it seduces my ear!

ALBERICH *touching her trustingly*
My heart flutters, flounders,
and sets itself on fire
at the mere smile of your exquisite praise.

FLOSSHILDE *gently fending him off*
How your elegance
pleases my eye,
your gentle laughter
replenishes my spirit!   150
   Tenderly she draws him towards her.
Man most blessed!

ALBERICH
Young woman most sweet!

FLOSSHILDE
Were you my love!

ALBERICH
I'd hold you for ever.

FLOSSHILDE *holding him completely in her arms*
Your piercing look,
your scrubby beard,
could I but see it, constantly hold it!
The tight curling
of your prickly hair,
could it but engulf Flosshilde for ever!   160
Your toad-like form,
the croaking of your voice,
could I but hear and see them
in speechless amazement!
   Woglinde and Wellgunde have dived down to be nearer.

WOGLINDE, WELLGUNDE *laughing*
Hahahahahaha!

ALBERICH *starting up, shocked, out of Flosshilde's arms*
Are you evil things making fun of me?

FLOSSHILDE *suddenly wrenching herself away from him
    merrily*
Just how the song should end!

Sie taucht mit den Schwestern schnell auf.

WOGLINDE, WELLGUNDE *lachend*
Hahahahahaha!

ALBERICH *mit kreischender Stimme*
Wehe! Ach wehe!
170 O Schmerz! O Schmerz!
Die dritte, so traut,
betrog sie mich auch?
Ihr schmählich schlaues,
liederlich schlechtes Gelichter!
Nährt ihr nur Trug,
ihr treuloses Nickergezücht?

WOGLINDE, WELLGUNDE, FLOSSHILDE
Wallala! Wallala!
Lalaleia, leialalei!
Heia! Heia! Haha!
180 Schäme dich, Albe!
Schilt nicht dort unten!
Höre, was wir dich heißen!
Warum, du Banger,
bandest du nicht
das Mädchen, das du minnst?
Treu sind wir
und ohne Trug
dem Freier, der uns fängt.
Greife nur zu
190 und grause dich nicht:
in der Flut entfliehn wir nicht leicht:
Wallala! Lalaleia! Leialalei!
Heia! Heia! Hahei!

*Sie schwimmen auseinander, hierher und dorthin, bald
tiefer, bald höher, um Alberich zur Jagd auf sie zu reizen.*

ALBERICH
Wie in den Gliedern
brünstige Glut
mir brennt und glüht!
Wut und Minne,
wild und mächtig,

She dives up quickly with her sisters.

WOGLINDE, WELLGUNDE *laughing*

Hahahahahaha!

ALBERICH *his voice screaming*

Horror! Oh, horror!

The pain! The pain! 170

The third, so trusting,

she cheated me too?

You miserably sly,

slovenly, dissolute riff-raff!

Is breeding deceit all you do,

you fickle flock of water-sprites?

WOGLINDE, WELLGUNDE, FLOSSHILDE

Wallala! Wallala!

Lalaleia, leialalei!

Heia! Heia! Haha!

For shame, dwarf! 180

Don't tell us off down there!

Listen to what we're telling you to do!

Why, you worrier,

didn't you tie up

the girl you desire?

We're faithful

and don't lie

to the suitor tying us down.

Just take your pick

and don't dread it: 190

in these torrents, we can't easily escape:

Wallala! Lalaleia! Leialalei!

Heia! Heia! Hahei!

They swim apart, here and there, now deeper, now
higher, provoking Alberich into hunting them down.

ALBERICH

Like the unruly inferno

coursing through my limbs,

I'm burning and glowing!

Anger and love,

wild and strong,

wühlt mir den Mut auf. –

200   Wie ihr auch lacht und lügt,
lüstern lechz' ich nach euch,
und eine muß mir erliegen!

*Er macht sich mit verzweifelter Anstrengung zur Jagd
auf: mit grauenhafter Behendigkeit erklimmt er Riff für
Riff, springt von einem zum andern, sucht bald dieses,
bald jenes der Mädchen zu erhaschen, die mit lustigem
Gekreisch stets ihm ausweichen.*

*Er strauchelt, stürzt in den Abgrund und klettert dann
hastig wieder in die Höhe zu neuer Jagd.*

[Die Mädchen] neigen sich etwas herab.

*Fast erreicht er sie, stürzt abermals zurück und ver-
sucht es nochmals.*

*[Alberich] hält endlich, vor Wut schäumend, atemlos an
und streckt die geballte Faust nach den Mädchen hinauf.*

*Mit äußerster Heftgkeit**
kaum seiner mächtig

Fing' eine diese Faust!

*Er verbleibt in sprachloser Wut, den Blick aufwärts ge-
richtet, wo er dann plötzlich von dem folgenden Schau-
spiele angezogen und gefesselt wird.*

*Durch die Flut ist von oben her ein immer lichterer
Schein gedrungen, der sich an einer hohen Stelle des mit-
telsten Riffes allmählich zu einem blendend hell strahlen-
den Goldglanze entzündet; ein zauberisch goldenes Licht
bricht von hier durch das Wasser.*

*Ganz ruhige Bewegungen der Rheintöchter**

WOGLINDE
Lugt, Schwestern!
Die Weckerin lacht in den Grund.

WELLGUNDE
Durch den grünen Schwall
den wonnigen Schläfer sie grüßt.

FLOSSHILDE
Jetzt küßt sie sein Auge,
daß er es öffne.

are stirring up my being. –
Fool around and fib as you like,

200

I'm lusting lecherously after you,
and one of you must yield to me!

He starts chasing them with frantic strenuousness: with nightmarish alacrity he scrambles on reef after reef and leaps from one to another, trying to snatch one, then more of the girls, who keep dodging out of his way, screeching with laughter.

He trips up, falls into the abyss, and then clambers hurriedly back towards the top to start a new hunt.

[The girls] move a bit further down.

He nearly gets to them, only to fall back a second time and try again.

Foaming with rage and out of breath, [Alberich] eventually stops and shakes a clenched fist at the girls above.

With extreme ferocity*
scarcely in control of himself

This fist need catch only one!

He freezes in inchoate rage, his eyes fixed upwards, when he's suddenly attracted and riveted by the following spectacle.

An ever clearer glow has begun to permeate the torrents above at a high point on the central reef and gradually blazes up into a dazzlingly bright ray of brilliant gold; from this position a magically golden light penetrates the water.

The Rhinedaughters' movements completely calm*

WOGLINDE

Look, sisters!
The rising sun smiles into the river's bed.

WELLGUNDE

Through green waters
she greets the gold blissfully asleep.

FLOSSHILDE

She kisses his eyes now
that he may open them.

WELLGUNDE

210   Schaut, er lächelt
       in lichtem Schein.

WOGLINDE

       Durch die Fluten hin
       fließt sein strahlender Stern!

       Die drei Rheintöchter zusammen das Riff anmutig um-
       schwimmend:

WOGLINDE, WELLGUNDE, FLOSSHILDE

       Heiajaheia!
       Heiajaheia!
       Wallalalalala leiajahei!
       Rheingold!
       Rheingold!
       Leuchtende Lust,
220   wie lachst du so hell und hehr!
       Glühender Glanz
       entgleißet dir weihlich im Wag!
       Heiajahei!
       Heiajaheia!
       Wache, Freund!
       Wache froh!
       Wonnige Spiele
       spenden wir dir:
       flimmert der Fluß,
230   flammet die Flut,
       umfließen wir tauchend,
       tanzend und singend
       im seligem Bade dein Bett!
       Rheingold!
       Rheingold!
       Heiajaheia!
       Heiajaheia!
       Wallalalalalaleia jahei!

       Mit immer ausgelassenerer Lust umschwimmen die Mäd-
       chen das Riff. Die ganze Flut flimmert in hellem Gold-
       glanze.

WELLGUNDE
Look, he smiles   210
in the clear light.
WOGLINDE
His shining star streams
forth into the flood!
The three Rhinedaughters in consort swimming graceful-
ly around the reef:
WOGLINDE, WELLGUNDE, FLOSSHILDE
Heiajaheia!
Heiajaheia!
Wallalalalala leiajahei!
Rhinegold!
Rhinegold!
Radiant bliss,
how bright and regal your smile!   220
Blazing brilliance
flows from you wondrously in waves!
Heiajahei!
Heiajaheia!
Wake up, friend,
wake, be glad!
Entrancing games
are our gift to you:
the stream shimmers,
the flood's in flames,   230
we're surrounding your bed,
dancing and singing,
diving and bathing in bliss!
Rhinegold!
Rhinegold!
Heiajaheia!
Heiajaheia!
Wallalalalalaleia jahei!
With ever more uninhibited pleasure, the girls swim
around the reef. The entire floodwater shimmers in the
brightness of the shining gold.

ALBERICH *dessen Augen, mächtig von dem Glanze angezo-*
gen, starr auf dem Golde haften
Was ist's, ihr Glatten,
240   das dort so glänzt und gleißt?

WOGLINDE, WELLGUNDE, FLOSSHILDE
Wo bist du Rauher denn heim,
daß vom Rheingold nicht du gehört?

WELLGUNDE
Nichts weiß der Alb
von des Goldes Auge,
das wechselnd wacht und schläft?

WOGLINDE
Von der Wassertiefe
wonnigem Stern,
der hehr die Wogen durchhellt?

WOGLINDE, WELLGUNDE, FLOSSHILDE
Sieh, wie selig
250   im Glanze wir gleiten!
Willst du Banger
in ihm dich baden,
so schwimm und schwelge mit uns!
Wallalalalaleialalei!
Wallalalalaleia jahei!

ALBERICH
Eurem Taucherspiele
nur taugte das Gold?
Mir gält' es dann wenig!

WOGLINDE
Des Goldes Schmuck
260   schmähte er nicht,
wüßte er all seine Wunder!

WELLGUNDE
Der Welt Erbe
gewänne zu eigen,
wer aus dem Rheingold
schüfe den Ring,
der maßlose Macht ihm verlieh'.

ALBERICH *whose eyes, strongly attracted by its brightness,*
    are rigidly fixed on the gold
  You slippery ones, what's
  that there shining and glowing?   240

WOGLINDE, WELLGUNDE, FLOSSHILDE
  You hoodlum, where've you been living
  that you haven't heard of the Rhinegold?

WELLGUNDE
  Does the dwarf know nothing
  about the eye of the gold,
  swaying between waking and slumber?

WOGLINDE
  Or the entrancing star
  from the waters' deep,
  regally flooding the waves with light?

WOGLINDE, WELLGUNDE, FLOSSHILDE
  See, how happily
  we float in its shine!   250
  If you want to bathe in it,
  you lily-livered dwarf,
  come swimming and swirling with us!
  Wallalalalaleialalei!
  Wallalalalaleia jahei!

ALBERICH
  Are your diving antics
  all the gold's good for?
  That's no good to me!

WOGLINDE
  He wouldn't scorn
  the golden jewel,   260
  if he knew all its marvels!

WELLGUNDE
  He shall inherit
  the world for himself,
  whoever forges the ring
  from the Rhinegold
  that will grant him measureless power.

FLOSSHILDE
Der Vater sagt' es,
und uns befahl er,
klug zu hüten
270   den klaren Hort,
daß kein Falscher der Flut ihn entführe:
drum schweigt, ihr schwatzendes Heer!

WELLGUNDE
Du klügste Schwester,
verklagst du uns wohl?
Weißt du denn nicht,
wem nur allein,
das Gold zu schmieden, vergönnt?

WOGLINDE *Kein starkes Hervortreten individuellen Empfin-
dens* *
Nur wer der Minne
Macht versagt,
280   nur wer der Liebe
Lust verjagt,
nur der erzielt sich den Zauber,
zum Reif zu zwingen das Gold.

WELLGUNDE
Wohl sicher sind wir
und sorgenfrei,
denn, was nur lebt, will lieben,
meiden will keiner die Minne.

WOGLINDE
Am wenigsten er,
der lüsterne Alb;
290   vor Liebesgier
möcht' er vergehn.

FLOSSHILDE
Nicht fürcht' ich den,
wie ich ihn erfand:
seiner Minne Brunst
brannte fast mich.

WELLGUNDE
Ein Schwefelbrand
in der Wogen Schwall,

FLOSSHILDE
  Father said so,
  and commanded us
  to guard the gleaming hoard
  with guile, should a cheat   270
  want to abduct it from the waters:
  so lips sealed, you gossiping horde!

WELLGUNDE
  Are you blaming us,
  you brightest sister of all?
  Don't you know about
  the only being who
  will be granted the ability to forge the gold?

WOGLINDE *Showing no marked emergence of personal*
    *feelings**
  Whoever denies
  the power of love,
  whoever banishes   280
  the delights of the flesh,
  only he can conjure up the magic
  that turns the gold into the ring.

WELLGUNDE
  We're safe then
  and needn't worry,
  because what lives wants love,
  no one will ever shun that.

WOGLINDE
  Especially our
  horny dwarf;
  he'd like to die   290
  just craving it.

FLOSSHILDE
  I'm not afraid
  of how I imagined him:
  his carnal intensity
  almost touched me.

WELLGUNDE
  Like sulphurous surf
  in the swelling of the waves,

vor Zorn der Liebe
zischt er laut.

WOGLINDE, WELLGUNDE, FLOSSHILDE

300 Wallala! Wallaleialala!
Lieblichster Albe!
Lachst du nicht auch?
In des Goldes Scheine
wie leuchtest du schön!
O komm, Lieblicher, lache mit uns!
Heiajaheia! Heiajaheia!
Wallalalalalaleia jahei!

Sie schwimmen lachend im Glanze auf und ab.
[Alberich,] die Augen starr auf das Gold gerichtet, hat
dem Geplauder der Schwestern wohl gelauscht.

ALBERICH *wie in finsterem Brüten**
Der Welt Erbe
gewänn' ich zu eigen durch dich?

310 Erzwäng' ich nicht Liebe,
doch listig erzwäng' ich mir Lust?

furchtbar laut
Spottet nur zu!
Der Niblung naht eurem Spiel!

Wütend springt er nach dem mittleren Riff hinüber und
klettert in grausiger Hast nach dessen Spitze hinauf.
Die Mädchen fahren kreischend auseinander und tau-
chen nach verschiedenen Seiten hinauf.

WOGLINDE, WELLGUNDE, FLOSSHILDE
Heia! Heia! Heiajahei!
Rettet euch!
Es raset der Alb;
in den Wassern sprüht's,
wohin er springt:
die Minne macht ihn verrückt!

Sie lachen im tollsten Übermut.

320 Hahahahahahaha!

[Alberich] gelangt mit einem letzten Satze zur Spitze.

ALBERICH *mit furchtbar hervorbrechender Leidenschaft,*
die rhythmischen Akzente, desgleichen die Stabreime
hervorzuheben*

he hisses loudly
in anger about love.
WOGLINDE, WELLGUNDE, FLOSSHILDE
Wallala Wallaleialala!   300
Most darling of dwarfs!
Why not laugh too?
How radiant you look
in the glow of the gold!
O come, my darling, laugh with us!
Heiajaheia! Heiajaheia!
Wallalalalalaleia jahei!
    Laughing, they swim to and fro in the bright light.
        *[Alberich,] his eyes fixed on the gold, has been eaves-
        dropping, listening closely to the sisters' chit-chat.*
ALBERICH *brooding sinisterly**
I shall inherit
the world for myself through you?
I may not get love by force,   310
but enforce covetousness with cunning?
    terrifyingly loud
Just carry on mocking!
Unto your gold, the Nibelung is nigh!
    *He jumps furiously onto the reef in the middle and clam-
    bers up it with macabre rapidity towards the pinnacle.*
        *Screaming, the girls move apart and scatter, diving
        upwards on different sides.*
WOGLINDE, WELLGUNDE, FLOSSHILDE
Heia! Heia! Heiajahei!
Save your lives!
The dwarf's raving;
in the waters there's tumult
wherever he jumps:
Love's made him a madman!
    They laugh with the craziest recklessness.
Hahahahahahaha!   320
    [Alberich] reaches the pinnacle with a final effort.
ALBERICH *with a terrifying outburst of passion, stressing
    rhythmic accents as well as the alliterative structure of the
    verse**

Bangt euch noch nicht?
So buhlt nun im Finstern,
feuchtes Gezücht!
Er streckt die Hand nach dem Gold aus.
Das Licht lösch' ich euch aus,
entreiße dem Riff das Gold,
schmiede den rächenden Ring;
denn hör' es die Flut:
so verfluch' ich die Liebe!
Er reißt mit furchtbarer Gewalt das Gold aus dem Riffe
und stürzt dann hastig in die Tiefe, wo er schnell ver-
schwindet. Dichte Nacht bricht plötzlich überall herein.
Die Mädchen tauchen jach dem Räuber in die Tiefe nach.

FLOSSHILDE
Haltet den Räuber!

WELLGUNDE
330   Rettet das Gold!

WOGLINDE
Hilfe!

WOGLINDE, WELLGUNDE
Hilfe!

WOGLINDE, WELLGUNDE, FLOSSHILDE
Weh! Weh!
Die Flut fällt mit ihnen nach der Tiefe hinab.
Aus dem untersten Grunde hört man Alberichs gellen-
des Hohngelächter.
In dichtester Finsternis verschwinden die Riffe, die
ganze Bühne ist von der Höhe bis zur Tiefe von schwar-
zem Gewoge erfüllt, das eine Zeitlang immer nach ab-
wärts zu sinken scheint.
Allmählich sind die Wogen in Gewölk übergegangen,
welches, als eine immer heller dämmernde Beleuchtung
dahintertritt, zu feinerem Nebel sich abklärt.
Als der Nebel in zarten Wolkchen, sich gänzlich in der
Höhe verliert, wird, im Tagesgrauen eine freie Gegend
auf Bergeshöhen sichtbar. – Wotan und neben ihm Fricka,
beide schlafend, liegen zur Seite auf blumigem Grunde.

Not terrified yet?
Then tout for trade in darkness,
you clammy bunch!
   He stretches out his hand to the gold.
I'll extinguish your light,
extricate the gold from the reef,
forge the ring and exact revenge;
so let the waters listen:
love it is that I curse!
   *With terrifying violence he gouges the gold out of the reef
   and then rushes hastily into the deep, where he quickly dis-
   appears. Thick darkness suddenly descends everywhere.
   The girls dive abruptly after the thief into the deep.*

FLOSSHILDE
Stop this bandit!

WELLGUNDE
Save the gold!   330

WOGLINDE
Help!

WOGLINDE, WELLGUNDE
Help!

WOGLINDE, WELLGUNDE, FLOSSHILDE
Woe! Woe!
   The waters subside with them into the deep.
   *Alberich's ringingly scornful laughter can be heard
   from the lowest point out of the depths.*
   *In the thickest darkness, the reefs disappear; a black
   surging motion dominates the stage from top to bottom
   and for a time seems to keep sinking on a downward path.*
   *Gradually the waves turn into clouds, which resolve
   into a fine mist as an increasingly bright light emerges
   behind them.*
   *While the mist in the form of delicate wisps of cloud is
   completely fading away at the top, an open mountaintop
   area comes into view in the dawn light. – Wotan is lying
   on one side of it with Fricka next to him; both are asleep
   on a flowery bed.*

ZWEITE SZENE

Freie Gegend auf Bergeshöhen, am Rhein gelegen

Der hervorbrechende Tag beleuchtet mit wachsendem Glanze eine Burg mit blinkenden Zinnen, die auf einem Felsgipfel im Hintergrunde steht; zwischen diesem und dem Vordergrunde ist ein tiefes Tal, durch das der Rhein fließt, anzunehmen.
  Wotan und Fricka schlafend
  Die Burg ist ganz sichtbar geworden. – Fricka erwacht: ihr Auge fällt auf die Burg.
  Nicht zu heftig, sondern mehr großartig zu fassen*

FRICKA *erschrocken*
  Wotan, Gemahl! Erwache!
WOTAN *fortträumend*
  Der Wonne seligen Saal
  bewachen mir Tür und Tor:
  Mannes Ehre,
  ewige Macht
  ragen zu endlosem Ruhm!
FRICKA *rüttelt ihn*
340 Auf, aus der Träume
  wonnigem Trug!
  Erwache, Mann, und erwäge!
    Wotan erwacht und erhebt sich ein wenig; sein Blick wird
    sogleich vom Anblick der Burg gefesselt.
WOTAN
  Vollendet das ewige Werk!
  Auf Berges Gipfel
  die Götterburg;
  prächtig prahlt
  der prangende Bau!
  Wie im Traum ich ihn trug,
  wie mein Wille ihn wies,
350 stark und schön

SCENE TWO

An open mountaintop area, situated near the Rhine

The light of breaking day falls with growing splendour on a fortress with gleaming battlements visible on a rocky pinnacle in the background; between it and the foreground, a deep valley with the Rhine flowing through it is to be imagined.
  Wotan and Fricka sleeping
  The whole fortress can now be seen. – Fricka awakes: she catches sight of the fortress.
  Not to be too violently expressed, but with a touch of grandeur*

FRICKA *alarmed*
  Wotan, spouse! Wake up!
WOTAN *dreaming on*
  Over my joy in this happy building
  its portals stand guard:
  a husband's privilege,
  eternal power
  soar to infinite glory!
FRICKA *shakes him*
  Stop the dreams,   340
  the blissful lie!
  Wake up, husband, and think!
    Wotan wakes up and raises himself slightly; the sight of
    the fortress immediately captures his attention.
WOTAN
  Achieved, the immortal work!
  The gods' fortress,
  the mountain's crown,
  the superb swagger
  of the brilliant building!
  As I carried it in my dreams,
  as my will revealed it,
  strong and fine   350

steht er zur Schau:
hehrer, herrlicher Bau!

FRICKA *Alles nun folgende Dialogische mit besonderer Ver-*
meidung jedes Schleppens! 'Wenn ihr nicht so langweilige
Kerle wärt, müßte das "Rheingold" in zwei Stunden fertig
sein.'*

Nur Wonne schafft dir,
was mich erschreckt?
Dich freut die Burg,
mir bangt es um Freia!
Achtloser, laß mich erinnern
des ausbedungenen Lohns!
Die Burg ist fertig,
360   verfallen das Pfand:
vergaßest du, was du vergabst?

WOTAN

Wohl dünkt mich's, was sie bedangen,
die dort die Burg mir gebaut;
durch Vertrag zähmt' ich
ihr trotzig Gezücht,
daß sie die hehre
Halle mir schüfen;
die steht nun – dank den Starken: –
um den Sold sorge dich nicht.

FRICKA *das Tempo wie in der gesprochenen Rede!**
370   O lachend frevelnder Leichtsinn!
Liebelosester Frohmut!
Wußt' ich um euren Vertrag,
dem Truge hätt' ich gewehrt;
doch mutig entfernet
ihr Männer die Frauen,
um taub und ruhig vor uns
allein mit den Riesen zu tagen:
so ohne Scham
verschenktet ihr Frechen
380   Freia, mein holdes Geschwister,
froh des Schächergewerbs!
Was ist euch Harten

it's there for all to see:
an august, lofty edifice!

FRICKA *All the following dialogue with particular avoid-*
ance of any kind of dragging! 'If you weren't such boring
numbskulls, "Rhinegold" would be over within two
hours.' *

Is what terrifies me
only what you enjoy?
You rejoice in the fortress,
I tremble for Freia!
Foolhardy man, let me recall
what you agreed to pay!
The fortress is built,
the pledge overdue: 360
did you forget what you promised?

WOTAN

I recall indeed the promise extracted
by the builders of my fortress;
I held their hostile race
in check with contract law,
stipulating that they create
my regal palace;
that's in place – due to their power: –
so don't worry about the price.

FRICKA *the tempo the same as in a spoken monologue!* *

O ludicrously lawless negligence!   370
Joy without the slightest compassion!
I'd have stopped the lies
if I'd had an inkling of your contract;
but you men had the nerve
to keep the women at bay,
so you could quietly meet the giants
ahead of us, alone, deaf to our view:
you brass-necked creatures
shamelessly bartered away
Freia, my dear sibling,   380
cocky about your shady dealings!
What is still sacred

    doch heilig und wert,
    giert ihr Männer nach Macht?
WOTAN *ruhig*
    Gleiche Gier
    war Fricka wohl fremd,
    als selbst um den Bau sie mich bat?
FRICKA *Sehr innig, aber den Sprechton nicht verlassen* *
    Um des Gatten Treue besorgt
    muß traurig ich wohl sinnen,
390   wie an mich er zu fesseln,
    zieht's in die Ferne ihn fort:
    herrliche Wohnung,
    wonniger Hausrat
    sollten dich binden
    zu säumender Rast.
    Doch du bei dem Wohnbau sannst
    auf Wehr und Wall allein:
       energisch hervorzuheben *
    Herrschaft und Macht
    soll er dir mehren;
400   nur rastlosern Sturm zu erregen,
    erstand dir die ragende Burg.
WOTAN *lächelnd*
    Wolltest du Frau
    in der Feste mich fangen,
    mir Gotte mußt du schon gönnen,
    daß, in der Burg
    gefangen, ich mir
    von außen gewinne die Welt:
    Wandel und Wechsel
    liebt, wer lebt;
410   das Spiel drum kann ich nicht sparen!
FRICKA *sehr heftig* *
    Liebeloser,
    leidigster Mann!
    Um der Macht und Herrschaft
    müßigen Tand
    verspielst du in lästerndem Spott
    Liebe und Weibes Wert?

and dear to thugs like you,
once you men crave power?
WOTAN *calmly*
Fricka of course was innocent
of the same craving
when she asked me for the building?
FRICKA *Very heartfelt, but not losing the sense of speech**
Concern about my husband's fidelity
is sadly what I have to keep in mind,
how to keep him tied to me   390
when he's drawn to distant lands:
a lofty home,
a happy household
were to commit you
to staying longer.
But you thought of the house
solely as defence and reinforcement:
   the following to be thrown into sharp relief*
to extend your rule and power
is why it's there;
to unleash storms more unsettling still   400
is why the towering fortress was built.
WOTAN *smiling*
Wife, if you want me
confined to barracks,
you must at least allow me
as a god, a prisoner
in this fortress,
to win the world from outside:
whoever's alive, loves
transformation and change;
it's a sport I can't do without!   410
FRICKA *very violently**
Compassionless,
most irksome man!
For power and rule and its
pointless playthings
you fritter away with abusive scorn
the worth of love and wife?

WOTAN *ernst*
   Um dich zum Weib zu gewinnen,
   mein eines Auge
   setzt' ich werbend daran;
420   wie törig tadelst du jetzt!
   Ehr' ich die Frauen
   doch mehr, als dich freut;
   und Freia, die Gute,
   geb' ich nicht auf;
   nie sann dies ernstlich mein Sinn.

FRICKA *mit ängstlicher Spannung in die Szene blickend*
   So schirme sie jetzt:
   in schutzloser Angst
   läuft sie nach Hilfe dort her!
     Freia tritt, wie in hastiger Flucht auf.

FREIA
   Hilf mir, Schwester!
430   Schütze mich, Schwäher!
   Vom Felsen drüben
   drohte mir Fasolt,
   mich Holde käm' er zu holen.

WOTAN
   Laß ihn drohn!
   Sahst du nicht Loge?

FRICKA
   Daß am liebsten du immer
   dem Listigen traust!
   Viel Schlimmes schuf er uns schon,
   doch stets bestrickt er dich wieder.

WOTAN
440   Wo freier Mut frommt,
   allein frag' ich nach keinem.
   Doch des Feindes Neid
   zum Nutz sich fügen,
   lehrt nur Schlauheit und List,
   wie Loge verschlagen sie übt.
   Der zum Vertrage mir riet,
   versprach mir, Freia zu lösen:
   auf ihn verlass' ich mich nun.

WOTAN *seriously*
To win you as my wife,
I put at stake
the one eye I had left;
how stupid to chide me now!   420
I revere women
even more than would please you;
and I'll not surrender Freia,
the dear good soul;
never did I seriously consider that.

FRICKA *stiff with fear, glancing into the wings*
Then guard her this instant;
vulnerable and afraid,
she's running to us for help!
    Freia enters, as if fleeing in haste.

FREIA
Help me, sister!
Protect me, brother-in-law!   430
From the rocks over there
Fasolt threatened to come
and fetch me, the lovely Freia.

WOTAN
Let him threaten!
Didn't you see Loge?

FRICKA
You're always preferring
to trust that trickster!
He's harmed us a lot already,
yet charms you again and again.

WOTAN
Where free thinking reigns,   440
I simply ask nobody.
But to take advantage
of the enemy's hostility,
only the slyness and stealth
Loge's so good at will help us.
The contract was his advice,
and he promised Freia's release:
I'm relying on him now.

FRICKA

Und er läßt dich allein!
450 Dort schreiten rasch
die Riesen heran:
wo harrt dein schlauer Gehilf'?

FREIA

Wo harren meine Brüder,
daß Hilfe sie brächten,
da mein Schwäher die Schwache verschenkt!
Zu Hilfe, Donner!
  *Freia begleitet ihre Rufe nach Hülfe mit jammernden
  Gebärden* *
Hierher, hierher!
Rette Freia, mein Froh!

FRICKA

Die in bösem Bund dich verrieten,
460 sie alle bergen sich nun.
  *Fasolt und Fafner, beide in riesiger Gestalt, mit starken
  Pfählen bewaffnet, treten auf.*

FASOLT

Sanft schloß
Schlaf dein Aug';
wir beide bauten
Schlummers bar die Burg.
Mächt'ger Müh'
müde nie,
stauten starke
Stein' wir auf;
steiler Turm,
470 Tür und Tor,
deckt und schließt
im schlanken Schloß den Saal.
  auf die Burg deutend
Dort steht's,
was wir stemmten,
schimmernd hell,
bescheint's der Tag:
zieh nun ein,
uns zahl den Lohn!

FRICKA

And he's letting you down!
The giants are over there,   450
striding fast towards us:
where's your clever sidekick now?

FREIA

And where's my brothers' help
for their poor sister, thrown to
the dogs by her brother-in-law!
Help me, Donner!
  *Freia accompanies her cries for help with woebegone
  gestures**
Come here, come here!
My dear Froh, save Freia!

FRICKA

Your betrayers in this evil bunch
are all making themselves scarce.   460
  *Fasolt and Fafner enter, both immense figures armed with
  thick poles.*

FASOLT

Gentle sleep
closed your eyes;
devoid of sleep we both
built the fortress.
Straining every muscle,
never tired,
we piled up
massive stones;
steeply rising towers,
doors and gates   470
protect and secure
the elegant castle's hall.
  pointing at the castle
There it stands,
our handiwork,
gleaming and bright,
lit by the day:
now move in,
and pay us our wages!

WOTAN *Wie kurz abgebrochen zu sprechen, im gleichgültigen*
    *Tone**

    Nennt, Leute, den Lohn;

480   was dünkt euch zu bedingen!

FASOLT

    Bedungen ist,

    was tauglich uns dünkt:

    gemahnt es dich so matt?

    Freia, die Holde,

    Holda, die Freie –

        Mit entschlossenem Ausdruck, etwas rascher als das Vor-
        *angegangene**

    vertragen ist's,

    sie tragen wir heim.

WOTAN *schnell*

    Seid ihr bei Trost

    mit eurem Vertrag?

490   Denkt auf andern Dank:

    Freia ist mir nicht feil!

        Fasolt steht, in höchster Bestürzung, eine Weile sprachlos.

FASOLT *Die Worte heftig hervorzustoßen**

    Was sagst du? Ha!

    Sinnst du Verrat?

    Verrat am Vertrag?

        *Von hier mit festem Ausdruck**

    Die dein Speer birgt,

    sind sie dir Spiel,

    des berat'nen Bundes Runen?

FAFNER *höhnisch*

    Getreuster Bruder,

    merkst du Tropf nun Betrug?

        *Fasolt beginnt erst ruhig mit wie verhaltener Erregtheit**

FASOLT

500   Lichtsohn du,

    leicht gefügter!

    Hör und hüte dich;

    Verträgen halte Treu'!

    Was du bist,

WOTAN *In a clipped and abrupt manner with an indifferent tone**

   Name your price, comrades:

   what you think you should get!   480

FASOLT

   Agreed is that

   which seems right to us:

   you only vaguely remember?

   Freia, the fair,

   Holda, the free –

      With decisive expression, somewhat faster than the previous passage*

   as we agreed,

   we carry her home.

WOTAN *quickly*

   Has your contract

   driven you insane?

   Think of another idea: 490

   Freia's not for sale!

      Fasolt stands aghast, for a moment at a loss for words.

FASOLT *The words to be uttered fiercely**

   What are you saying? Ha!

   Thinking of betrayal?

   Breaching the contract?

      From here with firm expression*

   Those runes of solemn covenant

   enshrined in your spear,

   are they just playthings to you?

FAFNER *mockingly*

   Trustiest brother,

   dolt, don't you smell a rat?

      Fasolt begins quietly at first, as if restraining his rage*

FASOLT

   You son of the light,   500

   easy to persuade!

   Listen and watch your back;

   stay true to contracts!

   Contracts define who you are,

bist du nur durch Verträge;
bedungen ist,
wohl bedacht deine Macht:
bist weiser du,
als witzig wir sind,
510 bandest uns Freie
zum Frieden du:
  etwas beeilend. Mit Leidenschaft*
all' deinem Wissen fluch' ich,
fliehe weit deinen Frieden,
  *ein weinig zurückhaltend und mit deutlichster Betonung
  jedes Wortes**
weißt du nicht offen,
ehrlich und frei,
Verträgen zu wahren die Treu'!
Ein dummer Riese
rät dir das:
du Weiser, wiss' es von ihm!

WOTAN

520 Wie schlau für Ernst du achtest,
was wir zum Scherz nur beschlossen!
Die liebliche Göttin,
licht und leicht,
was taugt euch Tölpeln ihr Reiz?

FASOLT

Höhnst du uns?
Ha, wie unrecht!
Die ihr durch Schönheit herrscht,
schimmernd hehres Geschlecht,
wie töricht strebt ihr
530 nach Türmen von Stein,
setzt um Burg und Saal
Weibes Wonne zum Pfand!
Wir Plumpen plagen uns
schwitzend mit schwieliger Hand,
ein Weib zu gewinnen,
das wonnig und mild
bei uns Armen wohne:

you're only that;
everything considered,
your power is conditional:
because you've more
wisdom than we do,
you pledged us free   510
spirits to peace:
    *somewhat hastily. With passion**
but I'll curse all your wisdom,
and desert your peace,
    *holding back a little and with the clearest accentuation
    of each word**
if you don't openly,
honestly and freely
preserve your faith in contracts!
A stupid giant's
telling you that:
take it from him, wise that you are!

WOTAN

You're clever to take seriously   520
what we decided just in fun!
That lovely dear goddess,
pale and gentle,
of what use is she to you yokels?

FASOLT

Sneering at us?
Ha, it's not right!
You use splendour to rule,
you're a glitteringly regal race,
how foolish that you strive
after towers of stone,   530
pledge the loveliness of woman
in exchange for fortress and hall!
We crude ones slave away,
sweating with calloused hands,
to win a woman,
who'd lovingly and softly
live with us lowly mortals:

sehr heftig*
und verkehrt nennst du den Kauf?

FAFNER
Schweig dein faules Schwatzen;
540 Gewinn werben wir nicht:
Freias Haft
hilft wenig;
doch viel gilt's,
den Göttern sie zu entreißen.
leise
Goldene Äpfel
wachsen in ihrem Garten,
sie allein
weiß, die Äpfel zu pflegen;
der Frucht Genuß
550 frommt ihren Sippen
zu ewig nie
alternder Jugend:
siech und bleich
doch sinkt ihre Blüte,
alt und schwach
schwinden sie hin,
müssen Freia sie missen.
grob
Ihrer Mitte drum sei sie entführt!

WOTAN *für sich*
Loge säumt zu lang!

FASOLT
560 Schlicht gib nun Bescheid!

WOTAN
Fordert andern Sold!

FASOLT
Kein andrer: Freia allein!

FAFNER
Du da! Folge uns!
*Fafner und Fasolt dringen auf Freia ein. Froh und Don-
ner kommen eilig.*

*very forcefully**
and you call our deal perverse?

FAFNER

Enough of your lazy twaddle;
we'll get nowhere with this: 540
detaining Freia
won't help;
but it is worth
snatching her from the gods.
   quietly
Golden apples
grow in her garden,
but how to tend those apples,
only she knows;
by relishing the fruit,
her own flesh and blood   550
enjoy eternally
ageless youth:
but wasted and wan
their prime will pass,
old and weak
they'll fade away,
if it's Freia they can't keep.
   roughly
So from their midst let her be torn!

WOTAN *aside*

Loge's taking too long!

FASOLT

Give a straight answer!   560

WOTAN

Demand different terms!

FASOLT

No others: just Freia!

FAFNER

You there! Follow us!
   Fafner and Fasolt push their way to Freia. Froh and Don-
   ner come in haste.

FREIA *fliehend*
Helft! Helft, vor den Harten!
FROH *Freia in seine Arme fassend*
Zu mir, Freia!
  zu Fafner
Meide sie, Frecher!
Froh schützt die Schöne!
DONNER *sich vor die beiden Riesen stellend*
Fasolt und Fafner,
fühltet ihr schon
570   meines Hammers harten Schlag?
FAFNER
Was soll das Drohn?
FASOLT
Was dringst du her?
Kampf kiesten wir nicht,
verlangen nur unsern Lohn.
DONNER
Schon oft zahlt' ich
Riesen den Zoll.
Kommt her, des Lohnes Last
wäg' ich mit gutem Gewicht!
  Er schwingt den Hammer.
WOTAN *seinen Speer zwischen die Streitenden ausstreckend*
      mit großartiger Gebärde und großem Ausdrucke*
Halt, du Wilder!
580   Nichts durch Gewalt!
      mehr im gewöhnlichen Sprechton*
Verträge schützt
meines Speeres Schaft: –
Spar deines Hammers Heft!
FREIA
Wehe! Wehe!
Wotan verläßt mich!
FRICKA
Begreif' ich dich noch,
grausamer Mann?
  Wotan wendet sich ab und sieht Loge kommen.

FREIA *fleeing*
   Help! Protect me from these thugs!
FROH *clasping Freia in his arms*
   To me, Freia!
      to Fafner
   Hands off, brazen bully!
   Froh's lovely sister is safe with him!
DONNER *blocking both giants' paths*
   Fasolt and Fafner,
   have you ever felt
   the heavy thud of my hammer?   570
FAFNER
   Why threaten us?
FASOLT
   Why all the fuss?
   Fighting isn't what we chose,
   we're just asking for our wages.
DONNER
   I've often paid
   giants their dues.
   Come here, I'll match the cost
   of the wage with good measure!
      He swings his hammer.
WOTAN *holding his spear out between the disputing parties
         with grand gestures and august expression**
   Stop, you hothead!
   Nothing with violence!   580
      *more like normal spoken dialogue**
   It's the shaft of my spear
   that holds contracts secure: –
   not the handle of your hammer!
FREIA
   I'm lost! I'm lost!
   Wotan's abandoning me!
FRICKA
   Do I still understand you,
   cold-blooded man?
      Wotan turns aside and sees Loge coming.

WOTAN
    Endlich Loge!
    Eiltest du so,
590   den du geschlossen,
    den schlimmen Handel zu schlichten?
  LOGE *ist im Hintergrunde aus dem Tale heraufgestiegen.*
    Wie? Welchen Handel
    hätt' ich geschlossen?
        Die Reden Loges sind durchweg im Tone leichter Ironie,
        dabei frei von jeder Affektation zu halten. *
    Wohl was mit den Riesen
    dort im Rate du dangst?
    In Tiefen und Höhen
    treibt mich mein Hang;
    Haus und Herd
    behagt mir nicht.
600   Donner und Froh,
    die denken an Dach und Fach;
    wollen sie frein,
    ein Haus muß sie erfreun.
    Ein stolzer Saal,
    ein starkes Schloß,
    danach stand Wotans Wunsch.
    Haus und Hof,
    Saal und Schloß,
    die selige Burg,
610   sie steht nun fest gebaut.
    Das Prachtgemäuer
    prüft' ich selbst;
    ob alles fest,
    forscht' ich genau:
    Fasolt und Fafner
    fand ich bewährt:
    kein Stein wankt in Gestemm'.
    Nicht müßig war ich,
    wie mancher hier;
620   der lügt, wer lässig mich schilt.
WOTAN
    Arglistig

WOTAN

    Loge, about time!

    In a rush

    to sort out   590

    that dreadful deal you closed?

LOGE *has climbed up in the background out of the valley*

    Huh? What deal

    am I supposed to have closed?

        Loge's utterances are to be delivered throughout in a

        lightly ironic tone, free of all affectation. *

    Perhaps the one you took on

    in consultation with the giants?

    In bad times and good

    I'm a creature of impulse;

    house and home

    give me the jitters.

    Donner and Froh,   600

    they think of getting things done;

    if they want to marry,

    they get a house to enjoy.

    A proud hall,

    a resilient castle,

    they were part of Wotan's generosity.

    A roof over their heads,

    a place to feel powerful,

    the heavenly fortress,

    it's all firmly built.   610

    I inspected the magnificent

    stonework myself,

    looking closely to see

    if it's all secure:

    Fasolt and Fafner

    I deemed first-rate:

    no stone's loose inside the frame.

    I didn't dawdle,

    like some here:

    it's a lie to scold me for being remiss.   620

WOTAN

    You're shrewdly

weichst du mir aus:
mich zu betrügen
hüte in Treuen dich wohl!
Von allen Göttern
dein einz'ger Freund
nahm ich dich auf
in der übel trauenden Troß:
Nun red' und rate klug!
  in lebhaft vordringendem Zeitmaß zu sprechen *

630 Da einst die Bauer der Burg
zum Dank Freia bedangen,
du weißt, nicht anders
willigt' ich ein,
als weil auf Pflicht du gelobtest,
zu lösen das hehre Pfand?

LOGE
Mit höchster Sorge
drauf zu sinnen,
wie es zu lösen,
das – hab' ich gelobt.
640 Doch, daß ich fände,
was nie sich fügt,
was nie gelingt –
wie ließ sich das wohl geloben?

FRICKA *zu Wotan*
Sieh, welch trugvollem
Schelm du getraut!

FROH *mit leidenschaftlichem Ausdruck* *
      zu Loge
Loge heißt du,
doch nenn' ich dich Lüge!

DONNER
Verfluchte Lohe,
dich lösch' ich aus!

LOGE
650 Ihre Schmach zu decken,
schmähen mich Dumme!
    Donner holt auf Loge aus.

missing my point:
make sure you trust yourself
not to deceive me!
Among the gods
your one remaining friend,
I took you up
as part of that hostile retinue:
so talk and counsel prudently!
  *to be spoken in a briskly urgent tempo**
Once the builders of the castle   630
had demanded Freia as thanks,
are you aware that I only agreed
to nothing else
because you'd promised, as a duty,
to free the noble one I'd pledged?

LOGE
To think
with the greatest care
about how to free her,
that – I did promise.
But I was to discover something   640
that never happens as it should,
that never succeeds –
how on earth could a promise work?

FRICKA *to Wotan*
Lo and behold your trusty
swindling scoundrel!

FROH *with passionate expression**
    to Loge
Your name's Loge,
but for me it's Liar!

DONNER
Damned flickering flame,
I'll stamp you out!

LOGE
To hush up their scandal,   650
idiots smear me!
  Donner lunges at Loge.

WOTAN *dazwischentretend*
In Frieden laßt mir den Freund!
Nicht kennt ihr Loges Kunst:
reicher wiegt
seines Rates Wert,
zahlt er zögernd ihn aus.

FAFNER
Nichts gezögert!
Rasch gezahlt!

FASOLT
Lang währt's mit dem Lohn!
        Wotan wendet sich hart zu Loge.

WOTAN *drängend*
660   Jetzt hör, Störrischer!
Halte Stich!
Wo schweiftest du hin und her?

LOGE *Mit dem Tone gekränkter Unschuld**
Immer ist Undank
Loges Lohn!
Für dich nur besorgt,
sah ich mich um,
durchstöbert' im Sturm
alle Winkel der Welt:
Ersatz für Freia zu suchen,
670   wie er den Riesen wohl recht.
Umsonst sucht' ich
und sehe nun wohl:
in der Welten Ring
nichts ist so reich,
        Fricka mit staunend betroffener Mi[e]ne*
als Ersatz zu muten dem Mann
für Weibes Wonne und Wert!
        *Alle geraten in Erstaunen und verschiedenartige Betrof-
        fenheit.*
So weit Leben und Weben
in Wasser, Erd und Luft,
viel frug ich,
680   forschte bei allen,
wo Kraft nur sich rührt,

WOTAN *stepping between them*
   Grant me peace for our friend!
   Loge's art isn't known to you:
   the worth of his wisdom
   is all the greater
   the more tentatively he parts with it.
FAFNER
   Delay nothing!
   Pay fast!
FASOLT
   A long wait for our reward!
       Wotan turns to Loge with a tough stance.
WOTAN *urgently*
   Now listen, restive man!   660
   Make some sense!
   Where did your wanderings take you?
LOGE *With a tone of hurt innocence**
   Rudeness is always
   Loge's reward!
   Caring just for you,
   I scouted around,
   scavenging all corners
   of the earth in the storm:
   searching for something acceptable
   to the giants in Freia's stead.   670
   I returned empty-handed
   and now realize:
   all around the world,
   nothing has allure enough
       *Fricka with flabbergasted amazement written on her face**
   to ask of a man that he exchange it
   for woman's loveliness and worth.
       *All react with astonishment and fall into different states
       of shock.*
   Where life and movement exist
   in water, earth and air,
   I asked something momentous,
   enquiring of everything   680
   that had even the slightest

und Keime sich regen:
was wohl dem Manne
mächt'ger dünk'
als Weibes Wonne und Wert?
Doch so weit Leben und Weben,
verlacht nur ward
meine fragende List:
in Wasser, Erd' und Luft
690 lassen will nichts
von Lieb und Weib.
   Gemischte Bewegung
Nur einen sah ich,
der sagte der Liebe ab;
um rotes Gold
entriet er des Weibes Gunst.
Des Rheines klare Kinder
klagten mir ihre Not:
der Nibelung,
Nacht-Alberich,
700 buhlte vergebens
um der Badenden Gunst;
das Rheingold da
raubte sich rächend der Dieb:
das dünkt ihm nun
das teuerste Gut,
hehrer als Weibes Huld.
Um den gleißenden Tand,
der Tiefe entwandt,
erklang mir der Töchter Klage:
710 an dich, Wotan,
wenden sie sich,
daß zu Recht du zögest den Räuber
   mit wachsender Wärme
das Gold dem Wasser
wiedergebest,
und ewig es bliebe ihr Eigen.
   Hingebende Bewegung aller
    Die Götter blicken sich wechselseitig wie verzaubert
an. *

stirring of vitality and growth:
what is a man likely
to think more powerful
than a woman's loveliness and worth?
But where life and movement exist,
my questioning guile
met only with ridicule:
in water, earth and air
nothing will forsake   690
love and woman.
   mixed reactions
Only one did I see,
who denied himself love;
he exchanged women's favours
for red gold.
The Rhine's plain-speaking children
told me they were beside themselves:
the Nibelung,
Night-Alberich,
tried in vain to enjoy   700
their services as they bathed;
then in revenge the felon
filched the Rhinegold for himself:
he now deems that
the most coveted property,
loftier than women's favours.
About those gaudy playthings,
pilfered from the deep,
the daughters moaned resoundingly:
they are turning   710
to you, Wotan,
to bring the robber to justice,
   with growing warmth
give the gold
back to the waters,
and let it remain theirs for ever.
   Unanimous approval
    *The gods look at each other as if they've been be-
witched.* *

Dir's zu melden,
gelobt' ich den Mädchen:
nun löste Loge sein Wort.

WOTAN

Törig du bist,
720   wenn nicht gar tückisch!
Mich selbst siehst du in Not:
wie hülf' ich andern zum Heil?

FASOLT *der aufmerksam zugehört, zu Fafner*

Nicht gönn' ich das Gold dem Alben;
viel Not schon schuf uns der Niblung,
doch schlau entschlüpfte unserm
Zwange immer der Zwerg.

FAFNER

Neue Neidtat
sinnt uns der Niblung,
gibt das Gold ihm Macht. –
730   Du da, Loge!
Sag ohne Lug:
was Großes gilt denn das Gold,
daß dem Niblung es genügt?

LOGE

Ein Tand ist's
in des Wassers Tiefe,
lachenden Kindern zur Lust;
doch ward es zum runden
Reife geschmiedet,
hilft es zu höchster Macht,
740   gewinnt dem Manne die Welt.
    Betretenes Erstaunen aller *

WOTAN *sinnend*

Von des Rheines Gold
hört' ich raunen:
Beute-Runen
berge sein roter Glanz;
Macht und Schätze
schüf ohne Maß ein Reif.

I solemnly promised the girls
I'd let you know:
now Loge's kept his word.

WOTAN

You're absurd,
if not downright duplicitous!   720
You see me in dire straits myself:
how could I help others to salvation?

FASOLT *who has listened attentively, to Fafner*
I won't allow the dwarf near the gold;
the Nibelung's already caused us grief,
yet the dwarf always did escape
our clutches with cunning.

FAFNER

The Nibelung is planning
new deeds of envy against us,
once the gold empowers him. –
You there, Loge!   730
Say it straight:
what great thing is the gold good for
that the Nibelung thinks he can get?

LOGE

It's a plaything
in the water's deep,
for laughing children to have fun;
but once forged
into a round ring,
it's an aid to supreme power,
winning its master the world.   740
    All react in embarrassed amazement*

WOTAN *musing*
Murmerings about the Rhine's
gold have reached my ears:
it's said that its red glow
conceals signs of plunder;
that limitless rule and riches
can be created by a ring.

FRICKA *leise zu Loge*
   Taugte wohl
   des goldnen Tandes
   gleißend Geschmeid'
750 auch Frauen zu schönem Schmuck?
LOGE
   Des Gatten Treu'
   ertrotzte die Frau,
   trüge sie hold
   den hellen Schmuck,
   den schimmernd Zwerge schmieden,
   rührig im Zwange des Reifs.
FRICKA *schmeichelnd zu Wotan*
   Gewänne mein Gatte
   sich wohl das Gold?
      [Wotan] *wie in einem Zustande wachsenden Bezaube-*
      rung
WOTAN *zu sich* *
   Des Reifes zu walten,
760 rätlich will es mich dünken.
   Doch wie, Loge,
   lernt' ich die Kunst?
   Wie schüf' ich mir das Geschmeid'?
LOGE
   Ein Runen-Zauber
   zwingt das Gold zum Reif;
      sehr deutlich *
   keiner kennt ihn;
   doch einer übt ihn leicht,
   der selger Lieb entsagt.
      Wotan wendet sich unmutig ab.
   Das sparst du wohl;
770 zu spät auch kämst du:
   Alberich zauderte nicht.
   Zaglos gewann er
   des Zaubers Macht:
      Äußerst grell zu singen. Einen Moment bricht das
      dämonische Element in Loge hervor, der aber gleich

FRICKA *quietly to Loge*
  Perhaps the glittering
  gems of the golden playthings
  too can serve
  as pretty jewellery for us women?   750
LOGE
  A wife could force
  her husband to be faithful
  if she fondly wore
  the bright jewellery,
  dazzlingly forged by dwarfs
  toiling under the yoke of the ring.
FRICKA *flatteringly, to Wotan*
  Might my husband win
  the gold for himself?
    [Wotan] looking more and more like someone in a state
    of rapture
WOTAN *aside**
  To prevail over the ring
  strikes me as advisable.   760
  But how, Loge,
  do I learn the art?
  What do I do to make the jewel mine?
LOGE
  A magic spell with runes
  turns the gold into a ring;
    *very clearly**
  nobody knows it;
  but someone can cast it easily,
  if he renounces happy love.
    Annoyed, Wotan turns away.
  You wouldn't, of course;
  you're too late anyway: 770
  Alberich didn't hesitate.
  He boldly acquired
  the magic's power:
    To be sung extremely harshly. For a moment the demonic
    element in Loge erupts, but straight away reverts to his

wieder seine scheinbare Gemütlichkeit hervorkehrt*
geraten ist ihm der Ring!

DONNER *zu Wotan*
  Zwang uns allen
  schüfe der Zwerg,
  würd' ihm der Reif nicht entrissen.

WOTAN *mit erregter Leidenschaft und der Gebärde fester*
    Entschlossenheit*
  Den Ring muß ich haben!

FROH
  Leicht erringt
780 ohne Liebesfluch er sich jetzt.

LOGE *grell*
  Spottleicht,
  ohne Kunst, wie im Kinderspiel!

WOTAN
  So rate, wie?

LOGE
  Durch Raub!
  Was ein Dieb stahl,
  das stiehlst du dem Dieb:
  ward leichter ein Eigen erlangt?
  Doch mit arger Wehr
  wahrt sich Alberich;
790 klug und fein
  mußt du verfahren,
  ziehst den Räuber du zu Recht,
  um des Rheines Töchtern
  den roten Tand,
    mit Wärme
  das Gold wiederzugeben;
  denn darum flehen sie dich.

WOTAN
  Des Rheines Töchter?
  Was taugt mir der Rat!

FRICKA
  Von dem Wassergezücht
800 mag ich nichts wissen;

   apparently easy-going friendliness*
now he's got the ring!

DONNER *to Wotan*
  We'll all be under
  the dwarf's yoke,
  if the ring's not pried away from him.

WOTAN *his passion aroused and with a gesture of firm deci-*
    siveness*
  I have to get that ring!

FROH
  Easy to get
  now without cursing love.   780

LOGE *harshly*
  Dead easy,
  no skill needed, mere child's play!

WOTAN
  So how then?

LOGE
  By theft!
  What a thief stole,
  from the thief you steal back:
  could a possession be easier to gain?
  But Alberich protects himself
  with evil means;
  your methods must   790
  have wit and finesse
  to bring the thief to justice,
  so that the red plaything,
  the gold, can be returned
    with warmth
  to the daughters of the Rhine;
  that's why they're imploring you.

WOTAN
  The daughters of the Rhine?
  What's all that to me!

FRICKA
  I don't want to know
  about that aquatic ménage: 800

schon manchen Mann
– mir zum Leid –
verlockten sie buhlend im Bad.

*Wotan steht stumm mit sich kämpfend, die übrigen Göt-
ter heften in schweigender Spannung die Blicke auf ihn.
– Währenddem hat Fafner beiseite mit Fasolt beraten.*

*Allen Vorgängen sieht Loge, der etwas entfernt von
den anderen steht, mit überlegenem Spotte zu.* *

FAFNER *zu Fasolt*
Glaub mir, mehr als Freia
frommt das gleißende Gold:
auch ew'ge Jugend erjagt,
wer durch Goldes Zauber sie zwingt.

*Fasolts Gebärde deutet an, daß er sich wider Willen
überredet fühlt.*

Fafner tritt mit Fasolt wieder an Wotan heran.

Hör', Wotan,
der Harrenden Wort!
810 Freia bleib' euch in Frieden;
leicht'ren Lohn
fand ich zur Lösung:
uns rauhen Riesen genügt
des Niblungen rotes Gold.

WOTAN *sehr heftig* *
Seid ihr bei Sinn?
Was nicht ich besitze,
soll ich euch Schamlosen schenken?

FAFNER
Schwer baute
dort sich die Burg:
820 leicht wird dir's
mit list'ger Gewalt
was im Neidspiel nie uns gelang:
den Niblungen fest zu fahn.

WOTAN *beschleunigend*
Für euch müht' ich
mich um den Alben?
Für euch fing' ich den Feind?
Unverschämt

many a man already
– to my regret –
was lured by those swimming sluts.

> *Wotan stands voicelessly wrestling with himself, while the other gods fix their eyes on him in tense silence. – Meanwhile Fafner confers with Fasolt to one side.*
>
> *Loge is standing somewhat apart from the others and sees everything going on with scornful superciliousness.* *

FAFNER *to Fasolt*

The glistening gold's worth
more than Freia, believe me:
eternal youth is captured anyway
by the force of the gold's magic.

> *Fasolt's demeanour suggests that he feels persuaded against his will.*
>
> *Fafner approaches Wotan again with Fasolt.*

Listen, Wotan,
to a word from those who wait!
Freia can stay with you in peace;   810
I found a simpler payment
in settlement:
we gruff giants are happy
with the Nibelung's red gold.

WOTAN *very forcefully* *

Are you crazy?
What I don't own,
I'm to give you shameless monsters?

FAFNER

Hard it was
to build that fortress:
easy it will be for you   820
with sly force,
which we were never good at in war,
to hunt the Nibelung down.

WOTAN *quickening the pace*

For you I make an effort
on account of the dwarf?
For you I capture the enemy?
My gratitude has turned you into

und überbegehrlich
macht euch Dumme mein Dank!

FASOLT *ergreift plötzlich Freia, und führt sie mit Fafner zur Seite.*

830   Hierher, Maid!
In unsre Macht!
Als Pfand folgst du uns jetzt,
bis wir Lösung empfahn!

FREIA *schreiend*
Wehe! Wehe! Weh!

FAFNER
Fort von hier
sei sie entführt!
Bis Abend – achtet's wohl! –
pflegen wir sie als Pfand;
wir kehren wieder;
840   doch kommen wir,
und bereit liegt nicht als Lösung
das Rheingold licht und rot –

FASOLT
Zu End' ist die Frist dann,
Freia verfallen:
für immer folge sie uns!

Freia wird von den hastig enteilenden Riesen fortgetragen.

FREIA *schreiend*
Schwester! Brüder!
Rettet! Helft!

FROH
Auf, ihnen nach!

DONNER
Breche denn alles!

Sie blicken Wotan fragend an.

FREIA *aus der Ferne*
850   Rettet! Helft!

LOGE *den Riesen nachsehend*
Über Stock und Stein zu Tal
stapfen sie hin:
durch des Rheines Wasserfurt

disgraceful,
overly covetous cretins!

FASOLT *suddenly takes firm hold of Freia and leads her with*
Fafner to one side.

Over here, young woman!   830
Into our power!
You follow us now as hostage,
until we get settlement.

FREIA *screaming*

I'm lost! I'm lost! Alas!

FAFNER

Let her be taken
away from here!
Until evening – take good note –
we care for her as hostage;
we'll be back;
but if we come,   840
and the bright, red Rhinegold
isn't there in settlement –

FASOLT

Time will be up,
and Freia forfeit:
she'll be with us for ever!

The giants hastily depart, dragging Freia along with them.

FREIA *screaming*

Sister! Brothers!
Save me! Help!

FROH

Let's go, after them!

DONNER

Smash everything!

They look searchingly at Wotan.

FREIA *in the distance*

Save me! Help!   850

LOGE *following the giants with his eyes*

They stomp along
up hill and down dale to the valley:
the giants wade

waten die Riesen:
fröhlich nicht
hängt Freia
den Rauhen über den Rücken! –
Heia! Hei!
Wie taumeln die Tölpel dahin!
860 Durch das Tal talpen sie schon;
wohl an Riesenheims Mark
erst halten sie Rast! –
Er wendet sich zu den Göttern.
Was sinnt nun Wotan so wild?
*Ein fahler Nebel erfüllt mit wachsender Dichtheit die
Bühne; in ihm erhalten die Götter ein zunehmend blei-
ches und ältliches Aussehen; alle stehen bang und erwar-
tungsvoll auf Wotan blickend, der sinnend die Augen an
den Boden heftet.*
Den sel'gen Göttern, wie geht's?
Trügt mich ein Nebel?
Neckt mich ein Traum?
Wie bang und bleich
verblüht ihr so bald!
Euch erlischt der Wangen Licht;
870 der Blick eures Auges verblitzt! –
Frisch, mein Froh!
Noch ist's ja früh! –
Deiner Hand, Donner,
entsinkt ja der Hammer!
Was ist's mit Fricka?
Freut sie sich wenig
ob Wotans grämlichem Grau,
das schier zum Greisen ihn schafft?

FRICKA
Wehe! Wehe!
880 Was ist geschehen?

DONNER
Mir sinkt die Hand!

FROH
Mir stockt das Herz!

through the Rhine like a ford:
not happy,
Freia is slung
over the backs of the brutes! –
Heia! Hei!
Yokels tumbling on their way!
Now they stomp through the valley,   860
probably stopping to rest only at
the entry to the land of the giants! –
   He turns to the gods.
What troubles the mind now, Wotan?
   A hazy fog fills the stage with increasing density; within
   it the gods turn pale, taking on the appearance of old age
   more and more; all stand with a worried and expectant
   gaze at Wotan, who, his mind elsewhere, fixes his eyes on
   the floor.
Happy Gods, how are you?
Is this a fog that deceives me?
Or a teasing dream?
Worried and pale,
you wilt so soon!
The light in your cheeks is dead;
the look in your eyes burnt out! –   870
Buck up, dear Froh!
It's hardly begun! –
Even your hammer, Donner,
glides out of your hand!
What about Fricka?
Is she less than delighted
at Wotan's sullen greyness,
that he's practically a very old man?

FRICKA
   Woe! Woe!
   What's happened?   880
DONNER
   My hand sinks!
FROH
   My heart stands still!

LOGE

Jetzt fand' ich's! Hört, was euch fehlt!
Von Freias Frucht
genosset ihr heute noch nicht.
Die gold'nen Äpfel
in ihrem Garten,
sie machten euch tüchtig und jung,
aßt ihr sie jeden Tag.
890   Des Gartens Pflegerin
ist nun verpfändet;
an den Ästen darbt
und dorrt das Obst,
bald fällt faul es herab.
Mich kümmert's minder;
an mir ja kargte
Freia von je
knausernd die köstliche Frucht:
denn halb so echt nur
900   bin ich wie, Selige, ihr!
    frei, doch lebhaft und grell
Doch ihr setztet alles
auf das jüngende Obst:
das wußten die Riesen wohl;
auf eurer Leben
legten sie's an:
    Der sehr belebt geworden[e] Ausdruck ist hier plötzlich
    zu mäßigen. *
nun sorgt, wie ihr das wahrt!
Ohne die Äpfel
alt und grau,
greis und grämlich,
910   welkend zum Spott aller Welt,
    sehr ernst vorzutragen *
erstirbt der Götter Stamm.

FRICKA *bang*

Wotan, Gemahl!
Unsel'ger Mann!
Sieh, wie dein Leichtsinn

LOGE
I've got it! Hear what you're missing!
Today you didn't yet partake
of Freia's fruit.
The golden apples
in her garden,
they made you healthy and young
each day you ate them.
The garden's keeper,   890
she's a hostage now;
the fruit on the branches
starves, shrivels, rots,
and soon will fall.
That bothers me little;
but Freia always was
mean to me, stinting
on the mouth-watering fruit:
after all I'm only half a god
compared, happy ones, with you!   900
    freely, yet feistily and loudly
But on the rejuvenating fruit
you staked everything:
the giants knew that of course;
they pitted it
against your life:
    *Expression has become very lively but must be suddenly
    moderated here.* *
so watch how you keep it alive!
Without the apples,
old and grey,
senile and sullen,
a wilting travesty to the entire world,   910
    to be stated very seriously *
the house of the gods will perish.
FRICKA *worried*
Wotan, spouse!
Unhappy husband!
Look how your levity

    lachend uns allen
    Schimpf und Schmach erschuf!

WOTAN *mit plötzlichem Entschluß auffahrend*
    Auf, Loge!
    Hinab mit mir!
    Nach Nibelheim fahren wir nieder:
920   gewinnen will ich das Gold!

LOGE *wieder leichthin**
    Die Rheintöchter
    riefen dich an:
    so dürfen Erhörung sie hoffen?

WOTAN *heftig*
    Schweige, Schwätzer!
    Freia, die Gute,
    Freia gilt es zu lösen!

LOGE
    Wie du befiehlst
    führ' ich dich gern:
    steil hinab
930   steigen wir denn durch den Rhein?

WOTAN
    Nicht durch den Rhein!

LOGE
    So schwingen wir uns
    durch die Schwefelkluft:
    dort schlüpfe mit mir hinein!
       Er geht voran und verschwindet seitwärts in einer Kluft,
       aus der sogleich ein schwefliger Dampf hervorquillt.

WOTAN
    Ihr andern harrt
    bis Abend hier:
    verlor'ner Jugend
    erjag' ich erlösendes Gold!
       Er steigt Loge nach in die Kluft hinab: der aus ihr drin-
       gende Schwefeldampf verbreitet sich über die ganze
       Bühne und erfüllt diese schnell mit dichtem Gewölk.
       Bereits sind die Zurückbleibenden unsichtbar.

DONNER
    Fahre wohl, Wotan!

    has flippantly brought
    shame and disgrace on us all!

WOTAN *flaring up with sudden decisiveness*
    Get up, Loge!
    Descend with me!
    Let's get down to Nibelheim:
    I need to win the gold!   920

LOGE *sounding glib again**
    The Rhine daughters
    appealed to you:
    are they allowed a hearing?

WOTAN *fiercely*
    Cut the smooth talk!
    Freia, dear good soul,
    it's about getting Freia back!

LOGE
    Just as you wish,
    I'd love to take you:
    shall we start our steep descent
    by climbing through the Rhine?   930

WOTAN
    Not through the Rhine!

LOGE
    Then let's jump
    through the sulphurous crack:
    Slip in there with me!
        He goes ahead and vanishes sideways inside a chasm out
        of which a sulphurous vapour immediately starts to seep.

WOTAN
    Everybody else wait
    here until evening:
    for lost youth
    I'll capture the redeeming gold!
        Following Loge, he climbs down into the chasm: the sul-
        phurous vapour gushing out of it spreads over the entire
        stage and quickly envelops it with a dense cloud. Already,
        the gods who have stayed behind are invisible.

DONNER
    Farewell, Wotan!

FROH

940   Glück auf! Glück auf!

FRICKA

O kehre bald
zur bangenden Frau!

*Der Schwefeldampf verdüstert sich zu ganz schwarzem
Gewölk, welches von unten nach oben steigt; dann ver-
wandelt sich dieses in festes, finstres Steingeklüft, das sich
immer aufwärts bewegt, so daß es den Anchein hat, als
sänke die Szene immer tiefer in die Erde hinab.*

*Von verschiedenen Seiten her dämmert aus der Ferne
dunkelroter Schein auf: wachsendes Geräusch wie von
Schmiedenden wird überall her vernommen.*

*Das Getöse der Ambosse verliert sich. Eine unab-
sehbar weit sich dahinziehende unterirdische Kluft wird
erkennbar, die sich nach allen Seiten hin in enge Schacht-
en auszumünden scheint.*

DRITTE SZENE

Die unterirdischen Klüfte Nibelheims

*Straff vordringende Energie, ohne unmotiviertes Verweilen
und Zögern bildete den Grundcharakter der Ausführung der
ganzen Szene.* *

*Alberich zerrt den kreischenden Mime an den Ohren aus
einer Seitenschluft herbei.*

ALBERICH

Hehe! Hehe!
Hierher! Hierher!
Tückischer Zwerg!
Tapfer gezwickt
sollst du mir sein,
schaffst du nicht fertig,
wie ich's bestellt,

950   zur Stund' das feine Geschmeid'!

FROH
  Good luck! Good luck!   940
FRICKA
  O return soon
  to this frightened wife!

  *The sulphurous vapour darkens into a completely black
  cloud rising from the bottom towards the top; it then
  changes into a hard, gloomy stone fissure that continu-
  ally moves upwards so as to give the impression that the
  stage is constantly sinking downwards into the earth.*

  *From various points in the distance, a dark red glow
  starts to get lighter: a growing noise like workers forging
  can be heard from all quarters.*

  *The din of the anvils peters out. A subterranean space
  becomes visible, stretching back infinitely into the dis-
  tance and opening out into what seem like narrow shafts
  on all sides in every direction.*

SCENE THREE

Nibelheim's underground chasms

*Tense, forward-moving energy without unmotivated pauses
and hesitancy should be the main feature of the way the whole
scene is executed.* *

  *Alberich hauls the yelping Mime by his ears out of a shaft
at the side.*

ALBERICH
  Hehe! Hehe!
  Over here! Over here!
  Cunning dwarf!
  I ought to
  pinch you hard,
  if you don't finish
  that fine piece of work
  on time as I told you to!   950

MIME *heulend*
  Ohe! Ohe!
  Au! Au!
  Lass mich nur los!
  Fertig ist's,
  wie du befahlst,
  mit Fleiß und Schweiß
  ist es gefügt: –
    grell
  nimm nur die Nägel vom Ohr!
ALBERICH *loslassend*
  Was zögerst du dann
960 und zeigst es nicht?
MIME
  Ich Armer zagte,
  daß noch was fehle.
ALBERICH
  Was wär' noch nicht fertig?
MIME *verlegen*
  Hier – und da –
ALBERICH
  Was hier und da?
  Her das Geschmeid'!
    *Er will ihm wieder an das Ohr fahren: vor Schreck läßt
    Mime ein metallnes Gewirke, das er krampfhaft in den
    Händen hielt, sich entfallen. Alberich hebt es hastig auf
    und prüft es genau.*
  Schau, du Schelm!
  Alles geschmiedet
  und fertig gefügt –
970 wie ich's befahl!
  So wollte der Tropf
  schlau mich betrügen?
  Für sich behalten
  das hehre Geschmeid',
  das meine List
  ihn zu schmieden gelehrt?
  Kenn' ich dich dummen Dieb?

MIME *whining*
> Oh no! Oh no!
> Ouch! Ouch!
> Just let me go!
> It's finished,
> as you instructed,
> with diligence and sweat
> it's all in place: –
>> *harshly*
> just take your nails out of my ears!

ALBERICH *letting go*
> Then why the delay
> and why not show it?   960

MIME
> Silly me, I was afraid
> something's still missing.

ALBERICH
> What couldn't be finished?

MIME *abashed*
> Here – and there –

ALBERICH
> Here and there – what?
> Give me the thing!
>> *He goes for Mime's ears again; Mime is so frightened that
>> he drops an elaborate metal object he has been holding
>> tightly in his hands. Alberich hastily picks it up and in-
>> spects it closely.*
> Look, you rascally dwarf!
> All hammered
> and fitted into place –
> just as I commanded!   970
> Did the sly devil
> try to deceive me?
> Keep for himself
> the fabulous piece of work
> that clever me
> taught him to make?
> I know you, filching fool, don't I?

Er setzt das Gewirk als Tarnhelm auf den Kopf.
Dem Haupt fügt sich der Helm:
ob sich der Zauber auch zeigt?
   sehr leise
980 'Nacht und Nebel –
niemand gleich!'
   Seine Gestalt verschwindet; statt ihrer gewahrt man eine
   Nebelsäule.
Siehst du mich, Bruder?
MIME *blickt sich verwundert um*
Wo bist du? Ich sehe dich nicht.
ALBERICH *unsichtbar*
So fühle mich doch,
du fauler Schuft!
   Mime windet sich unter empfangenen Geißelhieben,
   deren Fall man vernimmt, ohne die Geißel selbst zu sehen.
Nimm das für dein Diebesgelüst!
MIME
Ohe! Ohe!
Au! Au! Au!
ALBERICH *lachend, unsichtbar*
Hahahahahaha!
990 Hab Dank, du Dummer!
Dein Werk bewährt sich gut.
Hoho! Hoho!
Niblungen all,
neigt euch nun Alberich!
Überall weilt er nun,
euch zu bewachen;
Ruh' und Rast
ist euch zerronnen;
ihm müßt ihr schaffen,
1000 wo nicht ihr ihn schaut;
wo nicht ihr ihn gewahrt,
seid seiner gewärtig!
Untertan seid ihr ihm immer!
   grell
Hoho! Hoho!

He puts the metal object on his head as a magic helmet.
The helmet's right for my head:
will the spell work too?
    very softly
'Night and fog –   980
no one alike!'
    *His shape vanishes; in its place, a pillar of fog comes into
    view.*
Do you see me, brother?
MIME *looks around, puzzled*
Where are you? I don't see you.
ALBERICH *invisible*
So get a taste of me then,
you lazy wretch!
    *Mime writhes under the whiplashes he receives, the im-
    pact of which is heard without seeing the whip.*
For itching to steal it, take this!
MIME
Oh no! Oh no!
Ouch! Ouch! Ouch!
ALBERICH *laughing, invisible*
Hahahahahaha!
In gratitude, you dumb fool!   990
Your work's well up to scratch.
Hoho! Hoho!
All Nibelungs
bow now before Alberich!
He's everywhere,
watching your every move;
no respite
for you is left;
for him you must slave
where you see he's not there;   1000
where you feel he's not there,
be aware that he is!
His slaves you'll always be!
    harshly
Hoho! Hoho!

Hört ihn, er naht:
der Niblungen Herr!

> *Die Nebelsäule verschwindet dem Hintergrunde zu: man
> hört in immer weiterer Ferne die tobende Ankunft Al-
> berichs. – Mime ist vor Schmerz zusammengesunken.*
> *Wotan und Loge lassen sich aus einer Schluft von oben
> herab.*

LOGE

Nibelheim hier.
Durch bleiche Nebel,
was blitzen dort feurige Funken?

MIME *am Boden*

1010   Au! Au! Au!

WOTAN

Hier stöhnt es laut:
was liegt im Gestein?

LOGE *sich zu Mime neigend*

Was Wunder wimmerst du hier?

MIME

Ohe! Ohe!
Au! Au!

LOGE

Hei, Mime! Muntrer Zwerg!
Was zwingt und zwackt dich denn so?

MIME

Laß mich in Frieden!

LOGE

Das will ich freilich,
1020   und mehr noch, hör!
Helfen will ich dir, Mime!

> *Er stellt ihn mühsam aufrecht.*

MIME

Wer hälfe mir?
Gehorchen muß ich
dem leiblichen Bruder,
der mich in Bande gelegt.

LOGE

Dich, Mime, zu binden,

Hear him coming:
the Nibelungs' master!

The pillar of mist vanishes into the background: Alberich's blustering arrival can be heard further and further into the distance. – Mime has slumped to the ground in pain.

Wotan and Loge lower themselves down out of a shaft above.

LOGE

Nibelheim it is.
What are the fiery sparks flashing
in the bleary fog?

MIME *on the ground*

Ouch! Ouch! Ouch!   1010

WOTAN

Loud groaning here:
what's lying in the rocks?

LOGE *leaning towards Mime*

Is it small wonder you're whining?

MIME

Oh no! Oh no!
Ouch! Ouch!

LOGE

Hi, Mime! Sparky dwarf!
What prods and pinches you so?

MIME

Leave me in peace!

LOGE

I'll do that of course,
but more too, listen!   1020
Mime, I want to help you!
Laboriously, he gets him to his feet.

MIME

Help me? Who could?
I must obey
my own brother,
who has me in shackles.

LOGE

What gave him the power,

was gab ihm die Macht?

MIME

Mit arger List
schuf sich Alberich
1030   aus Rheines Gold
einem gelben Reif:
seinem starken Zauber
zittern wir staunend;
mit ihm zwingt er uns alle,
der Niblungen nächt'ges Heer.

Mit einer etwas tänzelnden Gebärde *

Sorglose Schmiede,
schufen wir sonst wohl
Schmuck unsern Weibern,
wonnig Geschmeid',
1040   niedlichen Niblungentand;
wir lachten lustig der Müh'! –
Nun zwingt uns der Schlimme,
in Klüfte zu schlüpfen,
für ihn allein
uns immer zu mühn.
Durch des Ringes Gold
errät seine Gier,
wo neuer Schimmer
in Schachten sich birgt:
1050   da müssen wir spähen,
spüren und graben,
die Beute schmelzen
und schmieden den Guß,
ohne Ruh' und Rast,
dem Herrn zu häufen den Hort.

LOGE

Dich Trägen soeben
traf wohl sein Zorn?

MIME

Mich Ärmsten, ach!
Mich zwang er zum Ärgsten.
1060   Ein Helmgeschmeid'

Mime, to hold you captive?
MIME
   With his evil wiles
   Alberich made himself
   a yellow ring   1030
   from the Rhine's gold:
   its awesome magic
   startles and stuns us;
   he uses it to enchain us,
   the night army of the Nibelungs.
     With somewhat dance-like demeanour *
   Once smiths without a care,
   we were used to fashioning
   jewellery for our women,
   delightful ornaments,
   dainty Nibelung playthings;   1040
   we laughed at the work it took! –
   Now this monster forces us
   to clamber into chasms,
   always to toil
   only for him.
   The ring's gold allows
   his greed to guess
   where a new streak's
   hiding in the shafts:
   there we must survey,   1050
   search and dig,
   melt the haul down
   and mould it into a cast,
   without respite,
   to amass the master's treasure.
LOGE
   Your sluggishness just now
   probably made him angry?
MIME
   Ah me, the most dejected of all!
   On me he forced the worst task.
   He told me to weld   1060

hieß er mich schweißen;
genau befahl er,
wie es zu fügen.
Wohl merkt' ich klug,
welch mächt'ge Kraft
zu eigen dem Werk,
das aus Erz ich wob;
für mich drum hüten
wollt' ich dem Helm;
1070 durch seinen Zauber
Alberichs Zwang mich entziehn:
vielleicht – ja vielleicht
den Lästigen selbst überlisten,
in meine Gewalt ihn zu werfen,
den Ring ihm zu entreißen,
daß, wie ich Knecht jetzt dem Kühnen
    grell
mir Freien er selber dann fröhn'!

LOGE
Warum, du Kluger,
glückte dir's nicht?

MIME
1080 Ach, der das Werk ich wirkte,
den Zauber, der ihm entzuckt,
den Zauber erriet ich nicht recht:
der das Werk mir riet
und mir's entriß,
der lehrte mich nun
– doch leider zu spät, –
welche List läg' in dem Helm.
Meinem Blick entschwand er;
doch Schwielen dem Blinden
1090 schlug unschaubar sein Arm.
    heulend und schluchzend
Das schuf ich mir Dummen
schön zu Dank!
    Er streicht sich den Rücken.
    'Sie dürfen das Streichen des Rückens wohl etwas

a precious helmet;
he told me exactly
how to put it in place.
Naturally I felt
the huge power
of the object I was
creating out of the ore;
I wanted the helmet
for self-protection;
using its magic I could   1070
escape from Alberich's shackles:
perhaps – yes perhaps
outfox the tiresome man himself,
get him under my control,
snatch the ring from him
so that I, the tyrant's servant,
    harshly
am in turn a free man he must serve!
LOGE
  You're clever, so why
  didn't you succeed?
MIME
  Ah, it was his object I worked on,   1080
  but it was the spell it contained,
  the spell I could never guess:
  he gave me advice about the object
  and snatched it from me,
  teaching me only now
  – but alas too late –
  what tricks the helmet has in store.
  He vanished from my sight;
  yet though I couldn't see him,
  he lacerated me with his invisible arm.   1090
    whimpering and snivelling
  That's the nice thanks I got,
  dolt that I am!
    He strokes his back.
      'You are certainly at liberty to spread the stroking of

weiter nach unten zu ausdehnen!'*
   Wotan und Loge lachen.

LOGE *zu Wotan*
   Gesteh, nicht leicht
   gelingt der Fang.

WOTAN
   Doch erliegt der Feind,
   hilft deine List!

MIME *von dem Lachen der Götter betroffen, betrachtet diese*
   aufmerksamer.
      Mime wird mißtrauisch*
   Mit eurem Gefrage,
   wer seid denn ihr Fremde?

LOGE
   Freunde dir;
   von ihrer Not
   befrein wir der Niblungen Volk!
      Mime schrickt zusammen, da er Alberich sich wieder
      nahen hört.

MIME
   Nehmt euch in acht;
   Alberich naht.
      Er rennt vor Angst hin und her.

WOTAN *ruhig sich auf einen Stein setzend*
   Sein' harren wir hier.
      Alberich, der den Tarnhelm vom Haupte genommen und
      an den Gürtel gehängt hat, treibt mit geschwungener
      Geißel aus der unteren, tiefer gelegenen Schlucht auf-
      wärts eine Schar Nibelungen vor sich her: diese sind mit
      goldenem und silbernem Geschmeide beladen, das sie,
      unter Alberichs steter Nötigung, all' auf einen Haufen
      speichern und so zu einem Horte häufen.

ALBERICH
   Hierher! Dorthin!
   Hehe! Hoho!
   Träges Heer!
   Dort zuhauf
   schichtet den Hort!

your back to a bit further down!' *
     Wotan and Loge laugh.

LOGE *to Wotan*

Admit it, the capture
won't be easy.

WOTAN

But the enemy will succumb,
helped by your tricks!

MIME *embarrassed by the laughing of the gods, observes them
     more closely.*
          Mime becomes suspicious. *

Who are you strangers with all
your interminable questions?

LOGE

Your friends;
in their moment of need,   1100
we'll liberate the Nibelung people!
     *Mime jumps nervously at the sound of Alberich coming
     back again.*

MIME

Look out for yourselves;
Alberich's getting closer.
     He scampers hither and thither in fear.

WOTAN *calmly sitting down on a rock*

We'll wait for him here.
     *Having taken the Tarnhelm off his head and hung it on
     his belt, Alberich uses the lashes of his whip to herd a
     crowd of Nibelungs upwards and onwards out of the
     low-lying shaft below: they are loaded down with orna-
     ments made of gold and silver, which Alberich constant-
     ly bullies them into piling in a heap so that it gradually
     accumulates into a stash of treasure.*

ALBERICH

Over here! Over there!
Hehe! Hoho!
Army of sluggards!
Pile the loot,
stash it there!

Alles mit herrisch-dämonischer Energie und schnei-
dender Schärfe zu singen*

1110 Du da, hinauf!

Willst du voran?

Schmähliches Volk!

Ab das Geschmeide!

Soll ich euch helfen?

Alles hierher!

    Er gewahrt plötzlich Wotan und Loge.

       Hastig, mit äußerster Vehemenz hervorzustoßen*

He! Wer ist dort?

Wer drang hier ein? –

Mime, zu mir!

Schäbiger Schuft!

1120 Schwatztest du gar

mit dem schweifenden Paar?

Fort, du Fauler!

Willst du gleich schmieden und schaffen?

    Er treibt Mime mit Geißelhieben in den Haufen der Ni-
    belungen hinein.

He! An die Arbeit!

Alle von hinnen!

Hurtig hinab!

Aus den neuen Schachten

schafft mir das Gold!

Euch grüßt die Geißel,

1130 grabt ihr nicht rasch!

Daß keiner mir müßig,

bürge mir Mime,

sonst birgt er sich schwer

meiner Geißel Schwunge!

Daß ich überall weile,

wo keiner mich wähnt,

das weiß er, dünkt mich, genau!

Zögert ihr noch?

Zaudert wohl gar? –

    Er zieht seinen Ring vom Finger, küßt ihn und streckt ihn
    drohend aus.

Everything to be sung with bullying, demonic energy and
  *wounding bite**

You there, on your pins!   1110
Want to go on?
Miserable bunch!
Dump the treasure!
Should I help you, then?
Over here, all of it!
  He is suddenly aware of Wotan and Loge.
    *In a rush, to be uttered with extreme vehemence**
Oi! Who's there?
Who's burst in here? –
Mime, come to heel!
Scabby scoundrel!
Did you gossip at all   1120
with the two scroungers?
Get lost, you layabout!
Go forge and work: want to start?
  He herds Mime with the lash of his whip into the Ni-
  belung crowd.
Oi! Get cracking!
Everyone out!
Down with you to the deep!
Get me gold
from the new shafts!
If you don't dig fast,
my whip will pay you a visit!   1130
Mime answers to me
for any slackers,
or it'll be hard for him as well
to hide from the crack of my whip!
That I lurk in every place
where no one thinks I am,
I think he knows only too well!
Still hesitating?
Even wavering at all? –
  He slips the ring off his finger, kisses it and holds it out
  threateningly.

Die Zwerge zucken zusammen, wenn sie sehen, wie
Alb[erich] d[en] Ring küßt.*
Mit gewaltiger Stimme*
1140   Zittre und zage,
gezähmtes Heer!
Rasch gehorcht
des Ringes Herrn!

Unter Geheul und Gekreisch stieben die Nibelungen –
unter ihnen Mime – auseinander und schlüpfen nach al-
len Seiten in die Schachten hinab.
Alberich betrachtet lange und mißtrauisch Wotan und
Loge.
Was wollt ihr hier?

WOTAN *mit ruhiger, sich selbst beherrschender Würde**
Von Nibelheims nächt'gem Land
vernahmen wir neue Mär':
mächt'ge Wunder
wirke hier Alberich;
daran uns zu weiden,
1150   trieb uns Gäste die Gier.

ALBERICH
Nach Nibelheim
führt euch der Neid:
so kühne Gäste,
glaubt, kenn' ich gut!

LOGE
Kennst du mich gut,
kindischer Alp?
Nun sag, wer bin ich,
daß du so bellst?
Im kalten Loch,
1160   da kauernd du lagst,
wer gab dir Licht
und wärmende Lohe,
wenn Loge nie dir gelacht?
Was hülf' dir dein Schmieden,
heizt' ich die Schmiede dir nicht?
Dir bin ich Vetter
und war dir Freund:

*The dwarfs recoil when they see how Alberich kisses
the ring.* *

With a powerful voice *

Shake and quake,   1140
fettered flock!
Submit, and quickly
to the lord of the ring!

*In the midst of their yelling and screaming, the Nibelungs
– Mime included – scatter and slip down into the sur-
rounding shafts.*

*Alberich takes a long and mistrustful look at Wotan
and Loge.*

What do you want here?

WOTAN *controlling himself with calm dignity* *

From Nibelheim, land of the night,
we've heard new rumours:
wondrous miracles
are said to be Alberich's work;
for we visitors to revel in them,
a burning compulsion led us here.   1150

ALBERICH

Envy of power led you
to Nibelheim:
so, venturesome guests,
believe me, it's old news!

LOGE

Do you know me well,
childish dwarf?
Tell me who you think I am
that you bark like that?
As you lay huddled
in a cold hole,   1160
who'd have given you light
and the warmth of a fire
if Loge had never smiled on you?
What help would you get from forging,
if I hadn't fired your forge?
I am your cousin
and was your friend:

nicht fein drum dünkt mich dein Dank!

ALBERICH

Den Lichtalben
1170   lacht jetzt Loge,
der list'ge Schelm.
Bist du Falscher ihr Freund,
wie mir Freund du einst warst: –
haha! – Mich freut's! –
Von ihnen fürcht' ich dann nichts.

LOGE

So denk' ich, kannst du mir traun.

ALBERICH

Deiner Untreu' trau' ich,
nicht deiner Treu'!
   Eine herausfordernde Stellung annehmend
Doch getrost trotz' ich euch allen!

LOGE

1180   Hohen Mut
verleiht deine Macht;
grimmig groß
wuchs dir die Kraft!

ALBERICH

Siehst du den Hort,
den mein Heer
dort mir gehäuft?

LOGE

So neidlichen sah ich noch nie.

ALBERICH

Das ist für heut,
ein kärglich Häufchen!
1190   Kühn und mächtig
soll er künftig sich mehren.

WOTAN

Zu was doch frommt dir der Hort,
da freudlos Nibelheim,
und nichts für Schätze hier feil?

ALBERICH

Schätze zu schaffen,

your thanks lack grace, I beg to think!

ALBERICH

Loge you smile
on the light-elves now,   1170
you wily scoundrel.
If a phoney like you is their friend,
as you were once a friend to me: –
haha! – I'm glad! –
No point then in being afraid of them.

LOGE

The way I see it, you can trust me.

ALBERICH

I trust your lack of trust,
not your loyalty!
    Assuming a challenging posture
But I can safely defy all of you!

LOGE

Your power bestows   1180
on you great courage:
your strength's grown
with ferocious tenacity!

ALBERICH

Can you see the hoard
that my army's
amassed for me there?

LOGE

I'm so jealous, never seen such a thing.

ALBERICH

That's only today's haul,
a mere molehill!
It's about to get bigger,   1190
a bold and mighty mountain.

WOTAN

But what's the hoard to you
in this joyless Nibelheim,
and where treasure buys nothing?

ALBERICH

The Nibelheim night helps me

und Schätze zu bergen,
nützt mir Nibelheims Nacht.
Doch mit dem Hort,
in der Höhle gehäuft,
1200   denk' ich dann Wunder zu wirken:
die ganze Welt
gewinn' ich mit ihm mir zu eigen!

WOTAN
Wie beginnst du, Gütiger, das?

ALBERICH
Die in linder Lüfte Weh'n
da oben ihr lebt,
lacht und liebt: –
mit goldner Faust
euch Göttliche fang' ich mir alle!
Wie ich der Liebe abgesagt,
1210   alles, was lebt,
soll ihr entsagen!
Mit Golde gekirrt,
nach Gold nur sollt ihr noch gieren!
Auf wonnigen Höh'n,
in seligem Weben
wiegt ihr euch;
den Schwarzalben
verachtet ihr ewigen Schwelger!
Habt acht!
1220   Habt acht!
Denn dient ihr Männer
erst meiner Macht,
    Mit lustgierigem, schneidendem Hohn*
eure schmucken Frau'n,
die mein Frei'n verschmäht,
sie zwingt zur Lust sich der Zwerg,
lacht Liebe ihm nicht!
    wild lachend
Hahahaha!
Habt ihr's gehört?
Habt acht!

to produce treasure,
and to stash treasure away.
But with that hoard
piled up in my lair,
I intend to make miracles happen: 1200
with its power
I'll win the whole world for myself!

WOTAN
Where, kind friend, will you start?

ALBERICH
You up there living,
laughing and loving
in soft breezes swaying: –
I'll catch you gods with my golden fist,
every one of you!
Just as I spurned love,
all that lives   1210
shall renounce it too!
Baited with gold,
gold's all you'll have left to crave!
On radiant heights
you've cradled yourselves
in a blissful cocoon;
you inveterate hedonists despise
the black dwarf!
Be on your guard!
Be on your guard!   1220
Once you men are yoked
to my power,
   *With lascivious, cutting derision**
the dwarf will ravish
your sassy women,
who mocked me when I wooed them:
love smiles on him no more!
   laughing wildly
Hahahaha!
Did you hear that?
Be on your guard!

1230　Habt acht vor dem nächtlichen Heer,
entsteigt des Niblungen Hort
aus stummer Tiefe zu Tag!
WOTAN *auffahrend*
　Vergeh, frevelnder Gauch!
ALBERICH
　Was sagt der?
LOGE *dazwischentretend*
　Sei doch bei Sinnen! –
　　zu Alberich
　Wen doch faßte nicht Wunder,
　erfährt er Alberichs Werk?
　Gelingt deiner herrlichen List,
　was mit dem Horte du heischest:
1240　den Mächtigsten muß ich dich rühmen;
　denn Mond und Stern'
　und die strahlende Sonne,
　sie auch dürfen nicht anders,
　dienen müssen sie dir.
　Doch – wichtig acht' ich vor allem,
　daß des Hortes Häufer,
　der Niblungen Heer,
　neidlos dir geneigt?
　Einen Reif rührtest du kühn;
1250　dem zagte zitternd dein Volk: –
　doch, wenn im Schlaf
　ein Dieb dich beschlich',
　den Ring schlau dir entriss' –
　wie wahrtest du Weiser dich dann?
ALBERICH
　Der Listigste dünkt sich Loge;
　andre denkt er
　immer sich dumm:
　daß sein' ich bedürfte
　zu Rat und Dienst,
1260　um harten Dank,
　das hörte der Dieb jetzt gern!
　Den hehlenden Helm

On guard against the night army,   1230
the steps of the Nibelung's horde
out of the voiceless depths into day!

WOTAN *flaring up*
Get lost, impertinent fool!

ALBERICH
What's he saying?

LOGE *coming between them*
Keep your temper! –
  to Alberich
Who wouldn't be amazed
at everything Alberich's done?
If, with the horde, your wonderful
wit gets you everything you demand:
I honour you as the mightiest of men;   1240
the moon and stars
and the shining sun,
they also may do no other
than serve you without fail.
Yet – I see this as crucial –
shouldn't the Nibelung army,
who get and amass the hoard,
regard you without envy?
You boldly touched a ring;
it made your people quake in terror: –   1250
but if you're asleep
and a thief steals in,
deftly to snatch the ring from you,
how, wise dwarf, do you prevent that?

ALBERICH
Loge thinks he's the cleverest of all;
everyone else
he takes for an idiot:
that I even need
your service and advice,
let alone your hard-won thanks,   1260
any thief would be glad to hear.
The helmet of disguise

ersann ich mir selbst;
der sorglichste Schmied,
Mime, mußt' ihn mir schmieden:
schnell mich zu wandeln,
nach meinem Wunsch
die Gestalt mir zu tauschen,
taugt der Helm.
1270 Niemand sieht mich,
wenn er mich sucht;
doch überall bin ich,
geborgen dem Blick.
So ohne Sorge
bin ich selbst sicher vor dir,
du fromm sorgender Freund!

LOGE
Vieles sah ich,
Seltsames fand ich,
doch solches Wunder
1280 gewahrt' ich nie.
Dem Werk ohne Gleichen
kann ich nicht glauben;
wäre dies eine möglich,
deine Macht währte dann ewig!

ALBERICH
Meinst du, ich lüg'
und prahle wie Loge?

LOGE
Bis ich's geprüft,
bezweifl' ich, Zwerg, dein Wort.

ALBERICH
Vor Klugheit bläht sich
1290 zum Platzen der Blöde!
Nun plage dich Neid!
Bestimm, in welcher Gestalt
soll ich jach vor dir stehn?

LOGE
In welcher du willst;
nur mach vor Staunen mich stumm!

is my own invention;
the most fastidious smith,
Mime, had to make it for me:
to change myself quickly
into anything I want,
into any shape I choose,
I use the helmet.
If someone looks for me,   1270
they won't see me;
yet I'm everywhere,
concealed from view.
So without caring a jot,
I feel safe, even from you,
my piously devoted friend!

LOGE
I've seen a lot,
I've found strange things,
but such a miracle
I've never witnessed.   1280
I can have no faith
in an object without peer;
if it possibly exists,
then your power prevails for ever!

ALBERICH
I'm fibbing, you think,
and preening like Loge?

LOGE
Until I've vetted it,
dwarf, I doubt your word.

ALBERICH
The idiot's so puffed out
with cleverness, he'll burst!   1290
May envy afflict you still!
Say, what shape should I
take on for you right now?

LOGE
Whatever you want;
just amaze me, make me speechless!

ALBERICH *setzt den Helm auf*
'Riesenwurm
winde sich ringelnd!'
Statt seiner windet sich eine ungeheure Riesenschlange
am Boden; sie bäumt sich und sperrt den aufgerissenen
Rachen auf Wotan und Loge zu.
LOGE *stellt sich von Furcht ergriffen*
Ohe! Ohe!
Schreckliche Schlange,
1300   verschlinge mich nicht!
Schone Logen das Leben!
WOTAN *lachend*
Hahaha! Hahaha!
Gut, Alberich!
Gut, du Arger!
Wie wuchs so rasch
zum riesigen Wurme der Zwerg!
Die Schlange verschwindet; statt ihrer erscheint sogleich
Alberich wieder in seiner wirklichen Gestalt.
ALBERICH
Hehe! Ihr Klugen!
Glaubt ihr mir nun?
LOGE *mit zitternder Stimme*
Mein Zittern mag dir's bezeugen!
1310   Zur großen Schlange
schufst du dich schnell:
weil ich's gewahrt,
willig glaub' ich dem Wunder.
Doch, wie du wuchsest,
kannst du auch winzig
und klein dich schaffen?
Das Klügste schien' mir das,
Gefahren schlau zu entfliehn:
das aber dünkt mich zu schwer!
ALBERICH
1320   Zu schwer dir,
weil du zu dumm!
Wie klein soll ich sein?

ALBERICH *puts on the helmet*
'Colossal dragon
curl, twist, coil!'
> *In his place a monstrous giant serpent goes through
> all sorts of contortions on the ground; it rears up, jaws
> gaping and snapping at Wotan and Loge.*
LOGE *feigning terror*
Oh my! Oh my!
Horrible serpent,
don't gobble me up!   1300
Spare Loge his life!
WOTAN *laughing*
Hahaha! Hahaha!
Good, Alberich!
Good, you wicked man!
How quickly the dwarf
changed into a huge dragon!
> *The serpent vanishes; straight away in its place Alberich
> appears in his real shape.*
ALBERICH
Hehe! You smart alecks!
Now do you believe me?
LOGE *his voice quivering*
I'm quivering all over: that proves it!
You changed yourself fast   1310
into a large serpent:
as I've seen it myself,
I'm minded to believe the marvel.
Yet just as you got bigger,
can you also get smaller,
shrink into a tiny little thing?
That seems to me the most prudent
way of escaping danger smartly:
but it's too difficult to do, in my view!
ALBERICH
Too difficult for you,   1320
because you're too stupid!
How small do I have to be?

LOGE

Daß die feinste Klinze dich fasse,
wo bang die Kröte sich birgt.

ALBERICH

Pah! Nichts leichter!
Luge du her!

Er setzt den Helm auf.

'Krumm und grau
krieche Kröte!'

*Er verschwindet: die Götter gewahren im Gestein eine
Kröte auf sich zukriechen.*

LOGE *zu Wotan*

Dort, die Kröte!
Greife sie rasch!

*Wotan setzt seinen Fuß auf die Kröte: Loge fährt ihr nach
dem Kopfe und hält den Tarnhelm in der Hand.*

ALBERICH *ist plötzlich in seiner wirklichen Gestalt sichtbar
geworden, wie er sich unter Wotans Fuße windet*

Ohe! Verflucht!
Ich bin gefangen!

LOGE

Halt' ihn fest,
bis ich ihn band.

Loge bindet ihm mit einem Bastseile Hände und Füße.

Nun schnell hinauf:
dort ist er unser!

*Den Geknebelten, der sich wütend zu wehren sucht,
fassen beide und schleppen ihn mit sich zu der Kluft, aus
der sie herabkamen. Dort verschwinden sie, aufwärts-
steigend.*

*Die Szene verwandelt sich, nur in umgekehrter Weise,
wie zuvor.*

*Die Verwandlung führt wieder an den Schmieden
vorbei.*

fortdauernde Verwandlung nach oben

*Wotan und Loge, den gebundenen Alberich mit sich
führend, steigen aus der Kluft herauf.*

LOGE
  So that finest fissures can harbour you,
  the sort where toads hide in fear.
ALBERICH
  Pah! Nothing's easier!
  You just watch me!
    He puts on the helmet.
  'Bent and grey,
  creepy-crawly toad!'
    He vanishes: the gods gradually notice a toad in the rocks
    creeping towards them.
LOGE *to Wotan*
  There, the toad!
  Grab it fast!   1330
    Wotan traps the toad with his foot: Loge goes for its head
    and holds the Tarnhelm in his hand.
ALBERICH *suddenly becomes visible in his own shape as he*
    flails around underneath Wotan's foot
  Oh no! Curse you!
  I'm trapped!
LOGE
  Hold him tightly,
  until I've tied him up.
    Loge ties up his hands and feet with a strong-fibred
    rope.
  Now fast to the top:
  there he's ours!
    Both take hold of the muzzled prisoner, who angrily tries
    to defend himself, and drag him to the chasm through
    which they first entered. Then they vanish, climbing up-
    wards.
      The scene undergoes transformation as before, but in
    reverse order.
      The transformation leads past the forging workers
    again.
      continuing transformation upwards
      Wotan and Loge climb out of the crevice with Alberich
    trussed up, dragging him with them.

VIERTE SZENE

Freie Gegend auf Bergeshöhen, am Rhein gelegen

*Die Aussicht ist noch in fahle Nebel verhüllt wie am Schlusse
der zweiten Szene.*

LOGE
Da, Vetter,
sitze du fest!
Luge, Liebster,
1340   dort liegt die Welt,
die du Lung'rer gewinnen dir willst: –
welch Stellchen, sag,
bestimmst du drin mir zu Stall?
   Er schlägt tanzend ihm Schnippchen.
ALBERICH
Schändlicher Schächer!
Du Schalk! Du Schelm!
Löse den Bast,
binde mich los;
den Frevel sonst büßest du Frecher!
WOTAN
Gefangen bist du,
1350   fest mir gefesselt;
wie du die Welt,
was lebt und webt,
in deiner Gewalt schon wähntest;
in Banden liegst du vor mir –
du Banger kannst es nicht leugnen!
Zu ledigen dich,
bedarf's nun der Lösung.
ALBERICH
O ich Tropf!
Ich träumender Tor!
1360   Wie dumm traut' ich
dem diebischen Trug!

SCENE FOUR

An open mountaintop area, situated near the Rhine

*The stage is still enveloped in hazy fog as at the end of the
second scene.*

LOGE
  There, cousin,
  you sit tight!
  Look, dearest friend,
  there lies the world   1340
  you want to win, you skulking brat: –
  which little spot, tell me,
  did you spy out for my hovel?
    He dances around him, playing tricks.
ALBERICH
  Treacherous thief!
  Poor wag! Prankster!
  Undo the rope,
  cut me loose;
  or burn in hell for this brazen outrage!
WOTAN
  I'm holding you captive,
  securely bound;   1350
  once you fondly thought
  that you'd have power over
  all that lives and moves in the world;
  now you lie in shackles before me –
  no quarrelling with that, you wimp!
  We just need a ransom
  to set you free.
ALBERICH
  I'm an imbecile!
  In a fool's paradise!
  What a numbskull I was   1360
  not to see the sly trick!

Furchtbare Rache
räche den Fehl!

LOGE

Soll Rache dir frommen,
vor allem rate dich frei:
dem gebundnen Manne
büßt kein Freier den Frevel.
Drum sinnst du auf Rache,
rasch ohne Säumen

1370   sorg um die Lösung zunächst!

*Er zeigt ihm, den Fingern schnalzend, die Art der Lösung
an.*

ALBERICH *barsch*

So heischt, was ihr begehrt!

WOTAN

Den Hort und dein helles Gold.

ALBERICH

Gieriges Gaunergezücht!

für sich

Doch behalt' ich mir nur den Ring,
des Hortes entrat' ich dann leicht;
denn von neuem gewonnen
und wonnig genährt
ist er bald durch des Ringes Gebot:

Etwas ruhiger (freier!) *

eine Witzigung wär's,

1380   die weise mich macht;
zu teuer nicht zahl' ich die Zucht,
lass' für die Lehre ich den Tand.

WOTAN

Erlegst du den Hort?

ALBERICH

Löst mir die Hand,
so ruf' ich ihn her.

Loge löst ihm die Schlinge an der rechten Hand.

*Alberich rührt den Ring mit den Lippen und murmelt
heimlich einen Befehl.*

Wohlan, die Nibelungen

Let vile vengeance
expiate my blunder!

LOGE

To benefit from vengeance,
it's vital that you're free:
no roped-up man ever gets
a free one to atone for an outrage.
So if you're aiming for revenge,
take care of the ransom first,
and fast – no dawdling!   1370

*He shows him by snapping his fingers the kind of ransom
he means.*

ALBERICH *brusquely*

Just ask what you're lusting after!

WOTAN

The hoard and your radiant gold.

ALBERICH

Piggish pack of hoodlums!
aside
Yet if I keep back the ring,
the hoard's easily dispensed with;
the ring will dictate soon enough
that it's won back again
and happily cared for:
Somewhat more calm (more freely!) *
it will be a lesson
to make me wise;   1380
the training's not too costly for me,
if I let the hoard pay for the tuition.

WOTAN

Putting the hoard down as payment?

ALBERICH

Free my hand,
so I can summon it.

Loge loosens the rope around his right hand.
*Alberich touches the ring with his lips and furtively
mutters a command.*

It's done, I've summoned

rief ich mir nah.
Ihrem Herrn gehorchend
hör' ich den Hort
1390 aus der Tiefe sie führen zu Tag: –
nun löst mich vom lästigen Band!

WOTAN
Nicht eh'r, bis alles gezahlt.
Die Nibelungen steigen aus der Kluft herauf, mit den
Geschmeiden des Hortes beladen.

ALBERICH
O schändliche Schmach!
Während des Folgenden schichten die Nibelungen den
Hort auf.
Daß die scheuen Knechte
geknebelt selbst mich erschaun!
zu den Nibelungen
Dorthin geführt,
wie ich's befehl'!
All' zuhauf
schichtet den Hort!
1400 Helf' ich euch Lahmen?
Hierher nicht gelugt!
Rasch da! Rasch!
Dann rührt euch von hinnen!
Daß ihr mir schafft!
Fort in die Schachten!
Weh' euch, treff' ich euch faul!
Auf den Fersen folg ich euch nach!
Er küßt seinen Ring und streckt ihn gebieterisch aus.
Wie von einem Schlage getroffen, drängen sich die
Nibelungen scheu und ängstlich der Kluft zu, in die sie
schnell hinabschlüpfen.
Gezahlt hab' ich;
nun laßt mich zieh'n:
1410 und das Helmgeschmeid',
das Loge dort hält,
das gebt mir nun gütlich zurück!

the Nibelungs to approach.
I hear them obeying their master,
carrying the hoard
out of the depths into day: –   1390
now free me from the wretched ropes!

WOTAN

Not before everything's paid.
> *The Nibelungs climb up out of the chasm, weighed down*
> *with the hoard's treasure.*

ALBERICH

O foul disgrace!
> *During the following passage, the Nibelungs pile up the*
> *hoard.*

That these timid slaves
should see that even I'm enslaved!
> *to the Nibelungs*

Carry it over there,
like I told you to!
The lot of it,
pile up the hoard!
Want any help, sluggards?   1400
Don't look here!
There, fast! Fast!
Now get the hell out!
Slave for me more!
Off into the shafts!
You'll be sorry if I catch you slacking!
I'll be after you, hard on your heels!
> *He kisses his ring and holds it out dictatorially.*
> *At one fell swoop, the Nibelungs all surge timidly and*
> *nervously towards the chasm through which they quickly*
> *slip down.*

I've paid;
so let me go:
and the metalwork helmet   1410
that Loge's got there in his hand,
be so good as to return it to me!

LOGE *den Tarnhelm auf den Hort werfend*
  Zur Buße gehört auch die Beute.
ALBERICH
  Verfluchter Dieb! –
  Doch nur Geduld!
  Der den alten mir schuf,
  schafft einen andern:
  noch halt' ich die Macht,
  der Mime gehorcht.
1420 Schlimm zwar ist's,
  dem schlauen Feind
  zu lassen die listige Wehr! –
  Nun denn! Alberich
  ließ euch alles;
  jetzt löst, ihr Bösen, das Band!
LOGE *zu Wotan*
  Bist du befriedigt?
  Lass' ich ihn frei?
WOTAN
  Ein goldner Ring
  ragt dir am Finger:
1430 hörst du, Alp?
  Der, acht' ich, gehört mit zum Hort.
ALBERICH *entsetzt*
  Der Ring?
WOTAN
  Zu deiner Lösung
  mußt du ihn lassen.
ALBERICH *bebend*
  Das Leben, doch nicht den Ring!
WOTAN *heftiger*
  Den Reif' verlang' ich:
  mit dem Leben mach, was du willst.
ALBERICH
  Lös' ich mir Leib und Leben,
  den Ring auch muß ich mir lösen;
1440 Hand und Haupt,
  Aug und Ohr

LOGE *throwing the Tarnhelm onto the hoard*
  This prize is forfeit too.
ALBERICH
  Damned thief! –
  But be patient!
  I'll have another made
  by the maker of the old one:
  Mime obeys the power
  that I still hold.
  Admittedly it's bad   1420
  to let a sophisticated weapon
  be taken by a shrewd enemy! –
  But then! Alberich's
  leaving you everything;
  now, you diabolical pair, cut the ropes!
LOGE *to Wotan*
  Happy with that?
  Shall I free him?
WOTAN
  A golden ring
  protrudes on your finger:
  are you listening, dwarf?   1430
  In my estimation, it's part of the hoard.
ALBERICH *aghast*
  The ring?
WOTAN
  If you want to be free,
  it must be forfeit.
ALBERICH *shaking*
  My life, but not the ring!
WOTAN *more violently*
  I'm claiming the ring:
  do what you like with your life.
ALBERICH
  If I cut off limb and life,
  I must cut off the ring too;
  hand and head,   1440
  eye and ear

sind nicht mehr mein eigen
als hier dieser rote Ring!

*Wotan tritt mit zwei Schritten energisch vor Alberich
hin.* *

WOTAN

Dein eigen nennst du den Ring?
Rasest du, schamloser Albe?
Nüchtern sag,
wem entnahmst du das Gold,
daraus du den schimmernden schufst?
War's dein eigen,
1450   was du Arger
der Wassertiefe entwandt?
Bei des Rheines Töchtern
hole dir Rat,
ob ihr Gold sie
zu eigen dir gaben,
das du zum Ring dir geraubt!

ALBERICH

Schmähliche Tücke!
Schändlicher Trug! –

*Mit eindringendem Ausdruck, im Tempo etwas verwei-
lend* *

Wirfst du Schächer
1460   die Schuld mir vor,
die dir so wonnig erwünscht?
Wie gern raubtest
du selbst dem Rheine das Gold,
war nur so leicht
die Kunst, es zu schmieden, erlangt?
Wie glückt es nun
dir Gleißner zum Heil,
daß der Niblung, ich,
aus schmählicher Not,
1470   in des Zornes Zwange,
den schrecklichen Zauber gewann,
dess' Werk nun lustig dir lacht?
Des Unseligen,

are no more my own
than this red ring here!
> *Wotan takes two vigorous strides to be in front of Al-*
> *berich**

WOTAN

You're claiming the ring for yourself?
Are you raving mad, shameless dwarf?
Tell us, soberly now,
from whom did you take the gold
to shape the shimmering object?
Was it yours,
you desperate man,   1450
to pilfer from the waters' deep?
Go to the daughters of the Rhine
and ask them
if they gave their gold
to you as your own,
the gold you robbed for the ring!

ALBERICH

Miserable malice!
Foul chicanery! –
> *With piercing expression, in a tempo that is somewhat*
> *lingering**

Are you blaming me,
thief, for something   1460
you happily wish you'd done?
Wouldn't you have gladly stolen
the gold from the Rhine yourself,
if you'd found an easy way
to learn the art of forging it?
Aren't you lucky with your
forked tongue to find salvation
in the fact that I, the Nibelung,
out of miserable need,
maddened by anger,   1470
won mastery of the formidable magic,
its work now smiling on you with glee?
Is this shocking deed,

Angstversehrten
fluchfertige,
furchtbare Tat,
zu fürstlichem Tand
soll sie fröhlich dir taugen,
zur Freude dir frommen mein Fluch?
1480 Hüte dich,
herrischer Gott! –
Frevelte ich,
so frevelt' ich frei an mir: –
doch an allem was war,
ist und wird,
frevelst, Ewiger, du –
entreißest du frech mir den Ring!

WOTAN
Her den Ring!
Kein Recht an ihm
1490 schwörst du schwatzend dir zu.
    Er ergreift Alberich und entzieht seinem Finger mit hef-
    tiger Gewalt den Ring.

ALBERICH *gräßlich aufschreiend*
Ha! – Zertrümmert! Zerknickt!
Der Traurigen traurigster Knecht!

WOTAN *den Ring betrachtend*
Nun halt' ich, was mich erhebt,
der Mächtigen mächtigsten Herrn!
    Er steckt den Ring an.

LOGE *zu Wotan*
Ist er gelöst?

WOTAN
Bind ihn los!
    Loge löst Alberich vollends die Bande.

LOGE *zu Alberich*
Schlüpfe denn heim!
Keine Schlinge hält dich:
frei fahre dahin!

ALBERICH *sich erhebend*
1500 Bin ich nun frei?
    wütend lachend

curse at the ready,
by someone ill-fated
and riddled with fear,
nicely suited to your purpose
of acquiring princely playthings,
of usefully finding joy in my curse?
Be on your guard,   1480
imperious god! –
If I've transgressed,
then only freely against myself: –
but it's against all things that were,
are and will be
that, eternal one, you transgress –
if you dare to wrench the ring from me!

WOTAN
The ring, hand it over!
Nothing you're babbling about
gives you a right to it.   1490
*He grips Alberich and pulls the ring from his finger with
ferocious violence.*

ALBERICH *screaming out horribly*
Aah! – Gutted! Crippled!
Most desolate of desolate slaves!

WOTAN *observing the ring*
Something ennobling I hold at last,
most powerful of powerful lords!
He puts on the ring.

LOGE *to Wotan*
Is he free?

WOTAN
Cut him loose!
Loge frees all the ropes tying Alberich.

LOGE *to Alberich*
Now skulk off home!
No rope's holding you back:
feel free to go!

ALBERICH *lifting himself up*
I'm free now?   1500
laughing angrily

Wirklich frei?
So grüß' euch denn
meiner Freiheit erster Gruß!
Wie durch Fluch er mir geriet,
verflucht sei dieser Ring!
Gab sein Gold
mir Macht ohne Maß,
nun zeug' sein Zauber
Tod dem, der ihn trägt!
1510   Kein Froher soll
seiner sich freun,
keinem Glücklichen lache
sein lichter Glanz!
Wer ihn besitzt,
den sehre die Sorge,
und wer ihn nicht hat,
den nage der Neid!
Jeder giere
nach seinem Gut,
1520   doch keiner genieße
mit Nutzen sein!
Ohne Wucher hüt' ihn sein Herr;
doch den Würger zieh' er ihm zu!
Dem Tode verfallen,
feßle den Feigen die Furcht:
so lang er lebt
sterb' er lechzend dahin,
des Ringes Herr
als des Ringes Knecht: –
1530   bis in meiner Hand
den geraubten wieder ich halte!
So segnet
in höchster Not
der Nibelung seinen Ring: –
behalt' ihn nun,
        lachend
hüte ihn wohl!
        grimmig

Really free?
Then let my freedom's
first greeting to you be this!
Just as a curse handed it to me,
so let this ring in turn be cursed!
To me, the gift of its gold
was power without precedent.
To all who wear it, its magic
now shall bring death!
No blithe spirit shall   1510
rejoice in it,
no glad soul bask
in its lucid brilliance!
Let those who own it
be plagued by sorrow,
and those who don't
by festering envy!
Let everyone ache
to own it,
but let no one enjoy   1520
what it brings!
Its protector shall amass no riches;
but attract his exterminator, it will!
A slave to death,
let his faint heart freeze with fear:
as long as he lives,
let the ring's lord,
as the ring's slave,
rot with longing: –
until I hold what's been stolen   1530
again in my hand!
With no way out now remotely in sight,
the Nibelung thus
consecrates his ring: –
just keep it,
    laughing
take good care of it!
    viciously

Meinem Fluch fliehest du nicht!
Er verschwindet schnell in der Kluft.
   Wotan einen Moment verwirrt, faßt sich gleich wieder. *
   Der dichte Nebelduft des Vordergrundes klärt sich allmählich auf.

LOGE
Lauschtest du
seinem Liebesgruß?

WOTAN *in den Anblick des Ringes an seiner Hand versunken*
1540 Gönn ihm die geifernde Lust!
   Es wird immer heller.

LOGE *nach rechts in die Szene blickend*
Fasolt und Fafner
nahen von fern:
Freia führen sie her.
   Aus dem sich immer mehr zerteilenden Nebel erscheinen Donner, Froh und Fricka und eilen dem Vordergrunde zu.

FROH
Sie kehren zurück!

DONNER
Willkommen, Bruder!

FRICKA *besorgt zu Wotan*
Bringst du gute Kunde?

LOGE *auf den Hort deutend*
Mit List und Gewalt
gelang das Werk:
dort liegt, was Freia löst.

DONNER
1550 Aus der Riesen Haft
naht dort die Holde.

FROH
Wie liebliche Luft
wieder uns weht,
wonnig Gefühl
die Sinne erfüllt!
Traurig ging' es uns allen,
getrennt für immer von ihr,

You will not flee from my curse!
He vanishes quickly inside the chasm.
Wotan is momentarily confused, but immediately pulls himself together. *
The thick haze of fog in the foreground gradually clears up.

LOGE
Were you listening
to his declaration of love?

WOTAN *looking at the ring on his finger with rapt attention*
Let him enjoy his rant!   1540
It is constantly growing lighter.

LOGE *looking into the wings on the right*
Fasolt and Fafner
are coming nearer:
they're bringing Freia.
As the fog dissipates more and more, Donner, Froh and Fricka emerge from it and hurry into the foreground.

FROH
They're coming back!

DONNER
Welcome, brother!

FRICKA *to Wotan, uneasily*
Are you bringing good news?

LOGE *pointing to the hoard*
With cunning and force,
we accomplished our task:
it's lying there, Freia's ransom.

DONNER
There comes our fair sister   1550
out of the giants' clutches.

FROH
How the soft breezes
sway over us again,
replenishing our senses
with feelings of happiness!
How sad for all of us
had we been parted for ever from her,

die leidlos ewiger Jugend
jubelnde Lust uns verleiht.

*Der Vordergrund ist wieder ganz hell geworden; das
Aussehen der Götter gewinnt durch das Licht wieder die
erste Frische: über dem Hintergrunde haftet jedoch noch
der Nebelschleier, so daß die ferne Burg unsichtbar bleibt.
Fasolt und Fafner treten auf, Freia zwischen sich
führend. Fricka eilt freudig auf die Schwester zu, um sie
zu umarmen.*

FRICKA *mit Wärme zu singen* *

1560   Lieblichste Schwester,
süßeste Lust!
Bist du mir wieder gewonnen?

FASOLT *ihr wehrend*
Halt! Nicht sie berührt!
Noch gehört sie uns. –
Auf Riesenheims
ragender Mark
rasteten wir;
mit treuem Mut
des Vertrages Pfand
1570   pflegten wir.
So sehr mich's reut,
zurück doch bring ich's,
erlegt uns Brüdern
die Lösung ihr.

WOTAN
Bereit liegt die Lösung:
des Goldes Maß
sei nun gütlich gemessen.

FASOLT
Das Weib zu missen,
wisse, gemutet mich weh:
1580   soll aus dem Sinn sie mir schwinden,
des Geschmeides Hort
häufe denn so,
daß meinem Blick
die Blühende ganz er verdeck'!

who bestows upon us the exultant
joy of youth, eternally free of pain.

> *The foreground is filled with brightness once more; the light restores to the appearance of the gods their original freshness: but a foggy haze still shrouds the background such that the fortress in the distance remains invisible.*
>
> *Fasolt and Fafner enter, shepherding Freia between them. Fricka rushes up to her sister with elation in order to embrace her.*

FRICKA *to be sung with warmth* *

Sister most darling,   1560
sweetest delight!
Have I won you back?

FASOLT *fending her off*

Stop! Hands off her!
She's still ours. –
We rested
at the lofty entrance
to the land of the giants;
with true tenacity
we attended to
the contract's pledge.   1570
Much as it pains me,
I'll still bring her back,
provided you pay us
brothers the ransom.

WOTAN

The ransom's all ready:
just let the amount of gold
be amicably measured.

FASOLT

You should know, doing without
the woman will be painful for me:
if I am to get her off my mind,   1580
the hoard's treasure
must be piled in such a way
that it totally conceals
her vivid presence from my sight!

WOTAN

So stellt das Maß
nach Freias Gestalt!

Freia wird von den beiden Riesen in die Mitte gestellt.
Darauf stoßen sie ihre Pfähle zu Freias beiden Seiten so
in den Boden, daß sie gleiche Höhe und Breite mit ihrer
Gestalt messen.

FAFNER

Gepflanzt sind die Pfähle
nach Pfandes Maß;
gehäuft nun füll' es der Hort!

WOTAN

1590   Eilt mit dem Werk:
widerlich ist mir's!

LOGE

Hilf mir, Froh!

FROH

Freias Schmach
eil' ich zu enden.

Loge und Froh häufen hastig zwischen den Pfählen das
Geschmeide.

FAFNER

Nicht so leicht
und locker gefügt!

Mit roher Kraft drückt er die Geschmeide dicht zusam-
men.

Fest und dicht
füll' er das Maß!

Er beugt sich, um nach Lücken zu spähen.

Hier lug' ich noch durch:
1600   verstopft mir die Lücken!

LOGE

Zurück, du Grober!

FAFNER

Hierher!

LOGE

Greif mir nichts an!

WOTAN

Then arrange it all
to fit Freia's shape!

Freia is placed in the middle by the two giants.

*They plunge their poles on each side of Freia into the
ground in such a way that they correspond with her shape
in height and breadth.*

FAFNER

The poles have been planted
to fit the size of the pledge;
heap the hoard, let the space be filled!

WOTAN

Get on with it: 1590
it makes me sick!

LOGE

Help me, Froh!

FROH

I'm quick to end
Freia's dishonour.

*Loge and Froh hurriedly heap up the treasure between
the poles.*

FAFNER

The pile's too flimsy
and wobbly!

*With brute force, he presses the treasure together to make
a tighter fit.*

Solid and tight
it's got to be!

He bends down to see if there are any chinks.

Here I still see through:
plug the gaps for me!   1600

LOGE

Back off, you ruffian!

FAFNER

Over here!

LOGE

Don't even touch me!

FAFNER
Hierher! Die Klinze verklemmt!

WOTAN *unmutig sich abwendend*
 alles fest im Tempo weiter. Ja kein sentimentales Zu-
 *rückhalten!**
Tief in der Brust
brennt mir die Schmach!

FRICKA *den Blick auf Freia geheftet*
Sieh, wie in Scham
schmählich die Edle steht:
um Erlösung fleht
1610 stumm der leidende Blick.
Böser Mann!
Der Minnigen botest du das!

FAFNER
Noch mehr!
Noch mehr hierher!

DONNER
Kaum halt' ich mich;
schäumende Wut
weckt mir der schamlose Wicht!
Hierher, du Hund!
Willst du messen,
1620 so miß dich selber mit mir!

FAFNER
Ruhig, Donner!
Rolle, wo's taugt:
hier nützt dein Rasseln dir nichts.

DONNER *ausholend*
Nicht dich Schmähl'chen zu zerschmettern?

WOTAN
Friede doch! –
Schon dünkt mich Freia verdeckt.
 Fafner mißt den Hort genau mit dem Blick und späht
 nach Lücken.

LOGE
Der Hort ging auf.

FAFNER
Noch schimmert mir Holdas Haar: –

FAFNER
   Over here! Fill the gap tight!
WOTAN *turning away with annoyance*
         everything to continue in strict tempo. Absolutely no
      sentimental dawdling! *
   Deep inside my breast
   dishonour burns!
FRICKA *her eyes riveted on Freia*
   Look how miserably
   the noble woman stands in shame:
   her plaintive countenance
   begs wordlessly for redemption.   1610
   Evil man!
   You offered this to the goddess of love!
FAFNER
   Still more!
   Still more over here!
DONNER
   I'm beside myself;
   the flagrant wretch
   has me seething with fury!
   Over here, you dog!
   Want to measure her out?
   Then measure yourself against me!   1620
FAFNER
   Steady, Donner!
   Be rough when it's right:
   raucousness will get you nowhere.
DONNER *lunging out*
   Not even to batter a little sod like you?
WOTAN
   Stop it! –
   I think Freia's already out of sight.
      Fafner scrutinizes the hoard with a sharp eye on the look-
      out for gaps.
LOGE
   The hoard's all gone.
FAFNER
   Holda's hair is still shimmering at me: –

dort das Gewirk
1630 wirf auf den Hort!

LOGE

Wie? Auch den Helm?

FAFNER

Hurtig, her mit ihm!

WOTAN

Laß ihn denn fahren!

Loge wirft den Tarnhelm auf den Hort.

LOGE

So sind wir denn fertig!
Seid ihr zufrieden?

FASOLT

Freia, die Schöne,
schau' ich nicht mehr: –
so ist sie gelöst?
muß ich sie lassen?

Er tritt nahe hinzu und späht durch den Hort.

1640 Weh! Noch blitzt
ihr Blick zu mir her;
des Auges Stern
strahlt mich noch an;
durch eine Spalte
muß ich's erspäh'n. –

außer sich

Seh' ich dies wonnige Auge,

Mit glutvoller Leidenschaft*

von dem Weibe laß ich nicht ab!

FAFNER *beschleunigend*

He! Euch rat' ich,
verstopft mir die Ritze!

LOGE

1650 Nimmer-Satte!
Seht ihr denn nicht,
ganz schwand uns der Hort?

*Fafner stößt seine Worte äußerst grob und entschieden
hervor.**

there, that metal object,
throw it on the hoard!   1630

LOGE

What? The helmet too?

FAFNER

Swiftly, let's have it!

WOTAN

Let them have it!
Loge flings the Tarnhelm onto the hoard.

LOGE

So now we're finished!
Are you pleased?

FASOLT

I look no more upon
the beautiful Freia: –
so is she free?
Must I leave her?
He steps over nearer to the hoard and squints through it.
Argh! She still looks   1640
at me with brilliant light;
the stars in her eyes
shine on me still:
and I have to see it
through a crack. –
beside himself
When I behold these blissful eyes,
With sultry passion *
I cannot let this woman go!

FAFNER *responding quickly*

Hey! You'd better
plug that gap for me!

LOGE

Never sated!   1650
The hoard's completely gone,
can't you see?
*Fafner forces out his words extremely coarsely and de-
cisively.* *

FAFNER
Mitnichten, Freund!
An Wotans Finger
glänzt von Gold noch ein Ring:
den gebt, die Ritze zu füllen!

WOTAN
Wie! Diesen Ring?

LOGE *immer lebhaft**
Laßt euch raten!
Den Rheintöchtern
1660   gehört dies Gold;
ihnen gibt Wotan es wieder.

WOTAN
Was schwatzest du da?
Was schwer ich mir erbeutet,
ohne Bangen wahr' ich's für mich!

LOGE
Schlimm dann steht's
um mein Versprechen,
das ich den Klagenden gab!

WOTAN
Dein Versprechen bindet mich nicht:
als Beute bleibt mir der Reif.

FAFNER
1670   Doch hier zur Lösung
mußt du ihn legen.

WOTAN
Fordert frech, was ihr wollt:
alles gewähr' ich;
um alle Welt, doch
nicht fahren lass' ich den Ring!

   Fasolt zieht wütend Freia hinter dem Horte hervor.

FASOLT
Aus denn ist's!
Beim alten bleibt's;
nun folgt uns Freia für immer!

FREIA
Hilfe!

FAFNER

No way, friend!
On Wotan's finger
there's still a ring of gleaming gold:
give it here to fill the gap!

WOTAN

What! This ring?

LOGE *always lively* *

Be advised!
The Rhinedaughters
own this gold; 1660
Wotan will give it back to them.

WOTAN

What are you gabbling about?
What was hard for me to get,
I'm not afraid to keep for myself!

LOGE

A bad omen, then,
for the promise I made
to the aggrieved daughters!

WOTAN

Your promise commits me to nothing:
the ring stays with me as trophy.

FAFNER

But you've got to put it here 1670
as part of the ransom.

WOTAN

Dare to ask what you want:
I'll concede anything;
but not for the life of me
will I let go of the ring!

In a rage, Fasolt drags Freia out from behind the hoard.

FASOLT

So be it!
It's just as we were;
Freia's with us now for ever!

FREIA

Help!

FRICKA

1680   Harter Gott!

FREIA

Hilfe!

FRICKA

Gib ihnen nach!

FROH

Spare das Gold nicht!

DONNER

Spende den Ring doch!

> *Fafner hält den fortdrängenden Fasolt noch auf: alle stehen bestürzt.*

WOTAN *Mit unbeugsamster Entschlossenheit**

Laßt mich in Ruh':

den Reif geb' ich nicht!

> *Wotan wendet sich zürnend zur Seite.*
>
> *Die Bühne hat sich von neuem verfinstert.*
>
> *Aus der Felskluft zur Seite bricht ein bläulicher Schein hervor: in ihm wird plötzlich Erda sichtbar, die bis zu halber Leibeshöhe aus der Tiefe aufsteigt; sie ist von edler Gestalt, weithin von schwarzem Haare umwallt.*

ERDA *sehr langsam und feierlich**

> *in geheimnisvoll verschleiertem Tone zu bringen**
>
> *die Hand mahnend gegen Wotan ausstreckend*

Weiche, Wotan! Weiche!

Flieh des Ringes Fluch!

Rettungslos

1690   dunklem Verderben

weiht dich sein Gewinn.

WOTAN *leise**

Wer bist du, mahnendes Weib?

ERDA

Wie alles war – weiß ich;

wie alles wird,

wie alles sein wird –

seh' ich auch:

der ew'gen Welt

Urwala,

FRICKA
  Callous god!
FREIA
  Help!
FRICKA
  Give way to them!
FROH
  Don't keep the gold!
DONNER
  Release the ring, no matter what!
      *Fafner stops Fasolt from rushing off: all are rooted to the
      spot aghast.*
WOTAN *With the most unrelenting resolve**
  Leave me in peace:
  I won't give up the ring!
      Wotan turns aside enraged.
        The stage has darkened again.
        *Out of a chasm in the rocks at the side a bluish ray of
      light bursts forth: in it Erda suddenly becomes visible as
      she rises up out of the deep to half her height; she is of
      noble stature, cloaked by waves of black hair.*
ERDA *very slowly and solemnly**
        *to be conveyed in a cryptically veiled tone of voice**
        raising an admonitory hand towards Wotan
  Go back, Wotan! Go back!
  Be gone from the ring's curse!
  Your trophy will doom you
  to dark destruction
  beyond rescue.
WOTAN *softly**
  Who are you, woman, to warn me?
ERDA
  All that was – I know;
  all that is,
  all that will be –
  I see that too:
  the eternal world's
  primal seeress,

Erda, mahnt deinen Mut. –
1700 Drei der Töchter,
urerschaff'ne,
gebar mein Schoß:
was ich sehe,
sagen dir nächtlich die Nornen.
Doch höchste Gefahr
führt mich heut
selbst zu dir her.
Höre! Höre! Höre!
Alles, was ist, – endet!
1710 Ein düstrer Tag
dämmert den Göttern: –
   mit entsetzenerfülltem Ausdruck *
dir rat' ich, meide den Ring!
WOTAN *Erda versinkt langsam bis an die Brust, während der*
   bläuliche Schein zu dunkeln beginnt.
Geheimnishehr
hallt mir dein Wort: –
weile, daß mehr ich wisse!
ERDA *im Versinken*
Ich warnte dich;
du weißt genug:
   In ruhigem ernst-bedeutsamem Tone *
sinn in Sorg' und Furcht!
   Sie verschwindet gänzlich.
     Wotan will der Verschwindenden in die Kluft nach, um
     sie zu halten: Froh und Fricka werfen sich ihm entgegen
     und halten ihn zurück.
WOTAN
Soll ich sorgen und fürchten,
1720 dich muß ich fassen,
alles erfahren!
FRICKA
Was willst du, Wütender?
FROH
Halt ein, Wotan!
Scheue die Edle,

Erda, cautions your conceit. –
Three daughters,   1700
primordially conceived,
my womb brought forth:
what I see,
the Norns tell you at night.
But today utmost peril
leads me to you
in person.
Pay heed! Pay heed! Pay heed!
All that is, – will end!
A dark day   1710
is dawning for the gods: –
  *with expression suffused with horror**
I advise you, avoid the ring!

WOTAN *Erda is sinking down slowly to chest height, while the
    bluish ray of light starts to fade.*
Noble and cryptic
to me is the echo of your Word: –
wait, that I may know more!

ERDA *continuing to sink down*
I've warned you;
you know enough:
  *In a calm tone of voice both serious and momentous**
ponder it with disquiet and dread!
  She completely disappears.
    *Wotan wants to follow her vanishing figure into the
    chasm in order to stop her: Froh and Fricka thrust them-
    selves into his path and hold him back.*

WOTAN
If I am to live in disquiet and dread,
I must catch you,   1720
learn everything!

FRICKA
What do you want, intemperate man?

FROH
Stop, Wotan!
Beware the noble goddess,

achte ihr Wort!
> *Wotan starrt sinnend vor sich hin.*

DONNER *sich entschlossen zu den Riesen wendend*
Hört, ihr Riesen!
Zurück, und harret!
Das Gold wird euch gegeben.

FREIA
Darf ich es hoffen?
1730 Dünkt euch Holda
wirklich der Lösung wert?
> *Alle blicken gespannt auf Wotan; dieser, nach tiefem Sinnen zu sich kommend, erfaßt seinen Speer und schwenkt ihn, wie zum Zeichen eines mutigen Entschlusses.*

WOTAN *Bei diesen Worten durchmißt er mit majestätischen Schritten den ganzen Bühnenraum.* *
Zu mir, Freia!
Du bist befreit!
Wieder gekauft
kehr' uns die Jugend zurück!
Ihr Riesen, nehmt euren Ring!
> *Er wirft den Ring auf den Hort. Die Riesen lassen Freia los: Sie eilt freudig auf die Götter zu, die sie abwechselnd längere Zeit in höchster Freude liebkosen.*
>
> *Fafner hat sogleich einen ungeheuren Sack ausgebreitet und macht sich über den Hort her, um ihn da hineinzuschichten.*
>
> *Fafner wirft ein altes, schlecht aussehendes, von ihm für wertlos gehaltenes Schwert, nach kurzer Besichtigung wieder weg.* *

FASOLT *dem Bruder sich entgegenwerfend*
Halt, du Gieriger!
Gönne mir auch was!
Redliche Teilung
1740 taugt uns beiden.

FAFNER
Mehr an der Maid als am Gold
lag dir verliebtem Geck!
Mit Müh' zum Tausch

respect her words!
   Wotan stares in front of him, thinking.
DONNER *addressing the giants with resolution*
  Hear this, you giants!
  Come back here, and wait!
  The gold will be given to you.
FREIA
  May I still hope?
  Do you think Holda   1730
  really worth the ransom?
   All look to Wotan in suspense; after losing himself in deep
   thought, he comes to himself, takes hold of the spear and
   swings it as a sign of spirited resolve.
WOTAN *In majestic strides he traverses the entire area of the*
   stage with these words. *
  To me, Freia!
  You're freed!
  Bring us back
  our repossessed youth!
  You giants, take your ring!
   He tosses the ring onto the hoard. The giants let Freia go
   free: elated, she rushes up to the gods, who for some time
   each hug her in turn in an outpouring of joy.
   At the same time Fafner has laid out a huge sack and
   delves right into the hoard, piling it into the sack layer by
   layer.
   Fafner throws away an old, badly worn-out sword
   again, after inspecting it briefly and judging it to be
   worthless. *
FASOLT *throwing himself in his brother's way*
  Stop, you pig!
  Let me have some too!
  Honest helpings
  are best for us both.   1740
FAFNER
  You were after the young woman more
  than the gold, you flirtatious fop!
  Much ado it cost me

vermocht' ich dich Toren;
ohne zu teilen,
hättest du Freia gefreit:
teil' ich den Hort,
billig behalt' ich
die größte Hälfte für mich!

FASOLT

1750   Schändlicher du!
Mir diesen Schimpf? –
    zu den Göttern
Euch ruf' ich zu Richtern:
teilet nach Recht
uns redlich den Hort!
    Wotan wendet sich verächtlich ab.

LOGE *zu Fasolt*
Den Hort laß ihn raffen;
halte du nur auf den Ring!
    Fasolt stürzt sich auf Fafner, der immerzu eingesackt hat.

FASOLT
Zurück! Du Frecher!
Mein ist der Ring;
mir blieb er für Freias Blick!
    Er greift hastig nach dem Ring: sie ringen.

FAFNER

1760   Fort mit der Faust!
Der Ring ist mein!
    Fasolt entreißt Fafner den Ring.

FASOLT
Ich halt' ihn, mir gehört er!

FAFNER *mit seinem Pfahle ausholend*
Halt ihn fest, daß er nicht fall'!
    Er streckt Fasolt mit einem Streiche zu Boden: dem Ster-
    benden entreißt er dann hastig den Ring.
      *zu Fasolt sich niederbückend, mit Hohn**
Nun blinzle nach Freias Blick!
An den Reif rührst du nicht mehr!
    Er steckt den Ring in den Sack und rafft dann gemächlich
    den Hort vollends ein. Alle Götter stehen entsetzt: feier-
    liches Schweigen.

to get you to barter, you fool;
Freia you'd have sued for love
without sharing her:
if I divide the hoard,
in fairness I keep
the bigger half for myself!

FASOLT

You traitor!   1750
For me, this affront? –
   to the gods
I appeal to you as judges:
divide the hoard lawfully
and honestly between us!
   Wotan turns aside in contempt.

LOGE *to Fasolt*

Let him hog the hoard:
just don't lose sight of the ring!
   Fasolt lunges at Fafner, who's continued filling his sack.

FASOLT

Back off! Brazen bully!
Mine is the ring;
left to me for Freia's gaze!
   He makes a hasty grab for the ring: they wrestle.

FAFNER

Keep your hands off!   1760
The ring's mine!
   Fasolt prises the ring away from Fafner.

FASOLT

I'm holding it, it belongs to me!

FAFNER *raising his arms with the pole ready to strike*

Hold it tightly, in case it drops!
   *He lays Fasolt low with a single stroke: then he hastily
   prises the ring away from his dying brother.*
     *Fafner mockingly bends down to Fasolt**

Squint at Freia's gaze now!
No ring on the finger any more for you!
   *He tucks the ring into the sack and leisurely gathers what
   remains of the hoard into it. All the gods are rooted to
   the spot in horror: portentous silence.*

WOTAN *erschüttert*
  Furchtbar nun
  erfind' ich des Fluches Kraft! –
LOGE *Mit scharf-ironischem Ton**
  Was gleicht, Wotan,
  wohl deinem Glücke?
1770 Viel erwarb dir
  des Ringes Gewinn;
  daß er nun dir genommen,
  nützt dir noch mehr:
  deine Feinde – sieh! –
  fällen sich selbst –
  um das Gold, das du vergabst.
WOTAN
  Wie doch Bangen mich bindet!
  Sorg' und Furcht
  fesseln den Sinn –
1780 wie sie zu enden,
  lehre mich Erda: –
  zu ihr muß ich hinab!
FRICKA *schmeichelnd sich an ihn schmiegend*
  Wo weilst du, Wotan?
  Winkt dir nicht hold
  die hehre Burg,
  die des Gebieters
  gastlich bergend nun harrt?
WOTAN *düster*
  Mit bösem Zoll
  zahlt' ich den Bau!
DONNER *auf den Hintergrund deutend, der noch in Nebel-
    schleier gehüllt ist.*
1790 Schwüles Gedünst
  schwebt in der Luft; –
  lästig ist mir
  der trübe Druck!
  Das bleiche Gewölk
  samml' ich zu blitzendem Wetter,
  das fegt den Himmel mir hell!

WOTAN *appalled*
>The terrible force of the curse
>dawns on me now! –

LOGE *With a sharply ironic tone**
>Aren't you, Wotan,
>incomparably lucky?
>By winning the ring   1770
>you won a great deal;
>now you've divested yourself of it,
>it'll be even more useful:
>your enemies – look! –
>they're killing each other –
>all because of the gold you gave away.

WOTAN
>But fear pins me down despite it!
>Disquiet and dread
>enchain my mind –
>let Erda teach me   1780
>how to end them: –
>I must go down to her!

FRICKA *snuggling up to him affectionately*
>Where are you, Wotan?
>Is not the fine fortress
>beckoning to you fondly,
>its hospitable haven
>awaiting its master?

WOTAN *bleakly*
>I paid for that building
>with tainted goods!

DONNER *pointing towards the background, which is still en-*
>*veloped by a veil of fog.*
>A humid haze   1790
>floats in the air; –
>the sunless blanket
>saps my spirits!
>The dull clouds
>I shall gather into stormy weather,
>and sweep the heavens clean!

> *Donner besteigt einen hohen Felsstein am Talabhange*
> *und schwingt dort seinen Hammer; mit dem Folgenden*
> *ziehen die Nebel sich um ihn zusammen.*

Heda! Heda! Hedo!
Zu mir, du Gedüft!
Ihr Dünste, zu mir!
Donner, der Herr,
ruft euch zu Heer!

> *Er schwingt den Hammer.*

Auf des Hammers Schwung
schwebet herbei!
Dunstig Gedämpf!
Schwebend Gedüft!
1800   Donner, der Herr,
ruft euch zu Heer!
Heda! Heda! Hedo!

> *Donner verschwindet völlig in einer immer finsterer sich*
> *ballenden Gewitterwolke.*
>
> *Man hört Donners Hammerschlag schwer auf den Fels-*
> *stein fallen.*
>
> *Ein starker Blitz entfährt der Wolke: ein heftiger Don-*
> *nerschlag folgt.*
>
> *Froh ist im Gewölk verschwunden.*
>
> *[Donner] unsichtbar*

Bruder, hierher!
1810   Weise der Brücke den Weg!

> *Plötzlich verzieht sich die Wolke; Donner und Froh*
> *werden sichtbar: von ihren Füßen aus zieht sich mit blen-*
> *dendem Leuchten, eine Regenbogen-Brücke über das Tal*
> *hinüber bis zur Burg, die jetzt im Glanze der Abendsonne*
> *strahlt.*
>
> *Fafner, der neben der Leiche seines Bruders endlich*
> *den ganzen Hort eingerafft, hat, den ungeheuren Sack*
> *auf dem Rücken, während Donners Gewitterzauber die*
> *Bühne verlassen.*

FROH *der der Brücke mit der ausgestreckten Hand den Weg*
      über das Tal angewiesen
           zu den Göttern

*Donner climbs onto a high rock on the valley slope where
he swings his hammer; during the following, clouds of
mist draw together around him.*

Heda! Heda! Hedo!
To me, you mist!
You clouds, to me!
Donner, your lord,
summons you to order!
   He swings the hammer.
At the swing of my hammer,
float over here!
Vaporous haze!
Floating mist!
Donner, your master,   1800
summons you to order!
Heda! Heda! Hedo!

*Donner completely disappears inside an increasingly dark
accumulation of thundercloud.*

   *Donner's hammer is heard hitting the rock with a
heavy blow.*

   *The cloud emits a powerful flash of lightning: a violent
clap of thunder follows.*

   Froh has vanished in the clouds.

   [Donner] invisible
Brother, over here!
Show the bridge where it must lead!   1810

*Suddenly the cloud disperses; Donner and Froh become
visible: a rainbow bridge with dazzlingly shining lights
stretches out from their feet across the valley towards
the fortress, now resplendent in the glow of the evening
sun.*

   *Fafner, who alongside the corpse of his brother has at
last finished packing away the hoard, has left the stage
during Donner's magic storm with the enormous sack on
his back.*

FROH *who with an outstretched hand has shown the bridge,
the path to be taken across the valley*
   to the gods

Zur Burg führt die Brücke,
leicht, doch fest eurem Fuß:
beschreitet kühn
ihren schrecklosen Pfad!
 Wotan und die andern Götter sind sprachlos in den
 prächtigen Anblick verloren.

WOTAN
Abendlich strahlt
der Sonne Auge;
in prächtiger Glut
prangt glänzend die Burg.
In des Morgens Scheine
1820 mutig erschimmernd,
lag sie herrenlos,
hehr verlockend vor mir.
Von Morgen bis Abend,
in Müh' und Angst,
nicht wonnig ward sie gewonnen!
Es naht die Nacht:
vor ihrem Neid
biete sie Bergung nun.
 Wotan ergreift das von Fafner liegend gelassene Schwert. *
 W[otan] deutet mit dem Schwert auf die Burg. *
 Wie von einem großen Gedanken ergriffen, sehr ent-
 schlossen
So grüß' ich die Burg,
1830 sicher vor Bang' und Grau'n!
 Er wendet sich feierlich zu Fricka.
Folge mir, Frau!
In Walhall wohne mit mir.

FRICKA
Was deutet der Name?
Nie, dünkt mich, hört' ich ihn nennen.

WOTAN
Was, mächtig der Furcht
mein Mut mir erfand,
wenn siegend es lebt,
leg' es den Sinn dir dar!

The bridge leads to the fortress,
airy, yet solid beneath your feet:
take its path unafraid,
it has no fright in store!
Wotan and the other gods are lost in speechless amaze-
ment at the glorious sight.

WOTAN

The eye of the sun
glows at evening time;
in its glorious embers
the fortress shines radiantly forth.
In the morning light,
glimmering valiantly,   1820
it lay adrift before me,
sublime and alluring.
From dawn to dusk,
in pain and terror,
it was unhappily won!
Night is drawing in:
from night's envy,
let it offer shelter now.
Wotan takes hold of the sword Fafner has left lying
around. *
    W[otan] points with the sword to the fortress. *
    As if carried away by a grand idea, very decisively
So I hail the fortress,
safe from fear and dread!   1830
He formally addresses Fricka.
Follow me, wife!
In Valhalla, live with me.

FRICKA

What is the meaning of the name?
I don't think I've ever heard it.

WOTAN

The idea that came to me,
a power against fear
if it lives in victory,
will show you the meaning!

Er faßt Fricka an der Hand und schreitet mit ihr langsam
der Brücke zu: Froh, Freia und Donner folgen.

LOGE *im Vordergrunde verharrend und den Göttern nach-*
blickend

Ihrem Ende eilen sie zu,
1840   die so stark im Bestehen sich wähnen.
Fast schäm' ich mich,
mit ihnen zu schaffen;
zur leckenden Lohe
mich wieder zu wandeln,
spür' ich lockende Lust:
sie aufzuzehren,
die einst mich gezähmt,
statt mit den Blinden
blöd zu vergehn,
1850   und wären es göttlichste Götter! –
Nicht dumm dünkte mich das!
Bedenken will ich's: –
wer weiß, was ich tu'!

Er geht, um sich den Göttern in nachlässiger Haltung
anzuschließen

WOGLINDE, WELLGUNDE, FLOSSHILDE *Die drei Rheintöch-*
ter in der Tiefe des Tales, unsichtbar

Rheingold! Rheingold!
Reines Gold!
Wie lauter und hell
leuchtetest hold du uns.

WOTAN *im Begriff, den Fuß auf die Brücke zu setzen, hält an*
und wendet sich um.

Welch Klagen dringt zu mir her?

WOGLINDE, WELLGUNDE, FLOSSHILDE

Um dich, du Klares,
1860   wir nun klagen:
gebt uns das Gold
gebt uns das Gold!
O gebt uns das reine zurück!

LOGE *späht in das Tal hinab*

Des Rheines Kinder
beklagen des Goldes Raub.

He takes Fricka by the hand and processes slowly with
her towards the bridge: Froh, Freia and Donner follow.
LOGE *lingering in the foreground and watching the gods go*
on their way

Speeding on to their destruction,
they suppose they'll always be strong.   1840
It almost makes me blush
to have any truck with them;
I feel pleasantly tempted
to turn myself back
into a flaming blaze:
that way I can engorge with fire those
who once tamed me,
instead of cravenly
going to pot with these blind beings,
and the godliest of gods at that! –   1850
It's not such a stupid thought!
I'll bear it in mind: –
who knows what I'll do!
In a lackadaisical frame of mind, he goes and falls in line
with the gods.

WOGLINDE, WELLGUNDE, FLOSSHILDE *The three Rhine-*
daughters in the depths of the valley, invisible

Rhinegold! Rhinegold!
Pure gold!
How innocent and clear
was the light you shed sweetly upon us.

WOTAN *about to set foot on the bridge, stops and turns*
round

What's the lament I'm hearing?

WOGLINDE, WELLGUNDE, FLOSSHILDE

For your innocence,
we now mourn: 1860
give us the gold,
give us the gold!
O give us back its purity!

LOGE *peers down into the valley*

The Rhine's children
lament the theft of the gold.

WOTAN
  Verwünschte Nicker!
    zu Loge
  Wehre ihrem Geneck!
LOGE *in das Tal hinabrufend*
  Ihr da im Wasser!
  Was weint ihr herauf?
1870 Hört, was Wotan euch wünscht: –
  Glänzt nicht mehr
  euch Mädchen das Gold,
  in der Götter neuem Glanze
  sonnt euch selig fortan!
    Die Götter lachen und beschreiten mit dem Folgenden
    die Brücke.
WOGLINDE, WELLGUNDE, FLOSSHILDE
  Rheingold! Rheingold!
  Reines Gold!
  O leuchtete noch
  in der Tiefe dein laut'rer Tand!
  Traulich und treu
1880 ist's nur in der Tiefe:
  falsch und feig
  ist, was dort oben sich freut!
    Während die Götter auf der Brücke der Burg zuschreiten,
    fällt der Vorhang.

WOTAN
    Accursed nixies!
     to Loge
    Stop their taunts!
LOGE *calling down into the valley*
    You there in the water!
    Why do you cry up to us here?
    Listen, Wotan wishes you this: –   1870
    as the gold no longer lends
    its brilliance to you young women,
    bathe now to your heart's content
    in the new brilliance of the gods!
      The gods laugh and during what follows take the path
      across the bridge.
WOGLINDE, WELLGUNDE, FLOSSHILDE
    Rhinegold! Rhinegold!
    Pure gold!
    O if only your innocent plaything
    could still cast a light in the deep!
    Trusting and faithful
    it only is in the deep: 1880
    up there, where it thrills, it is
    false and accursed!
      While the gods take the path over the bridge towards the
      castle, the curtain falls.

DIE WALKÜRE

(ERSTER TAG)

ERSTER AUFZUG

VORSPIEL UND ERSTE SZENE

Das Innere der Wohnung Hundings

Ein kurzes Orchestervorspiel von heftiger, stürmischer Bewegung leitet ein.

Der Vorhang geht auf [Takt 112]. – In der Mitte steht der Stamm einer mächtigen Esche, dessen stark erhabene Wurzeln sich weithin in den Erdboden verlieren; von seinem Wipfel ist der Baum durch ein gezimmertes Dach geschieden, welches so durchshnitten ist, daß der Stamm und die nach allen Seiten sich ausstreckenden Äste durch genau entsprechende Öffnungen hindurch gehen; von dem belaubten Wipfel wird angenommen, daß er sich über dieses Dach ausbreite. Um den Eschenstamm, als Mittelpunkt, ist nun ein Saal gezimmert; die Wände sind aus roh behauenem Holzwerk, hie und da mit geflochtenen und gewebten Decken behangen. Rechts im Vordergrunde steht der Herd, dessen Rauchfang seitwärts zum Dache hinausführt; hinter dem Herde befindet sich ein innerer Raum, gleich einem Vorratsspeicher, zu dem man auf einigen hölzernen Stufen hinaufsteigt: davor hängt, halb zurückgeschlagen, eine geflochtene Decke. Im Hintergrunde eine Eingangstüre mit schlichtem Holzriegel. Links die Türe zu einem inneren Gemache, zu dem gleichfalls Stufen hinaufführen; weiter vornen auf derselben Seite ein Tisch mit einer breiten,

THE VALKYRIE
(FIRST DAY)

ACT ONE

PRELUDE AND FIRST SCENE

Inside Hunding's house

A short orchestral prelude, stormy and agitated, introduces the scene.

The curtain rises [bar 112]. – The trunk of a mighty ash-tree occupies the middle of the stage. Its strongly protruding roots disappear all around into the ground. The tree trunk is separated from its top by a timber roof that has had holes bored into it so that the trunk and the branches growing out of it on all sides pass through exactly matching openings. The foliage of the treetop spreading out above the roof is left to the imagination. With the trunk in the middle, a wooden hall has been built around the ash-tree. Its walls are made of roughly hewn timbers with plaited and woven rugs hanging here and there. In the foreground on the right is the fireplace with its chimney leading up sideways to the outside of the roof. There is an inner space behind the fireplace like a loft cupboard with some wooden steps leading up to it and a plaited rug hung in front, half pulled back. The front door, fitted with a simple latch, is at the back, and a door leading to an inner bedroom is to the left, also with steps leading up to it. A table can be seen further forwards on the same side with a wide bench behind it fitted to the wall and wooden stools in front.

an der Wand angezimmerten Bank dahinter, und hölzernen Schemeln davor.

Die Bühne bleibt eine Zeitlang leer, außen Sturm, im Begriffe, sich gänzlich zu legen.

Siegmund öffnet von außen die Eingangstüre und tritt ein. Er hält den Riegel noch in der Hand und überblickt den Wohnraum; er scheint von übermäßiger Anstrengung erschöpft; sein Gewand und Aussehen zeigen, daß er sich auf der Flucht befinde. Da er niemand gewahrt, schließt er hinter sich, schreitet mit der äußersten Anstrengung eines Todmüden auf den Herd zu und wirft sich von dort auf eine Decke von Bärenfell nieder.

SIEGMUND

Wess' Herd dies auch sei,
hier muß ich rasten.

   Er sinkt zurück und bleibt regungslos ausgestreckt.

    Sieglinde tritt aus der Tür des inneren Gemaches. Sie glaubte ihren Mann heimgekehrt; ihre ernste Miene zeigt sich dann verwundert, als sie einen Fremden am Herde ausgestreckt sieht.

SIEGLINDE *noch im Hintergrunde*

Ein fremder Mann?
Ihn muß ich fragen.

   Sie tritt näher.

Wer kam ins Haus
und liegt dort am Herd?

   Da Siegmund sich nicht regt, tritt sie noch etwas näher und betrachtet ihn.

Müde liegt er
von Weges Müh'n.
Schwanden die Sinne ihm?
Wäre er siech?

   Sie neigt sich zu ihm herab und lauscht.

Noch schwillt ihm den Atem;
das Auge nur schloß er. –
Mutig dünkt mich der Mann,
sank er müd' auch hin.

   [Siegmund] fährt jäh mit dem Haupt in die Höhe.

For a time the stage remains empty; the storm is on the point of completely dying down.

Siegmund opens the front door from the outside and enters. Still keeping his hand on the latch, he takes stock of the living space; he has the appearance of someone overwrought by excessive struggle; his clothes and the way he looks suggest that he is a fugitive. Seeing that the coast is clear, he shuts the door behind him, walks towards the fireplace with the excessively belaboured movements of someone who is dog-tired, and hurls himself onto a bearskin rug.

SIEGMUND
Whoever's hearth this is,
I must rest here.
> *He slumps down and stays inertly sprawled out.*
>> *Sieglinde enters from the door of the inner bedroom. She thinks her husband has come home; the serious look on her face soon turns into one of surprise when she sees a stranger sprawled out in front of the hearth.*

SIEGLINDE *still in the background*
A man I don't know?
I'd better ask him.
> *She steps nearer.*
Who came in the house
and lies there in front of the hearth?
> *Siegmund still doesn't move, so she steps still closer to get a look at him.*
He lies there tired out
by the trials of his journey.
Has he fainted?
Is he very sick?   10
> *She bends over him and listens intently.*
He's still breathing;
his eyes are only closed. –
The man has courage,
even if he's collapsed with tiredness.
> *[Siegmund] suddenly lifts his head.*

SIEGMUND
  Ein Quell! Ein Quell!

SIEGLINDE
  Erquickung schaff' ich.

  *Sie nimmt schnell ein Trinkhorn und geht damit aus dem
  Haus.*

  *Sie kommt zurück und reicht das gefüllte Trinkhorn
  Siegmund.*

  Labung biet' ich
  dem lechzenden Gaumen:
  Wasser, wie du gewollt.

  *Siegmund trinkt und reicht ihr das Horn zurück. Als er
  ihr mit dem Haupte Dank zuwinkt, haftet sein Blick mit
  steigender Teilnahme an ihren Mienen.*

SIEGMUND
20 Kühlende Labung
  gab mir der Quell,
  des Müden Last
  machte er leicht;
  erfrischt ist der Mut,
  das Aug' erfreut
  des Sehens selige Lust.
  Wer ist's, der so mir es labt?

  *Sieglinde will antworten, besinnt sich aber und halt schwei-
  gend inne.* *

SIEGLINDE
  Dies Haus und dies Weib
  sind Hundings Eigen: –
30 gastlich gönn' er dir Rast;
  harre bis heim er kehrt!

SIEGMUND
  Waffenlos bin ich;
  dem wunden Gast
  wird dein Gatte nicht wehren.

  Sieglinde tritt näher zu Siegmund. *

SIEGLINDE *mit besorgter Hast*
  Die Wunden weise mir schnell!

SIEGMUND
    Water! Water!
SIEGLINDE
    I'll fetch refreshment.
        *She quickly takes a drinking-horn and goes out of the
        house to fill it.*
            *She returns with the drinking-horn now full and gives
            it to Siegmund.*
    I offer relief
    for those parched lips:
    water, as you wanted.
        *Siegmund drinks and gives the horn back to her. As he
        nods his head to her in thanks, he looks at her face with
        increasingly intense interest.*
SIEGMUND
    The drink has cooled   20
    and revived me,
    it's made light
    of my heavy tiredness;
    my spirits are refreshed,
    my eyes are rejoicing
    in the blissful pleasure of seeing.
    Who is it, who gives me new life?
        *Sieglinde wants to give an honest answer, but thinks better
        of it.* *
SIEGLINDE
    This house and this woman
    are Hunding's property: –
    as host, he will grant you rest;   30
    wait until he returns!
SIEGMUND
    I'm unarmed;
    your husband won't spurn
    a wounded guest.
        Sieglinde steps closer to Siegmund. *
SIEGLINDE *with concerned haste*
    Quickly show me your wounds!

SIEGMUND *Er schüttelt sich und springt lebhaft vom Lager*
    zum Sitz auf.
  Gering sind sie,
  der Rede nicht wert;
  noch fügen des Leibes
  Glieder sich fest.
40 Hätten halb so stark wie mein Arm
  Schild und Speer mir gehalten,
  nimmer floh ich dem Feind; –
  doch zerschellten mir Speer und Schild.
  Der Feinde Meute
  hetzte mich müd',
  Gewitter-Brunst
  brach meinen Leib;
  doch schneller, als ich der Meute,
  schwand die Müdigkeit mir:
50 sank auf die Lider mir Nacht,
  die Sonne lacht mir nun neu.
    Sieglinde geht nach dem Speicher, füllt ein Horn mit Met
    und reicht es Siegmund mit freundlicher Bewegtheit.
SIEGLINDE
  Des seimigen Metes
  süßen Trank
  mögst du mir nicht verschmähn.
SIEGMUND
  Schmecktest du mir ihn zu?
    Sieglinde nippt am Horn und reicht es ihm wieder.
    Siegmund tut einen langen Zug, indem er den Blick mit
    wachsender Wärme auf sie heftet. Er setzt so das Horn
    ab und läßt es langsam sinken, während der Ausdruck
    seiner Miene in starke Ergriffenheit übergeht.
    Er senkt den Blick düster zu Boden.
    mit bebender Stimme
  Einen Unseligen labtest du:
    lebhaft
  Unheil wende
  der Wunsch von dir!
    Er bricht auf.

SIEGMUND *He regains his composure and from his lying posi-*
tion sits up with alacrity.
They're slight,
not worth talking about;
I'm still sound
in body and limb.
Had my spear and shield held up   40
even half as strongly as my arm,
I'd never have fled the enemy; –
but spear and shield were smashed to pieces.
The enemy pack
hunted me until I dropped,
a raging storm
beat the life out of me;
now my tiredness has vanished faster
than I did from the enemy:
after night made my eyelids heavy,   50
the sun is smiling on me afresh.
    Sieglinde goes to the loft cupboard, fills the horn with
    mead and hands it to Siegmund with friendly emotion.

SIEGLINDE
May you forgive me for offering you
a sweet drink
of rich mead.

SIEGMUND
Would you taste it for me?
    Sieglinde sips from the horn and gives it back to him.
      Siegmund takes a long drink, looking at her with grow-
    ing warmth. He removes the horn from his mouth and
    lowers it slowly while the expression on his face shows
    greater and greater emotion.
      He looks bleakly down at the ground.
      his voice trembling
You've tended a fated man:
    animatedly
may the god of gifts
spare you calamity!
    He quickly gets up.

Gerastet hab' ich
60   und süß geruht.
Weiter wend' ich den Schritt.
   Er geht nach hinten.
SIEGLINDE *lebhaft sich umwendend*
Wer verfolgt dich, daß du schon flieh'st?
SIEGMUND *hat angehalten*
Mißwende folgt mir,
wohin ich fliehe;
Mißwende naht mir,
wo ich mich neige. –
Dir Frau doch bleibe sie fern!
Fort wend' ich Fuß und Blick.
   Er schreitet schnell bis zur Tür und hebt den Riegel.
SIEGLINDE *in heftigem Selbstvergessen ihm nachrufend*
So bleibe hier!
70   Nicht bringst du Unheil dahin,
wo Unheil im Hause wohnt!
   *Sieglinde ist von ihrem eigenen Geständniße im Tiefsten
   erschüttert.**
      *Siegmund bleibt tief erschüttert stehen: er forscht in
   Sieglindes Mienen; diese schlägt verschämt und traurig
   die Augen nieder. Siegmund kehrt zurück.*
SIEGMUND
Wehwalt hieß ich mich selbst: –
Hunding will ich erwarten.
   *Er lehnt sich an den Herd: sein Blick haftet mit ruhiger
   und entschlossener Teilnahme an Sieglinde: diese hebt
   langsam das Auge wieder zu ihm auf; beide blicken sich
   in tiefem Schweigen mit dem Ausdruck großer Ergriffen-
   heit in die Augen.*

I'm refreshed
and pleasantly rested.   60
Now I'll press onwards.
 He walks to the back.
SIEGLINDE *turning around briskly*
Who's after you, why flee so soon?
SIEGMUND *stopping*
Misfortune pursues me,
wherever I flee;
misfortune pulls me closer,
wherever I stay. –
You, woman, may it never reach!
On foot and alert, I must be gone.
 He goes quickly to the door and raises the latch.
SIEGLINDE *calling after him with passionate abandon*
So stay here!
You can't bring calamity   70
in the house where calamity lives!
 *Sieglinde is shaken by her own confession to the depths
 of her being.* *
  *Siegmund stops in his tracks, deeply shocked: he looks
 searchingly at Sieglinde's face; she lowers her eyes in
 shame and sadness. Siegmund comes back.*
SIEGMUND
I call myself Ruled by Sorrow: –
As for Hunding, I'll wait for him.
 *He leans against the hearth: his eyes fastened on Sieglinde
 with calm resolve: she slowly raises her eyes again to look
 at him; with an expression of great emotion, they look in
 long silence into each other's eyes.*

ZWEITE SZENE

[Takt 5 der Szene] Jetzt hört man das Klopfen an die Türe. *
*Sieglinde fährt plötzlich auf, lauscht und hört Hunding, der
sein Roß außen zum Stall führt.*
Sie geht hastig zur Tür und öffnet.
*Hunding, gewaffnet sein Schild und Speer, tritt ein und hält
unter der Tür, als er Siegmund gewahrt.*
*Hunding wendet sich mit einem ernst fragenden Blick an
Sieglinde.*

SIEGLINDE *dem Blicke Hundings entgegnend*
    Müd am Herd
    fand ich den Mann;
    Not führt' ihn ins Haus.
HUNDING *rasch hervorgestoßen* *
    Du labtest ihn?
SIEGLINDE *ruhig*
      nicht schnell und sehr unbefangen *
    Den Gaumen letzt' ich ihm,
    gastlich sorgt' ich sein'.
SIEGMUND *der ruhig und fest Hunding beobachtet*
80   Dach und Trank
    dank' ich ihr:
    willst du dein Weib drum schelten?
HUNDING
    Heilig ist mein Herd:
    heilig sei dir mein Haus.
      Er legt seine Waffen ab und übergibt sie Sieglinde.
      zu Sieglinde
    Rüst' uns Männern das Mahl!
      *Sieglinde hängt die Waffen an Ästen des Eschenstammes
      auf; dann holt sie Speise und Trank aus dem Speicher und
      rüstet auf dem Tische das Nachtmahl.*
        *Unwillkürlich heftet sie wieder den Blick auf Sieg-
      mund.*

SCENE TWO

[5th bar of the scene] Now knocks on the door can be heard. *
*   With a sudden start, Sieglinde pricks up her ears and hears Hunding outside, leading his horse to the stable.*
*   She walks quickly to the door and opens it.*
*   Hunding enters, armed with a shield and a spear, but stops in the doorway when he notices Siegmund.*
*   Hunding turns to Sieglinde with a seriously questioning look.*

SIEGLINDE *countering Hunding's gaze*
    I found the man tired out
    next to the hearth;
    hardship drove him into the house.
HUNDING *curtly* *
    You gave him refreshment?
SIEGLINDE *calmly*
        not fast and very naturally *
    I gave him nourishment,
    caring for his needs as our guest.
SIEGMUND *calmly fixing his attention on Hunding*
    For a roof and a drink   80
    I thank her:
    will you scold your wife for that?
HUNDING
    Blest is my hearth:
    blest to you be my house.
        He takes off his weapons and hands them to Sieglinde.
        to Sieglinde
    Make a meal for us men!
        Sieglinde hangs up the weapons on the branches of the ash-tree's trunk; she then fetches food and drink from the loft cupboard and gets the evening meal ready on the table.
        In spite of herself, she looks at Siegmund again.

Hunding mißt scharf und verwundert Siegmunds Züge,
die er mit denen seiner Frau vergleicht.
   für sich
Wie gleicht er dem Weibe!
der gleißende Wurm
glänzt auch ihm aus dem Auge. –
  Er birgt sein Befremden und wendet sich wie unbefangen
  zu Siegmund.
    Nicht zu stark, mehr im Sprechton. *
Weit her, traun!
90 kamst du des Wegs;
ein Roß nicht ritt,
der Rast hier fand:
welch schlimme Pfade
schufen dir Pein?

SIEGMUND
Durch Wald und Wiese,
Heide und Hain,
jagte mich Sturm
und starke Not:
nicht kenn' ich den Weg, den ich kam.
100 Wohin ich irrte,
weiß ich noch minder:
Kunde gewänn' ich dess' gern.

HUNDING *Hunding am Tisch, und Siegmund den Sitz bietend*
Dess' Dach dich deckt,
dess' Haus dich hegt –
Hunding heißt der Wirt;
wendest von hier du
nach West den Schritt,
in Höfen reich
hausen dort Sippen,
110 die Hundings Ehre behüten: –
gönnt mir Ehre mein Gast,
wird sein Name nun mir gennant.
   Siegmund, der sich am Tisch niedergesetzt, blickt nach-
   denklich vor sich hin.

*Hunding scrutinizes Siegmund's looks with surprise
and compares them with his wife's.*
    aside
How like the woman he is!
The glistening dragon
also gleams from his eye. –
    *He hides his uneasiness and turns to Siegmund as if noth-
    ing were amiss.*
        Not too strongly, more like speech. *
You have indeed come
a long way on your journey;   90
not riding a horse,
finding rest here:
what terrible paths
led to your distress?

SIEGMUND
Forest, meadow,
heath and grove,
everywhere I was plagued
by storms and great hardship:
I don't know the way I came.
Still less do I know   100
how I got here:
tidings about that, I'd be glad to hear.

HUNDING *Hunding at table, and offering Siegmund a seat*
He whose roof protects you,
whose household offers you care –
your host's name is Hunding;
if you turn from here
and travel west,
you'll find tribes living there
in courtly magnificence,
protecting Hunding's honour: –   110
if my guest honours me,
he will surely tell me his name.
    *Siegmund, who has sat down at the table, stares into
    space, lost in thought.*

Sieglinde, die sich neben Hunding, Siegmund gegen-
über gesetzt, heftet ihr Auge mit auffallender Teilnahme
und Spannung auf diesen.

[Hunding] der beide beobachtet

Trägst du Sorge
mir zu vertraun,
der Frau hier gib doch Kunde:
  *etwas heftig und unmutvoll**
sieh wie gierig sie dich frägt!

SIEGLINDE *unbefangen und teilnahmsvoll*

Gast, wer du bist,
wüßt' ich gern.

  Siegmund blickt auf, sieht ihr in das Auge und beginnt
  ernst.

SIEGMUND

Friedmund darf ich nicht heißen;
Frohwalt möcht' ich wohl sein:
  *mit schmerzlich erbebendem Tone**
doch Wehwalt muß ich mich nennen.
Wolfe, der war mein Vater;
zu zwei kam ich zur Welt,
  *einfach!**
eine Zwillingsschwester, und ich.
Früh schwanden mir
Mutter und Maid;
die mich gebar,
und die mit mir sie barg,
kaum hab' ich je sie gekannt. –
Wehrlich und stark war Wolfe;
der Feinde wuchsen ihm viel.
Zum Jagen zog
mit dem Jungen der Alte;
Von Hetze und Harst
einst kehrten wir heim,
da lag das Wolfsnest leer.
Zu Schutt gebrannt
der prangende Saal,
zum Stumpf der Eiche

Sieglinde, sitting next to Hunding, opposite Siegmund,
fastens her eyes on the latter with obvious involvement
and expectancy.

[Hunding] watching them both

If you're worried
about trusting me,
tell your news to the woman here:
    somewhat fiercely and displeased*
look how she can't wait to ask you!

SIEGLINDE *relaxed and involved*

Guest, I'd like to know
who you are.

Siegmund looks up, gazing into her eyes and beginning
in earnest.

SIEGMUND

I cannot be Protector of Peace;
I wish I were Ruled by Happiness: 120
    in a painfully trembling tone of voice*
but Ruled by Sorrow I must be called.
Wolf, he was my father;
I came into the world a twin,
    simply!*
a twin sister, and I.
Mother and girl
were soon lost to me;
the woman who bore me,
and the girl she sheltered with me,
I scarcely ever knew either. –
Wolf was valiant and strong;   130
his enemies grew to be many.
The old man
took the boy hunting:
one day we returned
from the thrill of the chase
to find Wolf's lair empty.
The fine hall
had been burnt to ashes,
the oak-tree's healthy trunk

140   blühender Stamm;
       mit vibrierender Stimme*
    erschlagen der Mutter
    mutiger Leib,
    verschwunden in Gluten
    der Schwester Spur.
    Uns schuf die herbe Not
    der Neidinge harte Schar.
    Geächtet floh
    der Alte mit mir,
    lange Jahre
150   lebte der Junge
    mit Wolfe im wilden Wald:
    manche Jagd
    ward auf sie gemacht;
    doch mutig wehrte
    das Wolfspaar sich.
       zu Hunding gewandt
    Ein Wölfing kündet dir das,
    den als Wölfing mancher wohl kennt.

HUNDING
    Wunder und wilde Märe
    kündest du, kühner Gast,
160   Wehwalt – der Wölfing!
    Mich dünkt, von dem wehrlichen Paar
    vernahm ich dunkle Sage,
    kannt' ich auch Wolfe
    und Wölfing nicht.

SIEGLINDE
    Doch weiter künde, Fremder:
    wo weilt dein Vater jetzt?

SIEGMUND
    Ein starkes Jagen auf uns
    stellten die Neidinge an.
    Der Jäger viele
170   fielen den Wölfen,
    in Flucht durch den Wald
    trieb sie das Wild:

turned into a stump;   140
  *with a shaky voice**
my mother was slain,
her fine body beaten to death;
all signs of my sister
had vanished in the flames.
Our bitter catastrophe was the work
of the Neidings' hard-bitten army.
Outlawed, the old man
fled with me,
for many long years
the young boy lived   150
with Wolf in the wild forest:
many a hunt
for them was launched;
but the wolf pair
bravely resisted.
  turning to Hunding
A wolf's offspring is telling you this,
known to many as the Son of Wolf.

HUNDING
  Of wonders and wild tales
  you tell, bold guest,
  Ruled by Sorrow – the Son of Wolf!   160
  I think I've heard sinister stories
  about the resilient pair,
  though Wolf I didn't know,
  nor Wolf's son.

SIEGLINDE
  Tell us more, stranger:
  where is your father now?

SIEGMUND
  The Neidings assembled
  a big hunt to get us.
  We wolves killed
  many of the hunters,   170
  as we, their prey, forced them
  to flee through the forest:

wie Spreu zerstob uns der Feind.
Doch ward ich vom Vater versprengt,
seine Spur verlor ich,
je länger ich forschte:
eines Wolfes Fell nur
traf ich im Forst;
> *Langsamer, mit wie schattenhaftem Ton. 'Ohne jede Sen-*
> *timentalität'**

leer lag das vor mir,
180 den Vater fand ich nicht.
Aus dem Wald trieb es mich fort;
mich drängt' es zu Männern und Frauen.
Wieviel ich traf,
wo ich sie fand,
ob ich um Freund,
um Frauen warb, –
immer doch war ich geächtet:
Unheil lag auf mir!
Was Rechtes je ich riet,
190 andern dünkte es arg;
was schlimm immer mir schien,
andre gaben ihm Gunst:
> *belebend*

in Fehde fiel ich,
wo ich mich fand;
Zorn traf mich,
wohin ich zog;
> *zögernd*

gehrt' ich nach Wonne,
weckt' ich nur Weh': –
drum mußt' ich mich Wehwalt nennen,
200 des Wehes waltet' ich nur.
> *Er sieht zu Sieglinde auf und gewahrt ihren teilnehmen-*
> *den Blick.*
> *Hunding finster blickend und [in] strengem Tone**

HUNDING
Die so leidig Los dir beschied,
nicht liebte dich die Norn':

we scattered them like chicken feed.
But I lost contact with my father,
the more I lost track of him,
the longer I tried to find him:
the only thing I stumbled on
in the forest was a wolfskin;
> More slowly, with a shadow-like tone. 'Without any sen-
> timentality'*

empty it lay in front of me,
father was nowhere to be found.   180
This made the forest repugnant to me;
I was drawn to men and women.
But no matter how many I met,
wherever I found them,
whether I sought friends,
or courted women, –
I was always the outlaw:
dogged by disaster!
What I ever thought to be right,
others took to be wrong;   190
what I always took to be bad,
others looked on with favour:
> bracingly

I got into a fight,
wherever I was;
I met with anger,
wherever I went;
> tentatively

if I longed for happiness,
I caused only sorrow: –
hence my name Ruled by Sorrow,
only over sorrow could I prevail.   200
> He looks up at Sieglinde and notices her concern.
> Hunding looking on sullenly and [in] an austere tone
> of voice*

HUNDING
If she gifted you such a luckless fate,
the Norn could not have loved you:

froh nicht grüsst dich der Mann,
dem fremd als Gast du nahst.

SIEGLINDE *etwas lebhaft*
    mit dem Ton leiser Verachtung (an Hunding gerichtet) *
Feige nur fürchten den,
der waffenlos einsam fährt. –
Künde noch, Gast,
wie du im Kampf
zuletzt die Waffe verlorst!

SIEGMUND *immer lebhafter*
    Die ganze Erzählung ist mit tiefer persönlicher Erregt-
    heit widerzugeben. *

210 Ein trauriges Kind
rief mich zum Trutz:
vermählen wollte
der Magen Sippe
dem Mann ohne Minne die Maid.
Wider den Zwang
zog ich zum Schutz;
der Dränger Troß
traf ich im Kampf:
dem Sieger sank der Feind.

220 Erschlagen lagen die Brüder;
die Leichen umschlang da die Maid,
den Grimm verjagt' ihr der Gram.
Mit wilder Tränen Flut
betroff sie weinend die Wal;
um des Mordes der eignen Brüder
klagte die unsel'ge Maid.
Der Erschlagnen Sippen
stürmten daher;
übermächtig

230 ächzten nach Rache sie:
rings um die Stätte
ragten mir Feinde.
Doch von der Wal
wich nicht die Maid;
mit Schild und Speer
schirmt' ich sie lang,

the man you, stranger, ask for shelter
is not happy to greet you as a guest.

SIEGLINDE *livening up somewhat*
with a tone of faint disdain (directed at Hunding) *

A lonely defenceless traveller
instils dread only in cowards. –
Guest, tell us more
about how and when
you lost your weapons in battle!

SIEGMUND *increasingly more lively*
*The whole narration is to be expressed with deeply
personal emotional turbulence.* *

A sad child   210
called me to arms:
tribal relatives
wanted to wed
a young woman to a man without love.
I rushed in protectively
to stave off the abuse;
meeting her entourage
head on in battle:
the victor crushed the enemy.
The brothers lay beaten to death;   220
the young woman hugged their bodies,
her grief vanquishing her fury.
With a wild storm of tears
she flooded the slain;
the abject young woman lamented
the murder of her own brothers.
The families of the dead men
gathered up a storm;
in dizzying numbers
they groaned for revenge: 230
surrounding me everywhere,
enemies reared up.
But the young woman did not budge
from the slain;
long did I protect her
with my shield and my spear,

bis Speer und Schild
im Harst mir zerhaun.
Wund und waffenlos stand ich,
240   sterben sah ich die Maid:
mich hetzte das wütende Heer.
Auf den Leichen lag sie tot.
> *mit einem Blicke voll schmerzlichen Feuers auf Sieglinde*

Nun weißt du, fragende Frau,
warum ich Friedmund nicht heiße!
> *Er steht auf und schreitet auf den Herd zu. Sieglinde*
> *blickt erbleicht und tief erschüttert zu Boden.*
> *[Hunding] erhebt sich.*

HUNDING *mäßig und verhalten*
Ich weiß ein wildes Geschlecht,
nicht heilig ist ihm,
was andern hehr:
> *heftiger*

verhaßt ist es allen und mir.
Zur Rache ward ich gerufen,
250   Sühne zu nehmen
für Sippenblut:
zu spät kam ich,
und kehrte nun heim,
des flücht'gen Frevlers Spur
im eignen Haus zu erspähn.
> *Er geht herab.*
> *[Und] geht mit starken Schritten auf Siegmund zu* *

Mein Haus hütet,
Wölfing, dich heut';
für die Nacht nahm ich dich auf:
> *belebter*

mit starker Waffe
260   doch wehre dich morgen;
zum Kampfe kies' ich den Tag:
für Tote zahlst du mir Zoll.
> *Sieglinde schreitet mit besorgter Gebärde zwischen die*
> *beiden Männer vor.*

until spear and shield were cut
from me in shatters in the chase.
Wounded and weaponless I stood,
I saw the young woman die: 240
a wild army hunted me.
On the dead, she lay lifeless.
   staring at Sieglinde with a look aflame with hurt
Now you know why, eager woman,
my name's not Protector of Peace!
    He stands up and walks to the hearth. Turning pale, Sieg-
    linde stares at the floor, deeply shaken.
    [Hunding] gets to his feet.
HUNDING *measured and composed*
I know of a savage race;
it holds nothing sacred
that others cherish:
   more fiercely
it's hated by all, including me.
I was called upon to seek revenge,
to exact retribution   250
for the spilling of tribal blood:
I came too late
and returned home,
only to scent in my own house
the trail of the culprit on the run.
   He walks downstage.
    *[And] goes to Siegmund with powerful strides**
My house protects you,
Son of Wolf, for today;
I'll take you in for the night:
   more lively
but defend yourself
tomorrow with strong weapons;   260
for the battle, I choose the day:
for the dead, you pay me a price.
   Sieglinde comes between both men, looking concerned.

[Hunding] mit dem Fuße auf den Boden stampfend*
Fort aus dem Saal!
Säume hier nicht;
den Nachttrunk rüste mir drin
und harre mein' zur Ruh'.

Sieglinde steht eine Weile unentschieden und sinnend.

Sie wendet sich langsam und zögernden Schrittes nach dem Speicher.

Dort hält sie wieder an und bleibt, in Sinnen verloren, mit halb abgewandtem Gesicht stehen.

Mit ruhigem Entschluß öffnet sie den Schrein, füllt ein Trinkhorn und schüttet aus einer Büchse Würze hinein.

Dann wendet sich das Auge auf Siegmund, um seinem Blicke zu begegnen, den dieser fortwährend auf sie heftet.

Sie gewahrt Hundings Spähen und wendet sich sogleich zum Schlafgemach.

Auf den Stufen kehrt sie sich noch einmal um, heftet das Auge sehnsuchtsvoll auf Siegmund und deutet mit dem Blicke andauernd und mit sprechender Bestimmtheit auf eine Stelle am Eschenstamme.

Hunding fährt auf und treibt sie mit einer heftigen Gebärde zum Fortgehen an.

Mit einem letzten Blick auf Siegmund geht sie in das Schlafgemach und schließt hinter sich die Türe.

Hunding nimmt seine Waffen vom Stamme herab.
Mit Waffen wahrt sich der Mann.

im Abgehen sich zu Siegmund wendend
Dich Wölfing treffe ich morgen;
mein Wort hörtest du:
270 hüte dich wohl.

Er geht in das Gemach; man hört ihn von innen den Riegel schließen.

[Hunding] stamping the ground with his foot*
Get out of the room!
Don't hang around here;
get my drink ready for the night
and wait for me to come to bed.

Sieglinde stands for a while, undecided and pensive.

She turns slowly and steps hesitantly towards the loft cupboard.

There she stops again and remains lost in thought, her face half turned away.

With calm decisiveness, she opens the cupboard, fills a drinking-horn and tips spices into it from a jar.

Then she turns her eyes towards Siegmund to meet his, as he continues to look at her.

She notices Hunding peering at her and turns straight away towards the bedroom.

On the steps she turns around once more, casting her eyes longingly on Siegmund, the whole time eloquently using her gaze to point exactly to a place on the trunk of the ash tree.

Hunding reacts sharply, violently pushing her on her way.

With a last look at Siegmund, she goes into the bedroom and closes the door behind her.

Hunding takes his weapons down from the tree.
With weapons a man is on his guard.

turning to Siegmund as he departs
I'll meet you tomorrow, Son of Wolf;
you heard what I said:
protect yourself with care.

He walks into the bedroom; he can be heard closing the bolt from inside.

270

DRITTE SZENE

*Siegmund allein. Es ist vollständig Nacht geworden; der Saal
ist nur noch von einem schwachen Feuer im Herde erhellt.*
    *Siegmund läßt sich nah' beim Feuer auf dem Lager nieder
und brütet in großer innerer Aufregung eine Zeitlang schwei-
gend vor sich hin.*

SIEGMUND *Mit hartem, wie starrem Ausdruck* *
Ein Schwert verhieß mir der Vater:
ich fänd' es in höchster Not.
Waffenlos fiel ich
in Feindes Haus;
seiner Rache Pfand,
raste ich hier:
ein Weib sah ich,
wonnig und hehr;
entzückend Bangen
280 zehrt mein Herz.
    Mit leidenschaftlich schmerzlicher Glut *
Zu der mich nun Sehnsucht zieht,
die mit süßem Zauber mich sehrt,
im Zwange hält sie der Mann,
der mich Wehrlosen höhnt! –
Wälse! Wälse!
Wo ist dein Schwert?
das starke Schwert,
das im Sturm ich schwänge,
bricht mir hervor aus der Brust,
290 was wütend das Herz noch hegt?
    *Das Feuer bricht zusammen; es fällt aus der aufsprühen-
den Glut plötzlich ein greller Schein auf die Stelle des
Eschenstammes, welche Sieglindes Blick bezeichnet hatte
und an der man jetzt deutlich einen Schwertgriff haften
sieht.*
Was gleißt dort hell
im Glimmerschein?

SCENE THREE

Siegmund alone. Night has completely fallen; the hall is lit only by the dying embers of a fire in the hearth.

Siegmund sets himself down on the bed near the fire and, clearly very upset, agonizes with himself in silence for some time.

SIEGMUND *With hard, as if fixed, expression**
Father pledged me a sword:
I'd find it in direst need.
Defenceless, I was thrown
into the house of a foe;
as forfeit in his revenge,
I shelter here:
I saw a woman,
lovely and radiant;
but fear feasts with
relish on my heart.   280
    *With passionately grief-stricken fervency**
Desire is now drawing me to her,
she who hurts me with sweet magic,
whose husband enslaves her,
and scorns me, a defenceless man! –
Wälse! Wälse!
Where is your sword?
the powerful sword
that I'm to flourish in battle,
will my breast disgorge all that
my heart still angrily feels?   290
    The fire collapses; out of the sparks flying up from the embers, a penetrating light suddenly falls on the spot on the trunk of the ash-tree that Sieglinde's gaze had pointed to and where the hilt of a sword can now be clearly seen embedded in it.
What's gleaming there brightly
in the shimmering light?

Welch ein Strahl bricht
aus der Esche Stamm?
Des Blinden Auge
leuchtet ein Blitz:
lustig lacht da der Blick.
Wie der Schein so hehr
das Herz mir sengt!
300   Ist es der Blick
der blühenden Frau,
den dort haftend
sie hinter sich ließ,
als aus dem Saal sie schied?
        Von hier an verlischt das Herdfeuer allmählich.
Nächtiges Dunkel
deckte mein Aug';
ihres Blickes Strahl
streifte mich da:
Wärme gewann ich und Tag.
310   Selig schien mir
der Sonne Licht;
den Scheitel umgliß mir
ihr wonniger Glanz –
bis hinter Bergen sie sank.
        Ein neuer schwacher Aufschein des Feuers.
Noch einmal da sie schied,
traf mich abends ihr Schein;
selbst der alten Esche Stamm
erglänzte in goldner Glut:
da bleicht die Blüte,
320   das Licht verlischt;
nächtiges Dunkel
deckt mir das Auge:
tief in des Busens Berge
glimmt nur noch lichtlose Glut.
        Das Feuer ist gänzlich verloschen; volle Nacht.
            Das Seitengemach öffnet sich leise.
            Sieglinde in weißem Gewande tritt heraus und schrei-
        tet leise, doch rasch auf den Herd zu.

What radiance streams
from the ash-tree's trunk?
A lightning flash in
the eyes of the blind:
the sight now lusty, laughing.
How gloriously the light
scorches my heart!
Is it the gaze   300
of that radiant woman,
fixed there
after she left it behind,
as she went out of the room?
   From here on, the fire in the hearth gradually dies out.
Abiding darkness
shrouded my eyes;
then her glowing look
touched me:
warmth was mine, and daylight.
I seemed to feel   310
the blissful rays of the sun;
the top of my head wreathed
by her sweet brilliance –
until she sank behind the hills.
   The fire gives some sign of weakly reviving.
As she left, her light struck
me again in the evening;
even the trunk of the old ash-tree
danced in its golden embers:
but the sparks are spent,
the light's extinguished;   320
abiding darkness
shrouds my eyes:
deep in the darkness of my breast
there flickers only heat without light.
   The fire is completely extinguished: the depth of night.
     The bedroom door opens quietly.
     *Sieglinde comes out in a white robe, moving softly yet
quickly over to the hearth.*

SIEGLINDE
Schläfst du, Gast?
SIEGMUND *freudig überrascht*
Wer schleicht daher?
SIEGLINDE *mit geheimnisvoller Hast*
Ich bin's: höre mich an!
In tiefem Schlaf liegt Hunding;
ich würzt' ihm betäubenden Trank.
330 Nütze die Nacht dir zum Heil!
SIEGMUND *hitzig unterbrechend*
Heil macht mich dein Nah'n!
SIEGLINDE
Eine Waffe laß mich dir weisen:
o wenn du sie gewännst!
Den hehrsten Helden
dürft' ich dich heißen:
dem Stärksten allein
ward sie bestimmt.
O merke wohl, was ich dir melde.
Der Männer Sippe
340 saß hier im Saal,
von Hunding zur Hochzeit geladen:
    *mußte erzählend, unpersönlich vorgetragen werden**
er freite ein Weib,
das ungefragt
Schächer ihm schenkten zur Frau.
Traurig saß ich,
während sie tranken:
ein Fremder trat da herein:
ein Greis in grauem Gewand;
tief hing ihm der Hut,
350 der deckt' ihm der Augen eines;
doch des andren Strahl,
Angst schuf es allen,
traf die Männer
sein mächtiges Dräu'n:
mir allein
weckte das Auge

SIEGLINDE
  Are you sleeping, guest?
SIEGMUND *happily surprised*
  Who's prowling here?
SIEGLINDE *in conspiratorial haste*
  It's me: listen to what I tell you!
  Hunding's sleeping deeply;
  I laced his drink to make him drowsy.
  Use the night for your salvation!   330
SIEGMUND *heatedly interrupting*
  Your return is my salvation!
SIEGLINDE
  Let me show you a weapon:
  oh, if only you could win it!
  I'd be right in calling you
  the most radiant of heroes:
  only for the mightiest of men
  was it destined.
  Take good note of what I tell you!
  The men of the tribe
  were sitting in this hall   340
  as guests at Hunding's wedding:
      has to be delivered impersonally, like a narration*
  he was marrying a woman
  thieves had given him as wife
  with no questions asked.
  Sadly I watched
  while they drank.
  Then in came a stranger:
  an old man in a grey robe;
  he'd pulled his hat down
  to cover one of his eyes;   350
  but the other radiated strength,
  making all the men
  afraid of meeting
  its powerful, threatening stare.
  Only in me
  did this eye awaken

süß sehnenden Harm,

Tränen und Trost zugleich.

Auf mich blickt' er,

360 und blitzte auf jene,

als ein Schwert in Händen er schwang;

das stieß er nun

in der Esche Stamm,

bis zum Heft haftet' es drin.

Dem sollte der Stahl geziemen,

der aus dem Stamm' es zög'.

Der Männer alle,

so kühn sie sich mühten,

die Wehr sich keiner gewann;

370 Gäste kamen

und Gäste gingen,

die stärksten zogen am Stahl;

keinen Zoll entwich er dem Stamm:

dort haftet schweigend das Schwert.

   mit bewußtem Ausdruck *

Da wußt' ich, wer der war,

der mich Gramvolle gegrüßt;

   mit gesteigerter Bestimmtheit und leidenschaftlich wer-
   dender Wärme *

ich weiß auch,

wem allein

im Stamm das Schwert er bestimmt.

380 O fänd' ich ihn hier'

und heut, den Freund;

käm' er aus Fremden

zur ärmsten Frau!

Was je ich gelitten

in grimmigem Leid;

was je mich geschmerzt

in Schande und Schmach:

süßeste Rache

sühnte dann alles:

390 erjagt hätt' ich,

was je ich verlor,

sweetly longing hurt,
tears and solace at once.
His gaze rested on me,
and flashed like lightning at the others,   360
as he flourished a sword in his grasp.
He then plunged it
into the trunk of the ash-tree,
embedding it up to the hilt.
The steel would befit the one
who pulls it from the trunk, he said.
Each and every man,
furiously as they tried,
failed to get the weapon out.
Guests came   370
and guests went,
the strongest pulling on the steel;
in the trunk it didn't budge an inch:
the sword stays there in silence.
   *with knowing expression**
Then I knew who had greeted me,
me, this woman laden with sorrow;
   *with intensifying certainty and passionately growing
   warmth**
I also know
to whom alone
he destined the sword in the tree.
Oh, if only I could find   380
that friend here today;
if only he'd come from afar
to the frailest of women!
For all I've ever suffered
in cruel affliction;
all that's ever caused me pain
in disgrace and dishonour:
let sweetest vengeance
pay me back:
I'd go after   390
all I ever lost,

was je ich beweint,
wär' mir gewonnen,
fänd' ich den heiligen Freund,
umfing' den Helden mein Arm!

SIEGMUND *mit Glut Sieglinde umfassend*
Dich selige Frau
hält nun der Freund,
dem Waffe und Weib bestimmt.
Heiß in der Brust
400 brennt mir der Eid,
der mich dir Edlen vermählt.
Was je ich ersehnt,
ersah ich in dir;
in dir fand ich,
was je mir gefehlt;
littest du Schmach,
und schmerzte mich Leid;
war ich geächtet,
und warst du entehrt:
410 freudige Rache
ruft nun den Frohen!
Auf lach' ich
in heiliger Lust,
halt' ich dich Hehre umfangen,
fühl' ich dein schlagendes Herz!
Die große Tür springt auf.

SIEGLINDE *fährt erschrocken zusammen und reißt sich los.*
Ha, wer ging? Wer kam herein?
Die Tür bleibt geöffnet: außen Frühlingsnacht; der Voll-
mond leuchtet herein und wirft sein helles Licht auf das
Paar, das so sich plötzlich in voller Deutlichkeit wahrneh-
men kann.

SIEGMUND *in leiser Entzückung*
Keiner ging;
doch Einer kam:
Siehe, der Lenz
420 lacht in den Saal.

all I ever mourned
I'd win again;
if I could find that cherished friend,
I'd take that hero into my arms!

SIEGMUND *embracing Sieglinde with glowing warmth*

You, blessed woman,
are now held by that friend,
weapon and woman are destined for him.
Burning in my breast
with passion is the oath   400
that weds you, noble wife, to me.
All I ever craved,
I saw in you;
in you I found
all I ever lacked;
you endured dishonour,
and I hurt with sorrow;
I was despised,
and you were humiliated;
now rapturous revenge   410
rouses us in joy!
I whoop with laughter
in divine pleasure,
wrapping you, noble wife, in my arms,
feeling your beating heart!
    The big door flies open.

SIEGLINDE *recoils in shock and tears herself away.*

Ha, who went? Who came inside?
    The door stays open: outside is a spring night; the full
    moon shines inside, throwing its bright light on the pair
    so that they are suddenly able to take each other in with
    complete clarity.

SIEGMUND *in quiet rapture*

No one left; –
but one thing came:
look, the spring
smiles into the hall.   420

Er zieht Sieglinde mit sanfter Gewalt zu sich auf das
Lager, so daß sie neben ihn zu sitzen kommt. Wachsende
Helligkeit des Mondscheines.

Winterstürme wichen
dem Wonnemond,
in mildem Lichte
leuchtet der Lenz;
auf linden Lüften
leicht und lieblich,
Wunder webend
er sich wiegt;
durch Wald und Auen
430   weht sein Atem,
weit geöffnet
lacht sein Aug':
aus sel'ger Vöglein Sange
süß er tönt,
holde Düfte
haucht er aus;
seinem warmen Blut entblühen
wonnige Blumen,
Keim und Sproß
440   entsprießt seiner Kraft.
Mit zarter Waffen Zier
bezwingt er die Welt;
Winter und Sturm wichen
der starken Wehr:
wohl mußte den tapfern Streichen
die strenge Türe auch weichen,
die trotzig und starr
uns – trennte von ihm.
Zu seiner Schwester
450   schwang er sich her:
          zart
die Liebe lockte den Lenz;
in unsrem Busen
barg sie sich tief:
nun lacht sie selig dem Licht.

Gently but firmly, he draws Sieglinde closer to him onto
the couch until she comes to sit beside him. The light of
the moon grows brighter.

Winter storms gave way
to the moon of joy,
the spring glistens
in the gentle light;
on wafting breezes,
lightly and lovingly,
weaving wonders
the spring sways;
through forest and meadow
its breathing drifts,   430
its eye wide open,
smiling: –
in the happy song of little birds,
it sweetly sounds,
fair fragrance
on its breath;
from its warm blood bloom
flowers of delight,
seed and shoot
blossom from its power.   440
Adorned with delicate armouries,
it subdues the world.
Winter and storm gave way
to its strong fight:
to its brave blows,
the stern door also had to yield,
stubbornly, stiffly,
dividing us – from its power.
But to its sister now
the spring has sped: 450
        tenderly
love enticed the spring;
in our breasts
it lay deep within:
now it smiles happily at the light.

Die bräutliche Schwester
befreite der Bruder;
zertrümmert liegt,
was je sie getrennt;
jauchzend grüßt sich
460 das junge Paar:
vereint sind Liebe und Lenz!

SIEGLINDE
Du bist der Lenz,
nach dem ich verlangte
in frostigen Winters Frist.
Dich grüßte mein Herz
mit heiligem Grau'n,
als dein Blick zuerst mir erblühte.
Fremdes nur sah ich von je,
freundlos war mir das Nahe;
470 als hätt' ich nie es gekannt,
war, was immer mir kam.
Doch dich kannt' ich
deutlich und klar;
als mein Auge dich sah,
warst du mein Eigen;
was im Busen ich barg,
was ich bin,
hell wie der Tag
taucht' es mir auf;
480 o wie tönender Schall
schlug's an mein Ohr,
als in frostig öder Fremde
zuerst ich den Freund ersah.

*Sie hängt sich entzückt an seinen Hals und blickt ihm
nahe ins Gesicht.*

SIEGMUND *mit Hingerissenheit*
O süßeste Wonne!
Seligstes Weib!

SIEGLINDE *dicht an seinen Augen*
O laß in Nähe
zu dir mich neigen,

The bridal sister's
brother set her free;
in smithereens lies
all that ever parted them;
cock-a-hoop the young couple
call to each other: 460
united are love and spring!

SIEGLINDE

You are the spring
I longed for
in frosty winter times.
My heart greeted you
with canny foreboding,
as your gaze on me first blossomed.
Everything I ever saw was strange,
my surroundings were friendless;
whatever came my way seemed like   470
something I'd never known.
But you I knew,
plainly and clearly;
when I laid eyes on you,
you were mine;
what I hid in my heart,
what I am,
bright as day,
came to me;
like a ringing sound   480
did it strike my ear,
in a foreign land, frosty and bleak,
when, friend, I saw you first.

> *Carried away, she puts her arms around his neck and
> looks closely into his face.*

SIEGMUND *with rapture*

O sweetest joy!
Woman most blessed!

SIEGLINDE *close to his eyes*

O let me lean
closer to you,

daß hell ich schaue
den hehren Schein,
490   der dir aus Aug'
und Antlitz bricht
und so süß die Sinne mir zwingt.

SIEGMUND

Im Lenzesmond
leuchtest du hell;
hehr umwebt dich
das Wellenhaar:
was mich berückt,
errat' ich nun leicht:
denn wonnig weidet mein Blick.

SIEGLINDE *Sie schlägt ihm die Locken von der Stirn zurück*
und betrachtet ihn staunend.

500   Wie dir die Stirn
so offen steht,
der Adern Geäst
in den Schläfen sich schlingt!
Mir zagt es vor der Wonne,
die mich entzückt.
Ein Wunder will mich gemahnen:
den heut zuerst ich erschaut,
mein Auge sah dich schon!

SIEGMUND

Ein Minnetraum
510   gemahnt auch mich:
in heißem Sehnen
sah ich dich schon.

SIEGLINDE

Im Bach erblickt' ich
mein eigen Bild,
und jetzt gewahr' ich es wieder;
wie einst dem Teich es enttaucht,
bietest mein Bild mir nun du!

SIEGMUND

Du bist das Bild,
das ich in mir barg.

to sense vividly
the radiant light
breaking forth   490
from your eyes and face,
and urging my senses so sweetly.

SIEGMUND
In the spring moon,
you seem luminous,
radiantly encircled
by the waves of your hair.
What beguiles me
I can easily guess:
I revel joyfully in what I see.

SIEGLINDE *She parts the locks of hair on his forehead and
      looks at him in astonishment.*
With your brow   500
as open as this,
how like a maze
the veins throng your temples!
I'm fearful of the joy
that transports me.
A miracle stirs in my mind:
the one I saw today for the first time
is you, someone I've already seen!

SIEGMUND
A dream of love
also stirs my mind: 510
in ardent longing
I've seen you before.

SIEGLINDE
I once caught sight
of my own likeness in a brook,
and now I see it again;
then it rose up from the water,
now my likeness comes from you!

SIEGMUND
You are the likeness
that I hid within me.

SIEGLINDE *den Blick schnell abwendend*

520   O still! Laß mich
der Stimme lauschen:
mich dünkt, ihren Klang
hört' ich als Kind;
   aufgeregt
– doch nein! Ich hörte sie neulich,
als meiner Stimme Schall
mir widerhallte der Wald.

SIEGMUND

O lieblichste Laute,
denen ich lausche!

SIEGLINDE *ihm wieder in die Augen spähend*

Deines Auges Glut
530   erglänzte mir schon:
so blickte der Greis
grüßend auf mich,
als der Traurigen Trost er gab.
An dem Blick
erkannt' ihn sein Kind –
schon wollt' ich beim Namen ihn nennen!
  Wie plötzlich erschreckend scheint Sieglinde verhindert
  zu sein ihr auf der Zunge liegendes Geheimniß auszu-
  sprechen. *
Wehwalt heißt du fürwahr?

SIEGMUND *die folgenden Worte in einfach schlichtestem*
  Tone*

Nicht heiß' mich so,
seit du mich liebst;
540   nun walt' ich der hehrsten Wonnen.

SIEGLINDE *wehmütig, aber ruhig ohne Akzente**

Und Friedmund darfst du
froh dich nicht nennen?

SIEGMUND

Nenne mich du,
wie du liebst, daß ich heiße:
den Namen nehm' ich von dir.

SIEGLINDE

Doch nanntest du Wolfe den Vater?

SIEGLINDE *quickly averting her gaze*
Quiet! Let me   520
listen to that voice:
I think it's a sound
I heard as a child;
   agitated
– no, I'm wrong! I heard it not long ago,
when the sound of my voice was
echoed back to me by the forest.

SIEGMUND
O tenderest sound
to reach my ear!

SIEGLINDE *looking intently again into his eyes*
The embers in your eyes have
shed their glow on me before: 530
just like that old man who
gazed on me, greeting me
to offer solace to a sad woman.
By the way he looked at her,
his child recognized him –
even then, I wanted to call him by name!
   Looking suddenly scared, Sieglinde seems to be prevent-
   ed from revealing a secret that is right on the tip of her
   tongue. *
Is your name really Ruled by Sorrow?

SIEGMUND *the following words in the simplest, plainest*
   tone of voice*
No, it's not,
now that you love me;
I bask in the most glorious happiness.   540

SIEGLINDE *wistfully, but calmly without emphases**
So if you're happy, why can't you
be called Friedmund, Protector of Peace?

SIEGMUND
Name me yourself
according to how you love me:
I'll take my name from you.

SIEGLINDE
Didn't you name your father Wolf?

SIEGMUND
Ein Wolf war er feigen Füchsen;
doch dem so stolz
strahlte das Auge,
550 wie, Herrliche, hehr dir es strahlt,
der war Wälse genannt.
SIEGLINDE *außer sich*
War Wälse dein Vater,
und bist du ein Wälsung;
stieß er für dich
sein Schwert in den Stamm –
so laß mich dich heißen
wie ich dich liebe: –
Siegmund –
so nenn' ich dich!
Siegmund springt auf.
SIEGMUND
560 Siegmund heiß' ich,
und Siegmund bin ich!
Bezeug' es dies Schwert,
das zaglos ich halte:
Wälse verhieß mir,
in höchster Not
fänd' ich es einst;
ich fass' es nun!
Heiligster Minne
höchste Not,
570 sehnender Liebe
sehrende Not,
brennt mir hell in der Brust,
drängt zu Tat und Tod:
Nothung! Nothung! –
so nenn' ich dich, Schwert: –
Nothung! Nothung!
neidlicher Stahl!
Zeig' deiner Schärfe
schneidenden Zahn!
580 Heraus aus der Scheide zu mir!

SIEGMUND
   To cowardly foxes he was a wolf;
   but to those proud people
   on whom his eye shone,
   as nobly, fine woman, as it did on you,   550
   his name was Wälse.

SIEGLINDE *beside herself*
   If Wälse was your father,
   and you're a Wälsung;
   if it was for you he plunged
   his sword into the trunk of the tree –
   so let me call you
   as I love you: –
   Siegmund, Protector of Victory –
   that is your name!
      Siegmund springs to his feet.

SIEGMUND
   Siegmund I'm called,   560
   and Siegmund I am!
   Let this sword I hold
   boldly be witness:
   Wälse pledged it to me,
   if ever I found it
   in direst extremity;
   I'm gripping it now!
   Supreme ecstasy's
   direst extremity,
   yearning love's   570
   aching need
   is ablaze in my breast,
   urging me to act and to die:
   Nothung! Nothung! –
   my sword, that's what I'm calling you: –
   Nothung! Nothung!
   pitiless steel!
   Show your sharp edge,
   your pointed tooth!
   Out from your sheath to me!   580

Er zieht mit einem gewaltigen Ruck das Schwert aus dem
Stamme und zeigt es der von Staunen und Entzücken
erfaßten Sieglinde.

Siegmund den Wälsung,
siehst du, Weib;
als Brautgabe
bringt er dies Schwert.
So freit er sich
die seligste Frau;
dem Feindeshaus
entführt er dich so.
Fern von hier
590   folge mir nun,
fort in des Lenzes
lachendes Haus!
Dort schützt dich Nothung, das Schwert,
wenn Siegmund dir liebend erlag.
        Er hat sie umfaßt, um sie mit sich fortzuziehen.
SIEGLINDE *reißt sich in höchster Trunkenheit von ihm los*
        und stellt sich ihm gegenüber.
Bist du Siegmund,
den ich hier sehe:
Sieglinde bin ich,
die dich ersehnt:
die eigne Schwester
600   gewannst du zueins mit dem Schwert!
        Sie wirft sich ihm an die Brust.
SIEGMUND
Braut und Schwester
bist du dem Bruder –
so blühe denn, Wälsungen-Blut!
        Er zieht sie mit wütender Glut an sich.
        Der Vorhang fällt schnell.

He heaves the sword out of the trunk with a colossal
effort and shows it to Sieglinde, who is carried away in
amazement and ecstasy.

Siegmund the Wälsung
you see, wife, before you;
he brings this sword
as a bridal gift.
That's how he won
the happiest woman;
and that's how he'll take you
out of the enemy's house.
It's time to follow me
far away from here   590
into springtime's
house full of laughter!
My sword Nothung will guard you there,
if Siegmund succumbs to you in love!
  He puts his arm around her to take her away with him.

SIEGLINDE *completely intoxicated, tears herself away from*
      him and stands opposite him.
Is this Siegmund
I see here:
I'm Sieglinde
who craves you:
your own sister
you've won with the sword at last!   600
  She throws herself onto his breast.

SIEGMUND
To your brother
you are bride and sister –
so may the Wälsungs' blood thrive!
  He pulls her close to him with unruly passion.
    The curtain falls quickly.

ZWEITER AUFZUG

VORSPIEL UND ERSTE SZENE

Der Vorhang geht auf [Takt 71].

Wildes Felsengebirge

*Im Hintergrund zieht sich von unten her eine Schlucht herauf,
die auf ein erhöhtes Felsjoch mündet; von diesem senkt sich
der Boden dem Vordergrunde zu wieder abwärts.*

*Wotan, kriegerisch gewaffnet, mit dem Speer: vor ihm
Brünnhilde, als Walküre, ebenfalls in voller Waffenrüstung*

WOTAN *Das Zwiegespräch zwischen Wotan und Brünnhilde
durchaus energisch und rasch vordringend* *
Nun zäume dein Roß,
reisige Maid!
Bald entbrennt
brünstiger Streit.
Brünnhilde stürme zum Kampf;
dem Wälsung kiese sie Sieg!
610 Hunding wähle sich,
wem er gehört;
nach Walhall taugt er mir nicht.
Drum rüstig und rasch,
reite zur Wal!
*[Brünnhilde] jauchzend von Fels zu Fels die Höhe rechts
hinaufspringend*
BRÜNNHILDE
Hojotoho! Hojotoho!
Heiaha! Heiaha!
Hojotoho! Hojotoho!
Heiaha! Heiaha!
Hojotoho! Hojotoho!
620 Hojotoho! Hojotoho!
Heiahaja! Hojoho!

ACT TWO

PRELUDE AND SCENE ONE

The curtain rises [bar 71].

Wild rocky mountains

In the background below, a ravine stretches upwards, merging into a high pass in the rocks from where the ground again dips down towards the front of the stage.

Wotan, armed for war, with his spear: in front of him Brünnhilde, also fully equipped with weapons in her role as a Valkyrie

WOTAN *The dialogue between* Wotan and Brünnhilde *really vigorous and fast-moving**
Now bridle your horse,
battle-ready young woman!
A frenzied fight
is about to be unleashed.
Let Brünnhilde storm to battle;
let her secure victory for the Wälsung!
Let Hunding decide
where he belongs;
he's no use to me in Valhalla.
So get ready for war,
ride fast into battle!
    [Brünnhilde] jumping up high on the right and whooping with joy from rock to rock

BRÜNNHILDE
Hojotoho! Hojotoho!
Heiaha! Heiaha!
Hojotoho! Heiaha!
Heiaha! Heiaha!
Hojotoho! Hojotoho!
Hojotoho! Hojotoho!
Heiahaja! Hojoho!

Sie hält auf einer hohen Felsenspitze an, blickt in die hintere Schlucht hinab und ruft zu Wotan zurück.

Dir rat' ich, Vater,
rüste dich selbst;
harten Sturm
sollst du bestehn:
Fricka naht, deine Frau,
im Wagen mit dem Widdergespann.
Hei! wie die goldne
Geißel sie schwingt!
630   Die armen Tiere
ächzen vor Angst;
wild rasseln die Räder:
zornig fährt sie zum Zank!
In solchem Strauße
streit' ich nicht gern,
lieb' ich auch mutiger
Männer Schlacht;
drum sieh wie den Sturm du bestehst:
ich Lustige lass' dich im Stich!
640   Hojotoho! Hojotoho!
Hojotoho! Hojotoho!
Heiaha! Heiaha!
Hojotoho! Hojotoho!
Hojotoho! Hojotoho!

Brünnhilde verschwindet hinter der Gebirgshöhe zur Seite.

Heiaha! ja!
verhallend

In einem mit zwei Widdern bespannten Wagen langt Fricka aus der Schlucht auf dem Felsjoche an: dort hält sie rasch an und steigt aus.

Fricka schreitet heftig in den Vordergrund auf Wotan zu.

WOTAN
Der alte Sturm,
die alte Müh'!
zurückhaltend

She stops on a high rocky peak, looks down into the ra-
vine behind her, and calls to Wotan in reply.

I advise you, father,
brace yourself too;
severe storms
will test you:
Fricka nears, your wife,
in the chariot with yoked rams.
Hey! how she cracks
the golden whip!
The poor animals   630
groan with terror;
wheels clatter wildly:
she's furious, looking for a fight!
Skirmishes like these
aren't for me,
love it as I do when brave
men fight;
so see how you weather the storm.
Fend for yourself – I want sport!
Hojotoho! Hojotoho!   640
Hojotoho! Hojotoho!
Heiaha! Heiaha!
Hojotoho! Hojotoho!
Hojotoho! Hojotoho!

Brünnhilde disappears behind the mountain peak at the
side.

Heiaha! ja!

fading away

In a chariot drawn by two rams, Fricka arrives out
of the ravine onto the pass in the rocks: there she stops
quickly and climbs out.

Fricka strides impetuously into the foreground to-
wards Wotan.

WOTAN

The old storm,
the old quarrelling!

holding back

Doch stand muß ich hier halten!

FRICKA *Je näher sie kommt, mäßigt sie den Schritt, und stellt*
    sich mit Würde vor Wotan hin.

      In dem ganzen Dialoge darf auch bei den gemütstiefen
    Stellen kein Zögern im Tempo erfolgen.*

    Wo in den Bergen du dich birgst,

650   der Gattin Blick zu entgehn,

    einsam hier

    such' ich dich auf,

    daß Hülfe du mir verhießest.

WOTAN *vornehm, wie ein König zu sprechen**

    Was Fricka kümmert,

    künde sie frei.

FRICKA

    Ich vernahm Hundings Not,

    um Rache rief er mich an:

    der Ehe Hüterin

    hörte ihn,

660   verhieß streng

    zu strafen die Tat

    des frech frevelnden Paars,

    das kühn den Gatten gekränkt.

WOTAN

    Was so Schlimmes

    schuf das Paar,

    das liebend einte der Lenz?

    Der Minne Zauber

    entzückte sie:

    wer büßt mir der Minne Macht?

FRICKA

670   Wie töricht und taub du dich stellst,

    als wüßtest fürwahr du nicht,

    daß um der Ehe

    heiligen Eid,

    den hart gekränkten, ich klage!

WOTAN

    Unheilig

    acht' ich den Eid,

But I mustn't waver now!

FRICKA *The closer she comes, the more she moderates her*
step and confronts Wotan with composure.
    In this entire dialogue there should be no slowing of
the tempo, even in moments of the profoundest feeling. *

Where you're hiding in the hills
to escape your wife's gaze,   650
all alone,
it's here that I've come looking for you
for the help you promised me.

WOTAN *stately, to be spoken like a king* *
Whatever troubles Fricka,
let her speak her mind.

FRICKA
I noticed Hunding's distress,
when he appealed to me for revenge:
I, the guardian of marriage,
heard him,
promising unconditionally   660
to punish the actions
of that brazen pair of upstarts,
who dare offend a husband.

WOTAN
What's so bad
about what the pair did,
united lovingly by spring?
The magic of love
carried them away:
who does penance for love's power?

FRICKA
How stupid and deaf you pretend to be,   670
as if you really didn't know
that this callous offence
against the solemn vow of marriage
is the reason for my complaint.

WOTAN
Godless
is the vow

der Unliebende eint;
und mir wahrlich
mute nicht zu,
680 daß mit Zwang ich halte,
was dir nicht haftet:
denn wo kühn Kräfte sich regen,
da rat' ich offen zum Krieg.
   *Fr[icka] will heftig entgegnen, faßt sich aber gleich wie-
   der.**

FRICKA
Achtest du rühmlich
der Ehe Bruch,
so prahle nun weiter
und preis es heilig,
daß Blutschande entblüht
dem Bund eines Zwillingspaars!
690 Mir schaudert das Herz,
es schwindelt mein Hirn:
bräutlich umfing
die Schwester den Bruder!
Wann ward es erlebt,
daß leiblich Geschwister sich liebten?

WOTAN
Heut hast du's erlebt.
Erfahre so,
was von selbst sich fügt,
sei zuvor auch noch nie es geschehn.
700 Daß jene sich lieben,
leuchtet dir hell;
drum höre redlichen Rat:
soll süße Lust
deinen Segen dir lohnen,
so segne, lachend der Liebe,
Siegmunds und Sieglindes Bund!

FRICKA *in höchste Entrüstung ausbrechend*
So ist es denn aus
mit den ewigen Göttern,
seit du die wilden

that seals a bond without love;
and you really
cannot expect me
to use force to stop   680
something that's none of your business:
bold powers are stirring here,
therefore I openly counsel war.
   *Fr[icka] wants to retort violently, but quickly pulls herself
   together again.* *

FRICKA
   If you think
   adultery's a good thing,
   just go on boasting
   and praise the godliness
   of incest shining forth
   from the bonding of twins!
   My heart shudders,   690
   my brain reels:
   a sister sleeps with
   her brother as his bride!
   Whoever heard of
   brother and sister making love?

WOTAN
   You've just seen it for yourself.
   Be alive
   to what happens of its own accord,
   to what may have never happened before.
   Those two are in love,   700
   that's obvious, even to you;
   take some frank advice:
   if sweet pleasure
   is worth your blessing,
   rejoice in love and bless
   Siegmund's and Sieglinde's bond.

FRICKA *erupting in high dudgeon*
   Does this mean the end
   of the eternal gods,
   now you've sired

710   Wälsungen zeugtest?
        *mit heftigem und hartem Tone**
      Heraus sagt' ich's;
      traf ich den Sinn?
      Nichts gilt dir der Hehren
      heilige Sippe;
      hin wirfst du alles,
      was einst du geachtet,
      zerreißest die Bande,
      die selbst du gebunden,
      lösest lachend
720   des Himmels Haft:
      daß nach Lust und Laune nur walte
        *Ganz nah an Wotan sehr leise ('Als wollte sie, daß dies
        niemand sonst hören könnte!')**
      dies frevelnde Zwillingspaar,
      deiner Untreue zuchtlose Frucht.
      O, was klag' ich
      um Ehe und Eid,
      da zuerst du selbst sie versehrt.
      Die treue Gattin
      trogest du stets;
      wo eine Tiefe,
730   wo eine Höhe,
      dahin lugte
      lüstern dein Blick,
      wie des Wechsels Lust du gewännest,
      und höhnend kränktest mein Herz.
      Trauernden Sinnes
      mußt' ich's ertragen,
      zogst du zur Schlacht
      mit den schlimmen Mädchen,
      die wilder Minne
740   Bund dir gebar:
      denn dein Weib noch scheutest du so,
      daß der Walküren Schar,
        *Fricka wendet sich wieder direkt an Wotan.**
      und Brünnhilde selbst,

the wild Wälsungs?   710
   with a fierce and hard tone of voice *
Let me be blunt;
am I right?
The godly family of the august
means nothing to you;
you're throwing overboard
what you once valued;
you're ripping bonds apart
that even you yourself forged,
while laughing as you dissolve
the power of the skies: 720
those twins act only on a whim,
   *Really close to Wotan and very softly ('as if she wants no
   one else to be able to hear!')* *
that capricious pair of sinners,
your perfidy's licentious fruit.
Oh, why do I mourn
marriage and vow,
when you yourself damaged them first.
You constantly betrayed
a faithful wife;
down here,
up there,   730
you poked around
with your lecherous gaze
to gratify your promiscuous cravings,
mocking, making me sick at heart.
I had to put up with it,
grieving
as you went to the slaughter
with the terrible daughters
born to you in a commune
of wild love: 740
at least you feared your wife enough
to order this brood of Valkyries,
   Fricka turns again to address Wotan directly. *
and Brünnhilde herself,

deines Wunsches Braut,
in Gehorsam der Herrin du gabst.
Doch jetzt, da dir neue
Namen gefielen,
als 'Wälse' wölfisch
im Walde du schweiftest,
750   jetzt, da zu niedrigster
Schmach du dich neigtest,
gemeiner Menschen
ein Paar zu erzeugen:
jetzt dem Wurfe der Wölfin
wirfst du zu Füßen dein Weib!
    Fricka tritt mit großer Heftigkeit zurück. *
So führ' es denn aus;
fülle das Maß!
Die Betrogne laß auch zertreten!

WOTAN *ruhig*
Nichts lerntest du,
760   wollt' ich dich lehren,
was nie du erkennen kannst,
eh' dir ertagte die Tat.
Stets Gewohntes
nur magst du verstehn:
doch was noch nie sich traf,
danach trachtet mein Sinn.
Eines höre!
Not tut ein Held,
der, ledig göttlichen Schutzes,
770   sich löse vom Göttergesetz;
so nur taugt er
zu wirken die Tat,
die, wie not sie den Göttern,
    *mit bedeutsamen Ausdruck und etwas gehalten**
dem Gott doch zu wirken verwehrt.

FRICKA
Mit tiefem Sinne
willst du mich täuschen:
was Hehres sollten

the apple of your eye,
to obey the spouse of their lord.
But now since your fad
for new names,
roaming the forest as 'Wälse'
like a wolf,
now prostrating yourself   750
in a gutter of disgrace
where you've sired a pair
of insidious human beings,
now that you've thrown your wife
on the mercies of the she-wolf's litter!
   With great ferocity Fricka steps back. *
Just finish it off;
fill the mug to the brim!
Let her you've cheated be crushed too!

WOTAN *calmly*
Nothing's sunk in,
despite my wanting to teach you   760
what you're never capable of knowing
until it dawns literally before your eyes.
Routine
is all you understand:
but what I'm striving to grasp
has never happened.
There's one thing you should hear!
This impasse requires a hero,
who, freed from the gods' protection,
is independent of their laws;   770
only he is capable
of taking the action
that the gods need,
   with momentous expression and somewhat dignified *
but which this god is forbidden to take.

FRICKA
You're misleading me
with profundity:
what great deed

Helden je wirken,
das ihren Göttern wäre verwehrt,
780 deren Gunst in ihnen nur wirkt?

WOTAN
Ihres eignen Mutes
achtest du nicht?

FRICKA
Wer hauchte Menschen ihn ein?
Wer hellte den Blöden den Blick?
In deinem Schutz
scheinen sie stark;
durch deinen Stachel
streben sie auf:
du reizest sie einzig,
790 die so mir Ew'gen du rühmst.
Mit neuer List
willst du mich belügen,
durch neue Ränke
mir jetzt entrinnen;
doch diesen Wälsung
gewinnst du dir nicht:
in ihm treff' ich nur dich,
denn durch dich trotzt er allein.

WOTAN
In wildem Leiden
    ergriffen
800 erwuchs er sich selbst,
mein Schutz schirmte ihn nie.

FRICKA
So schütz auch heut ihn nicht!
Nimm ihm das Schwert,
das du ihm geschenkt!

WOTAN
Das Schwert?

FRICKA
Ja, das Schwert –
das zauberstark
zuckende Schwert,
das du Gott dem Sohne gabst.

could heroes ever undertake
that is denied to the gods,
whose wish solely dictates their actions?   780

WOTAN
Don't you value
their own will?

FRICKA
Who breathed it into humans?
Who gave stupidity insight?
Shielded by you
they look strong;
stimulated by you
they're ambitious:
you alone excite those
whom I, eternal goddess, hear you praise.   790
You want to pull the wool over my eyes
with new trickery,
to elude me now
with new sophistry;
but you'll not win
this Wälsung for yourself:
in him I see only you;
he's defiant, but reliant on you alone.

WOTAN
With incalculable suffering
   deeply affected
he fended for himself,   800
my protective powers never shielded him.

FRICKA
Then don't protect him today!
Deprive him of the sword
you bestowed on him!

WOTAN
The sword?

FRICKA
Yes, the sword –
strong through magic,
the glinting sword
that a god, you, gave to your son.

WOTAN *heftig*

810 Siegmund gewann es sich
      mit unterdrücktem Beben
    selbst in der Not!
      Wotan drückt in seiner ganzen Haltung von hier an einen
      immer wachsenden unheimlichen, tiefen Unmut aus.

FRICKA *eifrig fortfahrend*
    Du schufst ihm die Not,
    wie das neidliche Schwert.
    Willst du mich täuschen,
    die Tag und Nacht
    auf den Fersen dir folgt?
    Für ihn stießest du
    das Schwert in den Stamm;
    du verhießest ihm
820 die hehre Wehr:
    willst du es leugnen,
    daß nur deine List
    ihn lockte, wo er es fänd'?
      Wotan fährt mit einer grimmigen Gebärde auf.
      [Fricka] immer sicherer, da sie den Eindruck gewahrt,
      den sie auf Wotan hervorgebracht hat
    Mit Unfreien
    streitet kein Edler;
    den Frevler straft nur der Freie.
    Wider deine Kraft
    führt' ich wohl Krieg:
    doch Siegmund verfiel mir als Knecht!
      neue heftige Gebärde Wotans, dann Versinken in das
      Gefühl seiner Ohnmacht
830 Der dir als Herren
    hörig und eigen,
    gehorchen soll ihm
    dein ewig Gemahl?
    Soll mich in Schmach
    der Niedrigste schmähen,
    dem Frechen zum Sporn,
    dem Freien zum Spott?

WOTAN *fiercely*

   Siegmund won it   810

     with suppressed trembling

   even when there was no way out!

     From here on, Wotan expresses with his whole demeanour
     an ever-growing, terrifying sense of utter wretchedness.

FRICKA *carrying on regardless*

   You invented that impasse for him,

   as you did the pitiless sword.

   Are you playing fast and loose with me,

   the one who's been pursuing you

   day and night, hard on your heels?

   For him you plunged

   the sword into the trunk of the tree;

   you promised him

   that illustrious weapon: 820

   will you deny

   that your deviousness alone lured him

   to where he was supposed to find it?

     Wotan bridles at the suggestion, gesturing angrily.

     [Fricka] ever more sure of herself as she notices the
     impression that she has made on Wotan

   With those who are not free,

   no noble will fight;

   an upstart is punished only by his master.

   I might make war

   to resist your power:

   but Siegmund remains my slave!

     Wotan gestures angrily again, then succumbs to the feel-
     ing of his own powerlessness.

   He is his lord's   830

   obedient servant and slave:

   should your eternal wife

   be subject to him?

   Should this lowest of the low

   denigrate me in my humiliation,

   turn me into an object of scorn

   for the brazen, of mockery for the free?

Das kann mein Gatte nicht wollen,
die Göttin entweiht er nicht so!
   Fricka bleibt regungslos, Wotan in's Auge schauend.
   Wotan abgewendet*
WOTAN *finster*
840 Was verlangst du?
FRICKA *furchtbar heraus, mit einer gebieterischen Handbe-*
      wegung*
   Laß von dem Wälsung!
WOTAN *mit gedämpfter [erbebender*] Stimme*
   Er geh' seines Wegs.
FRICKA
   Doch du, schütze ihn nicht,
   wenn zur Schlacht ihn der Rächer ruft!
WOTAN
   Ich schütze ihn nicht.
      Fricka steht immer nahe bei Wotan. *
FRICKA
   Sieh mir ins Auge;
   sinne nicht Trug:
   die Walküre wend' auch von ihm!
WOTAN
   Die Walküre walte frei.
FRICKA
850 Nicht doch! Deinen Willen
   vollbringt sie allein:
   verbiete ihr Siegmunds Sieg!
WOTAN *in heftigen inneren Kampf ausbrechend*
   Ich kann ihn nicht fällen,
   er fand mein Schwert!
FRICKA *sehr gebieterisch**
   Entzieh dem den Zauber,
   zerknick' es dem Knecht!
   Schutzlos schau' ihn der Feind!
      Man vernimmt Brünnhilde von der Höhe her.
BRÜNNHILDE
   Heiaha! Heiaha! Hojotoho!

My husband can't want this.
Profane a goddess: that he won't do!
  Fricka remains motionless, looking Wotan in the eye.
  *Wotan turning away**
WOTAN *bleakly*
What do you want?   840
FRICKA *terrifyingly expressed, with an imperious hand ges-*
    *ture**
Forswear the Wälsung!
WOTAN *in a hushed [trembling*] voice*
He's going his own way.
FRICKA
But not you: do not protect him,
if the avenger calls him to battle!
WOTAN
I won't protect him.
  *Fricka continues to stand close to Wotan.**
FRICKA
Look me in the eye;
don't think of cheating:
the Valkyrie must abandon him too!
WOTAN
The Valkyrie's free to do as she likes.
FRICKA
No, she isn't! Your will   850
alone she brings to fruition:
don't let her give Siegmund victory!
WOTAN *his angry inner conflict erupting into the open*
I can't strike him down;
he found my sword!
FRICKA *very imperiously**
Take away its magic,
smash it to pieces in his servile hands!
Let his foe see him bereft of protection!
  Brünnhilde can be heard high up in the distance.
BRÜNNHILDE
Heiaha! Heiaha! Hojotoho!

FRICKA
Dort kommt deine kühne Maid:
860   jauchzend jagt sie daher.

BRÜNNHILDE
Heiaha! Heiaha!
Hojohotojohotojoha!

WOTAN
Ich rief sie für Siegmund zu Roß!

*Brünnhilde erscheint mit ihrem Roß auf dem Felsenpfade
rechts.*

*Als sie Fricka gewahrt, bricht sie schnell ab, und gelei-
tet ihr Roß still und langsam während des Folgenden den
Felsweg herab: dort birgt sie es dann in einer Höhle.*

FRICKA
Deiner ew'gen Gattin
heilige Ehre
beschirme heut' ihr Schild!
Von Menschen verlacht,
verlustig der Macht,
gingen wir Götter zu Grund:
870   würde heut nicht hehr
und herrlich mein Recht
gerächt von der mutigen Maid.
Der Wälsung fällt meiner Ehre:
empfah' ich von Wotan den Eid?

WOTAN *in furchtbarem Unmut und innerem Grimm auf einen
       Felsensitz sich werfend*
           mit wie gebrochener Stimme*
Nimm den Eid!

FRICKA *schreitet dem Hintergrunde zu: dort begegnet sie
       Brünnhilden, und hält einen Augenblick vor ihr an.*
Heervater
harret dein:
laß ihn dir künden,
wie das Los er gekiest.

Sie fährt schnell davon.

*Brünnhilde tritt mit verwunderter und besorgter Miene
vor Wotan, der auf dem Felssitz zurückgelehnt in finstres
Brüten versunken ist.*

FRICKA
  Here comes your fearless young woman:
  galloping towards us, shouting for joy.   860

BRÜNNHILDE
  Heiaha! Heiaha!
  Hojohotojohotojoha!

WOTAN
  I ordered her to horse for Siegmund!

    Brünnhilde enters with her horse on the pathway in the
    rocks on the right.
      When she notices Fricka, she quickly breaks off and
    during the following leads her horse quietly and slowly
    down the path to a cave, where she lets it rest.

FRICKA
  Your eternal wife's
  sacred honour
  is protected for now by her shield!
  But we gods will go to our ruin,
  ridiculed by humankind,
  deprived of our power:
  that is, if my rights are not greatly   870
  and gloriously avenged today
  by that strong-minded young woman.
  The Wälsung is a sacrifice to my honour:
  can Wotan give me his oath?

WOTAN *hurling himself onto a seat in the rocks in terrible*
    wretchedness and inner turmoil
      *his voice sounding broken**
  Accept my oath!

FRICKA *strides towards the back: there she meets Brünnhilde,*
    pausing for a moment in front of her.
  The lord of the army
  awaits you:
  let him tell you
  how he has chosen his fate.

    She quickly drives off.
      Brünnhilde steps before Wotan, her features betraying
    concern and surprise. Wotan is leaning back in his seat,
    sunk in dark thought.

ZWEITE SZENE

BRÜNNHILDE

880 Schlimm, fürcht' ich,
schloß der Streit,
lachte Fricka dem Lose!
Vater, was soll
dein Kind erfahren?
Trübe scheinst du und traurig!

WOTAN *Er läßt den Arm machtlos sinken und den Kopf in den*
Nacken fallen.
In eigner Fessel
fing ich mich: –
ich Unfreiester aller.

BRÜNNHILDE

So sah ich dich nie:
890 was nagt dir das Herz?

WOTAN *Von hier an steigert sich Wotans Ausdruck und Ge-*
bärde bis zum furchtbarsten Ausbruch.
O heilige Schmach!
O schmählicher Harm!
Götternot!
Götternot!
Endloser Grimm!
Ewiger Gram!
Der Traurigste bin ich von Allen!
Brünnhilde wirft erschrocken Schild, Speer und Helm
von sich und läßt sich mit besorgter Zutraulichkeit zu
seinen Füßen nieder.

BRÜNNHILDE

Vater! Vater!
Sage, was ist dir?
900 Wie erschreckst du mit Sorge dein Kind!
Vertraue mir!
Ich bin dir treu:
sieh, Brünnhilde bittet.

SCENE TWO

BRÜNNHILDE
  I fear the quarrel   880
  went badly
  if Fricka laughs at its end!
  Father, what should
  your child know?
  You look dreary and desolate!

WOTAN *He lets his arm flop down helplessly and his head*
    slump forward.
  I'm caught
  in my own trap: –
  with less freedom than anyone.

BRÜNNHILDE
  Never have I seen you like this:
  what's gnawing at your heart?   890

WOTAN *Wotan's whole demeanour intensifies from here on*
    until it erupts with terrifying force.
  O godly disgrace!
  O inglorious sorrow!
  No way out for the gods!
  No way out for the gods!
  Endless rage!
  Eternal grief!
  I'm the unhappiest of beings!
    Brünnhilde throws off her spear, shield and helmet in
    shock and settles down, concerned and confidingly, at his
    feet.

BRÜNNHILDE
  Father! Father!
  Tell me, what's the matter?
  How your worrying frightens your child!   900
  Trust me!
  I'm loyal to you:
  look, Brünnhilde begs for an answer.

*Sie legt traulich und ängstlich Haupt und Hände ihm auf
Knie und Schoß.*

> *Wotan blickt ihr lange ins Auge; dann streichelt er ihr
> mit unwillkürlicher Zärtlichkeit die Locken.*

> *Wie aus tiefem Sinnen zu sich kommend, beginnt er
> endlich.*

WOTAN *sehr leise*

Lass' ich's verlauten,
lös' ich dann nicht
meines Willens haltenden Haft?

BRÜNNHILDE *sehr leise*

Zu Wotans Willen sprichst du,
sagst du mir, was du willst;
wer bin ich,
910   wär' ich dein Wille nicht?

WOTAN *sehr leise*

Was keinem in Worten ich künde,
unausgesprochen
bleib' es denn ewig:
mit mir nur rat' ich,
red' ich zu dir.

> *mit gänzlich gedämpfter Stimme*

Als junger Liebe
Lust mir verblich,
verlangte nach Macht mein Mut:
von jäher Wünsche
920   Wüten gejagt,
gewann ich mir die Welt.
Unwissend trugvoll
Untreue übt' ich,
band durch Verträge,
was Unheil barg:
listig verlockte mich Loge,
der schweifend nun verschwand.
Von der Liebe doch
mocht' ich nicht lassen,
930   in der Macht verlangt' ich nach Minne.
Den Nacht gebar,

*She rests her head and hands trustingly and anxiously on
his knees and lap.*

*Wotan looks into her eyes for a long time; he then
caresses her hair with instinctive tenderness.*

*As if coming to after being in a state of deep contem-
plation, he begins at last.*

WOTAN *very quietly*
If I utter it aloud,
don't I weaken
the enduring power of my will?

BRÜNNHILDE *very quietly*
You speak to Wotan's will
if you tell me what you want;
if I am not your will,
who am I?   910

WOTAN *very quietly*
What I tell no one in words,
let it be for ever
unspoken:
I only talk to myself,
if I speak to you.
  with a completely subdued voice
When the pleasures of being young
and in love began to pall on me,
my instinct longed for power:
driven by ruthless,
raging ambition,   920
I gained possession of the world.
Full of guile without knowing it,
I indulged in deceit,
binding with legal contract
all that hid disaster:
Loge, everywhere yet nowhere,
tricked me into it.
But though engrossed by power
I was loathe to relinquish love;
I longed for its intimacy.   930
The wary Nibelung,

der bange Nibelung,
Alberich, brach ihren Bund;
er fluchte der Lieb',
und gewann durch den Fluch
des Rheines glänzendes Gold,
und mit ihm maßlose Macht.
Den Ring, den er schuf,
entriß ich ihm listig;
940   doch nicht dem Rhein
gab ich ihn zurück:
mit ihm bezahlt' ich
Walhalls Zinnen,
der Burg, die Riesen mir bauten,
aus der ich der Welt nun gebot.
Die alles weiß,
was einstens war,
Erda, die weihlich
weiseste Wala,
950   riet mir ab von dem Ring,
warnte vor ewigem Ende.
        etwas heftiger
Von dem Ende wollt' ich
mehr noch wissen;
        zurückhaltend
doch schweigend entschwand mir das Weib.
        belebend
Da verlor ich den leichten Mut;
zu wissen begehrt' es den Gott:
in den Schoß der Welt
schwang ich mich hinab,
mit Liebeszauber
960   zwang ich die Wala,
stört' ihres Wissens Stolz,
daß sie Rede nun mir stand.
Kunde empfing ich von ihr;
von mir doch empfing sie ein Kind:
der Welt weisestes Weib
gebar mir, Brünnhilde, dich.

Alberich, offspring of the night,
broke love's binding power.
He cursed love,
and with the curse gained possession
of the Rhine's dazzling gold,
and with that power without limit.
I tore from him the ring he made
with a trick;
but I did not   940
give it back to the Rhine:
I used it to pay for
the battlements of Valhalla,
the fortress that giants built for me,
from where I now ruled the world.
She who knows all
that's ever been,
Erda, the seeress whose
ultimate knowledge is sacred,
advised me to discard the ring,   950
warning of eternal destruction.
    somewhat more vehemently
I wanted to know still more
about this destruction;
    holding back
but the woman vanished without a word.
    animatedly
My easy-going nature vanished too;
the god longed to know more:
I journeyed down
to the bowels of the earth.
I coerced the Wala
with erotic magic,   960
rattled her arrogant pride
to make her justify what she'd said.
I received important news from her;
but from me she received a child:
the world's wisest woman
bore me, Brünnhilde, you.

Mit acht Schwestern
zog ich dich auf;
durch euch Walküren
970   wollt' ich wenden,
was mir die Wala
zu fürchten schuf:
ein schmähliches Ende der Ew'gen.
Daß stark zum Streit
uns fände der Feind,
hieß ich euch Helden mir schaffen:
die herrisch wir sonst
in Gesetzen hielten,
die Männer, denen
980   den Mut wir gewehrt,
die durch trüber Verträge
trügende Bande
zu blindem Gehorsam
wir uns gebunden,
die solltet zu Sturm
    immer belebter, doch mit gemäßigter Stärke
und Streit ihr stacheln,
ihre Kraft reizen
zu rauhem Krieg,
daß kühner Kämpfer Scharen
990   ich sammle in Walhalls Saal.

BRÜNNHILDE
Deinen Saal füllten wir weidlich:
viele schon führt' ich dir zu.
Was macht dir nun Sorge,
da nie wir gesäumt?

WOTAN *wieder gedämpfter*
Ein andres ist's:
achte es wohl,
wess' mich die Wala gewarnt.
Durch Alberichs Heer
droht uns das Ende:
    der Schluß der Phrase ['Ende'] leise wie ins Leere verhal-
    *lend**

I nurtured you
with eight sisters;
through you, the Valkyries,
I wanted to reverse   970
what the Wala
made me fear:
an inglorious end of the immortals.
So the enemy would find us
well prepared for battle,
I asked you to bring me heroes:
those we'd have otherwise bullied
into subjection with laws,
men whose freedom of action
we would have curbed,   980
bound to us,
made blindly obedient
through the treacherous bonds
of spurious contracts.
All of you were to goad them
    always more animated, but with tempered force
into attack and battle,
to kindle their strength
for bitter war,
so that I could assemble a host of
bold warriors in Valhalla's hall.   990

BRÜNNHILDE

We worked hard to fill your hall:
I brought you many myself.
There has never been any delay,
so what's worrying you?

WOTAN *again more subdued*

It's something else:
take heed of
what the Wala warned me about.
Alberich's army
is threatening us with oblivion:
    *the conclusion of the phrase ['oblivion'] softly as if sound-
    ing into empty space ***

1000   mit neidischem Grimm
      grollt mir der Niblung;
        belebend
      doch scheu' ich nun nicht
      seine nächtigen Scharen,
      meine Helden schüfen mir Sieg.
        gedämpfter
      Nur wenn je den Ring
      zurück er gewänne –
        noch gedämpfter
      dann wäre Walhall verloren:
      der der Liebe fluchte,
      er allein
1010   nützte neidisch
      des Ringes Runen
      zu aller Edlen
      endloser Schmach;
      der Helden Mut
        belebend
      entwendet' er mir,
      die Kühnen selber
      zwäng' er zum Kampf,
      mit ihrer Kraft
      bekriegte er mich.
        gedämpft
1020   Sorgend sann ich nun selbst,
      den Ring dem Feind zu entreißen.
        gedämpft
      Der Riesen einer,
      denen ich einst
      mit verfluchtem Gold
      den Fleiß vergalt,
      Fafner hütet den Hort,
      um den er den Bruder gefällt.
      Ihm müßt' ich den Reif entringen,
      den selbst als Zoll ich ihm zahlte.
1030   Doch mit dem ich vertrug,
      ihn darf ich nicht treffen;

enraged with pitiless envy,   1000
the Nibelung wishes me ill;
  enlivened
but I'm no longer afraid
of his nocturnal hordes:
my heroes will ensure victory.
  more subdued
Only if he ever
wins back the ring –
  still more subdued
will Valhalla be lost:
only he
who cursed love
could ruthlessly exploit   1010
the ring's runes
to bring eternal disgrace
upon every noble being;
the loyal valour of my heroes
  enlivened
he'd steal from me,
he'd force these brave men
into battle himself,
with their strength
he'd wage war against me.
  subdued
I now carefully devised my own plan   1020
for wresting the ring from the enemy.
  subdued
One of the giants,
whom I once paid
for his work with gold
that was under a curse,
he, Fafner, is guarding the hoard
over which he killed his brother.
I'd have to fight him to get back
the ring I myself used to pay him off.
But the one with whom I had a contract   1030
is precisely the one I cannot meet;

machtlos vor ihm
erläge mein Mut;
   bitter
das sind die Bande
die mich binden:
der durch Verträge ich Herr,
den Verträgen bin ich nun Knecht.
Nur Einer könnte,
was ich nicht darf:
1040 ein Held, dem helfend
nie ich mich neigte,
der fremd dem Gotte,
frei seiner Gunst,
unbewußt,
ohne Geheiß,
aus eigner Not,
mit der eignen Wehr
schüfe die Tat,
die ich scheuen muß,
1050 die nie mein Rat ihm riet,
wünscht sie auch einzig mein Wunsch.
Der, entgegen dem Gott,
für mich föchte,
den freundlichen Feind,
wie fände ich ihn?
Wie schüf' ich den Freien,
den nie ich schirmte,
der im eignen Trotze
der trauteste mir?
1060 Wie macht' ich den andren,
der nicht mehr ich,
und aus sich wirkte,
was ich nur will?
O göttliche Not!
Gräßliche Schmach!
Zum Ekel find' ich
ewig nur mich
in allem was ich erwirke.

I'd be powerless in front of him,
my courage would fail;
   sardonically
these are the bonds
that are binding me:
the contracts that made me a master
have now turned me into their slave.
Only one man could do
what I cannot:
a hero I've never   1040
been inclined to help,
a stranger to the god,
free of his influence,
instinctive,
unprompted,
taking action
with his own weapons
to escape his own crises,
action I have to shun,
action I never told him to take,   1050
yet enacting the only thing I wish.
How could I find
this enemy without enmity,
a man opposed to the god,
who would fight for me?
How do I create the free man
whom I've never protected,
whose defiant independence
makes him closest to me?
How do I make another being   1060
who is no longer like me,
who does what he wants,
yet only what I want?
Alas no way out for the gods!
Dire disgrace!
To my disgust I find
in everything I do
only an eternal reflection of myself.

Das andre, das ich ersehne,
1070 das andre erseh' ich nie:
denn selbst muß der Freie sich schaffen;
Knechte erknet' ich mir nur.

BRÜNNHILDE *mit innigstem Blicke* Wotan *in die Augen*
*schauend**
Doch der Wälsung, Siegmund?
wirkt er nicht selbst?

WOTAN
Wild durchschweift' ich
mit ihm die Wälder;
gegen der Götter Rat
reizte kühn ich ihn auf:
gegen der Götter Rache
1080 schützt ihn nun einzig das Schwert,
    gedehnt und bitter
das eines Gottes
Gunst ihm beschied.
Wie wollt' ich listig
selbst mich belügen?
So leicht ja entfrug mir
Fricka den Trug:
zu tiefster Scham
durchschaute sie mich!
    *schmerzlich aufzuckend**
        rasch
Ihrem Willen muß ich gewähren.

BRÜNNHILDE
1090 So nimmst du von Siegmund den Sieg?

WOTAN
Ich berührte Alberichs Ring,
gierig hielt ich das Gold.
Der Fluch, den ich floh,
nicht flieht er nun mich.
Was ich liebe, muß ich verlassen,
morden, wen je ich minne!
Trügend verraten,
wer mir traut. –

I long for that other existence,
that other I can never envisage: 1070
a free man must bring himself into being;
slaves are all I can create.

BRÜNNHILDE *looking Wotan in the eye with the most heart-*
    *felt expression**
But the Wälsung, Siegmund?
aren't his actions his own?

WOTAN
I roamed with him wildly
through the forests;
daringly, I goaded him
into resisting the gods' counsel:
the only thing protecting him now
from the gods' vengeance is the sword,   1080
    slowly and sardonically
granted to him
at the behest of a god.
How did I manage
to lie to myself with such guile?
It was so easy for Fricka
to get me to admit that it was deceit:
to my deepest shame,
she saw right through me!
    *grimacing bitterly**
        briskly
I must accede to her will.

BRÜNNHILDE
And deprive Siegmund of victory?   1090

WOTAN
I touched Alberich's ring,
I relished holding the gold.
I escaped from the curse
that now won't escape from me.
I must abandon what I love,
murder the one I cherish most!
Treacherously betray
the one who trusts me. –

Wotans Gebärde geht aus dem Ausdruck des furcht-
barsten Schmerzes zu dem der Verzweiflung über.

Fahre denn hin,
1100   herrische Pracht!
Göttlichen Prunkes
prahlende Schmach!
Zusammenbreche,
was ich gebaut.
Auf geb' ich mein Werk!
nur Eines will ich noch:
das Ende!
Das Ende!
         Er hält sinnend ein.
Und für das Ende
1110   sorgt Alberich! –
Jetzt versteh' ich
den stummen Sinn
des wilden Wortes der Wala.
         Wie vor sich hinsinnend *
'Wenn der Liebe finstrer Feind
zürnend zeugt einen Sohn,
der Sel'gen Ende
säumt dann nicht.'
Vom Niblung jüngst
vernahm ich die Mär',
1120   daß ein Weib der Zwerg bewältigt,
dess' Gunst Gold ihm erzwang.
Des Hasses Frucht
hegt eine Frau;
des Neides Kraft
kreißt ihr im Schoß:
das Wunder gelang
dem Liebelosen;
doch der in Lieb' ich freite,
den Freien erlang' ich mir nicht.
         mit bittrem Grimm sich aufrichtend
1130   So nimm meinen Segen,
Niblungen-Sohn!

Wotan's bearing changes from an expression of direst
pain to one of desperation.
Away with
bullying brilliance!   1100
The preening shamefulness
of godly grandeur!
Let everything I've built
collapse.
I disown my work!
Only one thing do I still want:
destruction!
Destruction!
    He pauses to reflect.
And to achieve that destruction,
Alberich is scheming! –   1110
I now understand
the Wala's wild utterance
and its real meaning.
    *As if thinking to himself**
'If love's sinister enemy
angrily fathers a son,
the happy gods' destruction
will not wait.'
Not long ago I heard it said
of the Nibelung that this dwarf
had conquered a woman, using gold   1120
to force her to grant him her favours.
A woman is harbouring
the fruits of hatred;
the forces of envy
stir in her womb.
The man without love
achieved a miracle;
I was in love when I made love,
but sire a man who is free, I did not.
    rising up with sardonic bitterness
So take my blessing,   1130
son of the Nibelung!

Was tief mich ekelt,
dir geb' ich's zum Erbe;
der Gottheit nichtigen Glanz,
zernage ihn gierig der Neid!

BRÜNNHILDE *erschrocken*
   *mit leidenschaftlich heftiger Bewegung auf Wotan zu stürzend**

O sag! Künde,
was soll nun dein Kind?

WOTAN *bitter*

Fromm streite für Fricka,
hüte ihr Eh' und Eid!
   trocken

1140 Was sie erkor,
das kiese auch ich:
was frommte mir eigner Wille?
Einen Freien kann ich nicht wollen:
für Frickas Knechte
kämpfe nun du!

BRÜNNHILDE

Weh'! Nimm reuig
zurück das Wort!
Du liebst Siegmund:
dir zu Lieb' –

1150 ich weiß es, schütz' ich den Wälsung.

WOTAN *noch nicht zu heftig**

Fällen sollst du Siegmund,
für Hunding erfechten den Sieg!
Hüte dich wohl
und halte dich stark;
all deiner Kühnheit
entbiete im Kampf:
ein Siegschwert
schwingt Siegmund; –
schwerlich fällt er dir feig!

BRÜNNHILDE *mit leidenschaftliche Wärme**

1160 Den du zu lieben
stets mich gelehrt,

I bequeath to you
everything that profoundly sickens me;
the vacuous brilliance of godhood,
let hate greedily gnaw it to pieces!

BRÜNNHILDE *startled*
      rushing towards Wotan *with passionately impetuous
      emotion**
Say something! Tell me,
what is your child supposed to do?

WOTAN *bitterly*
Fight honourably for Fricka,
help her protect marriage and vows!
      drily
What she chose,   1140
I choose too:
how can a will of my own help me?
I can't wish for a free man:
so fight for Fricka's slaves,
yes, you!

BRÜNNHILDE
No! Rue your command
and retract it!
You love Siegmund;
for your sake –
that I know, I'll protect the Wälsung.   1150

WOTAN *not yet too fiercely**
Kill Siegmund: you must do it
to gain victory for Hunding!
Be vigilant
and keep yourself strong;
give all your bravery
to the fight:
Siegmund wields
a sword of victory; –
for you he'll hardly die a coward!

BRÜNNHILDE *with passionate warmth**
He whom you always   1160
taught me to love,

der in hehrer Tugend
dem Herzen dir teuer; –
gegen ihn zwingt mich nimmer
dein zwiespältig Wort!
  Brünnhilde wendet sich mit trotziger Gebärde ab. *
WOTAN *in furchtbarem Zornesausbruch* *
  Ha Freche du!
  Frevelst du mir?
  Wer bist du, als meines Willens
  blind wählende Kür?
1170 Da mit dir ich tagte,
  sank ich so tief,
  daß zum Schimpf der eignen
  Geschöpfe ich ward?
  Kennst du, Kind, meinen Zorn?
  Verzage dein Mut,
  wenn je zermalmend
  auf dich stürzte sein Strahl!
  In meinem Busen
  berg' ich den Grimm,
1180 der in Grau'n und Wust
  wirft eine Welt,
  die einst zur Lust mir gelacht.
  Wehe dem, den er trifft!
  Trauer schüf' ihm sein Trotz!
  Drum rat' ich dir,
  reize mich nicht!
  Besorge, was ich befahl:
  Siegmund falle!
  Dies sei der Walküre Werk!
    Er stürmt fort, und verschwindet schnell links im Ge-
    birge. – Brünnhilde steht lange erschrocken und betäubt.
BRÜNNHILDE *sucht wieder Fassung zu gewinnen.* *
1190 So – sah ich
  Siegvater nie,
  erzürnt' ihn sonst wohl auch ein Zank.
    Sie neigt sich betrübt und nimmt ihre Waffen auf, mit
    denen sie sich wieder rüstet.

who with his great virtue
is dear to your heart; –
your forked tongue will never
force me to turn against him.
    Brünnhilde turns away with a gesture of defiance. *
WOTAN *in a terrible outbreak of fury* *
    What outrageous cheek!
    Are you blaspheming me?
    Who are you but my will's
    conduit of blind choice?
    When I conferred with you,   1170
    did I sink so low
    that I became an object of scorn
    for my own offspring?
    Are you aware, child, of my anger?
    Your courage would shrivel
    if you were ever to get caught
    in its bruising glare!
    In my breast
    I hide the rage
    that can call up horror and chaos   1180
    in a world
    that once smiled on me in pleasure.
    Woe betide anyone who is its victim!
    Surliness would turn to sorrow!
    So take my advice,
    do not upset me!
    Carry out my order:
    Siegmund dies! –
    The Valkyrie's doing this shall be!
        He storms off and vanishes in the mountains on the left.
        – Brünnhilde is rooted to the spot, shocked and stunned.
BRÜNNHILDE *tries to pull herself together again.* *
    I have never seen   1190
    the father of victory – like that,
    even if a row always did annoy him.
        Saddened, she stoops to pick up her weapons and rearms
        herself.

Schwer wiegt mir
der Waffen Wucht!
Wenn nach Lust ich focht,
wie waren sie leicht!
Zu böser Schlacht
schleich' ich heut so bang.
   Sie sinnt vor sich hin.
      seufzend
Weh! mein Wälsung!
1200 Im höchsten Leid
muß dich treulos die Treue verlassen.
   Sie wendet sich langsam dem Hintergrunde zu.

DRITTE SZENE

*Auf dem Bergjoch angelangt, gewahrt Brünnhilde in die
Schlucht hinabblickend Siegmund und Sieglinde: sie betrachtet
die Nahenden einen Augenblick, dann wendet sie sich in die
Höhle zu ihrem Rosse, so daß sie dem Zuschauer gänzlich
verschwindet.*

   Siegmund und Sieglinde erscheinen auf dem Bergjoche.

   *Sieglinde schreitet Siegmund hastig voraus; Siegmund sucht
sie aufzuhalten.*

SIEGMUND
   Raste nun hier;
   gönne dir Ruh'!
SIEGLINDE
   Weiter! Weiter!
SIEGMUND *Er umfaßt sie mit sanfter Gewalt.*
   Nicht weiter nun!
      Er schließt sie fest an sich.
   Verweile, süßestes Weib!
   Aus Wonne-Entzücken
   zucktest du auf,
   mit jäher Hast
1210 jagtest du fort;

The weapons' load
weighs heavily upon me!
How light they were,
when I fought with zest!
Now I'm crawling into a dark fight,
such is my foreboding.
   She muses to herself.
     sighing
Alas! my Wälsung!
In deepest grief   1200
your loyal friend is forced to betray you.
   She turns around slowly towards the background.

SCENE THREE

*Having reached the mountain pass, Brünnhilde looks down
into the ravine and sees Siegmund and Sieglinde: she watches
them approaching for a moment, then completely disappears
out of the audience's sight by turning into the cave to find her
horse.*
   Siegmund and Sieglinde appear on the mountain pass.
   *Sieglinde is striding hastily ahead of Siegmund; Siegmund
tries to hold her back.*

SIEGMUND
   Take rest here;
   get some peace and quiet!
SIEGLINDE
   Keep going! Keep going!
SIEGMUND *He embraces her gently but firmly.*
   Don't keep going!
     He hugs her tightly.
   Stay here, sweetest woman!
   You awoke with a start
   after we'd been carried away by love,
   you stormed off
   in sudden haste;   1210

kaum folgt ich der wilden Flucht:
durch Wald und Flur,
über Fels und Stein,
sprachlos, schweigend
sprangst du dahin,
kein Ruf hielt dich zur Rast.
Sie starrt wild vor sich hin.
Ruhe nun aus:
rede zu mir,
ende des Schweigens Angst!
1220 Sieh, dein Bruder
hält seine Braut:
Siegmund ist dir Gesell'!
*Sie blickt Siegmund mit wachsendem Entzücken in die
Augen; dann umschlingt sie leidenschaftlich seinen Hals
und verweilt so.*
Dann fährt sie mit jähem Schreck auf.

SIEGLINDE
Hinweg! Hinweg!
Flieh die Entweihte!
Unheilig
umfängt dich ihr Arm;
entehrt, geschändet,
schwand dieser Leib:
flieh die Leiche,
1230 lasse sie los!
*Mit zu höchster Kraft gesteigertem Ausdruck des Jam-
mers und Entsetzens. 'Was Sieglinde gesagt hat, ist so
schrecklich, daß Siegmund dann lange, in tiefer Betrof-
fenheit den Blick zum Boden geheftet hält.'**
Der Wind mag sie verwehn,
die ehrlos dem Edlen sich gab.
Da er sie liebend umfing,
da seligste Lust sie fand,
mit ergreifender Liebesinnigkeit in Bild und Ton*
da ganz sie minnte der Mann,
der ganz ihre Minne geweckt: –
vor der süßesten Wonne

I've barely kept up the wild chase:
through woods and fields,
up hill and down dale,
not uttering a word,
you pressed on and on,
nothing I said could stop you.
She stares wildly in front of her.
You must rest:
talk to me,
end this fear that doesn't speak!
Look, your brother   1220
is at the side of his bride:
Siegmund is your husband!
*She looks into Siegmund's eyes with growing ecstasy;
eventually she throws her arms passionately around his
neck and remains like that for a moment.*
Then with a sudden shock, she flares up.

SIEGLINDE

Go! Go!
Flee this sullied woman!
Wickedly
her arm embraces you;
defiled, demeaned,
this body is gone:
flee the corpse,
let it go!   1230
*With an expression of wretchedness and horror wound
up to a point of extreme intensity and power. 'What Sieg-
linde has said is so terrible that Siegmund then fixes his
eyes to the ground for a long time in deep shock.'**
Let the wind blow it away,
it's surrendered to the hero in shame.
When he embraced her lovingly,
when she found supreme bliss,
with moving, loving intimacy in image and sound*
the man gave her all his passion,
all her passion was awoken by him: –
but beside sweetest love's

heiliger Weihe,
die ganz ihr Sinn
1240 und Seele durchdrang,
   *die alleräußerste, schrankenlose Heftigkeit der Akzente**
Grauen und Schauder
ob gräßlichster Schande
mußte mit Schreck
die Schmähliche fassen,
die je dem Manne gehorcht,
   *mit furchtbar verzweifeltem Ausdruck**
der ohne Minne sie hielt!
Laß die Verfluchte,
laß sie dich fliehn!
Verworfen bin ich,
1250 der Würde bar:
dir reinstem Manne
muß ich entrinnen,
dir Herrlichem darf ich
nimmer gehören.
Schande bring' ich dem Bruder,
Schmach dem freienden Freund.

SIEGMUND
Was je Schande dir schuf,
das büßt nun des Frevlers Blut.
Drum fliehe nicht weiter!
1260 Harre des Feindes;
hier soll er mir fallen:
   *mit eiserner Energie**
wenn Nothung ihm
das Herz zernagt,
Rache dann hast du erreicht.
   Es ist, als hätte Sieglinde die Trostesworte Siegmunds gar
   nicht gehört, wie von einer Vision beängstigt starrt sie zu
   *Boden.**

SIEGLINDE *schrickt auf und lauscht*
Horch, die Hörner!
Hörst du den Ruf?
Ringsher tönt

sacred blessing
that pulsed through
her senses and her soul,   1240
   accents of the very utmost, uninhibited vehemence*
the horror and dread
of the most monstrous disgrace
could not but take shocking hold
of the shamed woman,
ever obedient to that husband,
   with frighteningly distraught expression*
who had possessed her without love!
Abandon the damned,
let her desert you!
I'm an outcast,
deprived of dignity: 1250
I must leave you,
purest of husbands,
to you glorious man,
I cannot belong.
Shame I bring to my brother,
disgrace to my entreating friend.

SIEGMUND
That bad man's blood will atone
for all the disgrace brought upon you.
Don't keep running away!
Wait for the enemy;   1260
I'll kill him here:
   with implacable energy*
once Nothung
rips into his heart,
you'll be avenged.
   It is as if Sieglinde has heard none of Siegmund's com-
   forting words; she stares at the ground, as if frightened
   by some vision.*

SIEGLINDE *startled, pricking up her ears*
Listen, the horns!
You hear their call?
Deafening noise

wütend Getös';
aus Wald und Gau
1270 gellt es herauf.
Hunding erwachte
aus hartem Schlaf;
Sippen und Hunde
ruft er zusammen;
mutig gehetzt
heult die Meute,
wild bellt sie zum Himmel
um der Ehe gebrochenen Eid!
    Sie starrt wie wahnsinnig vor sich hin.
Wo bist du, Siegmund?
1280 Seh' ich dich noch?
Brünstig geliebter,
leuchtender Bruder!
    Sieglinde an Siegmund gelehnt mit inbrünstigem, in
    Schmerz und Seligkeit erbebendem Ausdruck*
Deines Auges Stern
laß noch einmal mir strahlen,
wehre dem Kuß
des verworf'nen Weibes nicht!
    Sie hat sich ihm schluchzend an die Brust geworfen: –
    dann schrickt sie ängstlich wieder auf.
Horch! O horch!
Das ist Hundings Horn.
Seine Meute naht
1290 mit mächtger Wehr:
kein Schwert frommt
vor der Hunde Schwall;
wirf es fort, Siegmund!
Siegmund – wo bist du?
    alles vor sich nach einer Stelle singend*
Ha dort! – Ich sehe dich: –
schrecklich Gesicht!
Rüden fletschen
die Zähne nach Fleisch;
sie achten nicht
1300 deines edlen Blicks;

rages around us;
it roars upward
out of forest and soil.   1270
Hunding's woken up
from deep sleep;
he's summoning
tribes and hounds;
their blood is up,
the pack howls,
wildly baying to heaven
at a broken marriage vow!
     She stares in front of her, as if demented.
Where are you, Siegmund?
Are you still there?   1280
Passionate lover,
radiant brother!
     Sieglinde leaning on Siegmund with ardent expressive-
     ness convulsed by pain and bliss *
Let the stars of your eyes
shine upon me once more,
do not resist the kiss
of this unrighteous woman!
     She has flung herself into his arms, sobbing: – then she
     flares up again, looking startled and anxious.
Listen! Listen hard!
That's Hunding's horn.
His pack nears
formidably armed: 1290
no sword can withstand
this onslaught of dogs;
throw it away, Siegmund!
Siegmund – where are you?
     singing everything in front of her to an imaginary place *
Ah, there! – I see you: –
terrible visions!
The hounds scent flesh,
bare their fangs;
they're oblivious
to your proud bearing;   1300

bei den Füßen packt dich
das feste Gebiß:
du fällst,
in Stücken zerstaucht das Schwert: –
die Esche stürzt –
es bricht der Stamm! –
Bruder! Mein Bruder!
 Sie sinkt ohnmächtig in Siegmunds Arme.
Siegmund! Ha!

SIEGMUND
Schwester! Geliebte.
 *Er lauscht ihrem Atem und überzeugt sich, daß sie noch
lebt.*

 *Er läßt sie an sich herabgleiten, so daß sie, als er sich
selbst zum Sitze niederläßt, mit ihrem Haupte auf seinem
Schoße zu ruhen kommt. In dieser Stellung verbleiben
beide bis zum Schlusse des folgenden Auftrittes.*

 *Langes Schweigen, während dessen Siegmund mit zärt-
licher Sorge über Sieglinde sich hinneigt, und mit einem
langen Kusse ihr die Stirne küßt.*

VIERTE SZENE

*Brünnhilde, ihr Roß am Zaume geleitend, tritt aus der Höhle
und schreitet langsam und feierlich nach vorne.*
 Sie hält an und betrachtet Siegmund von fern.
 Sie schreitet wieder langsam vor.
 Sie hält in größerer Nähe an.
 *Sie trägt Schild und Speer in der einen Hand, lehnt sich
mit der andren an den Hals des Rosses und betrachtet so mit
ernster Miene Siegmund:*

BRÜNNHILDE
1310 Siegmund!
 Sieh auf mich:
 Ich bin's,
 der bald du folgst.

they're gripping their teeth
around your ankles:
you fall,
the sword buckles and shatters: –
the ash-tree topples –
the trunk splits! –
Brother! My brother!
　　She sinks fainting into Siegmund's arms.
Siegmund! Ha!

SIEGMUND
Sister! Lover.
　　*He listens intently to her breathing and convinces himself
　　that she is still alive.*
　　　*He lets her sink down onto him so that as he sits down
　　himself her head comes to rest on his lap. Both of them
　　stay in this position until the end of the following scene.*
　　　*A long silence, during which Siegmund bends over
　　Sieglinde with tender care and kisses her forehead with a
　　long kiss.*

SCENE FOUR

*Brünnhilde comes out of the cave leading her horse by the
reins and walks with slow solemn steps towards the front.*
　　She stops to look at Siegmund from a distance.
　　She steps slowly forwards again.
　　She stops closer to him.
　　*Carrying her shield and spear in one hand and resting her
other hand on the neck of her horse, she faces Siegmund
gravely:*

BRÜNNHILDE
Siegmund!   1310
Look to me:
I'm the one
you're soon to follow.

SIEGMUND *richtet den Blick zu ihr auf*
  Wer bist du, sag',
  die so schön und ernst mir erscheint?
BRÜNNHILDE
  Nur Todgeweihten
  taugt mein Anblick;
  wer mich erschaut,
  der scheidet vom Lebenslicht.
1320 Auf der Walstatt allein
  erschein' ich Edlen;
  wer mich gewahrt,
  zur Wal kor ich ihn mir.
        Siegmund blickt ihr lange forschend und fest in das Auge,
        senkt dann sinnend das Haupt, und wendet sich endlich
        mit Ernste wieder zu ihr.
SIEGMUND
  Der dir nun folgt,
  wohin führst du den Helden?
BRÜNNHILDE
  Zu Walvater,
  der dich gewählt,
  führ' ich dich:
  nach Walhall folgst du mir.
SIEGMUND
1330 In Walhalls Saal
  Walvater find' ich allein?
BRÜNNHILDE
  Gefallner Helden
  hehre Schar
  umfängt dich hold
  mit hoch-heiligem Gruß.
SIEGMUND
  Fänd' ich in Walhall
  Wälse, den eignen Vater?
BRÜNNHILDE
  Den Vater findet
  der Wälsung dort!

SIEGMUND *raises his eyes to look at her*
  Tell me, who are you
  to appear before me so finely and sternly?
BRÜNNHILDE
  Only those destined to die
  are worthy of my gaze;
  if you lay eyes on me,
  you depart the light of life.
  Only on the field of slaughter   1320
  do I appear to noble heroes;
  whoever sees me,
  I choose him to be slaughtered.
    *Siegmund looks her in the eye for a long time intently
    and firmly, then lowers his head pensively, and eventually
    turns gravely towards her again.*
SIEGMUND
  If your hero follows you,
  where will you lead him?
BRÜNNHILDE
  I'll lead him
  to the father of battles
  who's chosen you:
  you'll follow me to Valhalla.
SIEGMUND
  Will the father of battles   1330
  be in Valhalla on his own?
BRÜNNHILDE
  A great galaxy
  of fallen heroes
  will warmly embrace you
  with a solemn salute.
SIEGMUND
  Will I find Wälse
  in Valhalla, my own father?
BRÜNNHILDE
  The Wälsung will find
  his father there!

SIEGMUND *zart*

1340 Grüßt mich in Walhall
      froh eine Frau?

BRÜNNHILDE

      Wunschmädchen
      walten dort hehr:
      Wotans Tochter
      reicht dir traulich den Trank!

SIEGMUND

      Hehr bist du,
      und heilig gewahr' ich
      das Wotanskind;
      doch Eines sag mir, du Ew'ge!

1350 Begleitet den Bruder
      die bräutliche Schwester?
      Umfängt Siegmund
      Sieglinde dort?

BRÜNNHILDE

      Erdenluft
      muß sie noch atmen:
      Sieglinde
      sieht Siegmund dort nicht.

      Siegmund neigt sich sanft über Sieglinde, küßt sie leise auf
      die Stirn und wendet sich ruhig wieder zu Brünnhilde.

SIEGMUND

      So grüße mir Walhall;
      grüße mir Wotan;

1360 grüße mir Wälse
      und alle Helden;
      grüß auch die holden
      Wunschesmädchen:
           sehr bestimmt
      zu ihnen folg' ich dir nicht!

BRÜNNHILDE

      Du sahst der Walküre
      sehrenden Blick:
      mit ihr mußt du nun ziehn.

SIEGMUND

      Wo Sieglinde lebt

SIEGMUND *tenderly*

 Can I expect a woman in Valhalla   1340
 to give me warm welcome?

BRÜNNHILDE

 There gifted young women
 have illustrious power:
 a daughter of Wotan
 will fondly prepare your drink!

SIEGMUND

 You are illustrious,
 and I solemnly behold
 Wotan's child;
 you are eternal, but tell me one thing!
 Will the brother's bride,   1350
 his sister, go with him?
 Will Siegmund embrace
 Sieglinde there?

BRÜNNHILDE

 She still has to breathe
 the earth's air:
 Sieglinde
 won't see Siegmund there.
  Siegmund leans gently over Sieglinde, kisses her softly on
  the brow and again turns calmly to Brünnhilde.

SIEGMUND

 So, send my tribute to Vahalla;
 my tribute to Wotan;
 my tribute to Wälse   1360
 and all heroes;
 send my tribute also to the fair,
 gifted young women:
  very decisively
 to them I'll not follow you!

BRÜNNHILDE

 You saw the Valkyrie's
 trenchant gaze:
 you must now go with her.

SIEGMUND

 Where Sieglinde lives

in Lust und Leid,
1370   da will Siegmund auch säumen:
noch machte dein Blick
nicht mich erbleichen;
vom Bleiben zwingt er mich nicht.

BRÜNNHILDE
Solang du lebst,
zwäng' dich wohl nichts;
doch zwingt dich Toren der Tod:
ihn dir zu künden
kam ich her.

SIEGMUND
Wo wäre der Held,
1380   dem heut ich fiel'?

BRÜNNHILDE
Hunding fällt dich im Streit.

SIEGMUND
Mit Stärk'rem drohe
als Hundings Streichen!
Lauerst du hier
lüstern auf Wal,
jenen kiese zum Fang;
ich denk ihn zu fällen im Kampf.

BRÜNNHILDE
Dir, Wälsung, –
höre mich wohl: –
1390   dir ward das Los gekiest.

SIEGMUND
Kennst du dies Schwert?
Der mir es schuf,
beschied mir Sieg:
deinem Drohen trotz' ich mit ihm.

BRÜNNHILDE *sehr stark betont*
Der dir es schuf,
beschied dir jetzt Tod:
seine Tugend nimmt er dem Schwert.

SIEGMUND *heftig*
Schweig, – und schrecke

in joy and grief,
there Siegmund wants to stay too: 1370
your gaze still doesn't
fill me with terror;
it'll not force me to leave.

BRÜNNHILDE
While you're alive,
nothing could probably force you;
but death, you simpleton, will:
to announce that to you
is why I came.

SIEGMUND
Where's the hero
who'll kill me today?   1380

BRÜNNHILDE
Hunding will kill you in battle.

SIEGMUND
Threaten me with stronger things
than Hunding's blows!
If you're lying here in wait,
lusting after slaughter,
choose him as your prey;
I intend to kill him in battle.

BRÜNNHILDE
For you, Wälsung, –
listen to me carefully: –
your destiny has been chosen.   1390

SIEGMUND
Do you know this sword?
He who made it for me
destined me for victory:
with it, I'll brave your threats.

BRÜNNHILDE *with very strong emphasis*
He who made it for you
destines you now for death:
he'll rob the sword of its virtue.

SIEGMUND *angrily*
Be still, – and don't scare

die Schlummernde nicht!
*Er beugt sich mit hervorbrechendem Schmerze zärtlich
über Sieglinde.*

1400   Weh! Weh!
Süßestes Weib,
du traurigste aller Getreuen!
Gegen dich wütet
in Waffen die Welt;
und ich, dem du einzig vertraut,
für den du ihr einzig getrotzt,
mit meinem Schutz
nicht soll ich dich schirmen,
die Kühne verraten im Kampf?

1410   Ha, Schande ihm,
der das Schwert mir schuf,
beschied er mir Schimpf für Sieg!
Muß ich denn fallen,
nicht fahr' ich nach Walhall:
Hella, halte mich fest!
Er neigt sich tief zu Sieglinde.
*'Die höchste Ehre des Helden: nach Walhall zu-
kommen achtet Siegmund für nichts; so etwas hat eine
Walküre nie gehört.'**

BRÜNNHILDE *erschüttert*
durchaus empfindungsvoll zu singen*
So wenig achtest du
ewige Wonne?
zögernd und zurückhaltend
Alles wär' dir
das arme Weib,

1420   das müd' und harmvoll
matt auf dem Schoße dir hängt?
Nichts sonst hieltest du hehr?

SIEGMUND *bitter zu ihr aufblickend*
So jung und schön
erschimmerst du mir,
doch wie kalt und hart
erkennt dich mein Herz!

the woman out of her sleep!
>   *With erupting signs of anguish, he bends tenderly over*
>   *Sieglinde.*

Alas! Alas!   1400
Sweetest woman,
you, the unhappiest of all loyal wives!
Against you rage the
weapons of the world;
and I, the only one you can trust,
for whom you alone defied the world,
who will not be allowed to shelter you
and keep you safe,
am I to betray your bravery in battle?
Ha, shame on him,   1410
who made me this sword;
he destined me for scorn, not victory.
If I have to die,
I'll not journey to Valhalla:
Hella, hold me firm!
>   *He leans down to Sieglinde.*
>   *'The highest honour for a hero, namely to come to*
>   *Valhalla: Siegmund places no value on it at all. Of this a*
>   *Valkyrie has never heard.'**

BRÜNNHILDE *shaken*
>   *absolutely to be sung full of feeling**

Do you value
eternal bliss so little?
>   *hesitating and holding back*
Is she everything to you,
this poor woman,
who, weary and sorrowful,   1420
clings to you limply on your lap?
Is nothing else dear to you?

SIEGMUND *bitterly looking up to her*
To me you shimmer
with youth and beauty,
but my heart can tell how
cold and hard you are!

Kannst du nur höhnen,
so hebe dich fort,
du arge, fühllose Maid!
1430 Doch mußt du dich weiden
an meinem Weh',
mein Leiden letze dich denn,
meine Not labe
dein neidvolles Herz: –
nur von Walhalls spröden Wonnen
sprich du wahrlich mir nicht.

BRÜNNHILDE
Ich sehe die Not,
die das Herz dir zernagt;
ich fühle des Helden
1440 heiligen Harm! –
Siegmund, befiehl mir dein Weib:
mein Schutz umfange sie fest!

SIEGMUND
Kein andrer als ich
soll die Reine lebend berühren;
verfiel ich dem Tod,
die Betäubte töt' ich zuvor!

BRÜNNHILDE *in wachsender Ergriffenheit*
Wälsung! Rasender!
Hör' meinen Rat:
befiehl mir dein Weib
1450 um des Pfandes willen,
das wonnig von dir es empfing!

SIEGMUND *Sein Schwert ziehend:*
Dies Schwert –
das dem Treuen ein Trugvoller schuf;
dies Schwert –
das feig vor dem Feind mich verrät:
frommt es nicht gegen den Feind,
so fromm' es denn wider den Freund!
    Er zückt das Schwert auf Sieglinde.
Zwei Leben
lachen dir hier:
1460 nimm sie, Nothung,

If all you can do is scoff,
then get on your way,
you evil, soulless young woman!
If you must revel   1430
in my regret,
let my pain at least succour you,
let my calamity brace
your envious heart: –
only please don't tell me
about Valhalla's feeble charms.

BRÜNNHILDE

I see the distress
gnawing at your heart;
I feel the sacred sorrow
of a hero! –   1440
Siegmund, entrust me with your wife:
under my guard she'll be safe!

SIEGMUND

No one but me
is to touch this pure woman alive;
if I'm to die,
I'll kill her first while she sleeps!

BRÜNNHILDE *in growing emotional turmoil*

Wälsung! Man of fury!
Hear what we must do:
entrust me with your wife
for the sake of the pledge   1450
she accepted from you in blissful love!

SIEGMUND *Drawing his sword:*

This sword –
made by a traitor for the trusted:
this sword –
cravenly betraying me to the enemy:
it's no use against a foe,
so let it be used against a friend!
    He brandishes the sword at Sieglinde.
Two lives
smile on you here:
take them, Nothung,   1460

neidischer Stahl!
Nimm sie mit einem Streich!

BRÜNNHILDE *im heftigsten Sturme des Mitgefühls*
        mit leidenschaftlicher Ektase, ohne Überhetzung des
        Tempos *

Halt ein! Wälsung!
Höre mein Wort!
Sieglinde lebe,
und Siegmund – lebe mit ihr!
Beschlossen ist's:
das Schlachtloos wend' ich;
dir, Siegmund,
1470   schaff' ich Segen und Sieg!

        Man hört aus dem fernen Hintergrunde Hornrufe er-
        schallen.

            diese Episode etwas ruhiger *

Hörst du den Ruf?
Nun rüste dich, Held!
Traue dem Schwert
und schwing es getrost:
treu hält dir die Wehr,
wie die Walküre treu dich schützt.
Leb wohl, Siegmund,
seligster Held!
Auf der Walstatt seh' ich dich wieder!

        Sie stürmt fort und verschwindet mit dem Rosse rechts
        in einer Seitenschlucht. Siegmund blickt ihr freudig und
        erhoben nach.

        Die Bühne hat sich allmählich verfinstert; schwarze
        Gewitterwolken senken sich auf den Hintergrund herab,
        und hüllen die Gebirgswände, die Schlucht und das er-
        höhte Bergjoch, nach und nach gänzlich ein.

        Er [Siegmund] neigt sich wieder über Sieglinde, dem
        Atem lauschend.

pitiless steel!
Take them at one stroke!

BRÜNNHILDE *in a fierce storm of compassionate feeling*
        with passionate ecstasy, but without rushing the tempo
    too much*

Stop! Wälsung!
Hear me out!
Let Sieglinde live,
and Siegmund – live with her!
The die is cast:
I reverse the battle's fate;
to you, Siegmund,
I give blessing and victory!   1470

    Horn calls can be heard resounding in the background
    from afar.

        this episode somewhat calmer*

Do you hear that sound?
Arm yourself, hero!
Trust in the sword
and wield it without fear:
the weapon will stay loyal to you,
as loyal as the Valkyrie's guard.
Farewell, Siegmund,
hero most happy!
On the field of slaughter we'll meet again!

    She storms away and with her horse vanishes into a ravine
    on the right-hand side. Happy and buoyant, Siegmund
    watches her go.

    The stage has become gradually darker; heavy storm
    clouds gather in the background and one by one settle
    down until they envelop, little by little, the mountain
    walls, the ravine, and the heightened mountain ridge.

    He [Siegmund] leans again over Sieglinde, listening to
    her breathing.

FÜNFTE SZENE

SIEGMUND

1480 Zauberfest
bezähmt ein Schlaf
der Holden Schmerz und Harm.
Da die Walküre zu mir trat,
schuf sie ihr den wonnigen Trost?
Sollte die grimmige Wahl
nicht schrecken ein gramvolles Weib?
Leblos scheint sie,
die dennoch lebt:
  mit zartestem Ausdruck *
der Traurigen kost
1490 ein lächelnder Traum.
So schlummre nun fort,
bis die Schlacht gekämpft
und Friede dich erfreu'!
  Er legt sie sanft auf den Steinsitz, und küßt ihr zum Ab-
  schied die Stirne.
    Siegmund vernimmt Hundings Hornruf, und bricht
  entschlossen auf.
Der dort mich ruft,
rüste sich nun;
was ihm gebührt,
biet' ich ihm:
  Er zieht das Schwert.
Nothung zahl' ihm den Zoll!
  Er eilt dem Hintergrunde zu, und verschwindet, auf dem
  Joche angekommen, sogleich in finstrem Gewittergewölk,
  aus welchem alsbald Wetterleuchten aufblitzt.

SIEGLINDE *beginnt, sich träumend unruhiger zu bewegen.*
Kehrte der Vater nur heim! –
1500 Mit dem Knaben noch weilt er im Wald.
Mutter! Mutter!
Mir bangt der Mut;
nicht freund und friedlich

SCENE FIVE

SIEGMUND
Sheer magic   1480
curbs pain and sorrow
in my handsome wife's sleep.
When the Valkyrie sided with me,
did she bring her this sweet comfort?
Should the fearsome choice
not have frightened a careworn wife?
Lifeless she looks,
yet lifeless she's not:
   *with the tenderest expression**
the sombre woman is being caressed
by a smiling dream.   1490
So let your slumber last
until the slaughter's finished
and you can relish peace!
   He places her carefully on the stone seat, kissing her farewell on the forehead.

     Siegmund notices Hunding's horn-call, and promptly leaves.
Whoever's sounding that call
should take to arms;
from me, he'll get
his just deserts.
   He draws his sword.
Nothung will exact the price!
   He goes hastily towards the back and, once he's arrived at the ridge, vanishes in dark storm clouds, out of which sheets of lightning immediately start to flash.
SIEGLINDE *still dreaming, starts becoming more restless.*
If only my father would come home! –
He's still with the boy in the forest.   1500
Mother! Mother!
I'm losing heart;
strangers seem

scheinen die Fremden:
Schwarze Dämpfe,
schwüles Gedünst!
Feurige Lohe
leckt schon nach uns:
es brennt das Haus!
1510   Zu Hilfe! Bruder!
Siegmund! Siegmund!
    Sie springt auf.
        Starker Blitz und Donner
Siegmund! Ha!
    Sie starrt in steigender Angst um sich her: fast die gan-
    ze Bühne ist in schwarze Gewitterwolken gehüllt. Der
    Hornruf Hundings ertönt in der Nähe.
HUNDING'S STIMME *im Hintergrunde vom Bergjoche her*
Wehwalt! Wehwalt!
Steh mir zum Streit,
sollen dich Hunde nicht halten!
SIEGMUND *Siegmunds Stimme von weiter hinten her aus der*
    Schlucht:
Wo birgst du dich,
daß ich vorbei dir schoß?
Steh, daß ich dich stelle!
SIEGLINDE *in furchtbarer Angst lauschend*
Hunding! Siegmund!
1520   Könnt' ich sie sehen!
HUNDING
Hieher, du frevelnder Freier!
Fricka fälle dich hier!
SIEGMUND *nun ebenfalls vom Joche her*
Noch wähnst du mich waffenlos,
feiger Wicht?
Drohst du mit Frauen,
so ficht nun selber,
sonst läßt dich Fricka im Stich!
Denn sieh, deines Hauses
heimischem Stamm
1530   entzog ich zaglos das Schwert:

not kind or calm:
black fumes,
humid haze!
Blazing flames
now on our heels:
the burning house!
Help me! Brother!   1510
Siegmund! Siegmund!
  She jumps up.
    Severe thunder and lightning.
Siegmund! Ha!
  She looks all around her with an increasingly terrified
  stare: black storm clouds envelop nearly the whole stage.
  Hunding's horn-call sounds near.

HUNDING'S VOICE *from the mountain pass in the background*
  Ruled by Sorrow! Ruled by Sorrow!
  Rear up for battle,
  if the dogs don't get you first!

SIEGMUND *Siegmund's voice coming from the ravine further*
    back:
  Where are you so hidden
  that I could pass you by?
  Show yourself, so I can hunt you down!

SIEGLINDE *listening intently in terrible fear*
  Hunding! Siegmund!
  if only I could see them!   1520

HUNDING
  Over here, you scabrous scum!
  Fricka'll kill you right here!

SIEGMUND *his voice now also coming from the pass*
  Do you still fancy I'm unarmed,
  you yellow-bellied imp?
  You've used women to threaten me,
  so now fight on your own,
  or Fricka'll leave you in the lurch!
  You see, fearlessly I drew the sword
  embedded in the trunk of the tree
  in your own house: 1530

seine Schneide schmecke jetzt du!

Ein Blitz erhellt für einen Augenblick das Bergjoch, auf welchem jetzt Hunding und Siegmund kämpfend gewahrt werden.

SIEGLINDE *mit höchster Kraft*

Haltet ein, ihr Männer!

Mordet erst mich!

Sie stürzt auf das Bergjoch zu: ein von rechts her über den Kämpfern ausbrechender Schein blendet sie aber plötzlich so heftig, daß sie wie erblindet zur Seite schwankt.

BRÜNNHILDE

Triff ihn, Siegmund!

Traue dem Schwert!

In dem Lichtglanze erscheint Brünnhilde, über Siegmund schwebend, und diesen mit dem Schilde deckend. – Als Siegmund soeben zu einem tödlichen Streiche gegen Hunding ausholt, bricht von links her ein glühend rötlicher Schein durch das Gewölk aus, in welchem Wotan erscheint, über Hunding stehend und seinen Speer Siegmund quer entgegenhaltend.

WOTAN

Zurück vor dem Speer!

In Stücken das Schwert!

Brünnhilde weicht erschrocken vor Wotan mit dem Schilde zurück: Siegmunds Schwert zerspringt an dem vorgehaltenen Speere.

Dem Unbewehrten stößt Hunding seinen Speer in die Brust.

Siegmund stürzt tot zu Boden: Sieglinde, die seinen Todesseufzer gehört, sinkt mit einem Schrei wie leblos zusammen.

Mit Siegmunds Fall ist zugleich von beiden Seiten der glänzende Schein verschwunden; dichte Finsternis ruht im Gewölk bis nach vorn: in ihm wird Brünnhilde undeutlich sichtbar, wie sie in jäher Hast sich Sieglinden zuwendet.

BRÜNNHILDE

Zu Roß, daß ich dich rette!

now it's your turn to taste its edge!

For a moment, a flash of lightning lights up the moun-
tain pass where Hunding and Siegmund can now be seen
fighting.

SIEGLINDE *with as much force as possible*

Stop, you men!

Murder me first!

She makes a dash for the pass. A bright light breaking out
from the right above the fighters suddenly dazzles her so
violently that, as if blinded, she stumbles sideways.

BRÜNNHILDE

Strike him, Siegmund!

Trust in the sword!

The blaze of light shows Brünnhilde hovering over Sieg-
mund, covering him with her shield. – Just as Siegmund
is about to get ready to deal Hunding a deadly blow, a
glowing red light coming from the left breaks through
the clouds, in which Wotan can be seen standing over
Hunding, holding out his spear in a horizontal position
towards Siegmund.

WOTAN

Back off the spear!

The sword must shatter!

Brünnhilde gives way to Wotan with her shield in shock:
Siegmund's sword splits into pieces on the outstretched
spear.

Hunding drives his own spear into his defenceless
opponent's breast.

Siegmund falls dead to the ground: after hearing the
sound of his dying breath, Sieglinde collapses with a
scream, as if lifeless.

At the point of Siegmund's death, the shining light
from both sides has vanished: a dense gloom in the clouds
stretches right up to the front of the stage: in the clouds
Brünnhilde is barely visible, as she turns to Sieglinde in
abrupt haste.

BRÜNNHILDE

If I'm to save you, get on the horse!

*Sie hebt Sieglinde schnell zu sich auf ihr, der Seiten-
schlucht nahe stehendes Roß, und verschwindet sogleich
mit ihr.*

*Alsbald zerteilt sich das Gewölk in der Mitte, so daß
man deutlich Hunding gewahrt, der soeben seinen Speer
dem gefallenen Siegmund aus der Brust gezogen. Wotan,
von Gewölk umgeben, steht dahinter auf einem Felsen
an seinen Speer gelehnt, und schmerzlich auf Siegmunds
Leiche blickend.*

WOTAN *zu Hunding*
Geh' hin, Knecht!
1540 Kniee vor Fricka!
Meld ihr, daß Wotans Speer
gerächt, was Spott ihr schuf.
Geh! Geh!

*Vor seinem verächtlichen Handwink sinkt Hunding tot
zu Boden.*

[Wotan] plötzlich in furchtbarer Wut auffahrend
Doch Brünnhilde!
Weh' der Verbrecherin!
Furchtbar sei
die Freche gestraft,
erreicht mein Roß ihre Flucht!

*Er verschwindet mit Blitz und Donner. – Der Vorhang
fällt schnell.*

*She hoists up Sieglinde quickly to be with her on her
horse, standing near the ravine on the side, and promptly
disappears with her.*

  *Straight away the clouds divide to create a gap in the
middle so that Hunding, who has just pulled his spear
out of the dead Siegmund's chest, can clearly be seen.
Wotan, surrounded by clouds, stands behind him on a
rock, leaning on his spear and gazing in distress at Sieg-
mund's corpse.*

WOTAN *to Hunding*
Go from here, slave!
Kneel before Fricka!   1540
Tell her, Wotan's spear
has avenged what mockery did to her.
Go! Go!

  *At a scornful wave of Wotan's hand, Hunding sinks to
the ground, dead.*

  [Wotan] suddenly bursting into a terrible rage
Now for Brünnhilde!
That delinquent will be sorry!
Let her cheek
be cruelly punished,
if my horse thwarts her escape!

  *He vanishes in thunder and lightning. – The curtain
quickly falls.*

DRITTER AUFZUG

VORSPIEL UND ERSTE SZENE

Auf dem Gipfel eines Felsenberges (des 'Brünnhildensteines')

Der Vorhang geht auf [T. 35].
 Rechts begrenzt ein Tannenwald die Szene. Links der Eingang einer Felshöhle, die einen natürlichen Saal bildet: darüber steigt der Fels zu seiner höchsten Spitze auf. Nach hinten ist die Aussicht gänzlich frei; höhere und niedere Felssteine bilden den Rand vor dem Abhange, der – wie anzunehmen ist – nach dem Hintergrund zu steil hinabführt. – Einzelne Wolkenzüge jagen, wie vom Sturm getrieben, am Felsensaume vorbei.
 Die Namen der acht Walküren, welche – außer Brünnhilde – in dieser Szene auftreten, sind: Gerhilde, Ortlinde, Waltraute, Schwertleite, Helmwige, Siegrune, Grimgerde, Rossweisse.
 Gerhilde, Ortlinde, Waltraute und Schwertleite haben sich auf der Felsspitze, an und über die Höhle gelagert: sie sind in voller Waffenrüstung.

GERHILDE *zu höchst gelagert, dem Hintergrunde zurufend,*
 wo ein starkes Gewölk herzieht
 [D]en Speer in der linken Hand haltend, [sie] winkt der
 herankommenden Genossin. *
 Hojotoho! Hojotoho!
1550 Heiaha! Heiaha!
 Helmwige! Hier!
 Hieher mit dem Roß!
HELMWIGE *Helmwiges Stimme im Hintergrunde*
 durch ein Sprachrohr
 Hojotoho! Hojotoho!
 Hojotoho! Hojotoho!
 Heiaha!
 In dem Gewölk bricht Blitzesglanz aus: eine Walküre zu
 Roß wird in ihm sichtbar; über ihrem Sattel hängt ein
 erschlagener Krieger.

ACT THREE

PRELUDE AND SCENE ONE

On the summit of a rocky mountain ('Brünnhilde's rock')

The curtain rises [b. 35].
On the right, the scene is bordered by a pine forest. On the left is the entrance to a cave forming a natural hall: above it, the rock rises to its highest peak. At the back, the view is wide open; higher and lower rocks form the edge of the slope which – it can be assumed – leads to a steep drop towards the background. – A few wispy clouds skirt the edges of the rock as if driven by a storm.

The names of the eight Valkyries who – apart from Brünnhilde – appear in this scene are: Gerhilde, Ortlinde, Waltraute, Schwertleite, Helmwige, Siegrune, Grimgerde, Rossweisse.

Gerhilde, Ortlinde, Waltraute and Schwertleite have camped on the top of the rock outside and above the cave: they are in full armour.

GERHILDE *camped highest up, calling into the background, where thick clouds are approaching*
> *Holding her spear in her left hand, she waves to her approaching comrade.* *
Hojotoho! Hojotoho!
Heiaha! Heiaha!   1550
Helmwige! Here!
This way with your horse!
HELMWIGE *Helmwige's voice in the background through a speaking-trumpet*
Hojotoho! Hojotoho!
Hojotoho! Hojotoho!
Heiaha!
> *Bright lightning flashes in the clouds: it reveals a Valkyrie on horseback; draped over her saddle is a slaughtered warrior.*

Die Erscheinung zieht, immer näher, am Felsensaume
von links nach rechts vorbei.

GERHILDE, WALTRAUTE, SCHWERTLEITE
Heiaha! Heiaha!

Die Wolke mit der Erscheinung ist rechts hinter dem
Tann verschwunden.

'Scharf im Akzent und mäßig in der Kraft', die Regel
für alle dialogischen Stellen der Walküren. In der drama-
tischen Aktion ist alles Schablonenhafte zu vermeiden
und darf bei aller Freiheit der Bewegung kein unmoti-
viertes Hin- und Herlaufen stattfinden; nie dürfen die
Walküren auf einen Haufen zusammengedrängt stehen. *

ORTLINDE *in den Tann hineinrufend*
Zu Ortlindes Stute
stell deinen Hengst:
mit meiner Grauen
1560 grast gern dein Brauner!

WALTRAUTE *hineinrufend*
Wer hängt dir im Sattel?

HELMWIGE *aus dem Tann auftretend*
Sintolt, der Hegeling!

SCHWERTLEITE
Führ deinen Braunen
fort von der Grauen:
Ortlindes Mähre
trägt Wittig, den Irming!

GERHILDE *ist etwas näher herabgestiegen.*
Als Feinde nur sah ich
Sintolt und Wittig!

ORTLINDE *springt auf*
Heiaha! Heiaha! Die Stute
1570 stößt mir der Hengst!

Sie läuft in den Tann.

GERHILDE, HELMWIGE, SCHWERTLEITE *lachend*
Ha, ha, ha, ha, ha,
ha, ha, ha, ha, ha!

GERHILDE
Der Recken Zwist
entzweit noch die Rosse!

> *The image moves from left to right, getting closer and closer past the edges of the rock.*

GERHILDE, WALTRAUTE, SCHWERTLEITE
Heiaha! Heiaha!

> *The cloud and the image have vanished behind the pine forest on the right.*
>
> *'Sharply accentuated and moderate in power', the rule for all the Valkyries' voices when they are in dialogue. Everything clichéd in the dramatic action is to be avoided and for all the freedom of movement there must be no unmotivated running around; never should the Valkyries stand crowded together in a pack.* *

ORTLINDE *calling into the pine forest*
Put your stallion
with Ortlinde's mare:
my grey and your bay
enjoy grazing together!   1560

WALTRAUTE *calling into the wood*
Who's draped over your saddle?

HELMWIGE *coming out of the pine forest*
Sintolt, the Hegeling!

SCHWERTLEITE
The bay must be led
away from the grey:
Ortlinde's mare
is carrying Wittig, the Irming!

GERHILDE *has climbed down somewhat closer.*
I know they're enemies,
Sintolt and Wittig!

ORTLINDE *leaps to her feet*
Heiaha! The mare's
being jostled by the stallion!   1570

> *She runs into the pine forest.*

GERHILDE, HELMWIGE, SCHWERTLEITE *laughing*
Ha, ha, ha, ha, ha,
ha, ha, ha, ha, ha!

GERHILDE
The warriors' quarrel
still riles the horses!

HELMWIGE *in den Tann zurückrufend*
Ruhig Brauner!
Brich nicht den Frieden!

WALTRAUTE *auf der Höhe, wo sie für Gerhilde die Wacht übernommen*
Hojoho! Hojoho!
nach rechts in den Hintergrund rufend
Siegrune, hier!
Wo säumst du so lang?
Sie lauscht nach rechts.

SIEGRUNE *Siegrunes Stimme durch ein Sprachrohr von der rechten Seite des Hintergrundes her*
1580 Arbeit gab's!
Sind die andren schon da?

SCHWERTLEITE *nach rechts in dem Hintergrund rufend*
Hojotoho!

WALTRAUTE *nach rechts in dem Hintergrund rufend*
Hojotoho!

GERHILDE, SCHWERTLEITE, WALTRAUTE *nach rechts in den Hintergrund rufend*
Heiaha!
Ihre Gebärden, sowie ein heller Glanz hinter dem Tann, zeigen an, daß soeben Siegrune dort angelangt ist.

GRIMGERDE *Stimme von links im Hintergrund durch ein Sprachrohr*
Hojotoho!

ROSSWEISSE *Stimme durch ein Sprachrohr von eben daher*
Hojotoho!

GRIMGERDE, ROSSWEISSE
Heiaha!

WALTRAUTE *nach links*
Grimgerd' und Rossweisse!

GERHILDE *ebenso*
Sie reiten zu zwei.
In einem blitz-erglänzenden Wolkenzuge, der von links her vorbeizieht, erscheinen Rossweisse and Grimgerde, ebenfalls auf Rossen, jede einen Erschlagenen im Sattel führend.

HELMWIGE *calling back into the pine forest*
  Stop it bay!
  Stop breaking the peace!
WALTRAUTE *on top of the rock, where she has replaced Ger-*
    hilde on watch
  Hojoho! Hojoho!
    calling into the background on the right
  Siegrune, here!
  What's taken you so long?
    She listens to the right.
SIEGRUNE *Siegrune's voice through a speaking-trumpet*
    coming from the background on the right
  Work kept me!   1580
  Are the others already here?
SCHWERTLEITE *calling into the background on the right*
  Hojotoho!
WALTRAUTE *calling into the background on the right*
  Hojotoho!
GERHILDE, SCHWERTLEITE, WALTRAUTE *calling into the*
    background on the right
  Heiaha!
    Their gestures and a brightly shining light behind the for-
    est show that Siegrune has just arrived there.
GRIMGERDE *voice from the left in the background*
    through a speaking-trumpet
  Hojotoho!
ROSSWEISSE *voice through a speaking-trumpet*
    from the same direction
  Hojotoho!
GRIMMGERDE, ROSSWEISSE
  Heiaha!
WALTRAUTE *to the left*
  Grimgerd' and Rossweisse!
GERHILDE *also to the left*
  They're riding abreast.
    In a bank of clouds lit by lightning and moving past
    from the left, Rossweisse and Grimgerde appear, also
    on horseback, each carrying a slaughtered body in her
    saddle.

*Helmwige, Ortlinde und Siegrune sind aus dem Tann
getreten und winken vom Felsensaume den Ankommen-
den zu:*

HELMWIGE, ORTLINDE, SIEGRUNE

1590 Gegrüßt, ihr Reisige!

Rossweiss' und Grimgerde!

ROSSWEISSE, GRIMGERDE *Rossweisses und Grimgerdes
Stimmen durch ein Sprachrohr*

Hojotoho! Hojotoho!

Die Erscheinung verschwindet hinter dem Tann.

Heiaha!

HELMWIGE, ORTLINDE, GERHILDE, WALTRAUTE,
SIEGRUNE, SCHWERTLEITE

Hojotoho! Hojotoho!

Heiaha! Heiaha!

Hojotoho! Hojotoho!

Heiaha! Heiaha!

HELMWIGE, ORTLINDE

Hojotoho! Hojotoho!

Hojotoho! Hojotoho!

1600 Heiaha!

GERHILDE, WALTRAUTE, SIEGRUNE, SCHWERTLEITE

Heiaha! Heiaha!

Heiaha! Heiaha!

Heiaha! Heiaha!

*Alle Walküren stürzen mit Ungestüm herunter und eilen
der Mitte der Bühne zu.* *

GERHILDE *in den Tann rufend*

In Wald mit den Rossen

zu Rast und Weid'!

ORTLINDE *ebenfalls in den Tann rufend*

Führet die Mähren

fern von einander,

bis unsrer Helden

Haß sich gelegt!

WALTRAUTE, SCHWERTLEITE

danach

GERHILDE, SIEGRUNE

lachend

Helmwige, Ortlinde and Siegrune have come out of the forest, and from the edges of the rock beckon to the arrivals:

HELMWIGE, ORTLINDE, SIEGRUNE

Greetings, you riders from battle!   1590
Rossweiss' and Grimgerde!

ROSSWEISSE, GRIMGERDE *the voices of Rossweisse and Grim-gerde through a speaking-trumpet*

Hojotoho! Hojotoho!

Their image disappears behind the forest.

Heiaha!

HELMWIGE, ORTLINDE, GERHILDE, WALTRAUTE,
SIEGRUNE, SCHWERTLEITE

Hojotoho! Hojotoho!
Heiaha! Heiaha!
Hojotoho! Hojotoho!
Heiaha! Heiaha!

HELMWIGE, ORTLINDE

Hojotoho! Hojotoho!
Hojotoho! Hojotoho!
Heiaha!   1600

GERHILDE, WALTRAUTE, SIEGRUNE, SCHWERTLEITE

Heiaha! Heiaha!
Heiaha! Heiaha!
Heiaha! Heiaha!

All the Valkyries storm down tumultuously and make haste towards the middle of the stage. *

GERHILDE *calling into the forest*

Get the horses into the forest
for resting and grazing!

ORTLINDE *also calling into the forest*

Keep the horses
well apart
until our heroes'
hate has died away!

WALTRAUTE, SCHWERTLEITE
then

GERHILDE, SIEGRUNE
laughing

1610 Ha, ha, ha, ha, ha,
      ha, ha, ha, ha, ha!

HELMWIGE
      Der Helden Grimm
      büßte schon die Graue!

WALTRAUTE, SCHWERTLEITE
      danach

HELMWIGE, GERHILDE
      danach

ORTLINDE, SIEGRUNE
      lachend
      Ha, ha, ha, ha, ha,
      ha, ha, ha, ha, ha!

ROSSWEISSE, GRIMGERDE *aus dem Tann tretend*
      Hojotoho! Hojotoho!

HELMWIGE, ORTLINDE, GERHILDE, WALTRAUTE,
SIEGRUNE, SCHWERTLEITE
      Willkommen! Willkommen!
      Willkommen!

SCHWERTLEITE
      Wart ihr Kühnen zu zwei?

GRIMGERDE
1620 Getrennt ritten wir
      und trafen uns heut.

ROSSWEISSE
      Sind wir alle versammelt,
      so säumt nicht lange:
      nach Walhall brechen wir auf,
      Wotan zu bringen die Wal.

HELMWIGE
      Acht sind wir erst:
      eine noch fehlt!

GERHILDE
      Bei dem braunen Wälsung
      weilt wohl noch Brünnhild'.

WALTRAUTE
1630 Auf sie noch harren
      müßen wir hier:

Ha, ha, ha, ha, ha,   1610
ha, ha, ha, ha, ha!

HELMWIGE
For the heroes' fury,
the grey's done penance already!

WALTRAUTE, SCHWERTLEITE
then

HELMWIGE, GERHILDE
then

ORTLINDE, SIEGRUNE
laughing
Ha, ha, ha, ha, ha,
ha, ha, ha, ha, ha!

ROSSWEISSE, GRIMGERDE *coming out of the forest*
Hojotoho! Hojotoho!

HELMWIGE, ORTLINDE, GERHILDE, WALTRAUTE,
SIEGRUNE, SCHWERTLEITE
Welcome! Welcome!
Welcome!

SCHWERTLEITE
Were you together, brave sisters?

GRIMGERDE
We rode separately   1620
and met up today.

ROSSWEISSE
As we're all here,
don't let's wait any longer:
let's make for Valhalla
and bring Wotan his slaughtered heroes.

HELMWIGE
There're only eight of us:
someone's missing!

GERHILDE
Brünnhilde's still likely to be
with that bay of a Wälsung.

WALTRAUTE
Then we must wait   1630
for her here:

Walvater gäb' uns
grimmigen Gruß,
säh' ohne sie er uns nahn.

SIEGRUNE *auf der Warte*
Hojotoho! Hojotoho!
   in den Hintergrund rufend
Hieher! Hieher!
   zu den andern
In brünstigem Ritt
jagt Brünnhilde her!
   alle oben auf der Warte

HELMWIGE, SIEGRUNE
Hojotoho! Hojotoho!
1640   Heiaha!

GERHILDE, ORTLINDE, WALTRAUTE, ROSSWEISSE
Hojotoho! Hojotoho!
Brünnhilde, hei!

GRIMGERDE, SCHWERTLEITE
Hojotoho!
Brünnhilde, hei!
   Sie spähen mit wachsender Verwunderung.

WALTRAUTE
Nach dem Tann lenkt sie
das taumelnde Roß.

GRIMGERDE
Wie schnaubt Grane
vom schnellen Ritt!

ROSSWEISSE
So jach sah ich nie
1650   Walküren jagen!

ORTLINDE
Was hält sie im Sattel?

HELMWIGE
Das ist kein Held!

SIEGRUNE
Eine Frau führt sie!

GERHILDE
Wie fand sie die Frau?

the father of battles
will be furious at us,
if he sees us coming without her.

SIEGRUNE *on the lookout point*
Hojotoho! Hojotoho!
  calling into the background
This way! This way!
  to the others
Brünnhilde's riding this way
at break-neck speed!
  all above on the lookout point

HELMWIGE, SIEGRUNE
Hojotoho! Hojotoho!
Heiaha!   1640

GERHILDE, ORTLINDE, WALTRAUTE, ROSSWEISSE
Hojotoho! Hojotoho!
Brünnhilde, hei!

GRIMGERDE, SCHWERTLEITE
Hojotoho!
Brünnhilde, hei!
  They look on with growing amazement.

WALTRAUTE
She's steering the floundering horse
towards the forest.

GRIMGERDE
How Grane snorts
from the fast ride!

ROSSWEISSE
I never saw Valkyries
gallop that wildly!   1650

ORTLINDE
What's she holding in her saddle?

HELMWIGE
That's no hero!

SIEGRUNE
It's a woman she's carrying!

GERHILDE
How did she find the woman?

SCHWERTLEITE
  Mit keinem Gruß
  grüßt sie die Schwestern!
WALTRAUTE *hinabrufend, sehr stark*
  Heiaha! Brünnhilde,
  hörst du uns nicht?
ORTLINDE
  Helft der Schwester
1660 vom Roß sich schwingen!
    Ortlinde herunter gehend *
HELMWIGE, GERHILDE *beide nach dem Tann laufend*
  Hojotoho! Hojotoho!
SIEGRUNE, ROSSWEISSE
  Hojotoho! Hojotoho!
    Sigrune und Rossweisse laufen ihnen [Helmwige,
    Gerhilde] nach.
WALTRAUTE, GRIMGERDE, SCHWERTLEITE
  Heiaho! Heiaha!
ORTLINDE
  Heiaha!
WALTRAUTE *in den Tann blickend*
  Zu Grunde stürzt
  Grane, der Starke!
GRIMGERDE
  Aus dem Sattel hebt sie
  hastig das Weib!
ORTLINDE, WALTRAUTE, GRIMGERDE, SCHWERTLEITE *alle*
  in den Tann laufend
  Schwester! Schwester!
1670 Was ist geschehn?
    Alle Walküren kehren auf die Bühne zurück; mit ihnen
    kommt Brünnhilde, Sieglinde unterstützend und herein-
    geleitend.
BRÜNNHILDE *atemlos*
  Schützt mich und helft
  in höchster Not!
GRIMGERDE, GERHILDE
  Wo rittest du her

SCHWERTLEITE
    She's giving no sign
    of greeting her sisters!
WALTRAUTE *calling down, very forcefully*
    Heiaha! Brünnhilde,
    can't you hear us?
ORTLINDE
    Help our sister
    get down from her horse!   1660
        *Ortlinde going down**
HELMWIGE, GERHILDE *both running towards the forest*
    Hojotoho! Hojotoho!
SIEGRUNE, ROSSWEISSE
    Hojotoho! Hojotoho!
        *Sigrune and Rossweisse run after them [Helmwige,
        Gerhilde].*
WALTRAUTE, GRIMGERDE, SCHWERTLEITE
    Heiaho! Heiaha!
ORTLINDE
    Heiaha!
WALTRAUTE *looking into the forest*
    Grane, the powerful horse,
    is falling to the ground!
GRIMGERDE
    She's hurriedly lifting
    the woman out of the saddle!
ORTLINDE, WALTRAUTE, GRIMGERDE, SCHWERTLEITE *all
    running into the forest*
    Sister! Sister!
    What's happened?   1670
        *All the Valkyrie sisters return back to the stage; Brünn-
        hilde comes with them, supporting and ushering in
        Sieglinde.*
BRÜNNHILDE *out of breath*
    Guard me and give help
    in this terrible emergency!
GRIMGERDE, GERHILDE
    Where did you ride from

in rasender Hast?

SIEGRUNE
Woher in rasender Hast?
Bist du in Flucht?

HELMWIGE
Woher in rasender Hast?

ORTLINDE, WALTRAUTE, ROSSWEISSE, SCHWERTLEITE
So flieht nur, wer auf der Flucht!

BRÜNNHILDE
Zum erstenmal flieh' ich
1680 und bin verfolgt:
Heervater hetzt mir nach!
alle Walküren heftig erschreckend

HELMWIGE, GERHILDE, SIEGRUNE, GRIMGERDE
Bist du von Sinnen?
Sage uns! Wie?
Fliehst du vor ihm?

ORTLINDE, WALTRAUTE, ROSSWEISSE, SCHWERTLEITE
Ha! Sprich!
Verfolgt dich Heervater?
O sag!
*Brünnhilde wendet sich ängstlich, um zu spähen, und
kehrt wieder zurück.*

BRÜNNHILDE
O Schwestern, späht
von des Felsens Spitze!
1690 Schaut nach Norden,
ob Walvater naht!
*Ortlinde und Waltraute springen auf die Felsspitze zur
Warte.*
Schnell! Seht ihr ihn schon?

ORTLINDE
Gewittersturm
weht von Norden!

WALTRAUTE
Starkes Gewölk
staut sich dort auf!

in such frantic haste?

SIEGRUNE
  Where from in such frantic haste?
  Are you a fugitive?

HELMWIGE
  Where from in such frantic haste?

ORTLINDE, WALTRAUTE, ROSSWEISSE, SCHWERTLEITE
  Only fugitives flee like that!

BRÜNNHILDE
  For the first time I'm fleeing
  and being pursued: 1680
  the army's lord is hounding me!
    all Valkyries sounding severely shocked

HELMWIGE, GERHILDE, SIEGRUNE, GRIMGERDE
  Have you lost your mind?
  Tell us! How?
  You're on the run from him?

ORTLINDE, WALTRAUTE, ROSSWEISSE, SCHWERTLEITE
  Ha! Speak!
  The army's lord pursues you?
  Just say!
    *Brünnhilde veers round nervously on the lookout, and
    returns to where she was.*

BRÜNNHILDE
  O sisters, take a look
  from the tip of the rock!
  Look north to see whether   1690
  the father of battles nears!
    *Ortlinde and Waltraute leap up to the lookout point on
    the top of the rock.*
  Fast! Do you see him or not?

ORTLINDE
  A thunder-storm
  gathers from the north!

WALTRAUTE
  Heavy cloud
  is gathering there!

HELMWIGE, GERHILDE, SIEGRUNE, ROSSWEISSE,
GRIMGERDE, SCHWERTLEITE
　　Heervater reitet
　　sein heiliges Roß!
BRÜNNHILDE
　　Der wilde Jäger,
1700　der wütend mich jagt,
　　er naht, er naht von Norden!
　　Schützt mich, Schwestern!
　　Wahret dies Weib!
HELMWIGE, GERHILDE, SIEGRUNE, ROSSWEISSE,
GRIMGERDE, SCHWERTLEITE
　　Was ist mit dem Weibe?
BRÜNNHILDE
　　Hört mich in Eile:
　　Sieglinde ist es,
　　Siegmunds Schwester und Braut:
　　gegen die Wälsungen
　　wütet Wotan in Grimm;
1710　dem Bruder sollte
　　Brünnhilde heut
　　entziehen den Sieg;
　　doch Siegmund schützt' ich
　　mit meinem Schild,
　　trotzend dem Gott:
　　der traf ihn da selbst mit dem Speer:
　　Siegmund fiel;
　　doch ich floh
　　fern mit der Frau:
1720　sie zu retten
　　eilt' ich zu euch,
　　ob mich Bange auch
　　　　kleinmütig
　　ihr berget vor dem strafenden Streich!
HELMWIGE, GERHILDE, SIEGRUNE, ROSSWEISSE,
GRIMGERDE, SCHWERTLEITE
　　Betörte Schwester!
　　was tatest du?

HELMWIGE, GERHILDE, SIEGRUNE, ROSSWEISSE,
GRIMGERDE, SCHWERTLEITE
  The army's lord rides
  his sacred horse!
BRÜNNHILDE
  The wild hunter
  hunts me in fury;   1700
  he nears, he nears from the north!
  Guard me, sisters!
  Safeguard that woman!
HELMWIGE, GERHILDE, SIEGRUNE, ROSSWEISSE,
GRIMGERDE, SCHWERTLEITE
  What about that woman?
BRÜNNHILDE
  Just listen, hurry:
  it's Sieglinde,
  Siegmund's sister and bride:
  Wotan's in a rage, furious
  at the Wälsungs;
  today Brünnhilde's   1710
  supposed to have
  stripped the brother of victory;
  instead I guarded Siegmund
  with my shield,
  defying the god:
  he struck him himself with his spear:
  Siegmund fell;
  but I fled
  far with the woman:
  to save her   1720
  I sped to you,
  and to ask, scared as I am,
     timidly
  if you'd hide me from punishment!
HELMWIGE, GERHILDE, SIEGRUNE, ROSSWEISSE,
GRIMGERDE, SCHWERTLEITE
  Deluded sister!
  what did you do?

Wehe! Wehe!
Brünnhilde, wehe!

HELMWIGE, SIGRUNE, GRIMGERDE
Brach ungehorsam
Brünnhilde
Heervaters heilig Gebot?

GERHILDE, ROSSWEISSE, SCHWERTLEITE
Brachst du
1730 Heervaters heilig Gebot?

WALTRAUTE *auf der Warte*
Nächtig zieht es
von Norden heran.

ORTLINDE *auf der Warte*
Wütend steuert
hieher der Sturm!

ROSSWEISSE, GRIMGERDE, SCHWERTLEITE
Wild wiehert
Walvaters Roß.

HELMWIGE, GERHILDE, SIEGRUNE
Schrecklich schnaubt es daher!

BRÜNNHILDE
1740 Wehe der Armen,
wenn Wotan sie trifft:
den Wälsungen allen
droht er Verderben!
Wer leiht mir von euch
das leichteste Roß,
das flink die Frau ihm entführ'?

SIEGRUNE
Auch uns rätst du
rasenden Trotz?

BRÜNNHILDE
Rossweisse, Schwester,
1750 leih mir deinen Renner!

ROSSWEISSE
Vor Walvater floh
der fliegende nie.

Alas! Alas!
Brünnhilde, alas!

HELMWIGE, SIGRUNE, GRIMGERDE
Did Brünnhilde
defiantly break
the lord of the army's sacred law?

GERHILDE, ROSSWEISSE, SCHWERTLEITE
Did you break
the lord of the army's sacred law?   1730

WALTRAUTE *on the lookout point*
Murkiness is coming
to us from the north.

ORTLINDE *on the lookout point*
Raging along its path,
the storm's getting closer!

ROSSWEISSE, GRIMGERDE, SCHWERTLEITE
The horse of the father of battles
is braying fiercely.

HELMWIGE, GERHILDE, SIEGRUNE
It's snorting hideously!

BRÜNNHILDE
Pity the wretched woman   1740
if Wotan meets her:
he's threatening all Wälsungs
with destruction!
Which one of you'll lend me
the nimblest of horses,
to whisk the woman out of his clutches?

SIEGRUNE
Are you recommending
frenzied defiance to us too?

BRÜNNHILDE
Rossweisse, sister,
lend me your fast horse!   1750

ROSSWEISSE
My sprightly steed never fled
from the father of battles.

BRÜNNHILDE

Helmwige, höre!

HELMWIGE

Dem Vater gehorch' ich.

BRÜNNHILDE

Grimgerde! Gerhilde!

Gönnt mir eu'r Roß!

Schwertleite! Siegrune!

Seht meine Angst!

O seid mir treu,

1760 wie traut ich euch war:

rettet dies traurige Weib!

Sieglinde, die bisher finster und kalt vor sich hingestarrt,
fährt, als Brünnhilde sie lebhaft – wie zum Schutze – um-
faßt, mit einer abwehrenden Gebärde auf.

SIEGLINDE

Nicht sehre dich Sorge um mich:

einzig taugt mir der Tod!

'Jedes Wort, jede einzelne Silbe deutlich heraus, sonst
geht alles verloren' *

Wer hieß dich Maid,

dem Harst mich entführen?

Im Sturm dort hätt' ich

den Streich empfah'n

von derselben Waffe,

der Siegmund fiel:

1770 das Ende fand ich

vereint mit ihm!

Fern von Siegmund –

Siegmund, von dir! –

[V]on tiefstem Leid bedrückt neigt [sie] sich mit abwärts
gerichtetem Blick zu Boden *

O deckte mich Tod,

daß ich's denke!

wendet sich aber rasch wieder zu Brün[n]hilde, im Aus-
druck mit steigender Leidenschaft. *

Soll um die Flucht

dir, Maid, ich nicht fluchen,

so erhöre heilig mein Flehen: –

BRÜNNHILDE
Helmwige, what about you!

HELMWIGE
I obey the father.

BRÜNNHILDE
Grimgerde! Gerhilde!
Give me your horse!
Schwertleite! Siegrune!
See my fear!
O keep faith with me,
as I kept faith with you: 1760
rescue this woebegone woman!

*Sieglinde, who has been glowering darkly and coldly into
space, flares up when Brünnhilde eagerly embraces her –
as if to protect her – and fends her off.*

SIEGLINDE
Don't harm yourself worrying about me:
I'm only good for death!

*'Each word, each individual syllable clearly enunciated,
otherwise everything will be lost'* *

Who asked you, young woman,
to abduct me from the throes of battle?
In that storm I'd have
been hit with a blow
from the same weapon
that felled Siegmund:
I'd have met my end   1770
at one with him!
I'm far from Siegmund –
Siegmund, from you! –

*Oppressed by deepest sorrow, she looks downwards,
stooping to the ground* *

O that death would smother me
when I think of it!

*but turns quickly again to Brünnhilde with an expression
of increasingly intense passion.* *

If I'm not to chide you
for my escape, young woman,
give solemn ear to what I implore: –

den Verzweiflungsausbruch mit dämonischer Leiden-
schaft hervorbrechend *

stoße dein Schwert mir ins Herz!

BRÜNNHILDE

1780 Lebe, o Weib,
um der Liebe willen!
Rette das Pfand,
das von ihm du empfingst:
stark und drängend
ein Wälsung wächst dir im Schoß!

Die Worte: 'ein Wälsung' etc. mit erschütternder Gewalt.
Der Meister sang sie selbst vor, im Tone seiner Stimme
lag eine von tiefem Ernste getragene wie prophetische
Begeisterung. *

Der Moment für die Entwickelung der Handlung
höchst wichtig: es überkömmt [sic] Sieglinde, daß sie zur
Erfüllung eines ungeheuren Schicksals auserkoren sei. *

Sieglinde erschrickt zunächst heftig: sogleich strahlt
aber ihr Gesicht in erhabener Freude auf.

SIEGLINDE

Rette mich, Kühne!
Rette mein Kind!
Schirmt mich, ihr Mädchen,
mit mächtigstem Schutz!

Immer finsteres Gewitter steigt im Hintergrunde auf.

WALTRAUTE *auf der Warte*

Der Sturm kommt heran!

ORTLINDE *auf der Warte*

1790 Flieh, wer ihn fürchtet!

GERHILDE, ROSSWEISSE, HELMWIGE, SIEGRUNE,
GRIMGERDE, SCHWERTLEITE

Fort mit dem Weibe,
droht ihm Gefahr!
Der Walküren keine
wag' ihren Schutz!

SIEGLINDE *auf den Knien vor Brünnhilde*

Rette mich Maid!
Rette die Mutter!

*the outburst of desperation breaking forth with demonic
passion**

plunge your sword into my heart!

BRÜNNHILDE

Live, dear woman,   1780
for love's sake!
Save the pledge
you accepted from him:
  strongly and urgently
a Wälsung is growing in your womb!
  *The words: 'a Wälsung' etc. with shattering power. The
  master sang them himself, and in the tone of his voice
  there was deep seriousness as well as a sense of prophetic
  vision.**
    *This moment in the development of the action is most
  important: it dawns on Sieglinde that she has been chosen
  for the fulfilment of an extraordinary destiny.**
    *Sieglinde is shocked and stunned at first: but almost
  immediately her face is flooded with sublime joy.*

SIEGLINDE

Rescue me, brave one!
Rescue my baby!
Shield me, you young women,
with the mightiest shelter!
  A dark storm in the background gathers strength.

WALTRAUTE *on the lookout point*

The storm's getting closer!

ORTLINDE *on the lookout point*

Flee, whoever fears it!   1790

GERHILDE, ROSSWEISSE, HELMWIGE, SIEGRUNE,
GRIMGERDE, SCHWERTLEITE

Get the woman out,
if danger threatens her!
None of the Valkyries
is going to dare guard her!

SIEGLINDE *on her knees in front of Brünnhilde*

Young woman, rescue me!
Rescue a mother!

BRÜNNHILDE *mit lebhaftem Entschluß hebt sie Sieglinde auf*
So fliehe denn eilig,
und fliehe allein!
Ich bleibe zurück,
1800   biete mich Wotans Rache:
an mir zögr' ich
den Zürnenden hier,
während du seinem Rasen entrinnst.

SIEGLINDE
Wohin soll ich mich wenden?
*Brünnhilde mit angstvoll fragender Gebärde sich nach
allen Seiten hin wendend**

BRÜNNHILDE
Wer von euch Schwestern
schweifte nach Osten?

SIEGRUNE
Nach Osten weithin
dehnt sich ein Wald:
der Niblungen Hort
1810   entführte Fafner dorthin.

SCHWERTLEITE
Wurmes Gestalt
schuf sich der Wilde,
in einer Höhle
hütet er Alberichs Reif.

GRIMGERDE
Nicht geheu'r ist's dort
für ein hilflos Weib.

BRÜNNHILDE
Und doch, vor Wotans Wut
schützt sie sicher der Wald;
ihn scheut der Mächt'ge
1820   und meidet den Ort.

WALTRAUTE *auf der Warte*
Furchtbar fährt
dort Wotan zum Fels!

BRÜNNHILDE *raises Sieglinde up with vigorous resolve*
    Then get out fast,
    and get out alone!
    I'll stay behind,
    offer myself up to Wotan's revenge: 1800
    I'll delay the angry god,
    confronting him here,
    while you escape his fury.

SIEGLINDE
    Where should I turn?
      Brünnhilde addressing everyone with an anxiously ques-
      tioning gesture *

BRÜNNHILDE
    Which of you sisters
    has traversed the east?

SIEGRUNE
    Extending to the east
    lies a forest
    to where Fafner carried off
    the Nibelung's hoard.   1810

SCHWERTLEITE
    The maniac's changed
    himself into a dragon,
    inside a cave
    he's nursing Alberich's ring.

GRIMGERDE
    That's not so good a place
    for a helpless woman.

BRÜNNHILDE
    And yet, in the face of Wotan's rage
    the forest's surely a shield;
    the mighty one's wary of it
    and avoids the place.   1820

WALTRAUTE *on the lookout point*
    Wotan's riding to the rock
    at a furious pace!

GERHILDE, HELMWIGE, ROSSWEISSE, SIEGRUNE,
GRIMGERDE, SCHWERTLEITE
   Brünnhilde! Hör
   seines Nahens Gebraus'!
BRÜNNHILDE *drängend*
   Fort denn eile,
   nach Osten gewandt!
   Mutigen Trotzes
   ertrag alle Müh'n;
     drängend
   Hunger und Durst,
1830   Dorn und Gestein;
   lache, ob Not,
   ob Leiden dich nagt;
   denn eines wiss'
   und wahr es immer:
   den hehrsten Helden der Welt
   hegst du, o Weib,
   im schirmenden Schoß.
     Sie zieht die Stücken von Siegmunds Schwert unter ihrem
     Panzer hervor, und überreicht sie Sieglinde.
   Verwahr ihm die starken
   Schwertesstücken;
1840   seines Vaters Walstatt
   entführt' ich sie glücklich: –
   der neugefügt
   das Schwert einst schwingt,
   den Namen nehm' er von mir:
   'Siegfried' erfreu' sich des Siegs!
SIEGLINDE *in größter Rührung*
   O hehrstes Wunder,
   herrlichste Maid!
   Dir Treuen dank' ich
   heiligen Trost!
1850   Für ihn, den wir liebten,
   rett' ich das Liebste:
   meines Dankes Lohn
   lache dir einst!

GERHILDE, HELMWIGE, ROSSWEISSE, SIEGRUNE,
GRIMGERDE, SCHWERTLEITE
  Brünnhilde! Listen
  to the roar as he nears!
BRÜNNHILDE *urgently*
  So hurry onwards,
  find a way to the east!
  Let your sheer guts
  brave all obstacles;
    urgently
  hunger and thirst,
  thorns and rocks;   1830
  smile when misery
  and suffering wear you down;
  just know one thing
  and never forget it:
  it's the world's noblest hero,
  dear woman, you're bearing
  in the refuge of your womb.
    *She takes the pieces of Siegmund's sword out from under
    her armour, and gives them to Sieglinde.*
  Keep these sturdy pieces
  of the sword safe for him;
  fortune favoured my escape with them   1840
  from where his father was slaughtered: –
  let him, who'll one day forge
  and flourish the sword anew,
  take the name I give him now:
  'Siegfried' – joyous in victory!
SIEGLINDE *with the greatest emotion*
  O noblest of miracles,
  loveliest young woman!
  I thank you, loyal friend,
  for solemn words of comfort!
  For him whom we loved,   1850
  I'll rescue the most cherished of things:
  may the reward of my thanks
  smile on you one day!

Lebe wohl!
Dich segnet Sieglindes Weh!
Sie eilt rechts im Vordergrunde von dannen.
 *Die Felsenhöhe ist von schwarzen Gewitterwolken
umlagert; furchtbarer Sturm braust aus dem Hintergrun-
de daher; wachsender Feuerschein rechts daselbst.*
WOTAN *Wotans Stimme durch ein Sprachrohr*
Steh! Brünnhild'!
 *Brünnhilde, nachdem sie eine Weile Sieglinde nachgese-
hen, wendet sich in den Hintergrund, blickt in den Tann
und kommt angstvoll wieder vor.*
ORTLINDE UND WALTRAUTE *von der Warte herabsteigend*
Den Fels erreichten
Roß und Reiter!
ORTLINDE, WALTRAUTE, HELMWIGE, GERHILDE,
SIEGRUNE, GRIMGERDE, ROSSWEISSE, SCHWERTLEITE
Weh'! Brünnhild'!
1860   Rache entbrennt!
BRÜNNHILDE
Ach, Schwestern, helft!
Mir schwankt das Herz:
sein Zorn zerschellt mich,
wenn euer Schutz ihn nicht zähmt!
 *Die Walküren flüchten ängstlich nach der Felsenspitze
hinauf; Brünnhilde läßt sich von ihnen nachziehen.*
HELMWIGE, ROSSWEISSE, SCHWERTLEITE, GERHILDE,
SIEGRUNE, GRIMGERDE, ORTLINDE, WALTRAUTE
Hieher, Verlorne!
Laß dich nicht sehn!
Schmiege dich an uns
und schweige dem Ruf!
 *Sie verbergen Brünnhilde unter sich, und blicken ängstlich
nach dem Tann, der jetzt von grellem Feuerschein erhellt
wird, während der Hintergrund ganz finster geworden
ist.*
Weh'!
1870   Wütend schwingt sich

Farewell!
Be blessed by Sieglinde's aching heart!
In the foreground, she hastens away to the right.
The top of the rocks is surrounded by black thunder-clouds; a terrible storm gathers in the background, and moves from there with a growing fiery glow to the right.
WOTAN *Wotan's voice through a speaking-trumpet*
Stop! Brünnhilde!
Having watched Sieglinde's departure for a while, Brünn-hilde turns towards the background, looks into the pine forest, and then comes to the front, full of anxiety.
ORTLINDE AND WALTRAUTE *climb down from the lookout*
Horse and rider
have reached the rock!
ORTLINDE, WALTRAUTE, HELMWIGE, GERHILDE,
SIEGRUNE, GRIMGERDE, ROSSWEISSE, SCHWERTLEITE
Alas, Brünnhilde!
Vengeance is ablaze!   1860
BRÜNNHILDE
Ah, sisters, help!
My heart falters:
his fury will shatter me,
unless your protection subdues him!
The Valkyries flee anxiously towards the top of the rock; Brünnhilde lets them drag her along with them.
HELMWIGE, ROSSWEISSE, SCHWERTLEITE, GERHILDE,
SIEGRUNE, GRIMGERDE, ORTLINDE, WALTRAUTE
This way, spurned sister!
Don't let yourself be seen!
Blend in with us
and ignore his call!
They surround Brünnhilde to conceal her and turn their gaze fearfully towards the pine forest, now lit by a harsh fiery glow, while the background has become completely dark.
Woe!
Wotan's leapt down   1870

Wotan vom Roß!
Hieher rast
sein rächender Schritt!

ZWEITE SZENE

*Wotan tritt in höchster zorniger Aufgeregtheit aus dem Tann
auf, und schreitet vor der Gruppe der Walküren auf der Höhe,
nach Brünnhilde spähend, heftig einher.*

WOTAN
  Wo ist Brünnhild',
  wo die Verbrecherin?
  Wagt ihr, die Böse
  vor mir zu bergen?
HELMWIGE, ORTLINDE, SIEGRUNE, GRIMGERDE
  Schrecklich ertost dein Toben!
  Was taten, Vater, die Töchter,
1880 daß sie dich reizten
  zu rasender Wut?
GERHILDE, WALTRAUTE, ROSSWEISSE, SCHWERTLEITE
  Schrecklich ertost dein Toben!
  Wer reizte dich
  zu rasender Wut?
WOTAN
  Wollt ihr mich höhnen?
  Hütet euch, Freche!
  Ich weiß, Brünnhilde
  bergt ihr vor mir.
  Weichet von ihr,
1890 der ewig Verworfnen,
  wie ihren Wert
  von sich sie warf!
    *Bei aller Empfindungswärme darf [der folgende] Gesang
    nicht den Charakter angstvoller Erregtheit verlieren und
    demgemäß nicht zu sehr ins Weichlich-lyrische überge-
    hen.* *

from his horse in a rage!
He's hurtling toward us
with unforgiving strides!

SCENE TWO

*Wotan comes out of the pine forest in a state of extreme rage
and strides furiously to and fro in front of the group of Val-
kyries on top of the rock, keenly looking out for Brünnhilde.*

WOTAN
  Where's Brünnhilde,
  where is she, the traitor?
  Dare you hide your
  bad sister from me?

HELMWIGE, ORTLINDE, SIEGRUNE, GRIMGERDE
  Your violent temper roars cruelly!
  What did your daughters do, father,
  to make you fly   1880
  into this frenzied rage?

GERHILDE, WALTRAUTE, ROSSWEISSE, SCHWERTLEITE
  Your violent temper roars cruelly!
  Who made you fly
  into this frenzied rage?

WOTAN
  Do you want to mock me?
  Take heed, impudent rascals!
  I know: you're hiding
  Brünnhilde from me.
  Turn away from her,
  she's been exiled for ever,   1890
  just as she spurned
  her own worth!
    *For all its warmth of expression, the singing in [the follow-
    ing] ensemble may not forgo a sense of anxious agitation
    and become too softly lyrical.* *

ROSSWEISSE
   Zu uns floh die Verfolgte;
   unsern Schutz flehte sie an:
   für die bange Schwester
   bitten wir nun;
   daß den ersten Zorn du bezähmst.

SIEGRUNE
   Unsern Schutz flehte sie an;
   Furcht und Zagen
1900 faßt die Verfolgte.
   Zähme den ersten Zorn!

GRIMGERDE, SCHWERTLEITE
   Unsern Schutz flehte sie an;
   mit Furcht und Zagen
   faßt sie dein Zürnen:
   für die Bange
   bitten wir dich!

WALTRAUTE
   Mit Furcht und Zagen
   faßt sie dein Zorn:
   für die bange Schwester,
      dringend
1910 bitten wir nun,
   daß den ersten Zorn du bezähmst.

ORTLINDE
   Vater, hör uns flehn!
   Laß dich erweichen!

GERHILDE
   Laß dich erweichen,
   Laß dich erweichen!

HELMWIGE
   Laß dich erweichen,
   für sie, zähme deinen Zorn!

WOTAN
   Weichherziges
   Weibergezücht!
1920 So matten Mut
   gewannt ihr von mir?

ROSSWEISSE
  The fugitive fled to us;
  she begged us to protect her:
  for our terror-stricken sister,
  we beg you
  to tame the anger you first felt.

SIEGRUNE
  She begged us to protect her;
  the fugitive's in the grip
  of fear and trembling.
  Tame the anger you first felt!   1900

GRIMGERDE, SCHWERTLEITE
  She begged us to protect her;
  with fear and trembling,
  she's in the grip of your wrath:
  for the one stricken with terror,
  we beg you!

WALTRAUTE
  With fear and trembling,
  she's in the grip of your anger:
  for our terror-stricken sister,
    urgently
  we beg you   1910
  to tame the anger you first felt.

ORTLINDE
  Father, hear our plea!
  Relent!

GERHILDE
  Relent,
  relent!

HELMWIGE
  Relent,
  for her, tame your anger!

WOTAN
  What a maudlin
  shrewish madhouse!
  Did you get this half-baked   1920
  bravery from me?

Erzog ich euch kühn,
zum Kampfe zu zieh'n,
schuf ich die Herzen
euch hart und scharf,
daß ihr Wilden nun weint und greint,
wenn mein Grimm eine Treulose straft?
So wißt denn, Winselnde,
was die verbrach,
um die euch Zagen
die Zähre entbrennt!
Keine wie sie
kannte mein innerstes Sinnen!
Keine wie sie
wußte den Quell meines Willens!
Sie selbst war
meines Wunsches schaffender Schoß:
und so nun brach sie
den seligen Bund,
daß treulos sie
meinem Willen getrotzt,
mein herrschend Gebot
offen verhöhnt,
gegen mich die Waffe gewandt,
die mein Wunsch allein ihr schuf.
Hörst du's, Brünnhilde?
Du, der ich Brünne,
Helm und Wehr,
Wonne und Huld,
Namen und Leben verlieh?
Hörst du mich Klage erheben,
und birgst dich bang dem Kläger,
daß feig du der Straf' entflöh'st?

*Brünnhilde tritt aus der Schar der Walküren hervor,
schreitet demütigen, doch festen Schrittes von der Felsen-
spitze herab und tritt so in geringer Entfernung vor Wotan.*

BRÜNNHILDE
Hier bin ich, Vater
gebiete die Strafe!

Didn't I bring you up
to go boldly into battle?
Did I harden your hearts,
and steel them,
just so you wild ones yowl and howl
the moment I angrily punish a traitor?
So, moaning daughters, hear
what that girl's done wrong,
that girl, for whose sake your tears   1930
engulf you and make you tremble!
None but she
knew my most intimate thoughts!
None but she
knew the source of my will!
She was herself the vessel
through which my wishes passed:
and then she broke
that sacred bond
by disloyally   1940
defying my will,
openly mocking
my command's authority,
and turning the weapon against me
that alone my generosity created for her.
Are you listening to this, Brünnhilde?
You, to whom I granted a coat of mail,
helmet and arms,
happiness and grace,
name and life?   1950
Do you hear me lodge my complaint?
Do you shy from your accuser and
flee like a coward from punishment?
> *Brünnhilde steps forward out of the Valkyrie throng,*
> *walking humbly yet firmly down from the top of the rock*
> *until she steps near to Wotan in front of him.*

BRÜNNHILDE
Here I am, father
pronounce sentence!

WOTAN

Nicht straf' ich dich erst;
deine Strafe schufst du dir selbst.
Durch meinen Willen
warst du allein:
1960   gegen ihn doch hast du gewollt;
meine Befehle nur
führtest du aus:
gegen ihn doch hast du befohlen;
Wunschmaid
warst du mir:
gegen mich doch hast du gewünscht;
Schildmaid
warst du mir:
gegen mich doch hobst du den Schild;
1970   Loskieserin
warst du mir:
gegen mich doch kiestest du Lose;
Heldenreizerin
warst du mir:
gegen mich doch reiztest du Helden.
Was sonst du warst,
sagte dir Wotan:
was jetzt du bist,
das sage dir selbst!
   gedehnt
1980   Wunschmaid bist du nicht mehr;
Walküre bist du gewesen:
   scharf
nun sei fortan,
was so du noch bist!

BRÜNNHILDE *heftig erschreckend*

Du verstößest mich;
versteh' ich den Sinn?

WOTAN

Nicht send' ich dich mehr aus Walhall;
   sehr getragen
nicht weis' ich dir mehr
Helden zur Wal,

WOTAN
  Not only do I punish you:
  you passed sentence on yourself.
  You only existed
  through my will:
  yet your will has been against mine;   1960
  you only carried
  out my orders:
  yet against them you've given your own;
  you were my
  gifted daughter:
  yet against me you used your gifts;
  you were my
  shield's bearer:
  yet against me you raised that shield;
  you were my   1970
  fate's arbiter:
  yet against me you turned fate;
  you were my
  hero's champion:
  yet you championed the hero to fight me.
  What you once were,
  Wotan's told you:
  what you now are,
  tell yourself that!
    sustained
  You're no longer my gifted daughter;   1980
  your Valkyrie days are gone:
    sharply
  be in future,
  whatever's still left of you!
BRÜNNHILDE *showing acute alarm*
  You're disowning me;
  is that what you mean?
WOTAN
  I'll dispatch you from Valhalla no more;
    very solemnly
  No longer will I direct you
  to heroes for slaughter,

nicht führst du mehr Sieger
1990 in meinen Saal:
bei der Götter trautem Mahle
das Trinkhorn nicht reichst
du traulich mir mehr;
nicht kos' ich dir mehr
den kindischen Mund;
von göttlicher Schar
bist du geschieden,
ausgestoßen
aus der Ewigen Stamm;
2000 gebrochen ist unser Bund;
aus meinem Angesicht bist du verbannt.

*Die Walküren verlassen in aufgeregter Bewegung ihre
Stellung, indem sie sich tiefer herabziehen.*

ORTLINDE, WALTRAUTE, HELMWIGE, GERHILDE,
SIEGRUNE, GRIMGERDE, ROSSWEISSE, SCHWERTLEITE
Wehe! Weh'!
Schwester, ach Schwester!

BRÜNNHILDE
Nimmst du mir alles,
was einst du gabst?

WOTAN
Der dich zwingt, wird dir's entziehn!
Hieher auf den Berg
banne ich dich;
in wehrlosen Schlaf
2010 schließ' ich dich fest,
der Mann dann fange die Maid,
der am Wege sie findet und weckt.

*In höchster Aufregung kommen sie [die Walküren] von
der Felsenhöhe ganz herab, und umgeben in ängstlichen
Gruppen Brünnhilde, welche halb knieend vor Wotan
liegt.*

WALTRAUTE
Halt ein! Halt ein!
O Vater!
Soll die Maid verblühn

no longer will you lead victors
into my hall: 1990
no more those intimate moments
when you hand me the drinking horn
at the congenial feasts of the gods;
no more will I caress
your childlike mouth:
you've been divorced
from the company of the gods,
disowned
by the immortal lineage;
our bond is rent asunder; 2000
from my presence, you're banished.
The Valkyries leave their position with agitated movements by moving further down.

ORTLINDE, WALTRAUTE, HELMWIGE, GERHILDE,
SIEGRUNE, GRIMGERDE, ROSSWEISSE, SCHWERTLEITE
All's lost! Lost!
Sister, ah sister!

BRÜNNHILDE
Are you depriving me
of all you ever gave?

WOTAN
Your finder will force it from you!
Up the mountain over here
I'll put you under a magic spell;
I'll enclose you tightly
in an unguarded sleep, 2010
so a man may capture the young woman,
if in passing he finds and wakes her.
In a state of extreme excitement they [the Valkyries] come right down from the top of the rock, and in anxious groups surround Brünnhilde, who lies half-kneeling in front of Wotan.

WALTRAUTE
Stop there! Stop there!
O father!
Should the young woman wilt

und verbleichen dem Mann?
Ach wende die Schmach!
Ach, wende die schreiende Schmach!
Wende die Schmach!
2020   Ach wende, Schrecklicher, die Schmach!
Ach wende, wende die Schmach!
Wie die Schwester träf' uns auch ihr Schimpf,

ORTLINDE
O Vater! Halt ein!
Halt ein! Hör unser Flehn!
Ach wende von ihr die schreiende Schmach!
Schrecklicher Gott!
Wende die Schmach!
Schrecklicher, ach wende,
wende die Schmach von ihr!
2030   Wie sie träf' uns auch ihr Schimpf,

GRIMGERDE
O Vater!
Soll die Maid verblühn
und verbleichen dem Mann?
Ach wende ab die schreiende Schmach!
Erhöre uns!
Ach, wende, du Schecklicher, wende,
ach wende von ihr diese schreiende Schmach,
wend' ab die Schmach!
Wie die Schwester träf' uns selber der Schimpf,
2040   soll die heilige Maid verblühn
und verbleichen dem Mann;

SCHWERTLEITE
O Vater!
Soll die Maid verblühn
und verbeichen dem Mann?
Soll die Maid verblühn und verbleichen?
Ach wende ab die Schmach!
Ach, wende, du Schrecklicher, wende,
ach wende von ihr diese schreiende Schmach
ach wende die Schmach,
2050   ach wende, wende die Schmach!
Wie sie träf' uns ihr Schimpf,

and fade for a man!
Ah spare the disgrace!
Ah, spare the outrageous disgrace!
Spare the disgrace!
Ah terrible one, spare the disgrace!   2020
Ah spare, spare the disgrace!
Insult our sister and you also insult us,

ORTLINDE
O father! Stop there!
Stop there! Hear our plea!
Spare her from outrageous disgrace!
Terrible god!
Avert the disgrace!
Terrible god, spare her,
spare her from disgrace!
Insult her and you also insult us,   2030

GRIMGERDE
O father!
Should the young woman wilt
and fade for a man?
Avert the outrageous disgrace!
Answer our plea!
Spare, you terrible god, spare,
spare her from outrageous disgrace,
avert the disgrace!
Insult our sister and you insult us all,
should this divine young woman wilt   2040
and fade for a man;

SCHWERTLEITE
O father!
Should the young woman wilt
and fade for a man?
Should the young woman wilt and fade?
Avert the disgrace!
Spare, you terrible god, spare,
spare her from outrageous disgrace,
avert the disgrace,
avert, avert the disgrace!   2050
Insult her and you insult us,

HELMWIGE
> Halt ein den Fluch!
> Halt ein! Hör unser Flehn!
> Wende von ihr die schreiende Schmach!
> Schrecklicher Gott!
> Wende von ihr die schreiende Schmach!
> Wie die Schwester träf' uns auch ihr Schimpf,

GERHILDE
> Halt ein den Fluch!
> O Vater!
2060
> Soll die Maid verblühn
> und verbleichen dem Mann?
> Du Schrecklicher, schrecklicher Gott!
> Wende die Schmach!
> Schrecklicher, ach wende die Schmach!
> Wie die Schwester träf' uns auch der Schimpf,
> soll die heilige Maid verblühn
> und verbleichen dem Mann;

ROSSWEISSE
> Halt ein den Fluch!
> Soll die Maid verblühn
2070
> und verbleichen dem Mann?
> Schrecklicher Vater!
> wende die Schmach!
> Schrecklicher, wende,
> ach wende die schreiende Schmach von ihr!
> Ach wende, wende die Schmach!
> Wie sie auch träf' uns auch ihr Schimpf,

SIGRUNE
> Halt ein den Fluch!
> Soll die Maid verblühn
> und verlbleichen dem Mann?
2080
> Wende von ihr die schreiende Schmach;
> Schrecklicher,
> wende von ihr die schreiende Schmach!
> Ach wende die Schmach!
> Wie die Schwester träf' uns selber der Schimpf,
> soll die heilige Maid verblühn
> und verbleichen dem Mann;

HELMWIGE
   Stay your curse!
   Stop there! Hear our plea!
   Spare her from outrageous disgrace!
   Terrible god!
   Spare her from outrageous disgrace!
   Insult our sister and you also insult us,

GERHILDE
   Stay your curse!
   O father!
   Should the young woman wilt   2060
   and fade for a man?
   You terrible, terrible god!
   Avert the disgrace!
   Terrible god, avert the disgrace!
   Insult our sister and you also insult us,
   should this divine young woman wilt
   and fade for a man;

ROSSWEISSE
   Stay your curse!
   Should the young woman wilt
   and fade for a man?   2070
   Terrible father!
   avert the disgrace!
   Terrible god, spare,
   spare her from outrageous disgrace!
   Avert, avert the disgrace!
   Insult her and you also insult us,

SIGRUNE
   Stay your curse!
   Should the young woman wilt
   and fade for a man?
   Spare her from outrageous disgrace;   2080
   terrible god,
   spare her from outrageous disgrace!
   Avert the disgrace!
   Insult our sister and you insult us all,
   should this divine young woman wilt
   and fade for a man;

ALLE ACHT WALKÜREN
wie die Schwester träf uns selbst auch ihr Schimpf!

WOTAN
Hörtet ihr nicht,
was ich verhängt?
2090 Aus eurer Schar
ist die treulose Schwester geschieden;
mit euch zu Roß
durch die Lüfte nicht reitet sie länger;
die magdliche Blume
verblüht der Maid;
ein Gatte gewinnt
ihre weibliche Gunst,
dem herrschenden Manne
gehorcht sie fortan;
    grell und etwas gedehnt
2100 am Herde sitzt sie und spinnt,
aller Spottenden Ziel und Spiel.
    Brünnhilde sinkt mit einem Schrei zu Boden. Die Walküren
    weichen entsetzt mit heftigem Geräusch von ihrer Seite.
Schreckt euch ihr Los?
So flieht die Verlorne;
weichet von ihr,
und haltet euch fern!
Wer von euch wagte
bei ihr zu weilen,
wer mir zum Trotz
zu der Traurigen hielt',
2110 die Törin teilte ihr Los:
das künd' ich der Kühnen an.
Fort jetzt von hier;
meidet den Felsen.
Hurtig jagt mir von hinnen;
sonst erharrt Jammer euch hier!
    Die Walküren fahren mit wildem Wehschrei auseinander
    und stürzen in hastiger Flucht in den Tann.

ALLE ACHT WALKÜREN
Weh'! Weh'!

ALL EIGHT VALKYRIES
   insult our sister and you insult us all too!
WOTAN
   Are you all deaf
   to my demand?
   Your treacherous sister   2090
   is banished from your company;
   no longer shall she ride the skies
   with you on horseback;
   the young woman's youthful bloom
   will go to seed;
   a husband shall win
   her womanly favours,
   from then on she'll belong
   to that domineering man;
     harshly and somewhat sustained
   at the fireside, she'll sit and spin,   2100
   the object and sport of all who sneer.
     Brünnhilde collapses to the floor with a scream. The
     Valkyries recoil from her in horror with a violent din.
   Her fate makes you panic?
   Abandon your forlorn sister;
   get away from her,
   and stay well away!
   If any of you dare
   to be with her,
   if any of you snub me
   by falling for her melancholy,
   let the fool share her fate: 2110
   that I declare to my bold daughters.
   Now get out of here;
   keep off the rock.
   Get out of my sight – fast;
   you'll find only misery here!
     The Valkyries disperse with wild screams of woe and
     rush headlong into the pine forest.
ALL EIGHT VALKYRIES
   Woe! Woe!

Schwarzes Gewölk lagert sich dicht am Felsenrande; man
hört wildes Geräusch im Tann.

Ein greller Blitzesglanz bricht in dem Gewölk aus; in
ihm erblickt man die Walküren mit verhängtem Zügel, in
einer Schar zusammengedrängt, wild davon jagen.

Bald legt sich der Sturm; die Gewitterwolken verzie-
hen sich allmählich. In der folgenden Szene bricht, bei
endlich ruhigem Wetter, Abenddämmerung ein, der am
Schlusse Nacht folgt.

DRITTE SZENE

Wotan und Brünnhilde, die noch zu seinen Füßen hingestreckt
liegt, sind allein zurückgeblieben. Langes feierliches Schwei-
gen: unveränderte Stellung.

BRÜNNHILDE *Sie beginnt das Haupt langsam ein wenig zu*
    erheben.
     schüchtern beginnend und steigernd
    War es so schmählich,
    was ich verbrach,
    daß mein Verbrechen so schmählich du bestrafst?
2120   War es so niedrig,
    was ich dir tat,
    daß du so tief mir Erniedrigung schaffst?
    War es so ehrlos,
    was ich beging,
    daß mein Vergehn nun die Ehre mir raubt?
     Sie erhebt sich allmählich bis zur knieenden Stellung.
    O sag, Vater!
    Sieh mir ins Auge;
    schweige den Zorn,
    zähme die Wut
2130   und deute mir klar
    die dunkle Schuld,
    die mit starkem Trotze dich zwingt,
    zu verstoßen dein trautestes Kind?

*Black clouds are forming near the edge of the rock: a
wild din can be heard in the forest.*

*The clouds discharge a garish flash of lightning that re-
veals an image of the Valkyries in tight formation storm-
ing off wildly at full speed.*

*Soon the storm abates; the storm clouds clear away
little by little. In the following scene, the weather having
calmed down at last, twilight falls, followed at the end by
night.*

SCENE THREE

*Wotan and Brünnhilde, who still lies prostrate at his feet, are
left behind on their own. Long solemn silence: their position
unchanged.*

BRÜNNHILDE *She slowly begins to raise her head up just a
little.*

  starting shyly and growing in intensity
Was my wrongdoing
so vile
that you so vilely punish my crime?
Was what I did to you   2120
so humiliating
that you humiliate me so profoundly?
Was what I did
so without honour
that I forfeit honour for my offence?
  She gets up gradually to a kneeling position.
Say something, father!
Look me in the eye;
silence your rage,
tame your anger
and tell me plainly   2130
of the murky guilt
that compels you with icy defiance
to spurn the child you cherish most?

WOTAN *in unveränderter Stellung, ernst und düster*
Frag deine Tat,
sie deutet dir deine Schuld!

BRÜNNHILDE
Deinen Befehl
führte ich aus.

WOTAN
Befahl ich dir,
für den Wälsung zu fechten?

BRÜNNHILDE
2140   So hießest du mich
als Herrscher der Wal!

WOTAN
Doch meine Weisung
nahm ich wieder zurück!

BRÜNNHILDE *belebt*
Als Fricka den eignen
Sinn dir entfremdet;
da ihrem Sinn du dich fügtest,
warst du selber dir Feind.

WOTAN *leise und bitter*
Daß du mich verstanden, wähnt' ich,
und strafte den wissenden Trotz:
2150   doch feig und dumm
dachtest du mich!
So hätt' ich Verrat nicht zu rächen;
zu gering wärst du meinem Grimm?

BRÜNNHILDE
Nicht weise bin ich,
doch wußt' ich das eine,
daß den Wälsung du liebtest.
    bewegt
Ich wußte den Zwiespalt,
der dich zwang,
dies eine ganz zu vergessen.
2160   Das andre mußtest
einzig du sehn,
was zu schaun so herb

WOTAN *in an unchanged position, seriously and sombrely*
  Consider your actions,
  they tell you why you're guilty!
BRÜNNHILDE
  I obeyed
  your order.
WOTAN
  Did I order you
  to fight for the Wälsung?
BRÜNNHILDE
  Yes you did,   2140
  as lord of battles!
WOTAN
  But then I declared
  my decree null and void!
BRÜNNHILDE *animated*
  When Fricka set
  your own mind against you,
  the moment you caved in to her,
  you were your own enemy.
WOTAN *quiet and embittered*
  I felt you did understand that
  I would punish conscious contempt:
  but you simply thought me   2150
  craven and foolish!
  If I did not have to avenge treason,
  would you be worth punishing at all?
BRÜNNHILDE
  I'm not wise,
  but one thing I did know:
  that you loved the Wälsung.
    agitated
  I sensed the divided loyalty
  that made you
  forget this one thing entirely.
  You had to see   2160
  only the other side,
  something that so bitterly

schmerzte dein Herz,
daß Siegmund Schutz du versagtest.

WOTAN *mit etwas plötzlich hervorbrechendem, aber doch*
    nicht leidenschaftlichem Tone zu sprechen *

Du wußtest es so,
und wagtest dennoch den Schutz?

BRÜNNHILDE *leise beginnend*

Weil für dich im Auge
das Eine ich hielt,
dem, im Zwange des andren
2170   schmerzlich entzweit,
ratlos den Rücken du wandtest!
Die im Kampfe Wotan
den Rücken bewacht,
die sah nun das nur,
was du nicht sahst.
Siegmund mußt' ich sehn.
Tod kündend
trat ich vor ihn,
gewahrte sein Auge,
2180   hörte sein Wort,
ich vernahm des Helden
heilige Not;
tönend erklang mir
des Tapfersten Klage:
freiester Liebe
furchtbares Leid;
traurigsten Mutes
mächtigster Trotz!
Meinem Ohr erscholl,
2190   mein Aug' erschaute,
was tief im Busen das Herz
zu heil'gem Beben mir traf!
Scheu und staunend
stand ich vor Scham:
ihm nur zu dienen
konnt' ich noch denken;
    belebend

pained your heart,
that you refused Siegmund protection.
WOTAN *to be uttered with a tone erupting somewhat sudden-*
   *ly, but nevertheless not passionately**
   You knew all this,
   and still dared to protect him?
BRÜNNHILDE *beginning softly*
   Because for you I kept
   the one thing in mind
   that you – baffled,
   cruelly torn, coerced –   2170
   turned your back on!
   She, who guards Wotan's
   back in battle,
   saw this time only
   what you did not see.
   I had to see Siegmund.
   I stepped up to him
   to announce death,
   noticed his eyes,
   heard his words,   2180
   the hero's sacred peril
   came home to me;
   the lamentation of the bravest
   resounded in my ears:
   the grim suffering
   of the freest love;
   the fiercest defiance
   of the gloomiest spirit!
   My ears were ringing,
   my eyes seeing all   2190
   that shook me to the core,
   my heart pounding heavenwards!
   Apprehensive and amazed,
   I stood so ashamed:
   just to serve him
   was all I could think;
      enlivened

Sieg oder Tod
mit Siegmund zu teilen:
dies nur erkannt' ich
2200   zu kiesen als Los!
       langsam
Der diese Liebe
mir ins Herz gelegt,
dem Willen, der
dem Wälsung mich gesellt,
ihm innig vertraut,
       breiter
trotzt' ich deinem Gebot.
WOTAN *im Tone düsterer Strenge**
So tatest du,
was so gern zu tun ich begehrt;
doch was nicht zu tun
2210   die Not zwiefach mich zwang?
So leicht wähntest du,
Wonne des Herzens erworben,
       *von hier an mit leidenschaftlich gesteigertem Ausdruck**
wo brennend' Weh'
in das Herz mir brach,
wo gräßliche Not
den Grimm mir schuf,
einer Welt zu Liebe
der Liebe Quell
im gequälten Herzen zu hemmen?
2220   Wo gegen mich selber
ich sehrend mich wandte,
aus Ohnmacht Schmerzen
schäumend ich aufschoß,
wütender Sehnsucht
sengender Wunsch
den schrecklichen Willen mir schuf,
in den Trümmern der eignen Welt
meine ew'ge Trauer zu enden:
       etwas frei
da labte süß

to share victory
with Siegmund, or death:
only this I knew
to choose as my fate!   2200
   slowly
You who put this love
into my heart,
whose will it was that
drove me to meet the Wälsung,
to confide in him,
   more broadly
it was your command I defied.
WOTAN *in a tone of sombre sternness* *
   So you acted,
in a way I dearly longed for;
but in not acting like that,
wasn't I doubly forced by danger?   2210
Were you so shallow to imagine
that I could win pleasure in my heart
   from here passionately increasing in expression *
when that heart was being broken
by burning grief,
when hideous necessity
was incurring my wrath,
making me stem
the flow of love in my tormented heart
for love of the world?
When I turned against myself,   2220
wounding myself,
foaming as I shot up
out of the pains of powerlessness,
of furious longing,
of the torrid desire to do good
that forged the terrible will
to bring my endless sorrow to an end
in the ruins of my own world:
   with some freedom
weren't you then

2230   dich selige Lust;
       wonniger Rührung
       üppigen Rausch
       enttrankst du lachend
       der Liebe Trank,
       als mir göttlicher Not
       nagende Galle gemischt?
           trocken und kurz
       Deinen leichten Sinn
       laß dich denn leiten:
       von mir sagtest du dich los.
2240   Dich muß ich meiden;
       gemeinsam mit dir
       nicht darf ich Rat mehr raunen;
       getrennt, nicht dürfen
       traut wir mehr schaffen,
       so weit Leben und Luft,
       darf der Gott dir nicht mehr begegnen!
       BRÜNNHILDE *einfach*
       Wohl taugte dir nicht
       die tör'ge Maid,
       die staunend im Rate
2250   nicht dich verstand,
       wie mein eigner Rat
       nur das eine mir riet:
       zu lieben, was du geliebt.
       Muß ich denn scheiden
       und scheu dich meiden,
       mußt du spalten
       was einst sich umspannt,
       die eigne Hälfte
       fern von dir halten,
2260   daß sonst sie ganz dir gehörte,
       du Gott, vergiß dess' nicht!
       Dein ewig Teil
       nicht wirst du entehren,
       Schande nicht wollen,
       die dich beschimpft:

enjoying blissful pleasure;   2230
weren't you gaily extracting
from the fountain of love
the wanton frenzy
of erotic feeling,
while for me divine necessity
mingled with corrosive bile?
   dryly and with short shrift
Then let your shallow mind
be your guide:
you've rid yourself of me.
And I must abandon you;   2240
no longer can I share
confidences with you;
apart, we can work
closely no more,
as long as life and breath exist,
the god cannot encounter you again!
BRÜNNHILDE *simply*
You didn't seem to like it
when the foolish young woman,
wide-eyed in astonishment
at a command she didn't grasp,   2250
decided on her own to do
the only thing she thought right:
to love what you loved.
If I must take my leave
and avoid you in dread,
if you must split asunder
what was once in harness,
then don't forget, you god,
that the half of your being
you keep far away from you   2260
was once entirely your own!
You'll not disown
this eternal part of you,
nor want that shame,
which will bring you abuse:

dich selbst ließest du sinken,
sähst du dem Spott mich zum Spiel!

WOTAN *ruhig*
Du folgtest selig
der Liebe Macht;
2270   folge nun dem,
den du lieben mußt!

BRÜNNHILDE
Soll ich aus Walhall scheiden,
nicht mehr mit dir schaffen und walten,
dem herrischen Manne
gehorchen fortan:
dem feigen Prahler
gib mich nicht preis;
nicht wertlos sei er,
der mich gewinnt.

WOTAN
2280   Von Walvater schiedest du;
nicht wählen darf ich für dich.

BRÜNNHILDE *leise mit vertraulicher Heimlichkeit*
Du zeugtest ein edles Geschlecht;
kein Zager kann je ihm entschlagen:
der weihlichste Held, ich weiß es,
entblüht dem Wälsungen Stamm!

WOTAN *mit Heftigkeit**
Schweig von dem Wälsungen Stamm!
Von dir geschieden,
schied ich von ihm;
vernichten mußt' ihn der Neid!

BRÜNNHILDE *den Sinn der Worte [riß, rettete] durch scharfe
        Betonung recht deutlich zu machen**
2290   Die von dir sich riß,
rettete ihn:
    heimlich
Sieglinde hegt
die heiligste Frucht;
    belebter
in Schmerz und Leid,

    you'd rather sink into oblivion
    than subject me to mockery and sport!

WOTAN *calmly*
    You joyfully pursued
    the allure of love;
    so follow him   2270
    if love him you must!

BRÜNNHILDE
    If I'm to be dismissed from Valhalla
    no longer to work and rule with you,
    subordinate for ever
    to a domineering man:
    don't abandon me
    to some cowardly show-off;
    let whoever wins me
    not be without worth.

WOTAN
    You parted from the father of battles;   2280
    for you I cannot choose.

BRÜNNHILDE *softly with a confiding air of mystery*
    You sired a noble race;
    no coward can it ever create:
    the most revered hero, I know,
    will emerge from the Wälsung clan!

WOTAN *with vehemence**
    Be silent about the Wälsung clan!
    Once parted from you,
    I parted from them;
    my pitilessness had to destroy them!

BRÜNNHILDE *the sense of the words [wrested, rescued] to be*
    *made really clear with sharp accentuation**
    She who wrested herself from you,   2290
    rescued them:
      secretively
    Sieglinde is bearing
    the most sacred fruit;
      more lively
    in pain and suffering

wie kein Weib sie gelitten,
wird sie gebären,
was bang sie birgt.

WOTAN
Nie suche bei mir
Schutz für die Frau,
2300   noch für ihres Schoßes Frucht!

BRÜNNHILDE *heimlich*
Sie wahret das Schwert,
das du Siegmund schufest.

WOTAN *heftig*
Und das ich ihm in Stücken schlug!
In den Mienen Brünnhilde's tiefste Niedergeschlagenheit*
lange Pause
Nicht streb, o Maid,
den Mut mir zu stören;
erwarte dein Los,
wie sich's dir wirft;
nicht kiesen kann ich es dir. –
Doch fort muß ich jetzt,
2310   fern mich verziehn;
zu viel schon zögert' ich hier:
von der Abwendigen
wend' ich mich ab;
nicht wissen darf ich,
was sie sich wünscht:
die Strafe nur
muß vollstreckt ich sehn!

BRÜNNHILDE
Was hast du erdacht,
daß ich erdulde?

WOTAN
2320   In festen Schlaf
verschließ' ich dich: –
wer so die Wehrlose weckt,
dem ward, erwacht, sie zum Weib!

BRÜNNHILDE
Soll fesselnder Schlaf

such as no woman has endured,
she will give birth
to what she shelters in fear.

WOTAN
Don't ever try to get me
to protect the woman,
or the fruit of her womb! 2300

BRÜNNHILDE *secretively*
She's keeping the sword safe
that you made for Siegmund.

WOTAN *vehemently*
And I smashed to pieces for him!
Utter despondency in Brünnhilde's features *
long pause
Don't get any ideas, young woman,
about shaking my confidence;
wait for what fate
has in store for you;
I can't choose it on your behalf. –
But now I have to go,
move far away: 2310
I've already stayed here too long:
from you, unfaithful woman,
I withdraw my faith;
I'm not to know
what you want:
it's my duty only
to see punishment carried out!

BRÜNNHILDE
What are you minded to do,
that I might suffer?

WOTAN
I shall embalm you 2320
in a deep sleep: –
who wakes the defenceless woman,
shall claim her, awoken, as wife!

BRÜNNHILDE
If sound sleep is to

fest mich binden,
dem feigsten Manne
zur leichten Beute:
dies eine mußt du erhören,
was heil'ge Angst zu dir fleht:
2330 die Schlafende schütze
mit scheuchenden Schrecken,
   bestimmt
daß nur ein furchtlos
freiester Held
hier auf dem Felsen
einst mich fänd'!

WOTAN
Zu viel begehrst du,
zu viel der Gunst!

BRÜNNHILDE *Wotan zu Füßen stürzend*
   Die Hände ringend schleppt sie sich zu Wotan und
   umfaßt seine Kniee. *
Dies eine
mußt du gewähren!
2340 Zerknicke dein Kind,
das dein Knie umfaßt,
zertritt die Traute;
zertrümmre die Maid;
ihres Leibes Spur
zerstöre dein Speer:
   mit einer alle Schranken sprengenden Leidenschaft *
doch gib, Grausamer, nicht
der gräßlichsten Schmach sie preis!
   mit wilder Begeisterung
Auf dein Gebot
entbrenne ein Feuer;
2350 den Felsen umglühe
lodernde Glut;
es leck' ihre Zung',
es fresse ihr Zahn
den Zagen, der frech sich wagte
dem freislichen Felsen zu nahn!

so entwine me that
I'm easy prey
to the most gutless coward:
then hear my plea about one thing,
my holy fear begs it of you:
guard the sleeping woman   2330
with terrors so daunting
   assertively
that only the most fearlessly
free of heroes
could ever find me
here on the rock!

WOTAN
You want too much,
ask too many favours!

BRÜNNHILDE *falling at Wotan's feet*
   Wringing her hands, she drags herself up to Wotan and
   clasps his knees. *
One thing
you must guarantee!
Break apart the child   2340
clutching at your knee,
crush her courage to pieces;
turn the young woman into a ruin;
erase all trace of her body
with your spear:
   with a passion beyond all restraint *
but do not, cruel father,
expose her to such monstrous disgrace!
   with wild enthusiasm
Unleash a fire
with your command;
let blazing heat   2350
light up the mountain;
its tongues shall lick,
and its teeth feast
on the weakling who insolently dares
to get anywhere near the lethal rock!

Wotan, überwältigt und tief ergriffen, wendet sich lebhaft
gegen Brünnhilde, erhebt sich von den Knieen, und blickt
ihr gerührt in das Auge.

WOTAN

Leb wohl, du kühnes,
herrliches Kind!
Du meines Herzens
heiligster Stolz!
2360   Leb wohl! Leb wohl! Leb wohl!
       sehr leidenschaftlich
Muß ich dich meiden,
und darf nicht minnig
mein Gruß dich mehr grüßen;
sollst du nun nicht mehr
neben mir reiten,
noch Met beim Mahl mir reichen;
muß ich verlieren
dich, die ich liebe,
du lachende Lust meines Auges:
2370   ein bräutliches Feuer
soll dir entbrennen,
wie nie einer Braut es gebrannt!
Flammende Glut
umglühe den Fels;
mit zehrenden Schrecken
scheuch' es den Zagen;
der Feige fliehe
Brünnhildes Fels!
Denn einer nur freie die Braut,
2380   der freier als ich, der Gott!
       Brünnhilde sinkt, gerührt und begeistert, an Wotans
       Brust: er hält sie lange umfangen.
          Sie schlägt das Haupt wieder zurück und blickt, immer
       noch ihn umfassend, feierlich ergriffen Wotan ins Auge.
          Der Grundton des Abschiedgesanges Wotans bildet bei
       aller leidenschaftlichen Innigkeit im Einzelnen doch die
       Ruhe elegischer Betrachtung*

*Overcome and deeply moved, Wotan turns energetically
towards Brünnhilde, raises her from her knees and looks
with emotion into her eyes.*

WOTAN

Farewell, you defiant,
magnificent child!
You, the most sacred
joy of my heart!
Farewell! Farewell! Farewell!   2360
  very passionately
If I have to abandon you,
and my greetings can
greet you lovingly no more;
if you are no longer
to ride at my side,
or pass mead to me at table;
if I must lose you,
the one I love,
my laughing joy, apple of my eye:
then a fire fit for a young bride   2370
shall burn for you,
as it's never burned for a bride before!
The rock will be aglow
with flaming heat;
let its daunting terrors
scatter the fainthearted;
cowards will shrink
from Brünnhilde's rock!
Only one is destined to wed the bride,
one freer than I, the god!   2380

*Touched and inspired, Brünnhilde sinks onto Wotan's
breast: he holds her in his arms for a long time.*

*She pulls her head back once more and, still in an
embrace with him, looks into Wotan's eyes, seized with
profound emotion.*

*The fundamental tone of Wotan's song of farewell, for
all the passionate intimacy of its details, should be the
calm of elegiac contemplation.* *

Der Augen leuchtendes Paar,
das oft ich lächelnd gekost,
wenn Kampfeslust
ein Kuß dir lohnte,
wenn kindisch lallend
der Helden Lob
von holden Lippen dir floß;
dieser Augen strahlendes Paar,
das oft im Sturm mir geglänzt,
2390   wenn Hoffnungssehnen
das Herz mir sengte,
nach Weltenwonne
mein Wunsch verlangte,
aus wild webendem Bangen:
zum letztenmal
letz' es mich heut
mit des Lebewohles
letztem Kuß!
Dem glücklichern Manne
2400   glänze sein Stern:
dem unseligen Ew'gen
muß es scheidend sich schließen.

> *Er faßt ihr Haupt in beide Hände.*
>> *Man muß es deutlich sehen, wie jetzt zum ersten Male
>> der Speer der Hand Wotans entfällt.* *

Denn so kehrt
der Gott sich dir ab,
so küßt er die Gottheit von dir!

> *Er küßt sie lange auf beide Augen.*
>> *Sie sinkt, mit geschlossenen Augen, sanft ermattend, in
>> seinen Armen zurück. Er geleitet sie zart auf einen nied-
>> rigen Mooshügel zu liegen, über den sich eine breitästige
>> Tanne ausstreckt.*
>> *Er betrachtet sie und schließt ihr den Helm: sein Auge
>> weilt dann auf der Gestalt der Schlafenden, die er nun
>> mit dem großen Stahlschilde der Walküre ganz zudeckt.*
>> *Langsam kehrt er sich ab; mit einem schmerzlichen
>> Blicke wendet er sich noch einmal um.*
>> *Wotan nimmt den Speer vom Boden auf.* *

The two radiant eyes
that I've often caressed with a smile,
when your zest for battle
found reward with a kiss,
when your praise of heroes
flowed from your fair lips
like the murmurings of a child;
these two gleaming eyes
that shone at me often in the storm,
when the yearning for hope   2390
wrenched my heart,
when I clamoured for
world happiness
out of wildly proliferating fear:
for the last time
I savour them today
with the last kiss
of my farewell!
May their star shine
out to a happier man: 2400
now they must close
on parting from this unhappy god.
He takes her head in both hands.

*It must clearly be seen that now is the first time the
spear slips from Wotan's hand.* *
This is how
the god renounces you,
kissing your godhood away!
He places a long kiss on both her eyes.

*With eyes closed, she sinks back into his arms, gently
falling asleep. He leads her tenderly to a low mossy bank
beneath a pine tree with long outstretched branches and
lays her down.*

*He looks at her and closes her helmet: his eye then lin-
gers on her sleeping body, drawing her big Valkyrie shield
made of steel over her until she is completely covered.*

*Slowly he turns his back on her; but once more he turns
around with a look aching with sorrow.*

Wotan picks up the spear from the ground. *

> *Dann schreitet er mit feierlichem Entschlusse in die*
> *Mitte der Bühne und kehrt die Spitze seines Speeres*
> *gegen einen mächtigen Felsstein.*

Loge, hör!
Lausche hieher
Wie zuerst ich dich fand,
als feurige Glut,
wie dann einst du mir schwandest,
als schweifende Lohe;
wie ich dich band,
bann' ich dich heut!
Herauf, wabernde Lohe.
Umlodre mir feurig den Fels!

> *Er stößt mit dem folgenden dreimal mit dem Speer auf*
> *den Stein.*
>> *erster Stoß*

Loge!

> *zweiter Stoß*

Loge!

> *dritter Stoß*

Hieher!

> *Dem Stein entfährt ein Feuerstrahl, der zur allmählich*
> *immer helleren Flammenglut anschwillt.*
>> *Hier bricht die lichte Flackerlohe aus.*
>> *Lichte Brunst umgibt Wotan mit wildem Flackern. Er*
>> *weist mit dem Speere gebieterisch dem Feuermeere den*
>> *Umkreis des Felsenrandes zur Strömung an; alsbald zieht*
>> *es sich nach dem Hintergrunde, wo es nun fortwährend*
>> *den Bergsaum umlodert.*

Wer meines Speeres
Spitze fürchtet,
durchschreite das Feuer nie!

> *Er streckt den Speer wie zum Banne aus.*
>> *Er blickt schmerzlich auf Brünnhilde zurück.*
>> *Er wendet sich langsam zum Gehen.*
>> *Er wendet sich nochmals mit dem Haupte und blickt*
>> *zurück.*
>> *Er verschwindet durch das Feuer.*
>> *Vorhang fällt.*

2410

2420

> *With formal resolution, he then steps towards the mid-*
> *dle of the stage and turns the tip of his spear towards a*
> *mighty stone in the rock.*

Loge, listen!
Take heed, over here!
The way I first found you,
as fiery heat,
the way you then vanished from me,   2410
like a roving inferno;
the way I bound you,
I bind you now with a spell!
Arise, swirling inferno.
Girdle the rock for me with flame!

> *During the following, he strikes the stone three times*
> *with his spear.*
>> *first strike*

Loge!

>> *second strike*

Loge!

>> *third strike*

Come here!

> *A jet of fire spurts out of the stone, gradually swelling in*
> *size into a gradually ever-brighter fiery glow.*
>> *At this point, bright tongues of flame break out.*
>> *Bright heat surrounds Wotan with wild flickering. With*
>> *his spear, he peremptorily directs the ocean of fire to flow*
>> *towards the area around the edge of the rock; at once*
>> *it moves towards the background where it continuously*
>> *encircles the foot of the mountain with a blaze.*

Whoever fears
the tip of my spear,   2420
never through this fire shall they walk!

> *He stretches out his spear as though casting a spell.*
>> *He looks back sorrowfully at Brünnhilde.*
>> *He turns around slowly to leave.*
>> *He turns his head back again and looks behind him.*
>> *He vanishes through the fire.*
>> *Curtain falls.*

SIEGFRIED

(ZWEITER TAG)

ERSTER AUFZUG

VORSPIEL UND ERSTE SZENE

Eine Felsenhöhle im Wald

Der Vorhang geht auf [Takt 133]. Den Vordergrund bildet ein Teil einer Felsenhöhle, die sich links tiefer nach innen zieht, nach rechts aber gegen drei Vierteile der Bühne einnimmt. Zwei natürlich gebildete Eingänge stehen dem Walde zu offen: der eine nach rechts, unmittelbar im Hintergrunde, der andere, breitere, ebenda seitwärts. An der Hinterwand, nach links zu, steht ein großer Schmiedeherd, aus Felsstücken natürlich geformt; künstlich ist nur der große Blasebalg: die rohe Esse geht – ebenfalls natürlich – durch das Felsendach hinauf. Ein sehr großer Amboß und andre Schmiedegerätschaften.

Am Amboß [vor dem Schmiedeherd] sitzt Mime, eifrig an einem Schwerte hämmernd.

MIME *hämmernd mit einem kleinen Hammer*
    einhaltend
  Zwangvolle Plage!
  Müh' ohne Zweck!
  Das beste Schwert,
  das je ich geschweißt,
  in der Riesen Fäusten
  hielte es fest:
  doch dem ich's geschmiedet,

SIEGFRIED

(SECOND DAY)

ACT ONE

PRELUDE AND FIRST SCENE

A rock cave in the forest

The curtain rises [bar 133]. Part of a rock cave is in the fore-ground, stretching on the left further into the background, but on the right it takes up roughly three-quarters of the stage. Two naturally formed entrances open out into the forest: one towards the right, directly in the background, the second broader, also in the background to one side. A large forge, formed naturally out of pieces of rock, stands against the back wall towards the left; only the large bellows is man-made. The crude chimney-pipe – likewise naturally formed – passes up-wards through the roof of the rocks. An extremely large anvil and other forging appliances.

    Mime is sitting at the anvil [in front of the forge] hammer-ing away intently at a sword.

MIME *hammering with a small hammer*
    pausing
  Slaving, slogging!
  No end to the grind!
  In the fists of giants,
  the finest sword
  that I ever welded
  could stay in one piece:
  but whenever I've forged it

der schmähliche Knabe,
er knickt und schmeißt es entzwei,
10 als schüf' ich Kindergeschmeid! –
    Mime wirft das Schwert unmutig auf den Amboß, stem-
    mt die Arme ein und blickt sinnend zu Boden.
        Hier hebt Mime leise den Kopf, wie wenn er einen
        Gedanken gefaßt hätte. *
Es gibt ein Schwert,
das er nicht zerschwänge; –
Nothung's Trümmern
zertrotzt' er mir nicht:
könnt' ich die starken
Stücken schweißen,
die meine Kunst
nicht zu kitten weiß!
Könnt' ich's dem Kühnen schmieden,
20 meiner Schmach erlangt' ich da Lohn! –
    Er sinkt tiefer zurück, das Haupt nachdenklich neigend.
Fafner, der wilde Wurm,
lagert im finstren Wald;
mit des furchtbaren Leibes Wucht
der Niblungen Hort
hütet er dort.
Siegfrieds kindischer Kraft
erläge wohl Fafners Leib:
des Niblungen Ring
erränge ich mir; –
30 ein Schwert nur taugt zu der Tat,
nur Nothung nützt meinem Neid,
wenn Siegfried sehrend ihn schwingt. –
    ist halb aufgesprungen, sehr leidenschaftliche gierige
    Gebärde *
        sinkt wieder auf den Sitz. *
Und ich kann's nicht schweißen,
Nothung das Schwert!
    Er hat das Schwert wieder zurechtgelegt und hämmert in
    höchstem Unmute daran weiter.
Zwangvolle Plage!

for that odious boy,
he snaps it in two and throws it out,
as if I'm making toys for a child! –   10

> *Mime throws the sword on the anvil in a huff, puts his
> hands on his hips and stares pensively at the ground.*
>
> *Here Mime gently raises his head, as if an idea had
> occurred to him.* *

A sword exists
that even he can't wreck; –
he'd not thumb his nose
at Nothung's remains:
I could weld its
powerful pieces,
if only I had the knack
of fitting one to the other!
Forging it for that daredevil if I could,
my humiliation would find some reward! –   20

> *He slumps further back, tilting his head in meditation.*

Fafner, the savage dragon,
has his lair in the lightless forest;
with the brunt of his hideous body
he keeps vigil there
over the Nibelung hoard.
Fafner's bulk may well succumb
to Siegfried's naive vigour:
the ring of the Nibelung
I'd win for myself; –
one sword only will do the trick,   30
only Nothung will serve my design,
once Siegfried uses its lethal force. –

> *makes an effort to leap up with a passionately covetous
> gesture* *
>
> *then falls back on his seat* *

And I can't weld it together,
Nothung the sword!

> *He gets the sword ready again and, greatly upset, goes on
> hammering on it.*

Slaving, slogging!

Müh' ohne Zweck!
Das beste Schwert,
das je ich geschweißt,
nie taugt es je
40 zu der einzigen Tat: –
ich tapp're und hämm're nur,
weil der Knabe es heischt:
er knickt und schmeißt es entzwei,
und schmäht doch, schmied' ich ihm nicht!

> *Siegfried, in wilder Waldkleidung, mit einem silbernen*
> *Horn an einer Kette, kommt mit jähem Ungestüm aus*
> *dem Walde herein; er hat einen großen Bären mit einem*
> *Bastseile gezäumt und treibt diesen mit lustigem Über-*
> *mute gegen Mime an.*

SIEGFRIED *noch außen*

Hoiho!
> *auftretend*
        Hoiho!
Hau ein! Hau ein!

> *Mime'n entsinkt vor Schreck das Schwert; er flüchtet*
> *hinter den Herd; Siegfried treibt ihm den Bären überall*
> *nach.*

Friß ihn! friß ihn,
den Fratzenschmied!

> *Er lacht unbändig.*

Hahaha hahahahahaha
50 hahahahahaha ha!

MIME

Fort mit dem Tier!
Was taugt mir der Bär?

SIEGFRIED

Zu zwei komm' ich,
dich besser zu zwicken.
Brauner! frag' nach dem Schwert!

MIME

He! laß das Wild!
Dort liegt die Waffe;
fertig fegt' ich sie heut'.

No end to the grind!
For the one vital deed,
the best sword
that I ever welded
won't ever be right: –
I hash it up and hammer away,
only because the boy insists:
he snaps it in two and throws it out,
only to fume, if I don't forge another!

> *Siegfried, in rough-and-tumble forest apparel, with a silver horn on a chain, makes an abruptly boisterous entrance out of the forest; with a strong-fibred rope, he has a big bear on a leash and goads it on with blithe exuberance in Mime's direction.*

SIEGFRIED *still outside*
Hoiho!

> *coming in*

Hoiho!
Get him! Get him!

> *The sword slips out of a terrified Mime's hand; he dives for cover behind the forge; Siegfried sets the bear on his heels wherever he goes.*

Gorge on him! Gorge
on the smith with the hideous face!

> *He laughs with abandon.*

Hahaha hahahahahaha
hahahahahaha ha!

MIME
Get the creature out!
What use is a bear to me?

SIEGFRIED
We came, the pair of us,
to torment you better.
Grizzly! Ask about the sword!

MIME
Hey! Stop that savage!
The sword's right there;
spick and span, finished today.

SIEGFRIED

So fährst du heute noch heil.
*Er löst dem Bären den Zaum, und gibt ihm damit einen
Schlag auf den Rücken.*

60   Lauf, Brauner!
dich brauch' ich nicht mehr.
*Der Bär läuft in den Wald zurück; Mime kommt zitternd
hinter dem Herde hervor.*

MIME

Wohl leid' ich's gern,
erlegst du Bären:
Siegfried setzt sich, um sich vom Lachen zu erholen.
was bringst du lebend
die braunen heim?

SIEGFRIED

Nach bess'rem Gesellen sucht' ich,
als daheim mir einer sitzt;
im tiefen Walde mein Horn
ließ ich hallend da ertönen:
70   ob sich froh mir gesellte
ein guter Freund? –
Das frug ich mit dem Getön'.

Aus dem Busche kam ein Bär,
der hörte mir brummend zu;
er gefiel mir besser als du,
doch bess're fänd' ich wohl noch!
Mit dem zähen Baste
zäumt' ich ihn da,
dich Schelm nach dem Schwerte zu fragen.
Er springt auf und geht auf den Amboß zu.

MIME *nimmt das Schwert auf, um es Siegfried zu reichen.*
80   Ich schuf die Waffe scharf,
ihrer Schneide wirst du dich freun.
*Er hält das Schwert ängstlich in der Hand fest, das Sieg-
fried ihm heftig entwindet.*

SIEGFRIED

Was frommt seine helle Schneide,
ist der Stahl nicht hart und fest?

SIEGFRIED

You'll stay in one piece for now then.

He frees the bear from the leash, and smacks him on the back with it.

Scram, grizzly!   60
I've no more use for you.

The bear lumbers back into the forest; Mime comes out trembling from behind the forge.

MIME

I'm really happy,
if you kill bears:

Siegfried sits down to get over his fits of laughter.

but why do you bring
grizzlies home alive?

SIEGFRIED

I'm looking for a better mate
than the one I've got at home;
there in the deep forest
I let my horn echo around:
any good friend out there   70
happy to join me? –
That's what I asked with the sound.

A bear came out of the bushes,
growling as he listened to me;
I liked him more than I like you,
and still I could do better!
Then with a tough rope,
I put him on a leash,
to ask you, creep, about the sword.

He jumps up and makes for the anvil.

MIME *picks up the sword in order to hand it to Siegfried.*

I made the weapon sharp,   80
you'll like its razor edge.

He grips the sword nervously in his hand; Siegfried violently pries it away from him.

SIEGFRIED

What's the point of its shiny edge,
if the steel's not hard and tough?

Er prüft es mit der Hand.
Hei! Was ist das
für müß'ger Tand!
Den schwachen Stift
nennst du ein Schwert?
Er zerschlägt es auf dem Amboß, daß die Stücken ring-
um fliegen; Mime weicht erschrocken aus.
Da hast du die Stücken,
schändlicher Stümper!
90   Hätt' ich am Schädel
dir sie zerschlagen! –
Soll mich der Prahler
länger noch prellen?
Schwatzt mir von Riesen
und rüstigen Kämpfen,
von kühnen Taten
und tüchtiger Wehr;
will Waffen mir schmieden,
Schwerte schaffen;
100 rühmt seine Kunst,
als könnt' er was recht's:
nehm' ich zur Hand nun,
was er gehämmert,
mit einem Griff
zergreif' ich den Quark!
Wär' mir nicht schier
zu schäbig der Wicht,
ich zerschmiedet' ihn selbst
mit seinem Geschmeid,
110 den alten albernen Alp: –
des Ärgers dann hätt' ich ein End'!
Siegfried wirft sich wütend auf eine Steinbank zur Seite
rechts. Mime ist ihm immer vorsichtig ausgewichen.
MIME
Nun tobst du wieder wie toll!
Dein Undank, traun, ist arg!
Mach ich dem bösen Buben
nicht alles gleich zu best,
was ich ihm Gutes schuf,

He tests it with his hand.
Hey! What kind of
stupid toy is this!
You call this piffling
peg a sword?
He smashes it on the anvil, so that the pieces fly every-
where; aghast, Mime ducks out of the way.
Bits and pieces for you,
shabby bungler!
If only I'd smashed   90
your skull with them! –
Is this swaggerer to
swindle me more?
He blabs about giants
and frisky fights,
about derring-do
and trusty defence;
wants to forge me weapons,
make swords;
lauds his skill   100
as if he could do something:
but as soon as I get hold
of what he's hammering,
with one swing
I've smashed the crap to bits!
If I didn't find the wretch
so utterly revolting,
I'd clobber him myself
with his own metal toys,
the silly old cretin: –   110
that'd put a stop to my fretting!
In a rage, Siegfried hurls himself onto a stone seat on the
right. Mime takes care always to keep his distance.
MIME
You're ranting and raving again!
Your rudeness, truly, is terrible!
The minute I don't give
the nasty boy all he wants,
he forgets only too fast

vergißt er gar zu schnell!
Willst du denn nie gedenken,
was ich dich lehrt' vom Danke:
120   dem sollst du willig gehorchen,
der je sich wohl dir erwies.

> *Siegfried wendet sich unmutig um, mit dem Gesicht nach*
> *der Wand, so daß er Mime den Rücken kehrt.*

Das willst du wieder nicht hören!

> *Er [Mime] steht verlegen; dann geht er in die Küche am*
> *Herd.*

Doch speisen magst du wohl?
Vom Spieße bring' ich den Braten:
versuchtest du gern den Sud?
Für dich sott ich ihn gar.

> *Er reicht Siegfried Speisen hin; dieser, ohne sich umzu-*
> *wenden, schmeißt ihm Topf und Braten aus der Hand.*

SIEGFRIED
Braten briet ich mir selbst:
deinen Sudel sauf allein!

MIME *stellt sich empfindlich. Mit kläglich kreischender Stimme*
Das ist nun der Liebe
130   schlimmer Lohn!
Das der Sorgen
schmählicher Sold!

> *Mime begleitet alles Erzählte mit charakteristischen*
> *Gebärden.* *

Als zullendes Kind
zog ich dich auf,
wärmte mit Kleiden
den kleinen Wurm:
Speise und Trank
trug ich dir zu,
hütete dich
140   wie die eig'ne Haut.
Und wie du erwuchsest,
wartet' ich dein,
dein Lager schuf ich,
daß leicht du schliefst.

the good I've done him!
You don't ever want to remember
what I taught you about gratitude:
you should be eager to obey anyone   120
who turns out to wish you well.

*Siegfried turns around in resentment, his face to the wall,
his back turned to Mime.*

Again you don't want to hear it!

*He [Mime] stands there sheepishly; then he goes into the
kitchen by the forge.*

Want something to eat then?
Shall I get the roast from the spit:
do you want to try the broth?
For you I'll heat it up till it's done.

*He hands the food to Siegfried, who without turning
around knocks the saucepan and roast out of his hands.*

SIEGFRIED
I'll do my own roast:
swig your swill on your own!

MIME *feigning offence. In a shrill woebegone voice*
All you need is hate
for love's unfair reward!   130
All you need is lousy pay
for all the pains you take!

*Mime accompanies everything he relates with gestures to
illustrate the story.* *

I brought you up
a child unweaned,
with clothes I warmed
the tiny tot:
for you I fetched
food and drink,
I cared for you
like my own kin.   140
And as you grew up,
over you I watched:
your bed I made,
so you slept well.

Dir schmiedet' ich Tand
und ein tönend Horn;
dich zu erfreun,
müht' ich mich froh:
mit klugem Rate
150 riet ich dir klug,
mit lichtem Wissen
lehrt' ich dich Witz.
Sitz' ich daheim
in Fleiß und Schweiß,
nach Herzenslust
jagst du umher:
für dich nur in Plage,
in Pein nur für dich
verzehr' ich mich alter,
160 armer Zwerg!
     schluchzend
Und aller Lasten
ist das nun mein Lohn,
daß der hastige Knabe
mich quält
     schluchzend
          und haßt!
*Siegfried hat sich wieder umgewendet und ruhig in
Mimes Blick geforscht.*
     *[Mime] begegnet Siegfrieds Blick und sucht den seini-
gen scheu zu bergen.*
SIEGFRIED
Vieles lehrtest du, Mime,
und manches lernt' ich von dir;
doch was du am liebsten mich lehrtest,
zu lernen gelang mir's nie: –
wie ich dich leiden könnt'!
170 Trägst du mir Trank
und Speise herbei, –
der Ekel speist mich allein;
schaffst du ein leichtes
Lager zum Schlaf, –

For you I built toys
and a ringing horn;
to make you happy
I happily toiled:
with clever advice
I advised you cleverly,   150
with lucid wisdom
I honed your wit.
If I sit at home,
and slave and sweat,
you're out hunting
to your heart's content:
I eat out my heart
for you only in pain,
in torment only for you,
poor dwarf that I am!   160
    snivelling
And after all this,
all I get in return
is a boy who in a flash
baits
    snivelling
        and hates me!
*Siegfried has turned round again and calmly looks search-
ingly into Mime's eyes.*
    *[Mime] meets Siegfried's gaze and tries shyly to hide
his own.*

SIEGFRIED
You taught me a lot, Mime,
and from you I've learnt something;
but what you most wanted to teach me
I've never been able to learn: –
how I could like you!
If you bring me   170
drink and food, –
revulsion's all that feeds me;
if you make a soft
bed to sleep on, –

der Schlummer wird mir da schwer;
willst du mich weisen,
witzig zu sein, –
gern bleib' ich taub und dumm.
Seh' ich dir erst
180 mit den Augen zu,
zu übel erkenn' ich,
was alles du tust!

> *Unmittelbar nach diesen mit steigendem Unmuth her-*
> *vorgestoßenen Worten, springt Siegfried von seinem*
> *Lager auf**

Seh' ich dich stehn,
gangeln und gehn,
knicken und nicken,
mit den Augen zwicken:

> *und Mimes jämmerliches Gebahren mit verspottender*
> *Gebärde nachahmend, fährt er dann bei den [folgenden]*
> *Worten auf den Zwerg los.**

beim Genick möcht' ich
den Nicker packen,
den Garaus geben
190 dem garst'gen Zwicker! –
So lernt' ich, Mime, dich leiden. –

Bist du nun weise,
so hilf mir wissen,
worüber umsonst ich sann: –
in den Wald lauf' ich,
dich zu verlassen; –
wie kommt das, kehr' ich zurück?
Alle Tiere sind
mir teurer als du,
200 Baum und Vogel,
die Fische im Bach,
lieber mag ich sie
leiden als dich: –
wie kommt das nun, kehr' ich zurück?
Bist du klug, so tu mir's kund.

> *Siegfried sitzt.**

insomnia's all I get;
if you show me
how to be clever, –
deaf and dumb I'll gladly stay.
Once I set
eyes on you,   180
I see the evil
in all you do!

    *Straight after these words, which Siegfried has spluttered
    out with increasing ill humour, he jumps up from where
    he is seated* *

Once I see you stand,
traipse and tread,
bend and nod,
with twitching eyes:

    *and then, imitating Mime's pitiful behaviour with deri-
    sive gestures, lets fly at the dwarf with the [following]
    words.* *

I'd like to take
your nodding neck,
and put an end
to that hideous twitch! –   190
So I'd learn, Mime, to abide you. –

If you're so wise,
then help me with something
I've racked my brains about: –
I run into the forest
to abandon you; –
so how is it that I come back?
You're not as dear to me
as all the animals are,
trees and birds,   200
fishes in the stream,
who I can put up with
more than with you: –
so how is it really that I come back?
You're so clever, tell me why.

    Siegfried sits down. *

Mime sucht sich ihm traulich zu nähern.

MIME

Mein Kind, das lehrt dich kennen,
wie lieb ich am Herzen dir lieg'.

SIEGFRIED *lacht*

Ich kann dich ja nicht leiden: –
vergiß das nicht so leicht!

MIME *fährt zurück und setzt sich weiter abseits, Siegfried
gegenüber.*

210   Dess' ist deine Wildheit schuld,
die du Böser bänd'gen sollst! –
Jammernd verlangen Junge
nach ihrer Alten Nest:
Liebe ist das Verlangen; –
so lechzest du auch nach mir,
so liebst du auch deinen Mime –
     wie befehlend*
so mußt du ihn lieben!
Was dem Vögelein ist der Vogel,
wenn er im Nest es hegt –
220   eh' das flügge mag fliegen,
das ist dir kind'schem Sproß
der kundig sorgende Mime, –
das muß er dir sein!

SIEGFRIED

Ei, Mime! Bist du so witzig,
so laß mich eines noch wissen. –

     einfach
Es sangen die Vöglein
so selig im Lenz,
     zart
das eine lockte das andre; –
du sagtest selbst,
230   da ich's wissen wollt', –
das wären Männchen
     zart
                    und Weibchen:
Sie kosten so lieblich,

Confidingly, Mime tries to get closer to him.

MIME

My child, that only goes to show you
how much you really care for me.

SIEGFRIED *laughs*

But I can't stand you: –
don't forget that in a hurry!

MIME *backs off and sits down opposite Siegfried further to
the side.*

It's because you're uncouth,   210
a bad boy's got to control it! –
Bellyaching youngsters yearn
for the nest of their elders:
that yearning is love; –
so you long for me as well,
so you love your Mime too –
    as if giving an order*
so love him you must!
What a bird is to its chicks,
when it nurtures them in its nest –
before the chicks are able to fly,   220
so to you, young sprout,
is your carefully caring Mime, –
for you he must be that!

SIEGFRIED

Eh, Mime! If you're so brainy,
help me with something else. –

    simply
The little birds sang
so happily in spring,
    tenderly
the one wooed the other; –
you said so yourself,
'cos I was curious, –   230
they were cocks
    tenderly
          and hens:
they cooed so lovingly,

und ließen sich nicht;
sie bauten ein Nest
und brüteten drin;
da flatterte junges
Geflügel auf,
und beide pflegten der Brut.
So ruhten im Busch
240   auch Rehe gepaart,
selbst wilde Füchse und Wölfe;
Nahrung brachte
zum Neste das Männchen;
das Weibchen säugte die Welpen: –
Da lernt' ich wohl,
was Liebe sei,
der Mutter entwandt' ich
die Welpen nie.
Wo hast du nun, Mime,
250   dein minniges Weibchen,
daß ich es Mutter nenne?

MIME *ärgerlich*
Was ist dir, Tor?
Ach, bist du dumm!
Bist doch weder Vogel noch Fuchs?

SIEGFRIED
Das zullende Kind
zogest du auf,
wärmtest mit Kleiden
den kleinen Wurm: –
wie kam dir aber
260   der kindische Wurm?
Du machtest wohl gar
ohne Mutter mich?

MIME *in großer Verlegenheit*
Glauben sollst du,
was ich dir sage:
ich bin dir Vater
und Mutter zugleich.

and without leaving each other;
they built a nest
and sat on their eggs in it;
then young wings
started to flap,
and both tended their brood.
In the shrubbery rested
pairs of deer,   240
even wild foxes and wolves;
the little father brought
food to the nest;
the little wife breastfed the babies: –
There I really learnt
what love is,
I never stole
the babies from their mother.
Where then, Mime, is
that loving little wife of yours   250
I can call mother?

MIME *annoyed*

What's wrong with you, idiot?
Ah, how stupid you are!
You're not a bird or a fox, are you?

SIEGFRIED

You raised the
unweaned child,
you warmed the tiny
tot with clothes: –
but how did the infant
come to be with you?   260
Did you really make
me without a mother?

MIME *greatly embarrassed*

You've got to believe
what I'm telling you:
I'm father and mother
to you at the same time.

SIEGFRIED

  Das lügst du, garstiger Gauch!
  Wie die Jungen den Alten gleichen,
  das hab' ich mir glücklich ersehn.
    *Mit höchster Ruhe und Gleichmäßigkeit, die friedselige
    Stille des Naturlebens objektiv darstellend**
270 Nun kam ich zum klaren Bach:
  da erspäht' ich die Bäum'
  und Tier' im Spiegel;
  Sonn' und Wolken,
  wie sie nur sind,
  im Glitzer erschienen sie gleich.
    *vor sich hinblickend, als ob er in den Bach schaute**
  Da sah ich denn auch
  mein eigen Bild: –
  ganz anders als du
  dünkt' ich mir da;
280 so glich wohl der Kröte
  der glänzender Fisch;
  doch kroch nie ein Fisch aus der Kröte!

MIME *höchst ärgerlich*

  Gräulichen Unsinn
  kramst du da aus!

SIEGFRIED *immer lebendiger*

  Siehst du! Nun fällt
  auch selbst mir ein,
  was zuvor umsonst ich besann:
  wenn zum Wald ich laufe,
  dich zu verlassen,
290 wie das kommt, kehr' ich doch heim?
    Er springt auf.
  Von dir erst muß ich erfahren,
  wer Vater und Mutter mir sei!

MIME *weicht ihm aus*

  Was Vater! Was Mutter!
  Müßige Frage!

SIEGFRIED *Er springt auf Mime los und faßt ihn bei der Kehle.*

  So muß ich dich fassen,
  um 'was zu wissen;

SIEGFRIED
> You're fibbing, you filthy cuckoo!
> Luckily I've learnt to see for myself
> how the young look like the old.
>> *With exceptional calmness and evenness objectively describing the blissfully calm stillness of natural life* *
> Once I came to clear water: 270
> I espied there the trees
> and animals on its surface;
> sun and clouds,
> as only they can be,
> appeared in the glistening waters too.
>> *looking straight ahead, as if seeing himself in the stream* *
> Then I saw
> myself as well: –
> I thought right there
> that I'm completely unlike you;
> a gleaming fish   280
> compared to a toad;
> yet out of a toad a fish never crawled!

MIME *extremely annoyed*
> You're dredging up
> ghoulish drivel!

SIEGFRIED *constantly getting livelier*
> You see! I used to rack
> my brains about it,
> now I get it, I really do:
> if I run into the forest
> to abandon you,
> how is it that I come back home?   290
>> *He jumps up.*
> From you I first have to learn
> who my father and mother are!

MIME *evasively*
> Father this! Mother that!
> Pointless question!

SIEGFRIED *He jumps onto Mime and grabs him by the throat.*
> I've got to grab you like this
> to get to know anything;

gutwillig
erfahr' ich doch nichts!
So mußt' ich alles
300   ab dir trotzen:
kaum das Reden
hätt' ich erraten,
entwand ich's mit Gewalt
nicht dem Schuft!
Heraus damit,
räudiger Kerl!
Wer ist mir Vater und Mutter?

MIME *nachdem er mit dem Kopfe genickt und mit den Hän-*
den gewinkt, ist von Siegfried losgelassen worden.

Ans Leben gehst du mir schier!
Nun laß! Was zu wissen dich geizt,
310   erfahr es, ganz wie ich's weiß.
O undankbares,
arges Kind!
jetzt hör', wofür du mich hassest!
Nicht bin ich Vater
noch Vetter dir,
und dennoch verdankst du mir dich;
ganz fremd bist du mir,
dem einzigen Freund;
aus Erbarmen allein
320   barg ich dich hier:
nun hab' ich lieblichen Lohn! –
Was verhofft' ich Tor mir auch Dank! –

Mime blickt mehr hinaus als in Siegfrieds Auge. Er hat
Angst und Scheu vor Siegfrieds Blick. *

Einst lag wimmernd ein Weib
da draußen im wilden Wald;
zur Höhle half ich ihr her,
am warmen Herd sie zu hüten.
Ein Kind trug sie im Schoße;
traurig gebar sie's hier;
sie wand sich hin und her, –
330   ich half, so gut ich konnt': –

if I'm nice
I'll get nowhere for sure!
I've got to drag everything
out of you: 300
I'd have hardly ever guessed
how to speak,
if I hadn't wrung it from
you, wretch, by force!
Out with it,
you scabby rascal!
Who are my father and mother?

MIME *after jerking his head and waving his hands, he is set*
    free by Siegfried.
You practically killed me!
Stop it! If you're greedy
to learn, just listen to what I know.   310
O ungrateful,
bad child!
now listen to why you hate me!
I'm not your father
nor related to you,
and still you owe me your life;
you're totally different from me,
the only friend you have;
only out of pity
did I harbour you here: 320
and a fat lot of good it did me!
How silly of me to expect gratitude! –

    Mime looks more away from than into Siegfried's eyes.
    He is anxious and shy about Siegfried looking at him. *

A long time ago there was a woman
lying out there in the forest, moaning;
I helped her here to the cave
where I nursed her by the warm fire.
She carried a child in her womb;
in sorrow she gave birth to it here;
she twisted and turned, –
I did my best to help: –   330

groß war die Not! Sie starb: –
doch Siegfried, der genas.

SIEGFRIED *langsam*

So starb meine Mutter an mir?

MIME

Meinem Schutz übergab sie dich;
  [Siegfried] steht sinnend.
ich schenkt’ ihn gern dem Kind.
Was hat sich Mime gemüht,
was gab sich der gute für Not!
‘Als zullendes Kind
zog ich dich auf’ –

SIEGFRIED

340 Mich dünkt, dess’ gedachtest du schon!
Jetzt sag’, – woher heiß’ ich ‘Siegfried’?

MIME

So hieß mich die Mutter
möcht’ ich dich heißen;
als ‘Siegfried’ würdest
du stark und schön.
‘Ich wärmte mit Kleiden
den kleinen Wurm.’ –

SIEGFRIED

Nun melde, wie hieß meine Mutter?

MIME

Das weiß ich wahrlich kaum! –

350 ‘Speise und Trank
trug ich dir zu’ –

SIEGFRIED *belebt*

Den Namen sollst du mir nennen!

MIME

Entfiel er mir wohl? Doch halt!
Sieglinde mochte sie heißen,
die dich in Sorge mir gab: –
‘Ich hütete dich
wie die eig’ne Haut’ –

SIEGFRIED *immer dringender*

Dann frag’ ich, wie hieß mein Vater?

Her distress was great! She died: –
as for Siegfried, he recovered.

SIEGFRIED *slowly*

So I caused my mother's death?

MIME

She committed you to my care;
   [Siegfried] stands and ponders.
I happily bestowed it on the child.
The things Mime did,
the pains the good soul took!
'I brought you up
a child unweaned' –

SIEGFRIED

I think you've said that already!   340
So tell me – why call me 'Siegfried'?

MIME

That's what your mother said
I should call you;
as 'Siegfried' you'd become
strong and handsome.
'With clothes I warmed
the tiny tot.' –

SIEGFRIED

Tell me, what was my mother called?

MIME

I honestly don't know exactly! –
'For you I fetched   350
food and drink' –

SIEGFRIED *briskly*

You've got to tell me her name!

MIME

Did I really forget it? Just a second!
Maybe it was Sieglinde, the one who
anxiously gave you into my care: –
'I cared for you
like my own kin' –

SIEGFRIED *increasingly more insistent*

What was my father's name then?

MIME *barsch*
    Den hab' ich nie gesehn!
SIEGFRIED
360 Doch die Mutter nannte den Namen?
MIME
    Erschlagen sei er, –
    das sagte sie nur: –
    dich Vaterlosen
    befahl sie mir da.
    'Und wie du erwuchsest,
    wartet' ich dein',
    dein Lager schuf ich,
    daß leicht du schliefst!'
SIEGFRIED *mit energisch auffahrender Gebärde* *
    Still mit dem alten
370 Starenlied!
    Soll ich der Kunde glauben,
    hast du mir nichts gelogen,
    so laß mich Zeichen sehn!
MIME
    Was soll dir's noch bezeugen?
SIEGFRIED
    Dir glaub' ich nicht mit dem Ohr',
    dir glaub' ich nur mit dem Aug':
    welch' Zeichen zeugt für dich?
        Er [Mime] holt nach einigem Besinnen die zwei Stücke
        eines zerschlagenen Schwertes herbei.
MIME
    Das gab mir deine Mutter;
    für Mühe, Kost und Pflege
380 ließ sie's als schwachen Lohn:
        mit sehr geringschätzendem Ausdruck *
    sieh her, ein zerbroch'nes Schwert;
    dein Vater, sagte sie, führt' es,
    als im letzten Kampf er erlag.
SIEGFRIED *begeistert*
    Und diese Stücken
    sollst du mir schmieden:

MIME *curtly*
    I've never seen him!
SIEGFRIED
    Mother spoke his name, didn't she?   360
MIME
    All she said was, –
    he'd been slain: –
    because you had no father
    she entrusted you to me.
    'And as you grew up,
    on you I watched:
    your bed I made,
    so you slept well!'
SIEGFRIED *with a vigorously hot-tempered gesture.* *
    Stop singing that old
    starling's song!   370
    If I'm to believe this news,
    if you're not lying to me,
    then show me it's true!
MIME
    What other proof do you want?
SIEGFRIED
    I don't believe you with my ears,
    I'll only believe you with my eyes:
    what proves that you're right?
        After some thought, he [Mime] fetches two pieces of a
        splintered sword.
MIME
    This your mother handed to me;
    she left it as meagre compensation
    for the trouble, food and care I'd provide: 380
        with very disdainful expression *
    so look, a broken sword;
    your father, she said, was wielding it
    when he fell in his final battle.
SIEGFRIED *inspired*
    And these pieces
    you're meant to forge for me:

dann schwing' ich mein rechtes Schwert!
Auf! Eile dich, Mime!
Mühe dich rasch!
Kannst du was recht's,
390   nun zeig deine Kunst:
täusche mich nicht
mit schlechtem Tand!
Den Trümmern allein
trau' ich was zu!
Find' ich dich faul,
fügst du ihn schlecht,
flickst du mit Flausen
den festen Stahl:
dir Feigem fahr' ich zu Leib;
400   das Fegen lernst du von mir!
Denn heute noch, schwör' ich,
will ich das Schwert,
die Waffe gewinn' ich noch heut'!

MIME *ängstlich*

Was willst du noch heut' mit dem Schwert?

SIEGFRIED

Aus dem Wald fort
in die Welt ziehn,
nimmer kehr' ich zurück!
Wie ich froh bin,
daß ich frei ward,
410   nichts mich bindet und zwingt!
Mein Vater bist du nicht;
in der Ferne bin ich heim;
dein Herd ist nicht mein Haus,
meine Decke nicht dein Dach:
wie der Fisch froh
in der Flut schwimmt,
wie der Fink frei
sich davon schwingt,
flieg' ich von hier,
420   flute davon,
wie der Wind über'n Wald

then I'll brandish my rightful sword!
Get up! Hurry, Mime!
Get cracking now!
If you can do something right,
then show what you can do: 390
no tricks now
with paltry toys!
Only in these pieces
do I put my trust!
If I see you flag,
foul up the fitting,
finish the firm steel
with fancy ideas:
I'll flog your funky body;
I'll teach you to beat a thing into shape! 400
I want the sword, I swear,
before the day's out,
I'll carry off the weapon today!

MIME *fearfully*

What do you want with the sword today?

SIEGFRIED

Out of the woods
away into the world,
never to return!
How happy I am
to be freed,
no ties and nothing to keep me back! 410
My father you're not;
far away I'm at home;
your hearth's not my house,
nor my refuge your roof:
glad as a fish
gliding through water,
free as a finch
flying up and away,
from here I flee,
surging forth, 420
breezing far

weh' ich dahin: –
dich, Mime, nie wieder zu sehn!
> *Er läuft in den Wald.*

MIME *in höchster Angst*
Halte! Halte!
> *läuft dem fortstürzenden Siegfried nach, läßt aber von sein-*
> *em als vergeblich erkannten Beginnen schnell wieder ab. **
Halte! Wohin?
> *Er ruft mit der größten Anstrengung in den Wald.*
He! Siegfried!
Siegfried! He!
> *Er sieht dem Fortstürmenden eine Weile staunend nach.*
> *Er kehrt in die Schmiede zurück und setzt sich hinter*
> *den Amboß.*
Da stürmt er hin!
Nun sitz' ich da; –
zur alten Not
430 hab' ich die neue: –
vernagelt bin ich nun ganz! –
Wie helf' ich mir jetzt?
Wie halt' ich ihn fest?
Wie führ' ich den Huien
zu Fafners Nest?
Wie füg' ich die Stücken
des tückischen Stahls?
Keines Ofens Glut
glüht mir die echten;
440 keines Zwergen Hammer
zwingt mir die harten!
Des Niblungen Neid,
Not und Schweiß
nietet mir Notung nicht,
schweißt mir das Schwert nicht zu ganz!
> *schluchzend*
> *Mime knickt verzweifelnd auf dem Schemel hinter dem*
> *Amboß zusammen.*

over the forest like flurries of wind: –
never, Mime, to see you again!
   He runs into the forest.
MIME *in a state of extreme anxiety*
Stop! Stop!
   runs after Siegfried as he storms off, but quickly gives up
   after realizing that it was futile from the start. *
       Stop! Where are you going?
   With huge exertion, he shouts into the forest.
Hey! Siegfried!
Siegfried! Hey!
   Stunned, he watches for a while as Siegfried storms into
   the distance.
     He returns to the forge and sits down behind the anvil.
Off he storms!
Just leaving me here; –
the hard times of old
give way to new: –
I'm totally stumped for sure! –
Now what do I do?
How do I pin him down?
How do I get the youth in a hurry
to Fafner's lair?
How do I match the pieces
of this elusive steel?
Find me a furnace
with the fire to fuse them;
find me a dwarf's hammer
that dents their iron will!
The Nibelung's schemes,
stress and sweat
won't let me rivet Nothung together,
weld the sword into a whole!
   snivelling
     Mime collapses in despair on the stool behind the
   anvil.

ZWEITE SZENE

*Der Wanderer (Wotan) tritt aus dem Wald an das hintere Tor
der Höhle heran. – Er trägt einen dunkelblauen, langen Man-
tel; einen Speer führt er als Stab. Auf dem Haupte hat er einen
großen Hut mit breiter runder Krämpe, die über das fehlende
eine Auge tief hereinhängt.*

WANDERER
   Heil dir, weiser Schmied!
   Dem wegmüden Gast
   gönne hold
   des Hauses Herd!

MIME *erschrocken auffahrend*
450   Wer ist's, der im wilden
   Walde mich sucht?
   Wer verfolgt mich im öden Forst?

WANDERER *sehr langsam, immer nur um einen Schritt, sich
    nähernd*
   'Wandrer' heißt mich die Welt;
   weit wandert' ich schon:
   auf der Erde Rücken
   rührt' ich mich viel!

MIME
   So rühre dich fort
   und raste nicht hier, –
   heißt dich 'Wandrer' die Welt!

WANDERER
460   Gastlich ruht' ich bei Guten,
   Gaben gönnten viele mir:
   denn Unheil fürchtet,
   wer unhold ist.

MIME
   Unheil wohnte
   immer bei mir;
   willst du dem Armen es mehren?

WANDERER *langsam immer näherschreitend*
   Viel erforscht' ich,

SCENE TWO

The Wanderer (Wotan) appears out of the forest at the back entrance to the cave. – He is dressed in a long dark blue coat and uses his spear as a walking stick. There is a large hat on his head with a broad, round brim hanging down low over his missing eye.

WANDERER
I salute you, wise smith!
Be so kind as to grant
a travel-worn visitor the favour
of your house and hearth!
MIME *looking up with a start*
Who's this calling on me   450
in these wooded wilds?
Tracking me down in this empty forest?
WANDERER *very slowly, always approaching only one step at
    a time*
The world calls me 'Wanderer';
already I've wandered far:
over the surface of the earth
I did and saw much!
MIME
Then see your way out
and don't stop here, –
if it's 'Wanderer' the world calls you!
WANDERER
Good people bade me stay,   460
many granted me gifts:
disaster is feared only
by those who aren't kind.
MIME
I live disaster
all the time;
do you want poor me to have more of it?
WANDERER *constantly stepping closer*
I studied many things,

    erkannte viel;
    wicht'ges konnt' ich
470 manchem künden,
    manchem wehren,
    was ihn mühte,
    nagende Herzensnot.
        Der unruhig gewordene Mime weicht etwas zurück. *

MIME
    Spürtest du klug
    und erspähtest du viel,
    hier brauch' ich nicht Spürer noch Späher.
    Einsam will ich
    und einzeln sein:
    Lungerern laß' ich den Lauf.

WANDERER *wieder etwas näher tretend*
480 Mancher wähnte,
    weise zu sein;
    nur was ihm not tat,
    wußte er nicht:
        geht mit großen Schritten mehr nach vorwärts. *
    was ihm frommte,
    ließ ich erfragen:
    lohnend lehrt' ihn mein Wort.

MIME *immer ängstlicher, da er den Wanderer sich nähern*
        sieht
    Müß'ges Wissen
    wahren manche;
    ich weiß mir g'rade genug:
        Wanderer vollends bis an den Herd vorschreitend
490 mir genügt mein Witz;
    ich will nicht mehr!
    Dir Weisem weis' ich den Weg!
        [Der Wanderer] stößt den Speer auf den Boden. *

WANDERER *am Herd sich setzend*
    Hier sitz' ich am Herd,
    und setze mein Haupt
    der Wissenswette zum Pfand.
    Mein Kopf ist dein,
    du hast ihn erkiest,

many things I understood;
I've been able to impart weighty
news to many people,   470
many people I've been able to shield
from the worry
consuming their stricken hearts.
    Mime has become restless and backs off a little. *

MIME
You've cleverly probed
and pried into much,
I need no probing or prying here.
Solitary and separate
I want to be:
I'll leave idlers to their own devices.

WANDERER *steps a bit closer again*
Many men imagined   480
they were prudent;
but they did not know,
what held a man back:
    walks forwards some more with big strides. *
I inquired of men
about what they ought to know:
my words brought benefit to them.

MIME *increasingly more frightened as he sees the Wanderer
    getting closer*
Many fill themselves
with futile knowledge;
I know exactly enough:
    the Wanderer walking the whole way to the hearth
my own wit suffices;   490
more I don't want!
I'll show you, wise man, on your way!
    [The Wanderer] strikes the ground with his spear. *

WANDERER *taking a seat by the hearth*
I sit here by your hearth,
and pledge my head
as forfeit in a battle of wits.
My head is yours,
it's destined for you,

*[Mime], der zuletzt den Wanderer mit offenem Munde
angestarrt hat, schrickt jetzt zusammen.*

erfrägst du dir nicht,
was dir frommt,
500 lös' ich's mit Lehren nicht ein.

MIME *kleinmütig für sich*

Wie werd' ich den Lauernden los? –
Verfänglich muß ich ihn fragen.

    Er ermannt sich wie zu Strenge.
     laut

Dein Haupt pfänd' ich
für den Herd:
nun sorg', es sinnig zu lösen!
Drei der Fragen
stell' ich mir frei.

WANDERER

Dreimal muß ich's treffen.

MIME *sammelt sich zum Nachdenken*

Du rührtest dich viel
510 auf der Erde Rücken,
die Welt durchwandertest du weit; –
nun sage mir schlau:
welches Geschlecht
tagt in der Erde Tiefe?

WANDERER

In der Erde Tiefe
tagen die Nibelungen;
Nibelheim ist ihr Land;
Schwarzalben sind sie;
Schwarz-Alberich
520 hütet' als Herrscher sie einst.
Eines Zauberringes
zwingende Kraft
zähmt' ihm das fleißige Volk.
Reicher Schätze
schimmernden Hort
häuften sie ihm:
der sollte die Welt ihm gewinnen.

[*Mime*], *who has just been staring at the Wanderer with
his mouth wide open, flinches with shock.*

if you don't find out
what's of use to you,
if my instruction is of no avail.   500

MIME *aside, timidly*

How do I get rid of the predator? –
I must be politic in my questioning.

He plucks up the courage to appear strict.
out loud

Your head I declare as forfeit
for my hearth:
take pains to redeem it with care!
I'll put three questions
at your disposal.

WANDERER

Three exact answers I must give.

MIME *concentrates to collect his thoughts*

You did and saw much
over the face of the earth,   510
you travelled the world far and wide; –
so tell me prudently:
which race
does its work in the earth's depths?

WANDERER

In the earth's depths
the Nibelungs do their work;
Nibelheim is their country;
they are black elves;
long ago they were ruled by their lord,
Black Alberich.   520
The coercive power
of a magic ring
held his industrious people in thrall.
For him they amassed
a gleaming hoard
of rich treasures:
it was supposed to win him the world.

Zum zweiten, was frägst du, Zwerg?
  Mime 'der Philolog und Antiquar'*
MIME *versinkt in immer tieferes Nachsinnen*
  Viel, Wanderer,
530 weißt du mir
  aus der Erde Nabelnest:
  nun sage mir schlicht:
  welches Geschlecht
  wohnt auf der Erde Rücken?
WANDERER
  Auf der Erde Rücken
  wuchtet der Riesen Geschlecht:
  Riesenheim ist ihr Land.
  Fasolt und Fafner,
  der Rauhen Fürsten,
540 neideten Nibelungs Macht;
  den gewaltigen Hort
  gewannen sie sich,
  errangen mit ihm den Ring.
  Um den entbrannte
  den Brüdern Streit:
  der Fasolt fällte,
  als wilder Wurm
  hütet nun Fafner den Hort.

  Die dritte Frage nun droht.
MIME *ganz entrückt und nachsinnend*
    von seinem antiquarischen Wissen wie entzückt und
    reibt sich darob froh die Hände*
550 Viel, Wanderer,
  weißt du mir
  von der Erde rauhem Rücken.
  Nun sage mir wahr,
  welches Geschlecht
  wohnt auf wolkigen Höh'n?
WANDERER
  Auf wolkigen Höhn
  wohnen die Götter:
  Walhall heißt ihr Saal.

What is your second question, dwarf?
  Mime 'the philologist and antiquarian'*
MIME *sinks into increasingly profound reflection*
  I see you know
  much, Wanderer,   530
  from the nest in the navel of the earth:
  so tell me simply:
  which race
  lives on the earth's surface?
WANDERER
  Over the earth's surface
  the giants' race towers with might:
  their country is Riesenheim.
  Fasolt and Fafner,
  the rough creatures' rulers,
  coveted the Nibelung's power;   540
  they took possession
  of the prodigious hoard,
  and with it won the ring.
  Over that the brothers
  fought in a fiery exchange:
  Fasolt was felled
  by Fafner, who now nurses the hoard
  as a ferocious dragon.

  The third question now looms.
MIME *thinking hard and utterly enraptured*
       as if infatuated with his own antiquarian knowledge
    and consequently rubbing his hands in glee*
  I see you know   550
  much, Wanderer,
  of the earth's unruly surface.
  Now tell me for sure,
  which race
  lives in the cloudy heights?
WANDERER
  In the cloudy heights
  live the gods:
  Valhalla is where they reside.

Lichtalben sind sie;
560 Licht-Alberich,
Wotan, waltet der Schar.
Aus der Welt-Esche
weihlichstem Aste
schuf er sich einen Schaft:
dorrt der Stamm,
nie verdirbt doch der Speer;
mit seiner Spitze
sperrt Wotan die Welt.
Heil'ger Verträge
570 Treue-Runen
schnitt in den Schaft er ein.
Den Haft der Welt
hält in der Hand,
wer den Speer führt,
den Wotans Faust umspannt:
ihm neigte sich
der Niblungen Heer;
der Riesen Gezücht
zähmte sein Rat:
580 ewig gehorchen sie alle
des Speeres starkem Herrn.
    Er stößt wie unwillkürlich mit dem Speer auf den Boden,
    wovon Mime heftig erschrickt.
Nun rede, weiser Zwerg!
wußt' ich der Fragen Rat?
Behalte mein Haupt ich frei?
MIME *nachdem er den Wanderer mit dem Speer aufmerksam*
    beobachtet hat, gerät nun in große Angst, sucht verwirrt
    nach seinen Gerätschaften, und blickt scheu zur Seite.
Fragen und Haupt
hast du gelöst:
nun, Wandrer, geh deines Weg's!
WANDERER
Was zu wissen dir frommt,
solltest du fragen:
590 Kunde verbürgte mein Kopf.

They are light elves;
over their multitude,   560
Light-Alberich, Wotan, holds sway.
He carved a shaft for himself
out of the most sacrosanct bough
of the world ash-tree:
its trunk may wither,
but the spear will never perish;
with its tip
Wotan secures the world.
Into the shaft he etched
symbols of fidelity   570
to solemn treaties.
Whoever carries the spear
in Wotan's grasp,
will hold the custody
of the world in their hands:
the Nibelung's army
would stoop before him;
the gang of giants
would be in thrall to his counsel:
all will submit for all time   580
to the spear's strong master.
　　He strikes the ground with his spear with a seemingly
　　arbitrary gesture, to which Mime reacts in violent shock.
Say something, wise dwarf!
did I know how to answer?
Am I free to keep my head?
MIME *after he has taken a good look at Wotan with his spear,*
　　he now gets extremely frightened, searching frantically
　　for his appliances and shyly looking to one side.
You've won
the contest and your head:
it's time, Wanderer, to get out!
WANDERER
You were supposed to inquire
after the knowledge you need:
staking my head guaranteed instruction.   590

belebter
Daß du nun nicht weißt,
was dir frommt,
dess' fass' ich jetzt deines als Pfand. –
   Mime erschrickt sichtlich. *
Gastlich nicht
galt mir dein Gruß;
mein Haupt gab ich
in deine Hand,
um mich des Herdes zu freun.
Nach Wettens Pflicht,
600   pfänd' ich nun dich,
lösest du drei
der Fragen nicht leicht.
Drum frische dir, Mime, den Mut!
MIME *sehr schüchtern und zögernd, endlich in furchtsamer*
      Ergebung sich fassend
Lang schon mied ich
mein Heimatland,
lang' schon schied ich
aus der Mutter Schoß:
   verstohlen zum Wanderer ein wenig aufblickend
mir leuchtete Wotans Auge,
zur Höhle lugt' er herein:
610   vor ihm magert
mein Mutterwitz.
Doch frommt mir's nun weise zu sein, –
Wand'rer, frage denn zu!
Vielleicht glückt mir's – gezwungen –
zu lösen des Zwerges Haupt.
WANDERER *wieder gemächlicher sich niederlassend*
Nun, ehrlicher Zwerg!
Sag mir zum ersten!
Welches ist das Geschlecht,
dem Wotan schlimm sich zeigte,
   sehr leise, doch vernehmbar
620   und das doch das liebste ihm lebt?

more lively
As forfeit I now claim your head,
because you haven't a clue
about what it is that you need. –
   Mime is visibly taken aback. *
As guest I think you gave me
a grudging welcome;
I put my head
into your hands
to enjoy your hospitality.
According to the rules of the wager
I now consider you forfeit,   600
if you don't answer these
three questions with ease.
So, Mime, screw up your courage!
MIME *very shyly and hesitantly, finally regaining his poise in*
   timid humility
I've long forgone
my native land,
I've long bid farewell
to my mother's womb:
   furtively glancing up a little at the Wanderer
Wotan's eye shone on me,
he looked into the cave:
my native wit   610
shrinks under his gaze.
Still, it's time to use my wit wisely, –
just ask then, Wanderer!
Perhaps – when pushed – I'm fortunate
to redeem my dwarf's head.
WANDERER *sitting again to make himself more comfortable*
Well, honest dwarf!
Tell me this first!
Which race is it
that Wotan treated so badly,
   very quietly, yet audibly
yet lives as the one he loves most?   620

MIME *sich ermunternd*
> Wenig hört' ich
> von Heldensippen;
> der Frage doch mach' ich mich frei. –
> Die Wälsungen sind
> das Wunschgeschlecht,
> das Wotan zeugte
> und zärtlich liebte,
> zeigt' er auch Ungunst ihm.
>> *sehr lebhaft**
> Siegmund und Sieglind

630
> stammten von Wälse,
> ein wild verzweifeltes
> Zwillingspaar:
>> *mit bedeutungsvoll erhobenem Finger**
> Siegfried zeugten sie selbst,
> den stärksten Wälsungensproß. –

> Behalt' ich, Wandrer,
> zum ersten mein Haupt?
WANDERER *gemütlich*
> Wie doch genau
> das Geschlecht du mir nennst!
> Schlau eracht' ich dich Argen. –

640
> Der ersten Frage
> wardst du frei:
> zum zweiten nun sag mir, Zwerg!
> Ein weiser Niblung
> wahret Siegfried;
> Fafnern soll er ihm fällen,
> daß den Ring er erränge,
> des Hortes Herrscher zu sein.
> Welches Schwert
> muß Siegfried nun schwingen
>> *etwas zurückhaltend*

650
> taug' es zu Fafners Tod?
MIME *seine gegenwärtige Lage immer mehr vergessend, reibt*
> *sich vergnügt die Hände.*
> Nothung heißt

MIME *cheering himself up*
　The lineage of heroes
　I know little about;
　but this question I'll get out of the way. –
　The Wälsungs are
　the gifted race
　that Wotan fathered
　and tenderly loved,
　but treated with disfavour.
　　*very lively**
　Siegmund and Sieglinde,
　that wildly despairing   630
　twin brother and sister,
　are Wälse's children:
　　*raising his finger portentously**
　they begat Siegfried themselves,
　the strongest Wälsung offspring. –

　For the moment, Wanderer,
　do I keep my head?
WANDERER *good-naturedly*
　With such precision
　you've named the race for me!
　I deem you shrewd, but spiteful. –
　The first question   640
　you've got out of the way:
　for the second, dwarf, tell me this!
　A wise Nibelung
　protects Siegfried;
　his charge is to kill Fafner for him,
　that he may get the ring
　and be ruler of the hoard.
　Which sword
　must Siegfried now wield
　　holding back somewhat
　that's fit for Fafner's death?   650
MIME *forgetting his present situation more and more, rubs his
　　hands in delight.*
　Nothung's the name

ein neidliches Schwert;
in einer Esche Stamm
stieß es Wotan:
dem sollt' es geziemen,
der aus dem Stamm es zög'.
Der stärksten Helden
keiner bestand's;
Siegmund, der Kühne
660 konnt's allein:
fechtend führt' er's im Streit,
bis an Wotans Speer es zersprang.
Nun verwahrt die Stücken
ein weiser Schmied;
denn er weiß, daß allein
mit dem Wotansschwert
ein kühnes dummes Kind,
Siegfried, den Wurm versehrt.
     ganz vergnügt
Behalt' ich Zwerg
670 auch zweitens mein Haupt?
WANDERER *lachend*
     Haha, haha, hahahaha!
     Der witzigste bist du
     unter den Weisen;
     wer käm' dir an Klugheit gleich?
     Doch bist du so klug,
     den kindischen Helden
     für Zwergenzwecke zu nützen, –
     mit der dritten Frage
     droh' ich nun.
680 Sag mir, du weiser
     Waffenschmied:
     wer wird aus den starken Stücken
     Nothung, das Schwert, wohl schweißen?
          [Mime] fährt im höchsten Schrecken auf.
MIME *kreischend*
     Die Stücken! Das Schwert!
     O weh, mir schwindelt! –
     Was fang' ich an?

of a pitiless sword;
Wotan plunged it
into the trunk of an ash-tree:
it was deemed to belong to the one
who could pull it out of the trunk.
None of the mightiest
heroes passed muster;
Siegmund, the dauntless hero,
he alone could do it: 660
as warrior he wielded it in combat,
until it shattered on Wotan's spear.
Its pieces are now kept safe
by a wise smith;
he well knows that only
with Wotan's sword
will a dauntless stupid child,
Siegfried, damage the dragon.
   quite breezily
As dwarf do I still keep
my head the second time around?   670
WANDERER *laughing*
Haha, haha, hahahaha!
You're the canniest
among the wise;
who can match your cleverness?
As you are so clever
in using the callow hero
for your dwarf's purposes, –
I'll up the stakes now
with the third question.
Tell me, you wise   680
welder of weapons:
out of Nothung's powerful pieces,
who will actually forge the sword?
   [Mime] jumps up in extreme terror.
MIME *screeching*
The pieces! The sword!
Oh no, I'm getting dizzy! –
How to begin?

Was fällt mir ein?
Verfluchter Stahl!
Daß ich dich gestohlen!
690   Er hat mich vernagelt
in Pein und Not!
Mir bleibt er hart,
ich kann ihn nicht hämmern;
Niet' und Löte
läßt mich im Stich!
Der weiseste Schmied

> *Er wirft wie sinnlos sein Gerät durcheinander und bricht in helle Verzweiflung aus.*

weiß sich nicht Rat!
Wer schweißt nun das Schwert,
schaff' ich es nicht?
700   Das Wunder, wie soll ich's wissen?

> *[Der Wanderer] ist ruhig vom Herd aufgestanden.*

WANDERER
Dreimal solltest du fragen,
dreimal stand ich dir frei: –
nach eitlen Fernen
forschtest du;
doch was zunächst dir sich fand,
was dir nützt, fiel dir nicht ein;
nun ich's errate,
wirst du verrückt:
gewonnen hab' ich
710   das witzige Haupt! –
Jetzt, Fafners kühner Bezwinger,
hör', verfall'ner Zwerg!
'Nur wer das Fürchten
nie erfuhr,
schmiedet Nothung neu.'

> *Mime starrt ihn groß an: er [der Wanderer] wendet sich zum Fortgange.*

Dein weises Haupt
wahre von heut': –

How to think?
Damned steel!
If only I'd never stolen you!
It's nailed me down   690
in agony with no way out!
To me it refuses to yield,
I can't hammer it:
riveting and soldering
get me nowhere!
The wisest smith
   He flings his tools all over the place looking demented
   and erupts in sheer despair.
hasn't a clue!
Who'll forge the sword then,
if I don't?
Am I supposed to know about miracles?   700
   [The Wanderer] has calmly stood up from the hearth.

WANDERER
You were to ask me three questions,
three times I agreed to cooperate: –
your questions
were self-absorbed and remote:
but your most immediate concern,
what you needed, didn't occur to you;
the minute I guessed it,
you went mad:
I've scooped
your canny head! –   710
Now, as for Fafner's bold conqueror,
listen, forfeited dwarf!
'Only he who's
never felt fear,
shall forge Nothung anew.'
   Mime gapes at him open-mouthed: he [the Wanderer]
   turns to go.
From today take care
of your wise head: –

verfallen, laß' ich es dem,
der das Fürchten nicht gelernt.
> *Er wendet sich lächelnd ab und verschwindet schnell im*
> *Walde.*
> *Mime ist wie vernichtet auf den Schemel hinter dem*
> *Amboß zurückgesunken.*

DRITTE SZENE

MIME *Er stiert, grad' vor sich aus, in den sonnig beleuchteten*
Wald hinein, und gerät zunehmend in heftiges Zittern.
720 Verfluchtes Licht!
Was flammt dort die Luft?
Was flackert und lackert, –
was flimmert und schwirrt, –
was schwebt dort und webt,
und wabert umher?
Dort glimmert's und glitzt's
in der Sonne Glut!
Was säuselt und summt,
und saust nun gar?
730 Es brummt und braus't, –
und prasselt hieher!
Dort bricht's durch den Wald,
will auf mich zu!
> *Er bäumt sich vor Entsetzen auf.*
Ein gräßlicher Rachen
reißt sich mir auf:
der Wurm will mich fangen!
Fafner! Fafner!
> *Siegfried bricht aus dem Waldgesträuch hervor.*
> *Mime sinkt schreiend hinter dem Amboß zusammen.*
SIEGFRIED *noch hinter der Szene, während man seine Bewe-*
gung an dem zerkrachenden Gezweige des Gesträuches
gewahrt.
Heda! Du Fauler!
Bist du nun fertig?

it's forfeit; but I'll leave that
to him who's never learned fear!
    With a smile, he turns his back and quickly vanishes in
    the forest.
        Looking annihilated, Mime slumps down on the stool
        behind the anvil.

SCENE THREE

MIME *He stares blankly ahead into the sun-drenched forest,*
        increasingly falling into a state of violent shuddering.
Light be damned!   720
What's setting the air alight?
What's kindling and crackling, –
what's burning and buzzing, –
what's there wafting and weaving,
and swirling around?
It's there glimmering and glittering
in the heat of the sun!
What's rustling and rumbling,
and even starting to rush?
It hums and hurtles, –   730
and clatters this way!
It's there, crashing through the forest,
and making for me!
    He works himself up into a state of terror.
Its hideous jaws
are snapping:
the dragon wants me in its snare!
Fafner! Fafner!
    Siegfried comes stomping out of the forest undergrowth.
    Mime slumps down screaming behind the anvil.
SIEGFRIED *still off-stage, while the audience becomes aware*
        of his movements as he tramples over the branches in the
        undergrowth.
Heda! You idler!
Are you finished yet?

tritt in die Höhle herein
740 Schnell, wie steht's mit dem Schwert?
    Er hält verwundert an.
    Wo steckt der Schmied?
    Stahl er sich fort? –
    Hehe! Mime, du Memme!
    Wo bist du? Wo birgst du dich?
MIME *mit schwacher Stimme hinter dem Amboß*
    Bist du es, Kind?
    Kommst du allein?
SIEGFRIED *lachend*
    Hinter dem Amboß?
    Sag', was schufest du dort?
    Schärftest du mir das Schwert?
MIME *höchst verstört und zerstreut hervorkommend*
750 Das Schwert? Das Schwert?
    Wie möcht' ich's schweißen?
       halb für sich
    'Nur wer das Fürchten
    nie erfuhr,
    schmiedet Nothung neu.' –
    Zu weise ward ich
    für solches Werk.
SIEGFRIED *heftig*
    Wirst du mir reden?
    Soll ich dir raten?
MIME *wie zuvor*
    Wo nähm' ich redlichen Rat?
760 Mein weises Haupt
    hab' ich verwettet:
       vor sich hin starrend
    verfallen, verlor ich's an den,
    der das Fürchten nicht gelernt! –
SIEGFRIED *ungestüm*
    Sind mir das Flausen?
    Willst du mir fliehn?
MIME *allmählich sich etwas fassend*
    Wohl flöh' ich dem,

steps inside the cave

Quick, how's the sword going?   740

Puzzled, he comes to a halt.

Where's the smith?

Did he steal away? –

Hehe! Mime, you coward!

Where are you? Where're you hiding?

MIME *with a weak voice behind the anvil*

Is it you, child?

Are you on your own?

SIEGFRIED *laughing*

Behind the anvil?

Say, what have you been doing there?

Whetting the sword for me?

MIME *coming into the open, highly strung and bewildered*

The sword? The sword?   750

How do I weld it?

in a half-whisper

'Only he who's

never felt fear,

shall forge Nothung anew.' –

I'm too wise

for such work.

SIEGFRIED *vehemently*

Will you talk to me?

Am I supposed to tell you something?

MIME *as before*

Where can I get honest help?

I've forfeited   760

my head, wise as it is:

staring in front of him

it's all over, I've lost it to him

who's not learned fear! –

SIEGFRIED *impetuously*

Are these fancy ideas?

Do you want to fly the coop?

MIME *gradually pulling himself together somewhat*

Of course I'd fly from him

'der's Fürchten kennt.' –
Doch das ließ ich dem Kinde zu lehren;
ich Dummer vergaß,
770   was einzig gut.
Liebe zu mir
sollt' er lernen;
das gelang nun leider faul! –
Wie bring' ich das Fürchten ihm bei?

SIEGFRIED *packt ihn*
He! Muß ich helfen?
Was fegtest du heut'?

MIME
Um dich nur besorgt,
versank ich in Sinnen,
wie ich dich Wichtiges wiese.

SIEGFRIED *lachend*
780   Bis unter den Sitz
warst du versunken:
was Wichtiges fandest du da?

MIME *sich immer mehr fassend*
Das Fürchten lernt' ich für dich,
daß ich's dich Dummen lehre.

SIEGFRIED *mit ruhiger Verwunderung*
Was ist's mit dem Fürchten?

MIME
Erfuhrst du's noch nie,
und willst aus dem Wald
doch fort in die Welt?
Was frommte das festeste Schwert,
790   blieb dir das Fürchten fern.

SIEGFRIED *ungeduldig*
Faulen Rat
erfindest du wohl.

MIME *immer zutraulicher Siegfried näher tretend*
Deiner Mutter Rat
redet aus mir,
was ich gelobte,
muß ich nun lösen:

'who knows what fear is'. –
But that I omitted to teach the child;
stupid me, I forgot
the vital thing.   770
He was supposed to learn
how to love me;
it's a rotten success, that we know! –
How do I teach him fear?

SIEGFRIED *grabbing hold of him*
Hey! Do I have to help?
What have you been polishing today?

MIME
I've been mired in thought,
worried only about you,
how to guide you in vital matters.

SIEGFRIED *laughing*
You were slumped down   780
right under the seat:
what vital matters did you find there?

MIME *pulling himself together more and more*
I was learning fear on your behalf,
so I can teach it to a dunce like you.

SIEGFRIED *with calm surprise*
What's all this about fear?

MIME
You've never felt it,
and yet you want to abandon
the forest for the world?
The best-built sword's of little use,
if fear's given you a wide berth.   790

SIEGFRIED *impatiently*
You're just inventing
addled advice.

MIME *stepping closer to Siegfried more and more confidingly*
It's your mother
speaking through me,
I've got to deliver
what I promised her:

in die listige Welt
dich nicht zu entlassen,
eh' du nicht das Fürchten gelernt. –

SIEGFRIED *heftig*

800   Ist's eine Kunst,
was kenn' ich sie nicht?
Heraus! Was ist's mit dem Fürchten?

MIME

Fühltest du nie
im finstren Wald,
bei Dämmerschein
am dunklen Ort,
wenn fern es säuselt,
summt und saust,
wildes Brummen
810   näher braust: –
wirres Flackern
um dich flimmert,
schwellend Schwirren
zu Leib' dir schwebt: –
        zitternd
fühltest du dann nicht grieselnd
        bebend
Grausen die Glieder dir fahen?
Glühender Schauer
schüttelt die Glieder,
        mit schütternder Stimme
in der Brust bebend und bang
820   berstet hämmernd das Herz?
Fühltest du das noch nicht,
das Fürchten blieb dir dann fremd.

SIEGFRIED *nachsinnend*

Sonderlich seltsam
muß das sein!
Hart und fest,
fühl' ich, steht mir das Herz.
Das Grieseln und Grausen,
das Glühen und Schauern,

not to free you
into the fickle world,
when you've not learned fear. –

SIEGFRIED *vehemently*

If it's a knack,   800
how come I don't know it?
Come on! What's all this about fear?

MIME

Have you never felt
in murky forests,
at twilight dusk
in sunless places,
if there's distant rustling,
rumbling and rushing,
wild humming
hurtling nearer: –   810
chaotic flames
around you swirling,
waves of whirring
wafting upon you: –
    shivering
haven't you then felt a cold sweat
    trembling
of horror taking your limbs in its grip?
Your limbs racked
by scorching terror,
    in a thin quavery voice
your heaving and hammering heart
bursting with anxiety in your breast?   820
If you still don't feel that,
fear to you will for ever be unknown.

SIEGFRIED *pondering*

That's got to be
weirdly strange!
I feel my heart to be
stalwart and strong.
The shuddering and horrifying,
the simmering and shivering,

Hitzen und Schwindeln,
830 Hämmern und Beben:
Gern begehr' ich das Bangen,
 zart
sehnend verlangt mich der Lust! –
Doch wie bringst du,
Mime, mir's bei?
Wie wärst du, Memme mir Meister?

MIME
Folge mir nur,
ich führe dich wohl:
sinnend fand ich es aus.
Ich weiß einen schlimmen Wurm,
840 der würgt' und schlang schon viel:
Fafner lehrt dich das Fürchten,
folgst du mir zu seinem Nest.

SIEGFRIED
Wo liegt er im Nest?

MIME
Neidhöhle
wird es genannt:
im Ost, am Ende des Walds.

SIEGFRIED
Dann wär's nicht weit von der Welt?

MIME
Bei Neidhöhle liegt sie ganz nah'.

SIEGFRIED
Dahin denn sollst du mich führen:
850 lernt' ich das Fürchten,
dann fort in die Welt!
Drum schnell! Schaffe das Schwert,
in der Welt will ich es schwingen.

MIME
Das Schwert? O Not!

SIEGFRIED
Rasch in die Schmiede!
Weis', was du schufst!

sweltering and tottering,
hammering and heaving: 830
I'd love to covet those feelings of fright,
    tenderly
to longingly crave their pleasures! –
But how will you,
Mime, teach me that?
How can a milksop like you be a master?

MIME

Just follow me,
I'll guide you of course:
I've pondered and found a way.
I know of a terrible dragon,
who's choked and chewed up many: 840
Fafner will teach you fear,
if you follow me to his nest.

SIEGFRIED

Where's he lying in his nest?

MIME

Neidhöhle
is its name,
in the east, at forest's end.

SIEGFRIED

So it's not far from the world?

MIME

Neidhöhle's really quite close.

SIEGFRIED

You must take me to this place:
once I've learnt fear,   850
I'm away into the world!
Make it snappy! Make the sword now,
in the world I want to flaunt it.

MIME

The sword? O my!

SIEGFRIED

To the forge, fast!
Let's see what you've done!

MIME

Verfluchter Stahl!
Zu flicken versteh' ich ihn nicht:
den zähen Zauber
860 bezwingt keines Zwergen Kraft.
Wer das Fürchten nicht kennt,
der fänd' wohl eher die Kunst.

SIEGFRIED

Feine Finten
weiß mir der Faule;
daß er ein Stümper,
sollt' er gestehn:
nun lügt er sich listig heraus!
Her mit den Stücken,
fort mit dem Stümper!
    auf den Herd zuschreitend
870 Des Vaters Stahl
fügt sich wohl mir:
ich selbst schweiße das Schwert!
    *Er macht sich, Mimes Gerät durcheinander werfend, mit
    Ungestüm an die Arbeit.*

MIME

Hättest du fleißig
die Kunst gepflegt,
jetzt käm' dir's wahrlich zu gut:
doch läßig warst du
stets in der Lehr';
was willst du Rechtes nun rüsten?

SIEGFRIED

Was der Meister nicht kann,
880 vermöcht' es der Knabe,
hätt' er ihm immer gehorcht?
    Er dreht ihm eine Nase.
Jetzt mach dich fort;
misch dich nicht drein,
sonst fällst du mir mit ins Feuer!
    *Er hat eine große Menge Kohlen auf dem Herd aufge-
    häuft und unterhält in einem fort die Glut, während er*

MIME

Damned steel!
Piecing it together's beyond me:
no dwarf has the power to counter
its stern spell.   860
Someone who doesn't know fear
is more likely to find the knack.

SIEGFRIED

Lofty lies
are all the layabout knows;
admit he's an addle-brain,
that's what he should do:
now he's fibbing, faking a way out!
Bring the pieces here,
bungler, be off!
    striding towards the forge
My father's steel   870
will submit to me:
I'll forge the sword myself!
    *Impetuously, he gets to work, throwing Mime's tools all
    over the place.*

MIME

If you'd worked hard
to hone your skills,
it would surely have served you well:
but you were always
idle at learning;
so how can you get it right now?

SIEGFRIED

If a boy always obeyed his master,
would he ever achieve anything   880
the master can't do?
    He turns his nose up at him.
Now make yourself scarce;
don't interfere,
otherwise you'll fall in my fire as well!
    *He has heaped a large quantity of charcoal onto the forge
    in one go to keep the flame alight, while at the same time*

*die Schwertstücke in den Schraubstock einspannt und sie
zu Spänen zerfeilt.*

*[Mime,] der sich etwas abseits niedergesetzt hat und
Siegfried bei der Arbeit zusieht*

MIME

Was machst du denn da?
Nimm doch die Löte;
den Brei braut' ich schon längst.

SIEGFRIED

Fort mit dem Brei,
ich brauch' ihn nicht;
890 mit Bappe back' ich kein Schwert!

MIME

Du zerfeilst die Feile,
zerreibst die Raspel!
Wie willst du den Stahl zerstampfen?

SIEGFRIED

Zersponnen muß ich
in Späne ihn sehn:
was entzwei ist, zwing' ich mir so.
Er feilt mit großem Eifer fort.

MIME *für sich*

Hier hilft kein Kluger,
das seh' ich klar;
hier hilft dem Dummen
900 die Dummheit allein. –
Wie er sich rührt,
und mächtig regt!
lhm schwindet der Stahl,
doch wird ihm nicht schwül. –
Siegfried hat das Herdfeuer zur hellsten Glut angefacht.
Nun ward ich so alt
wie Höhl' und Wald,
und hab' nicht so was gesehn! –
*Während Siegfried mit ungestümem Eifer fortfährt, die
Schwertstücken zu zerfeilen, setzt sich Mime noch mehr
beiseite.*
Mit dem Schwert gelingt's;
das lern' ich wohl:

securing the pieces of the sword in a vice and filing them
down.

    [Mime] sitting down to one side and watching Siegfried
    as he gets to work

MIME

What are you playing at?
Get the solder right now;
I made the filler ages ago.

SIEGFRIED

Get rid of the filler,
I don't need it;
I don't smelt swords with crap!   890

MIME

You're filing the file smooth,
rubbing the rasp into nothing!
How do you want to crush the steel?

SIEGFRIED

I must grind it down
and look at the bits:
ground asunder, it's for me more pliant.

    He carries on filing with great zeal.

MIME *aside*

Experts can't help here,
that's clear, I see;
here only ignorance
helps the ignorant. –   900
How he exerts himself,
and works at it hard!
He grinds the steel into nothing,
but it's no sweat for him. –

    Siegfried has stoked up the forge fire to maximum heat.

Now I'm as old
as cave and wood,
this all my life I've never seen! –

    While Siegfried carries on filing the pieces of the sword
    into bits with impetuous assiduousness, Mime sits down
    still further to one side.

With the sword it'll all work out;
that much I've learned:

910   furchtlos fegt er's zu ganz.
       Der Wand'rer wußt' es gut. –
       Wie berg' ich nun
       mein banges Haupt?
       Dem kühnen Knaben verfiel's,
       lehrt' ihn nicht Fafner die Furcht!
           mit wachsender Unruhe aufspringend und sich beugend
       Doch weh' mir Armen!
       Wie würgt' er den Wurm,
       erführ' er das Fürchten von ihm?
       Wie erräng' er mir den Ring?
920   Verfluchte Klemme!
       Da klebt' ich fest,
       fänd' ich nicht klugen Rat,
       wie den Furchtlosen selbst ich bezwäng'.
           *[Siegfried] hat nun die Stücken zerfeilt und in einem
           Schmelztiegel gefangen, den er jetzt in die Herdglut stellt.*
   SIEGFRIED
       He, Mime! Geschwind!
           Er [Mime] fährt zusammen und wendet sich zu Siegfried.
       Wie heißt das Schwert,
       das ich in Späne zersponnen?
   MIME
       Nothung nennt sich
       das neidliche Schwert:
           *Mime erzählt das mit einer gewissen Behaglichkeit. 'Wie
           ein Antiquar, der ein Buch anpreist.'**
       deine Mutter gab mir die Mär.
   SIEGFRIED *Unter dem folgenden Gesange nährt Siegfried die
           Glut mit dem Blasebalg.*
930   Nothung! Nothung!
       Neidliches Schwert!
       Was mußtest du zerspringen?
       Zu Spreu nun schuf ich
       die scharfe Pracht,
       im Tiegel brat' ich die Späne.
       Hoho! Hoho!
       Hahei! Hahei! Hoho!

fearlessly he'll polish it into a whole.   910
The Wanderer well knew. –
How to conceal
my harried head?
To the dauntless boy it will be forfeit
if he doesn't learn fear from Fafner!
   jumping up with growing unease and bowing down
But pity poor me!
If he does learn fear from the dragon,
how will he kill it?
How can he get me the ring?
Damned mess!   920
I'm really stuck,
if I don't find a clever way
of getting rid of the bold boy himself.
   [Siegfried] has filed down the pieces and put them in a
   melting-pot, which he now places on the fire in the hearth.

SIEGFRIED
   Hey, Mime! Quickly!
   He [Mime] looks startled and turns to Siegfried.
   What's the name of the sword
   I've been shaving to shreds?

MIME
   Nothung's the name
   of the pitiless sword:
      Mime tells the story with a certain relish. 'Like an anti-
      quarian bookseller going into raptures about a book.'*
   it's a fable your mother passed on to me.

SIEGFRIED *Siegfried stokes the flames with the bellows as he*
   sings the following passage.
   Nothung! Nothung!   930
   Pitiless sword!
   What demanded your destruction?
   Your piercing majesty
   I've turned to chaff,
   the shavings I smelt in the pot.
   Hoho! Hoho!
   Hahei! Hahei! Hoho!

Blase, Balg!
Blase die Glut!
940 Wild im Walde
wuchs ein Baum,
den hab' ich im Forst gefällt:
die braune Esche
brannt' ich zur Kohl';
auf dem Herd nun liegt sie gehäuft.

Hoho! Hoho!
Hahei! Hahei! Hoho!
Blase, Balg!
Blase die Glut!
950 Des Baumes Kohle,
wie brennt sie kühn;
wie glüht sie hell und hehr!
In springenden Funken
sprühet sie auf:
hahei, hoho, hahei! –
zerschmilzt mir des Stahles Spreu.

Hoho! Hoho!
Hahei! Hahei! Hoho!
Blase, Balg!
960 Blase die Glut!
MIME *immer für sich, entfernt sitzend*
Er schmiedet das Schwert,
und Fafner fällt er:
das seh' ich nun deutlich voraus.
Hort und Ring
erringt er im Harst:
wie erwerb' ich mir den Gewinn?
Mit Witz und List
gewinn' ich beides,
und berge heil mein Haupt.
SIEGFRIED *nochmals am Blasebalg*
970 Hoho! Hoho!
Hoho! Hahei! Hahei!

Bellows, blow!
Stoke up the flames!
In the forests I cut down   940
a tree growing
wild in the wood:
by burning the brown ash
I turned it to charcoal;
there it now lies, heaped on the forge.

Hoho! Hoho!
Hahei! Hahei! Hoho!
Bellows, blow!
Stoke up the flames!
The coals from the tree,   950
how boldly they burn;
how clearly and nobly they glow!
They give out sparks,
spraying and leaping:
hahei, hoho, hahei! –
melting for me the chaff of the steel.

Hoho! Hoho!
Hahei! Hahei! Hoho!
Bellows, blow!
Stoke up the flames!   960

MIME *always aside, sitting at a distance*
The sword he'll forge,
and Fafner he'll kill:
that much I can safely predict.
In the rough and tumble,
the hoard and the ring will be his:
but how do I land the loot for myself?
Coolly and cleverly
I'll get my hands on them both,
and recover my head in one piece.

SIEGFRIED *again at the bellows*
Hoho! Hoho!   970
Hoho! Hahei! Hahei!

MIME *im Vordergrunde, für sich*
  Rang er sich müd' mit dem Wurm,
  von der Müh' erlab' ihn ein Trunk:
  aus würz'gen Säften,
  die ich gesammelt,
  brau' ich den Trank für ihn;
  wenig Tropfen nur
  braucht er zu trinken,
  sinnlos sinkt er in Schlaf.
980 Mit der eig'nen Waffe,
  die er sich gewonnen,
      immer belebter
  räum' ich ihn leicht aus dem Weg,
  erlange mir Ring und Hort.
      Er reibt sich vergnügt die Hände.

SIEGFRIED
  Nothung! Nothung!
  Neidliches Schwert!
  Nun schmolz deines Stahles Spreu!
  Im eignen Schweiße
  schwimmst du nun.
      *Er gießt den glühenden Inhalt des Tiegels in eine
      Stangenform und hält diese in die Höhe.*

MIME
  Hei, weiser Wandrer!
990 Dünkt' ich dich dumm?
  Wie gefällt dir nun
  mein feiner Witz?
  Fand ich mir wohl
  Rat und Ruh?

SIEGFRIED
  Bald schwing' ich dich als mein Schwert!
      *Er stößt die gefüllte Stangenform in den Wassereimer:
      Dampf und lautes Gezisch der Kühlung erfolgen.*
  In das Wasser floß
  ein Feuerfluß:
  grimmiger Zorn
  zischt ihm da auf!
1000 Wie sehrend er floß,

MIME *in the foreground, aside*
> Worn out after fighting the dragon,
> he may need a drink to fend off fatigue:
> from the spicy juices
> in my possession,
> I'll prepare a potion for him;
> he needs to drink
> just a few drops
> to sink into a numbing sleep.
> With his own weapon,   980
> which he won for himself,
> > *more and more animated*
> I'll easily put him out of the way,
> and claim the ring and the hoard as mine.
> > *He rubs his hands in delight.*

SIEGFRIED
> Nothung! Nothung!
> Pitiless sword!
> Let your steel's chaff be melted!
> In your own sweat
> you're starting to swim.
> > *He pours the molten contents of the pot into a mould*
> > *and holds it up high.*

MIME
> Hey, wise Wanderer!
> Did I seem to you stupid?   990
> How do you like
> my keen wit now?
> Have I, at last, found
> a way without worry?

SIEGFRIED
> Soon I'll brandish you as my sword!
> > *He plunges the filled-up mould into a bucket of water:*
> > *steam and a loud hissing sound as it cools ensue.*
> Into the water flowed
> a river of fire:
> with ire most fierce
> it hissed up a storm!
> It did flow and wound,   1000

in des Wassers Flut
fließt er nicht mehr.
Starr ward er und steif,
herrisch der harte Stahl:
heißes Blut doch
fließt ihm bald.

> *Er stößt den Stahl in die Herdglut.*

> *Mime ist vergnügt aufgesprungen; er holt verschiedene Gefäße hervor, schüttet aus ihnen Gewürz und Kräuter in einen Kochtopf, und sucht diesen auf dem Herd anzubringen.*

> *Siegfried der die Blasebälge wieder mächtig anzieht*

Nun schwitze noch einmal,
daß ich dich schweiße!
Nothung, neidliches Schwert!

> *Er beobachtet während der Arbeit Mime, welcher vom andern Ende des Herdes her seinen Topf sorgsam an die Glut stellt.*

1010 Was schafft der Tölpel
dort mit dem Topf?
Brenn' ich hier Stahl,
braust du dort Sudel?

MIME

Zuschanden kam ein Schmied;
den Lehrer sein Knabe lehrt:
mit der Kunst nun ist's beim Alten aus,
als Koch dient er dem Kind.
Brennt es das Eisen zu Brei,
aus Eiern braut
1020 der Alte ihm Sud.

> *Er fährt fort zu kochen.*

SIEGFRIED

Mime, der Künstler,
lernt jetzt kochen;
das Schmieden schmeckt ihm nicht mehr.
Seine Schwerter alle
hab' ich zerschmissen:
was er kocht, ich kost' es ihm nicht!

but in the waters' great stream,
it flows no more.
It's become rigid and stiff,
its steel hard and haughty:
but on its blade soon
hot blood will flow.

He thrusts the sword into the forge fire.

Mime has jumped up in delight; he brings out different receptacles and out of them shakes spices and herbs into a saucepan, which he tries to place over the fire in the forge.

Siegfried who is strenuously operating the bellows again

Now start sweating again,
so I can weld you together!
Nothung, pitiless sword!

While he is working, he observes Mime, who at the other end of the forge is carefully putting his saucepan on the fire.

What's the dolt doing   1010
there with that pan?
As I'm melting steel here,
are you brewing swill there?

MIME

What dishonour for the smith;
teacher's being taught by his junior:
the old man's really lost it
now he serves the child as cook.
A boy burns iron into soup,
as his old tutor brews him
soup out of eggs.   1020

He continues to cook.

SIEGFRIED

Mime, the artist,
learns how to cook;
his taste for forging gone.
As for his swords,
I've smashed the lot:
and whatever he cooks, I won't taste!

Unter dem Folgenden zieht Siegfried die Stangenform aus
der Glut, zerschlägt sie und legt den glühenden Stahl auf
dem Amboß zurecht.

Das Fürchten zu lernen
will er mich führen,
ein Ferner soll es mich lehren:
was am besten er kann,
mir bringt er's nicht bei:
als Stümper besteht er in Allem!
    während des Schmiedens
Hoho! Hoho! Hahei!
Schmiede, mein Hammer,
ein hartes Schwert!
Hoho! Hahei!
Hoho! Hahei!

Einst färbte Blut
dein falbes Blau,
sein rotes Rieseln
rötete dich;
kalt lachtest du da,
das warme lecktest du kühl!
Heiaho! Haha!
Haheiaha!
Nun hat die Glut
dich rot geglüht;
deine weiche Härte
dem Hammer weicht:
zornig sprühst du mir Funken,
daß ich dich Spröden gezähmt.
Heiaho! Heiaho!
Heiahohohohohoho!
Hahei! Hahei! Hahei!
MIME *beiseite*
Er schafft sich ein scharfes Schwert,
Fafner zu fällen,
der Zwerge Feind;
ich braut' ein Truggetränk,
Siegfried zu fangen,

1030

1040

1050

During the following passage, Siegfried pulls the mould
out of the fire and breaks it off to get the red-hot steel
ready on the anvil.

He wants to lead me
to someone remote,
who'll teach me how to learn fear:
me he can't teach   1030
even what he does best:
he bungles all he touches!
   while forging
Hoho! Hoho! Hahei!
Forge, my hammer,
a ruthless sword!
Hoho! Hahei!
Hoho! Hahei!

Blood did once stain
your faded blue,
its red trickles   1040
making you blush;
coldly you laughed,
coolly licking the warmth!
Heiaho! Haha!
Haheiaha!
Now you glow red
from the burning coals;
your hard core softened,
it yields to my hammer:
you spit sparks at me in anger,   1050
as I temper your brittle ways.
Heiaho! Heiaho!
Heiahohohohoho!
Hahei! Hahei! Hahei!

MIME *aside*
He's making a sharp sword of his own
to fell Fafner,
the dwarfs' enemy;
I've brewed a potion of tricks
to trap Siegfried

1060   dem Fafner fiel.
         Gelingen muß mir die List;
         lachen muß mir der Lohn!
              Mime beschäftigt sich während des folgenden damit, den
              Inhalt des Topfes in eine Flasche zu gießen.
         SIEGFRIED
         Hoho! Hoho!
         Hoho! Hahei!
         Schmiede, mein Hammer,
         ein hartes Schwert!
         Hoho! Hahei!
         Hoho! Hahei!
         Der frohen Funken
1070   wie freu' ich mich;
         es ziert den Kühnen
         des Zornes Kraft.
         Lustig lachst du mich an,
         stellst du auch grimm dich und gram!
         Heiaho, haha,
         haheia ha!
         Durch Glut und Hammer
         glückt' es mir;
         mit starken Schlägen
1080   streckt' ich dich:
         nun schwinde die rote Scham,
         werde kalt und hart, wie du kannst!
              Er schwingt den Stahl und stößt ihn in den Wasser-
              eimer.
         Heiaho! Heiaho!
         Heiahohohohoho!
         Heiah!
              Er lacht bei dem Gezisch laut auf.
              Während Siegfried die geschmiedete Schwertklinge
              in dem Griffhefte befestigt, treibt sich Mime mit der
              Flasche im Vordergrund umher.
         MIME
         Den der Bruder schuf,
         den schimmernden Reif,

when Fafner falls.1060
My ruse must work;
my reward must come laughing my way!

*During the following passage, Mime is busy with pour-
ing the contents of the saucepan into a bottle.*

SIEGFRIED

Hoho! Hoho!
Hoho! Hahei!
Forge, my hammer,
a ruthless sword!
Hoho! Hahei!
Hoho! Hahei!
How I rejoice
in those happy sparks;1070
the force of wrath
enhances the bold.
Happy with laughter I see you,
though you pretend to be fierce and sad!
Heiaho, haha,
haheia ha!
The heat and the hammer
helped me carry it off;
striking with might
I've laid you out straight:1080
away now with blushful shame,
be as cold and hard as you can!

*He brandishes the steel and plunges it into a bucket of
water.*

Heiaho! Heiaho!
Heiahohohohoho!
Heiah!

At the sound of the hissing, he bursts out laughing.

*As Siegfried is fastening the forged blade of the sword
to its hilt, Mime is busy roaming around with his bottle
in the foreground.*

MIME

The gleaming ring
made by my brother,

in den er gezaubert
zwingende Kraft,
1090 das helle Gold,
das zum Herrscher macht,
ihn hab' ich gewonnen,
ich walte sein!
> *Er trippelt, mit zunehmender Vergnügtheit, lebhaft um-*
> *her.*
>> *Siegfried mit dem kleinen Hammer arbeitend*
>> *Er feilt und schleift.*

Alberich selbst,
der einst mich band,
> *Falsett*

zur Zwergenfrone
zwing' ich ihn nun;
als Niblungenfürst
fahr' ich darnieder,
1100 gehorchen soll mir
alles Heer.
> *Siegfried wieder hämmernd*

Der verachtete Zwerg,
wie wird er geehrt!
Zu dem Horte hin drängt sich
Gott und Held.
> *mit immer lebhafteren Gebärden*

Vor meinem Nicken
neigt sich die Welt;
> *Siegfried glättet mit den letzten Schlägen die Nieten des*
> *Griffheftes und faßt das Schwert nun.*

vor meinem Zorne
zittert sie hin!

SIEGFRIED
1110 Nothung! Nothung!
Neidliches Schwert!
Jetzt haftest du wieder im Heft.

MIME
Dann wahrlich müht sich
Mime nicht mehr:

who magically endowed it
with bludgeoning strength,
its shining gold   1090
making me ruler:
I've won it,
I shall prevail!
> *He breezily scurries around increasingly pleased with*
> *himself.*
>> *Siegfried working with the small hammer*
>> *He files and whets [the blade].*

Alberich himself,
who once made me his slave,
> *falsetto*

I'll force in an instant
to toil like a dwarf;
as Nibelung ruler,
I'll go down there,
where his forces will   1100
all have to obey me.
>> *Siegfried hammering again*

As a dwarf once scorned,
how honoured I'll be!
Gods and heroes
will flock to the hoard.
> *with gestures that are constantly more animated*

At a nod from me,
the world will bow before me;
> *Siegfried smooths down the rivets of the hilt with the*
> *last strokes of his hammer and then grabs the sword.*

at my fury,
it will quake in its boots!

SIEGFRIED
Nothung! Nothung!   1110
Pitiless sword!
Now you're home in your hilt again.

MIME
Then Mime truly bids
farewell to the grind:

SIEGFRIED
   Warst du entzwei,
   ich zwang dich zu ganz;
   kein Schlag soll nun dich mehr zerschlagen.

MIME
   ihm schaffen andre
   den ew'gen Schatz.

SIEGFRIED
1120   Dem sterbenden Vater
   zersprang der Stahl;
   der lebende Sohn
   schuf ihn neu:
   nun lacht ihm sein heller Schein,
   seine Schärfe schneidet ihm hart.

MIME
   Mime, der Kühne,
   Mime ist König,
      [Siegfried] das Schwert vor sich schwingend
   Fürst der Alben,
   Walter des Alls!

SIEGFRIED
1130   Nothung! Nothung!
   Neidliches Schwert!
   Zum Leben weckt' ich dich wieder.
   Tot lagst du
   in Trümmern dort,
   jetzt leuchtest du trotzig und hehr.

MIME
   Hei, Mime! Wie glückte dir das!

SIEGFRIED
   Zeige den Schächern
   nun deinen Schein!

MIME
   Wer hätte wohl das gedacht!

SEIGFRIED
1140   Schlage den Falschen,
   fälle den Schelm!

SIEGFRIED

In pieces you were,
whole now I've made you;
no blows again shall rent you asunder.

MIME

others must nurture
the infinite hoard.

SIEGFRIED

My dying father   1120
saw the steel snap;
his living son
made it new:
now its brilliance laughs,
its edge will cut sharply.

MIME

Mime, the undaunted,
Mime is king,
   [Siegfried] outwardly brandishing the sword
prince of elves,
ruler of the universe!

SIEGFRIED

Nothung! Nothung!   1130
Pitiless sword!
I've returned you to life anew.
Lifeless you lay
there in ruins,
now you emit stubbornness and pride.

MIME

Hey, Mime! How fortunate you are!

SIEGFRIED

Show the murderers
now what you're like!

MIME

Who'd have thought it possible!

SIEGFRIED

Death to the deceivers,   1140
kill the rogue!

Schau, Mime, du Schmied: –

Er holt mit dem Schwert aus.

So schneidet Siegfrieds Schwert!

Er schlägt auf den Amboß, welchen er, von oben bis unten, in zwei Stücken zerspaltet, so daß er unter großem Gepolter auseinander fällt. Mime, welcher in höchster Verzückung sich auf einen Schemel geschwungen hatte, fällt vor Schreck sitzlings zu Boden. Siegfried hält jauchzend das Schwert in die Höhe.

Der Vorhang fällt [schnell*].

Look, Mime, smith that you are: –
> *He raises the sword, getting ready to strike.*

Siegfried's sword cuts like this!
> *He strikes the anvil, slashing it from top to bottom into two pieces so that it falls apart with a deafening noise. Mime, who has swung himself onto a stool in heady rapture, falls with his rear end first to the ground in fright. Siegfried holds the sword jubilantly aloft.*

> *The curtain falls [quickly*].*

ZWEITER AUFZUG

VORSPIEL UND ERSTE SZENE

Tiefer Wald

Der Vorhang geht auf [Takt 96]. – Ganz im Hintergrunde die Öffnung einer Höhle. Der Boden hebt sich bis zur Mitte der Bühne, wo er eine kleine Hochebene bildet; von da senkt er sich nach hinten, der Höhle zu, wieder abwärts, so daß von dieser nur der obere Teil der Öffnung dem Zuschauer sichtbar ist. Links gewahrt man durch Waldbäume eine zerklüftete Felsenwand. – Finstere Nacht, am dichtesten über dem Hintergrunde, wo anfänglich der Blick des Zuschauers gar nichts zu unterscheiden vermag. Alberich, an der Felsenwand gelagert, duster brütend.

ALBERICH
   In Wald und Nacht
   vor Neidhöhl' halt ich Wacht:
   es lauscht mein Ohr,
   mühvoll lugt mein Aug'. –
   Banger Tag,
   bebst du schon auf?
1150   Dämmerst du dort
   durch das Dunkel auf?
     Aus dem Walde von rechts her erhebt sich Sturmwind;
     ein bläulicher Glanz leuchtet von eben daher.
   Welcher Glanz glitzert dort auf? –
   Näher schimmert
   ein heller Schein: –
   es rennt wie ein leuchtendes Roß,
   bricht durch den Wald
   brausend daher? –
   Naht schon des Wurmes Würger?
   Ist's schon, der Fafner fällt?
     Der Sturmwind legt sich wieder. Der Glanz verlischt.

ACT TWO

PRELUDE AND SCENE ONE

Deep in the forest

The curtain rises [bar 96]. – The opening of a cave can be seen far into the background. The ground gets steeper towards the middle of the stage, where it forms a small plateau; it sinks lower from there and slopes down towards the cave in such a way that only the upper part of the cave is visible to the audience. On the left, through the trees of the forest, a fissured rock-face can be seen. – The night is sombre and at its darkest envelops the background, where the audience at first is unable to make anything out. Alberich, situated at the cliff-face, darkly brooding.

ALBERICH
In woodland at night
I keep watch before Neidhöhle:
my ears alert,
my eyes straining to see. –
Day of unease,
do you wake with a shudder so soon?
There through the dark
are you dawning?
   A storm wind gathers force from the forest on the right; a
   bluish light is shining from the same direction.
What light flickers from afar? –
A bright gleam
dances closer: –
it races like a shining horse;
is it breaking through woodland,
hurtling this way? –
Is the dragon's slayer so near?
Is it Fafner's killer already?
   The storm wind dies down. The light fades away.

1160 Das Licht erlischt, –
der Glanz barg sich dem Blick:
Nacht ist's wieder. –

*Der Wanderer tritt aus dem Wald und hält Alberich ge-
genüber an.*

Wer naht dort schimmernd im Schatten?

DER WANDERER
Zur Neidhöhle
fuhr ich bei Nacht: –
wen gewahr' ich im Dunkel dort?

*Wie aus einem plötzlich zerreißenden Gewölk bricht
Mondschein herein und beleuchtet des Wanderers Ge-
stalt.*

*Alberich erkennt den Wanderer, fährt erschrocken zu-
rück, bricht aber sogleich in höchste Wut gegen ihn aus.*

ALBERICH
Du selbst läßt dich hier sehn? –
Was willst du hier?
Fort, aus dem Weg!
1170 Von dannen, schamloser Dieb!

WANDERER *ruhig*
Schwarz-Alberich,
schweifst du hier?
Hütest du Fafners Haus?

ALBERICH
Jagst du auf neue
Neidtat umher?
Weile nicht hier,
weiche von hinnen!
Genug des Truges
tränkte die Stätte mit Not;
1180 drum, du Frecher,
laß sie jetzt frei!

WANDERER
Zu schauen kam ich,
nicht zu schaffen:
wer wehrte mir Wandrers Fahrt?

The light's going out, –   1160
its glow is hidden from sight:
night's upon me again. –
> *The Wanderer comes out of the forest and stops opposite*
> *Alberich.*
Who's there glinting in the shadows?

THE WANDERER
During the night I've travelled
to Neidhöhle: –
who's that I see there in darkness?
> *As if from the sudden parting of a cloud, moonlight*
> *streams in and lights up the Wanderer's figure.*
>
>   *Alberich recognizes the Wanderer, pulls back in shock,*
> *but at the same time flies into an intense rage directed*
> *against him.*

ALBERICH
You dare show your face here? –
What is it you want?
Leave, out of the way!
Just scram, unscrupulous thief!   1170

WANDERER *calmly*
Black Alberich,
hanging about here?
Minding Fafner's house?

ALBERICH
Are you hunting around
for new pitiless deeds?
Don't loiter here,
turn around and be gone!
Enough of your lies
soaking this place with desperation;
for this reason, brazen bully,   1180
leave it well alone!

WANDERER
I came to observe,
not to interfere:
do you deny me a Wanderer's travels?

ALBERICH

Du Rat wütender Ränke!
Wär' ich dir zu Lieb'
doch noch dumm, wie damals,
als du mich Blöden bandest:
wie leicht geriet es,
1190   den Ring mir
    wütend
         nochmals zu rauben? –
Hab Acht! Deine Kunst
kenne ich wohl; –
   höhnisch
doch wo du schwach bist,
blieb mir auch nicht verschwiegen: –
  Bleibt im Tempo (auch in den ruhigeren Momenten muß
  die dämonische, wie verhaltene Wuth Alberichs immer
  fühlbar bleiben). *
mit meinen Schätzen
zahltest du Schulden,
mein Ring zahlte
der Riesen Müh',
die deine Burg dir gebaut.
1200 Was mit den Trotz'gen
einst du vertragen,
dess' Runen wahrt noch heut
deines Speeres herrischer Schaft:
nicht du darfst,
was als Zoll du gezahlt,
den Riesen wieder entreißen:
du selbst zerspelltest
deines Speeres Schaft;
in deiner Hand
1210 der herrische Stab,
der starke, zerstiebte wie Spreu!

WANDERER

Durch Vertrages Treuerunen
band er dich
Bösen mir nicht:

ALBERICH

You godfather of insidious gimmicks!
If I were to do you a favour,
just as stupidly as I did
when you tied me up, dolt that I was:
how easy would it be
to let my ring   1190
  furiously
            be stolen again? –
Take heed! I know well
the way you work; –
  sardonically
but your weakness
is no secret to me either: –
  *Stays in tempo (even at calmer moments Alberich's de-
  monic as well as suppressed rage must always be palp-
  able).* *
you paid off debts
with my treasures,
my ring paid for
the giants' sweat
that built your castle.
What you contracted   1200
once with that hostile pair
is still preserved today
in the runes of your imperious spear:
you cannot
wrest back from the giants
the dues you've settled:
you'd smash the shaft
of your spear yourself;
the haughty staff,
that power in your hand,   1210
would turn to dust!

WANDERER

Its contractual runes of trust
did not bind
your evil ways to me:

dich beugt er mir durch seine Kraft:
zum Krieg drum wahr' ich ihn wohl.

ALBERICH

Wie stark du dräu'st
in trotziger Stärke,
und wie dir's im Busen doch bangt! –
1220 Verfallen dem Tod
durch meinen Fluch
ist des Hortes Hüter: –
wer wird ihn beerben?
Wird der neidliche Hort
dem Niblungen wieder gehören?
Das sehrt dich mit ew'ger Sorge!
Denn fass' ich ihn wieder
einst in der Faust,
anders als dumme Riesen,
1230 üb' ich des Ringes Kraft: –
dann zittre der Helden
ewiger Hüter!
Walhalls Höhen
stürm' ich mit Hellas Heer:
der Welt walte dann ich. –

> *Nach seinen mit äußerster Heftigkeit hervorgestoßenen*
> *Worten macht Alberich eine trotzig triumphirende Ge-*
> *bärde in der er einen Moment lang verharrt.* *

WANDERER *ruhig*

Deinen Sinn kenn' ich wohl,
doch sorgt er mich nicht.
Des Ringes waltet,
wer ihn gewinnt.

ALBERICH *belebter*

1240 Wie dunkel sprichst du,
was ich deutlich doch weiß! –
An Heldensöhne
hält sich dein Trotz,
> *höhnisch*
die traut deinem Blute entblüht?
Pflegtest du wohl eines Knaben,
der klug die Frucht dir pflücke,

you bow to me through its force:
for that good reason I keep it for war.

ALBERICH

How strongly you loom
with stubborn force,
and how fear still stalks your heart! –
Consequent on my curse,   1220
a slave to death
is he who guards the hoard: –
who will inherit it?
Will the hoard, craved for by all,
be the Nibelung's once more?
That eternal fear cuts you to the quick!
Forget stupid giants;
once I ever hold it
again in my grasp,
I shall use the ring's power: –   1230
be afraid,
eternal champion of heroes!
With Hella's armies,
I'll storm the heights of Valhalla:
then the world will be my domain. –

> *After these words, which he has spewed out with extreme*
> *violence, Alberich indulges for a moment in a defiant ges-*
> *ture of triumph.* *

WANDERER *calmly*

Of course I know your plan:
but it doesn't worry me.
Whoever wins the ring,
its domain is his.

ALBERICH *livelier*

How ominously you speak   1240
of what I obviously know! –
In your defiance, do you abide
by the sons of heroes,
    sardonically
that comforting offspring of your blood?
Isn't it true that you've fostered a boy,
who'll discreetly pluck the fruit

 immer heftiger
 die du nicht brechen darfst? –
WANDERER
 Mit mir nicht,
 hadre mit Mime;
  leicht
1250 dein Bruder bringt dir Gefahr:
 einen Knaben führt er daher,
 der Fafner ihm fällen soll.
 Nichts weiß der von mir,
 der Niblung nützt ihn für sich.
 Drum sag' ich dir, Gesell:
 tue frei, wie dir's frommt!
  Alberich macht eine Gebärde heftiger Neugierde.
 Höre mich wohl,
 sei auf der Hut!
 Nicht kennt der Knabe den Ring;
1260 doch Mime kundet' ihn aus.
ALBERICH *heftig*
 Deine Hand hieltest du vom Hort?
WANDERER
 Wen ich liebe,
 lass' ich für sich gewähren:
 er steh' oder fall',
 sein Herr ist er;
 Helden nur können mir frommen.
ALBERICH
 Mit Mime räng' ich
 allein um den Ring?
WANDERER
 Außer dir begehrt er
1270 einzig das Gold.
ALBERICH
 Und dennoch gewänn' ich ihn nicht?
WANDERER *ruhig näher tretend*
 Ein Helde naht,
 den Hort zu befrei'n;
 zwei Niblungen geizen das Gold;

getting more violent
that you're not allowed to touch? –
WANDERER
Your quarrel's with Mime,
not with me;
   lightly
your brother's bringing you danger: 1250
he's bringing a boy
who's to kill Fafner on his behalf.
The Nibelung knows nothing about me;
he's exploiting the boy for himself.
Therefore I say to you, friend:
do exactly as you see fit!
   Alberich gives off signs of ferocious curiosity.
Hear me out,
watch your back!
The boy doesn't know what the ring is;
but Mime could tell him.   1260
ALBERICH *vehemently*
You'll keep your hands off the hoard?
WANDERER
I'll let the one I love
fend for himself:
whether he stands or falls,
he's his own master;
I have use only for heroes.
ALBERICH
Is Mime my only
rival for the ring?
WANDERER
Only he craves the gold,
except you.   1270
ALBERICH
And still I won't capture it?
WANDERER *calmly stepping closer*
A hero's close,
who'll cut the hoard loose;
two Nibelungs lust for the gold;

Fafner fällt,
der den Ring bewacht: –
wer ihn rafft, hat ihn gewonnen. –
Willst du noch mehr?
Dort liegt der Wurm: –
Er wendet sich nach der Höhle.

1280 warnst du ihn vor dem Tod,
willig wohl ließ' er den Tand; –
ich selber weck' ihn dir auf.
Er stellt sich auf die Anhöhe vor der Höhle und ruft hinein.
Fafner! Fafner!
Erwache, Wurm!

ALBERICH *mit gespanntem Erstaunen, für sich*
Was beginnt der Wilde?
Gönnt er mir's wirklich?

FAFNERS STIMME *durch ein starkes Sprachrohr*
Wer stört mir den Schlaf?

WANDERER *der Höhle zugewandt*
Gekommen ist einer,
Not dir zu künden;
1290 er lohnt dir's mit dem Leben,
lohnst du das Leben ihm
mit dem Horte, den du hütest.
Er beugt sein Ohr lauschend der Höhle zu.

FAFNERS STIMME
Was will er?

ALBERICH *Er ist dem Wanderer zur Seite getreten und ruft in die Höhle.*
Wache, Fafner!
Wache, du Wurm!
Ein starker Helde naht:
dich heil'gen will er bestehn. –

FAFNERS STIMME
Mich hungert sein'.

WANDERER
Kühn ist des Kindes Kraft,
1300 scharf schneidet sein Schwert.

Fafner guards the ring,
and falls: –
who grabs it wins it. –
What more do you want?
The dragon's lying there: –
   He turns towards the cave.
perhaps he'll be keen to let the toy go,   1280
if you warn him he's going to die; –
I'll rouse him for you myself.
   He stands on the plateau in front of the cave and shouts
   inside.
Fafner! Fafner!
Dragon, wake up!

ALBERICH *with eager astonishment, aside*
What's the wild god up to?
Will he really let me have it?

FAFNER'S VOICE *through a loud speaking-trumpet*
Who stirs me from my sleep?

WANDERER *facing the cave*
Someone's come
to tell you tales of disaster;
he'll reward you with your life,   1290
if you reward his life
with the hoard you're guarding.
   He cocks an ear towards the cave, listening intently.

FAFNER'S VOICE
What's his wish?

ALBERICH *He walks to the Wanderer's side and shouts into*
   the cave.
Wake up, Fafner!
You dragon, wake up!
A powerful hero's closing in:
he wishes to outwit Your Holiness. –

FAFNER'S VOICE
I'm hungry for him.

WANDERER
The boy is strong and intrepid,
the cut of his sword is sharp.   1300

ALBERICH

    Den goldnen Reif
    geizt er allein:
    laß mir den Ring zum Lohn,
    so wend' ich den Streit;
    du wahrest den Hort,
    und ruhig lebst du lang. –

FAFNERS STIMME

    Ich lieg' und besitz': –
      gähnend
    laßt mich schlafen! –
      Er [der Wanderer] lacht auf und wendet sich dann wieder
      zu Alberich.

WANDERER

    Nun, Alberich! Das schlug fehl!
1310   Doch schilt mich nicht mehr Schelm!
    Dies eine, rat' ich,
    achte noch wohl! –
      vertraulich zum ihm [Alberich] tretend
    Alles ist nach seiner Art:
    an ihr wirst du nichts ändern. –
      Ganz leichthin zu sprechen*
    Ich lass' dir die Stätte,
    stelle dich fest:
    versuch's mit Mime, dem Bruder;
    der Art ja versiehst du dich besser.
      zum Abgange gewendet
    Was anders ist, –
1320   das lerne nun auch!
      Er verschwindet schnell im Walde. Sturmwind erhebt
      sich, heller Glanz bricht aus: dann vergeht beides schnell.
      Alberich blickt dem davonjagenden Wanderer nach.

ALBERICH

    Da reitet er hin
    auf lichtem Roß;
    mich läßt er in Sorg' und Spott.
    Doch lacht nur zu,
    ihr leichtsinniges,

ALBERICH
  The golden ring
  is all he lusts for:
  if you reward me with that,
  I'll turn the fight around;
  you'll keep the hoard,
  and live in peace ever after. –

FAFNER'S VOICE
  Here is my place and here I prevail: –
    yawning
  let me sleep! –
    He [the Wanderer] bursts out laughing and then turns
    again to Alberich.

WANDERER
  Well, Alberich! What a flop!
  But berate me no more, rogue!   1310
  I'll tell you one thing,
  and take careful note! –
    approaching him [Alberich] in confidence
  All and sundry are of their kind:
  nothing you do can change it. –
    *To be said quite offhandedly**
  I cede this place to you,
  stand your ground:
  try it with Mime, your brother;
  you surely know his kind better.
    turns to leave
  What's not your kind, –
  learn that too while you're about it!   1320
    He vanishes quickly into the forest. A storm wind gathers
    force, a bright light shines out: then both rapidly disap-
    pear. Alberich looks on as the Wanderer speeds away.

ALBERICH
  Away he rides
  on his sprightly steed;
  he's left me tormented and taunted.
  Just laugh away,
  you frivolous,

lustgieriges
Göttergelichter!
Euch seh' ich
noch alle vergehn!
1330 Solang' das Gold
am Lichte glänzt,
hält ein Wissender Wacht: –
trügen wird euch sein Trotz!
> *Er schlüpft zur Seite in das Geklüft. – Die Bühne bleibt*
> *leer. –*
> *Morgendämmerung*

ZWEITE SZENE

Bei anbrechendem Tage treten Siegfried und Mime auf. Sieg-
fried trägt das Schwert in einem Gehenke von Bastseil. Mime
erspäht genau die Stätte; er forscht endlich dem Hintergrunde
zu, welcher, während die Anhöhe im mittleren Vordergrunde
später immer heller von der Sonne beleuchtet wird, in finstrem
Schatten bleibt; dann bedeutet er Siegfried.

MIME
Wir sind zur Stelle;
bleib hier stehn!
> *[Siegfried] setzt sich unter der Linde nieder und schaut*
> *sich um.*
SIEGFRIED
Hier soll ich das Fürchten lernen?
Fern hast du mich geleitet;
eine volle Nacht im Walde
selbander wanderten wir.
1340 Nun sollst du, Mime,
mich meiden!
Lern' ich hier nicht,
was ich lernen soll,
allein zieh' ich dann weiter:
dich endlich werd' ich da los!

godly vermin
avid for pleasure!
I'll see you
all vanish yet!
As long as the gold   1330
shines in the light,
someone who knows keeps watch: –
his defiance will deceive you!

> *He slips to one side into the chasms. – The stage stays empty. –*
> *daybreak*

SCENE TWO

Siegfried and Mime enter as day begins to break. Siegfried is carrying his sword in a belt made of strong fibre. Mime takes a good look at the area; eventually he starts finding out what is towards the back of it, a place which remains in dark shadow while the plateau in the centre foreground later catches the sun and is more and more brightly lit; he then gives Siegfried a sign.

MIME

We're there;
stop here!

> *[Siegfried] sits down under the linden-tree and looks around.*

SIEGFRIED

Is this where I'm supposed to learn fear?
You've led me a long way;
we've spent all night
wandering in the wood together.
It's about time, Mime,   1340
to leave me!
If I don't learn here
what I'm supposed to learn,
then I'll go on alone:
I'll be done with you at last!

MIME *setzt sich ihm gegenüber, so daß er die Höhle immer*
   noch im Auge behält.
   Glaube, Liebster,
   lernst du heut' und hier
   das Fürchten nicht,
   an andrem Ort,
1350   zu andrer Zeit,
   schwerlich erfährst du's je. –
   Siehst du dort
   den dunklen Höhlenschlund?
   Darin wohnt
   ein gräulich wilder Wurm:
   unmaßen grimmig
   ist er und groß,
   ein schrecklicher Rachen
   reißt sich ihm auf;
1360   mit Haut und Haar,
   auf einen Happ,
   verschlingt der Schlimme dich wohl.
SIEGFRIED *immer unter der Linde sitzend*
   Gut ist's, den Schlund ihm zu schließen:
   drum biet' ich mich nicht dem Gebiß.
MIME
   Giftig gießt sich
   ein Geifer ihm aus:
   wen mit des Speichels
   Schweiß er bespeit,
   dem schwinden wohl Fleisch und Gebein.
SIEGFRIED
1370   Daß des Geifers Gift mich nicht sehre,
   weich' ich zur Seite dem Wurm.
MIME
   Ein Schlangenschweif
   schlägt sich ihm auf:
   wen er damit umschlingt
   und fest umschließt,
   dem brechen die Glieder wie Glas!

MIME *sits opposite him, so that he can always keep an eye on
    the cave.*

  Rest assured, dearest,
  that if you don't learn fear
  here and now,
  you'll find it hard to learn it
  somewhere else,   1350
  some other time. –
  There, do you see
  the cave's dark throat?
  In it dwells
  an atrociously savage dragon:
  he's big and cruel
  beyond belief,
  with monstrous jaws
  gaping wide;
  the beast will swallow you soon enough,   1360
  skin and bone,
  in one big bite.

SIEGFRIED *remaining seated under the linden-tree*
  So it'll be good to stuff up his throat:
  then his chops won't feel I'm on offer.

MIME
  Poisonous sputum
  spouts from his mouth:
  whoever gets spat on
  with pockets of spit,
  truly their flesh and bone will shrivel.

SIEGFRIED
  The sputum's poison won't harm me,   1370
  once I move to the dragon's side.

MIME
  He's got the tail of a snake
  that he opens and uses to strike:
  whoever he gets in its coil
  and gripped in its vice,
  their limbs will break like glass!

SIEGFRIED

Vor des Schweifes Schwang mich zu wahren,
halt’ ich den Argen im Aug’. –
Doch heiße mich das:
1380   hat der Wurm ein Herz?

MIME

Ein grimmiges, hartes Herz!

SIEGFRIED

Das sitzt ihm doch,
wo es jedem schlägt,
trag’ es Mann oder Tier?

MIME

Gewiß, Knabe,
da führt’s auch der Wurm.
Jetzt kommt dir das Fürchten wohl an?
    *Siegfried, der bisher nachlässig ausgestreckt, erhebt sich
    rasch zum Sitz.*

SIEGFRIED

Nothung stoß’ ich
dem Stolzen ins Herz!
1390   Soll das etwa Fürchten heißen? –
He! Du Alter!
Ist das alles,
was deine List
mich lehren kann?
Fahr’ deines Wegs dann weiter:
das Fürchten lern’ ich hier nicht.

MIME

Wart’ es nur ab!
Was ich dir sage,
dünke dich tauber Schall:
1400   ihn selber mußt du
hören und sehn,
die Sinne vergehn dir dann schon.
Wenn dein Blick verschwimmt,
der Boden dir schwankt,
im Busen bang
dein Herz erbebt:

SIEGFRIED

For protection from the swing of his tail,
I'll keep the malicious beast in sight. –
But tell me something:
has the dragon a heart?   1380

MIME

A cruel, hard heart!

SIEGFRIED

That beats, does it,
in the same place as everyone else's,
human or animal?

MIME

That's true, boy,
that's indeed where the dragon's is.
Now fear's getting to you, is it?
    Siegfried, who until now was lying stretched out and re-
    laxed, sits up suddenly with a jolt.

SIEGFRIED

I'll drive Nothung
into the braggart's heart!
Perhaps you call that fear? –   1390
Hey! You old buzzard!
Is that all
your tricks
can teach me?
If so you'd better get packing:
here I'm not going to learn fear.

MIME

Just wait a bit!
You think what I said
is all sound and no sense:
you must hear and see   1400
the dragon itself,
that'll make you giddy soon enough.
Your sight will swim,
as the ground sways beneath you,
your heart will pound,
as your breast fills with fear:

> *sehr freundlich*
> dann dankst du mir, der dich führte,
> gedenkst, wie Mime dich liebt.

SIEGFRIED
> Du sollst mich nicht lieben!

1410 Sagt' ich's dir nicht?
> Fort aus den Augen mir!
> Laß mich allein,
> sonst halt' ich's hier länger nicht aus,
> fängst du von Liebe gar an!
> Das eklige Nicken
> und Augenzwicken,
> wann endlich soll ich's
> nicht mehr sehn,
> > *ungeduldig*
> wann werd' ich den Albernen los?

MIME
1420 Ich lass' dich schon.
> Am Quell dort lagr' ich mich;
> steh' du nur hier:
> steigt dann die Sonne zur Höh',
> merk' auf den Wurm:
> aus der Höhle wälzt er sich her,
> hier vorbei
> biegt er dann,
> am Brunnen sich zu tränken.

SIEGFRIED *lachend*
> Mime, weilst du am Quell,
> > *belebter*
> > > aber ohne Leidenschaftlichkeit.*
1430 dahin lass' ich den Wurm wohl gehn:
> Nothung stoß' ich
> ihm erst in die Nieren,
> wenn er dich selbst dort
> mit 'weg gesoffen. –
> Darum, hör meinen Rat,
> raste nicht dort am Quell;
> kehre dich 'weg,

very amicably
then you'll thank me that I led you here,
to remind you of how Mime loves you.

SIEGFRIED

Me you shall not love!
Haven't I told you that?   1410
Get out of my sight!
Leave me alone,
or I won't bear it here any longer,
especially if you start on about love!
Your revolting nodding,
your twitching eyes,
when will they finally
be out of my sight,
    impatiently
when will I see the back of this fool?

MIME

I'm already leaving you.   1420
I'll set myself up there by the spring;
just stay right here:
once the sun is high in the sky,
watch for the dragon:
he'll waddle out of the cave this way,
go past here
then turn
to take a drink at the well.

SIEGFRIED *laughing*
Mime, if you're by the spring,
    livelier
        but sounding uninvolved *
that's where I'll let the dragon go: 1430
with Nothung,
I'll get him in the gut,
but only after he's swilled
you down too.
So take a tip from me,
don't stay there by the spring;
turn around and be off,

so weit du kannst,
und komm nie mehr zu mir! –

MIME

1440 Nach freislichem Streit
dich zu erfrischen,
wirst du mir wohl nicht wehren?
[Siegfried] wehrt ihn hastig ab.
Rufe mich auch,
darbst du des Rates. –
[Siegfried] wiederholt die Gebärde mit Ungestüm.
Oder, wenn dir das Fürchten gefällt?
Siegfried erhebt sich und treibt Mime mit wütender Geb-
ärde zum Fortgehen.
Mime im Abgehen für sich
Fafner und Siegfried,
Siegfried, und Fafner: –
oh! brächten beide sich um!
Er verschwindet rechts im Wald. – Siegfried streckt sich
behaglich unter der Linde aus und blickt dem davon-
gehenden Mime nach.

SIEGFRIED

Daß der mein Vater nicht ist,
1450 wie fühl' ich mich drob so froh!
Nun erst gefällt mir
der frische Wald;
nun erst lacht mir
der lustige Tag,
da der Garstige von mir schied,
und ich gar nicht ihn wiederseh'.
[Siegfried] verfällt in schweigendes Sinnen.
Wie sah mein Vater wohl aus? –
Ha! gewiß, wie ich selbst!
Denn wär' wo von Mime ein Sohn,
1460 müsst' er nicht ganz
Mime gleichen?
Grade so garstig,
griesig und grau,
klein und krumm,

as far away as you can,
and never darken my life again! –

MIME

After such a bruising fight,   1440
you won't stop me bringing
refreshment to you, will you?
    [Siegfried] spurns him abruptly.
Also call out to me
if you're desperate for help. –
    [Siegfried] does it again, this time vehemently.
Or, if you find that it's fear you like?
    Siegfried gets up and with a furious gesture forces Mime
    to leave.
        Mime as he leaves, aside
Fafner and Siegfried,
Siegfried and Fafner: –
oh! if only they'd kill each other!
    He disappears on the right into the forest. – Siegfried
    comfortably stretches himself out under the linden-tree
    and watches Mime go off.

SIEGFRIED

He is not my father –
I'm on top of the world about that!   1450
At last I can enjoy
the forest and its freshness;
at last the joyous day
is smiling upon me
now I'm rid of the filthy dwarf,
and needn't ever see him again.
    [Siegfried] gets lost in quiet reflection.
So what did my father look like? –
Ha! of course, like me!
If there ever was a son of Mime,
wouldn't he have to look   1460
like Mime exactly?
Just as filthy,
gruesome and grey,
small and stooped,

höckrig und hinkend,
mit hängenden Ohren,
triefigen Augen? ...
Fort mit dem Alp! –
Ich mag ihn nicht mehr sehn!
   [Siegfried] lehnt sich tiefer zurück und blickt durch den
   Baumwipfel auf. Tiefe Stille – Waldweben.
1470 Aber – wie sah
meine Mutter wohl aus? –
Das kann ich
nun gar nicht mir denken! –
   sehr zart
Der Rehhindin gleich
glänzten gewiß
ihr hell schimmernde Augen?
Nur noch viel schöner! –

   sehr leise
Da bang sie mich geboren,
warum aber starb sie da?
1480 Sterben die Menschenmütter
an ihren Söhnen
alle dahin? –
Traurig wäre das, traun!
Ach, möcht' ich Sohn
meine Mutter sehen! –
Meine Mutter – –
ein Menschenweib!
   [Siegfried] seufzt leise und streckt sich tiefer zurück.
   Große Stille. –
     Wachsendes Waldweben. – Siegfrieds Aufmerksamkeit
   wird endlich durch den Gesang der Waldvögel gefesselt.
     [Siegfried] lauscht mit wachsender Teilnahme einem
   Waldvogel in den Zweigen über ihm.
Du holdes Vöglein,
dich hört' ich noch nie:
1490 bist du im Wald hier daheim?
Verstünd' ich sein süßes Stammeln!
Gewiß sagt' es mir 'was, –

humped and hobbling,
with droopy ears,
drooling eyes? . . .
Away with the dwarf! –
I don't want to see him ever again!
 [Siegfried] settles down more and looks up through the
 tops of the trees. Profound stillness – forest murmurs.
But – what did   1470
my mother look like? –
That's hard
for me even to think about! –
 very tenderly
Did her bright shimmering eyes
shine the same way
as those of a doe?
But still more beautifully! –

 very quietly
Beset by fear when she bore me,
why did she die then?
Do the mothers of men   1480
all pass away
giving birth to their sons? –
Truly that would be sad!
Ah, if I, my mother's son,
could only see her! –
My mother – –
a man's wife!
 [Siegfried] lets out a soft sigh and leans further back.
 Complete stillness. –
  The sounds of forest murmurs grow louder. – The sing-
 ing of the forest birds catches Siegfried's attention at last.
  [Siegfried] starts listening more and more intently to a
 forest bird in the branches above him.
You pretty little bird,
I've never heard you:
is the forest your home?   1490
If only I understood its sweet stammer!
Could it be saying something, –

vielleicht – von der lieben Mutter?

Ein zankender Zwerg
hat mir erzählt,
der Vöglein Stammeln
gut zu verstehn,
dazu könnte man kommen.
Wie das wohl möglich wär'? –

> *Er sinnt nach. Sein Blick fällt auf ein Rohrgebüsch un-*
> *weit der Linde.*

1500 Hei! – ich versuch's,
sing' ihm nach;
auf dem Rohr tön' ich ihm ähnlich:
entrat ich der Worte,
achte der Weise,
sing' ich so seine Sprache,
versteh' ich wohl auch, was es spricht.

> *Er springt an den nahen Quell, schneidet mit dem Schwerte*
> *ein Rohr ab und schnitzt sich hastig eine Pfeife daraus.*
> > *Während dem lauscht er wieder.*

Er schweigt und lauscht: –
so schwatz' ich denn los!

> *Er [Siegfried] bläst auf dem Rohr.*
> > *Er setzt ab, schnitzt wieder und bessert.*
> > *Er bläst wieder.*
> > *Er schüttelt mit dem Kopfe und bessert wieder.*
> > *Er versucht.*
> > *Er wird ärgerlich, drückt das Rohr mit der Hand und*
> > *versucht wieder.*
> > *Er setzt lächelnd ganz ab.*

Das tönt nicht recht;
1510 auf dem Rohre taugt
die wonnige Weise mir nicht.
Vöglein, mich dünkt,
ich bleibe dumm;
von dir lernt sich's nicht leicht.

> *Er hört den Vogel wieder und blickt zu ihm auf.*

Nun schäm' ich mich gar
vor dem schelmischen Lauscher;

perhaps – about my dear mother?

A quarrelsome dwarf
once told me that
the little birds' stammer
is something we can get
to understand well.
Can that really be true? –

> *He ponders. His eyes fall on a bush of reeds not far from
> the linden-tree.*

Hey! – I'll try   1500
to sing its song;
with the pipe I'll sound just like it:
if I ignore the words,
and attend to the tune,
I'll be singing its language in any case,
and grasping for sure what it means.

> *He hurries to the nearby spring, cutting off a reed with
> his sword and hastily whittling it into a pipe.*
>
> *While he is doing this, he listens intently again.*

It's silent and listens: –
so I'll start blabbing away!

> *He [Siegfried] blows his pipe.*
>
> *He stops, whittles more so it gets better.*
>
> *He blows it again.*
>
> *He shakes his head and adjusts it once more.*
>
> *He has another go.*
>
> *He gets annoyed, squeezes the pipe with his hand and
> tries again.*
>
> *Smiling, he gives up completely.*

That didn't sound good;
my pipe isn't right   1510
for playing the happy tune.
Little bird, I think
I'm still stupid;
it isn't easy learning from you.

> *He listens to the bird again and looks up to it.*

Now even I feel ashamed
in front of the mischievous eavesdropper;

er lugt,
  sehr zart
    und kann nichts erlauschen. –
Heida! So höre
nun auf mein Horn!
  Er schwingt das Rohr und wirft es weit fort.
1520   Auf dem dummen Rohre
gerät mir nichts.
Einer Waldweise,
wie ich sie kann,
der lustigen sollst du nun lauschen:
nach liebem Gesellen
lockt' ich mit ihr:
nichts bess'res kam noch
als Wolf und Bär.
Nun laß mich sehn,
1530   wen jetzt sie mir lockt,
ob das mir ein lieber Gesell?
  Siegfried lehnt sich nachsinnend zurück. *
   Er nimmt das silberne Hüfthorn und bläst darauf.
   Bei den lang gehaltenen Tönen blickt Siegfried immer
erwartungsvoll auf den Vogel.
   Im Hintergrunde regt es sich. Fafner, in der Gestalt
eines ungeheuren eidechsenartigen Schlangenwurmes,
hat sich in der Höhle von seinem Lager erhoben; er bricht
durch das Gesträuch und wälzt sich aus der Tiefe nach
der höheren Stelle vor, so daß er mit dem Vorderleibe be-
reits auf ihr angelangt ist, als er jetzt einen starken, gäh-
nenden Laut ausstößt.
   Siegfried sieht sich um und heftet den Blick verwun-
dert auf Fafner.
   Fafner hat beim Anblick Siegfrieds auf der Höhe ange-
halten und verweilt nun daselbst.
Haha! – Da hätte mein Lied
mir 'was liebes erblasen!
Du wärst mir ein saub'rer Gesell!
  Der Leib des Riesenwurms wird durch eine bekleidete
Maschine dargestellt: als diese zur Höhe gelangt ist, wird

it can see,
  very tenderly
        but hear nothing that makes sense. –
Heya! So listen out
for my horn then!
  He brandishes the reed and throws it far away.
Nothing doing   1520
with that stupid reed.
Now you'll be hearing
a merry forest tune
I really can play:
I've used it
to attract dear friends:
nothing's turned up so far
better than wolves and bears.
But let me see,
who can I lure now,   1530
another of my dear mates?
  Siegfried leans back lost in thought. *
  He takes his silver hunting horn and blows it.
  While he is holding the long sustained sounds, Siegfried looks up at the bird, expectantly as ever.
  In the background, something starts to move. Fafner, in the shape of an enormous serpentine, lizard-like dragon, has roused himself from his lair in the cave; he tramples through the undergrowth and waddles his way out of the depths towards the higher plateau, so that the front part of his torso has already landed on it as he now indulges in a big noisy yawn.
  Siegfried looks around and fastens his eyes on Fafner in amazement.
  Fafner has stopped on the plateau as he catches sight of Siegfried and stays there himself.
Haha! – It looks as if my tune's
blown something nice my way!
You'd make a fine mate for me!
  The body of the huge dragon is a machine in disguise: when it reaches the plateau, a trapdoor is opened, out of

daselbst eine Versenkung geöffnet, aus welcher der Sänger
des Fafner durch ein, dem Rachen des Ungeheuers von
innen her zugeführtes Sprachrohr, das Folgende singt. **

FAFNER

Was ist da?

SIEGFRIED

Ei, bist du ein Tier,
das zum Sprechen taugt,
wohl ließ' sich von dir 'was lernen?
Hier kennt einer
1540 das Fürchten nicht:
kann er's von dir erfahren?

FAFNER

Hast du Übermut?

SIEGFRIED

Mut oder Übermut, –
was weiß ich!
Doch dir fahr' ich zu Leibe,
lehrst du das Fürchten mich nicht.

FAFNER *stößt einen lachenden Laut aus.*

Trinken wollt' ich,
nun treff' ich auch Fraß!
      Er öffnet seinen Rachen und zeigt die Zähne.

SIEGFRIED

Eine zierliche Fresse
1550 zeigst du mir da,
lachende Zähne
im Leckermaul!
Gut wär' es, den Schlund dir zu schließen;
dein Rachen reckt sich zu weit.

FAFNER

Zu tauben Reden
taugt er schlecht:
dich zu verschlingen,
frommt der Schlund. –
      Er droht mit dem Schweife.

SIEGFRIED

Hoho! Du grausam,

which the singer representing Fafner sings the following
through a speaking-trumpet threaded into the jaws of the
monster from the inside. **

FAFNER

What's there?

SIEGFRIED

Aha, a talking animal;
if that's what you are,
is there something you'll teach?
Here's someone who
knows nothing about fear: 1540
can he learn it from you?

FAFNER

Are you crazy?

SIEGFRIED

Courageous or crazy, –
that I don't know!
But assault you I shall,
if you don't teach me fear.

FAFNER *emits a noise that sounds like a laugh.*

I wanted a drink,
now there's grub as well!
    He opens his jaws and shows his teeth.

SIEGFRIED

A nice set of choppers
you're showing me there,   1550
beaming teeth
in a mouth of good taste!
It would be great to stuff up your throat;
your yawning jaw's too wide.

FAFNER

It's not suited
to silly talk:
gobbling you up,
that's what my throat's for. –
    He moves his tail threateningly.

SIEGFRIED

Ho ho! You violent,

1560   grimmiger Kerl!
        Von dir verdaut sein
        dünkt mich übel.
        Rätlich und fromm doch scheint's,
        du verrecktest hier ohne Frist.
FAFNER *brüllend*
        Pruh! Komm,
        prahlendes Kind!
SIEGFRIED
        Hab acht, Brüller!
        Der Prahler naht!

Er zieht sein Schwert, springt Fafner an und bleibt herausfordernd stehen.

Fafner wälzt sich weiter auf die Höhe herauf und sprüht aus den Nüstern auf Siegfried. –

Siegfried weicht dem Geifer aus, springt näher zu und stellt sich zur Seite.

Fafner sucht ihn mit dem Schweife zu erreichen.

Siegfried, welchen Fafner fast erreicht hat, springt mit einem Satze über diesen hinweg und verwundet ihn in dem Schweife.

Fafner brüllt, zieht den Schweif heftig zurück und bäumt den Vorderleib, um mit dessen voller Wucht sich auf Siegfried zu werfen; so bietet er diesem die Brust dar; Siegfried erspäht schnell die Stelle des Herzens und stößt sein Schwert bis an das Heft hinein. Fafner bäumt sich vor Schmerz noch höher und sinkt, als Siegfried das Schwert losgelassen und zur Seite gesprungen ist, auf die Wunde zusammen.

        Da lieg', neidischer Kerl!
1570   Nothung trägst du im Herzen!

Die Maschine, welche den Wurm dartellt, ist während des Kampfes etwas weiter in den Vordergrund gerückt worden; jetzt ist unter ihr eine neue Versenkung geöffnet, aus welcher der Sänger des Fafner durch ein schwächeres Sprachrohr singt.**

FAFNER *mit schwächerer Stimme*
        Wer bist du, kühner Knabe,
        der das Herz mir traf?

vicious wretch!
How disgusted I'd feel
being digested by you.
But fitting and fair it is
that you croak right here and now.

FAFNER *bellowing*
Boo! Bring it on,
braggart of a child!

SIEGFRIED
Take care, bellowing beast!
The braggart's closing in!

>*He draws his sword, springing towards Fafner and stand-ing defiantly.*
>
>*Fafner waddles further up onto the plateau and sprays Siegfried out of his nostrils. –*
>
>*Siegfried dodges the venomous sputum, jumps closer and moves to one side.*
>
>*Fafner tries to swipe him with his tail.*
>
>*Siegfried, whom Fafner has now almost reached, springs over him at a single bound and wounds him in the tail.*
>
>*Fafner bellows, pulls his tail violently back and heaves the front of his body up so he can throw his full weight on Siegfried; but in doing so he exposes his breast to the latter. Siegfried quickly sees where the dragon's heart is and plunges his sword into it right up to the hilt. Fafner heaves himself up still higher in pain, collapsing onto his wound as Siegfried lets go of the sword and dodges out of the way.*

Lie there, murderous wretch!
You're carrying Nothung in your heart!

>*During the fight, the machine that represents the dragon has been shifted a little further into the foreground; now a new trapdoor is opened underneath it, out of which the singer of Fafner sings through a weaker speaking-trumpet.* **

FAFNER *with a weaker voice*
Who are you, dauntless boy,
to strike at my heart?

Wer reizte des Kindes Mut
zu der mordlichen Tat?
Dein Hirn brütete nicht,
was du vollbracht.

SIEGFRIED
Viel weiß ich noch nicht,
noch nicht auch, wer ich bin: –
mit dir mordlich zu ringen,
1580   reiztest du selbst meinen Mut. –

FAFNER
Du helläugiger Knabe,
unkund deiner selbst,
wen du gemordet,
meld' ich dir.
Der Riesen ragend Geschlecht,
Fasolt und Fafner,
die Brüder – fielen nun beide.
Um verfluchtes Gold,
von Göttern vergabt,
1590   traf ich Fasolt zu tot:
der nun als Wurm
den Hort bewachte,
Fafner, den letzten Riesen, –
    *etwas nachlassend mit der Stimme. Die Pausen drücken
    aus, daß er entkräftet ist, dies muß dann im Ausdruck der
    Stimme hervortreten, sie muß nach und nach wie gebro-
    chen klingen.* *
fällte ein rosiger Held. –
Blicke nun hell,
blühender Knabe!
Der dich Blinden reizte zur Tat,
berät jetzt des Blühenden Tod.
Merk', wie's endet! –
    ersterbend
1600   Acht auf mich!

SIEGFRIED *Ist nicht langsam zu sprechen und jede Spur von
    Sentimentalität zu vermeiden.* *
Woher ich stamme,
rate mir noch;

Who drove the child's spirit
to this murderous act?
It was not your mind that devised
what you've accomplished.

SIEGFRIED

I don't know much yet,
not even who I am: –
it was you who drove me on
to fight you to the death.   1580

FAFNER

You boy with clear eyes,
ignorant of yourself,
I'll tell you
whom you've murdered.
Fasolt and Fafner,
brothers from the towering giant race,
have now both fallen.
I struck Fasolt dead
because of gold under a curse,
gold forgone by gods: 1590
as for the dragon
guarding the hoard,
Fafner, the last of the giants, –
     *the voice weakening somewhat. The pauses show that he
     is enfeebled, and that must then be made obvious by the
     expression of the voice, which little by little has to sound
     as if it is broken.* *
was slain by a pink-faced hero. –
Now get this clear,
brilliant boy!
Who put you, blind one, up to this,
now covets the brilliant boy's death.
Mark how it will end! –
     in his final death throes
Respect me!   1600

SIEGFRIED *not to be spoken slowly and avoiding all trace of
     sentimentality.* *
Tell me my origin
while you still can;

weise ja scheinst du,
Wilder im Sterben:
rat es nach meinem Namen, –
Siegfried bin ich genannt.

FAFNER *tief seufzend*
Siegfried! . . .
Er hebt sich und stirbt.

SIEGFRIED
Zur Kunde taugt kein Toter.
So leite mich denn
1610   mein lebendes Schwert!

*Fafner hat sich im Sterben zur Seite gewälzt. Siegfried
zieht ihm jetzt das Schwert aus der Brust; dabei wird
seine Hand vom Blute benetzt; er fährt heftig mit der
Hand auf.*

Wie Feuer brennt das Blut! –

*Er führt unwillkürlich die Finger zum Munde, um das
Blut von ihnen abzusaugen. Wie er sinnend vor sich hin-
blickt, wird seine Aufmerksamkeit immer mehr von dem
Gesange der Waldvögel angezogen.*

Ist mir doch fast,
als sprächen die Vöglein zu mir?
Nützte mir das
des Blutes Genuß?
Das selt'ne Vöglein hier,
horch! Was singt es mir?

WALDVOGEL *von einer Knabenstimme zu singen
          aus den Zweigen der Linde über Siegfried*
Hei! Siegfried gehört
nun der Niblungen Hort!
1620   O, fänd' in der Höhle
den Hort er jetzt!
Wollt' er den Tarnhelm gewinnen,
der taugt' ihm zu wonniger Tat:
doch wollt' er den Ring sich erraten,
der macht' ihn zum Walter der Welt!

*Siegfried hat mit verhaltenem Atem und verzückter Miene
gelauscht.*

you seem all the wiser,
wild one, now that you're dying:
guess it from my name, –
Siegfried is what I'm called.

FAFNER *sighing deeply*
Siegfried! . . .
   He raises himself up and dies.

SIEGFRIED
The dead tell you nothing.
But my sword's alive,
so let it lead me instead!   1610
   In the throes of death, Fafner has rolled over to one side.
   Siegfried now extracts the sword from his breast; as he
   does so, his hand is bathed in blood. He whisks his hand
   away violently.
The blood burns like fire! –
   He instinctively puts his fingers into his mouth to suck
   off the blood. Wondering to himself what it is all about,
   he begins to be attracted more and more by the singing
   of the forest birds.
Am I dreaming it,
or are the birds speaking to me?
Is tasting the blood
helping me?
This rare little bird here,
listen! What is it singing to me?

FOREST BIRD *to be sung by a boy's voice*
      from the branches of the linden-tree above Siegfried
Hey! The Nibelung hoard
is Siegfried's now!
Oh, if only he'd find   1620
the hoard in the cave!
The Tarnhelm's his if he wants it,
he'll use it for many a marvellous deed:
but if it's the ring he wants to find,
that will allow him to rule the world!
   Siegfried has been listening with bated breath and an
   ecstatic look on his face.

SIEGFRIED *leise und gerührt*
>Dank, liebes Vöglein,
>für deinen Rat!
>Gern folg' ich dem Ruf!
>>*Er wendet sich nach hinten und steigt in die Höhle hinab,*
>>*wo er alsbald gänzlich verschwindet.*

DRITTE SZENE

Mime schleicht heran, scheu umherblickend, um sich von
Fafners Tod zu überzeugen. – Gleichzeitig kommt von der
anderen Seite Alberich aus dem Geklüft hervor; er beobachtet
Mime genau. Als dieser Siegfried nicht mehr gewahrt, und
vorsichtig sich nach hinten der Höhle zuwendet, stürzt
Alberich auf ihn zu und vertritt ihm den Weg.

ALBERICH
>Wohin schleichst du
1630>eilig und schlau,
>schlimmer Gesell?

MIME
>Verfluchter Bruder,
>dich braucht' ich hier!
>Was bringt dich her?

ALBERICH
>Geizt es dich, Schelm,
>nach meinem Gold?
>Verlangst du mein Gut?

MIME
>Fort von der Stelle!
>Die Stätte ist mein:
1640>was stöberst du hier?

ALBERICH
>Stör' ich dich wohl
>im stillen Geschäft,
>wenn du hier stiehlst?

SIEGFRIED *quietly and movingly*
  Thank you, dear little bird,
  for your counsel!
  I'll gladly answer your call!
    He turns to the back and climbs down into the cave,
    where he quickly disappears.

SCENE THREE

Mime sidles back into sight, looking around warily to make
sure that Fafner is really dead. – At the same time Alberich
slips out of the chasms on the other side; he takes a sharp
look at Mime. Once Mime notices that Siegfried is not there,
he turns with caution towards the cave, whereupon Alberich
bears down on him and bars his way.

ALBERICH
  Where are you slinking to
  so fast and fox-like,   1630
  wicked friend?
MIME
  Damned brother,
  just who I need!
  What brings you here?
ALBERICH
  Do you lust, rascal,
  after my gold?
  Long for my wealth?
MIME
  Get out of here!
  This place is mine:
  why poke around here?   1640
ALBERICH
  Do I disturb you,
  if stealing is
  what you're secretly doing?

MIME

    Was ich erschwang
    mit schwerer Müh',
    soll mir nicht schwinden.

ALBERICH

    Hast du dem Rhein
    das Gold zum Ringe geraubt?
    Erzeugtest du gar
1650   den zähen Zauber im Reif?

MIME

    Wer schuf den Tarnhelm,
    der die Gestalten tauscht?
    Der sein bedurfte,
    erdachtest du ihn wohl?

ALBERICH

    Was hättest du Stümper
    je wohl zu stampfen verstanden?
    Der Zauberring
    zwang mir den Zwerg erst zur Kunst.

MIME

    Wo hast du den Ring?
1660   Dir Zagem entrissen ihn Riesen.
    Was du verlorst,
    meine List erlangt' es für mich.

ALBERICH

    Mit des Knaben Tat
    will der Knicker nun knausern?
    Dir gehört sie gar nicht,
    der Helle ist selbst ihr Herr.

MIME

    Ich zog ihn auf;
    für die Zucht zahlt er mir nun:
    für Müh' und Last
1670   erlauert' ich lang meinen Lohn.

ALBERICH

    Für des Knaben Zucht
    will der knickrige,
    schäbige Wicht

MIME

    What I have earned
    with sheer hard work,
    I won't let slip through my fingers.

ALBERICH

    Did you rob the Rhine
    of its gold for the ring?
    Let alone lend
    the ring its implacable spell?   1650

MIME

    Who made the Tarnhelm
    that changes living shapes?
    You needed it,
    but did you really think it up?

ALBERICH

    How could a bungler like you
    have ever understood what to do?
    The magic ring
    obliged you, dwarf, to create for me.

MIME

    What did you do with the ring?
    Giants forced it from you, weakling.   1660
    What you lost,
    I'll use my wits to get back for myself.

ALBERICH

    Is old skinflint now skimpy
    with the boy's winnings?
    The treasure's not even yours,
    the fair boy himself is its boss.

MIME

    I brought him up;
    it's time for him to pay me back:
    to be rewarded for toil and trouble,
    long have I lain in wait for that!   1670

ALBERICH

    For rearing the boy,
    does this mangy
    scoundrel of a skinflint,

keck und kühn
wohl gar König nun sein?
Dem räudigsten Hund
wäre der Ring
geratner als dir,
nimmer erringst
1680   du Rüpel den Herrscherreif!
MIME *kratzt sich den Kopf*
Behalt ihn denn,
und hüt' ihn wohl,
den hellen Reif;
sei du Herr,
doch mich heiße auch Bruder!
Um meines Tarnhelms
lustigen Tand
tausch' ich ihn dir,
uns beiden taugt's,
1690   teilen die Beute wir so.
        Er reibt sich zutraulich die Hände.
ALBERICH *mit Hohnlachen*
Teilen mit dir?
Und den Tarnhelm gar?
Wie schlau du bist!
Sicher schlief' ich
niemals vor deinen Schlingen!
MIME *ausser sich*
Selbst nicht tauschen?
Auch nicht teilen?
Leer soll ich gehn?
Ganz ohne Lohn?
        kreischend
1700   Gar nichts willst du mir lassen?
ALBERICH
Nichts von allem!
Nicht einen Nagel
sollst du mir nehmen!
MIME *in höchster Wut*
Weder Ring noch Tarnhelm

cheeky and bold,
now even want to be king?
The ring's better
in the paws of the scabbiest dog
than in yours,
never will a lout like you
win the right to be the ring's master! 1680
MIME *scratches his head*
Then just hold on
to the lustrous ring,
and look after it well;
but if you're its boss,
I'm also your brother!
I'll trade it with you
for my amusing toy,
the Tarnhelm,
so that both of us
can split the proceeds. 1690
He rubs his hands confidingly.
ALBERICH *with mocking laughter*
Split the proceeds?
And the Tarnhelm, with you?
How sneaky you are!
With your snares all around,
I'd never sleep safely!
MIME *beside himself*
Not even swap?
Or share?
Go empty-handed, me?
No prize at all?
screeching
You'd leave me absolutely nothing? 1700
ALBERICH
Nothing at all!
Not even a nail
will you get out of me!
MIME *utterly enraged*
Neither ring nor Tarnhelm

soll dir denn taugen,
nicht teil' ich nun mehr!
Gegen dich doch ruf' ich
Siegfried zu Rat
und des Recken Schwert;
1710   der rasche Held,
der richte, Brüderchen, dich.
   Siegfried erscheint im Hintergrund.

ALBERICH
   Kehre dich um!
   Aus der Höhle kommt er daher.

MIME *sich umblickend*
   Kindischen Tand
   erkor er gewiß.

ALBERICH
   Den Tarnhelm hält er.

MIME
   Doch auch den Ring.

ALBERICH
   Verflucht! Den Ring?

MIME *hämisch lachend*
   Laß ihn den Ring dir doch geben!
1720   Ich will ihn mir schon gewinnen.
   Er schlüpft mit den letzten Worten in den Wald zurück.

ALBERICH
   Und doch seinem Herrn
   soll er allein noch gehören.
   Er verschwindet im Geklüfte.
      *Siegfried ist mit Tarnhelm und Ring, während des Letz-
      teren langsam und nachsinnend aus der Höhle vorge-
      schritten: er betrachtet gedankenvoll seine Beute und hält,
      nahe dem Baume, auf der Höhe des Mittelgrundes wieder
      an.*

SIEGFRIED
   Was ihr mir nützt,
   weiß ich nicht;
   doch nahm ich euch
   aus des Horts gehäuftem Gold,

will be useful to you,
if I don't share them!
I'll call on Siegfried
and his warrior's sword
to fight you;
the nimble hero, little brother,   1710
will make mincemeat of you!
    Siegfried appears in the background.

ALBERICH
Turn around!
He's coming here out of the cave!

MIME *looking back*
Childish playthings
he's chosen for sure.

ALBERICH
He's got the Tarnhelm.

MIME
The ring as well.

ALBERICH
Damn! The ring?

MIME *laughing gleefully*
Just ask him to give you the ring!
I'm still determined to get it.   1720
    With these last words, he slips back into the forest.

ALBERICH
And yet to its master alone
it shall belong.
    He disappears inside the fissures of the rock-face.
    *During the preceding passage, Siegfried has stepped
slowly and meditatively out of the cave, holding the Tarn-
helm and the ring: he looks thoughtfully at his winnings
and stops again at the top of the middle of the plateau
near the tree.*

SIEGFRIED
I don't know
what you're good for;
but I did take you
from that pile of gold

weil guter Rat mir es riet.
So taug' eure Zier
als des Tages Zeuge,
1730 es mahne der Tand,
daß ich kämpfend Fafner erlegt;
doch das Fürchten noch nicht gelernt.

> *Er steckt den Tarnhelm sich in den Gürtel und den Reif*
> *an den Finger. – Stillschweigen. – Wachsendes Wald-*
> *weben. – Siegfried achtet unwillkürlich wieder des Vogels,*
> *und lauscht ihm mit verhaltenem Atem.*

WALDVOGEL

Hei! Siegfried gehört
nun der Helm und der Ring.
O! traute er Mime,
dem treulosen, nicht!
Hörte Siegfried nur scharf
auf des Schelmen Heuchlergered'!
Wie sein Herz es meint,
1740 kann er Mime verstehn:
so nützt' ihm des Blutes Genuß.

> *Siegfrieds Miene und Gebärde drücken aus, daß er den*
> *Sinn des Vogelgesanges wohl vernommen. Er sieht Mime*
> *sich nähern und verbleibt, ohne sich zu rühren, auf sein*
> *Schwert gestützt, beobachtend und in sich geschlossen,*
> *in seiner Stellung auf der Anhöhe bis zum Schlusse des*
> *folgenden Auftrittes.*
>
> *Mime schleicht heran und beobachtet vom Vordergrund*
> *aus Siegfried.*

MIME

Er sinnt und erwägt
der Beute Wert: –
weilte wohl hier
ein weiser Wandrer,
schweifte umher,
beschwatzte das Kind
mit list'ger Runen Rat?
Zwiefach schlau
1750 sei nun der Zwerg;

on good advice.
So may your pride
be witness to this day,
and this junk a reminder   1730
that I slew Fafner fighting him,
but still didn't learn about fear.

> *He sticks the Tarnhelm into his belt and puts the ring on his finger. – Silence. – The sounds of forest murmurs grow louder. – Again the bird attracts the attention of Siegfried, who listens hard to it with bated breath.*

FOREST BIRD

Hey! Helmet and ring
are Siegfried's now.
Oh! let him not trust
the perfidious Mime!
Let Siegfried truly hear
the rogue's fraudulent talk!
Then he can understand
what Mime thinks in his heart: 1740
may tasting the blood help him.

> *Siegfried's face and demeanour show that he has well understood the meaning of the bird's song. He sees Mime getting closer and remains where he is without showing any reaction, leaning on his sword, watching everything for himself, and staying in this position on the plateau until the end of the scene.*
>
> *Mime sidles into view and observes Siegfried in the foreground.*

MIME

He muses and mulls over
the worth of his winnings: –
did a wise Wanderer
wait around here,
roaming about,
cajoling the boy
with crafty runes and their yarns?
Let the dwarf be
doubly smart;   1750

die listigste Schlinge
leg' ich jetzt aus,
daß ich mit traulichem
Truggerede
betöre das trotzige Kind.
> *Er tritt näher an Siegfried heran und bewillkommt diesen*
> *mit schmeichelnden Gebärden.*
Willkommen, Siegfried!
Sag', du Kühner,
hast du das Fürchten gelernt?

SIEGFRIED

Den Lehrer fand ich noch nicht!

MIME

1760   Doch den Schlangenwurm,
du hast ihn erschlagen?
Das war doch ein schlimmer Gesell?

SIEGFRIED

So grimm und tückisch er war,
sein Tod grämt mich doch schier,
da viel üblere Schächer
unerschlagen noch leben.
Der mich ihn morden hieß,
den hass' ich mehr als den Wurm!

MIME *sehr freundlich*

Nur sachte! Nicht lange
1770   siehst du mich mehr:
zum ew'gen Schlaf
> *süßlich*
schließ' ich dir die Augen bald.
Wozu ich dich brauchte,
> *wie belobend*
hast du vollbracht;
jetzt will ich nur noch
die Beute dir abgewinnen;
mich dünkt, das soll mir gelingen,
zu betören bist du ja leicht.

SIEGFRIED

So sinnst du auf meinen Schaden?

I'll snare him now
in the wiliest trap,
and with sweet
beguiling words,
sweep the stubborn boy off his feet.
> *He steps closer to Siegfried and welcomes him with ingratiating gestures.*
Welcome, Siegfried!
You, bold as you are,
can you say if you've learned fear?

SIEGFRIED

I've not found a teacher yet!

MIME

But didn't you slaughter   1760
the winding, crawling dragon?
That was a wicked companion, surely?

SIEGFRIED

Full of wrath and spite as he was,
his death grieves me even so,
because far worse thieves
are still at large, escaping slaughter.
I hate the dragon less than I do
the one who told me to kill him!

MIME *very amicably*

Steady on! Not much longer
will you see me: 1770
soon I'll be closing your eyes
> *smarmily*
in eternal sleep.
All I needed you for,
> *feigning praise*
you have accomplished;
all I have to do now
is claw back your winnings;
it seems to me I ought to succeed,
as it's so easy to lead you astray.

SIEGFRIED

Plotting to do me damage, are you?

MIME *verwundert*

1780 Wie sagt' ich denn das? –
        zärtlich fortfahrend
      Siegfried! Hör doch, mein Söhnchen!
      Dich und deine Art
      haßt' ich immer von Herzen;
        zärtlich
      aus Liebe erzog ich
      dich lästigen nicht:
      dem Horte in Fafners Hut,
      dem Golde galt meine Müh'.
        als verspräche er ihm hübsche Sachen
      Gibst du mir das
      gutwillig nun nicht,
        als wäre er bereit, sein Leben für ihn zu lassen
1790 Siegfried, mein Sohn,
      das siehst du wohl selbst,
        mit freundlichem Scherze
      dein Leben mußt du mir lassen. –

SIEGFRIED

      Daß du mich hassest,
      hör' ich gern:
      doch auch mein Leben muß ich dir lassen?

MIME *ärgerlich*

      Das sagt' ich doch nicht?
      Du verstehst mich ja falsch! –
        Er sucht sein Fläschchen hervor. – Er gibt sich die ersicht-
        lichste Mühe zur Verstellung.
      Sieh', du bist müde
      von harter Müh'.
1800 Brünstig wohl brennt dir der Leib;
      dich zu erquicken
      mit queckem Trank
      säumt' ich sorgender nicht:
      als dein Schwert du dir branntest,
      braut' ich den Sud;
      trinkst du nun den,
      gewinn' ich dein trautes Schwert,

MIME *puzzled*

  How could I have ever said that? –							1780
    carrying on tenderly
  Siegfried! Listen to me, my little son!
  From the bottom of my heart,
  I always hated you and your kind;
    tenderly
  I did not foster
  a pest like you out of love:
  the hoard and gold in Fafner's care
  were the reason I kept grinding on.
    as if promising him nice things
  If you don't give them
  to me in good faith,
    as if he were prepared to lose his life for him
  you can surely see yourself,							1790
  Siegfried, my son,
    in friendly fun
  that you must lose your life to me. –

SIEGFRIED

  I like to hear
  that you hate me:
  but why lose my life to you as well?

MIME *angrily*

  That's not what I said, is it?
  You're getting me wrong! –
    *He looks for his flask. – He makes a very visible effort to
    hide his real feelings.*
  Look, you're tired
  from hard work.
  Your body probably feels it's on fire;							1800
  caring for your every need,
  I wasn't slow making a tonic
  to refresh you:
  as you held your sword in the flames,
  I made this broth;
  if you drink it now,
  your trusty sword's mine,

und mit ihm Helm und Hort. –
> *kichernd*

Hihihihihihi!

SIEGFRIED

1810 So willst du mein Schwert
und was ich erschwungen,
Ring und Beute, mir rauben?

MIME *heftig*

Was du doch falsch mich verstehst!
Stamml' ich, fasl' ich wohl gar?
Die größte Mühe
geb' ich mir doch,
mein heimliches Sinnen
heuchelnd zu bergen,
und du dummer Bube

1820 deutest alles doch falsch!
Öffne die Ohren!
Und vernimm genau!
Höre, was Mime meint. –
> *wieder sehr freundlich, mit ersichtlicher Mühe*

Hier nimm, und trinke dir Labung;
mein Trank labte dich oft:
tat'st du wohl unwirsch,
stelltest dich arg,
was ich dir bot –
erbost auch – nahmst du doch immer.

SIEGFRIED *ohne eine Miene zu verziehen*

1830 Einen guten Trank
hätt' ich gern:
wie hast du diesen gebraut?

MIME *lustig scherzend, als schildere er ihm einen angenehm
berauschten Zustand, den ihm der Saft bereiten solle*

Hei! So trink nur,
trau meiner Kunst!
In Nacht und Nebel
sinken die Sinne dir bald;
ohne Wach' und Wissen
stracks streckst du die Glieder.

the helmet and hoard as well. –
  giggling
Hihihihihihi!

SIEGFRIED

So you want to rob me   1810
of my sword and the ring
and the rest of my winnings?

MIME *violently*

How you keep getting me wrong!
Do I stammer, drivel or something?
I really am making
great efforts
to dissemble and hide
my secret thoughts,
and you, stupid boy,
still don't know what I mean!   1820
Open your ears!
And listen exactly! –
Hear what Mime's saying. –
  regaining his friendly composure, with visible effort
Take this, and drink to your health;
my drinks often revived you:
even at your surliest,
acting spitefully,
angrily too –
what I offered, you still always took.

SIEGFRIED *with a completely straight face*

I'd really like   1830
a good drink:
how did you make this one?

MIME *cheerfully light-hearted, as if to give an idea of the pleas-
    antly inebriated state the juice is supposed to put him in*

Hey! Just drink it,
trust in my skill!
Your wits will soon recede
in night and fog:
without waking and knowing
you'll stretch your limbs straight out.

Liegst du nun da,
1840   leicht könnt' ich
die Beute nehmen und bergen:
doch erwachtest du je,
nirgends wär' ich
sicher vor dir,
hätt' ich selbst auch den Ring.
Drum mit dem Schwert,
das so scharf du schufst,
   mit einer Gebärde ausgelassener Lustigkeit
hau' ich dem Kind
den Kopf erst ab:
1850   dann hab' ich mir Ruh' und auch den Ring! –
   kichernd
Hihihihihihihihihihihi!

SIEGFRIED
Im Schlafe willst du mich morden?

MIME *wütend ärgerlich*
Was möcht' ich? Sagt' ich denn das? –
   Er bemüht sich, den zärtlichsten Ton anzunehmen.
Ich will dem Kind
   mit sorglichster Deutlichkeit
nur den Kopf abhaun!
   *mit dem Ausdruck herzlicher Besorgtheit für Siegfrieds
   Gesundheit*
Denn haßte ich dich
auch nicht so sehr,
und hätt' ich des Schimpfs
und der schändlichen Mühe
1860   auch nicht so viel zu rächen,
   sanft
aus dem Wege dich zu räumen
darf ich doch nicht rasten:
   wieder scherzend
wie käm' ich sonst anders zur Beute,
da Alberich auch nach ihr lugt?
   *Er gießt den Saft in das Trinkhorn und führt dieses Sieg-
   fried mit aufdringlicher Gebärde zu.*

Once you're lying there,
I could easily   1840
take and hide your winnings:
but if you ever awoke,
I'd never be safe
from you anywhere,
even if I did have the ring.
So first I'll chop
the child's head off
   gesturing in boisterous amusement
with the sword which
you shaped so sharply:
then I'll have my peace and also the ring! –   1850
   giggling
Hihihihihihihihihihihi!

SIEGFRIED

You want to murder me in my sleep?

MIME *furiously angry*

I want to do what? Is that what I said?
   He tries hard to adopt the gentlest tone of voice.
All I want from the child
   with the most considerate clarity
is to chop off his head!
   *with an expression of heartfelt concern for Siegfried's
   well-being*
Even if I didn't hate
you quite so much,
and didn't have to take
revenge for all your insults
and the ignominious grind,   1860
   silkily
I still couldn't rest until
I'd put you out of the way:
   light-heartedly again
how else could I get to the loot,
especially as Alberich is after it too?
   *He pours the juice into a drinking-horn and offers it to
   Siegfried with importunate gestures.*

Nun, mein Wälsung!
Wolfssohn du!
Sauf, und würg dich zu tot:
Nie tust du mehr 'nen Schluck! –
hihihihihi!

> *Siegfried holt mit dem Schwert aus.*
> *Er führt, wie in einer Anwandlung heftigen Ekels einen jähen Streich nach Mime; dieser stürzt sogleich tot zu Boden.*

SIEGFRIED

1870 Schmeck' du mein Schwert,
ekliger Schwätzer!

ALBERICH *hohnlachend, aus dem Geklüfte*
Hahahahahahahahaha ha!

SIEGFRIED *Er henkt, auf den am Boden Liegenden blickend, ruhig sein Schwert wieder ein.*

Neides Zoll
zahlt Nothung:
dazu durft' ich ihn schmieden.

> *Er rafft Mimes Leichnam auf und trägt ihn auf die Anhöhe vor den Eingang der Höhle.*
> *während er den Leichnam in die Höhle hinab wirft*

In der Höhle hier
lieg auf dem Hort!
Mit zäher List
erzieltest du ihn;
1880 jetzt magst du des wonnigen walten!
Einen guten Wächter
geb' ich dir auch,
daß er vor Dieben dich deckt.

> *Er wälzt mit großer Anstrengung den Leichnam des Wurmes vor den Eingang der Höhle, so daß er diesen ganz damit verstopft.*

Da lieg' auch du,
dunkler Wurm!
Den gleißenden Hort
hüte zugleich
mit dem beuterührigen Feind:
so fandet beide ihr nun Ruh'.

So, my Wälsung!
You son of the Wolf!
Guzzle it down, gag on it till you die:
you'll never take another gulp! –
hihihihihi!

> *Siegfried raises his sword ready to strike.*
>
> *With the look of someone overcome with a fit of violent repulsion, he aims a sudden sharp blow at Mime, who falls lifeless to the ground at once.*

SIEGFRIED

Taste a drop of my sword,   1870
you sickening windbag!

ALBERICH *laughing mockingly from the rock's fissures*
Hahahahahahahahaha ha!

SIEGFRIED *Looking at the body flat on the ground, he calmly puts his sword back into place.*

Nothung pays
the wages of pitilessness:
that's why I was able to forge it.

> *He snatches up Mime's corpse and carries it up to the plateau in front of the entrance to the cave.*
>
> *while he is throwing the corpse into the cave below*

Lie on the hoard
in this cave!
With dogged cunning
you've got what you wanted;
now may you rule your pretty domain!   1880
A good guardian
I'll give you as well,
that he may protect you from thieves.

> *He heaves the corpse of the dragon with great effort towards the entrance of the cave so that he can completely block it off.*

You lie there too,
dark-minded dragon!
Let both of you guard
the gaudy treasure,
you and your light-fingered foe:
so may the two of you rest in peace.

Er blickt eine Weile sinnend in die Höhle hinab und wen-
det sich dann langsam, wie ermüdet, in den Vordergrund.
Er führt sich die Hand über die Stirn.

1890 Heiß ward mir –
von der harten Last.
Brausend jagt
mein brünst'ges Blut!
Die Hand brennt mir am Haupt. –
Hoch steht schon die Sonne;
aus lichtem Blau
blickt ihr Aug'
auf den Scheitel steil mir herab. –
Linde Kühlung
1900 erkies' ich unter der Linde.

Er streckt sich unter der Linde aus und blickt wieder die
Zweige hinauf.

Noch einmal, liebes Vöglein, –
da wir so lang
lästig gestört, –
lauscht' ich gerne deinem Sange:
auf dem Zweige seh' ich
wohlig dich wiegen;
zwitschernd umschwirren
dich Brüder und Schwestern,
umschweben dich lustig und lieb. –

1910 Doch ich – bin so allein,
hab' nicht Brüder noch Schwestern:
meine Mutter schwand, –
mein Vater fiel:
nie sah sie der Sohn!
Mein einz'ger Gesell
war ein garstiger Zwerg;
warm
Güte zwang
uns nie zu Liebe:
listige Schlingen
1920 warf mir der schlaue;
nun mußt' ich ihn gar erschlagen!

*Thinking hard, he gazes into the cave for a while and
then, looking tired, slowly turns to the front of the stage.
    He wipes his hand over his brow.*

I'm getting hot –   1890
from the heavy load.
My blood's on fire,
roaring through my veins!
My hand burns touching my head. –
Already the sun is high in the sky;
its eye stares
out of limpid blue,
steep rays fall on my head's crown. –
Under the linden-tree,
I'll choose pleasant coolness.   1900

*He stretches out under the linden-tree and looks up again
    into the branches.*

Dear little bird, –
as it's been so long
before we were so rudely disturbed, –
I'd like to hear your song once more:
I see you rocking on the branches
to your heart's content;
twittering, buzzing
brothers and sisters
hover about you, droll and sweet. –

As for me – I'm so alone,   1910
have no brothers or sisters:
my mother died away, –
my father was slain:
their son never saw them!
My only companion
was a foul dwarf;
    warmly
no love or kindness
was lost between us:
the crafty creature
flung wily traps in my way;   1920
so I really had to slay him!

*Er blickt schmerzlich bewegt wieder nach den Zweigen
auf.*

Freundliches Vöglein,
dich frage ich nun.
Gönntest du mir
wohl ein gut Gesell?
Willst du mir das Rechte raten?
Ich lockte so oft,
und erlost' es mir nie.
Du, mein Trauter,
1930   träfst es wohl besser;
so recht ja rietest du schon.
         immer leise
Nun sing! Ich lausche dem Gesang.

WALDVOGEL

Hei! Siegfried erschlug
nun den schlimmen Zwerg!
Jetzt wüßt' ich ihm noch
das herrlichste Weib:
auf hohem Felsen sie schläft,
Feuer umbrennt ihren Saal:
durchschritt' er die Brunst,
1940   weckt' er die Braut,
Brünnhilde wäre dann sein!
         Siegfried fährt mit Heftigkeit vom Sitze auf.

SIEGFRIED

O holder Sang!
Süßester Hauch!
Wie brennt sein Sinn
mir sehrend die Brust!
Wie zückt er heftig,
zündend mein Herz?
Was jagt mir so jach
durch Herz und Sinne?
1950   Sag' es mir, süßer Freund!
         Er lauscht.

WALDVOGEL

Lustig im Leid
sing' ich von Liebe.

*Feeling disturbed, he looks up again into the branches
  above.*

Friendly little bird,
let me ask you.
Will you tell me how
I can find a good mate?
Tell me the correct thing to do?
I've tried to attract one so often,
and never had any luck.
You, my dear one,
are better placed to get it right;   1930
after all you've been right so far.
   always softly
Now sing! I'm listening to your song.

FOREST BIRD

Hey! The wicked dwarf
Siegfried's now slain!
Now I still have to point him
to the most glorious woman of all:
she sleeps high on a rock,
her space surrounded by fire:
pass through the inferno,
waken the bride,   1940
then Brünnhilde will be his!
   Siegfried leaps up frantically from where he is sitting.

SIEGFRIED

O sweet singing!
Sweetest breath!
How its spirit is aflame,
searing through my breast!
How does it tug forcefully
and rousingly at my heart?
What rushes so wildly
through my heart and mind?
Tell me that, my sweet friend!   1950
   He listens intently.

FOREST BIRD

Smiling in sorrow
I sing of love.

Wonnig aus Weh'
web' ich mein Lied: –
nur Sehnende kennen den Sinn.

SIEGFRIED
Fort jagt mich's
jauchzend von hinnen,
fort aus dem Wald auf den Fels!
Noch einmal sage mir,
1960 holder Sänger:
werd' ich das Feuer durchbrechen?
Kann ich erwecken die Braut?
  Siegfried lauscht nochmals.

WALDVOGEL
Die Braut gewinnt,
Brünnhild' erweckt
ein Feiger nie:
nur wer das Fürchten nicht kennt.

SIEGFRIED *aufjauchzend*
Der dumme Knab',
der das Fürchten nicht kennt,
mein Vöglein, der bin ja ich!
1970 Noch heute gab ich
vergebens mir Müh',
das Fürchten von Fafner zu lernen:
nun brenn' ich vor Lust,
es von Brünnhild' zu wissen!
Wie find' ich zum Felsen den Weg?
  *Der Vogel flattert auf, kreist über Siegfried und fliegt ihm
  zögernd voran.*
So wird mir der Weg gewiesen:
wohin du flatterst,
folg' ich dir nach!
  *Er läuft dem Vogel, welcher ihn neckend einige Zeit lang
  unstet nach verschiedenen Richtungen hinleitet, nach und
  folgt ihm endlich, als dieser, mit einer bestimmten Wen-
  dung nach dem Hintergrunde, davon fliegt.*
  Der Vorhang fällt.

Making pleasure from pain
I ply my song: –
only seekers of passion can grasp it.

SIEGFRIED

It drives me up and away,
on top of the world,
out of the forest and up to the rock!
Tell me once more,
sweet singer: 1960
will I break through the fire?
Can I waken the bride?
   Again, Siegfried listens intently.

FOREST BIRD

Winning the bride,
waking Brünnhilde
a coward never can:
only the one who doesn't know fear.

SIEGFRIED *whooping with joy*

The stupid boy,
who doesn't know fear,
my little bird, that's just who I am!
Only today I made   1970
a fruitless effort
to learn all about fear from Fafner:
now I'm dying to know
from Brünnhilde what it is!
How do I find the way to the rock?
   The bird flies into the air, circles over Siegfried and con-
   tinues on hesitantly in front of him.
So that's how I'll be shown the way:
wherever you flutter,
I'll be in pursuit!
   He pursues the bird, which for a time teasingly leads
   him astray in different directions, only to follow it at last
   when it starts flying off on a clear course into the back-
   ground.
      The curtain falls.

DRITTER AUFZUG

VORSPIEL UND ERSTE SZENE

Wilde Gegend am Fuße eines Felsenberges

Hier geht der Vorhang auf [Takt 55].

*Am Fuße eines Felsenberges, welcher nach links hin steil auf-
steigt. – Nacht. Sturm und Wetter. Blitz und heftiger Donner,
welcher letztere dann schweigt, während Blitze noch längere
Zeit die Wolken durchkreuzen. –*
    [Takt 66] Hier tritt der Wanderer auf.
    *Er schreitet entschlossen auf ein gruftähnliches Höhlentor
in einem Felsen des Vordergrundes zu und nimmt dort, auf
seinen Speer gestützt, eine Stellung ein, während er das Fol-
gende dem Eingange der Höhle zuruft.*

WANDERER
    Wache, Wala!
1980   Wala! Erwach'!
    Aus langem Schlaf
    weck' ich dich Schlummernde auf.
    Ich rufe dich auf:
    herauf! herauf!
    Aus nebliger Gruft,
    aus nächtigem Grunde herauf!
    Erda! Erda!
    Ewiges Weib!
    Aus heimischer Tiefe
1990   tauche zur Höh!
    Dein Wecklied sing' ich,
    daß du erwachest;
    aus sinnendem Schlafe
    weck' ich dich auf!
    Allwissende!
    Urweltweise!

ACT THREE

PRELUDE AND SCENE ONE

A wild region at the foot of a rocky mountain

The curtain rises here [bar 55].

At the foot of a rocky mountain, which towards the left to
the back rises steeply upwards. Lightning and violent thunder,
which falls silent as the lightning continues to flash through
the clouds for quite a bit longer. –
   [bar 66] The Wanderer enters here.
   He marches decisively towards the vault-like mouth of a
cave in the rock in the foreground and positions himself there,
leaning on his spear while he sings the following passage into
the cave's entrance.

WANDERER
   Waken, seeress!
   Seeress! Awaken!   1980
   I'm waking you,
   slumbering woman, from a long sleep.
   I'm summoning you:
   get up! get up!
   Out of your foggy vault,
   out of those murky depths, get up!
   Erda! Erda!
   Woman eternal!
   Ascend to the heights,
   from the provincial deep!   1990
   I sing you a song of awakening,
   so you may leave slumber behind;
   I'm waking you up
   from thoughtful sleep!
   The one who knows all!
   Primeval and wise!

Erda! Erda!
Ewiges Weib!
Wache, erwache, du Wala! Erwache!

Die Höhlengruft erdämmert. Bläulicher Lichtschein: von ihm beleuchtet steigt mit dem Folgenden Erda sehr allmählich aus der Tiefe auf. Sie erscheint wie von Reif bedeckt; Haar und Gewand werfen einen glitzernden Schimmer von sich.

ERDA

2000   Stark ruft das Lied;
kräftig reizt der Zauber.
Ich bin erwacht
aus wissendem Schlaf:
wer scheucht den Schlummer mir?

WANDERER

Der Weckrufer bin ich,
und Weisen üb' ich,
daß weithin wache,
was fester Schlaf verschließt.
Die Welt durchzog ich,
2010   wanderte viel,
Kunde zu werben,
urweisen Rat zu gewinnen.
Kundiger gibt es
keine als dich;
bekannt ist dir,
was die Tiefe birgt,
was Berg und Tal,
Luft und Wasser durchwebt:
wo Wesen sind,
2020   wehet dein Atem;
wo Hirne sinnen,
haftet dein Sinn:
Alles, sagt man,
sei dir bekannt.
Daß ich nun Kunde gewänne,
weck' ich dich aus dem Schlaf!

Erda! Erda!
Woman eternal!
Wake, awake, you, seeress! Awaken!

A bluish ray of light gradually begins to dawn in the vault
of the cave: it illuminates Erda, who very gradually rises
from the deep during the following passage. She looks as
if she is covered with hoar frost; her hair and the garment
she is wearing have a glittering shimmer about them.

ERDA

The song's call is strong;   2000
its magic has pungent allure.
I'm awakened
from insightful sleep:
who's chasing my slumber away?

WANDERER

I'm your awakener,
and I sing melodies
that far and wide waken
what deep sleep locks away.
I've traversed the world,
wandered widely   2010
to solicit news,
to harvest primal wisdom.
There is no one
as informed as you;
you know
what the deep hides,
what courses through hill and dale,
air and water:
where beings are,
your breath stirs;   2020
where minds think,
you vouch for it:
it is said you are
aware of All.
To reap the rewards of wisdom,
I wake you from your sleep!

ERDA

Mein Schlaf ist Träumen,
mein Träumen Sinnen,
mein Sinnen Walten des Wissens.
2030 Doch, wenn ich schlafe,
wachen Nornen:
sie weben das Seil,
und spinnen fromm, was ich weiß:
was frägst du nicht die Nornen?

WANDERER

Im Zwange der Welt
weben die Nornen,
sie können nichts wenden noch wandeln.
Doch deiner Weisheit
dankt' ich den Rat wohl,
2040 wie zu hemmen ein rollendes Rad?

ERDA

Männertaten
umdämmern mir den Mut;
mich Wissende selbst
bezwang ein Waltender einst.
Ein Wunschmädchen
gebar ich Wotan:
der Helden Wal
hieß für sich er sie küren.
Kühn ist sie
2050 und weise auch:
was weckst du mich
und frägst um Kunde
nicht Erdas und Wotans Kind?

WANDERER

Die Walküre meinst du,
Brünnhild', die Maid?
Sie trotzte dem Stürmebezwinger,
wo er am stärksten selbst sich bezwang:
was den Lenker der Schlacht
zu tun verlangte,
2060 doch dem er wehrte

ERDA

I dream when I sleep,
I think when I dream,
my thought is where wisdom prevails.
Still, when I sleep,   2030
the Norns stay alert:
they weave the rope,
and valiantly tell all that I know:
why don't you ask the Norns?

WANDERER

The world constrains
the weaving of the Norns;
they cannot reverse or change anything.
But I'd still be grateful for
your sage advice:
how can a rolling wheel be stopped?   2040

ERDA

Deeds of men
darken my spirit;
once a ruling god
broke even me, wise as I am.
I bore to Wotan
a girl to carry out his wishes:
he told her to choose
for him heroes slain in battle.
She is dauntless
and wise too: 2050
why not ask for news
from the child of Erda and Wotan
instead of waking me?

WANDERER

You mean the Valkyrie,
Brünnhilde, the young woman?
She defied the vanquisher of storms,
when he decisively vanquished himself:
what was demanded of
the arbiter of the battle,
but which against his own instincts   2060

zuwider sich selbst, –
allzu vertraut
wagte die Trotzige
das für sich zu vollbringen, –
Brünnhild' – in brennender Schlacht.
Streitvater
strafte die Maid:
in ihr Auge drückte er Schlaf;
auf dem Felsen schläft sie fest:

2070 erwachen wird
die Weihliche nur,
um einen Mann zu minnen als Weib. –
Frommten mir Fragen an sie?
　　'ganz geisterhaft' *

ERDA

Wirr wird mir,
seit ich erwacht:
wild und kraus
kreist die Welt! –
Die Walküre,
der Wala Kind,

2080 büßt' in Banden des Schlafs,
als die wissende Mutter schlief?
Der den Trotz lehrte,
straft den Trotz?
Der die Tat entzündet,
zürnt um die Tat?
Der die Rechte wahrt,
der die Eide hütet,
wehret dem Recht,
herrscht durch Meineid?
　　Es muß im Ausdruck fühlbar werden, wie Erda von dem
　　Willen Wotan's in Banden gehalten wird. *

2090 Laß mich wieder hinab! –
Schlaf verschließe mein Wissen!

WANDERER

Dich Mutter lass' ich nicht ziehn,
da des Zaubers mächtig ich bin. –

he bridled at doing, –
the defiant girl – Brünnhilde –
all too trustingly
dared in a blazing battle
to carry out for herself.
The father of disputes
punished the young woman:
into her eyes, he induced sleep;
she is sound asleep on the rock:
the revered girl   2070
will only be woken
to love a man as his wife. –
What's the point of asking her?
  'very eerily' *

ERDA

I am bewildered
since I woke:
savage and askew
is the orbit of the world! –
Did the Valkyrie,
child of the seeress,
as her knowing mother slept,   2080
suffer in the shackles of sleep?
You would teach defiance,
yet it's defiance you punish?
You incite an act,
yet against that act you rage?
You preserve rights,
you protect vows,
yet rights you oppose,
and through perjury you rule?

  The extent to which Erda is enslaved by Wotan's will
  must be palpable in the expression of this passage. *

Let me return to the deep! –   2090
Let sleep lock my wisdom away!

WANDERER

As I'm empowered by magic,
mother, I'll not let you leave. –

Urwissend
stachest du einst
der Sorge Stachel
in Wotans wagendes Herz:
mit Furcht vor schmachvoll
feindlichem Ende
2100   füllt' ihn dein Wissen,
daß Bangen band seinen Mut.
Bist du der Welt
weisestes Weib,
sage mir nun:
wie besiegt die Sorge der Gott?

ERDA
Du bist nicht,
was du dich nennst!
   mit äusserst schmerzlichem Ausdruck *
Was kamst du, störrischer Wilder,
zu stören der Wala Schlaf?

WANDERER
2110   Du bist nicht,
was du dich wähnst!
Urmütter-Weisheit
geht zu Ende:
dein Wissen verweht
vor meinem Willen. –
Weißt du, was Wotan will? –
   langes Schweigen
Dir Unweisen
ruf' ich in's Ohr,
daß sorglos ewig du nun schläfst!

2120   Um der Götter Ende
grämt mich die Angst nicht,
seit mein Wunsch es will.
Was in des Zwiespalts wildem Schmerze
verzweifelnd einst ich beschloß,
froh und freudig
führe frei ich nun aus.
   immer etwas gedehnt

Primal knowledge
led you to strike
a barb of fear
into Wotan's bold heart:
fearing a humiliatingly
hostile end,
he was consumed by your insight,   2100
unnerved to his core.
As you are the wisest
woman of the world,
tell me this:
how does a god conquer dread?

ERDA

You are not
what you say you are!
    *with extremely bitter expression**
Why did you come, restive savage,
to disturb the seeress's sleep?

WANDERER

You are not   2110
what you imagine you are!
The wisdom of ancient mothers
comes to a close:
your insight fades
before my will. –
Do you know what Wotan wants? –
    long silence
Unwise as you are,
let my words ring in your ears,
so you can sleep eternally without care!

I do not fret about   2120
the destruction of the gods,
now that I want to see it happen.
Once on the horns of a dilemma,
deciding under frantic duress,
I can now act freely
in gladness and in joy.
    always somewhat drawn out

Weiht' ich in wütendem Ekel
des Niblungen Neid schon die Welt;
dem herrlichsten Wälsung
2130 weis' ich mein Erbe nun an.
Der von mir erkoren,
doch nie mich gekannt,
ein kühnester Knabe,
bar meines Rates,
errang den Niblungenring.
Liebesfroh,
ledig des Neides,
erlahmt an dem Edlen
Alberichs Fluch:
2140 denn fremd bleibt ihm die Furcht.
Die du mir gebarst,
Brünnhild',
weckt sich hold der Held: –
wachend wirkt
dein wissendes Kind
erlösende Weltentat.
       etwas gedehnt
Drum schlafe nun du,
schließe dein Auge,
träumend erschau mein Ende!
2150 Was Jene auch wirken,
dem ewig Jungen
weicht in Wonne der Gott.
Hinab denn, Erda!
Urmütterfurcht!
Ursorge!
Hinab! Hinab
zu ew'gem Schlaf!

Nachdem Erda bereits die Augen geschlossen hat und all-
mählich tiefer versunken ist, verschwindet sie jetzt gänz-
lich; auch die Höhle ist jetzt wiederum durchaus verfins-
tert. Monddämmerung erhellt die Bühne, der Sturm hat
aufgehört.

In an act of furious revulsion, I once
left the world to the Nibelung's hate;
I leave my legacy now
to the greatest Wälsung.   2130
Chosen by me,
but to me a stranger,
a dauntless boy,
but without my help,
has won the Nibelung's ring.
Lucky in love,
free of ill-will,
his grace enfeebles
Alberich's curse:
he is, after all, still impervious to fear.   2140
The hero will gently wake
Brünnhilde,
whom you bore to me: –
wide awake
your witting child will carry out
the deed that redeems the world.
   somewhat drawn out
So you may sleep now,
shut your eyes,
and as in a dream, witness my end!
Regardless of what they do,   2150
this god yields in delight
to the eternally young man.
Go down then, Erda!
Primordial fear of ancient mothers!
Primordial dread!
Go down! Down
to eternal sleep!
   After Erda has already closed her eyes and gradually sunk
   deeper down, she now totally disappears; the cave is also
   now completely dark again. The storm has abated and the
   rising moon begins to cast its light over the stage.

ZWEITE SZENE

*Der Wanderer ist dicht an die Höhle getreten und lehnt sich
dann mit dem Rücken an sie, das Gesicht der Szene zugewandt.*

WANDERER
Dort seh' ich Siegfried nahn. –
Er verbleibt in seiner Stellung an der Höhle.
Siegfrieds Waldvogel flattert dem Vordergrunde zu.
*Plötzlich hält der Vogel in seiner Richtung ein, flattert
ängstlich hin und her und verschwindet hastig dem Hin-
tergrunde zu.*
Siegfried tritt auf und hält an.

SIEGFRIED
Mein Vöglein schwebte mir fort.

2160   Mit flatterndem Flug
und süßem Sang
wies es mich wonnig des Weg's:
nun schwand es fern mir davon! –
Am besten find' ich mir
selbst nun den Berg:
wohin mein Führer mich wies,
dahin wandr' ich jetzt fort. –
Er schreitet nach hinten.

WANDERER *immer in seiner Stellung verbleibend*
Wohin, Knabe,
heißt dich dein Weg?

SIEGFRIED *Er hält an und wendet sich um.*

2170   Da redet's ja?
wohl rät das mir den Weg? –
Er tritt dem Wanderer näher.
Einen Felsen such' ich,
von Feuer ist der umwabert:
dort schläft ein Weib,
das ich wecken will.

WANDERER
Wer sagt' es dir

SCENE TWO

The Wanderer has stepped close to the cave and leans his back
against it while facing towards the stage.

WANDERER
  I can see Siegfried approaching. –
      He remains in his place by the cave.
          Siegfried's forest bird flutters into the foreground.
          Suddenly the bird stops in its tracks, fluttering nervous-
          ly to and fro, and disappears in haste towards the back-
          ground.
          Siegfried enters and stands still.
SIEGFRIED
  My little bird's flown off.
  Flapping its wings   2160
  and singing sweetly,
  it happily showed me the way:
  it's far from me now, gone! –
  So if I find the mountain
  myself, that's best:
  I'll now travel on to where
  my leader showed me to go.
      He strides to the back.
WANDERER *always remaining in place*
  In which direction, boy,
  does your path take you?
SIEGFRIED *He stands still and turns round.*
  Someone talking?   2170
  probably telling me the way? –
      He steps closer to the Wanderer
  I'm looking for a rock
  with fire swirling around it:
  a woman's asleep there,
  and I want to wake her.
WANDERER
  Who told you

den Fels zu suchen?
Wer nach der Frau dich zu sehnen?

SIEGFRIED
Mich wies ein singend
2180   Waldvöglein,
das gab mir gute Kunde.

WANDERER
Ein Vöglein schwatzt wohl manches,
kein Mensch doch kann's verstehn:
wie mochtest du Sinn
dem Sang entnehmen?

SIEGFRIED
Das wirkte das Blut
eines wilden Wurms,
der mir vor Neidhöhl' erblaßte:
kaum netzt' es zündend
2190   die Zunge mir,
da verstand ich der Vöglein Gestimm'.

WANDERER
Erschlugst den Riesen du,
wer reizte dich,
den starken Wurm zu bestehn?

SIEGFRIED
Mich führte Mime,
ein falscher Zwerg;
das Fürchten wollt' er mich lehren:
zum Schwertstreich aber,
der ihn erstach,
2200   reizte der Wurm mich selbst:
seinen Rachen riß er mir auf.

*Der ganze Dialog zwischen Wotan und Siegfried 'ohne jede Leidenschaftlichkeit' auszuführen, was natürlich charakteristische Lebendigkeit des Ausdrucks nicht ausschließt. ***

WANDERER
Wer schuf das Schwert
so scharf und hart,
daß der stärkste Feind ihm fiel?

to look for the rock?
To pine after the woman?

SIEGFRIED

A little forest bird
showed me in song: 2180
it had good news to tell me.

WANDERER

A little bird chatters away,
but nobody can understand it:
how did you make
sense of its song?

SIEGFRIED

That was the work
of the savage dragon's blood
I spilled in front of Neidhöhle:
the moment I felt its fire
on my tongue,   2190
the little bird's tune made sense.

WANDERER

If you slew the giant,
who spurred you on
to tackle the powerful dragon?

SIEGFRIED

A duplicitous dwarf,
Mime, got me into it;
he wanted to teach me fear:
but it was the dragon
that goaded me on
to deliver the fatal blow: 2200
his wide-open jaws were for me.

*The whole dialogue between Wotan and Siegfried is to
be played 'without any kind of passionate engagement',
which of course does not exclude appropriate liveliness
of expression.* *

WANDERER

Who created a sword
so sharp and ruthless
that the mightiest foe is its victim?

SIEGFRIED

Das schweiß' ich mir selbst,
da's der Schmied nicht konnte:
schwertlos noch wär' ich wohl sonst.

WANDERER

Doch, wer schuf
die starken Stücken,
2210   daraus das Schwert du dir geschweißt?

SIEGFRIED

Was weiß ich davon?
Ich weiß allein,
daß die Stücke mir nichts nützten,
schuf ich das Schwert mir nicht neu.
   Der Wanderer bricht in ein freudig gemütliches Lachen
   aus.

WANDERER

Das mein' ich wohl auch!
   Er betrachtet Siegfried wohlgefällig.

SIEGFRIED *verwundert*

Was lachst du mich aus?
Alter Frager!
Hör' einmal auf,
laß mich nicht länger hier schwatzen.
2220   Kannst du den Weg
mir weisen, so rede:
vermagst du's nicht,
so halte dein Maul!

WANDERER

Geduld, du Knabe!
Dünk' ich dich alt,
so sollst du Achtung mir bieten.

SIEGFRIED

Das wär' nicht übel!
Solang' ich lebe,
stand mir ein Alter
2230   stets im Wege,
den hab' ich nun fort gefegt.
Stemmst du dort länger

SIEGFRIED

I welded it together myself,
because the smith couldn't:
otherwise I'd still be without a sword.

WANDERER

But who made
the powerful pieces
welded by you to make the sword?   2210

SIEGFRIED

How should I know?
I just know
that the pieces would have been useless
if I'd made the sword the old way.

*The Wanderer breaks out in cheerfully complacent laugh-
ter.*

WANDERER

That's what I think too!

He looks at Siegfried, pleased with what he sees.

SIEGFRIED *puzzled*

Are you making fun of me?
Old busybody!
Just stop it,
don't let me gossip here any longer.
If you can show   2220
me the way, tell me:
if you can't,
shut your mouth!

WANDERER

You boy, be patient!
If I look old to you,
you ought to show me respect.

SIEGFRIED

Not a bad idea!
All my life
an old man was
always in my way,   2230
and now I've swept him aside.
If you stand there much

steif dich mir entgegen,
sieh dich vor, sag' ich,
   mit entsprechender Gebärde
daß du wie Mime nicht fährst!
   Er tritt noch näher an den Wanderer hinan.
Wie siehst du denn aus?
Was hast du gar
für 'nen großen Hut?
Warum hängt er dir so in's Gesicht?

WANDERER *immer ohne seine Stellung zu verlassen*
2240 Das ist so Wand'rers Weise,
wenn dem Wind entgegen er geht.
   Siegfried immer näher ihn betrachtend

SIEGFRIED
Doch darunter fehlt dir ein Auge!
Das schlug dir einer
gewiß schon aus,
dem du zu trotzig
den Weg vertratst?
Mach dich jetzt fort,
sonst könntest du leicht
das andere auch noch verlieren.

WANDERER *sehr ruhig*
2250 Ich seh', mein Sohn,
wo du nichts weißt,
da weißt du dir leicht zu helfen. –
Mit dem Auge,
das als andres mir fehlt,
erblickst du selber das eine,
das mir zum Sehen verblieb.

SIEGFRIED *der sinnend zugehört hat, bricht jetzt unwill-*
   kürlich in ein helles Lachen aus.
Hahahaha!
Zum Lachen bist du mir lustig. –
Doch hör', nun schwatz' ich nicht länger:
2260 geschwind, zeig' mir den Weg, –
deines Weges ziehe dann du;
zu nichts andrem

longer blocking my path,
watch out, I warn you,
   with an appropriate gesture
don't come a cropper like Mime!
   He steps still closer to the Wanderer.
Aren't you a bit of a sight?
What's that big
hat you're wearing?
Why's it hanging over your face?

WANDERER *always without moving from where he stands*
That's what happens to the Wanderer   2240
when he walks against the wind.
   Siegfried constantly observing him more closely

SIEGFRIED
But under it you're missing an eye!
Someone surely gouged
it out, didn't they,
when you pig-headedly
stood in their way?
Now get off with you,
otherwise you'll quickly
lose the other one too.

WANDERER *very calmly*
I see, my son,   2250
that when you know nothing,
you're ready with easy answers. –
You yourself are
looking with my
missing eye at the one
I have left to see with.

SIEGFRIED *who has been listening thoughtfully, now spon-*
   taneously bursts out in ringing laughter.
Hahahaha!
You make me laugh, you're funny. –
But listen, I can't stand here chatting:
hurry up, show me the way, –   2260
and you get moving too;
I can't see what else

acht' ich dich nütz':
drum sprich, sonst spreng' ich dich fort!
WANDERER *weich*
  Kenntest du mich,
  kühner Sproß, –
  den Schimpf spartest du mir.
  Dir so vertraut,
  trifft mich schmerzlich dein Dräuen.
2270 Liebt' ich von je
  deine lichte Art,
  Grauen auch zeugt' ihr
  mein zürnender Grimm.
  Dem ich so hold bin,
  Allzuhehrer!
  Heut' nicht wecke mir Neid:
  er vernichtete dich und mich!
SIEGFRIED
  Bleibst du mir stumm,
  störrischer Wicht?
2280 Weich von der Stelle,
  denn dorthin, ich weiß,
  führt es zur schlafenden Frau:
  so wies es mein Vöglein,
  das hier erst flüchtig entfloh.
      Es wird schnell wieder ganz finster.
WANDERER *in Zorn ausbrechend und in gebieterischer Stel-*
      lung
  Es floh dir zu seinem Heil!
  Den Herrn der Raben
  erriet es hier:
  weh' ihm, holen sie's ein! –
  Den Weg, den es zeigte,
2290 sollst du nicht ziehn!
      Siegfried tritt mit Verwunderung in trotziger Stellung
      zurück.
SIEGFRIED
  Hoho! – Du Verbieter!
  Wer bist du denn,

you're useful for:
so speak, or I'll throw you out!

WANDERER *softly*

  If, my bold heir,
  you knew me, –
  you'd spare me your abuse.
  Close to you as I am,
  I feel hurt by your threats.
  From the start I've loved   2270
  your clear-sighted ways,
  even if my raging wrath
  sowed seeds of dread.
  I truly mean you well,
  hero all too sublime!
  Don't arouse my fury today:
  it could indeed crush you and me!

SIEGFRIED

  Won't you tell me,
  mealy-mouthed wretch?
  Then get out of the way,   2280
  because that path, I know,
  leads to the sleeping woman:
  the little bird, the one that flew
  away fast, told me as much.
    It is quickly getting quite dark again.

WANDERER *fulminating angrily and assuming a dictatorial stance*

  It fled you for its salvation!
  It sensed that the lord
  of the ravens was here:
  woe to it, if they catch up with it! –
  You are not to take
  the way it showed!   2290
    Siegfried steps back in amazement but in a defiant posture.

SIEGFRIED

  Hoho! – You tyrant!
  So who are you

daß du mir wehren willst?

WANDERER

Fürchte des Felsens Hüter!
Verschlossen hält
meine Macht die schlafende Maid: –
wer sie erweckte,
wer sie gewänne,
machtlos macht' er mich ewig.

2300 Ein Feuermeer
umflutet die Frau:
glühende Lohe
umleckt den Fels:
wer die Braut begehrt,
dem brennt entgegen die Brunst. –

Er winkt mit dem Speere nach der Felsenhöhe.

Blick' nach der Höh'!
Erlugst du das Licht?
Es wächst der Schein,
es schwillt die Glut:
2310 sengende Wolken,
wabernde Lohe,
wälzen sich brennend
und prasselnd herab:
ein Lichtmeer
umleuchtet dein Haupt;

*Mit wachsender Helle zeigt sich von der Höhe des Felsens
her ein wabernder Feuerschein.*

bald frißt und zehrt dich
zündendes Feuer. –
Zurück denn, rasendes Kind!

SIEGFRIED

Zurück, du Prahler, mit dir!
2320 Dort, wo die Brünste brennen,
zu Brünnhilde muß ich dahin!

Er schreitet weiter. Der Wanderer stellt sich ihm entgegen.

WANDERER

Fürchtest das Feuer du nicht,
so sperre mein Speer dir den Weg! –

to want to stop me?

WANDERER

Dread the defender of the rock!
My power
seals off the sleeping young woman: –
who wakes her,
who wins her,
ruins my power for ever.

A sea of fire   2300
encircles the woman:
a fiery furnace
engulfs the rock:
scorching heat will surge
towards the wooer of the bride. –
    He points with his spear to the top of the rock.
Look to the top!
Do you see the light?
The glow brightens,
the heat swells:
storms of fire,   2310
swirling infernos
tumble burning
and blasting downwards:
your head is haloed
in a sea of light;
    *A swirling glow of fire appears from the direction of the
    top of the rock with growing brightness.*
consuming fire is soon
to devour you, to sap your daring. –
So retreat, raving boy!

SIEGFRIED

You retreat, you show-off!
Where the heat is ablaze, there   2320
I must go to Brünnhilde!
    He steps further along. The Wanderer stands in his way.

WANDERER

For you, the fire holds no fear,
so my spear will block your way! –

Noch hält meine Hand
der Herrschaft Haft:
das Schwert, das du schwingst,
zerschlug einst dieser Schaft:
noch einmal denn
zerspring' es am ew'gen Speer!
   Er streckt den Speer vor.
SIEGFRIED *das Schwert ziehend*
2330   Meines Vaters Feind,
find' ich dich hier?
Herrlich zur Rache
geriet mir das!
Schwing deinen Speer:
in Stücken spalt' ihn mein Schwert!
   *Er haut dem Wanderer mit einem Schlage den Speer in
   zwei Stücken: ein Blitz fährt daraus nach der Felsenhöhe
   zu, wo von nun an der bisher mattere Schein in immer
   helleren Feuerflammen zu lodern beginnt. Starker Don-
   ner, der schnell sich abschwächt, begleitet den Schlag.*
      *Die Speerstücken rollen zu des Wanderers Füssen. Er
   rafft sie ruhig auf.*
WANDERER *zurückweichend*
Zieh hin! Ich kann dich nicht halten! –
   Er verschwindet plötzlich in völliger Finsternis.
SIEGFRIED
Mit zerfocht'ner Waffe
wich mir der Feige?
   *Wagner sprach die [vorangehenden] Worte vor mit einem
   wie naiv-verwunderten Ausdruck.* *
      *Die wachsende Helle der immer tiefer sich senkenden
   Feuerwolken trifft Siegfrieds Blick.*
Ha! Wonnige Glut!
2340   Leuchtender Glanz!
Strahlend nun offen
steht mir die Straße.
Im Feuer mich baden!
Im Feuer zu finden die Braut!
Hoho! Hahei!
Jetzt lock' ich ein liebes Gesell!

I still hold in my hand
the symbol of sovereignty:
this shaft did once shatter
the sword you now flourish:
so yet again
my eternal spear will rent it asunder!
  He stretches out his spear.
SIEGFRIED *drawing his sword*
  My father's enemy,   2330
  I've found you here?
  Now's my chance
  for superb revenge!
  Wield your spear:
  my sword will cut it apart!
    *At a single stroke, he cuts the Wanderer's spear in two:
    the impact produces a flash of lightning right up to the
    top of the rock, where a hitherto dull glow now begins to
    flare up with constantly brighter tongues of fire. The loud
    thunder accompanying the impact quickly subsides.*
      *The pieces of the spear roll towards the Wanderer's feet.
    He calmly picks them up.*
WANDERER *backing off*
  Move on! I can't stop you! –
    He vanishes instantly in total gloom.
SIEGFRIED
  With his weapon smashed,
  has the coward relented?
    *Wagner recited the [preceding] words with an expression
    that gave a sense of naïve wonderment.* *
      *The growing brilliance of the fire clouds constantly bil-
    lowing down towards him catches Siegfried's attention.*
  Ha! My darling fire!
  The radiance of your glow!   2340
  My road now lies open
  in glorious light.
  To bathe in fire!
  In fire to find the bride!
  Hoho! Hahei!
  Now I can attract a dear friend!

[Siegfried] setzt sein Horn an und stürzt sich in das wo-
gende Feuer, welches sich, von der Höhe herabdringend,
nun auch über den Vordergrund ausbreitet.
    [Takt 776] Siegfried, den man bald nicht mehr erblickt,
scheint sich nach der Höhe zu entfernen.
    [Takt 787] Hellstes Leuchten der Flammen
    [Takt 999] Von hier an, wo die Glut am stärksten war,
beginnt sie zu erbleichen und löst sich allmählich in ein
immer feineres, wie durch die Morgenröte beleuchtetes
Gewölk auf.

DRITTE SZENE

Auf dem Gipfel des 'Brünnhildensteines'

Das immer zarter gewordene Gewölk hat sich in einen feinen
Nebelschleier von rosiger Färbung aufgelöst und zerteilt sich
nun in der Weise, daß der Duft sich gänzlich nach oben ver-
zieht und dort endlich nur noch den heitren, blauen Tageshim-
mel erblicken läßt, während am Saume der nun sichtbar wer-
denden Felsenhöhe ganz die gleiche Szene wie im 3. Akte der
'Walküre' ein morgenrötlicher Nebelschleier haften bleibt,
welcher zugleich an die in der Tiefe noch lodernde Zauberlohe
erinnert. – Die Anordnung der Szene ist durchaus dieselbe wie
am Schlusse der 'Walküre': im Vordergrunde, unter der breit-
ästigen Tanne, liegt Brünnhilde, in vollständiger, glänzender
Panzerrüstung, mit dem Helm auf dem Haupte, den langen
Schild über sich gedeckt, in tiefem Schlafe.
    Siegfried gelangt von außen her auf den felsigen Saum der
Höhe und zeigt sich dort zuerst nur mit dem Oberleibe: so
blickt er lange staunend um sich. –

SIEGFRIED *leise*
  Selige Öde
  auf wonniger Höhe!

[Siegfried] raises his horn to his lips and dives hell for leather into the billowing fire as it surges downwards from the heights and even spreads into the foreground.

[bar 776] Siegfried, who will soon disappear from sight, appears to recede into the distance towards the summit.

[bar 787] the flames burning at their brightest

[bar 999] From here on, the blaze at its most intense begins to die down and gradually dissolves into an increasingly delicate cloud that looks as if it is lit up by a sunrise.

SCENE THREE

On the summit of 'Brünnhilde's rock'

The cloud formation that was steadily becoming softer and softer has now dissolved into a fine veil of rose-coloured mist, dissipating in such a way that the clouds are dispersing towards the top. Eventually only clear blue sky can be seen there. Meanwhile along the edge of the increasingly visible top of the rocks – exactly like the scene in the third act of The Valkyrie – there hangs a veil of reddish morning mist, which at the same time resembles the magic fire still swirling in the deep. – The arrangement of the stage picture is exactly the same as that at the end of The Valkyrie: in the foreground under the long outstretched branches of the pine-tree, Brünnhilde is lying in a deep sleep in full brilliant armour, with her helmet on her head and her long shield covering her body.

Coming from outside, Siegfried reaches the rocky edge of the top, at first only with his upper body showing: astonished, he takes a long look at his surroundings. –

SIEGFRIED *quietly*
Divine solitude
on rapturous heights!

*Er steigt vollends ganz herauf und betrachtet, auf einem
Felsensteine des hinteren Abhanges stehend, mit Verwun-
derung die Szene.*

    Er blickt zur Seite in den Tann und schreitet etwas vor.

Was ruht dort schlummernd

2350   im schattigen Tann?

Ein Roß ist's,

rastend in tiefem Schlaf!

    *Langsam näher kommend, hält er verwundert an, als er
noch aus einiger Entfernung Brünnhildes Gestalt wahr-
nimmt.*

Was strahlt mir dort entgegen?

Welch glänzendes Stahlgeschmeid'?

Blendet mir noch

die Lohe den Blick? –

    Er tritt näher hinzu.

Helle Waffen? –

Heb' ich sie auf? –

    *Er hebt den Schild ab und erblickt Brünnhildes Gestalt,
während ihr Gesicht jedoch noch zum großen Teil vom
Helm verdeckt ist.*

Ha! – In Waffen ein Mann? –

2360   Wie mahnt mich wonnig sein Bild! –

Das hehre Haupt

drückt wohl der Helm? –

Leichter würd' ihm,

löst' ich den Schmuck?

    *Vorsichtig löst er den Helm und hebt ihn der Schlafen-
den vom Haupte ab: langes lockiges Haar bricht hervor.
– Siegfried erschrickt.*

     zart

Ach! Wie schön!

    Er bleibt im Anblick versunken.

Schimmernde Wolken

säumen in Wellen

den hellen Himmels-See;

    ohne Steigerung in Stärke und Ausdruck*

*He climbs up until he is completely visible. Standing on
a rocky precipice at the back, he surveys the scene with
amazement.*

    He looks sideways into the forest and advances slightly.
What's lying there dozing
in the cool of the forest?   2350
It's a horse
sound asleep, resting!
    *Approaching slowly, he stops in wonderment when, still
    somewhat at a distance, he becomes aware of Brünnhilde's
    shape.*
What's the radiant light I see?
That brilliantly shining metal?
Are the flames
dazzling me still? –
    He steps closer.
Shining weaponry? –
Shall I lift it off? –
    *He lifts off Brünnhilde's shield. While her face for the
    most part is still hidden by her helmet, he takes a good
    look at her body.*
Ha! Is it a man in armour? –
How his image happily stirs me! –   2360
Isn't the helmet pressing
on his fine head? –
Won't it be easier for him
if I take that part off?
    *He carefully loosens the helmet and lifts it away from the
    sleeping Brünnhilde's head: long curly hair tumbles out.
    – Siegfried is startled.*
      tenderly
Ah! How lovely!
    He remains absorbed in what he sees.
Gleaming mists
garland the bright
lake of the heavens;
    without intensification of volume and expression*

leuchtender Sonne
2370 lachendes Bild
strahlt durch das Wogengewölk!
   Er neigt sich tiefer zu der Schlafenden hinab.
Von schwellendem Atem
schwingt sich die Brust: –
brech' ich die engende Brünne?
   Er versucht, die Brünne zu lösen.
Komm, mein Schwert!
Schneide das Eisen!
   Er zieht sein Schwert, durchschneidet mit zarter Vorsicht
   die Panzerringe zu beiden Seiten der Rüstung und hebt
   dann die Brünne und die Schienen ab, so daß nun Brünn-
   hilde in einem weichen weiblichen Gewande vor ihm
   liegt. Er fährt erschreckt und staunend auf.
Das ist kein Mann! –
   Er starrt mit höchster Aufgeregtheit auf die Schlafende
   hin.
Brennender Zauber
zückt mir in's Herz;
2380 feurige Angst
faßt meine Augen:
mir schwankt und schwindelt der Sinn.
   Er gerät in höchste Beklemmung.
Wen ruf' ich zum Heil,
daß er mir helfe?
Mutter! Mutter!
Gedenke mein'!
   Er sinkt, wie ohnmächtig, an Brünnhildes Busen.
      langes Schweigen
         Er fährt seufzend auf.
Wie weck' ich die Maid,
daß sie ihr Auge mir öffne? –
Das Auge mir öffnen?
2390 Blende mich auch noch der Blick?
Wagt' es mein Trotz?
Ertrüg' ich das Licht?
Mir schwebt und schwankt

the laughing image
of the radiant sun   2370
shines through swelling cloud!
He bends down closer to the sleeping figure.
With puffs of breath
his chest is moving: –
should I cut the tight coat of mail?
He tries to loosen the coat of mail.
Come, my sword!
Sever the iron!
*He pulls out his sword, cuts through some metal rings in
the coat on both sides with tender care and then lifts off
a whole piece of the chainmail and the shin guards. He
then sees Brünnhilde lying before him in soft feminine
clothing. He reacts with shock and astonishment.*
That's not a man! –
*In an extremely flustered state, he stares at the sleeping
woman.*
Stinging sorcery
stabs at my heart;
fervid fear   2380
takes hold of my eyes:
my mind falters and flounders.
He falls into a state of extreme anxiety.
Who's there to help me,
to grant me salvation?
Mother! Mother!
Think of me!
He sinks onto Brünnhilde's bosom as if passing out.
   long silence
   He gets up with a sigh.
How do I wake the young woman
that she may open her eyes to me? –
Open her eyes to me?
Will her look bedazzle me too?   2390
I'm defiant, but am I that brave?
Could I stand the light?
I'm teetering and tottering

und schwirrt es umher!
> *Muß 'wunderschön' gesungen werden. 'Als ob es aus einer*
> *recht schönen italienischen Oper wäre.'* *

Sehrendes Sehnen
zehrt meine Sinne;
am zagenden Herzen
zittert die Hand!
Wie ist mir Feigem?
2400   Ist dies das Fürchten?
O Mutter! Mutter!
Dein mutiges Kind!
> *sehr zart*

Im Schlafe liegt eine Frau, –
die hat ihn das Fürchten gelehrt.
Wie end' ich die Furcht?
Wie fass' ich Mut? –
Daß ich selbst erwache,
muß die Maid ich erwecken. –
> *Indem er sich der Schlafenden von neuem nähert, wird*
> *er wieder von zarteren Empfindungen an ihren Anblick*
> *gefesselt.*
> > *Er neigt sich tiefer hinab.*

Süß erbebt mir
2410   ihr blühender Mund. –
Wie mild erzitternd
mich Zagen er reizt! –
Ach! Dieses Atems
wonnig warmes Gedüft'!
> *wie in Verzweiflung*

Erwache! Erwache!
Heiliges Weib!
> *Er starrt auf sie hin.*

Sie hört mich nicht. –
> *gedehnt, mit gepreßtem, drängendem Ausdruck*

So saug' ich mir Leben
aus süßesten Lippen, –
> *nachlassend*

2420   sollt' ich auch sterbend vergehn!

and my mind's a wreck!
> *The following has to be sung 'gorgeously.' 'As if it's come*
> *from a really beautiful Italian opera.'* *

Aching longing
saps my senses;
my hands shake
on my limping heart!
Why such a coward?
Is this what fear is?   2400
O mother! Mother!
Your intrepid child!
> *very tenderly*

A woman lies asleep, –
she's taught him the meaning of fear.
How do I end fear?
Where do I find courage? –
I must wake the young woman,
so I myself can wake up. –
> *Nearing the sleeping woman for a second time, he is cap-*
> *tivated again by the more delicate sensitivities of her*
> *appearance.*
> > *He bends down closer.*

Her beautiful mouth
imparts a sweet shudder. –   2410
How its gentle trembling
excites me in my fear!
Ah! The lovely warm scent
of her breath!
> *with a look of despair*

Awaken! Awaken!
Sacred wife!
> *He stares at her.*

She can't hear me. –
> *slowly, with strained, urgent expression*

So I'll suck life
from those lips most sweet, –
> *flagging*

even should my life seep away!   2420

Er sinkt, wie ersterbend, auf die Schlafende und heftet,
mit geschlossenen Augen, seine Lippen auf ihren Mund.
Brünnhilde schlägt die Augen auf. – Siegfried fährt auf
und bleibt vor ihr stehen.
Brünnhilde richtet sich langsam zum Sitze auf.
Sie begrüßt mit feierlichen Gebärden der erhobenen
Arme ihre Rückkehr zur Wahrnehmung der Erde und des
Himmels.

BRÜNNHILDE

Heil dir, Sonne!
Heil dir, Licht!
Heil dir, leuchtender Tag! –
Lang war mein Schlaf;
ich bin erwacht:
wer ist der Held,
der mich erweckt'?

Siegfried von ihrem Blicke und ihrer Stimme feierlich
ergriffen, steht wie fest gebannt.

SIEGFRIED

Durch das Feuer drang ich,
das den Fels umbrann:
2430   ich erbrach dir den festen Helm:
Siegfried bin ich,
der dich erweckt.

BRÜNNHILDE *hoch aufgerichtet sitzend*

Heil euch, Götter!
Heil dir, Welt!
Heil dir, prangende Erde!
Zu End' ist nun mein Schlaf;
erwacht, seh' ich:
Siegfried ist es,
der mich erweckt.

SIEGFRIED *in erhabenste Verzückung ausbrechend*

2440   O Heil der Mutter,
die mich gebar!
Heil der Erde,
die mich genährt!
Daß ich das Aug' erschaut,

Looking as if he is about to die, he sinks onto the sleeping woman and with eyes shut presses his lips on her mouth.

Brünnhilde opens her eyes. – Siegfried gets up and stands still in front of her.

Brünnhilde slowly draws herself up into a sitting position.

Making solemn gestures with raised arms, she celebrates her return to a sense of the earth and the heavens.

BRÜNNHILDE

I greet you, sun!
I greet you, light!
I greet you, glorious day! –
My sleep was long;
I have been woken:
who is the hero,
who woke me?

Powerfully moved by her gaze and her voice, Siegfried stands looking as if he is being charmed by a magic spell.

SIEGFRIED

I passed through the blaze
surrounding the rock:
I prised your tight helmet open: 2430
I am Siegfried,
who woke you.

BRÜNNHILDE *sitting up straight*

I greet you, gods!
I greet you, world!
I greet you, glorious earth!
My sleep is ended;
now woken, I see:
it is Siegfried,
who woke me.

SIEGFRIED *breaking out in the most enraptured delight*

Let us greet the mother,   2440
who bore me!
Greet the earth,
which fed me!
Because they let me see the eyes,

das jetzt mir Seligem lacht!

BRÜNNHILDE *mit größter Bewegtheit*

O Heil der Mutter,
die dich gebar!
Heil der Erde,
die dich genährt!

2450 Nur dein Blick durfte mich schaun,
erwachen durft' ich nur dir!

*Beide bleiben voll strahlenden Entzückens in ihren ge-
genseitigen Anblick verloren.*

O Siegfried! Siegfried!
Seliger Held,
du Wecker des Lebens,
siegendes Licht!
O wüßtest du, Lust der Welt,
wie ich dich je geliebt!
Du warst mein Sinnen,
mein Sorgen du.

2460 Dich Zarten nährt' ich,
noch eh' du gezeugt,
noch eh' du geboren,
barg dich mein Schild.

wie eine zu ihrem Kinde sprechende Mutter*

So lang lieb' ich dich, Siegfried!

SIEGFRIED *leise und schüchtern*

So starb nicht meine Mutter?
Schlief die minnige nur?

*Brünnhilde lächelt, freundlich die Hand nach ihm aus-
streckend.*

BRÜNNHILDE

Du wonniges Kind!
zögernd
Deine Mutter kehrt dir nicht wieder.
Du selbst bin ich,
mit Wärme*

2470 wenn du mich Selige liebst.
dies wieder ruhig*
Was du nicht weißt,

which laugh now into my soul!

BRÜNNHILDE *with the deepest emotion*
Let us greet the mother,
who bore you!
Greet the earth,
which fed you!
Only your eyes were ever to see me,   2450
only you were ever to wake me!
  At the sight of each other, they remain transfixed, brim-
  ming with vibrant rapture.
O Siegfried! Siegfried!
Divine hero,
you restorer of life,
victorious light!
Oh, if you, the world's pleasure,
knew how I always loved you!
You were my mind,
my only care.
I fostered your delicate being,   2460
even before you were conceived.
Even before you were born,
my shield was your shelter.
  *like a mother speaking to her child**
I've loved you, Siegfried, that long!

SIEGFRIED *softly and shyly*
So my mother didn't die?
Was my love just asleep?
  Brünnhilde smiles, amiably stretching out her hand to
  him.

BRÜNNHILDE
You sweet child!
  hesitantly
You'll not see your mother return.
I am you, your very being,
  *with warmth**
if I am the blessed woman you love.   2470
  *restoring her calm**
What you do not know,

weiß ich für dich;
doch wissend bin ich
nur, weil ich dich liebe!

O Siegfried! Siegfried!
Siegendes Licht!
Dich liebt' ich immer,
denn mir allein
erdünkte Wotans Gedanke:
2480 der Gedanke, den ich nie
nennen durfte,
den ich nicht dachte,
sondern nur fühlte;
für den ich focht,
kämpfte und stritt,
für den ich trotzte
dem, der ihn dachte;
für den ich büßte,
Strafe mich band,
2490 weil ich nicht ihn dachte,
und nur empfand, –
denn, – der Gedanke –
dürftest du's lösen! –
mir war er nur Liebe zu dir!

*'Bis hierher waren Siegfried und Brünnhilde im Zustande
der Entrücktheit, wie im Reiche der Götterwelt, von jetzt
beginnt erst ihre Position von Mensch zu Mensch.' . . . Die
ganze Rede muß vom Darsteller des Siegfried als zart-
ester Dialog erfaßt werden.* *

SIEGFRIED
Wie Wunder tönt,
was wonnig du singst,
doch dunkel dünkt mich der Sinn.
   zart
Deines Auges Leuchten
seh' ich licht;
2500 deines Atems Wehen
fühl' ich warm,
deiner Stimme Singen

I know in your stead;
yet I know
only because I love you!

O Siegfried! Siegfried!
Victorious light!
You I've always loved,
because only I
could sense Wotan's idea:
an idea, which I was   2480
never to name,
which I did not think,
but only felt;
I fought for the idea,
in battle and in strife,
in its spirit I defied
the god who thought it;
I atoned for the idea,
locked in punishment,
because I sensed it,   2490
and did not think it, –
because – that idea –
you can probably guess! –
was for me only my love for you!

> *'Until now Siegfried and Brünnhilde have been in a state
> of heavenly rapture, as well as in the realm of the gods;
> from here their existence as one human being to another
> begins.' . . . The whole conversation must be seen by the
> one playing Siegfried as the tenderest of dialogues.* *

SIEGFRIED
What you sweetly sing
sounds like a miracle,
but to me its meaning is murky.
> *tenderly*
In the brilliance of your eyes
I see light;
in the waft of your breath   2500
I feel warmth;
in the singing of your voice

hör' ich süß: –
doch was du singend mir sagst,
staunend versteh' ich's nicht.
Nicht kann ich das Ferne
sinnig erfassen,
wenn alle Sinne
dich nur sehen und fühlen! –
2510 Mit banger Furcht
fesselst du mich:
du Einz'ge hast
ihre Angst mich gelehrt;
den du gebunden
in mächtigen Banden,
birg meinen Mut mir nicht mehr!

> *Er verweilt in großer Aufregung, sehnsuchtsvollen Blick*
> *auf sie heftend.*
>> *Brünnhilde wendet sanft das Haupt zur Seite und rich-*
>> *tet ihren Blick nach dem Tann.*

BRÜNNHILDE
Dort seh' ich Grane,
mein selig Ross:
wie weidet er munter,
2520 der mit mir schlief! –
Mit mir hat ihn Siegfried erweckt.

SIEGFRIED *in der vorigen Stellung verbleibend*
Auf wonnigem Munde
weidet mein Auge;
in brünstigem Durst
doch brennen die Lippen,
daß der Augen Weide sie labe! –

> *Brünnhilde deutet ihm mit der Hand nach ihren Waffen,*
> *die sie gewahrt.*

BRÜNNHILDE
Dort seh' ich den Schild,
der Helden schirmte.
Dort seh' ich den Helm,
2530 der das Haupt mir barg:
er schirmt, er birgt mich nicht mehr. –

I hear sweetness: –
but what you tell me in song,
I'm amazed to say I don't grasp.
I cannot relate to things
that aren't there,
if all I can see
and feel is you! –
You hold me captive   2510
with morbid fright:
you alone have
taught me fear;
you shackled me
in powerful bonds,
so hide my spirit from me no more!

    Fixing her with an impassioned look, he remains in a
    state of great excitement.

      Brünnhilde turns her head gently to one side and dir-
    ects her attention to the pine forest.

BRÜNNHILDE

There I see Grane,
my glorious horse:
he slept alongside me,
and now grazes in high spirits!   2520
With me, Siegfried woke him.

SIEGFRIED *staying in the same position*

My eyes graze
on your delightful mouth;
but let this feast for my eyes
refresh my lips,
burning with erotic thirst! –

    With her hand, Brünnhilde shows him that she has no-
    ticed her weapons.

BRÜNNHILDE

There I see my shield,
the protector of heroes.
There I see my helmet,
the guardian of my head: 2530
it protects, it guards me no more. –

SIEGFRIED *feurig*
  Eine selige Maid
  versehrte mein Herz;
  Wunden dem Haupte
  schlug mir ein Weib:
  ich kam ohne Schild und Helm!

BRÜNNHILDE *mit gesteigerter Wehmut*
  Ich sehe der Brünne
  prangenden Stahl:
  ein scharfes Schwert
2540 schnitt sie entzwei,
  von dem maidlichen Leibe
  löst' es die Wehr!
  Ich bin ohne Schutz und Schirm,
  ohne Trutz ein trauriges Weib!

SIEGFRIED *feurig*
  Durch brennendes Feuer
  fuhr ich zu dir,
  nicht Brünne noch Panzer
  barg meinen Leib:
  nun brach die Lohe
2550 mir in die Brust;
  es braust mein Blut
  in blühender Brunst;
  ein zehrendes Feuer
  ist mir entzündet:
  die Glut, die Brünnhilds
  Felsen umbrann,
  die brennt mir nun in der Brust! –
  O Weib! Jetzt lösche den Brand!
  Schweige die schäumende Wut!
    Er hat sie heftig umfaßt. Brünnhilde springt auf, wehrt
    ihm mit höchster Kraft der Angst und entflieht nach der
    anderen Seite.

BRÜNNHILDE
2560 Kein Gott nahte mir je!
    etwas gedehnter
  Der Jungfrau neigten

SIEGFRIED *passionately*
  A glorious young woman
  damaged my heart;
  a wife inflicted
  a wound to my head:
  I came without shield or helmet!
BRÜNNHILDE *with increasingly intense moroseness*
  I see the shining metal
  of the coat of mail:
  a sharp sword
  cut it apart;   2540
  from my young woman's body
  all armoured clothing is gone!
  I am without protection and a guard,
  a doleful woman, without defence!
SIEGFRIED *passionately*
  I made my way to you
  through burning fire,
  no coat of mail or suit of armour
  sheltered my body:
  but flames broke
  out in my breast;   2550
  my blood roars
  at white heat;
  a ravaging fire
  rages inside me:
  the blaze that burnt
  round Brünnhilde's rock
  now lays siege to my breast! –
  O wife! Put the fire out now!
  Silence this seething passion!
      He has embraced her impetuously. Brünnhilde jumps up,
      pushes him away with extreme force brought on by fear,
      and escapes to the other side.
BRÜNNHILDE
  Even gods never neared me!   2560
      somewhat more measured
  Heroes bowed down

scheu sich die Helden:
Heilig schied sie aus Walhall! –
Wehe! Wehe!
Wehe der Schmach,
der schmählichen Not!
Verwundet hat mich,
der mich erweckt!
Er erbrach mir Brünne und Helm:
2570   Brünnhilde bin ich nicht mehr.

SIEGFRIED *mit bebender Stimme wie der eines Leidenden* *
Noch bist du mir
die träumende Maid;
Brünnhildes Schlaf
brach ich noch nicht. –
Erwache, sei mir ein Weib!

BRÜNNHILDE *in Betäubung*
Mir schwirren die Sinne, –
mein Wissen schweigt:
soll mir die Weisheit schwinden?

SIEGFRIED
Sangst du mir nicht,
2580   dein Wissen sei
das Leuchten der Liebe zu mir?

BRÜNNHILDE *vor sich hinstarrend*
Trauriges Dunkel
trübt mir den Blick.
Mein Auge dämmert,
mein Licht verlischt:
Nacht wird's um mich.
Aus Nebel und Graun
windet sich wütend
ein Angstgewirr:
2590   Schrecken schreitet
und bäumt sich empor! –
    Sie birgt heftig die Augen mit den Händen.

SIEGFRIED *indem er ihr sanft die Hände von den Augen löst*
Nacht umfängt
gebund'ne Augen.

in awe before the virgin:
when I left Valhalla, I was sacred! –
Alas! Alas!
Alas for my disgrace,
for my inglorious state!
My wakener
inflicted my wounds!
He cut off my helmet and coat of mail:
I am Brünnhilde no more.   2570

SIEGFRIED *with a tremulous voice, like someone suffering**
You are for me still
the dreaming young woman;
not yet have I interrupted
Brünnhilde's sleep. –
Awaken, be a wife to me!

BRÜNNHILDE *in a daze*
I'm losing my head, –
my mind is a blank:
is my reason about to desert me?

SIEGFRIED
Didn't I hear you sing:
your wisdom is   2580
your radiant love for me?

BRÜNNHILDE *staring straight ahead of her*
Sunless and sad,
my sight is dulled.
My eyes grow dimmer,
my light goes out:
I feel deranged.
Out of fog and horror
comes a maze of fear,
curling and raving:
terror marches   2590
and rises aloft! –
    Wildly she covers her eyes with her hands.

SIEGFRIED *gently prising her hands away from her eyes*
Night envelops
blindfolded eyes.

Mit den Fesseln schwindet
das finst're Graun.
Tauch aus dem Dunkel, und sieh: –
sonnenhell leuchtet der Tag!

BRÜNNHILDE *in höchster Ergriffenheit*
  [Wagner] sprach diese Stelle mit erschütternder Macht
  des Ausdrucks vor: 'Ein furchtbarer Moment.'*

Sonnenhell
leuchtet der Tag meiner Schmach! –
2600 O Siegfried! Siegfried!
Sieh meine Angst!
  Brünnhildes Miene verrät, daß ihr ein anmutiges Bild vor
  die Seele tritt, von welchem ab sie den Blick mit Sanftmut
  wieder auf Siegfried richtet.

Ewig war ich,
ewig bin ich,
ewig in süß
sehnender Wonne,
doch ewig zu deinem Heil. –
  feurig, doch zart
O Siegfried! Herrlicher!
Hort der Welt!
Leben der Erde,
2610 lachender Held!
Laß, ach, laß!
Lasse von mir!
Nahe mir nicht
mit der wütenden Nähe,
zwinge mich nicht
mit dem brechenden Zwang,
zertrümm're die Traute dir nicht! –

Sahst du dein Bild
im klaren Bach?
2620 Hat es dich Frohen erfreut?
Rührtest zur Woge
das Wasser du auf,
zerflösse die klare

With the folds
the sombre dread will vanish.
Plunge out of the dark, and look: –
the day is radiant from the shining sun!

BRÜNNHILDE *in extreme emotional turmoil*
    [Wagner] recited these words with an upsetting power
    of expression: 'A terrible moment.'* [See Introduction]

Bright as the sun
shines the day of my disgrace! –
O Siegfried! Siegfried!   2600
See my fear!

    Brünnhilde's face inadvertently shows an image of grace
    in her soul that prompts her to look at Siegfried again
    with sweetly tempered feeling.

For ever I was,
for ever I am,
for ever in sweetly
yearning delight,
but also for ever to save you. –

    passionately, yet tenderly

O Siegfried! Glorious man!
World's treasure!
Earth's life,
laughing hero!   2610
Leave, ah, leave!
Leave me be!
Near me not
with your searing presence,
force me not
with your fractious constraints,
do not crush the woman you love! –

Did you see your reflection
in clear water?
Weren't you happy to see it?   2620
If you disturb the water
to make waves,
the streams's clear

Fläche des Bachs; –
dein Bild sähst du nicht mehr,
nur der Welle schwankend Gewog'! –
So berühre mich nicht,
trübe mich nicht!

2630 Ewig licht,
lachst du selig dann
aus mir dir entgegen,
froh und heiter, ein Held! –
O Siegfried!
Leuchtender Sproß!
Liebe dich,
und lasse von mir:
vernichte dein Eigen nicht!

SIEGFRIED
Dich lieb' ich:
dies furchtbar heraus, mit größter Emphase*

2640 o, liebtest mich du!
Nicht hab' ich mehr mich:
oh! hätte ich dich!
Ein herrlich Gewässer
wogt vor mir:
mit allen Sinnen
seh' ich nur sie,
die wonnig wogende Welle.
Brach sie mein Bild,
so brenn' ich nun selbst,

2650 sengende Glut
in der Flut zu kühlen!
Ich selbst, wie ich bin,
spring' in den Bach:
oh, daß seine Wogen
mich selig verschlängen,
mein Sehnen schwänd' in der Flut!
Erwache, Brünnhilde,
wache, du Maid!
Lache und lebe,

2660 süßeste Lust!

surface melts away; –
you'll see your reflection no more,
only the ebb and flow of the ripples! –
So do not touch me,
do not vex me!
Vividly for ever   2630
then will your divine laughter
be a reflection of mine,
you joyous, high-spirited hero!
O Siegfried!
My radiant heir!
Love yourself,
and let me be:
do not destroy who you are!

SIEGFRIED

I love you:
    bursting this out with the greatest emphasis *
if only you loved me!   2640
I am not who I am any more:
oh, if I only had you!
Glorious torrents
are surging before me:
my whole being
sees only those
waves that surge in delight.
Ruin my reflection they will,
but I'm fired up myself
to cool my torrid fervour   2650
in the floods!
I'll jump, just as I am,
into the waters:
so may their waves
consume me in glory,
may my longing fade in the flood!
Awaken, Brünnhilde,
young woman, wake up!
Laugh and live,
sweetest joy!   2660

Sei mein! Sei mein! Sei mein!

BRÜNNHILDE *sehr innig*

Oh, Siegfried! Dein
war ich von je!

SIEGFRIED *feurig*

Warst du's von je,
so sei es jetzt!

BRÜNNHILDE

Dein werd' ich
ewig sein!

SIEGFRIED

Was du sein wirst,
sei es mir heut'!
2670   Faßt dich mein Arm,
umschling' ich dich fest,
schlägt meine Brust
brünstig die deine,
zünden die Blicke,
zehren die Atem sich,
Aug' in Auge,
Mund an Mund!
Dann bist du mir,
was bang du mir warst und wirst:
Dann brach sich die brennende Sorge,
2680   ob jetzt Brünnhilde mein?

BRÜNNHILDE

Ob jetzt ich dein?

Göttliche Ruhe
rast mir in Wogen,
keuschestes Licht
lodert in Gluten:
himmlisches Wissen
stürmt mir dahin,
Jauchzen der Liebe
jagt es davon!

2690   Ob jetzt ich dein? –

Be mine! Be mine! Be mine!

BRÜNNHILDE *very sincerely*

O Siegfried! Yours
I have been for ever!

SIEGFRIED *passionately*

If you've been mine for ever,
then be that now!

BRÜNNHILDE

I will be yours
for ever!

SIEGFRIED

Be for me today
what you will be!
If I take you in my arms,   2670
if I embrace you,
if my heart beats
in heat with yours,
if our glances catch fire,
if breathing consumes us,
eye to eye,
mouth to mouth!
Then you are to me
what you were, will be and with fear:
won't that then rid me of searing care
about whether Brünnhilde is now mine?   2680

BRÜNNHILDE

Whether I'm now yours?

Waves of divine peace
surge into my being,
a light most chaste
blazes forth:
heavenly wisdom
storms away from me,
hounded out by
exultations of love!

Whether I'm now yours? –   2690

Siegfried! Siegfried!
Siehst du mich nicht?
Wie mein Blick dich verzehrt,
erblindest du nicht?
Wie mein Arm dich preßt –
entbrennst du mir nicht?
Wie in Strömen mein Blut
entgegen dir stürmt,
das wilde Feuer,
2700   fühlst du es nicht?
Fürchtest du, Siegfried,
fürchtest du nicht
das wild wütende Weib?
   Sie umfaßt ihn heftig.
SIEGFRIED *in freudigem Schreck*
  Ha!
Wie des Blutes Ströme sich zünden,
wie der Blicke Strahlen sich zehren;
wie die Arme brünstig sich pressen, –
kehrt mir zurück
mein kühner Mut;
2710   und das Fürchten, ach!
das ich nie gelernt, –
das Fürchten, das du
mich kaum gelehrt:
das Fürchten, mich dünkt,
ich Dummer vergaß es nun ganz!
   Er hat bei den letzten Worten Brünnhilde unwillkürlich
   losgelassen.
BRÜNNHILDE *freudig wild auflachend*
  Oh! Kindischer Held!
Oh, herrlicher Knabe!
Du hehrster Taten
törichter Hort!
2720   Lachend muß ich dich lieben,
lachend will ich erblinden,
lachend laß uns verderben,
lachend zu Grunde gehn!

Siegfried! Siegfried!
Don't you see me?
Don't you go blind
when my eyes devour you?
Don't I ignite your fire
when my arms squeeze you tightly? –
Don't you feel it
when my blood
rages like wildfire,
whirling towards you?   2700
Are you afraid, Siegfried,
don't you fear
this wildly passionate wife?
   She embraces him impetuously.
SIEGFRIED *happily taking fright*
Ah!
As our whirling blood catches fire,
as our eyes in heat devour each other;
as our arms lock in lustful embrace,
my dauntless self
returns to me;
and the fear, ah!   2710
the fear I never learned, –
the fear you
scarcely taught me:
that fear, how stupid of me,
I've now completely forgotten!
   With these last words, he has instinctively let go of
   Brünnhilde.
BRÜNNHILDE *happily bursting into wild laughter*
Oh! You naïve hero!
Oh, you brilliant boy!
You the fatuous hoard
of deeds most sublime!
Laughing I must love you;   2720
laughing I want to be blinded,
laughing let's go to ruin,
meet our destruction!

Fahr' hin, Walhalls
leuchtende Welt!
Zerfall' in Staub
deine stolze Burg!
Leb' wohl, prangende
Götterpracht!
2730   End' in Wonne,
du ewig Geschlecht!
Zerreißt, ihr Nornen,
das Runen-Seil!
Götterdämm'rung,
dunkle herauf!
Nacht der Vernichtung,
neb'le herein!
Mir strahlt zur Stunde
Siegfrieds Stern:
2740   er ist mir ewig,
ist mir immer
Erb' und Eigen,
Ein' und All':
leuchtende Liebe,
lachender Tod!

SIEGFRIED
Lachend erwachst
du Wonnige mir!
Brünnhilde lebt,
Brünnhilde lacht!
2750   Heil dem Tage,
der uns umleuchtet!
Heil der Sonne,
die uns bescheint!
Heil dem Licht,
das der Nacht enttaucht!
Heil der Welt,
der Brünnhilde lebt!
Sie wacht, sie lebt,
sie lacht mir entgegen:

Pass away, radiant
world of Valhalla!
May your proud fortress
crumble to dust!
Farewell, glorious
grandeur of the gods!
May your eternal race   2730
end in happiness!
Tear asunder, you Norns,
the rope of the runes!
Twilight of the gods,
let darkness arise!
Night of annihilation,
let the fog in!
I'm instantly lit
by Siegfried's star:
for me he's for ever,   2740
my proper heir,
eternally mine,
one and all:
radiant love,
laughing death!

SIEGFRIED

For me you awake,
laughing and happy!
Brünnhilde lives,
Brünnhilde laughs!
I greet the day   2750
shining around us!
I greet the sun
shining upon us!
I greet the light
from night emerging!
Hail to the world
where Brünnhilde lives!
She's awake, she's alive,
she's laughing with me:

2760 prangend strahlt
     mir Brünnhildes Stern!
     Sie ist mir ewig,
     ist mir immer,
     Erb' und Eigen,
     Ein und All!
     Leuchtende Liebe,
     lachender Tod!

> *Brünnhilde stürzt sich in Siegfrieds Arme.*
> *Der Vorhang fällt.*

I'm gloriously lit   2760
by Brünnhilde's star!
For me she's for ever,
my proper heir,
eternally mine,
one and all:
radiant love,
laughing death!

Brünnhilde throws herself into Siegfried's arms.
The curtain falls.

GÖTTERDÄMMERUNG

(DRITTER TAG)

VORSPIEL

Der Vorhang öffnet sich langsam [Takt 19]. – Die Szene ist die-
selbe wie am Schlusse des zweiten Tages, auf dem Walküren-
felsen. – Nacht. Aus der Tiefe des Hintergrundes leuchtet Feu-
erschein. – Die drei Nornen, hohe Frauengestalten in langen
dunklen und schleierartigen Faltengewändern. Die erste (ältes-
te) lagert im Vordergrunde rechts unter der breitästigen Tan-
ne; die zweite (jüngere) ist an einer Steinbank vor dem Felsen-
gemache hingestreckt; die dritte (jüngste) sitzt in der Mitte des
Hintergrundes auf einem Felssteine des Höhensaumes. Düs-
teres Schweigen und Bewegungslosigkeit.

ERSTE NORN
  Welch Licht leuchtet dort?
ZWEITE NORN
  Dämmert der Tag schon auf?
DRITTE NORN
  Loges Heer
  lodert feurig um den Fels.
  Noch ist's Nacht.
  Was spinnen und singen wir nicht?
ZWEITE NORN *zu der ersten*
  Wollen wir spinnen und singen,
  woran spannst du das Seil?
ERSTE NORN *während sie ein goldenes Seil von sich löst, und*
    mit dem einen Ende es an einen Ast der Tanne knüpft
  So gut und schlimm es geh',
10 schling' ich das Seil und singe. –

TWILIGHT OF THE GODS

(THIRD DAY)

PROLOGUE

The curtain rises slowly [bar 19]. – The scene is on the Val-
kyries' rock, the same as at the end of the second day. – Night.
Glowing fire shines out of the deep in the background. –
The three Norns, statuesque women in long, richly pleated
dark robes. The first (oldest) is positioned at the front under
the long outstretched branches of the pine-tree; the second
(younger) reclines on a stone seat in front of a cave in the
rock; the third (youngest) sits at the centre in the background
on a prominent rock along the high edge of the mountain.
Ominous silence and no movement at all.

FIRST NORN
    What light is shining there?
SECOND NORN
    Is it already dawn?
THIRD NORN
    Loge's garrisons
    girdle the rock with fire.
    Night's upon us still.
    Why not sing as we spin?
SECOND NORN *to the first*
    If we are to sing and spin,
    where will you attach the rope?
FIRST NORN *as she unwraps a golden rope from her body and*
    fastens one of its ends to a branch of the pine-tree
    Through thick and thin,
    I'll wrap the rope around and sing. –

vom Seil lesend*
An der Weltesche
wob ich einst,
da groß und stark
dem Stamm entgrünte
weihlicher Äste Wald.
Im kühlen Schatten
rauscht' ein Quell:
Weisheit raunend
rann sein Gewell';
20 da sang ich heil'gen Sinn.

Ein kühner Gott
trat zum Trunk an den Quell;
seiner Augen eines
zahlt' er als ewigen Zoll.
Von der Weltesche
brach da Wotan einen Ast;
eines Speeres Schaft
entschnitt der Starke dem Stamm.

In langer Zeiten Lauf
30 zehrte die Wunde den Wald;
falb fielen die Blätter,
dürr darbte der Baum;
traurig versiegte
des Quelles Trank:
trüben Sinnes
ward mein Gesang.
Doch, web' ich heut'
an der Weltesche nicht mehr,
muß mir die Tanne
40 taugen zu fesseln das Seil, –
Singe, Schwester,
dir werf' ich's zu;
weißt du, wie das wird?

ZWEITE NORN *Die zweite Norn windet das ihr zugeworfene
Seil um einen hervorspringenden Felsstein am Eingang
des Gemachs.*

*reading from the rope**
I did once weave
at the world ash-tree,
when verdant limbs,
blessed, big and strong,
blossomed forth from its trunk.
In the cool of the shadows
there bubbled a spring:
it welled up and flowed,
murmuring wisdom;
what I sang had sacred meaning.   20

To quench his thirst,
an indomitable god came to the spring;
of his eyes, he'd paid one
as eternal forfeit.
Then Wotan broke off
from the world ash-tree a bough;
from the trunk, the towering god cut
the shaft of a spear.

For many a year
the gash drained the forest's strength;   30
leaves fell, yellowed and dull,
the tree rotted, arid and starved;
the spring's water
dried up in distress:
cheerless in meaning
was my song.
Still, though I weave
at the world ash-tree no more,
the pine must suffice
to fasten the rope, –   40
Sing, sister,
I'll throw it to you;
do you know what will happen?
SECOND NORN *The second Norn winds the rope thrown to
her around a prominently protruding rock at the mouth
of the cave.*

'Sie liest, was sie singt gleichsam vom Seile ab.' *

Treu berat'ner
Verträge Runen
schnitt Wotan
in des Speeres Schaft: –
den hielt er als Haft der Welt.
Ein kühner Held
50 zerhieb im Kampfe den Speer;
in Trümmer sprang
der Verträge heiliger Haft.
Da hieß Wotan
Walhall's Helden
der Weltesche
welkes Geäst
mit dem Stamm in Stücke zu fällen:
die Esche sank;
ewig versiegte der Quell.
60 Fess'le ich heut'
an den scharfen Fels das Seil,
Singe, Schwester,
dir werf' ich's zu:
weißt du, wie das wird?

DRITTE NORN *das Seil auffangend und dessen Ende hinter*
    sich werfend
       [III. Norn] aufstehend liest ebenfalls von dem Seile das
       Kommende ab. *

Es ragt die Burg,
von Riesen gebaut:
mit der Götter und Helden
heiliger Sippe
sitzt dort Wotan im Saal.
70 Gehau'ner Scheite
hohe Schicht
ragt zu Hauf'
rings um die Halle:
die Weltesche war dies einst! –
Brennt das Holz

'She reads off what she sings as if from the rope.' *

Wotan notched
the runes of contracts,
honestly agreed,
into the shaft of his spear: –
that he took as security for the world.
An indomitable hero
shattered the spear in combat;   50
the contracts' sacred security
fell apart in ruin.
Then Wotan told
Valhalla's heroes
to cut in pieces
the withered boughs
and the world ash-tree's trunk:
the ash-tree fell;
the spring dried up for good.
Today once I've fastened   60
the rope to the rock's sharp edge,
Sing, sister,
I'll throw it to you:
do you know what will happen?

THIRD NORN *catching the rope and throwing the end of it
        behind her*

        [*IIIrd Norn*] *standing up, likewise reads from the rope
        about what is to come.* *

The fortress built by giants
towers over all:
with its revered clan
of gods and heroes,
Wotan sits there in its grand hall.
Hewn logs   70
heaped high
soar up in stacks
all around the hall:
the world ash-tree it used to be! –
But once the wood burns,

heilig brünstig und hell,
sengt die Glut
sehrend den glänzenden Saal,
der ewigen Götter Ende
80 dämmert ewig da auf. –
Wisset ihr noch?
So windet von Neuem das Seil;
von Norden wieder
werf' ich's dir nach.
    Sie wirft das Seil der zweiten Norn zu;
    diese schwingt es der ersten hin, welche das Seil vom
    Zweige löst, und es an einen andern Ast wieder anknüpft.
Spinne, Schwester, und singe!
ERSTE NORN *bei ihrer Beschäftigung nach hinten blickend*
Dämmert der Tag?
Oder leuchtet die Lohe?
Getrübt trügt sich mein Blick;
    [I. Norn] hat einen Blick in das Seil geworfen, woraus sie
    während der Arbeit wie aus alten Zeiten die Ereignisse
    heraus liest. *
nicht hell eracht' ich
90 das heilig Alte,
da Loge einst
entbrannte in lichter Glut.
Weißt du, was aus ihm ward?
ZWEITE NORN *das zugeworfene Seil wieder um den Stein*
    windend
Durch des Speeres Zauber
zähmte ihn Wotan;
Räte raunt' er dem Gott:
An des Schaftes Runen,
frei sich zu raten,
nagte zehrend sein Zahn:
100 da mit des Speeres
zwingender Spitze
bannte ihn Wotan,
Brünnhildes Fels zu umbrennen. –
Weißt du, was aus ihm wird?

holy, fervent and bright,
the blaze will scorch
and consume the splendid hall,
as then dawns for eternity
the eternal gods' destruction. –   80
Do either of you know more?
Then wind the rope afresh;
once more from the north
I'll cast it to you.

She throws the rope to the second Norn;
the latter tosses it to the first [Norn], who unties the rope
from the branch, and attaches it to another bough.

Spin, sister, and sing!

FIRST NORN *looking behind her as she works at her task*
Is it dawn?
Or is it light from the inferno?
My sight is bleary and deceiving;

[1st Norn] has cast a look into the rope, from which,
while she works, she discerns events that appear to be
from olden times. *

I cannot judge clearly
the sacred wisdom of old,   90
a time when Loge
burst into bright flame.
Do you know what became of him?

SECOND NORN *taking the rope thrown to her and winding it*
again round the rock
Wotan brought him under control
with the magic of the spear;
many a hint did he whisper to the god:
giving advice to wriggle free,
his tooth gnawed at the notches
in the shaft, draining their power:
then with the pitiless   100
point of the spear,
Wotan bewitched him:
Brünnhilde's rock was locked in fire. –
Do you know what will become of him?

Sie wirft das Seil der dritten Norn zu; diese wirft es
wieder hinter sich.

DRITTE NORN

Des zerschlag'nen Speeres
stechende Splitter
taucht einst Wotan
dem Brünstigen tief in die Brust:
zehrender Brand
110 zündet da auf;
den wirft der Gott
in der Weltesche
zu Hauf geschichtete Scheite. –

    Sie wirft das Seil zurück; die zweite Norn windet es auf
    und wirft es der ersten wieder zu.

Wollt ihr wissen
wann das wird?
Schwinget, Schwestern, das Seil! –

ERSTE NORN *das Seil von Neuem anknüpfend*

Die Nacht weicht;
nichts mehr gewahr' ich:
des Seiles Fäden
120 find' ich nicht mehr;
verflochten ist das Geflecht.
Ein wüstes Gesicht
wirrt mir wütend den Sinn: -
das Rheingold
raubte Alberich einst:
weißt du was aus ihm ward?

ZWEITE NORN *Sie windet mit mühvoller Hast das Seil um den*
    zackigen Stein des Gemaches.
       hastig wie verwirrt werdend *

Des Steines Schärfe
schnitt in das Seil;
nicht fest spannt mehr
130 der Fäden Gespinst;
verwirrt ist das Geweb':
aus Not und Neid
ragt mir des Niblungen Ring:

She throws the rope to the third Norn, who again throws it behind her.

THIRD NORN

The day will come when Wotan
plunges the keen-edged splinters
of the smitten spear deep into
the heart of the frenzied god of fire:
a ravenous inferno
will then be unleashed;   110
into the heaped scores
of logs from the world ash-tree,
the god will throw it. –

She throws the rope back; the second Norn lifts it up and throws it again to the first.

Do you want to know
when that will happen?
Sisters, toss the rope to me! –

FIRST NORN *attaching the rope anew*

Night is receding;
nothing more can I see:
nor can I find the rope's
threads any longer;   120
the weave's tangled up.
A chaotic visage
maddeningly confuses my senses: –
Alberich once stole
the Rhinegold:
Do you know what became of him?

SECOND NORN *She coils the rope with laborious haste around the jagged stone by the cave.*

hastily as if becoming confused *

The stone's sharp edge
cuts into the rope;
the threads in the weave
are no longer taut;   130
its warp and weft are frayed:
out of danger and pitilessness
I saw the rise of the Nibelung's ring:

ein rächender Fluch
nagt meiner Fäden Geflecht.
    Das Seil der dritten Norn zuwerfend.
Weißt du was daraus wird?

DRITTE NORN *das zugeworfene Seil hastig fassend*
Zu locker das Seil, –
mir langt es nicht!
Soll ich nach Norden
140   neigen das Ende,
straffer sei es gestreckt! –
    Sie zieht gewaltsam das Seil an; dieses reißt.
Es riß!

ZWEITE NORN
Es riß!

ERSTE NORN
Es riß!

DIE DREI NORNEN *Sie fassen die Stücken des zerrissenen
    Seiles und binden damit ihre Leiber aneinander*
Zu End' ewiges Wissen!
Der Welt melden
Weise nichts mehr. –

DRITTE NORN
Hinab!

ZWEITE NORN
    Zur Mutter!

ERSTE NORN
        Hinab!
Sie verschwinden.
   TAGESGRAUEN
    *Wachsende Morgenröte; immer schwächeres Leuchten
des Feuerscheines aus der Tiefe.*
    *Siegfried und Brünnhilde treten aus dem Steingemache
auf. Er ist in vollen Waffen, sie führt ihr Roß am Zaume.*

BRÜNNHILDE
Zu neuen Taten,
150   teurer Helde,
wie lieb' ich dich,
liess' ich dich nicht?

an avenging curse
gnaws at the weave of my threads.
  Throwing the rope to the third Norn.
Do you know what will come of it?

THIRD NORN *hastily grasping the rope thrown to her*
  The rope's too loose, –
  I can't make it work!
  If I'm to tilt its end
  northwards, let it be
  stretched more tautly! –
    She pulls on the rope violently until it breaks.
  It broke!

SECOND NORN
  It broke!

FIRST NORN
  It broke!

THE THREE NORNS *They take hold of the broken rope's
    pieces and use them to tie their bodies together.*
  Eternal knowing at an end!
  Nothing more have the wise
  to say to the world. –

THIRD NORN
  Down!

SECOND NORN
      To mother!

FIRST NORN
        Down!
    They vanish.
    DAWN
    *The red sky of morning begins to emerge; the signs of
    fire in the deep become increasingly weaker.*
    *Siegfried and Brünnhilde appear out of the cave in the
    rock. He is fully armed; she leads her horse by the reins.*

BRÜNNHILDE
  New feats await,
  dear hero,
  how could I love you,
  and not let you go?

140

150

Ein einzig Sorgen
läßt mich säumen,
daß dir zu wenig
mein Wert gewann.

Was Götter mich wiesen,
gab ich dir:
heiliger Runen
160 reichen Hort;
doch meiner Stärke
magdlichen Stamm
nahm mir der Held,
dem ich nun mich neige.

Des Wissens bar,
doch des Wunsches voll:
an Liebe reich,
doch ledig der Kraft,
mög'st du die Arme
170 nicht verachten,
die dir nur gönnen
nicht geben mehr kann.

SIEGFRIED
Mehr gabst du, Wunderfrau,
als ich zu wahren weiß.
Nicht zürne, wenn dein Lehren
mich unbelehret ließ!
Ein Wissen doch wahr' ich wohl –
    feurig
daß mir Brünnhilde lebt;
eine Lehre lernt' ich leicht –
180 Brünnhilde's zu gedenken!

BRÜNNHILDE
Willst du mir Minne schenken,
gedenke deiner nur,
gedenke deiner Taten:
gedenk' des wilden Feuers,
das furchtlos du durchschrittest,
da den Fels es rings umbrann –

A single worry
gives me pause,
that from my worth
you've won too little.

What gods taught me,
I gave to you:
a hoard rich
in sacred runes;   160
but you, my hero,
have taken my virginity,
the source of my strength,
you, whom I now honour.

Devoid of wisdom,
yet brimming with need:
do not despise
this poor creature
rich in love,
yet freed of her power,   170
who just wants to give,
but can give you no more.

SIEGFRIED
You've given more, wondrous woman,
than I know how to keep.
Don't be angry if your teaching
left me untaught!
Yet one thing I do know and cherish –
    fervently
that Brünnhilde lives for me;
that lesson I easily learnt –
to think of Brünnhilde!   180

BRÜNNHILDE
If you want to love me,
think only of yourself,
think of your deeds:
think of the savage fire,
through which you passed without fear
as its flames encircled the rock –

SIEGFRIED

Brünnhilde zu gewinnen!

BRÜNNHILDE

Gedenk' der beschildeten Frau,
die in tiefem Schlaf du fandest,
190   der den festen Helm du erbrachst!

SIEGFRIED

Brünnhilde zu erwecken.

BRÜNNHILDE

Gedenk' der Eide,
die uns einen;
gedenk' der Treue,
die wir tragen;
gedenk' der Liebe,
der wir leben:
Brünnhilde brennt dann ewig
heilig dir in der Brust! –
    Sie umarmt Siegfried.

SIEGFRIED

200   Lass' ich, Liebste, dich hier
in der Lohe heiliger Hut,
    Er hat den Ring Alberichs von seinem Finger gezogen
    und reicht ihn jetzt Brünnhilde dar.
zum Tausche deiner Runen
reich' ich dir diesen Ring.
Was der Taten je ich schuf,
dess' Tugend schließt er ein.
Ich erschlug einen wilden Wurm,
der grimmig lang ihn bewacht:
nun wahre du seine Kraft,
als Weihegruß meiner Treu'!

BRÜNNHILDE *voll Entzücken den Ring sich ansteckend*

210   Ihn geiz' ich als einziges Gut!
Für den Ring nimm nun auch mein Roß!
Ging sein Lauf mit mir
einst kühn durch die Lüfte, –
mit mir
verlor es die mächt'ge Art;

SIEGFRIED
  to win Brünnhilde!
BRÜNNHILDE
  Think of the shielded woman,
  fast asleep when you found her,
  the tight helmet you took off her!   190
SIEGFRIED
  To waken Brünnhilde!
BRÜNNHILDE
  Think of the vows,
  which unite us;
  think of the trust,
  on which we build;
  think of the love,
  for which we live:
  Brünnhilde will then for ever be
  a sacred flame in your breast! –
      She embraces Siegfried.
SIEGFRIED
  Before I leave you here, dearest woman,   200
  in the fire's sacred shelter,
      *He has pulled off Alberich's ring from his finger and prof-
      fers it now to Brünnhilde.*
  let me give you this ring
  in exchange for your runes.
  It retains the virtue of my deeds,
  all that I ever accomplished.
  I laid waste a savage dragon,
  who guarded it grimly and long:
  preserve its power well,
  as a solemn pledge of my faith!
BRÜNNHILDE *putting on the ring, full of rapture*
  With my only possession I'll never part!   210
  Take my horse for the ring now too!
  With me he once rode
  undaunted through air, –
  with me
  he lost that formidable gift;

über Wolken hin
auf blitzenden Wettern
nicht mehr
schwingt es sich mutig des Weg's;
220   doch wohin du ihn führst,
sei es durchs Feuer,
grauenlos folgt dir Grane:
denn dir, o Helde,
soll er gehorchen!
Du hüt' ihn wohl;
er hört dein Wort:
O, bringe Grane
oft Brünnhildes Gruß!

SIEGFRIED
Durch deine Tugend allein
230   soll so ich Taten noch wirken?
Meine Kämpfe kiesest du,
meine Siege kehren zu dir:
auf deines Rosses Rücken,
in deines Schildes Schirm; –
nicht Siegfried acht' ich mich mehr,
ich bin nur Brünnhildes Arm.

BRÜNNHILDE
O wäre Brünnhild' deine Seele!

SIEGFRIED
Durch sie entbrennt mir der Mut.

BRÜNNHILDE
So wärst du Siegfried und Brünnhild?

SIEGFRIED
240   Wo ich bin, bergen sich beide.

BRÜNNHILDE *lebhaft*
So verödet mein Felsensaal?

SIEGFRIED
Vereint, faßt er uns zwei!

BRÜNNHILDE *in großer Ergriffenheit*
O! heilige Götter!
Hehre Geschlechter!
Weidet eu'r Aug'

over clouds and away,
in weathers most foul,
no longer
does he soar bravely on paths like those;
but take him where you will,   220
be it through fire,
Grane will follow you unafraid:
you, O hero,
he shall obey!
Take good care of him;
he'll respect your word:
give Grane often
Brünnhilde's greetings!

SIEGFRIED

Am I now to take action
through your virtue alone?   230
You'll choose my battles,
my triumphs will be yours:
on the back of your horse,
protected by your shield, –
I feel I'm Siegfried no more,
I'm only Brünnhilde's arm.

BRÜNNHILDE

If only Brünnhilde were your soul!

SIEGFRIED

She's set my whole being on fire.

BRÜNNHILDE

So are you Siegfried and Brünnhilde?

SIEGFRIED

Wherever I am, I'm a refuge for both.   240

BRÜNNHILDE *in a lively manner*

So my home will be empty?

SIEGFRIED

It's for the two of us, together!

BRÜNNHILDE *in great emotional turmoil*

O! sacred gods!
Noble tribes!
Feast your eyes

an dem weihvollen Paar.
Getrennt – wer will uns scheiden?
Geschieden – trennt es sich nie!

SIEGFRIED
Heil dir, Brünnhilde,
250   prangender Stern!

BRÜNNHILDE
Heil dir, Siegfried,
siegendes Licht!

SIEGFRIED
Heil, strahlende Liebe!

BRÜNNHILDE
Heil, strahlendes Leben!

SIEGFRIED
Heil, strahlender Stern!

BRÜNNHILDE
Heil, siegendes Licht!

SIEGFRIED
Heil, Brünnhild'!

SIEGFRIED *und* BRÜNNHILDE
Heil! Heil! Heil! Heil!

*Siegfried geleitet schnell das Roß dem Felsenabhange zu,
wohin ihm Brünnhilde folgt.*

*Hier ist, während der vorangehenden drei Takte [646–
8], Siegfried mit dem Rosse hinter dem Felsenvorsprunge
abwärts verschwunden, so daß der Zuschauer ihn nicht
mehr sieht: Brünnhilde steht so plötzlich allein am Ab-
hange und blickt Siegfried in die Tiefe nach.*

*Brünnhilds Gebärde zeigt, daß jetzt Siegfried ihrem
Blicke entschwindet.*

Man hört Siegfrieds Horn aus der Tiefe.

Brünnhilde lauscht.

Sie tritt weiter auf den Abhang hinaus.

*Jetzt erblickt sie Siegfried nochmals in der Tiefe: sie
winkt ihm mit entzückter Gebärde zu. Aus ihrem freu-
digen Lächeln deutet sich der Anblick des lustig davon-
ziehenden Helden.*

*[Takt 717] Hier muß der Vorhang soeben schnell
herabgelassen worden sein.*

on this celebrated pair!
Apart – who'd make us estranged?
Estranged – we'll never part!

SIEGFRIED
I greet you, Brünnhilde,
glorious star!

BRÜNNHILDE
I greet you, Siegfried,
victorious light!

SIEGFRIED
Hail, glorious love!

BRÜNNHILDE
Hail, glorious life!

SIEGFRIED
Hail, glorious star!

BRÜNNHILDE
Hail, victorious light!

SIEGFRIED
Hail, Brünnhilde!

SIEGFRIED *and* BRÜNNHILDE
Hail! Hail! Hail! Hail!

> *Siegfried quickly leads the horse to the rocky slope, where Brünnhilde follows him.*
>
> *At this point, during the previous three bars [646–8], Siegfried has vanished with the horse downwards behind the rocky promontory, no longer to be seen by the audience: Brünnhilde is thus left standing suddenly alone on the slope, watching Siegfried as he descends into the valley.*
>
> *Brünnhilde's demeanour shows that Siegfried is now receding out of sight.*
>
> *Siegfried's horn is heard from below.*
>
> *Brünnhilde listens intently.*
>
> *She steps further out along the slope.*
>
> *She catches sight of Siegfried again in the valley: she waves to him with rapturous gestures. From her joyful smile one can tell that she is looking at a hero happily going on his way.*
>
> *[bar 717] Here the curtain must have just been quickly lowered.*

ERSTER AUFZUG

*Während der letzen vier Takte [889–892] ist der Vorhang
wieder aufgezogen worden.*

ERSTE SZENE

Gunthers Hofhalle am Rhein

*Diese ist dem Hintergrunde zu ganz offen. Den Hintergrund
selbst nimmt ein freier Uferraum bis zum Flusse hin ein; fel-
sige Anhöhen umgrenzen das Ufer.*
   *Gunther und Gutrune auf dem Hochsitze zur Seite, vor
welchem ein Tisch mit Trinkgerät steht; davor sitzt Hagen.*

GUNTHER
  Nun hör', Hagen;
260 sage mir, Held:
  sitz' ich herrlich am Rhein,
  Gunther zu Gibich's Ruhm?
HAGEN
  Dich ächt genannten
  acht' ich zu neiden;
  die beid' uns Brüder gebar,
  Frau Grimhild' ließ mich's begreifen.
GUNTHER
  Dich neide ich;
  nicht neide mich du.
  Erbt' ich Erstlings Art,
270 Weisheit ward dir allein:
  Halbbrüderzwist
  bezwang sich nie besser.
  Deinem Rat nur red' ich Lob,
  frag' ich dich nach meinem Ruhm.
HAGEN
  So schelt' ich den Rat,

ACT ONE

*During the last three bars [889–92] the curtain
has been raised again.*

SCENE ONE

The hall of Gunther's court near the Rhine

*This is pretty much open at the back. The back itself is taken
up with an open bank leading to the river; small rocky hills
border the shoreline.*

*Gunther and Gutrune on thrones to one side, a table with
drinking vessels on it in front of them; Hagen sits to the fore.*

GUNTHER

    So listen, Hagen;
    hero, tell me this:
    does Gunther's august throne on
    the Rhine match Gibich's glory?

    260

HAGEN

    I'm mindful that your authentic
    pedigree is to be envied;
    Grimhilde, mother of us brothers,
    gave me to understand that it is.

GUNTHER

    I envy you;
    do not envy me.
    I inherited the breed of the firstborn,
    but wisdom was yours alone:
    bad blood between half-brothers
    has never been better restrained.
    To your advice alone I give praise
    when asking you about my repute.

    270

HAGEN

    Then I'll grumble about my advice,

da schlecht noch dein Ruhm;
denn hohe Güter weiß ich,
die der Gibichung noch nicht gewann.

GUNTHER

Verschwiegest du sie,
280   so schelt' auch ich.

HAGEN

In sommerlich reifer Stärke
seh' ich Gibichs Stamm,
dich, Gunther, unbeweibt, –
dich, Gutrun', ohne Mann.

 Gunther und Gutrune sind in schweigendes Sinnen ver-
 loren

GUNTHER

Wen rät'st du nun zu frei'n,
daß uns'rem Ruhm' es fromm'?

HAGEN

Ein Weib weiß ich,
das herrlichste der Welt:
auf Felsen hoch ihr Sitz;
290   ein Feuer umbrennt ihren Saal:
nur wer durch das Feuer bricht,
darf Brünnhildes Freier sein.

GUNTHER

Vermag das mein Mut zu besteh'n?

HAGEN

Einem Stärk'ren noch ist's nur bestimmt.

GUNTHER

Wer ist der streitlichste Mann?

HAGEN

Siegfried, der Wälsungen Sproß,
der ist der stärkste Held.
Ein Zwillingspaar,
von Liebe bezwungen,
300   Siegmund und Sieglinde,
zeugten den ächtesten Sohn.
Der im Walde mächtig erwuchs, –
den wünsch' ich Gutrun' zum Mann.

as your repute is still bad;
I know of major resources,
as yet out of the Gibichung's reach.

GUNTHER

If you keep these quiet,
I too will start grumbling.   280

HAGEN

I'm witnessing the Gibich tribe
in the summer of its maturity,
you, Gunther, without a wife, –
you, Gutrune, without a husband.
> *Gunther and Gutrune have lapsed into silent contem-*
> *plation.*

GUNTHER

Who's to be sought in marriage,
do you think, to furbish our repute?

HAGEN

I know of a woman,
the world's most glorious:
high on a rock is her home,
her hall is surrounded by fire: 290
only he who breaks through the fire
shall be Brünnhilde's suitor.

GUNTHER

Do I have the guts for that?

HAGEN

There's still only one stronger in sight.

GUNTHER

Who is this most contentious man?

HAGEN

Siegfried, the Wälsungs' offspring,
he is the strongest hero.
Siegmund and Sieglinde,
twin brother and sister
driven by love,   300
conceived this purest of sons.
Reared in a forest to be strong, –
he is my choice as Gutrune's spouse.

GUTRUNE *schüchtern beginnend*
Welche Tat schuf er so tapfer,
daß als herrlichster Held er genannt?

HAGEN
Vor Neidhöhle
den Niblungenhort
bewachte ein riesiger Wurm:
Siegfried schloß ihm
310 den freislichen Schlund,
erschlug ihn mit siegendem Schwert.
Solch ungeheurer Tat
enttagte des Helden Ruhm.

GUNTHER *in Nachsinnen*
Vom Niblungenhort vernahm ich:
er birgt den neidlichsten Schatz?

HAGEN
Wer wohl ihn zu nützen wüßt',
dem neigte sich wahrlich die Welt.

GUNTHER
Und Siegfried hat ihn erkämpft?

HAGEN
Knecht sind die Niblungen ihm.

GUNTHER
320 Und Brünnhild' gewänne nur er?

HAGEN
Keinem andren wiche die Brunst.
    Gunther erhebt sich unwillig vom Sitze.

GUNTHER *schreitet vom Sitze herunter.* *
Was weck'st du Zweifel und Zwist?
Was ich nicht zwingen soll,
danach zu verlangen
machst du mir Lust?
    Er schreitet bewegt in der Halle auf und ab.
        Hagen, ohne seinen Sitz zu verlassen, hält Gunther, als
    dieser wieder in seine Nähe kommt, durch einen geheim-
    nisvollen Wink fest.

HAGEN
Brächte Siegfried

GUTRUNE *beginning shyly*
What brave deeds has he done
to be named the most glorious hero?
HAGEN
A huge dragon
before Neidhöhle
guarded the Nibelung hoard:
Siegfried closed
its baleful gullet,   310
slaying it with his conquering sword.
Such an unheard-of exploit
was the dawn of his repute as hero.
GUNTHER *immersed in thought*
I did hear tell of the Nibelung hoard:
it hides the most sought-after wealth?
HAGEN
Whoever knows how to use it
is indeed on their way to win the world.
GUNTHER
And did Siegfried win it?
HAGEN
The Nibelungs are slaves to him.
GUNTHER
And he alone can win Brünnhilde?   320
HAGEN
The inferno lets no other pass.
    Gunther rises indignantly from his seat.
GUNTHER *Gunther strides down from his throne**
Why stir up doubt and bad blood?
Why create a longing
in me for something
I cannot make happen?
    Upset, he paces up and down the hall.
        *Without leaving his seat, Hagen stops Gunther in his
    tracks with a cryptic sign when the latter comes close to
    him again.*
HAGEN
What if Siegfried

die Braut dir heim,
wär' dann nicht Brünnhilde dein?
    Gunther wendet sich wieder zweifelnd und unmutig ab.

GUNTHER
Was zwänge den frohen Mann,
330   für mich die Braut zu frei'n?

HAGEN *wie vorher*
Ihn zwänge bald deine Bitte,
bänd' ihn Gutrun' zuvor.

GUTRUNE
Du Spötter, böser Hagen!
Wie sollt' ich Siegfried binden?
Ist er der herrlichste
Held der Welt,
der Erde holdeste Frauen
friedeten längst ihn schon.

HAGEN *sehr vertraulich zu Gutrune hinneigend*
Gedenk' des Trankes im Schrein;
    heimlicher
340   vertraue mir, der ihn gewann:
Den Helden, dess' du verlangst,
bindet er liebend an dich.
    Gunther ist wieder an den Tisch getreten und hört, auf
    ihn gelehnt, jetzt aufmerksam zu.
Träte nun Siegfried ein,
genöss' er des würzigen Tranks,
daß vor dir ein Weib er ersah,
daß je ein Weib ihm genaht,
vergessen müßt' er dess' ganz.
Nun redet:
wie dünkt euch Hagens Rat?

GUNTHER *lebhaft auffahrend*
350   Gepriesen sei Grimhild',
die uns den Bruder gab!

GUTRUNE
Möcht' ich Siegfried je erseh'n!

GUNTHER
Wie fänden ihn wir auf?

brought your bride home,
wouldn't Brünnhilde then be yours?
>*Despairing and displeased, Gunther turns away again.*

GUNTHER
What would make this happy man
woo a bride in my stead?   330

HAGEN *as before*
Your plea will soon persuade him,
if he falls for Gutrune first.

GUTRUNE
You mocker, evil Hagen!
How do I make Siegfried fall for me?
If he's the most glorious
hero of the world,
the fairest women of the earth
have by now surely been his lovers.

HAGEN *leaning to Gutrune very confidentially*
Think of the potion in the cupboard;
>*more secretly*
trust me, the one who got hold of it: 340
it will create a loving bond
between you and the hero you long for.
>*Gunther has reached the table again, leans on it and lis-*
>*tens, this time attentively.*
If Siegfried entered now,
enjoyed the herbal potion,
he would totally forget
any woman he'd seen before,
or any woman who'd neared him.
Say something:
what do you think of Hagen's plan?

GUNTHER *reacting with enthusiasm*
Praise be to Grimhilde,   350
who gave us our brother!

GUTRUNE
If only I could see Siegfried!

GUNTHER
How do we find him?

Ein Horn auf dem Theater; aus dem Hintergrunde von
links her
> *sehr stark, aber fern*
> *Hagen lauscht.*
> *Siegfrieds Hornruf hat nur Hagen gehört.* *

HAGEN *wendet sich zu Gunther*
Jagt er auf Taten
wonnig umher,
zum engen Tann
wird ihm die Welt:
wohl stürmt er in rastloser Jagd
auch zu Gibichs Strand an den Rhein. –

GUNTHER
360 Willkommen hieß' ich ihn gern!
> *Horn auf dem Theater*
> *näher, aber immer noch fern*
> *Beide lauschen.*
> *Hagen eilt nach dem Ufer.*
Vom Rhein her tönt das Horn.
> *Hagen späht den Fluß hinab und ruft zurück:*

HAGEN
In einem Nachen Held und Roß! –
Der bläst so munter das Horn!
> *'Je mehr Bewegung auf der Bühne, desto schöner'* *
> *Horn auf dem Theater*
> *näher*
> *Gunther bleibt auf halbem Wege lauschend zurück.*

HAGEN *wie vorher*
Ein gemächlicher Schlag
wie von müßiger Hand
treibt jach den Kahn
wider den Strom:
so rüstiger Kraft
in des Ruders Schwung
370 rühmt sich nur der,
der den Wurm erschlug:
Siegfried ist es, sicher kein And'rer!

> *A horn off-stage; in the background on the left*
> *very strong, but distant*
> *Hagen listens intently.*
> *Hagen is the only one to have heard Siegfried's horn*
> *call.* *

HAGEN *turns to Gunther*
  Happy hunting
  ground for him
  is the pine forest's
  narrow world:
  but his restive hunt makes him storm
  up the Rhine to Gibich's shores too. –

GUNTHER
  I'll gladly welcome him.   360
> *horn off-stage*
>   *closer, but still distant*
>   *Both listen intently.*
>   *Hagen hastens to the shore.*
  The horn's coming from the Rhine.
> *Hagen peers down the river and shouts back:*

HAGEN
  A hero with a horse in a boat! –
  He's blithely blowing his horn!
> *'The more movement on stage, the better'* *
>   *horn off-stage*
>   *nearer*
>   *Half-way [down to the river] Gunther stops, listening.*

HAGEN *as before*
  He rows the boat hard
  against the stream
  with leisurely strokes,
  as if just passing the time:
  such vigorous power
  in the sweep of the oars
  can only mean that the   370
  dragon-slayer's at work:
  it's Siegfried, no one else!

GUNTHER
   Jagt er vorbei?
HAGEN *ruft durch die hohlen Hände nach dem Flusse zu.*
   Hoiho! Wohin,
   du heit'rer Held?
SIEGFRIED *aus der Ferne*
   Zu Gibich's starkem Sohne.
HAGEN
   Zu seiner Halle entbiet' ich dich. –
      Siegfried erscheint im Kahn am Ufer.
   Hieher! Hier lege an!

ZWEITE SZENE

Siegfried legt mit dem Kahne an.
   Hagen schließt den Kahn mit der Kette am Ufer fest.
Siegfried springt mit dem Rosse auf den Strand.

HAGEN
   Heil! Siegfried, teuer Held!
      Gunther ist zu Hagen an das Ufer getreten.
      Gutrune blickt vom Hochsitze aus in staunender Be-
      wunderung auf Siegfried. Gunther will freundlichen
      Gruß bieten. Alle sind in gegenseitiger stummer Betrach-
      tung gefesselt.
      Siegfried, auf sein Roß gelehnt, bleibt ruhig am Kahne
      stehen.
SIEGFRIED
380 Wer ist Gibichs Sohn?
GUNTHER
   Gunther, ich, den du suchst.
SIEGFRIED
   Dich hört' ich rühmen
   weit am Rhein:
   nun ficht mit mir,
   oder sei mein Freund!

GUNTHER
Will he rush past?
HAGEN *shouts through cupped hands towards the river.*
Hoiho! Where are you bound for,
blithe hero?
SIEGFRIED *in the distance*
For Gibich's sturdy son.
HAGEN
Then I invite you into his hall. –
Siegfried appears in his boat on the riverbank.
This way! Moor the boat here!

SCENE TWO

Siegfried moors his boat.
Hagen secures the boat to the riverbank with a chain.
Siegfried jumps ashore with his horse.

HAGEN
Hail! Siegfried, cherished hero!
Gunther has joined Hagen on the riverbank.
From her throne, Gutrune catches sight of Siegfried in wide-eyed amazement. Gunther is prepared to offer friendly greetings. Rooted to the spot, everyone looks speechlessly at each other.
Siegfried stays calmly next to his boat, leaning on his horse.
SIEGFRIED
Which one's Gibich's son? 380
GUNTHER
I'm Gunther, you're looking for me.
SIEGFRIED
I've heard you praised
along the Rhine:
do battle with me,
or be my friend!

GUNTHER
Lass' den Kampf!
Sei willkommen!
Siegfried sieht sich ruhig um.

SIEGFRIED
Wo berg' ich mein Roß?

HAGEN
Ich biet' ihm Rast.

SIEGFRIED *zu Hagen gewendet*
390   Du rief'st mich Siegfried:
sah'st du mich schon?

HAGEN
Ich kannte dich nur
an deiner Kraft.

SIEGFRIED *indem er an Hagen das Roß übergibt*
Wohl hüte mir Grane:
Du hieltest nie
von edlerer Zucht
am Zaume ein Roß.

Hagen führt das Ross. Während Siegfried ihm gedanken-
voll nachblickt, entfernt sich auch Gutrune, durch einen
Wink Hagens bedeutet, von Siegfried unbemerkt, nach
links durch eine Tür in ihr Gemach.
Gunther schreitet mit Siegfried, den er dazu einlädt, in
die Halle vor.

GUNTHER
Begrüße froh, o Held,
die Halle meines Vaters:
400   wohin du schreitest,
was du ersieh'st,
das achte nun dein Eigen;
dein ist mein Erbe,
Land und Leut',
hilf, mein Leib, meinem Eide!
Mich selbst geb' ich zum Mann. –

SIEGFRIED
Nicht Land noch Leute biete ich,
noch Vaters Haus und Hof:

GUNTHER
Forget the fighting!
Feel welcome!
Siegfried calmly looks around.

SIEGFRIED
Where do I put my horse?

HAGEN
I'll find him rest.

SIEGFRIED *having turned to Hagen*
You called me Siegfried: 390
have you seen me before?

HAGEN
From your strength alone,
I knew it was you.

SIEGFRIED *while handing over the horse to Hagen*
Look after Grane for me.
Take the reins:
you've never held any
horse of nobler breed.
Hagen leads the horse away. While Siegfried follows
him thoughtfully with his eyes, Gutrune, at a sign from
Hagen unobserved by Siegfried, retires to her room
through a door on the left.
Gunther invites Siegfried to walk over with him into
the hall.

GUNTHER
Give welcome, hero,
to the hall of my father:
where you set foot,   400
where you cast your eyes,
consider it now yours;
yours is my heritage,
my land and my people;
may my body give succour to my oath!
I pledge myself as your vassal. –

SIEGFRIED
I offer no land or people,
or a father's house and court:

einzig erbt' ich
410 den eig'nen Leib; –
lebend zehr' ich den auf,
nur ein Schwert hab' ich,
selbst geschmiedet:
hilf, mein Schwert, meinem Eide!
Das biet' ich mit mir zum Bund.

HAGEN *der zurückgekommen ist und jetzt hinter Siegfried steht*
Doch des Niblungenhortes
nennt die Märe dich Herrn?

SIEGFRIED *sich zu Hagen umwendend*
Des Schatzes vergaß ich fast;
so schätz' ich sein müß'ges Gut!
420 In einer Höhle ließ ich's liegen,
wo ein Wurm es einst bewacht.

HAGEN
Und nichts entnahmst du ihm?

SIEGFRIED
Dies Gewirk, unkund seiner Kraft.

HAGEN
Den Tarnhelm kenn' ich,
der Niblungen künstliches Werk:
er taugt, bedeckt er dein Haupt,
dir zu tauschen jede Gestalt;
verlangt dich's an fernsten Ort,
er entführt flugs dich dahin. –
430 Sonst nichts entnahm'st du dem Hort?

SIEGFRIED
Einen Ring.

HAGEN
Den hütest du wohl?

SIEGFRIED
Den hütet ein hehres Weib. –

HAGEN *für sich*
Brünnhild'!

GUNTHER
Nicht, Siegfried, sollst du mir tauschen,
Tand gäb' ich für dein Geschmeid',

I'm heir to just
this body of mine; –   410
and I wear that out just living,
with only one sword,
forged by myself:
may my sword give succour to my oath!
I commit it and myself to our covenant.

HAGEN *who has returned and now stands behind Siegfried*
But aren't there rumours of you
as lord of the Nibelung hoard?

SIEGFRIED *turning around to face Hagen*
I nearly forgot about the treasure;
so much for that shoddy stuff!
I left it behind in a cave,   420
once guarded by a dragon.

HAGEN
And you took nothing with you?

SIEGFRIED
Just this metal thing, whatever it's for.

HAGEN
It's the Tarnhelm, I know,
an ingenious Nibelung device:
if you cover your head with it,
it can change you into any shape;
if you long for a distant place,
it'll take you there in a flash. –
That's all you took from the hoard?   430

SIEGFRIED
A ring.

HAGEN
You're looking after it?

SIEGFRIED
A glorious woman is. –

HAGEN *aside*
Brünnhilde!

GUNTHER
Siegfried, we've nothing to exchange;
even if you took all I have,

nähm'st all mein Gut du dafür:
ohn' Entgelt dien' ich dir gern.

> *Hagen ist zu Gutrunes Türe gegangen und öffnet sie jetzt.*
> *Gutrune tritt heraus: sie trägt ein gefülltes Trinkhorn*
> *und nähert sich damit Siegfried.*

GUTRUNE

Willkommen, Gast,

440 in Gibich's Haus!

Seine Tochter reicht dir den Trank.

> *Siegfried neigt sich ihr freundlich und ergreift das Horn.*
> *Er hält das Horn gedankenvoll vor sich hin.*

SIEGFRIED *leise, doch sehr bestimmt*

Vergäß' ich Alles,
was du mir gabst,
von einer Lehre
lass' ich doch nie:
den ersten Trunk
zu treuer Minne,
Brünnhilde, bring' ich dir!

> *Er setzt das Trinkhorn an und trinkt in einem langen*
> *Zuge.*
> *Er reicht das Horn an Gutrune zurück, die verschämt*
> *und verwirrt, die Augen vor ihm niederschlägt.*
> *Siegfried heftet den Blick mit schnell entbrannter*
> *Leidenschaft auf sie.*

Die so mit dem Blitz

450 den Blick du mir seng'st,
was senk'st du dein Auge vor mir?

> *Gutrune schlägt errötend das Auge zu ihm auf.*
> *[Siegfried] heftig*

Ha, schönstes Weib!
Schließe den Blick;
das Herz in der Brust
brennt mir sein Strahl:
zu feurigen Strömen fühl' ich
ihn zehrend zünden mein Blut!

> *mit bebender Stimme*

Gunther, wie heißt deine Schwester?

I'd be giving junk for your jewels:
I'll happily serve you for nothing.
> *Hagen has gone to Gutrune's door and now opens it.*
>> *Gutrune appears: she is carrying a vessel filled with drink and approaches Siegfried with it.*

GUTRUNE

Guest, feel welcome
in Gibich's house!
I'm his daughter and offer this drink.
> *Siegfried bows to her courteously and takes the horn.*
> *He holds the horn thoughtfully in front of him.*

SIEGFRIED *quietly, but with great certainty*

If I ever forget
all you gave me,
still I'll never
forget one thing:
to you, Brünnhilde, I bring
this first drink,
to loyal love!
> *He raises the horn to his lips and empties it in one long go.*
>> *He hands the horn back to Gutrune, who bashfully lowers her eyes in confusion.*
>> *Siegfried fastens his eyes on her, his passion quickly catching fire.*

With such lightning
in your look that burns into mine,
why lower your eyes in front of me?
> *Gutrune looks up at him, blushing.*
>> *[Siegfried] forcefully*

Ah, most beautiful of women!
Close your eyes;
their flash is charring
the heart in my breast:
in fervid torrents I feel
my blood ruinously alight!
> *with a quivering voice*

Gunther, what's your sister's name?

440

450

GUNTHER
  Gutrune.
SIEGFRIED *leise*
    'mit etwas bebender Stimme' *

460 Sind's gute Runen,
  die ihrem Aug' ich entrate?
    Er faßt Gutrune feurig bei der Hand.
  Deinem Bruder bot ich mich zum Mann:
  der Stolze schlug mich aus;
  trüg'st du, wie er, mir Übermut,
  böt' ich mich dir zum Bund?
    Gutrune trifft unwillkürlich auf Hagens Blick; sie neigt
    demütig das Haupt, und mit einer Gebärde, als fühle sie
    sich seiner nicht wert, verläßt sie wankenden Schrittes
    wieder die Halle. Siegfried, von Hagen und Gunther auf-
    merksam beobachtet, blickt, wie festgezaubert, Gutrune
    nach.
      [Siegfried] ohne sich umzuwenden
  Hast du, Gunther, ein Weib?
GUNTHER
  Nicht freit' ich noch,
  und einer Frau
  soll ich mich schwerlich freu'n:
470 auf Eine setzt' ich den Sinn,
  die kein Rat mir je gewinnt.
SIEGFRIED *wendet sich lebhaft zu Gunther*
  Was wär' dir versagt,
  steh' ich zu dir?
GUNTHER
  Auf Felsen hoch ihr Sitz;
SIEGFRIED *mit verwunderungsvoller Hast einfallend*
  Auf Felsen hoch ihr Sitz?
GUNTHER
  ein Feuer umbrennt den Saal.
SIEGFRIED
  Ein Feuer umbrennt den Saal?
GUNTHER
  Nur wer durch das Feuer bricht,

GUNTHER
  Gutrune.
SIEGFRIED *quietly*
    'with a somewhat tremulous voice'
  Are those good runes   460
  I can unlock from her eyes?
    He fervently takes Gutrune by the hand.
  I offered to be your brother's vassal:
  but the proud man refused;
  would you, as he, think me too bold,
  if I offered myself to you in marriage?
    *Gutrune cannot help but catch Hagen's eye; she humbly
    bows her head and, with a demeanour suggesting that
    she feels unworthy of Siegfried, leaves the hall again, this
    time with faltering steps. Siegfried, keenly observed by
    Hagen and Gunther, gazes after her as if frozen to the
    spot by a magic spell.*
    [Siegfried] without turning round
  Do you have a wife, Gunther?
GUNTHER
  I am not married yet,
  and a wife
  I am not likely to enjoy:
  I did set my mind on one,   470
  but there's no way she'll ever be mine.
SIEGFRIED *turning quickly to Gunther*
  What can be denied to you,
  if I'm at your side?
GUNTHER
  High on a rock is her home;
SIEGFRIED *hastily interrupting, full of astonishment*
  High on a rock is her home?
GUNTHER
  the hall is surrounded by fire.
SIEGFRIED
  The hall is surrounded by fire?
GUNTHER
  Only he who breaks through the fire,

SIEGFRIED *mit der heftigsten Anstrengung, um eine Erinne-*
     rung festzuhalten
  Nur wer durch das Feuer bricht?

GUNTHER
480   darf Brünnhildes Freier sein.
     Siegfried verrät durch eine Gebärde, daß bei Nennung
     von Brünnhildes Namen die Erinnerung ihm vollends
     gänzlich schwindet.
        [Gunther] etwas weniger zögernd
        wie aus dem Leeren ins Leere verklingend. *
  Nun darf ich den Fels nicht erklimmen;
  das Feuer verglimmt mir nie!
     Siegfried kommt aus einem traumartigen Zustand zu sich
     und wendet sich mit übermütiger Lustigkeit zu Gunther.

SIEGFRIED
  Ich fürchte kein Feuer,
  für dich frei' ich die Frau:
  denn dein Mann bin ich,
  und mein Mut ist dein, –
  gewinn' ich mir Gutrun' zum Weib.

GUNTHER
  Gutrune gönn' ich dir gerne.

SIEGFRIED
  Brünnhilde bring' ich dir.

GUNTHER
490   Wie willst du sie täuschen?

SIEGFRIED
  Durch des Tarnhelms Trug
  tausch' ich mir deine Gestalt.

GUNTHER
  So stelle Eide zum Schwur!

SIEGFRIED
  Blutbrüderschaft
  schwöre ein Eid!
     Hagen füllt ein Trinkhorn mit frischem Wein; dieses hält
     er dann Siegfried und Gunther hin, welche sich mit ihren
     Schwertern die Arme ritzen und diese eine kurze Zeit
     über die Öffnung des Trinkhornes halten.

SIEGFRIED *with the most strenuous of efforts to focus his
memory*
Only he who breaks through the fire?

GUNTHER
can be Brünnhilde's suitor. 480
*Siegfried's demeanour shows that with the mention of
Brünnhilde's name all recollection of her has completely
deserted him.*
*[Gunther] somewhat less hesitantly
like empty words fading into emptiness* *
I cannot scale that rock;
the fire will never die out for me!
*Out of his dreamlike condition, Siegfried comes to and
turns to Gunther with boisterous confidence.*

SIEGFRIED
I fear no fire,
I'll woo the woman for you:
I am your vassal,
and my spirit is yours, –
if I can have Gutrune as my wife.

GUNTHER
I'll gladly give you Gutrune.

SIEGFRIED
I'll fetch you Brünnhilde.

GUNTHER
How do you want to trick her? 490

SIEGFRIED
I'll change my shape into yours
with the Tarnhelm's devious power.

GUNTHER
Then let oaths be sworn!

SIEGFRIED
Blood-brotherhood
shall swear an oath!
*Hagen fills a drinking-horn with new wine. He holds it
out to Siegfried and Gunther, who make incisions in their
arms with their swords and hold them for a short while
over the top of the drinking-horn.*

Beide legen zwei ihrer Finger auf das Horn, welches
Hagen fortwährend in ihrer Mitte hält.

Blühenden Lebens
labendes Blut
träufelt' ich in den Trank.

GUNTHER

Bruderbrünstig
500   mutig gemischt,
blüh' im Trank unser Blut.

SIEGFRIED *und* GUNTHER

Treue trink' ich dem Freund.
Froh und frei
entblühe dem Bund
Blutbrüderschaft heut'.

GUNTHER

Bricht ein Bruder den Bund: –

SIEGFRIED

Trügt den Treuen der Freund, –

GUNTHER *und* SIEGFRIED

Was in Tropfen heut'
hold wir tranken,
510   in Strahlen ström' es dahin,
fromme Sühne dem Freund!

Gunther trinkt und reicht das Horn Siegfried.

GUNTHER

So biet' ich den Bund!

SIEGFRIED

So –

Er trinkt und hält das geleerte Trinkhorn Hagen hin.
trink' ich dir Treu'.

Hagen zerschlägt mit seinem Schwerte das Horn in zwei
Stücke.

Gunther und Siegfried reichen sich die Hände.

Siegfried betrachtet Hagen, welcher während des
Schwures hinter ihm gestanden.

SIEGFRIED

Was nahmst du am Eide nicht teil?

*Both put two fingers on the horn, which Hagen has
been holding between them and continues to do so.*

Into this drink I've spilled
the invigorating blood
of my burgeoning life.

GUNTHER

Brothers with passion,
proudly mixed,   500
may our blood thrive in this drink.

SIEGFRIED *and* GUNTHER

I drink in faith to my friend.
Happily and in freedom
may the blood of our brotherhood
flourish from our bond today.

GUNTHER

If a brother breaks this bond: –

SIEGFRIED

If one friend betrays the other's trust, –

GUNTHER *and* SIEGFRIED

What today we drank
to good fortune,
shall stream forth in floods   510
as just punishment of that friend !

Gunther drinks and hands the horn to Siegfried.

GUNTHER

With this I enter into the covenant!

SIEGFRIED

With this –

He drinks and holds out the empty horn to Hagen.

I pledge allegiance to you.

*Hagen shatters the horn into two fragments with his
sword.*

Gunther and Siegfried shake hands.

*Siegfried looks at Hagen, who has been standing be-
hind him during the oath.*

SIEGFRIED

Why didn't you take part in the oath?

HAGEN

Mein Blut verdürb' euch den Trank;
nicht fließt mir's ächt
und edel wie euch: –
störrisch und kalt
stockt's in mir,
520   nicht will's die Wange mir röten.
D'rum bleibt ich fern
vom feurigen Bund. –

GUNTHER *zu Siegfried*

Lass' den unfrohen Mann!

Siegfried hängt sich den Schild wieder über.

SIEGFRIED

Frisch auf die Fahrt!
Dort liegt mein Schiff: –
schnell führt es zum Felsen.

Er tritt näher zu Gunther und bedeutet diesen.

Eine Nacht am Ufer
harr'st du im Nachen;
die Frau fährst du dann heim.

*Er wendet sich zum Fortgehen und winkt Gunther, ihm
zu folgen.*

GUNTHER

530   Rastest du nicht zuvor?

SIEGFRIED

Um die Rückkehr ist's mir jach!

Er geht an das Ufer, um das Schiff loszubinden.

GUNTHER

Du, Hagen, bewache die Halle!

*Er folgt Siegfried zum Ufer. – Während Siegfried und
Gunther, nachdem sie ihre Waffen darin niedergelegt, im
Schiff das Segel aufstecken und alles zur Abfahrt bereit
machen, nimmt Hagen seinen Speer und Schild.*

   *Gutrune erscheint an der Tür ihres Gemachs, als jetzt
soeben [Takt 828] Siegfried das Schiff abstößt, welches
sogleich der Mitte des Stromes zutreibt.*

GUTRUNE

Wohin eilen die Schnellen?

HAGEN
My blood would debase your drink;
what flows in me is not pure
and noble like both of you: –
cantankerous and cold,
it rots inside me,
won't redden my cheeks.   520
So I'm staying away
from this covenant of fire. –

GUNTHER *to Siegfried*
Forget that mirthless man!
Siegfried slings his shield over his body again.

SIEGFRIED
Let's get going!
There's my boat: –
we'll be at the rock in no time.
He steps closer to Gunther and tells him what to do.
You'll wait in the boat
for one night on the shore;
then you'll take your wife home.
*He turns to go on his way and gives Gunther a sign to
follow him.*

GUNTHER
Won't you rest first?   530

SIEGFRIED
I'm in a hurry to get back!
He goes to the riverbank to untie the boat.

GUNTHER
You, Hagen, guard the hall!
*He follows Siegfried to the riverbank. – After Siegfried
and Gunther have laid down their arms in the boat, and
while they hoist the sail and make everything ready for
departure, Hagen takes up his spear and shield.*
*Gutrune appears at the door of her room just when
[bar 828] Siegfried has pushed away the boat, which
heads at once towards the middle of the river.*

GUTRUNE
Where are the men going so fast?

HAGEN *während er sich gemächlich mit Schild und Speer vor*
der Halle niedersetzt.

Zu Schiff – Brünnhild' zu frei'n.

GUTRUNE

Siegfried?

HAGEN

Sieh, wie's ihn treibt,
zum Weib dich zu gewinnen!

GUTRUNE

Siegfried – mein!

Sie geht lebhaft erregt in ihr Gemach zurück.

Siegfried hat das Ruder erfaßt und treibt jetzt mit
dessen Schlägen den Nachen stromabwärts, so daß dieser
bald gänzlich außer Gesicht kommt.

Hagen sitzt mit dem Rücken an den Pfosten der Halle
gelehnt, bewegungslos.

HAGEN

Hier sitz' ich zur Wacht,
540   wahre den Hof,
wehre die Halle dem Feind.
Gibich's Sohne
wehet der Wind,
auf Werben fährt er dahin. –
Ihm führt das Steuer
ein starker Held,
Gefahr ihm will er besteh'n:
die eigne Braut
ihm bringt er zum Rhein;
mir aber bringt er den Ring! –
550   Ihr freien Söhne,
frohe Gesellen,
segelt nur lustig dahin: –
dünkt er euch niedrig,
ihr dient ihm doch,
des Niblungen Sohn.

Ein Teppich, welcher dem Vordergrunde zu die Halle
einfaßte, schlägt zusammen und schließt die Bühne vor
dem Zuschauer ab.

HAGEN *while he gets comfortably settled with his shield and*
    spear in front of the hall.
  By boat – to woo Brünnhilde.
GUTRUNE
  Siegfried?
HAGEN
  Look how keen he is
  to win you as wife!
GUTRUNE
  Siegfried – mine!
    She goes back into her room visibly excited.
    Siegfried has taken hold of the oars and with their
    strokes propels the boat downstream so that it soon
    recedes completely out of sight.
    Hagen sits without moving, his back leaning against a
    pillar in the hall.
HAGEN
  Here I sit on watch,
  protect the palace,   540
  defend the hall from its foes.
  Gibich's son
  is blown by the wind,
  he travels to find a wife. –
  Steering him is
  a strong hero,
  eager for him to survive peril:
  for him he'll bring
  a special bride to the Rhine;
  but for me he'll bring the ring! –
  You free sons,   550
  spirited friends,
  just sail happily along: –
  the Nibelung's son
  seems servile to you,
  but it's you who are serving him.
    The curtain that had girded the front part of the hall
    closes and shuts off the stage from the audience.

DRITTE SZENE

Der Walkürenfelsen

Der Vorhang wird wieder aufgezogen. Die Felsenhöhe wie im Vorspiel.

Brünnhilde sitzt am Eingange des Steingemaches in stummen Sinnen Siegfrieds Ring betrachtend.

Von wonniger Erinnerung ergriffen, bedeckt sie ihn mit Küssen.

Ferner Donner läßt sich vernehmen; sie blickt auf und lauscht.

Sie wendet sich wieder zu dem Ring.

ein ferner Blitz

Brünnhilde lauscht von Neuem und späht nach der Ferne, von woher eine finstre Gewitterwolke dem Felsensaume zuzieht.

BRÜNNHILDE
Altgewohntes Geräusch
raunt meinem Ohr die Ferne.
560 Ein Luftroß jagt
im Laufe daher;
auf der Wolke fährt es
wetternd zum Fels.
Wer fand mich Einsame auf?
WALTRAUTES STIMME *aus der Ferne:*
Brünnhilde! Schwester!
Schläfst oder wachst du?
Brünnhilde fährt vom Sitze auf.
BRÜNNHILDE
Waltrautes Ruf,
so wonnig mir kund! –
in die Szene rufend:
Kommst du Schwester?
Schwingst dich kühn zu mir her?
Sie eilt nach dem Felsrande.
570 Dort im Tann –

SCENE THREE

The Valkyries' rock

The curtain is raised again. High on the rock, as in the Prologue.

Brünnhilde is sitting at the entrance to her cave in the rock, looking in silent contemplation at Siegfried's ring.

Emotionally affected by happy memories, she covers it with kisses.

Distant thunder can be heard; she looks up and listens intently.

Then she turns back to the ring.

a distant flash of lightning

Listening out again, Brünnhilde peers into the distance, out of which a dark thundercloud looms towards the edge of the rock.

BRÜNNHILDE
Familiar noises of old
murmur from afar in my ear.
A horse storms through air,   560
galloping this way;
on the cloud it travels
thundering to the rock.
Who's found me, alone?

WALTRAUTE'S VOICE *in the distance:*
Brünnhilde! Sister!
Are you asleep or awake?
Brünnhilde leaps out of her seat.

BRÜNNHILDE
Waltraute's voice,
such a happy memory! –
calling into the wings:
Are you coming, sister?
Are you flying undaunted towards me?
She goes quickly to the edge of the rock.
There in the forest –   570

dir noch vertraut –
steige vom Roß
und stell' den Renner zur Rast!

*Sie stürmt in den Tann, von wo ein starkes Geräusch,
gleich einem Gewitterschlage, sich vernehmen läßt.*

*Brünnhilde kommt in heftiger Bewegung mit Waltraute
zurück; sie bleibt freudig erregt, ohne Waltrautes ängst-
liche Scheu zu beachten.*

Kommst du zu mir?
Bist du so kühn,
magst ohne Grauen
Brünnhild' bieten den Gruß?

WALTRAUTE

Einzig dir nur
galt meine Eil'!

BRÜNNHILDE

580   So wagtest du, Brünnhild' zu Lieb,
Walvaters Bann zu brechen?
Oder wie? – O sag'! –
wär' wider mich
Wotans Sinn erweicht? –
Als dem Gott entgegen
Siegmund ich schützte,
fehlend – ich weiß es –
erfüllt' ich doch seinen Wunsch.
Daß sein Zorn sich verzogen,
590   weiß ich auch.
Denn, verschloß er mich gleich in Schlaf,
fesselt' er mich auf den Fels,
wies er dem Mann mich zur Magd,
der am Weg mich fänd' und erweckt', –
meiner bangen Bitte
doch gab er Gunst:
mit zehrendem Feuer
umzog er den Fels,
dem Zagen zu wehren den Weg.
600   So zur Seligsten
schuf mich die Strafe:

you still know it –
get off the horse
and give your steed a rest!
> *She rushes into the forest, from where a powerful noise*
> *like a thunderclap can be heard.*
>
> *Brünnhilde returns with Waltraute in emotional tur-*
> *moil; she remains in her joyfully excited state, not no-*
> *ticing Waltraute's anxious wariness.*

You've come to me?
Are you that brave,
can you give to Brünnhilde
your greetings unafraid?

WALTRAUTE
My haste was
only about you!

BRÜNNHILDE
So you defied battle-father's   580
banishment of Brünnhilde for her sake?
Or what? – Tell me! –
Is it that Wotan has softened
his stance against me? –
In protecting Siegmund
against the god's wishes,
not very well – I know –
I was actually doing what he wanted.
I also know
that his anger was assuaged.   590
Yes, he did then embalm me in sleep,
he did imprison me on this rock,
so any man happening to find and wake
me could treat me as a handmaid, –
but he did pay heed
to my restive request:
he surrounded the rock
with a ravenous fire,
to deny any coward access.
So my punishment   600
made me the happiest of women:

der herrlichste Held
gewann mich zum Weib!
In seiner Liebe
leucht' und lach' ich heut' auf!
 Sie umarmt Waltraute unter stürmischen Freudenbezei-
 gungen, welche diese mit scheuer Ungeduld abzuwehren
 sucht.
Lockte dich Schwester mein Los?
An meiner Wonne
willst du dich weiden,
teilen, was mich betraf?
WALTRAUTE *heftig*

610　Teilen den Taumel,
der dich Törin erfaßt? –
Ein And'res bewog mich in Angst,
zu brechen Wotans Gebot.
 Brünnhilde gewahrt hier erst mit Befremdung die wild-
 aufgeregte Stimmung Waltrautes.
BRÜNNHILDE
Angst und Furcht
fesseln dich Arme?
So verzieh der Strenge noch nicht?
Du zag'st vor des Strafenden Zorn?
WALTRAUTE *düster*
Dürft' ich ihn fürchten,
meiner Angst fänd' ich ein End'!
BRÜNNHILDE

620　Staunend versteh' ich dich nicht.
WALTRAUTE
Wehre der Wallung,
achtsam höre mich an!
Nach Walhall wieder
treibt mich die Angst,
die von Walhall hierher mich trieb.
BRÜNNHILDE *erschreckt*
  taumelt zurück*
Was ist's mit den ewigen Göttern?

the most glorious of heroes
won me for his wife!
I bask and laugh today
in his love!

> *She embraces Waltraute with rapturous displays of joy,*
> *which the latter tries to fend off with frightened im-*
> *patience.*

Did my fate tempt you, sister?
Do you want to feast
on my happiness,
share in what's happened to me?

WALTRAUTE *forcefully*

Share the delirium, you fool,   610
which has you in its grip?
A different matter moved me in fear
to defy Wotan's command.

> *With surprise and displeasure, Brünnhilde notices Wal-*
> *traute's wildly agitated mood only now.*

BRÜNNHILDE

Poor thing: do fear
and dread inhibit you?
Is the austere god still not relenting?
Do you fear the austere god's wrath?

WALTRAUTE *darkly*

If I dreaded that alone,
my fear would be at an end!

BRÜNNHILDE

I'm amazed, I don't understand.   620

WALTRAUTE

Stay calm,
listen to me carefully!
Fear is driving me
again to Valhalla,
as from Valhalla it drove me here.

BRÜNNHILDE *shocked*
         reeling back *

What's happening to the eternal gods?

WALTRAUTE
    Höre mit Sinn, was ich dir sage!
    Seit er von dir geschieden,
    zur Schlacht nicht mehr
630   schickte uns Wotan:
    irr' und ratlos
    ritten wir ängstlich zu Heer;
    Walhall's mutige Helden
    mied Walvater.
    Einsam zu Roß,
    ohne Ruh' noch Rast,
    durchschweift' er als Wand'rer die Welt.
    Jüngst kehrte er heim;
    in der Hand hielt er
640   seines Speeres Splitter, –
    die hatte ein Held ihm geschlagen.
    Mit stummem Wink
    Walhall's Edle
    wies er zum Forst,
    die Weltesche zu fällen.
    Des Stammes Scheite
    hieß er sie schichten
    zu ragendem Hauf
    rings um der Seligen Saal.
650   Der Götter Rat
    ließ er berufen;
    den Hochsitz nahm
    heilig er ein:
    ihm zu Seiten
    hieß er die Bangen sich setzen,
    in Ring und Reih'
    die Hall' erfüllen die Helden. –
    So sitzt er,
    sagt kein Wort,
660   auf hehrem Sitze
    stumm und ernst;
    des Speeres Splitter
    fest in der Faust;
    Holdas Äpfel

WALTRAUTE

Listen to the point of what I'm saying!
Since he parted from you,
Wotan has sent us
into battle no more: 630
crazed and clueless,
we anxiously rode to arms;
Father of Battles shunned
Valhalla's spirited heroes.
On horseback in solitude,
never at peace,
he traversed the world as Wanderer.
He came back not long ago;
in his hand he held
the broken pieces of his spear, –   640
after a hero had slashed its shaft.
With a voiceless gesture
he instructed Valhalla's elite
to go to the wood
and cut the world ash-tree down.
The logs of the trunk
he ordered to be piled
in soaring stacks
around the sacred hall.
The gods' council   650
gathered at his behest;
solemnly he took
his place on the throne:
he asked the troubled gods
to sit on either side of him,
as the heroes filled the hall
in circles and in rows.
There he sits
on his august seat,
voiceless and unsmiling,   660
no word from his lips;
the spear's broken pieces
tightly in his hand;
no longer touching

rührt er nicht an.
Staunen und Bangen
binden starr die Götter.
Seine Raben beide
sandt' er auf Reise;
670 kehrten die einst
mit guter Kunde zurück; –
dann noch einmal –
zum letzten Mal! –
lächelte ewig der Gott.
Seine Knie' umwindend,
liegen wir Walküren, –
blind bleibt er
den flehenden Blicken:
uns alle verzehrt
680 Zagen und endlose Angst. –
An seine Brust
preßt' ich mich weinend; –
    zögernd
da brach sich sein Blick; –
er gedachte, Brünnhilde, dein'!
Tief seufzt' er auf,
schloß das Auge,
und wie im Traume
raunt' er das Wort:
'des tiefen Rheines Töchtern
690 gäbe den Ring sie wieder zurück, –
von des Fluches Last
erlöst wär' Gott und Welt!' –
Da sann ich nach: –
von seiner Seite,
durch stumme Reihen
stahl ich mich fort;
in heimlicher Hast
bestieg ich mein Roß, –
und ritt im Sturme zu dir. –
700 Dich, o Schwester,
beschwör' ich nun:

Holda's apples.
Dismay and disquiet
are paralysing the gods.
He despatched his two
ravens on a journey;
if they should ever come   670
back with good news; –
then just once more –
for the last time! –
the god would smile for ever.
We Valkyries lie around
his knees like a wreath, –
he stays blind
to our beseeching gaze:
consuming us all
are our faint hearts and endless fear. –   680
Crying, I pressed myself close
to his breast; –
     tentatively
his expression softened a little; –
you, Brünnhilde, he remembered!
He let out a deep sigh,
closed his eye,
and murmured these words
as if in a dream:
'if she returns the ring to the Rhine
and the daughters in its depths, –   690
god and world are redeemed
from the burden of the curse!' –
That I pondered: –
I slipped away
from his side
through silent echelons;
in covert haste
I got on my horse, –
and rode to you like fury. –
You, my sister,   700
I implore you now:

was du vermagst,
vollend’ es dein Mut;
ende der Ewigen Qual!
    Sie hat sich vor Brünnhilde niedergeworfen.

BRÜNNHILDE *ruhig*
Welch’ banger Träume Mären
meldest du Traurige mir!
Der Götter heiligem
Himmelsnebel
bin ich Törin enttaucht;
710 nicht fass’ ich, was ich erfahre.
Wirr und wüst
scheint mir dein Sinn:
in deinem Aug’,
so übermüde,
glänzt flackernde Glut.
Mit blasser Wange,
du bleiche Schwester,
    Brünnhilde läßt die Hand Waltraute’s, die sie bis dahin
    gehalten hat, fahren. *
was willst du Wilde von mir?

WALTRAUTE *heftig*
An deiner Hand, der Ring, –
720 er ist’s; – hör’ meinen Rat:
für Wotan wirf ihn von dir!

BRÜNNHILDE
Den Ring – von mir?

WALTRAUTE
Den Rheintöchtern gib ihn zurück!

BRÜNNHILDE
Den Rheintöchtern – ich – den Ring?
Siegfrieds Liebespfand?
Bist du von Sinnen?

WALTRAUTE
Hör’ mich! Hör’ meine Angst!
Der Welt Unheil
haftet sicher an ihm.
730 Wirf ihn von dir,

what is in your power to do,
may your spirit bring it to a close;
end the immortals' ordeal!
   She prostrates herself before Brünnhilde.
BRÜNNHILDE *calmly*
Sad woman: what bad dreams
and tales you're telling me!
I'm just a foolish girl
who's emerged from the mists
of the gods' sacred sky;
I see nothing in what I'm learning.   710
To me your point seems
tangled and desolate:
in your eyes,
deprived of sleep,
flickers a quivering flame.
You pale sister,
with ashen cheeks,
   *Brünnhilde lets go of Waltraute's hand, which she has
   been holding up to now.* *
wild woman: what do you want of me?
WALTRAUTE *forcefully*
On your hand, the ring, –
there it is; – hear me out: 720
rid yourself of it, for Wotan!
BRÜNNHILDE
The ring – get rid of it?
WALTRAUTE
Return it to the Rhinedaughters!
BRÜNNHILDE
To the Rhinedaughters – I – the ring?
Siegfried's token of love?
Are you mad?
WALTRAUTE
Listen to me! Listen to why I'm afraid!
Its fate is inseparable
from the calamity of the world.
Rid yourself of it,   730

fort in die Welle,
Walhall's Elend zu enden,
den verfluchten wirf in die Flut!
BRÜNNHILDE
Ha! Weißt du, was er mir ist?
Wie kannst du's fassen,
fühllose Maid! –
*immer starr den Ring ansehend**
Mehr als Walhall's Wonne,
mehr als der Ewigen Ruhm
ist mir der Ring:
740   ein Blick auf sein helles Gold,
ein Blitz aus dem hehren Glanz
gilt mir werter
als aller Götter
ewig währendes Glück.
Denn selig aus ihm
leuchtet mir Siegfrieds Liebe, –
Siegfrieds Liebe! –
O, ließ' sich die Wonne dir sagen! –
Sie wahrt mir der Reif. –

750   Geh' hin zu der Götter
heiligem Rat!
Von meinem Ringe
raune ihnen zu:
die Liebe ließe ich nie,
mir nähmen nie sie die Liebe,
stürzt' auch in Trümmern
Walhall's strahlende Pracht!
*Waltraute ist ganz außer sich geraten.**
WALTRAUTE
Dies deine Treue?
So in Trauer
760   entlässest du lieblos die Schwester?
BRÜNNHILDE
Schwinge dich fort,
fliege zu Roß!
Den Reif entführst du mir nie!

away with it into the waters
to end Valhalla's affliction;
fling the cursed object into the flood!
BRÜNNHILDE
Ha! Do you know what it means to me?
Not that it can ever dawn on you,
callous virgin! –
   constantly staring at the ring*
To me this ring is worth
more than Valhalla's bliss,
more than glory among eternal gods:
one glimpse of its bright gold,   740
one glint of its sublime brilliance
is more valuable to me
than all of the gods'
never-ending fortune.
Out of it pours for me
the beatific light of Siegfried's love, –
Siegfried's love! –
O, were that bliss to touch you! –
For me it's preserved in this ring. –

Go along to the gods'   750
holy council!
Moan to them
about my ring:
tell them I'll never stop loving,
that they'll never deprive me of love,
even if the lustrous swagger
of Valhalla collapses in ruins!
   Waltraute is completely beside herself.*
WALTRAUTE
Your loyalty's this?
Coldly leaving
your grieving sister in the lurch?   760
BRÜNNHILDE
Fly out of here,
back on your horse!
You'll never capture my ring!

WALTRAUTE
Wehe! Wehe!
Weh' dir, Schwester!
Walhall's Göttern Weh'!
Sie stürzt fort. – Bald erhebt sich unter Sturm eine Ge-
witterwolke aus dem Tann.
BRÜNNHILDE *während sie der davonziehenden, hell erleuch-*
teten Gewitterwolke, die sich bald gänzlich in der Ferne
verliert, nachblickt
Blitzend Gewölk,
vom Wind getragen,
stürme dahin:
770   zu mir nie steure mehr her!
Es ist Abend geworden. Aus der Tiefe leuchtet der Feuer-
schein allmählich heller auf.
Brünnhilde blickt ruhig in die Landschaft hinaus.
Abendlich Dämmern
deckt den Himmel;
heller leuchtet
die hütende Lohe herauf.
Der Feuerschein nähert sich aus der Tiefe.
Immer glühendere Flammenzungen lecken über den
Felsensaum auf.
Was leckt so wütend
die lodernde Welle zum Wall?
Zur Felsenspitze
wälzt sich der feurige Schwall.
Man hört aus der Tiefe Siegfrieds Hornruf nahen. Brünn-
hilde lauscht, und fährt dann entzückt auf.
Siegfried!
780   Siegfried zurück!
Seinen Ruf sendet er her!
Auf! Auf! Ihm entgegen!
In meines Gottes Arm!
Sie eilt in höchstem Entzücken dem Felsrande zu.
Feuerflammen schlagen herauf: aus ihnen springt Sieg-
fried auf einen hochragenden Felsstein empor, worauf die
Flammen sogleich wieder zurückweichen und abermals
nur aus der Tiefe herauf leuchten.

WALTRAUTE
  Alas! Alas!
  Beware, sister!
  Valhalla's gods, beware!
    She rushes away. – Soon a thundercloud from a storm
    arises out of the forest.
BRÜNNHILDE *as she watches the thundercloud blazing with*
    light moving away and soon completely disappearing in
    the distance
  Thunderous cloud,
  thrust by the wind,
  storm on your way:
  never steer towards me again!   770
    It is now evening. The light of the flames below gradually
    starts to get brighter.
        Brünnhilde gazes calmly at the surrounding scenery.
  Dusk has fallen
  blanketing the sky;
  brighter shines
  the vigilant fire below.
    From below the light of the fire draws nearer.
      Increasingly fierce tongues of flame lick up over the
    edge of the rock.
  Why does this wave of flame
  so furiously encroach on my refuge?
  The torrent of fire is rolling
  right up to the top of the rock.
    Siegfried's horn-call can be heard approaching from be-
    low. Brünnhilde listens and then leaps up in joy.
  Siegfried!
  Siegfried's back!   780
  He's sending his call up here!
  Up! Up! Go to meet him!
  Into the arms of my god!
    She rushes with utmost rapture to the edge of the rock.
      Tongues of fire ascend: Siegfried jumps out of them
    and upwards onto a prominent high rock, at which point
    the flames immediately recede again and once more blaze
    only upwards from beneath.

Verrat! –

*Siegfried, auf dem Haupte den Tarnhelm, der ihm bis zur
Hälfte das Gesicht verdeckt und nur die Augen frei läßt,
erscheint in Gunthers Gestalt.*

*Brünnhilde weicht voll Entsetzen zurück, flieht bis in
den Vordergrund und heftet von da aus, in sprachlosem
Erstaunen, ihren Blick auf Siegfried.*

      Wer drang zu mir?

*Siegfried, im Hintergrunde auf dem Steine verweilend,
betrachtet Brünnhilde, regungslos auf seinen Schild ge-
lehnt.*

   Langes Schweigen.

SIEGFRIED *mit verstellter (rauherer) Stimme*

Brünnhild'! Ein Freier kam, –
den dein Feuer nicht geschreckt.
Dich werb' ich nun zum Weib:
du folge willig mir!

BRÜNNHILDE *heftig zitternd*

Wer ist der Mann,
790   der das vermochte,
was dem Stärksten nur bestimmt?

SIEGFRIED *unverändert, wie zuvor*

Ein Helde, der dich zähmt,
bezwingt Gewalt dich nur.

BRÜNNHILDE *von Grausen erfaßt*

Ein Unhold schwang sich
auf jenen Stein!
Ein Aar kam geflogen,
mich zu zerfleischen!
Wer bist du, Schrecklicher?
  langes Schweigen
Stammst du von Menschen?
800   Kommst du von Hellas
nächtlichem Heer?

SIEGFRIED *wie zuvor, mit etwas bebender Stimme beginnend,
alsbald aber wieder sicherer fortfahrend*

Ein Gibichung bin ich, –
und Gunther heißt der Held,

Treason! –

With the Tarnhelm on his head hiding half his face and leaving only his eyes visible, Siegfried appears in Gunther's shape.

Brünnhilde cowers in total horror, escapes to the front of the stage and stands there dumbfounded with her eyes riveted on Siegfried.

Who's invaded my world?

Siegfried lingers in the background on the rock and leans stiffly without moving on his shield looking at Brünnhilde.

Long silence.

SIEGFRIED *with an altered (rougher) voice*

Brünnhilde! A wooer's come, –
not wavering through your fire.
I claim you now as my wife:
show willing and follow me!

BRÜNNHILDE *shaking heavily*

Who is this man
capable of doing   790
what only the strongest can do?

SIEGFRIED *inertly, as before*

A hero will bring you to heel,
be it violence alone that breaks you.

BRÜNNHILDE *gripped by utter dread*

An ogre's vaulted
onto that rock!
An eagle's swooped down
to tear me limb from limb!
Who are you, cruel being?
    long silence
Are you human?
Or from Hella's   800
nocturnal army?

SIEGFRIED *starting with a somewhat quavering voice as before, but quickly continuing again more securely*

I am a Gibichung, –
and Gunther is the name,

dem, Frau, du folgen sollst.

BRÜNNHILDE *in Verzweiflung ausbrechend*

Wotan! Ergrimmter,
grausamer Gott!
Weh'! Nun erseh' ich
der Strafe Sinn!
Zu Hohn und Jammer
810   jagst du mich hin!

> *Siegfried springt vom Stein herab und tritt näher heran.*

SIEGFRIED

Die Nacht bricht an: –
in deinem Gemach
mußt du dich mir vermählen!

BRÜNNHILDE *indem sie den Finger, an dem sie Siegfrieds
Ring trägt, drohend ausstreckt*

Bleib' fern! Fürchte dies Zeichen!
Zur Schande zwingst du mich nicht,
so lang' der Ring mich beschützt.

SIEGFRIED

Mannesrecht gebe er Gunther:
durch den Ring sei ihm vermählt!

BRÜNNHILDE

Zurück, du Räuber!
820   Frevelnder Dieb!
Erfreche dich nicht, mir zu nah'n!
Stärker als Stahl
macht mich der Ring:
nie raubst du ihn mir!

SIEGFRIED

Von dir ihn zu lösen,
lehrst du mich nun!

> *Er dringt auf sie ein. Sie ringen miteinander.*
>
> *Brünnhilde windet sich los, flieht und wendet sich um,
> wie zur Wehr.*
>
> *Siegfried greift sie von neuem an. Sie flieht; er erreicht
> sie. Beide ringen heftig miteinander. Er faßt sie bei der
> Hand und entzieht ihrem Finger den Ring.*
>
> *Brünnhilde schreit heftig auf. Als sie, wie zerbrochen,*

woman, of the hero you're to obey.

BRÜNNHILDE *in a despairing outburst*

Wotan! Ferocious,
barbaric god!
Alas! Now I see
the point of my punishment!
To hunt me down until
I'm derided and disgraced! 810

Siegfried jumps down from the rock and steps closer.

SIEGFRIED

Night is closing in: –
in your cave
you must marry me!

BRÜNNHILDE *pointing threateningly with the finger on which*
she wears Siegfried's ring

Stay away! Be afraid of this sign!
You'll not force disgrace upon me,
as long as I'm protected by the ring.

SIEGFRIED

It affords Gunther a husband's rights:
you must wed him because of the ring!

BRÜNNHILDE

Get back, you bandit!
Outrageous thief! 820
Don't even dare to get near me!
I am stronger than steel
because of the ring:
rob me of it you never will!

SIEGFRIED

You're teaching me now
to relieve you of it!

He closes in on her. They wrestle with one another.

Brünnhilde prises herself free, runs off and turns around, looking for a fight.

Siegfried attacks her again. She flees; he catches her. Both wrestle violently with each other. He grabs her hand and removes the ring from her finger.

Brünnhilde lets out a violent scream. As she sinks into

*in seinen Armen niedersinkt, streift ihr Blick bewußtlos
die Augen Siegfrieds.*

   *Er läßt die Machtlose auf die Steinbank vor dem Fel-
sengemache niedergleiten.*

Jetzt bist du mein,
Brünnhilde, Gunthers Braut, –
gönne mir nun dein Gemach!

   Brünnhilde starrt ohnmächtig vor sich hin.

BRÜNNHILDE *erhebt sich ein wenig, bleibt aber wie geknickt
in ihrem ganzen Wesen.* *

   matt

830 Was könntest du wehren,
elendes Weib!

   Siegfried treibt sie mit einer gebietenden Gebärde an.

   *Zitternd und wankenden Schrittes geht sie in das Ge-
mach.*

   Siegfried zieht sein Schwert.

SIEGFRIED *mit seiner natürlichen Stimme*

Nun, Nothung, zeuge du,
daß ich in Züchten warb.
Die Treue wahrend dem Bruder,
trenne mich von seiner Braut!

   Er folgt Brünnhilde nach.

   Der Vorhang fällt.

his arms, looking shattered, her swooning eyes fleetingly
meet Siegfried's.

    He lowers the powerless woman onto the stone seat in
front of the cave in the rock.

Now you're mine,
Brünnhilde, Gunther's bride, –
allow me the use of your cave!

    Brünnhilde stares helplessly in front of her.

BRÜNNHILDE *raises herself up a little, but still looks as if her*
    entire being has been crushed. *

    dully

Ward him off you can't,   830
unhappy woman!

    Siegfried pushes her on with a dictatorial gesture.

    With shaking and faltering steps, she walks into the
cave.

    Siegfried draws his sword.

SIEGFRIED *with his normal voice*

You, Nothung, bear witness
that my suit is above reproach.
In bounden duty to my brother,
keep me separate from his bride!

    He follows Brünnhilde.

    The curtain falls.

ZWEITER AUFZUG

VORSPIEL UND ERSTE SZENE

Vor Gunthers Halle

Der Vorhang geht auf [Takt 30]. – Uferraum vor der Halle der Gibichungen: rechts der offene Eingang zur Halle; links das Rheinufer; von diesem aus erhebt sich eine, durch verschiedene Bergpfade gespaltene, felsige Anhöhe, quer über die Bühne, nach rechts dem Hintergrunde zu aufsteigend. Dort sieht man einen der Fricka errichteten Weihstein, welchem, höher hinauf, ein größerer für Wotan, sowie seitwärts ein gleicher dem Donner geweihter entspricht. – Es ist Nacht. – Hagen, den Speer im Arme, den Schild zur Seite, sitzt schlafend an einen Pfosten der Halle angelehnt.

Hier [Takt 39] tritt der Mond plötzlich hervor und wirft ein grelles Licht auf Hagen und seine nächste Umgebung: man gewahrt Alberich vor Hagen kauernd, die Arme auf dessen Knie gelehnt.

ALBERICH *leise*
    Schläfst du, Hagen, mein Sohn? –
    Du schläfst und hörst mich nicht,
    den Ruh' und Schlaf verriet?
HAGEN *leise, ohne sich zu rühren, so daß er immer fort zu schlafen scheint, obwohl er die Augen offen hat.*
    Ich höre dich, schlimmer Albe:
840   was hast du meinem Schlaf zu sagen?
ALBERICH
    Gemahnt sei der Macht,
    der du gebietest,
    bist du so mutig,
    wie die Mutter dich mir gebar!
HAGEN *immer wie zuvor*
    Gab mir die Mutter Mut,

ACT TWO

PRELUDE AND SCENE ONE

In front of Gunther's hall

The curtain rises [bar 30]. – A space on the riverbank in front of the hall of the Gibichungs: on the right is the open entrance to the hall; on the left the shore of the Rhine. A small rocky hill ascends from the shore diagonally across the stage, crisscrossed by a number of mountain paths and rising upwards on the right into the background. There, an altar stone dedicated to Fricka is visible in a group with two others: a larger one higher up dedicated to Wotan and to the side of that one of the same size dedicated to Donner. – It is night. – Hagen, his arms around his spear and his shield by his side, sits leaning against one of the hall's pillars, asleep.

At this point [bar 39], the moon suddenly comes out, throwing a harsh light on Hagen and his immediate surroundings: Alberich can be seen crouching in front of Hagen and resting his arms on Hagen's knees.

ALBERICH *quietly*
Are you asleep, Hagen, my son? –
Do you sleep and not hear me,
me whom rest and sleep betrayed?

HAGEN *quietly, not moving, so that he seems to keep on sleeping, even though his eyes are open.*
I hear you, wicked dwarf:
what do you have to say to my sleep?   840

ALBERICH
May I recall the power
that you command,
if you're as spirited as the mother,
who rewarded me with your birth!

HAGEN *always as before*
If my mother gave me spirit,

nicht mag ich ihr doch danken,
daß deiner List sie erlag:
frühalt, fahl und bleich,
hass' ich die Frohen,
850   freue mich nie!
ALBERICH *wie zuvor*
Hagen, mein Sohn!
Hasse die Frohen!
Mich Lustfreien,
Leidbelasteten,
liebst du so wie du sollst!
Bist du kräftig,
kühn und klug:
die wir bekämpfen
mit nächtigem Krieg,
860   schon gibt ihnen Not unser Neid.
Der einst den Ring mir entriß,
Wotan, der wütende Räuber,
vom eig'nen Geschlechte
ward er geschlagen:
an den Wälsung verlor er
Macht und Gewalt:
mit der Götter ganzer Sippe
in Angst ersieht er sein Ende.
Nicht ihn fürcht' ich mehr:
870   fallen muß er mit allen! –

Schläfst du, Hagen, mein Sohn?
HAGEN *bleibt unverändert, wie zuvor*
Der Ewigen Macht, –
wer erbte sie?
ALBERICH
Ich – und du!
Wir erben die Welt, –
trüg' ich mich nicht
in deiner Treu',
teilst du meinen Gram und Grimm.
Wotans Speer

I'm not minded to thank her
for falling victim to your cunning:
old too soon, sickly and pale,
I loathe the lively,
never rejoice!   850
ALBERICH *as before*
Hagen, my son!
Loathe the lively!
Love me as you think fit,
lacking joy as I do,
loaded down with hurt.
Stay powerful,
undaunted and smart:
then those we fight
with nocturnal war
will feel the brunt of our pitiless quest.   860
Wotan, that raging bandit,
who once tore the ring from me,
was rendered helpless
by his own race:
he lost power and authority
to the Wälsung:
with the entire clan of the gods,
he sees his end coming with alarm.
He frightens me no more:
sink he must with the lot of them! –   870

Are you asleep, Hagen, my son?
HAGEN *stays exactly the same as before*
The eternal gods' power, –
who will inherit it?
ALBERICH
I – and you!
We'll inherit the world, –
provided I'm not led
astray by your loyalty,
and you share my hostility and hate.
The Wälsung broke Wotan's

880 zerspellte der Wälsung,
der Fafner, den Wurm,
im Kampfe gefällt,
und kindisch den Reif sich errang;
jede Gewalt
hat er gewonnen:
Walhall und Nibelheim
    immer heimlich
neigen sich ihm.
An dem furchtlosen Helden
erlahmt selbst mein Fluch;
890 denn nicht kennt er
des Ringes Wert,
zu nichts nützt er
die neidlichste Macht.
Lachend, in liebender Brunst,
brennt er lebend dahin.
Ihn zu verderben,
taugt uns nun einzig! –

Schläfst du, Hagen, mein Sohn?
HAGEN *wie zuvor*
    Zu seinem Verderben
900 dient er mir schon.
ALBERICH
    Den gold'nen Ring,
    den Reif – gilt's zu erringen!
    Ein weises Weib
    lebt dem Wälsung zu Lieb':
    riet' es ihm je,
    des Rheines Töchtern,
    – die in Wassers Tiefen
    einst mich betört, –
    zurück zu geben den Ring:
910 verloren ging' mir das Gold,
    keine List erlangte es je.
    D'rum, ohne Zögern
    ziel' auf den Reif!

spear apart,   880
Fafner, the dragon,
he felled in combat,
and the ring he gained like a child;
every fight for power
he's won:
Valhalla and Nibelheim
    continuing in a cryptic manner
are in thrall to him.
Even my curse falters
with the fearless hero;
he has no idea   890
of the ring's worth,
nor does he do anything
with its most pitiless power.
Heady with laughter, making love,
he burns away his life.
Now it's up to us alone
to destroy him! –

Are you asleep, Hagen, my son?
HAGEN *as before*
  He's already useful
  to my plan to destroy him.   900
ALBERICH
  The golden ring,
  the ring – our object is to get it!
  A wise woman
  lives for the sake of the Wälsung:
  if she ever tells him
  to return the ring
  to the daughters of the Rhine,
  – who once bedevilled me
  in the waters' deep, –
  then the gold's lost to me,   910
  no trick could ever retrieve it.
  So go for the ring
  with not a second to lose!

Dich Zaglosen
zeugt' ich mir ja,
daß wider Helden
hart du mir hieltest.
Zwar – stark nicht genug
den Wurm zu besteh'n,
920   was allein dem Wälsung bestimmt, –
zu zähem Haß doch
erzog ich Hagen;
der soll mich nun rächen,
den Ring gewinnen,
dem Wälsung und Wotan zum Hohn!
Schwörst du mir's, Hagen, mein Sohn?

> *Von hier an bedeckt ein immer finsterer werdender Schatten wieder Alberich. Zugleich beginnt das erste Tagesgrauen.*

HAGEN *immer wie zuvor*
Den Ring soll ich haben; –
harre in Ruh'!

ALBERICH
Schwörst du mir's, Hagen, mein Held?

> *Wie mit dem Folgenden Alberichs Gestalt immer mehr dem Blicke entschwindet, wird auch seine Stimme immer unvernehmbarer.*

HAGEN
930   Mir selbst schwör' ich's; –
schweige die Sorge!

ALBERICH
Sei treu, Hagen, mein Sohn!
Trauter Helde – sei treu!
Sei treu! – Treu! –

> *Alberich ist gänzlich verschwunden. Hagen, der unverändert in seiner Stellung verblieben, blickt regungslos und starren Auges nach dem Rheine hin, auf welchem sich die Morgendämmerung ausbreitet.*

That's the reason I sired you,
fearless creature,
mercilessly to maintain my fight
against heroes.
Yes – I was not strong enough
to overcome the dragon,
as the Wälsung was destined to do, –   920
but I did teach Hagen
bitter hate;
he is to avenge me now,
get the ring,
and defy the Wälsung and Wotan!
Do you swear to me, Hagen, my son?
   From here, a growing, ever-darkening shadow obscures
   Alberich from view. At the same time the first signs of
   dawn begin to appear.

HAGEN *still as before*
I'll get the ring in due course; –
be patient and calm!

ALBERICH
Do you swear to me, Hagen, my hero?
   As Alberich's figure increasingly recedes out of sight
   during the following passage, his voice is constantly
   harder to hear.

HAGEN
I've sworn it to myself; –   930
away with your alarm!

ALBERICH
Stay loyal, Hagen, my son!
Trusted hero – stay loyal!
Stay loyal! – Loyal! –
   Alberich is completely out of sight. Hagen, who has
   stayed in place unchanged, stares without moving, and
   with his eyes frozen on the Rhine as the dawn gradually
   casts its light upon it.

ZWEITE SZENE

*Von hier an [Takt 205] färbt sich der Rhein von immer stärker
erglühendem Morgenrot.*
   Hagen macht eine zuckende Bewegung.
   *Siegfried tritt plötzlich, dicht am Ufer, hinter einem Busche
hervor.*

SIEGFRIED
   Hoi-ho, Hagen!
   Müder Mann!
   Siehst du mich kommen?
       *Siegfried ist in seiner eignen Gestalt; nur den Tarnhelm
       hat er noch auf dem Haupte; diesen zieht er jetzt ab und
       hängt ihn, während er hervorschreitet, in den Gürtel.*
HAGEN *gemächlich sich erhebend*
       *geht mit schweren Schritten. Wie ein Seeman**
   Hei! Siegfried!
   Geschwinder Helde!
940   Wo brausest du her?
SIEGFRIED
   Vom Brünnhildenstein:
   dort sog ich den Atem ein,
   mit dem ich dich rief,
   so schnell war meine Fahrt.
   Langsamer folgt mir ein Paar,
   zu Schiff gelangt das her!
HAGEN
   So zwangst du Brünnhild'?
SIEGFRIED
   Wacht Gutrune?
HAGEN *in die Halle rufend*
   Hoi-ho! Gutrune!
950   Komm' heraus!
   Siegfried ist da:
   was säumst du drin?

SCENE TWO

*From here onwards [bar 205], the incandescent red glow of
dawn colouring the Rhine constantly deepens.*
   Hagen moves with a jolt.
   *Close to the riverbank, Siegfried steps out suddenly from
behind a bush.*

SIEGFRIED
   Hoi-ho, Hagen!
   Tired man!
   Did you see me coming?
      *Siegfried's body is his own again; only the Tarnhelm is
      still on his head. He now takes it off and straps it into his
      belt while he keeps walking into the open.*
HAGEN *sedately getting up*
         *walks with lumbering, dragging steps. Like a sailor**
   Hey! Siegfried!
   Hero in a hurry!
   Blazing in from where?   940
SIEGFRIED
   From Brünnhilde's rock:
   there I breathed in,
   breathed out and called you,
   my trip was that fast.
   The two following are slower,
   they're getting here by boat.
HAGEN
   You made Brünnhilde submit?
SIEGFRIED
   Is Gutrune waking up?
HAGEN *calling into the hall*
   Hoi-ho! Gutrune!
   Come out here!
   Siegfried's back: 950
   what are you waiting for?

SIEGFRIED *sich zur Halle wendend*
  Euch beiden meld' ich,
  wie ich Brünnhild' band.
      Gutrune tritt ihm aus der Halle entgegen.
  Heiß' mich willkommen,
  Gibichskind!
  Ein guter Bote bin ich dir.
GUTRUNE
  Freia grüße dich
  zu aller Frauen Ehre!
SIEGFRIED
960 Frei und hold
  sei nun mir Frohem!
  Zum Weib gewann ich dich heut'.
GUTRUNE
  So folgt Brünnhild' meinem Bruder?
SIEGFRIED
  Leicht ward die Frau ihm gefreit.
GUTRUNE
  Sengte das Feuer ihn nicht?
SIEGFRIED
  Ihn hätt' es auch nicht versehrt;
  doch ich durchschritt es für ihn, –
  da dich ich wollt' erwerben.
GUTRUNE
  Doch dich hat es verschont.
SIEGFRIED
970 Mich freute die schwelende Brunst.
GUTRUNE
  Hielt Brünnhild' dich für Gunther?
SIEGFRIED
  Ihm glich ich auf ein Haar:
  der Tarnhelm wirkte das,
  wie Hagen tüchtig es wies.
HAGEN
  Dir gab ich guten Rat.
GUTRUNE
  So zwangst du das kühne Weib?

SIEGFRIED *turning towards the hall*
Let me tell you both
how I got Brünnhilde.
    Gutrune comes out of the hall towards him.
Make me welcome,
Gibich's child!
I bring you good news.

GUTRUNE
May Freia extend you greetings
in honour of all women!

SIEGFRIED
Be candid and kind   960
to me now I'm so happy!
Today I've made you my wife!

GUTRUNE
So Brünnhilde's with my brother?

SIEGFRIED
It was easy to win her for him.

GUTRUNE
Didn't the fire scorch him?

SIEGFRIED
He'd not have been hurt by it;
I went through it for him anyway, –
as it was you I wanted to win.

GUTRUNE
But it did you no harm.

SIEGFRIED
I enjoyed the simmering heat.   970

GUTRUNE
Brünnhilde took you for Gunther?

SIEGFRIED
I was like him to a tee:
the Tarnhelm did it,
as old Hagen told us it would.

HAGEN
I gave you good advice.

GUTRUNE
You made the bold woman submit?

SIEGFRIED
  Sie wich – Gunthers Kraft.

GUTRUNE
  Und vermählte sie sich dir?

SIEGFRIED
  Ihrem Mann gehorchte Brünnhild'
980 eine volle bräutliche Nacht.

GUTRUNE
  Als ihr Mann doch galtest du?

SIEGFRIED
  Bei Gutrune weilte Siegfried.

GUTRUNE
  Doch zur Seite war ihm Brünnhild'?

SIEGFRIED
  Zwischen Ost und West
    auf sein Schwert deutend
                        der Nord:
  so nah' – war Brünnhild' ihm fern.

GUTRUNE
  Wie empfing Gunther sie nun von dir?

SIEGFRIED
  Durch des Feuers verlöschende Lohe,
  im Frühnebel vom Felsen
  folgte sie mir zu Tal;
990 dem Strande nah',
  flugs die Stelle
  tauschte Gunther mit mir:
  durch des Geschmeides Tugend
  wünscht' ich mich schnell hieher.
  Ein starker Wind nun treibt
  die Trauten den Rhein herauf.
  D'rum rüstet jetzt den Empfang!

GUTRUNE
  Siegfried! Mächtigster Mann!
  Wie faßt mich Furcht vor dir!

HAGEN *vom Ufer her rufend*
1000 In der Ferne seh' ich ein Segel!
    *Das Ganze ist immer als 'lebhafte Conversation', 'im
    Stile der komischen Oper' zu halten.* *

SIEGFRIED
  She gave in – to Gunther's power.
GUTRUNE
  And she slept with you?
SIEGFRIED
  For her entire bridal night,
  Brünnhilde was her husband's wife.   980
GUTRUNE
  But she took you for her husband?
SIEGFRIED
  With Gutrune, Siegfried stayed.
GUTRUNE
  With Brünnhilde at his side?
SIEGFRIED
  Between east and west
    pointing to his sword
                          is the north:
  Brünnhilde was that far – from him.
GUTRUNE
  How did you return her to Gunther?
SIEGFRIED
  In the dawn mist, past the rock's dying
  embers down to the valley,
  she followed me;
  near the shore   990
  I changed places
  in an instant with Gunther:
  my virtuous metal toy
  got me here in a trice, as I wished.
  A strong wind now steers
  the lovers up the Rhine.
  So get ready for their welcome now!
GUTRUNE
  Siegfried! Strongest man!
  How you fill me with awe!
HAGEN *calling out from the riverbank*
  I see a sail in the distance!   1000
    The whole thing must always be a 'lively conversation',
    delivered 'in the manner of a comic opera'. *

SIEGFRIED

So sagt dem Boten Dank!

GUTRUNE

Lasset uns sie hold empfangen,
daß heiter sie und gern hier weile!
Du, Hagen, minnig
rufe die Mannen
nach Gibich's Hof zur Hochzeit!
Frohe Frauen
ruf' ich zum Fest,
der Freudigen folgen sie gern.

Nach der Halle zuschreitend, wendet sie sich wieder um.

1010   Rastest du, schlimmer Held?

SIEGFRIED

Dir zu Helfen –

Er reicht ihr die Hand und geht mit ihr in die Halle.

            ruh' ich aus.

*Hagen hat einen Felsstein in der Höhe des Hintergrundes
ersteigen; dort setzt er jetzt sein Stierhorn zum Blasen an.*

DRITTE SZENE

HAGEN

Hoiho! Hoihohoho!
Ihr Gibich's-Mannen,
machet euch auf!
Wehe! Wehe!
Waffen! Waffen!
Waffen durch's Land!
Gute Waffen!
Starke Waffen!
1020   Scharf zum Streit!
Not ist da!
Not! Wehe! Wehe!
Hoiho! Hoihohoho!

*Hagen bleibt immer in seiner Stellung auf der Anhöhe.
Er bläst abermals. Auf den verschiedenen Höhenpfa-*

SIEGFRIED
  Give thanks to the messenger!
GUTRUNE
  We should welcome her kindly,
  so she feels at ease among us!
  You, Hagen, use your charm
  to call the vassals
  to Gibich's hall for a wedding!
  I'll invite joyous
  women to the feast,
  glad to join in my happiness.
    As she strides towards the hall, she turns around again.
  Will you rest, incorrigible hero?   1010
SIEGFRIED
  Helping you –
    He offers her his hand and walks with her into the hall.
              is rest for me.
    *Hagen has climbed onto a rock high in the background;
    there he now gets ready to play his cowhorn.*

SCENE THREE

HAGEN
  Hoiho! Hoihohoho!
  Vassals of Gibich,
  make yourselves ready!
  Woe! Woe!
  Weapons! Weapons!
  Weapons throughout the land!
  Good weapons!
  Strong weapons!
  Spoil for a fight!   1020
  We're in peril!
  Peril! Woe! Woe!
  Hoiho! Hoihohoho!
    Hagen remains in his position on the hill.
      He blows the horn again. Vassals pour in haste down

den stürmen in Hast und Eile gewaffnete Mannen herbei;
erst einzelne, dann immer mehrere zusammen, welche
sich dann auf dem Uferraum vor der Halle anhäufen.

MANNEN [T=TENOR; B=BASS]
Ein Manne [B2]
  Was tos't das Horn?
Ein Manne [T2]
  Was ruft es zu Heer?
Zwei Mannen [B1]
  Was tos't das Horn?
Zwei Mannen [T1]. *Ein anderer Manne* [T2]
  Was ruft es zu Heer?
Zwei Mannen [B2]
  Wir kommen mit Wehr.
Zwei Mannen [T2]
  Wir kommen mit Waffen!
Zwei Mannen [B1]
1030 Wir kommen mit Waffen!
Drei Mannen [B2]
  Was tos't das Horn?
Zwei andere [T2]
  Wir kommen mit Wehr.
Drei Mannen [B1]
  Was tos't das Horn?
Zwei Mannen [T2]
  Wir kommen mit Wehr.
Drei andere [B2]
  Wir kommen mit Waffen.
Zwei Mannen [T1]
  Wir kommen mit Wehr.
Drei andere [B1]
  Wir kommen mit Waffen.
Drei Mannen [T2]
  Hagen!
Drei Mannen [T1]
  Hagen!

the different mountain paths with their weapons; at first
just a few, then increasingly more of them as they crowd
together on the banks of the river in front of the hall.

VASSALS [T=TENOR; B=BASS]
One vassal [B2]
  Why the blaring horn?
One vassal [T2]
  Why call us to arms?
Two vassals [B1]
  Why the blaring horn?
Two vassals [T1]. *One other vassal* [T2]
  Why call us to arms?
Two vassals [B2]
  We come armed.
Two vassals [T2]
  We come with weapons!
Two vassals [B1]
  We come with weapons!   1030
Three vassals [B2]
  Why the blaring horn?
Two others [T2]
  We come armed.
Three vassals [B1]
  Why the blaring horn?
Two vassals [T2]
  We come armed.
Three others [B2]
  We come with weapons.
Two vassals [T1]
  We come armed.
Three others [B1]
  We come with weapons.
Three vassals [T2]
  Hagen!
Three vassals [T1]
  Hagen!

Drei andere [B1], *drei andere* [B2]

1040   Hoiho! Hoiho!
       Hagen! Hagen!

Drei andere [T1], *drei andere* [T2]

       Hagen! Hagen!
       Hoiho!

Alle [T1, T2, B1, B2]

       Hoiho! Hagen!
       Hoiho! Hagen!
       Hagen! Hoiho!

[*Alle* B1, B2]

       Welche Not ist da?
       Welcher Feind ist nah'?
       Wer gibt uns Streit?

1050   Hagen!

[*Alle* T1, T2]

       Wer gibt uns Streit?

[*Alle* B2]

       Ist Gunther in Not?
       Wer gibt uns Streit?
       Wer ist in Not?
       Welcher Feind ist nah'?
       Welche Not?
       Welche Not,
       welcher Feind?
       Hoiho!

[*Alle* T2]

1060   Ist Gunther in Not?
       Welche Not ist da?
       Welcher Feind ist nah'?
       Wir kommen mit Waffen,
       mit schneidiger Wehr.
       Welcher Streit?
       Hoiho!

[*Alle* B1]

       Ist Gunther in Not?
       Wer gibt uns Streit?
       Wer ist in Not,

Three others [B1], *three others* [B2]

   Hoiho! Hoiho!   1040

   Hagen! Hagen!

Three others [T1], *three others* [T2]

   Hagen! Hagen!

   Hoiho!

All [T1, T2, B1, B2]

   Hoiho! Hagen!

   Hoiho! Hagen!

   Hagen! Hoiho!

[*All* B1, B2]

   What peril's at hand?

   Which enemy's close?

   Who wants to fight us?

   Hagen!   1050

[*All* T1, T2]

   Who wants to fight us?

[*All* B2]

   Is Gunther in peril?

   Who wants to fight us?

   Who's in peril?

   Which enemy's close?

   What peril?

   What peril,

   which enemy?

   Hoiho!

[*All* T2]

   Is Gunther in peril?   1060

   What peril's at hand?

   Which enemy's close?

   We come with weapons,

   lethally armed.

   What fight?

   Hoiho?

[*All* B1]

   Is Gunther in peril?

   Who wants to fight us?

   Who's in peril,

1070   wer gibt uns Streit?
        Wer ist in Not?
        Welche Not,
        welcher Feind ist uns nah'?
        Hoiho!
        [*Alle* T1]
           Welche Not ist da?
           Welcher Feind ist nah'?
           Mit scharfer Wehr.
           Wir kommen mit Waffen.
           Wer gibt uns Not?
1080   Hoiho!
        [*Alle* T1, T2, B1, B2]
           Ho! Hagen!
        HAGEN *immer von der Anhöhe herab*
           Rüstet euch wohl,
           und rastet nicht!
           Gunther sollt ihr empfah'n:
           ein Weib hat der gefreit.
        MANNEN
           Drohet ihm Not?
           Drängt ihn der Feind?
        HAGEN
           Ein freisliches Weib
           führet er heim.
        MANNEN
1090   Ihm folgen der Magen
           feindliche Mannen?
        HAGEN
           Einsam fährt er,
           keiner folgt.
        MANNEN
           So bestand er die Not?
           So bestand er den Kampf?
           Sag' es an!
        HAGEN
           Der Wurmtöter
           wehrte der Not:

who wants to fight us?   1070
Who's in peril?
What peril,
which enemy's close to us?
Hoiho!
[*All* T1]
What peril's at hand?
Which enemy's close?
Armed to the teeth.
We come with weapons.
Who's putting us in peril?
Hoiho!   1080
[*All* T1, T2, B1, B2]
Ho! Hagen
HAGEN *still down from the hill*
Be well prepared,
and do not rest!
You are to welcome Gunther:
he's got himself a wife.
VASSALS
Is he in peril?
Hounded by the enemy?
HAGEN
It's a baleful wife
he's bringing home.
VASSALS
Are his in-laws' hostile   1090
vassals in pursuit?
HAGEN
No one's in pursuit,
he's on his own.
VASSALS
He's survived danger?
He's won his fight?
Let's hear more!
HAGEN
The dragon-slayer
fought off peril:

Siegfried der Held,
1100 der schuf ihm Heil!

MANNEN
Ein Manne [B1]
    Was soll ihm das Heer nun noch helfen?
Nur zwei [B2], *drei* [T2], *vier* [T1] *Mannen*
    Was hilft ihm nun das Heer?

HAGEN
    Starke Stiere
    sollt ihr schlachten;
    am Weihstein fließe
    Wotan ihr Blut!

MANNEN
Einer [B1]
    Was, Hagen, – was heißest du uns dann?
Acht Mannen [T1, T2]
    Was heißest du uns dann?
Vier Mannen [B2]
    Was soll es dann?
Alle [B1]
1110 Was heißest du uns dann?

HAGEN
    Einen Eber fällen
    sollt ihr für Froh,
    einen stämmigen Bock
    stechen für Donner:
    Schafe aber
    schlachtet für Fricka,
    daß gute Ehe sie gebe!

MANNEN *in immer mehr ausbrechender Heiterkeit*
Zwei [B2], *zwei* [B1], *acht* [T1, T2] *Mannen*
    Schlugen wir Tiere,
    was schaffen wir dann?

HAGEN
1120 Das Trinkhorn nehmt,
    von trauten Frau'n
    mit Met und Wein
    wonnig gefüllt!

Siegfried our hero
was his salvation.   1100

VASSALS
One vassal [B1]
So how can his army still help him?
Only two [B2], *three* [T2], *four* [T1] *vassals*
How can his army help him?

HAGEN
You've to slaughter
strong bulls;
let their blood gush
on that altar for Wotan!

VASSALS
One vassal [B1]
What, Hagen – will you ask of us then?
Eight vassals [T1, T2]
What will you ask of us then?
Four vassals [B2]
What's supposed to happen?
All [B1]
What will you ask of us then?   1110

HAGEN
Hunt and kill
a hog for Froh,
stab a sturdy
deer for Donner:
be sure to slay
sheep for Fricka,
that she may grant a good marriage!

VASSALS *with exhilaration erupting more and more*
Two [B2], *two* [B1], *eight* [T1, T2] *vassals*
After we've killed the animals,
what do we do next?

HAGEN
Take to your drinking-horn,   1120
happily filled
by your dear wives
with mead and wine!

MANNEN
[*Alle*]
  Das Trinkhorn zur Hand,
  wie halten wir es dann?

HAGEN
  Rüstig gezecht,
  bis der Rausch euch zähmt:
  Alles den Göttern zu Ehren,
  daß gute Ehe sie geben!
  Die Mannen brechen in ein schallendes Gelächter aus.

MANNEN
1130 Groß Glück und Heil
  lacht nun dem Rhein,
  da Hagen, der Grimme,
  so lustig mag sein!
  Der Hagedorn
  sticht nun nicht mehr;
  zum Hochzeitsrufer
  ward er bestellt.
  Groß Glück und Heil
  lacht dem Rhein,
1140 da Hagen, da Hagen,
  der Grimme, der Grimme,
  so lustig, so lustig mag sein!
    Hagen, der immer sehr ernst verblieben, ist zu den Man-
    nen herabgestiegen und steht jetzt unter ihnen.

HAGEN
  Nun laßt das Lachen,
  mut'ge Mannen!
  Empfa't Gunthers Braut:
  Brünnhilde naht dort mit ihm.
    Er deutet die Mannen nach dem Rhein hin: diese eilen
    zum Teil nach der Anhöhe, während andere sich am Ufer
    aufstellen, um die Ankommenden zu erblicken.
      näher zu einigen Mannen tretend
  Hold seid der Herrin,
  helfet ihr treu:
  traf sie ein Leid,

VASSALS
[*All*]
Drinking-horn in hand,
how do we behave?

HAGEN
Drink to your heart's content,
till drunkenness makes you compliant:
all to the glory of the gods,
that they grant a good marriage!
The vassals break into raucous laughter.

VASSALS
Great fortune and good   1130
now smile on the Rhine,
if Hagen, the hateful,
can be so much fun!
The haggard thorn
pricks now no more;
he's been told
to call a wedding.
Great fortune and good
smile on the Rhine,
if Hagen, if Hagen,   1140
the hateful, the hateful,
can be, can be so much fun!
Hagen, who has remained very serious the whole time,
climbs down to the vassals and now stands among them.

HAGEN
That's enough laughter,
high-spirited vassals!
Greet Gunther's bride:
Brünnhilde's approaching with him.
He directs the vassals' attention to the Rhine: some of
them make haste to the hill, while others stand along the
bank of the river to catch sight of who is arriving on shore.
stepping nearer to a few of the vassals
Be kind to our lady,
assist her with devotion:
if she should be wronged,

1150   rasch seid zur Rache!

      Er wendet sich langsam zur Seite in den Hintergrund.

MANNEN

Ein Manne [B], *auf der Höhe*

    Heil!

      Während des Folgenden kommt der Nachen mit Gunther
      und Brünnhilde auf dem Rheine an.

Einige [T1, T2, B1]

    Heil! Heil!

      Diejenigen, welche von der Höhe ausgeblickt hatten,
      kommen zum Ufer herab.

Andere [B1]

    Heil!

Alle [B2, T1, T2, B1]

    Willkommen! Willkommen!

      Einige Mannen springen in das Wasser und ziehen den
      Kahn an das Land. Alles drängt sich immer dichter an
      das Ufer.

[*Alle* B2]

    Heil!

[*Alle* T1, T2, B1]

    Willkommen!

[*Alle* B2]

    Willkommen, Gunther!

[*Alle* T1, T2, B1, B2]

    Heil! Heil! Heil!

VIERTE SZENE

Gunther steigt mit Brünnhilde aus dem Kahne: die Mannen
reihen sich ehrerbietig zu ihrem Empfange. Während des Fol-
genden geleitet Gunther Brünnhilde feierlich an der Hand.

DIE MANNEN

    Heil dir, Gunther!

1160   Heil dir, und deiner Braut!

    Heil sei Gunther dir und deiner Braut!

be quick to take revenge! 1150
> *He turns slowly to one side in the background.*

THE VASSALS
One vassal [B], on high
Hail!
> *The boat with Gunther and Brünnhilde appears on the
> Rhine during the following passage.*

A few [T1, T2, B1]
Hail! Hail!
> *Those who had been witnessing events from the hill come
> down to the bank of the river.*

Others [B1]
Hail!

All [B2, T1, T2, B1]
Welcome! Welcome!
> *A few vassals jump into the water and pull the boat in
> to land. All crowd together more and more closely along
> the shore.*

[All B2]
Hail!

[All T1, T2, B1]
Welcome!

[All B2]
Welcome, Gunther!

[All T1, T2, B1, B2]
Hail! Hail! Hail!

SCENE FOUR

*Gunther gets out of the boat with Brünnhilde: the vassals line
up reverentially to welcome them. During the following Gun-
ther takes Brünnhilde by the hand and escorts her ashore.*

THE VASSALS
Hail to you, Gunther!
Hail to you, and your bride! 1160
All hail to you Gunther and your bride!

Willkommen!
> *Sie schlagen die Waffen tosend zusammen.*

GUNTHER *Brünnhilde, welche bleich und gesenkten Blickes*
> *ihm folgt, den Mannen vorstellend*

Brünnhild', die hehrste Frau,
bring' ich euch her zum Rhein.
Ein edleres Weib
ward nie gewonnen.
Der Gibichungen Geschlecht,
gaben die Götter ihm Gunst,
zum höchsten Ruhm
1170 rag' es nun auf!
> *Die Mannen schlagen feierlich an ihre Waffen.*

DIE MANNEN
Heil dir,
glücklicher Gibichung!
> *Gunther geleitet Brünnhilde, welche nie aufblickt, zur*
> *Halle, aus welcher jetzt Siegfried und Gutrune, von Frau-*
> *en begleitet, heraustreten.*

GUNTHER *hält vor der Halle an.*
Gegrüßt sei, teurer Held;
gegrüßt, holde Schwester!
Dich seh' ich froh ihm zur Seite,
der dich zum Weib gewann.
Zwei sel'ge Paare
seh' ich hier prangen: –
> *Er führt Brünnhilde näher heran.*

Brünnhild' und Gunther, –
1180 Gutrun' und Siegfried! –
> *Brünnhilde schlägt erschreckt die Augen auf, und erblickt*
> *Siegfried; wie in Erstaunen bleibt ihr Blick auf ihn ge-*
> *richtet.*

> *Gunther, welcher Brünnhildes heftig zuckende Hand*
> *losgelassen hat, sowie alle Übrigen zeigen starre Betrof-*
> *fenheit über Brünnhildes Benehmen.*

MANNEN
Zwei Mannen [B2] *leise*
Was ist ihr?

Welcome!
> *They thunderously clash their weapons together.*

GUNTHER *introducing Brünnhilde to the vassals as she fol-*
> *lows him looking pale with downcast eyes*

Brünnhilde, woman most sublime,
I bring to you here on the Rhine.
Never was
a nobler wife won.
The gods' favour was given
to the Gibichung race
so that its fame may soar
to unheard of heights!   1170
> *The vassals strike their weapons solemnly.*

THE VASSALS
Hail to you,
fortunate Gibichung!
> *Gunther ushers Brünnhilde, who never looks up, to the*
> *hall just as Siegfried and Gutrune with their women at-*
> *tendants are coming out of it.*

GUNTHER *stops in front of the hall.*
Greetings to you, dear hero;
greetings, sweet sister!
I'm glad to see you at the side
of the hero who won you as wife.
Two divine couples
I see in all their radiance: –
> *He brings Brünnhilde nearer.*

Brünnhilde and Gunther, –
Gutrune and Siegfried! –   1180
> *Brünnhilde looks up, shocked, and lays eyes on Siegfried;*
> *she keeps on gazing at him with a look full of astonish-*
> *ment.*
>
> *Gunther has let go of Brünnhilde's violently twitching*
> *hand, showing the same stunned shock at Brünnhilde's*
> *demeanour as everyone else.*

VASSALS
Two vassals [B2] *quietly*
What's wrong with her?

Vier Mannen [B1]
   Was ist ihr?
Sechs Mannen [T]
   Ist sie entrückt?
      Brünnhilde beginnt zu zittern.
SIEGFRIED *geht einige Schritte auf Brünnhilde zu.*
   Was müht Brünnhildens Blick?
BRÜNNHILDE *kaum ihrer mächtig*
   Siegfried ... hier? Gutrune ... ?
SIEGFRIED
   Gunthers milde Schwester,
   mir vermählt,
   wie Gunther du.
BRÜNNHILDE *furchtbar heftig*
   Ich ... ? Gunther ... ? Du lügst!
      Sie schwankt und droht umzusinken.
         Siegfried stützt sie.
1190   Mir schwindet das Licht ...
      Sie blickt in seinen Armen matt [Siegfried] auf.
   Siegfried ... – kennt mich nicht!
SIEGFRIED
   Gunther, deinem Weib ist übel!
      Gunther tritt hinzu.
   Erwache, Frau!
   Hier steht dein Gatte.
      Brünnhilde erblickt am ausgestreckten Finger Siegfrieds
      den Ring und schrickt mit furchtbarer Heftigkeit auf.
BRÜNNHILDE
   Ha! ... Der Ring ...
   an seiner Hand! –
   Er ... ? Siegfried ... ?
      [Hagen] aus dem Hintergrunde unter die Mannen tretend
MANNEN
Einige [B]
   Was ist?
Einige [T]
         Was ist?

Four vassals [B1]
  What's wrong with her?
Six vassals [T]
  Is she in a trance?
    Brünnhilde begins to shudder.
SIEGFRIED *takes a few steps towards Brünnhilde.*
  Why does Brünnhilde look upset?
BRÜNNHILDE *nearly out of control*
  Siegfried ... here? Gutrune ... ?
SIEGFRIED
  Gunther's gentle sister
  is getting married to me,
  as you are to Gunther.
BRÜNNHILDE *with terrible violence*
  I ... ? Gunther ... ? You're lying!
    She totters on the verge of fainting.
      Siegfried props her up.
  Light is deserting me ...   1190
    She looks up at [Siegfried] wearily in his arms.
  Siegfried ... – doesn't know me!
SIEGFRIED
  Gunther, your wife's ill!
    Gunther steps forward.
  Pull yourself together, woman!
  It's your spouse standing here.
    Brünnhilde catches sight of the ring on Siegfried's out-
    stretched finger and reacts with shocking forcefulness.
BRÜNNHILDE
  Ah! ... The ring ...
  on his hand! –
  He ... ? Siegfried ... ?
    [Hagen] appearing from the back to join the vassals
VASSALS
A few [B]
  What's happening?
A few [T]
                          What's happening?

HAGEN

Jetzt merket klug,
1200 was die Frau euch klagt!

Brünnhilde sucht sich zu ermannen, indem sie die schrecklichste Aufregung gewaltsam zurückhält.

BRÜNNHILDE

Einen Ring sah ich
an deiner Hand; –
nicht dir gehört er,
ihn entriß mir –

auf Gunther deutend:

dieser Mann.
Wie mochtest von ihm
den Ring du empfah'n?

Siegfried betrachtet aufmerksam den Ring an seiner Finger.

SIEGFRIED

Den Ring empfing ich
nicht von ihm.

BRÜNNHILDE *zu Gunther*

1210 Nahmst du von mir den Ring,
durch den ich dir vermählt,
so melde ihm dein Recht,
ford're zurück das Pfand!

GUNTHER *in grosser Verwirrung*

Den Ring? – Ich gab ihm keinen:
doch – kennst du ihn auch gut?

BRÜNNHILDE

Wo bärgest du den Ring,
den du von mir erbeutet?

*Gunther schweigt in höchster Betroffenheit.
Brünnhilde fährt wütend auf.*

Ha! Dieser war es,
der mir den Ring entriß:
1220 Siegfried, der trugvolle Dieb!

Alles blickt erwartungsvoll auf Siegfried, welcher über der Betrachtung des Ringes in fernes Sinnen verloren ist.

HAGEN

Be wily now and notice
this woman's complaint to you! 1200
*Brünnhilde tries to regain her self-control by forcibly
repressing her worst anxieties.*

BRÜNNHILDE

I saw a ring
on your hand; –
it's not yours,
it was torn from me –
pointing at Gunther:
by this man.
How did you manage
to get the ring from him?
*Siegfried contemplates the ring on his finger with attent-
iveness.*

SIEGFRIED

I didn't get the ring
from him.

BRÜNNHILDE *to Gunther*

As you deprived me of the ring 1210
that proves I'm married to you,
why don't you tell him your rights
and insist he return our pledge!

GUNTHER *utterly baffled*

The ring? – I didn't give him one:
but – you know it well too?

BRÜNNHILDE

Where did you hide the ring,
the one you fought me to get?
*Gunther falls silent in extreme shock.
Brünnhilde erupts in rage.*
Ah! He's the one,
who prised the ring away from me:
Siegfried, that swindling thief! 1220
*Everyone looks with eager anticipation at Siegfried, still
lost in distant thought as he contemplates the ring.*

SIEGFRIED
  Von keinem Weib
  kam mir der Reif,
  noch war's ein Weib,
  dem ich ihn abgewann:
  genau erkenn' ich
  des Kampfes Lohn,
  den vor Neidhöhl' einst ich bestand,
  als den starken Wurm ich erschlug.
HAGEN *zwischen sie tretend*
  Brünnhild', kühne Frau!
1230 Kennst du genau den Ring?
  Ist's der, den du Gunthern gabst,
  so ist er sein, –
  und Siegfried gewann ihn durch Trug, –
  den der Treulose büßen sollt'!
BRÜNNHILDE *in furchtbarstem Schmerze aufschreiend*
        Mit diesen wiederholten Versuchen scheint sie den ver-
        sagenden Atem bewältigen zu wollen. * *
  Betrug! Betrug!
  Schändlichster Betrug!
  Verrat! Verrat! –
  Wie noch nie er gerächt!
FRAUEN, GUTRUNE, MANNEN
  Verrat? An wem?
BRÜNNHILDE
1240 Heil'ge Götter,
  himmlische Lenker!
  Rauntet ihr dies
  in eurem Rat?
  Lehrt ihr mich Leiden,
  wie keiner sie litt?
  Schuft ihr mir Schmach,
  wie nie sie geschmerzt?
        [Sie] erscheint wie ganz losgelöst von ihrer Umgebung …
        Nach einem innerlichen, furchtbar schmerzlichen Ringen
        bricht sie dann hervor. *
  Ratet nun Rache,

SIEGFRIED
The ring didn't come
to me from a woman,
nor was it wrested
from a woman by me:
I know it exactly
as the prize of a battle
I once won in front of Neidhöhle,
when I slaughtered the huge dragon.

HAGEN *stepping between them*
Brünnhilde, dauntless woman!
Do you know this exact ring?   1230
If it is the one you gave to Gunther,
it's his, –
and Siegfried cheated to win it, –
for that the swindler must pay a price!

BRÜNNHILDE *screaming out in the most appalling pain*
> *With these constant efforts she appears to be strug-
> gling to conquer her failing breath.* **
Trickery! Trickery!
Vilest trickery!
Treason! Treason! –
To be avenged as never before!

WOMEN, GUTRUNE, VASSALS
Treason? Against whom?

BRÜNNHILDE
Sacred gods,   1240
arbiters of the skies!
Is this what you muttered
to yourselves in council?
Teach her sorrows
as none have suffered?
Design her disgrace
to give unimagined pain?
> *[She] appears to be utterly unglued from her surround-
> ings . . . After an inner, hugely painful struggle, she then
> erupts.* *
Then tell me of vengeance,

wie nie sie gerast!
1250 Zündet mir Zorn,
wie noch nie er gezähmt!
Heißet Brünnhild'
ihr Herz zu zerbrechen,
den zu zertrümmern,
der sie betrog!

GUNTHER

Brünnhild', Gemahlin!
Mäß'ge dich!

BRÜNNHILDE

Weich' fern, Verräter!
Selbst Verratner!
　　Brünnhilde wendet sich wieder zu den Mannen. *
1260 Wisset denn alle: –
nicht ihm,
dem Manne dort
bin ich vermählt.

FRAUEN
Einige

Siegfried?

Andere

Gutruns Gemahl?

MANNEN

Gutruns Gemahl?

BRÜNNHILDE

Er zwang mir Lust
und Liebe ab.

SIEGFRIED

Achtest du so
1270 der eig'nen Ehre?
Die Zunge, die sie lästert,
muß ich der Lüge sie zeihen?
Hört ob ich Treue brach! –
Blutbrüderschaft
hab' ich Gunther geschworen.
Nothung, das werte Schwert,
wahrte der Treue Eid:

such as it has never raged!
Fire in me a fury 1250
never before restrained!
Instruct Brünnhilde
to shatter her heart,
that she may rip apart the man,
who cheated her!

GUNTHER
Brünnhilde, wife!
Be reasonable!

BRÜNNHILDE
Keep your distance, betrayer!
Yourself betrayed!
Brünnhilde turns once more to the vassals. *
To all of you I say: – 1260
I'm married,
not to him,
but to that man there.

WOMEN
A few
Siegfried?
The others
Gutrune's husband?

VASSALS
Gutrune's husband?

BRÜNNHILDE
He forced pleasure
and love from me.

SIEGFRIED
Is that what you
call self-respect? 1270
Your tongue maligns that:
must I accuse it of lying?
Hear if I'm a betrayer! –
I have sworn
blood-brotherhood to Gunther.
Nothung, my valued sword,
kept my oath of loyalty alive:

mich trennte seine Schärfe
von diesem traur'gen Weib. –

BRÜNNHILDE

1280 Du listiger Held,
sieh', wie du lügst,
wie auf dein Schwert
du schlecht dich berufst!
Wohl kenn' ich seine Schärfe,
doch kenn' auch die Scheide,
darin so wonnig
ruht an der Wand
Nothung, der treue Freund,
als die Traute sein Herr sich gewann.

*Die Mannen und Frauen treten in lebhafter Entrüstung
zusammen.*

MANNEN

1290 Wie? Brach er die Treue?
Trübte er Gunthers Ehre?

FRAUEN

Brach er die Treue?

GUNTHER *zu Siegfried*

Geschändet wär' ich,
schmählich bewahrt,
gäbst du die Rede
nicht ihr zurück!

GUTRUNE

Treulos, Siegfried,
sännest du Trug?
Bezeuge, daß jene

1300 falsch dich zeiht!

MANNEN

[*Alle* T2]

Reinige dich,
bist du im Recht!

[*Alle* B1, B2]

Schweige die Klage!

[*Alle* T1, T2]

Schwöre den Eid!

it was its sharp blade that divided me
from this unhappy woman. –

BRÜNNHILDE

You swindler of a hero,   1280
look how you lie,
how you call on your sword
to bear false witness!
I know its sharp blade well,
but I know its sheath too,
inside it Nothung,
your faithful friend,
resting nonchalantly against a wall
while its master ravishes his bride.

Vassals and women join together in a vigorous demon-
stration of outrage.

VASSALS

What? Was he unfaithful?   1290
Has he blackened Gunther's honour?

WOMEN

Was he unfaithful?

GUNTHER *to Siegfried*

I'd feel defiled,
shamefully treated,
if you didn't hurl
that insult back at her!

GUTRUNE

Are you a cheat, Siegfried,
plotting treachery?
Testify that her
charge is false!   1300

THE VASSALS

[*All* T2]

Show your innocence,
if you've done no wrong!

[*All* B1, B2]

Refute the charge!

[*All* T1, T2]

Swear an oath!

SIEGFRIED

Schweig' ich die Klage,
schwör' ich den Eid:
wer von euch wagt
seine Waffe daran?

HAGEN

Meines Speeres Spitze
1310   wag' ich daran:
sie wahr' in Ehren den Eid!

> *Die Mannen schließen einen Ring um Siegfried und Hagen.*
>
> *Hagen hält den Speer hin; Siegfried legt zwei Finger seiner rechten Hand auf die Speerspitze.*

SIEGFRIED

Helle Wehr,
heilige Waffe:
hilf meinem ewigen Eide!
Bei des Speeres Spitze
sprech' ich den Eid:
Spitze, achte des Spruchs!
Wo Scharfes mich schneide,
schneide du mich;
1320   wo der Tod mich soll treffen,
treffe du mich:
klagte das Weib dort wahr,
brach ich dem Bruder den Eid.

> *Brünnhilde tritt wütend in den Ring, reißt Siegfrieds Hand vom Speere hinweg und faßt dafür mit der ihrigen die Spitze.*

BRÜNNHILDE

Helle Wehr!
Heilige Waffe!
Hilf meinem ewigen Eide!
Bei des Speeres Spitze
sprech' ich den Eid: –
Spitze! Achte des Spruchs!
1330   Ich weihe deine Wucht,
daß sie ihn werfe!

SIEGFRIED

If I refute the charge
by swearing an oath:
who among you will
wager their weapon on it?

HAGEN

I'll wager the tip
of my spear on it: 1310
may it safeguard the oath's integrity!

> *The vassals close around Siegfried and Hagen in ring
> formation.*
>
> *Hagen holds out his spear; on its tip, Siegfried lays two
> fingers of his right hand.*

SIEGFRIED

Shining guardian,
sacred weapon:
give succour to my undying oath!
By the tip of this spear,
I swear the oath:
the tip, may it mark my words!
If a sharp point is to pierce me,
let it be you;
if death is to meet me,   1320
let it be you whom I meet:
if that woman's charge is just,
I did break the oath with my brother.

> *Brünnhilde strides in a fury into the ring, whips Sieg-
> fried's hand away from the spear and in his stead grasps
> the tip herself.*

BRÜNNHILDE

Shining guardian!
Sacred weapon!
Give succour to my undying oath!
By the tip of this spear
I swear the oath: –
The tip! May it mark my words!
I dedicate your force   1330
to his undoing!

Seine Schärfe segne ich,
daß sie ihn schneide!
Denn, brach seine Eide er all',
Schwur Meineid jetzt dieser Mann.

Die Mannen im höchsten Aufruhr

MANNEN

[*Alle* B2]
   Hilf, Donner!

[*Alle* B1, B2]
   Tose dein Wetter!

[*Alle* T1, T2, B1, B2]
   Hilf, Donner!
   Tose dein Wetter,
1340   zu schweigen die wütende Schmach!

SIEGFRIED

   Gunther! Wehr' deinem Weibe,
   das schamlos Schande dir lügt!
   Gönnt ihr Weil' und Ruh',
   der wilden Felsenfrau,
   daß ihre freche Wut sich lege,
   die eines Unholds
   arge List
   wider uns alle erregt! –
   Ihr Mannen, kehret euch ab!
1350   Laßt das Weibergekeif!
   Als Zage weichen wir gern,
   gilt es mit Zungen den Streit.

Er tritt dicht zu Gunther.

   Glaub', mehr zürnt es mich als dich,
   daß schlecht ich sie getäuscht;
   der Tarnhelm, dünkt mich fast,
   hat halb mich nur gehehlt.
   Doch Frauengroll
   friedet sich bald;
   daß ich dir es gewann, –
1360   dankt dir gewiß noch das Weib.

Er wendet sich wieder zu den Mannen.

   Munter, ihr Mannen!

I consecrate your cutting edge
that you may lacerate him!
all the oaths he swore are broken,
now this man's perjured himself.
   The vassals in complete turmoil

VASSALS
[*All* B2]
  Help, Donner!
[*All* B1, B2]
  Unleash your storms!
[*All* T1, T2, B1, B2]
  Help, Donner!
  Unleash your storms,
  to silence this disgraceful rampage!   1340

SIEGFRIED
Gunther! Resist your wife's
shameless slandering of you!
Allow this rampant woman of the rock
some peace and quiet,
so she can calm her insolent rage,
the evil tricks
of an ogre
ranged against us all.
Vassals, all of you, leave it be!
Forget bitches' nagging!   1350
We men gladly back off timidly,
when it's just a battle of tongues.
   He steps close to Gunther.
Believe me, I'm angrier than you are
that I botched my deception of her;
I almost think the Tarnhelm
only half hid me.
But women's tempers
soon calm down;
it was for you I won her; –
your wife's sure to thank you for that.   1360
   He turns again to address the vassals.
Lighten up, you vassals!

Folgt mir zum Mahl! –
   zu den Frauen
Froh zur Hochzeit,
helfet, ihr Frauen!
Wonnige Lust
lache nun auf!
In Hof und Hain,
heiter vor allen,
sollt ihr heute mich seh'n.
1370   Wen die Minne freut,
meinem frohen Mute
tu es der Glückliche gleich!

   *Siegfried schlingt in ausgelassenem Übermute seinen Arm
um Gutrune und zieht sie mit sich in die Halle fort. Die
Mannen und Frauen, von seinem Beispiele hingerissen,
folgen ihm nach.*
   Die Bühne ist leer geworden.
   *Nur Brünnhilde, Gunther und Hagen bleiben zurück.
– Gunther hat sich, in tiefer Scham und furchtbarer Ver-
stimmung, mit verhülltem Gesichte abseits niedergesetzt.
– Brünnhilde, im Vordergrunde stehend, blickt Siegfried
und Gutrune noch eine Zeitlang schmerzlich nach und
senkt dann das Haupt.*

FÜNFTE SZENE

Brünnhilde in starrem Nachsinnen befangen

BRÜNNHILDE
Welches Unholds List
liegt hier verhohlen?
Welches Zaubers Rat
regte dies auf?
Wo ist nun mein Wissen
gegen dies Wirrsal?
Wo sind meine Runen
1380   gegen dies Rätsel?

Follow me to the feast! –
   to the women
Go happily to the wedding,
you women, and help!
Let blissful pleasure
burst out laughing!
In halls and havens,
you'll see me today
as exuberant as ever.
So you fortunate men,   1370
who revel in love,
share my ebullient mood!

   *In uninhibited high spirits, he throws his arm around
Gutrune and takes her with him out of the hall. The vas-
sals and women follow him, bowled over by his enthu-
siasm.*

   The stage is empty.

   *Only Brünnhilde, Gunther and Hagen are still there.
– Gunther is now seated on one side, covering his face
in deep shame and in a terrible mood. – Standing in the
foreground, Brünnhilde looks at Siegfried and Gutrune
ruefully for a time as they depart from the hall, and then
sinks her head.*

SCENE FIVE

Brünnhilde preoccupied with bleak contemplation

BRÜNNHILDE
What ogre's tricks
are here concealed?
What reserves of sorcery
conjured this into being?
Where's my wisdom now
to calm this chaos?
Where's my runic lore
to unlock this riddle?   1380

Ach Jammer! Jammer!
Weh', ach Wehe!
All' mein Wissen
wies ich ihm zu! –
In seiner Macht
hält er die Magd,
in seinen Banden
hält er die Beute,
die, jammernd ob ihrer Schmach,
1390 jauchzend der Reiche verschenkt!
 *Wie mit beklemmender Brust nach Atem ringend**
Wer bietet mir nun das Schwert,
mit dem ich die Bande zerschnitt?

HAGEN *dicht an sie herantretend*
Vertraue mir,
betrog'ne Frau!
Wer dich verriet,
das räche ich.

BRÜNNHILDE *matt sich umblickend*
An wem?

HAGEN
An Siegfried, der dich betrog.

BRÜNNHILDE
An Siegfried? . . . du? . . .
 bitter lächelnd
1400 Ein einz'ger Blick
seines blitzenden Auges, –
das selbst durch die Lügengestalt
leuchtend strahlte zu mir, –
deinen besten Mut
machte er bangen.

HAGEN
Doch meinem Speere
spart' ihn sein Meineid?

BRÜNNHILDE
Eid, und Meineid,
müßige Acht!
1410 Nach Stärk'rem späh',

Ah the pity! the pity!
Alas, ah, alas!
I entrusted him
with all my wisdom! –
The young woman
he has in his power,
the prize
he has in shackles:
the rich man gives it exultantly away,
deaf to her disgrace and cries of pity!   1390
    Struggling for breath, her breast tightening *
Who's now to offer me a sword
that I may rid myself of this bondage?

HAGEN *moving very close to Brünnhilde*

Trust me,
scorned woman!
I'll take revenge
on your betrayer.

BRÜNNHILDE *dully looking around her*

On whom?

HAGEN

On Siegfried, who betrayed you.

BRÜNNHILDE

On Siegfried? . . . you? . . .
    with a wry smile
The lightning in his eyes –   1400
their radiance I felt
even behind that treacherous disguise, –
need strike you just once
to turn your bravest
spirit into cowering fear.

HAGEN

But doesn't his perjury
destine him for my spear?

BRÜNNHILDE

Oaths, perjuries,
straws in the wind!
Find stronger ways   1410

deinen Speer zu waffnen,
willst du den Stärksten besteh'n!

HAGEN

Wohl kenn' ich Siegfrieds
siegende Kraft,
wie schwer im Kampf er zu fällen;
d'rum raune nun du
mir guten Rat,
wie doch der Recke mir wich?

BRÜNNHILDE

O Undank, Schändlichster Lohn!
1420 Nicht eine Kunst
war mir bekannt,
die zum Heil nicht half seinem Leib:
unwissend zähmt' ihn
mein Zauberspiel, –
das ihn vor Wunden nun gewahrt.

HAGEN

So kann keine Wehr ihm schaden?

BRÜNNHILDE

Im Kampfe nicht! Doch –
träf'st du im Rücken ihn. –

Es erwachen in ihr schöne Erinnerungen. *

Niemals – das wußt ich –
1430 wich' er dem Feind,
nie reicht' er fliehend ihm den Rücken:
an ihm d'rum spart' ich den Segen.

HAGEN

Und dort trifft ihn mein Speer! –

Er wendet sich rasch von Brünnhilde ab zu Gunther.

Auf, Gunther,
edler Gibichung!
Hier steht dein starkes Weib:
was hängst du dort in Harm?

GUNTHER *leidenschaftlich auffahrend*

O Schmach!
O Schande!
1440 Wehe mir,
dem jammervollsten Manne!

to arm your spear,
if you want to beat the strongest man!

HAGEN
Of course I know Siegfried's
indomitable strength,
how hard it is to fight and kill him;
so can you whisper
good advice to me
on how to get the better of the warrior?

BRÜNNHILDE
O thankless, most shameful reward!
There isn't an art   1420
known to me
that didn't hone his well-being:
my magic arts innocently
calmed his body, –
thus shielding him from every wound.

HAGEN
No weapons can damage him?

BRÜNNHILDE
Not in battle! Unless –
you were to strike him from behind. –
    Happy memories return to her thoughts. *
Never – and I knew this –
would he cede to his enemy,   1430
or flee from him, exposing his back:
so on that I didn't bestow my blessing.

HAGEN
My spear will get him right there! –
    He turns in a flash from Brünnhilde to Gunther.
Up, Gunther,
noble Gibichung!
Your strong wife stands right here:
why slump around in sorrow?

GUNTHER *erupting in passion*
What shame!
What disgrace!
Have pity on me,   1440
the most pitiable of men!

HAGEN

  In Schande liegst du;
  leugn' ich das?

BRÜNNHILDE *zu Gunther*

  O feiger Mann!
  Falscher Genoss'!
  Hinter dem Helden
  hehltest du dich,
  daß Preise des Ruhmes
  er dir erränge!

1450 Tief wohl sank
  das teure Geschlecht,
  das solche Zagen gezeugt.

GUNTHER *außer sich*

  Betrüger ich – und betrogen!
  Verräter ich – und verraten! –
  Zermalmt mir das Mark!
  Zerbrecht mir die Brust!
  Hilf, Hagen!
  Hilf meiner Ehre!
  Hilf deiner Mutter,

1460 die mich auch ja gebar!

HAGEN

  Dir hilft kein Hirn,
  dir hilft keine Hand;
  dir hilft nur Siegfrieds Tod!

GUNTHER *von Grausen erfaßt*

  Siegfrieds Tod! . . .

HAGEN

  Nur der sühnt deine Schmach!

GUNTHER *vor sich hinstarrend*

  Blutbrüderschaft
  schwuren wir uns!

HAGEN

  Des Bundes Bruch
  sühne nun Blut!

GUNTHER

1470 Brach er den Bund?

HAGEN

    You're in disgrace;

    who am I to deny it?

BRÜNNHILDE *to Gunther*

    O cowardly man!

    Craven comrade!

    Concealing yourself

    behind the hero

    so he could win for you

    fame and fortune!

    Your valued race   1450

    sank low indeed

    to beget such a coward.

GUNTHER *beside himself*

    A deceiver I am – and one deceived!

    A betrayer I am – and one betrayed! –

    Crushed and broken I am!

    In the marrow of my being!

    Help, Hagen!

    Help my honour!

    Help your mother,

    who after all bore me too!   1460

HAGEN

    Help you won't get from any brain,

    help you won't get from any hand;

    Siegfried's death alone will help you!

GUNTHER *consumed with terror*

    Siegfried's death! . . .

HAGEN

    The only atonement for your shame!

GUNTHER *staring dead ahead*

    We each swore

    blood-brotherhood!

HAGEN

    Then let blood atone

    for the covenant's collapse!

GUNTHER

    He broke the covenant?   1470

HAGEN
  Da er dich verriet.
GUNTHER
  Verriet er mich?
BRÜNNHILDE
  Dich verriet er,
  und mich verrietet ihr alle!
  Wär' ich gerecht,
  alles Blut der Welt
  büßte mir nicht eure Schuld!
  Doch des Einen Tod
  taugt mir für alle:
1480 Siegfried falle,
  zur Sühne für sich und euch!
HAGEN *zu Gunther gewendet*
  Er falle –
      heimlich
              dir zum Heil!
  Ungeheure Macht wird dir,
  gewinnst von ihm du den Ring,
  den der Tod ihm wohl nur entreißt.
GUNTHER *leise*
  Brünnhildes Ring?
HAGEN
  Des Nibelungen Reif!
GUNTHER *schwer seufzend*
  So wär' es Siegfrieds Ende!
HAGEN
  Uns allen frommt sein Tod.
GUNTHER
1490 Doch – Gutrune, ach! –
  der ich ihn gönnte!
  Straften den Gatten wir so,
  wie bestünden wir vor ihr?
BRÜNNHILDE *wütend auffahrend*
  Was riet mir mein Wissen?
  Was wiesen mich Runen?
  Im hilflosen Elend

HAGEN
  Because he betrayed you.
GUNTHER
  He betrayed me?
BRÜNNHILDE
  He betrayed you,
  and all of you have betrayed me!
  If I am just,
  I could not make you pay for your guilt
  with all the blood in the world!
  Only one man's death
  will be enough for me:
  Siegfried shall die,   1480
  as atonement for him and you!
HAGEN *turning to Gunther*
  He shall die –
      furtively
                for your salvation!
  Huge power will be yours,
  if from him you win the ring,
  of which death alone will deprive him.
GUNTHER *quietly*
  Brünnhilde's ring?
HAGEN
  The Nibelung's ring!
GUNTHER *sighing deeply*
  So Siegfried's to be killed!
HAGEN
  We'll all gain from his death.
GUNTHER
  But – Gutrune, ah! –   1490
  I gave him to her!
  If we punish her husband like this,
  how will she react to what we've done?
BRÜNNHILDE *erupting furiously*
  What did I harvest from my wisdom?
  What did my runes show me?
  In my helpless misery

achtet mir's hell:
Gutrune heißt der Zauber,
der den Gatten mir entzückt!
1500 Angst treffe sie!
HAGEN *zu Gunther*
Muß sein Tod sie betrüben,
verhehlt sei ihr die Tat.
Auf munt'res Jagen
ziehen wir morgen;
der Edle braust uns voran: –
ein Eber bracht' ihn da um.
GUNTHER
So soll es sein!
Siegfried falle!
BRÜNNHILDE
So soll es sein:
1510 Siegfried falle!
GUNTHER
Sühn' er die Schmach,
die er mir schuf!
HAGEN
Sterb' er dahin,
der strahlende Held!
Mein ist der Hort,
mir muß er gehören.
Mir muß er gehören:
BRÜNNHILDE
Sühn' er die Schmach,
die er mir schuf!
1520 Eidtreue
hat er getrogen:
GUNTHER
Des Eides Treue
hat er getrogen:
BRÜNNHILDE, GUNTHER
mit seinem Blut
büß' er die Schuld!
Allrauner,

it came to me:
Gutrune is the name of the witchcraft
that lures my husband from me!
May her blood run cold!   1500

HAGEN *to Gunther*
   If she must be upset by his death,
   then let the deed be hidden from her.
   We'll move out tomorrow
   on a hunting jaunt;
   the gallant hero will race ahead: –
   let's just say a boar then killed him.

GUNTHER
   Let it be so!
   Siegfried shall die!

BRÜNNHILDE
   Let it be so:
   Siegfried shall die!   1510

GUNTHER
   May he atone for the shame
   he caused me!

HAGEN
   And so he'll die,
   the hero of light!
   The hoard is mine,
   it's mine by rights.
   It's mine by rights:

BRÜNNHILDE
   May he atone for the shame
   he caused me!
   He has betrayed
   his oath of loyalty: 1520

GUNTHER
   He has betrayed
   his oath of loyalty:

BRÜNNHILDE, GUNTHER
   with his blood
   he shall pay for his crime!
   All-seeing,

rächender Gott!
Schwurwissender
Eideshort!
1530 Wotan!
Wende dich her!
Weise die schrecklich
heilige Schar,
hieher zu horchen
dem Racheschwur!

HAGEN
d'rum sei der Reif
ihm entrissen.

Albenvater,
gefall'ner Fürst!
1540 Nachthüter!
Niblungenherr!
Alberich!
Achte auf mich!
Weise von neuem
der Niblungen Schar,
dir zu gehorchen,
des Ringes Herrn!

*Als Gunther mit Brünnhilde heftig der Halle sich zuwen-
det, tritt ihnen der von dort herausschreitende Brautzug
entgegen. Knaben und Mädchen, Blumenstäbe schwin-
gend, springen lustig voraus. Siegfried wird auf einem
Schilde, Gutrune auf einem Sessel von den Männern
getragen. – Auf der Anhöhe des Hintergrundes führen
Knechte und Mägde auf verschiedenen Bergpfaden Op-
fergeräte und Opfertiere zu den Weihsteinen herbei und
schmücken diese mit Blumen.*

*Siegfried und die Männer blasen auf ihren Hörnern den
Hochzeitsruf.*

*Die Frauen fordern Brünnhilde auf, an Gutrunes Seite
sie zu geleiten. – Brünnhilde blickt starr zu Gutrune auf,
welche ihr mit freundlichem Lächeln zuwinkt.*

god of vengeance!
Our steadfast oath's
sacred vessel!
Wotan!   1530
Pay heed to us!
Command your stern
and holy throng
this way to hear
our oath of revenge!

HAGEN
    so shall the ring
    be torn from him.

    Father, dwarf,
    ruler no more!
    Keeper of night!   1540
    The Nibelungs' lord!
    Alberich!
    Pay heed to me!
    Command anew
    the Nibelungs' throng,
    to obey you,
    lord of the ring!

As Gunther turns boisterously with Brünnhilde in the dir-
ection of the hall, they meet a bridal procession coming
out of it towards them. Boys and girls waving flowers on
sticks are jumping lustily at its head. Siegfried on a shield
and Gutrune on a chair are being carried aloft by the
men. – On different mountain paths across the hill in the
background, young men and women servants bring sac-
rificial implements and animals for sacrifice to the altar
stones, which they bedeck with flowers.

    Siegfried and the vassals blow the wedding-call on their
horns.

    The women invite Brünnhilde to join them in escorting
Gutrune at her side. – Brünnhilde looks up stony-faced at
Gutrune, who waves back with a friendly smile.

Als Brünnhilde heftig zurücktreten will, tritt Hagen rasch dazwischen und drängt sie an Gunther, der jetzt von Neuem ihre Hand erfaßt und sie den Frauen zuführt, worauf er selbst von den Männern sich auf einen Schild erheben läßt.

Während der Zug, kaum unterbrochen, schnell der Höhe zu sich wieder in Bewegung setzt, fällt der Vorhang.

As Brünnhilde violently attempts to withdraw, Hagen rapidly intervenes, forcing her on Gunther, who grasps her hand once more and leads her towards the women. At this point he is himself lifted onto a shield by the men.

As the procession quickly starts moving again towards the hill after its short stop, the curtain falls.

DRITTER AUFZUG

VORSPIEL UND ERSTE SZENE

Waldige Gegend am Rheine

Hörner auf dem Theater:
 Ein Horn – fern
 Ein Stierhorn – auf der entgegengesetzten Seite – fern
 Mehrere Hörner – ferner
 Ein Stierhorn
 Mehrere Hörner
 Ein Horn
 *[Takt 50] Der Vorhang geht auf. – Wildes Wald- und Fel-
sental am Rheine, welcher im Hintergrunde an einem stei-
len Abhange vorbei fließt. – Die drei Rheintöchter (Woglin-
de, Wellgunde und Floßhilde) tauchen aus der Flut auf und
schwimmen, wie im Reigentanze, im Kreise umher.*

WOGLINDE, WELLGUNDE, FLOSSHILDE *im Schwimmen
 mäßig einhaltend*
 Frau Sonne
 sendet lichte Strahlen;
1550 Nacht liegt in der Tiefe:
 einst war sie hell,
 da heil und hehr
 des Vaters Gold noch in ihr glänzte!
 Rheingold,
 klares Gold,
 wie hell du einstens strahltest,
 hehrer Stern der Tiefe!
  Sie schließen wieder den Schwimmreigen.
 Weialala,
 weialala
1560 leia leia wallalalaleilalala
 leilalala
 la (lei)la la

ACT THREE

PRELUDE AND SCENE ONE

A forest region near the Rhine

Off-stage horns:
 A horn – in the distance
 A cowhorn – on the opposite side – in the distance
 Several horns – further in the distance
 A cowhorn
 Several horns
 A horn
 [bar 50] The curtain rises. – A valley with wild forests and rocks on the Rhine, which flows past a steep cliff in the background. – The three Rhinedaughters (Woglinde, Wellgunde and Flosshilde) dive up out of the water and swim to and fro in a circle like a round dance.

WOGLINDE, WELLGUNDE, FLOSSHILDE *stopping their swimming for a moment*
 Mother sun
 sends her limpid radiance;
 night lies in the deep: 1550
 light once was there,
 when father's gold still shone out,
 safe and sound!
 Rhinegold,
 innocent gold,
 how bright your beams were once,
 regal star of the deep!
   They close the circle for their round dance once more.
 Weialala,
 weialala
 leia leia wallalalaleilalala   1560
 leilalala
 la (lei)la la

lei, walalalala
weiala walala
weiala lala
walala lala
leia leia leia
leila la la la!
> *Sie lauschen.*
>> *Horn auf dem Theater*
>> *rechts, fern*
>> *im Echo links*
>> *[Die Rheintöchter] schlagen jauchzend das Wasser.*

Frau Sonne,
1570 sende uns den Helden,
der das Gold uns wieder gebe!
Ließ' er es uns,
dein lichtes Auge
neideten dann wir nicht länger!
Rheingold!
Klares Gold,
wie froh du dann strahltest,
freier Stern der Tiefe!
> *Horn auf dem Theater, näher als zuvor*

WOGLINDE
Ich höre sein Horn.

WELLGUNDE
1580 Der Helde naht.

FLOSSHILDE
Laßt uns beraten!
> *Sie tauchen alle drei schnell unter.*
>> *Siegfried erscheint auf dem Abhange in vollen Waffen.*

SIEGFRIED
Ein Albe führte mich irr,
daß ich die Fährte verlor. –
He, Schelm! In welchem Berge
barg'st du so schnell mir das Wild?
> *Die drei Rheintöchter tauchen wieder auf und schwimmen im Reigen.*

lei, walalalala
weiala walala
weiala lala
walala lala
leia leia leia
leila la la la!
   They listen intently.
      horn off-stage
      to the right, in the distance.
      echoing from the left
      [The Rhinedaughters] splash the water joyfully.
Mother sun,
send us the hero,					1570
who'd give us back our gold!
If he'd let us have it,
we'd no longer envy
your limpid eye.
Rhinegold!
Innocent gold,
how blithe your beams were then,
freedom's star of the deep!
   horn off-stage, closer than before

WOGLINDE

I hear his horn.

WELLGUNDE

Our hero's coming.					1580

FLOSSHILDE

Let's have a talk!
   All three quickly dive under.
      Siegfried appears on the cliff fully armed.

SIEGFRIED

A dwarf distracted me,
and I lost my way. –
Hey, prankster! Which mountain
did you hide my prey in so fast?
   The three Rhinedaughters dive up again and swim their
   round dance.

WOGLINDE, WELLGUNDE, FLOSSHILDE
  Siegfried!
FLOSSHILDE
  Was schilt'st du so in den Grund?
WELLGUNDE
  Welchem Alben bist du gram?
WOGLINDE
  Hat dich ein Nicker geneckt?
WOGLINDE, WELLGUNDE, FLOSSHILDE
1590 Sag' es, Siegfried, sag' es uns!
SIEGFRIED *sie lächelnd betrachtend*
  Entzücktet ihr zu euch
  den zottigen Gesellen,
  der mir verschwand?
  Ist's euer Friedel,
  euch lustigen Frauen
  lass' ich ihn gern.
    Die Mädchen lachen.
WOGLINDE
  Siegfried, was gibst du uns,
  wenn wir das Wild dir gönnen?
SIEGFRIED
  Noch bin ich beutelos;
1600 so bittet, was ihr begehrt!
WELLGUNDE
  Ein gold'ner Ring
  glänzt dir am Finger:
WOGLINDE, WELLGUNDE, FLOSSHILDE
  Den gib uns!
SIEGFRIED
  Einen Riesenwurm
  erschlug ich um den Reif, –
  für eines schlechten Bären Tatzen
  böt' ich ihn nun zum Tausch?
WOGLINDE
  Bist du so karg?
WELLGUNDE
  So geizig beim Kauf?

WOGLINDE, WELLGUNDE, FLOSSHILDE
  Siegfried!
FLOSSHILDE
  Why rail at the ground like that?
WELLGUNDE
  Which dwarf's annoying you?
WOGLINDE
  Did a sprite tease you?
WOGLINDE, WELLGUNDE, FLOSSHILDE
  Say it, Siegfried, tell us all!   1590
SIEGFRIED *smiling as he looks at them*
  Did you lure away
  my shaggy little mate,
  the one who vanished on me?
  If he's your lover,
  you funny girls
  can have him.
    The girls laugh.
WOGLINDE
  Siegfried, what can you give us,
  if we get you your prey?
SIEGFRIED
  I've no prey yet;
  so ask for what you wish!   1600
WELLGUNDE
  A golden ring
  gleams on your finger:
WOGLINDE, WELLGUNDE, FLOSSHILDE
  give us that!
SIEGFRIED
  To get this ring I killed
  an enormous dragon, –
  so am I supposed to offer it
  in exchange for a rotten bear's paw?
WOGLINDE
  Are you that cheap?
WELLGUNDE
  A stingy customer?

FLOSSHILDE

1610   Freigebig
solltest Frauen du sein!

SIEGFRIED

Verzehrt' ich an euch mein Gut,
dess' zürnte mir wohl mein Weib.

FLOSSHILDE

Sie ist wohl schlimm?

WELLGUNDE

Sie schlägt dich wohl?

WOGLINDE

Ihre Hand fühlt schon der Held!
Sie lachen unmäßig.

SIEGFRIED

Nun lacht nur lustig zu!
In Harm lass' ich euch doch:
denn giert ihr nach dem Ring,

1620   euch Neckern geb' ich ihn nie!
Die Rheintöchter haben sich wieder zum Reigen gefaßt.

FLOSSHILDE

So schön!

WELLGUNDE

So stark!

WOGLINDE

So gehrenswert!

WOGLINDE, WELLGUNDE, FLOSSHILDE

Wie schade, daß er geizig ist!
Sie lachen und tauchen unter.
Siegfried steigt tiefer in den Grund hinab.

SIEGFRIED

Was leid' ich doch
das karge Lob?
Lass' ich so mich schmäh'n?
Kämen sie wieder
zum Wasserrand,

1630   den Ring könnten sie haben. –
Laut rufend:
He! Hehe! Ihr munt'ren

FLOSSHILDE
You ought to spend freely 1610
on women!
SIEGFRIED
If I squander my fortune on you,
my wife will be livid.
FLOSSHILDE
Is she really bad?
WELLGUNDE
She slaps you, does she?
WOGLINDE
Already our hero's feeling her hand!
They laugh recklessly.
SIEGFRIED
Just carry on laughing!
You'll have long faces yet:
you're greedy for the ring,
but you needling girls won't ever get it! 1620
The Rhinedaughters focus again on their round dance.
FLOSSHILDE
So gorgeous!
WELLGUNDE
So strong!
WOGLINDE
So hot!
WOGLINDE, WELLGUNDE, FLOSSHILDE
Shame he's such a skinflint!
They laugh and dive under.
Siegfried climbs further down towards the river.
SIEGFRIED
But why put myself through
such mealy-mouthed praise?
Let myself in for such abuse?
If they resurfaced
at the water's edge,
they could have the ring. – 1630
Calling loudly:
Hey! Hey-ey! You feisty

Wasserminnen!
Kommt rasch! Ich schenk' euch den Ring!
> *Er hat den Ring vom Finger gezogen und hält ihn in die*
> *Höhe. Die Rheintöchter tauchen wieder auf.*
>> *Sie zeigen sich ernst und feierlich.*

FLOSSHILDE
Behalt' ihn, Held,
und wahr' ihn wohl,
bis du das Unheil errätst, –

WOGLINDE, WELLGUNDE
das in dem Ring du hegst,

FLOSSHILDE
froh fühlst du dich dann,

WOGLINDE, WELLGUNDE
froh fühlst du dich,

WOGLINDE, WELLGUNDE, FLOSSHILDE
1640   befrei'n wir dich von dem Fluch.

SIEGFRIED *steckt gelassen den Ring wieder an seinen Finger.*
So singet, was ihr wißt!

WOGLINDE, WELLGUNDE, FLOSSHILDE
Siegfried! Siegfried! Siegfried!
Schlimmes wissen wir dir.

WELLGUNDE
Zu deinem Unheil
wahr'st du den Ring.

WELLGUNDE, FLOSSHILDE
Aus des Rheines Gold

WOGLINDE, WELLGUNDE, FLOSSHILDE
ist der Ring geglüht:

WELLGUNDE
der ihn listig geschmiedet –

WOGLINDE
und schmählich verlor,

WOGLINDE, WELLGUNDE
1650   der verfluchte ihn,

WOGLINDE, WELLGUNDE, FLOSSHILDE
in fernster Zeit
zu zeugen den Tod
dem, der ihn trüg'.

mermaids!
Get here fast! The ring's a present from me!
He has pulled the ring off his finger
and holds it up high. The Rhinedaughters dive up again.
They appear stern and grave.

FLOSSHILDE
Keep it, hero,
and be sure to look after it,
until you sense the calamity, –

WOGLINDE, WELLGUNDE
that's in your cherished ring,

FLOSSHILDE
then you'll feel glad,

WOGLINDE, WELLGUNDE
you'll feel glad,

WOGLINDE, WELLGUNDE, FLOSSHILDE
when we free you from the curse.   1640

SIEGFRIED *puts the ring back on his finger unperturbed.*
So sing of what you know!

WOGLINDE, WELLGUNDE, FLOSSHILDE
Siegfried! Siegfried! Siegfried!
We know bad things about your fate.

WELLGUNDE
Keeping the ring
will do you harm.

WELLGUNDE, FLOSSHILDE
From the gold of the Rhine

WOGLINDE, WELLGUNDE, FLOSSHILDE
the ring was formed:

WELLGUNDE
the trickster who forged it –

WOGLINDE
and lost it ingloriously,

WOGLINDE, WELLGUNDE
put a curse on it,   1650

WOGLINDE, WELLGUNDE, FLOSSHILDE
in order to doom to death
in the furthest reaches of time
any person who wears it.

FLOSSHILDE
   Wie den Wurm du fälltest,
WELLGUNDE, FLOSSHILDE
   so fällst auch du,
WOGLINDE, WELLGUNDE, FLOSSHILDE
   und heute noch:
   so heißen wir's dir,
   tauschest den Ring du uns nicht,
WELLGUNDE, FLOSSHILDE
   im tiefen Rhein ihn zu bergen:
WOGLINDE, WELLGUNDE, FLOSSHILDE
1660   nur seine Flut
   sühnet den Fluch!
SIEGFRIED
   Ihr listigen Frauen,
   laßt das sein!
   Traut' ich kaum eurem Schmeicheln,
   euer Drohen schreckt mich noch minder!
WOGLINDE, WELLGUNDE, FLOSSHILDE
   Siegfried! Siegfried!
   Wir weisen dich wahr.
   Weiche! Weiche dem Fluch!
   Ihn flochten nächtlich
1670   webende Nornen
   in des Urgesetzes Seil!
SIEGFRIED *mit energisch-trotziger, furchtloser Gebärde**
   Mein Schwert zerschwang einen Speer: –
   des Urgesetzes
   ewiges Seil,
   flochten sie wilde
   Flüche hinein, –
   Nothung zerhaut es den Nornen! –
   Wohl warnte mich einst
   vor dem Fluch ein Wurm, –
      wegwerfend, ironisch*
1680   doch das Fürchten lehrt' er mich nicht!
      Er betrachtet den Ring.
   Der Welt Erbe

FLOSSHILDE
  Just as you killed the dragon,
WELLGUNDE, FLOSSHILDE
  so you shall be killed,
WOGLINDE, WELLGUNDE, FLOSSHILDE
  and on this day:
  that's how we read your fate,
  if you don't give us the ring
WELLGUNDE, FLOSSHILDE
  to hide in the depths of the Rhine:
WOGLINDE, WELLGUNDE, FLOSSHILDE
  only its waters   1660
  can dissolve the curse!
SIEGFRIED
  Stop this now,
  you women tricksters!
  Your pretty speeches I scarcely believe,
  your foreboding scares me still less!
WOGLINDE, WELLGUNDE, FLOSSHILDE
  Siegfried! Siegfried!
  We show you what's true.
  Get away! Get away from the curse!
  Every night the Norns
  have woven it   1670
  into the rope of primordial law!
SIEGFRIED *with a vigorously defiant, fearless gesture**
  A swing of my sword broke a spear: –
  who cares if the Norns
  wove wild curses
  into the eternal rope
  of primordial law, –
  Nothung can shred it anyway! –
  Yes, a dragon did once
  warn me of the curse, –
    *dismissively, ironically**
  but did nothing to teach me fear!   1680
    He looks at the ring.
  A ring shall win me

gewänne mir ein Ring: –
für der Minne Gunst
miss' ich ihn gern;
ich geb' ihn euch, gönnt ihr mir Gunst.
Doch, bedroht ihr mir Leben und Leib, –
faßte er nicht
eines Fingers Wert, –
den Reif entringt ihr mir nicht.
1690 Denn, Leben und Leib,
seht:

> *Er hebt eine Erdscholle vom Boden auf, hält sie über sei-*
> *nem Haupte und wirft sie mit den letzten Worten hinter*
> *sich.*

so,
werf' ich sie weit von mir!

WOGLINDE, WELLGUNDE, FLOSSHILDE
Kommt, Schwestern!
Schwindet dem Toren!
So weise und stark
verwähnt sich der Held,
als gebunden und blind er doch ist!

> *Sie schwimmen, wild aufgeregt, in weiten Schwenkungen*
> *dicht an das Ufer heran.*

Eide schwur er,
und achtet sie nicht!

> *wieder heftige Bewegung*

1700 Runen weiß er,
und rät sie nicht!

FLOSSHILDE, *danach* WOGLINDE
Ein hehrstes Gut
ward ihm gegönnt:

WOGLINDE, WELLGUNDE, FLOSSHILDE
daß er's verworfen,
weiß er nicht;

FLOSSHILDE
nur den Ring,

WELLGUNDE
der zum Tod ihm taugt,

world inheritance: –
for the kindness of love
I'd gladly do without it;
show me kindness and it's yours.
But as you bully me body and soul, –
not that it's worth
even a finger, –
you'll not wrest the ring from me!
As for body and soul,   1690
look:

*He takes a clump of earth out of the ground, holds it
above his head and uttering the following words throws
it behind him.*

   this way
I just toss them far from me!

WOGLINDE, WELLGUNDE, FLOSSHILDE
Sisters, come!
Slip away from this joker!
The hero thinks he's
so high and mighty,
but really he's just boring and blind!

*Frantically nervous, they swerve to and fro as they swim
close to the riverbank.*

Oaths he swore,
and doesn't keep!

more frantic movement

Runes he knows,   1700
and can't unlock!

FLOSSHILDE, *then* WOGLINDE
A glorious gift
was given him:

WOGLINDE, WELLGUNDE, FLOSSHILDE
he doesn't know
that he's squandered it;

FLOSSHILDE
only the ring,

WELLGUNDE
which will be his death,

WOGLINDE, WELLGUNDE, FLOSSHILDE
den Reif nur will er sich wahren!

Leb' wohl, Siegfried!
1710   Ein stolzes Weib
wird noch heut' dich Argen beerben;
sie beut uns bess'res Gehör:
zu ihr! zu ihr! zu ihr!
> *Sie wenden sich schnell zum Reigen, mit welchem sie*
> *gemächlich, dem Hintergrunde zu, fortschwimmen.*
Weialala weiala la
> *Siegfried sieht ihnen lächelnd nach, stemmt ein Bein auf*
> *ein Felsstück am Ufer und verweilt mit auf die Hand*
> *gestütztem Kinne.*
leia leia walla la la
lei la la la
lei la la la
la la la (la la)

SIEGFRIED
Im Wasser wie am Lande
1720   lernte nun ich Weiber Art:
wer nicht ihrem Schmeicheln traut,
den schrecken sie mit Drohen;
wer dem nun kühnlich trotzt, –

WOGLINDE, WELLGUNDE, FLOSSHILDE *immer ferner*
lei, wallalalala
weia la wallala
weiala la lei
wallala la la
leia leia leia (leia) la la
la la (la la la la)
> *Die Rheintöchter sind hier gänzlich verschwunden.*

SIEGFRIED
1730   dem kommt dann ihr Keifen dran! –
Und doch, –
trüg' ich nicht Gutrun' Treu',
> *Die Rheintöchter werden aus größerer Entfernung nur*
> *gehört.*

WOGLINDE, WELLGUNDE, FLOSSHILDE
  it's only the ring he wants to keep!

  Goodbye, Siegfried!
  A proud woman   1710
  today will inherit your dolorous legacy;
  she hopes to give us a better hearing:
  to her! To her! To her!
      They quickly resume their round dance, and with that
      continue swimming unhurriedly into the background.
  Weialala weiala la
      Siegfried watches them go with a smile, lifts one leg onto a
      rock on the riverbank and stays there with his chin resting
      on his hand.
  leia leia walla la la
  lei la la la
  lei la la la
  la la la (la la)
SIEGFRIED
  Now I've learnt how women are
  in water and on land: 1720
  if you don't trust their flattery,
  they scare you by threatening you;
  and if you dare to defy that, –
WOGLINDE, WELLGUNDE, FLOSSHILDE *ever more distant*
  lei, wallalalala
  weia la wallala
  weiala la lei
  wallala la la
  leia leia leia (leia) la la
  la la (la la la la)
      The Rhinedaughters are here completely out of sight.
SIEGFRIED
  they'll give you a piece of their mind! –   1730
  Even so, –
  if I wasn't committed to Gutrune,
      The Rhinedaughters by now can scarcely be heard in the
      distance.

WOGLINDE, WELLGUNDE, FLOSSHILDE
La la!

SIEGFRIED
der zieren Frauen eine
hätt' ich mir – frisch gezähmt!
Er blickt ihnen unverwandt nach.
Hörner auf dem Theater aus dem Hintergrund

HAGENS STIMME *von fern*
Hoi-ho!
Siegfried fährt aus einer träumerischen Entrücktheit
auf, und antwortet dem vernommenen Rufe auf seinem
Horne.

ZWEITE SZENE

STIMME DER MANNEN *außerhalb der Szene*
Mehrere [B]
Hoiho?

SIEGFRIED *antwortend*
Hoiho!
Hagen kommt auf der Höhe hervor. Gunther folgt ihm.

MANNEN
Andere [B], *danach alle* [T, B]
Hoiho? Hoiho?

SIEGFRIED
1740   Hoiho! Hoihe!

HAGEN *Siegfried erblickend*
Finden wir endlich,
wohin du flogest?

SIEGFRIED
Kommt herab! Hier ist frisch und kühl!
Die Mannen kommen alle auf der Höhe an und steigen
nun, mit Hagen und Gunther, herab.

HAGEN
Hier rasten wir,
und rüsten das Mahl!
Jagdbeute wird zuhauf gelegt.

WOGLINDE, WELLGUNDE, FLOSSHILDE
La la!

SIEGFRIED
I'd take one of the pretty women
for myself – and bring her to heel!
His eyes are still glued to where they left.
onstage horns sounding in the background

HAGEN'S VOICE *in the distance*
Hoi-ho!
Siegfried snaps out of his enraptured state and, using his
horn, answers the call he has just heard.

SCENE TWO

VASSALS' VOICES *off-stage*
Several [B]
Hoiho?

SIEGFRIED *answering*
Hoiho!
Hagen enters on top of the cliff. Gunther follows him.

VASSALS
Others [B], *then all* [T, B]
Hoiho? Hoiho?

SIEGFRIED
Hoiho! Hoihe!   1740

HAGEN *spotting Siegfried*
Have we found where
you escaped to at last?

SIEGFRIED
Come down! Here it's fresh and cool!
All the vassals arrive on the cliff top and proceed to climb
down with Hagen and Gunther.

HAGEN
We'll rest here
and get our meal ready!
The dead quarry is piled in a heap.

Laßt ruhn die Beute,
und bietet die Schläuche!
  Schläuche und Trinkhörner werden hervorgeholt.
  Alles lagert sich.
Der uns das Wild verscheuchte,
nun sollt ihr Wunder hören,
1750 was Siegfried sich erjagt.

SIEGFRIED *lachend*
Schlimm steht es um mein Mahl:
von eurer Beute
bitte ich für mich.

HAGEN
Du beutelos?

SIEGFRIED
Auf Waldjagd zog ich aus, –
doch Wasserwild zeigte sich nur:
war ich dazu recht beraten,
drei wilde Wasservögel
hätt' ich euch wohl gefangen,
  Alle haben sich, nachdem Ruhe eingetreten ist, bequem
  gelagert. *
1760 die dort auf dem Rhein mir sangen,
erschlagen würd' ich noch heut'.
  Bestürzte Bewegung der Mannen. Einige erheben sich. *
  Gunther erschrickt und blickt düster auf Hagen.
  Er [Siegfried] lagert sich zwischen Gunther und Ha-
  gen.

HAGEN
Das wäre üb'le Jagd,
wenn den Beutelosen selbst
ein lauernd Wild erlegte.

SIEGFRIED
Mich dürstet!

HAGEN *indem er für Siegfried ein Trinkhorn füllen läßt und es*
  diesem dann darreicht
Ich hörte sagen, Siegfried,
der Vögel Sangessprache
verstündest du wohl: –
so wäre das wahr?

Leave our catch in peace,
and bring the wineskins out!
> *Wineskins and drinking-horns are fetched.*
> > *They all set up camp.*
He frightened off our game,
so now you'll hear the miracle
of Siegfried hunting his own. 1750

SIEGFRIED *laughing*

Things look bad for my meal:
I beg you for some
of your quarry.

HAGEN

You, no quarry?

SIEGFRIED

I set out to hunt in the forest, –
but all I found was waterfowl:
if I'd had good advice,
I could at least have caught
three wild aquatic birds for you,
> *Now all is calmer, everyone has settled down comfortably.* *
who sang to me there on the Rhine 1760
that I'd be slain this very day.
> *The vassals react with shock. Some stand up.* *
> > *Gunther, startled, looks grimly at Hagen.*
> > *He [Siegfried] sets himself down between Gunther and Hagen.*

HAGEN

That's a vicious hunt,
when the hunter without a catch
is himself killed by lurking game!

SIEGFRIED

I'm parched!

HAGEN *while having a drinking-horn filled for Siegfried and then handing it to him*

There's hearsay, Siegfried,
that you really do understand
the meaning of birdsong: –
how true is that?

SIEGFRIED

1770   Seit lange acht' ich
        des Lallens nicht mehr.
            Er erfaßt das Trinkhorn und wendet sich damit zu
            Gunther.
                Er trinkt und reicht das Horn Gunther hin.
        Trink, Gunther, trink':
        dein Bruder bringt es dir!
            Gunther blickt mit Grausen in das Horn.

GUNTHER *dumpf*
        Du mischtest matt und bleich: –
            noch gedämpfter
        dein Blut allein darin!

SIEGFRIED *lachend*
        So misch' es mit dem deinen!
            Er gießt aus Gunthers Horn in das seinige, so daß dieses
            überläuft.
        Nun floß gemischt es über:
        der Mutter Erde
        lass' das ein Labsal sein!

GUNTHER *mit einem heftigen Seufzer*
1780   Du überfroher Held!

SIEGFRIED *leise zu Hagen*
        Ihm macht Brünnhilde Müh'?

HAGEN *leise zu Siegfried*
        Verstünd' er sie so gut,
        wie du der Vögel Sang!

SIEGFRIED
        Seit Frauen ich singen hörte,
        vergaß ich der Vöglein ganz.

HAGEN
        Doch einst vernahmst du sie?

SIEGFRIED *sich lebhaft zu Gunther wendend*
        Hei! Gunther,
        grämlicher Mann!
        Dankst du es mir,
1790   so sing' ich dir Mären
        aus meinen jungen Tagen.

SIEGFRIED

  For ages I've no longer   1770
  noticed their babbling.
    He takes hold of the drinking-horn and with it turns to
    Gunther.
      He drinks and hands Gunther the horn.
  Drink, Gunther, drink:
  your brother urges you to take it!
    Gunther looks into the horn, horror-stricken.

GUNTHER *numbly*

  You've mixed feebly and faintly: –
    still more muted
  only your blood's in there!

SIEGFRIED *laughing*

  Mix it with yours like this!
    He pours enough from Gunther's horn into his own for
    it to overflow.
  Now mixed it's brimming over:
  let it rejuvenate
  our Mother Earth!

GUNTHER *with a very heavy sigh*

  Hero, you're too happy!   1780

SIEGFRIED *to Hagen, lowering his voice*

  Is Brünnhilde bothering him?

HAGEN *to Siegfried, lowering his voice*

  Were it so that he understood her,
  as well you do the songs of the birds!

SIEGFRIED

  Once I started hearing women's voices,
  I totally forgot about the little birds.

HAGEN

  But you did once understand them?

SIEGFRIED *turning to Gunther in high spirits*

  Hey! Gunther,
  peevish man!
  Show some grace,
  and I'll sing you tales   1790
  about when I was young.

GUNTHER

Die hör' ich gern.

Alle lagern sich nah an Siegfried, welcher allein aufrecht
sitzt, während die andern tiefer gestreckt liegen.

HAGEN

So singe, Held!

SIEGFRIED

Mime hieß
ein mürrischer Zwerg;
in des Neides Zwang
zog er mich auf,
daß einst das Kind,
wann kühn es erwuchs,
1800   einen Wurm ihm fällt' im Wald,
der lang' schon hütet' einen Hort.
Er lehrte mich schmieden
und Erze schmelzen;
doch was der Künstler
selber nicht konnt',
des Lehrlings Mute
mußt' es gelingen:
eines zerschlag'nen Stahles Stücken
neu zu schmieden zum Schwert.
1810   Des Vaters Wehr
fügt' ich mir neu,
nagelfest
schuf ich mir Nothung.
Tüchtig zum Kampf
dünkt' er dem Zwerg;
der führte mich nun zum Wald:
dort fällt' ich Fafner, den Wurm.

Jetzt aber merkt
wohl auf die Mär':
1820   Wunder muß ich euch melden.
Von des Wurmes Blut
mir brannten die Finger;
sie führt' ich kühlend zum Mund: –

GUNTHER
I'd like to hear them.
Everyone settles close to Siegfried, who is the only one
to sit up straight, the others stretching out lower down.

HAGEN
Sing away, hero!

SIEGFRIED
Once there was
a dour-looking dwarf
called Mime; he raised
me with pitiless purpose,
so that the child, once
he'd grown big and bold,
could kill a dragon in the forest.   1800
It had sat on a hoard for years.
The dwarf taught me
to forge and smelt metal;
but when my master
could cope no more,
his spirited student
leapt into the breach:
to forge a new sword
from the shattered pieces of another.
My father's blade it was,   1810
that I pieced together afresh,
hammering it down
to make myself Nothung.
The dwarf seemed to think
we were suited for battle;
so with him I went to the forest:
I killed Fafner, the dragon, right there.

Now notice with care
how the tale unfolds:
though first I must tell of a miracle.   1820
From the dragon's blood,
my fingers burnt;
so I sucked them to cool them: –

kaum netzt' ein wenig
die Zunge das Naß, –
was da die Vöglein sangen,
das konnt' ich flugs versteh'n.
Auf den Ästen saß es und sang:
'Hei! Siegfried gehört nun
1830   der Niblungen Hort!
Oh! fänd' in der Höhle
den Hort er jetzt!
Wollt' er den Tarnhelm gewinnen,
der taugt' ihm zu wonniger Tat!
Doch wollt' er den Ring sich erraten,
der macht' ihn zum Walter der Welt!'

HAGEN

Ring und Tarnhelm
trugst du nun fort?

EIN MANNE

Das Vöglein hörtest du wieder?

SIEGFRIED

1840   Ring und Tarnhelm
hatt' ich gerafft:
da lauscht' ich wieder
dem wonnigen Laller;
der saß im Wipfel und sang:
'Hei, Siegfried gehört nun
der Helm und der Ring.
Oh! traute er Mime,
dem Treulosen, nicht!
Ihm sollt' er den Hort nur erheben;
1850   nun lauert er listig am Weg;
nach dem Leben trachtet er Siegfried:
oh, traute Siegfried nicht Mime!'

HAGEN

Es mahnte dich gut?

VIER MANNEN

Vergaltest du Mime?

SIEGFRIED

Mit tödlichem Tranke

the fluid had barely
wet my tongue, –
when the little birds' songs
made sense all at once.
One sat there singing on branches aloft:
'Heya! The Nibelungs' hoard
is Siegfried's now!   1830
Oh! if only he'd find
the hoard in the cave!
The Tarnhelm's his if he wants it,
he'll use it for many a marvellous deed!
But if it's the ring he wants to find,
that will allow him to rule the world!'

HAGEN

The ring and the Tarnhelm:
did you get them?

ONE VASSAL

Did you listen to the bird some more?

SIEGFRIED

Ring and Tarnhelm,   1840
I grabbed them both:
then I listened once more
to the happy babbler,
who sat singing at the top of a tree:
'Heya, the helmet and the ring
are Siegfried's now.
Oh! let him not trust
the perfidious Mime,
who used him only to win the hoard!
The wily dwarf awaits his chance,   1850
to put an end to Siegfried's life:
oh, let Siegfried not trust Mime!'

HAGEN

Was it a good warning?

FOUR VASSALS

Did you get your own back on Mime?

SIEGFRIED

He came up to me

trat er zu mir;
bang und stotternd
gestand er mir Böses:
Nothung streckte den Strolch!

HAGEN *grell lachend*
1860 Was nicht er geschmiedet,
schmeckte doch Mime!
> *Hagen läßt ein Trinkhorn neu füllen und träufelt den Saft*
> *eines Krautes hinein.*

EIN MANNE, *danach* EIN ANDERER
Was wies das Vöglein dich wieder?

HAGEN
Trink' erst, Held,
aus meinem Horn:
ich würzte dir holden Trank,
die Erinnerung hell dir zu wecken,
> *Er reicht Siegfried das Horn.*
daß Fernes nicht dir entfalle!

SIEGFRIED *blickt gedankenvoll in das Horn und trinkt dann*
> *langsam*
In Leid zu dem Wipfel
lauscht' ich hinauf;
1870 da saß es noch und sang:
'Hei! Siegfried erschlug nun
den schlimmen Zwerg!
Jetzt wüßt' ich ihm noch
das herrlichste Weib:
auf hohem Felsen sie schläft,
Feuer umbrennt ihren Saal:
durchschritt' er die Brunst,
weckt' er die Braut,
Brünnhilde wäre dann sein!' –
> *Bei dem Worte 'Brünnhilde' heftige Bewegung aller Man-*
> *nen**

HAGEN
1880 Und folgtest du
des Vögleins Rate?

with a poisoned potion;
solicitous and stammering
he declared his evil intent:
Nothung cut the thug down!

HAGEN *laughing garishly*

What he'd tried to forge,   1860
Mime tasted after all!

    Hagen has a drinking-horn freshly filled and adds a dash
    of herbal juice.

ONE VASSAL, *then* ANOTHER

Did the little bird tell you more?

HAGEN

Hero, take a sip first
out of my horn:
I've spiced a tasty drink for you,
to keep your memories so alive,

    He hands the horn to Siegfried.

that old ones may not slip your mind!

SIEGFRIED *looks thoughtfully into the horn, then drinks out*
    of it slowly

With sorrow I listened hard
right up to the top of the tree;
there it sat still singing: 1870
'Heya! The wicked dwarf
Siegfried's now slain!
Now I must point him
to the most glorious woman of all:
she sleeps high on a rock,
her space surrounded by fire:
pass through the inferno,
waken the bride,
then Brünnhilde will be his!' –

    Stormy reaction to the word 'Brünnhilde' from all the
    vassals*

HAGEN

And did you follow   1880
the little bird's advice?

SIEGFRIED
  Rasch ohne Zögern
  zog ich nun aus; –
    Gunther hört mit immer größerem Erstaunen zu.
  bis den feurigen Fels ich traf: –
    Hier steht Siegfried auf. *
  die Lohe durchschritt ich
  und fand zum Lohn –
    in immer größere Verzückung geratend
  schlafend ein wonniges Weib
  in lichter Waffen Gewand.
  Den Helm löst' ich
1890 der herrlichen Maid;
  mein Kuß erweckte sie kühn:
  oh! wie mich brünstig da umschlang
  der schönen Brünnhilde Arm!
GUNTHER *in höchstem Schrecken aufspringend*
  Was hör' ich!
    Zwei Raben fliegen aus einem Busche auf, kreisen über
    Siegfried und fliegen dann, dem Rheine zu, davon.
HAGEN
  Errätst du auch
  dieser Raben Geraun'?
    Siegfried fährt heftig auf und blickt, Hagen den Rücken
    zukehrend, den Raben nach.
  Rache rieten sie mir!
    Hagen stößt seinen Speer in Siegfrieds Rücken.
      Gunther und die Mannen stürzen sich über Hagen.
      Siegfried schwingt mit beiden Händen seinen Schild
    hoch empor, um ihn nach Hagen zu werfen: die Kraft
    verläßt ihn; der Schild entsinkt ihm rückwärts; er selbst
    stürzt über dem Schilde zusammen.
VIER MANNEN *welche vergebens Hagen zurückzuhalten ver-*
    suchen
1900 Hagen, was tust du?
ZWEI ANDERE MANNEN
  Was tatest du!
GUNTHER
  Hagen, – was tatest du?

SIEGFRIED

In a flash,
I moved on; –
Gunther listens with growing astonishment.
until I met with the rock on fire: –
Siegfried now stands up. *
I strode through the blaze
and was rewarded with –
succumbing to growing ecstasy
a beautiful woman asleep
in simple armoured dress.
I loosened the helmet
of the glorious young woman;   1890
my kiss wakened her boldly:
oh! how fervently
the arms of the lovely Brünnhilde embraced me!

GUNTHER *leaping up in total horror*

What's all this!
*Two ravens fly up out of a bush, circle above Siegfried and
then fly off towards the Rhine.*

HAGEN

Can you also unlock
these ravens' whispers?
*Siegfried eagerly leaps to his feet and, turning his back on
Hagen, follows the ravens with his eyes.*
Their advice to me is vengeance!
He plunges his spear into Siegfried's back.
Gunther and the vassals hurl themselves at Hagen.
*Siegfried swings his shield up high with both hands
in order to throw it at Hagen: his strength fails him; the
shield sinks backwards away from him; he collapses on
the top of the shield.*

FOUR VASSALS *who attempt to hold Hagen back, but to no
avail*

Hagen, what are you doing?   1900

TWO OTHER VASSALS

What have you done!

GUNTHER

Hagen, – what have you done?

HAGEN
    Meineid rächt' ich!

    Hagen wendet sich ruhig zur Seite ab und verliert sich
    dann über die Höhe, wo man ihn langsam durch die
    anbrechende Dämmerung von dannen schreiten sieht. –
    Gunther beugt sich schmerzergriffen zu Siegfrieds Seite
    nieder. – Die Mannen umstehen teilnahmsvoll den Ster-
    benden.

SIEGFRIED *von zwei Mannen sitzend erhalten, schlägt die*
    Augen glanzvoll auf.

Brünnhilde!
Heilige Braut!
Wach' auf! Öffne dein Auge!
Wer verschloß dich
wieder in Schlaf?
Wer band dich in Schlummer so bang?
Der Wecker kam: –
er küßt dich wach; –
und aber – der Braut
bricht er die Bande: –
da lacht ihm Brünnhildes Lust. –
Ach! Dieses Auge –
ewig nun offen!
Ach, dieses Atems
wonniges Wehen!
Süßes Vergehen, –
seliges Grauen!
Brünnhild' bietet mir Gruß! –

    Siegfried sinkt zurück und stirbt. – Regungslose Trauer
    der Umstehenden.

      Die Nacht ist hereingebrochen.

      Auf die stumme Ermahnung Gunthers erheben die
    Mannen Siegfrieds Leiche und geleiten sie, mit dem Fol-
    genden, in feierlichem Zuge über die Felsenhöhe langsam
    von dannen.

      Der Mond bricht durch die Wolken und beleuchtet im-
    mer heller den die Berghöhe erreichenden Trauerzug. –

      Aus dem Rheine sind Nebel aufgestiegen und erfüllen

1910

HAGEN

I've avenged perjury!

He calmly turns to one side and then starts to disappear over the top of the cliff, where he can be seen slowly walking away in the falling darkness. – Gunther is beside himself with grief and bends down to be at Siegfried's side. – Showing their affection for him, the vassals surround the dying man.

SIEGFRIED *sitting propped up by two vassals, opens his eyes in full splendour.*

Brünnhilde!

Sacred bride!

Awaken! Open your eyes!

Who embalmed you

in sleep once more?

Who shut you in such restless slumber?

Your awakener has come: –

he wakes you with a kiss; –

and again – he rends   1910

the bride's shackles asunder: –

so Brünnhilde's joy laughs to him. –

Ah! these eyes,

open for eternity!

Ah, these sweet

stirrings of breath!

Sweet sinking, –

peaceful shuddering!

Brünnhilde offers me her greeting! –

He collapses and dies. – Those standing around him are stunned with grief.

Night has fallen.

Gunther silently bids the vassals to lift Siegfried's body and, during the following passage, to escort it slowly away in solemn procession over the high rocks.

The moon breaks through the clouds and throws an increasingly brighter light on the funeral procession as it reaches the top of the hill. –

Mists have come in from the Rhine and gradually fill

*allmählich die ganze Bühne, auf welcher der Trauerzug
bereits unsichtbar geworden ist, bis nach vorne, so daß
diese, während des Zwischenspieles, gänzlich verhüllt
bleibt.*

*Von hier an [Takt 977] verteilen die Nebel sich wieder,
bis endlich die Halle der Gibichungen, wie im ersten Auf-
zuge, immer erkennbarer hervortritt. –*

DRITTE SZENE

Gunthers Halle

*Es ist Nacht. Der Mondschein spiegelt sich auf dem Rheine.
Gutrune tritt aus ihrem Gemache in die Halle heraus.*

GUTRUNE

1920   War das sein Horn?
    Sie lauscht.
Nein! Noch
kehrt' er nicht heim. –
Schlimme Träume
störten mir den Schlaf!
Wild wieherte sein Roß; –
Lachen Brünnhildes
weckte mich auf. –
Wer war das Weib,
das ich zum Ufer schreiten sah?
1930   Ich fürchte Brünnhild'.
Ist sie daheim?
    Sie lauscht an der Türe rechts und ruft:
Brünnhild'! Brünnhild'!
Bist du wach?
    Sie öffnet schüchtern und blickt in das innere Gemach.
Leer das Gemach.
So war es sie,
die ich zum Rheine schreiten sah? –
    Horn auf dem Theater – fern

the whole stage – on which the funeral procession has
already disappeared from view – up to the front. During
the interlude the stage is completely enveloped.

From here [bar 977] the mists disperse again until the
hall of the Gibichungs appears more and more as it was
in the first act. –

SCENE THREE

Gunther's Hall

It is night. The light of the moon is reflected in the Rhine.
Gutrune comes out of her room into the hall.

GUTRUNE

Was that his horn?   1920
  She listens.
No! Still
he's not home. –
Bad dreams
unsettled my sleep!
The wild whinnying of his horse; –
Brünnhilde's laughter
waking me up. –
Who was that woman
I saw striding to the bank of the river?
Brünnhilde makes me afraid.   1930
Is she still here?
  She listens at the door on the right and calls out:
Brünnhilde! Brünnhilde!
Are you awake?
  Shyly she opens the door and peers into the room.
The room's empty.
So was it she
I saw making her way to the Rhine? –
  Horn off-stage – in the distance

War das sein Horn?
Nein!
Öd' alles!
  Sie blickt ängstlich hinaus.
1940 Säh' ich Siegfried nur bald! –
  Hagens Stimme, von außen sich nähernd

HAGEN
Hoiho! Hoiho!
  Als Gutrune Hagens Stimme hört, bleibt sie, von Furcht
  gefesselt, eine Zeitlang unbeweglich stehen.
    Hagen sagt Alles mit derbem, wie nonchalantem Aus-
  druck, als wenn es sich um gar nichts handeln würde. *
Wacht auf! Wacht auf!
Lichte! Lichte,
helle Brände!
Jagdbeute
bringen wir heim.
Hoiho! Hoiho!
  wachsender Feuerschein von außen
    Hagen tritt in die Halle.
Auf, Gutrun'!
Begrüße Siegfried!
1950 Der starke Held,
er kehret heim!

GUTRUNE *im großer Angst*
Was geschah? Hagen!
Nicht hört' ich sein Horn!

HAGEN
Der bleiche Held,
nicht bläst er es mehr;
  Männer und Frauen, mit Lichtern und Feuerbränden,
  geleiten in großer Verwirrung den Zug der mit Siegfrieds
  Leiche Heimkehrenden
nicht stürmt er zur Jagd,
zum Streite nicht mehr,
noch wirbt er um wonnige Frauen.

GUTRUNE *mit wachsendem Entsetzen*
Was bringen die?

Was that his horn?
No!
Not a soul!
   Nervously she takes a look outside.
If only I could see Siegfried soon! –
   Hagen's voice outside, getting closer

HAGEN
   Hoiho! Hoiho!
      *The moment Gutrune hears Hagen's voice, she freezes up
      in fear and stays standing for a while rooted to the spot.
         Everything Hagen says, he says with coarse, at the same
      time nonchalant, expression as if it were nothing at all.* *
   Awaken! Awaken!
   Light! Light,
   bright torches!
   Our dead quarry
   we're bringing home.
   Hoiho! Hoiho!
      *growing firelight from outside
         Hagen enters the hall.*
   Up, Gutrune!
   Greet your Siegfried!
   Your mighty hero's
   coming back!

GUTRUNE *in great anxiety*
   What happened? Hagen!
   His horn, I didn't hear it!

HAGEN
   It'll be blown no more
   by our pasty-faced hero;
      *In great confusion, men and women with torches and
      firebrands accompany the procession of vassals returning
      with Siegfried's body.*
   nor to hunts or battles
   will he storm any longer,
   let alone ask sweet women for love.

GUTRUNE *with growing consternation*
   What are they bringing?

*Der Zug gelangt in die Mitte der Halle, und die Mannen
setzen dort die Leiche auf einer schnell errichteten Erhö-
hung nieder.*

'*Das ist kein Trauerzug mehr, sondern ein Schreckens-
zug.*'*

HAGEN

1960   Eines wilden Ebers Beute:
Siegfried, deinen toten Mann.

Gutrune schreit auf und stürzt über die Leiche hin.

*Allgemeine Erschütterung und Trauer; Gunther be-
müht sich um die Ohnmächtige.*

GUNTHER

Gutrun'! holde Schwester,
hebe dein Auge, – schweige mir nicht! –

GUTRUNE *wieder zu sich kommend*

Siegfried – Siegfried – erschlagen! –

Sie stößt Gunther heftig zurück.

Fort, treuloser Bruder,
du Mörder meines Mannes! –
O Hilfe! Hilfe!
Wehe! Wehe!
Sie haben Siegfried erschlagen!

GUNTHER

1970   Nicht klage wider mich,
dort klage wider Hagen.
Er ist der verfluchte Eber,
der diesen Edlen zerfleischt'.

HAGEN

Bist du mir gram darum?

GUNTHER

Angst und Unheil
greife dich immer!

Hagen, mit furchtbarem Trotze herantretend

HAGEN

Ja denn! Ich hab' ihn erschlagen.
Ich – Hagen –
schlug ihn zu tod. –

1980   Meinem Speer war er gespart,

*The procession reaches the middle of the hall and the
vassals set down the body on a hastily arranged resting
place.*

'*It's no longer a funeral procession; it's a procession of
horror.*'*

HAGEN

A wild boar's prey: 1960
Siegfried, your dead husband.

Gutrune screams and falls prostrate over the body.

*Everywhere trauma and sorrow; Gunther attends to
his sister, who has blacked out.*

GUNTHER

Gutrune! beloved sister,
open your eyes, – talk to me! –

GUTRUNE *coming to*

Siegfried – Siegfried – slaughtered! –

She rebuffs Gunther with force.

Get away, treacherous brother,
you, killer of my husband! –
O help! Help!
Alas! Alas!
They've murdered my Siegfried!

GUNTHER

Don't rail against me,   1970
rail against Hagen there.
He's the foul boar,
who mauled this noble man to death.

HAGEN

That's why you loathe me?

GUNTHER

Fear and calamity
shall give you no rest!

Hagen, stepping forward with ogre-like defiance

HAGEN

So be it! I killed him.
I – Hagen –
struck him down.
He was destined for my spear,   1980

bei dem er Meineid sprach. –
Heiliges Beuterecht
hab’ ich mir nun errungen: –
D’rum fordr’ ich hier diesen Ring.

GUNTHER

Zurück! Was mir verfiel,
sollst nimmer du empfah’n!

HAGEN

Ihr Mannen, richtet mein Recht!

GUNTHER

Rühr’st du an Gutrunes Erbe,
schamloser Albensohn?

HAGEN *zieht sein Schwert.*
　　'Der Kampf der Riesen im Rheingold erneuert sich.'*

1990　Des Alben Erbe
fordert so sein Sohn!

　　Er dringt auf Gunther ein; dieser wehrt sich; sie fechten.
　　Die Mannen werfen sich dazwischen. Gunther fällt von
　　einem Streiche Hagens tot darnieder.

Her den Ring!

　　Er greift nach Siegfrieds Hand; diese hebt sich drohend
　　empor. – Gutrune hat bei Gunthers Falle entsetzt aufge-
　　schrien. Alles bleibt in Schauder regungslos gefesselt.

　　　Aus dem Hintergrunde schreitet, fest und feierlich,
　　Brünnhilde, dem Vordergrunde zu.

BRÜNNHILDE *noch im Hintergrunde*

Schweigt eures Jammers
jauchzenden Schwall!
Das ihr alle verrietet,
zur Rache schreitet sein Weib! –

　　während sie ruhig weiter vorschreitet

Kinder hört’ ich
greinen nach der Mutter,
da süße Milch sie verschüttet:

2000　doch nicht erklang mir
würdige Klage,
des höchsten Helden wert.

on which he'd committed perjury. –
The sacred right of capture
I deem myself to have won: –
this ring I now demand forthwith.

GUNTHER

Hands off! You'll never receive
what's been passed on to me.

HAGEN

Vassals, you judge if I'm right!

GUNTHER

You brazen son of a dwarf,
are you eyeing Gutrune's heritage?

HAGEN *draws his sword.*

'The battle of the giants in The Rhinegold resumes.'*

It's the dwarf's heritage   1990
his son's now claiming!

He closes in on Gunther, who resists; they fight. The vassals hurl themselves between the two men. A single stroke of Hagen's sword kills Gunther.

The ring's mine!

He tries to grab Siegfried's hand, which ominously rises up. – Gutrune has screamed with shock at Gunther's demise. All are rooted to the spot in stunned horror.

Brünnhilde walks decisively and solemnly from the back of the stage into the foreground.

BRÜNNHILDE *still at the back*

Silence your misery's
delirious cries!
All of you betrayed his wife,
and now it's vengeance she seeks! –

while she calmly moves further forward

Over spilled milk
I've heard children
whine to their mothers:
but a grave lament,   2000
fit for the most noble of heroes,
has yet to reach my ears.

GUTRUNE *vom Boden heftig sich aufrichtend*
  Brünnhilde! Neiderboste!
  Du brachtest uns diese Not:
  die du die Männer ihm verhetztest, –
  weh', daß du dem Haus genaht!
BRÜNNHILDE
  Armsel'ge, schweig'!
    Ohne Bitterkeit. Bemitleidend!*
  Sein Eheweib warst du nie;
  als Buhlerin
2010 bandest du ihn.
  Sein Mannesgemahl bin ich,
  der ewige Eide er schwur,
  eh' Siegfried je dich ersah.
GUTRUNE *in jähe Verzweiflung ausbrechend*
  Verfluchter Hagen!
  Daß du das Gift mir rietest,
  das ihr den Gatten entrückt!
  Ach, Jammer!
  Wie jäh' nun weiß ich's: –
    Sie hat sich voll Scheu von Siegfried abgewendet und beugt sich nun ersterbend über Gunthers Leiche; so verbleibt sie regungslos bis zum Schlusse.
  Brünnhild' war die Traute,
2020 die durch den Trank er vergaß! –
    Hagen steht, trotzig auf Speer und Schild gelehnt, in finsteres Sinnen versunken, auf der entgegengesetzen Seite. – Brünnhilde allein in der Mitte; nachdem sie lange in den Anblick Siegfrieds versunken gewesen, wendet sie sich mit feierlicher Erhabenheit, an die Männer und Frauen.
BRÜNNHILDE *zu den Mannen*
  Starke Scheite
  schichtet mir dort
  am Rande des Rheins zu Hauf'!
  Hoch und hell
  lod're die Glut,
  die den edlen Leib
  des hehrsten Helden verzehrt.

GUTRUNE *getting up from the ground in a fury*
   Brünnhilde! Enraged and pitiless!
   You brought this calamity upon us:
   you made the men hate him, –
   I rue the day you came near this house!
BRÜNNHILDE
   Pitiful woman, be silent!
      Without bitterness. Showing sympathy! *
   You were never the woman he married;
   you ensnared him
   as his mistress.   2010
   I'm this man's real wife,
   to whom he swore eternal vows
   before he, Siegfried, ever saw you.
GUTRUNE *erupting in sudden exasperation*
   Foul Hagen!
   You told me to use the poison
   that took her husband from her!
   Ah, what disgrace!
   Now all of a sudden, I see the truth: –
      Full of dread, she turns away from Siegfried and – her life
      draining away – bends over Gunther's body; she remains
      without moving in this position until the end.
   Brünnhilde was his true haven of trust;
   only the drink made him forget her! –   2020
      Leaning defiantly on his spear and shield, Hagen stands
      on the opposite side of the stage sunk in dark thought. –
      Brünnhilde is alone in the centre; after having been lost
      herself in long contemplation of Siegfried, she turns to
      the men and women with solemn dignity.
BRÜNNHILDE *to the vassals*
   Heap heavy
   logs for me there
   to soar up on the edge of the Rhine!
   Set fires alight,
   bright to the sky,
   to wrap the fine limbs
   of our noblest hero in flame.

Sein Roß führet daher,
daß mit mir dem Recken es folge:
2030 denn des Helden heiligste
Ehre zu teilen
verlangt mein eigener Leib.
Vollbringt Brünnhildes Wort!

*Die jüngeren Männer errichten, während des Folgenden,
vor der Halle, nahe am Rheinufer, einen mächtigen Schei-
terhaufen: Frauen schmücken diesen dann mit Decken,
auf welche sie Kräuter und Blumen streuen. – Brünnhilde
versinkt von neuem in die Betrachtung des Antlitzes der
Leiche Siegfrieds.*

*Ihre Mienen nehmen eine immer sanftere Verklärung
an.*

Wie Sonne lauter
strahlt mir sein Licht;
der Reinste war er,
der mich verriet!
Die Gattin trügend –
treu dem Freunde, –
2040 von der eig'nen Trauten –
einzig ihm teuer, –
schied er sich durch sein Schwert.
Echter als er
schwur keiner Eide;
treuer als er
hielt keiner Verträge;
laut'rer als er
liebte kein and'rer!
Und doch, alle Eide,
2050 alle Verträge,
die treueste Liebe –
trog keiner wie er! –

Wißt ihr, wie das ward?
nach oben blickend
O ihr, der Eide
ewige Hüter!

Bring his horse here,
that with me it may follow the warrior:
it's truly the most sacred   2030
homage to our hero
that my own body yearns to share.
Do as Brünnhilde says!

*During the following, the younger men start building a
huge funeral pyre in front of the hall near the edge of
the Rhine: women then deck it out with blankets, over
which they scatter herbs and flowers. – Brünnhilde again
loses herself in rapt contemplation of the dead Siegfried's
countenance.*

*Her features undergo an increasingly tender transfigu-
ration.*

His light shines upon me
like the innocent sun;
yet I was betrayed
by this purest of men!
Unfaithful to his wife –
faithful to his friend, –
from the wife he could trust, –   2040
the only one close to him, –
he separated, using his sword.
Oaths were never taken
by a man more honest;
contracts never honoured
by a man more loyal;
no man ever loved
more innocently than he!
And yet, no one dishonoured
all oaths, all contracts,   2050
the most faithful love –
as this man did! –

Do you know, how it came about?
looking above
O you, immortal
keepers of oaths!

Lenkt euren Blick
auf mein blühendes Leid;
erschaut eure ewige Schuld!
Meine Klage hör',
2060 du hehrster Gott!
Durch seine tapferste Tat,
– dir so tauglich erwünscht, –
weihtest du den,
der sie gewirkt,
dem Fluche, dem du verfielest, –
mich mußte
der Reinste verraten,
daß wissend würde ein Weib!

Weiß ich nun, was dir frommt?

2070 Alles, Alles,
Alles weiß ich, –
Alles ward mir nun frei.
Auch deine Raben
hör' ich rauschen;
mit bang ersehnter Botschaft
send' ich die beiden nun heim. –
Ruhe, ruhe, du Gott!
　　Sie winkt den Mannen, Siegfrieds Leiche auf den Scheiter-
　　haufen zu tragen; zugleich zieht sie von Siegfrieds Finger
　　den Ring ab und betrachtet ihn sinnend.
Mein Erbe nun
nehm' ich zu eigen. –
2080 Verfluchter Reif!
Furchtbarer Ring!
Dein Gold fass' ich
und geb' es nun fort.
Der Wassertiefe
weise Schwestern,
des Rheines schwimmende Töchter, –
euch dank' ich redlichen Rat:
was ihr begehrt,

Cast your eyes
on my unfurling grief;
witness your guilt without end!
Hear my grievance,
you noblest of gods!   2060
With his bravest deed
– which you so rightly wanted –
you doomed him,
once he'd done it,
to the curse that doomed you, –
the purest of men
had to betray me,
that a woman might become wise!

Now do I know what you want?

All, all,   2070
I know all things, –
all freedom has now become mine.
Also I hear
your ravens' whispers;
this instant I send them both home
with their news, awaited in fear. –
Rest, rest, you god!
   She gives the vassals a sign to carry Siegfried's body
   onto the funeral pyre; at the same time she pulls the ring
   off Siegfried's finger and looks at it pensively.
I take possession
of my heritage now. –
The ring accursed!   2080
The abominable ring!
I'm capturing your gold
and now give it away.
Knowing sisters
of the water's depths,
swimming daughters of the Rhine, –
I thank you for honest advice:
to you I give

ich geb' es euch:
2090   aus meiner Asche
nehmt es zu eigen!
Das Feuer, das mich verbrennt,
rein'ge vom Fluche den Ring!
Ihr in der Flut,
löset ihn auf,
und lauter bewahrt
das lichte Gold,
das euch zum Unheil geraubt.

Sie hat den Ring sich angesteckt und wendet sich jetzt zu dem Scheitengerüste, auf welchem Siegfrieds Leiche ausgestreckt liegt. Sie entreißt einem Manne den mächtigen Feuerbrand.

den Feuerbrand schwingend und nach dem Hintergrunde deutend

Fliegt heim, ihr Raben!
2100   Raunt es eurem Herren,
was hier am Rhein ihr gehört!
An Brünnhildes Felsen
fahrt vorbei:
der dort noch lodert,
weiset Loge nach Walhall!
Denn der Götter Ende
dämmert nun auf.
So – werf' ich den Brand
in Walhall's prangende Burg.

Sie schleudert den Brand in den Holzstoß, welcher sich schnell hell entzündet.

Zwei Raben sind vom Felsen am Ufer aufgeflogen und verschwinden nach den Hintergrunde.

Sie [Brünnhilde] gewahrt ihr Roß, welches soeben zwei Männer hereinführen.

2110   Grane, mein Roß!
Sei mir gegrüßt!

Sie ist ihm entgegen gesprungen, faßt es und entzäumt es schnell; dann neigt sie sich traulich zu ihm.

*'Zu den Leuten sagt sie gar nichts, Alles ist wie eine großartige Vision.' **

what you seek:
take it from my ashes,   2090
it belongs to you!
The fire that burns me to death
shall purge the ring of its curse!
You in the waters,
dissolve it,
and keep pure
the luminous gold,
whose theft from you led to calamity.

> *She has slipped the ring onto her finger and now turns to the heap of logs with Siegfried's outstretched body lying on top of it. She wrests a massive firebrand from one of the vassals.*
>
>> *brandishing the firebrand and pointing it towards the background*

Fly home, you ravens!
Whisper to your master   2100
what you've heard here by the Rhine!
Fly past
Brünnhilde's rock:
Loge's still there ablaze:
point him towards Valhalla!
Now the destruction of the gods
is truly dawning.
Like this – I throw the firebrand
into Valhalla's brilliant fortress.

> *She slings the firebrand into the log heap, which quickly bursts into bright flames.*
>
> *Two ravens fly up from the rocks on the river bank and disappear into the distance at the back.*
>
> *She [Brünnhilde] catches sight of her horse just being led in by two young men.*

Grane, my horse!   2110
My greetings to you!

> *She jumps towards it, takes hold of it and quickly unbridles it; she then leans over to take it into her confidence.*
>
> *'She says absolutely nothing to the people: it is all like a magnificent vision.'**

Weißt du auch, mein Freund,
wohin ich dich führe?
Im Feuer leuchtend
liegt dort dein Herr,
Siegfried, mein seliger Held.
Dem Freunde zu folgen,
wieherst du freudig?
Lockt dich zu ihm
2120   die lachende Lohe?
Fühl' meine Brust auch,
wie sie entbrennt,
helles Feuer
das Herz mir erfaßt,
ihn zu umschlingen,
umschlossen von ihm,
in mächtigster Minne,
vermählt ihm zu sein!
Heiajoho! Grane!
2130   Grüß deinen Herren!
   *Sie hat sich auf das Roß geschwungen und hebt es jetzt
   zum Sprunge.*
Siegfried! Siegfried! Sieh!
Selig grüßt dich dein Weib!
   *Sie sprengt das Roß mit einem Satze in den brennenden
   Scheiterhaufen.*
     *Sogleich steigt prasselnd der Brand hoch auf, so daß
   das Feuer den ganzen Raum vor der Halle erfüllt und
   diese selbst schon zu ergreifen scheint.*
     *Entsetzt drängen sich Männer und Frauen nach dem
   äußersten Vordergrunde.*
     *Als der ganze Bühnenraum nur noch von Feuer erfüllt
   erscheint, verlischt plötzlich der Glutschein, so daß bald
   bloß ein Dampfgewölk zurückbleibt, welches sich dem
   Hintergrunde zu verzieht und dort am Horizonte sich als
   finstere Wolkenschicht lagert. – Zugleich ist vom Ufer her
   der Rhein mächtig angeschwollen und hat seine Flut über
   die Brandstätte gewälzt. Auf den Wogen sind die drei
   Rheintöchter herbeigeschwommen und erscheinen, jetzt*

Do you also know, my friend,
to where I shall lead you?
Radiant in fire,
there Siegfried lies,
your master, my hero divine.
Following our friend,
will you whinny with joy?
Will this boisterous blaze
entice you to join him?   2120
Feel too the passion
alight in my breast,
how this bright fire
has gripped my heart
to embrace him,
to be enveloped by him,
to be wedded to him
in mightiest love!
Heiajoho! Grane!
Greet your lord!   2130

*She has vaulted onto the horse and now holds it steady
to jump.*

Siegfried! Siegfried! Look!
Your wife greets you in bliss!

*At full speed, she rides the horse with a single leap into
the burning pyre.*

*The crackling fire climbs instantly to such a height that
its flames fill the entire space in front of the hall and even
appear to ravage the hall itself.*

*The horrified men and women surge into the fore-
ground as far as is possible.*

*At the point where the entire stage appears to be filled
only by fire, the glow suddenly fades, so that soon only
a cloud of smoke remains, drifting into the background
and there spreading over the horizon in a dark layer of
cloud. – At the same time the Rhine has burst its banks
with mighty force and heavily flooded the scene of the
fire. The three Rhinedaughters have been swimming
along on the waves and now appear above the scene of*

über der Brandstätte. – Hagen, der seit dem Vorgange mit dem Ringe Brünnhildes Benehmen mit wachsender Angst beobachtet hat, gerät beim Anblick der Rheintöchter in höchsten Schreck.

HAGEN *Er wirft hastig Speer, Schild und Helm von sich und stürzt, wie wahnsinnig, sich in die Flut. Woglinde und Wellgunde umschlingen mit ihren Armen seinen Nacken und ziehen ihn, so zurückschwimmend, mit sich in die Tiefe.*

Zurück vom Ring!

Flosshilde, den anderen voran dem Hintergrunde zu schwimmend, hält jubelnd den gewonnenen Ring in die Höhe.

Durch die Wolkenschicht, welche sich am Horizonte gelagert, bricht ein rötlicher Glutschein mit wachsender Helligkeit aus.

Von dieser Helligkeit beleuchtet, sieht man die drei Rheintöchter auf den ruhigeren Wellen des allmählich wieder in sein Bett zurückgetretenen Rheines, lustig mit dem Ringe spielend, im Reigen schwimmen.

Aus den Trümmern der zusammengestürzten Halle sehen die Männer und Frauen, in höchster Ergriffenheit, dem wachsenden Feuerscheine am Himmel zu. Als dieser endlich in lichtester Helligkeit leuchtet, erblickt man darin den Saal Walhall's, in welchem die Götter und Helden, ganz nach der Schilderung Waltrautes im ersten Aufzuge, versammelt sitzen. – Helle Flammen scheinen in dem Saal der Götter aufzuschlagen.

Als die Götter von den Flammen gänzlich verhüllt sind, fällt der Vorhang.

the fire. – Since the incident with the ring, Hagen has been noticing Brünnhilde's actions with increasing unrest and at the sight of the Rhinedaughters falls into a state of sheer panic.

HAGEN *He throws off his spear, shield and helmet in haste and plunges like a madman into the water. Woglinde and Wellgunde entwine his neck with their arms and swim off with him like that, pulling him along with them into the deep.*

Hands off the ring!

Swimming ahead of the others towards the background, Flosshilde jubilantly celebrates the recovery of the ring by holding it aloft.

Through the layer of cloud that has spread over the horizon a reddish blaze of fire is breaking out with growing brightness.

Illuminated by this brightness, the Rhinedaughters can be seen happily playing with the ring and swimming in circles on the calmer waves of the Rhine, which has gradually receded back into its bed.

The men and women, extremely moved, watch the growing glow of fire in the sky from the ruins of the collapsed hall. When this is at last at its brightest and most radiant, the assembled gods and heroes seated in the hall of Valhalla come into view, exactly as Waltraute described them in the first act. – Bright flames give the impression of blazing up in the hall of the gods.

When the gods are completely engulfed by the flames, the curtain falls.

Sources of the German Text

DIALOGUE, INCLUDING ENSEMBLES

The Rhinegold / Das Rheingold
  Orchestral score: *Sämtliche Werke*, vol. 10 / i–ii, ed. Egon Voss
  (Mainz, 1988–9).
  Vocal score: ed. Egon Voss (Mainz, 2010).

The Valkyrie / Die Walküre
  Orchestral score: *Sämtliche Werke*, vol. 11 / i–iii, ed. Christa Jost
  (Mainz, 2002–5).
  Vocal score: ed. Egon Voss (Mainz, 2013).

Siegfried
  Orchestral score: *Sämtliche Werke*, vol. 12 / i–iii, eds. Klaus Döge
  and Egon Voss (Mainz, 2006–14).
  Vocal score: ed. Egon Voss (Mainz, 2014).

Twilight of the Gods / Götterdämmerung
  Orchestral score: *Sämtliche Werke*, vol. 13 / i–iii, ed. Hartmut Fladt
  (Mainz, 1980–82).
  Vocal score: eds Klaus Döge and Eva Katharina Klein (Mainz,
  2013).

PERFORMANCE AND STAGE DIRECTIONS

All directions are from *Sämtliche Werke* unless otherwise stated. I
have retained – for the sake of simplicity in the midst of now more
diverse international practices and conventions – Wagner's original
voice specifications in the synopses and his use of 'left' and 'right'
from the audience's perspective in the stage directions. In the trans-
lation and notes I have used the following abbreviations and signs:

SSD   *Sämtliche Schriften und Dichtungen*, 16 vols (Leipzig, 1914–16): *Der Ring des Nibelungen*, v, pp. 199–268; vi, pp. 1–256. This version of the text first published by Wagner in 1872. I have retained the gaps in the verse he occasionally introduced to highlight junctures in the narrative, but not his systematic indentation of shorter lines. So many passages had to be diffently structured to get even approximately close to their original meaning, I felt that slavishly trying in English to reproduce Wagner's method of pointing visually to the difference between long and short lines was counter-productive. Both the original text and the translation in this edition are therefore printed flush left. For a modern German edition that reproduces Wagner's scheme, see: Reclam's *Universal-Bibliothek*, ed. Egon Voss (Stuttgart, 2009) with variants from SW in dialogue and ensembles, but not stage directions.

SW   *Sämtliche Werke*: orchestral and vocal scores of *The Ring* listed above.

WWV   John Deathridge, Martin Geck, Egon Voss (eds), *Wagner Werk-Verzeichnis (WWV): Verzeichnis der musikalischen Werke Richard Wagners und ihrer Quellen* (Mainz/London/New York/Tokyo, 1986).

*   indicates an entry (Wagner verbatim in inverted commas) made in one of the following: **1876** = printed vocal scores with entries by Julius Kniese, Hermann Levi, Felix Mottl and Heinrich Porges based on personal written records of the 1876 rehearsals and entered in 1896 at the invitation of Cosima Wagner as part of preparations for that year's Bayreuth production of *The Ring* (WWV 86A Musik VII-Id); **GLASENAPP** = printed vocal scores annotated principally by Henriette Glasenapp (WWV 86A Musik VIIIc); **PORGES 1** = printed vocal scores annotated in 1876 by Heinrich Porges (WWV 86B Musik Xa); **PORGES 2** = printed full score of *Siegfried* annotated in 1876 by Heinrich Porges (WWV 86C Musik Xa); **LEVI** = printed vocal scores of *The Rhinegold* and *The Valkyrie* annotated in 1876 by Hermann Levi (St. th. 887/8, Bavarian State Library, Munich); **KNIESE** = printed vocal score of *Twilight of the Gods* annotated in 1876 by Julius Kniese (KA S 52, National Archive Richard Wagner Foundation, Bayreuth); **MOTTL** = printed vocal scores, ed. Felix Mottl, with notes from the 1876 rehearsals (Leipzig, 1914). All transcriptions of entries in SW 29/iii, *Dokumente zur ersten Bayreuther Aufführung von Der Ring des Nibelungen*, ed. Christa Jost (Mainz, forthcoming in 2018). In most cases I have privileged the wording of 1876 for all directions appearing in two or more sources. Some but by no means all of the directions have already appeared in the relevant full and vocal scores of the critical edition.

**   indicates footnotes by Wagner in the orchestral score.

Notes

These notes reference sources and variants of performance and stage directions in SW and SSD and from the Bayreuth 1876 rehearsals. They also refer to points of translation, and on occasion to Wagner's literary allusions, but not to the detail of his radical reworking of his medieval sources, a subject that is too complex to be adequately gone into here. Some of the literature on Wagner's handling of Norse and German legend is worth consulting and relatively easy to access. Still rewarding are Jessie Weston's *The Legends of the Wagner Dramas* (London, 1896), Deryck Cooke's *I Saw the World End* (Oxford, 1979), and especially Elizabeth Magee's *Richard Wagner and the Nibelungs* (Oxford, 1990) and the introduction to Edward Haymes's *Wagner's* Ring *in 1848* (Rochester, NY, 2010) that also include material about the scholarly fascination for the Nibelung sagas among Wagner's contemporaries. Standard reference works like the *Wagner Handbook* (1992), *The Wagner Compendium* (2001), *The Cambridge Companion to Wagner* (2011) and *The Cambridge Wagner Encyclopedia* (2013) offer moments of sagacity, as do internet sites like Wikipedia. Readers who want to get a sense of the stark differences between Wagner's invented world-myth and the ancient tales that inspired it should consult A. T. Hatto's fine translation of *The Nibelungenlied* (1965), Jesse L. Byock's of *The Saga of the Volsungs* (2004) and *The Prose Edda* (2005), and Andy Orchard's of *The Elder Edda* (2013) in the Penguin Classics series.

THE RHINEGOLD

Scene 1

1 before   *With graceful . . . dawning light*: direction in SSD.
      SW specifies the Rhinedaughter as Woglinde.

1 after   **1876** Mottl p. 5: *The whole scene in an extremely*
      flowing tempo! No lingering anywhere. / Die ganze
      Szene äußerst fließend im Zeitmaß! Nirgends ein
      Verweilen.

7 after   **1876** Porges p. 6: *When the Rhinedaughters sing*
      individually, the character of a **dramatic dialogue**
      must be maintained / In den Einzel-Gesängen der
      Rheintöchter ist stets der **dramatisch-dialogische**
      Charakter festzuhalten. [Emphasis Porges.]

8 after   *She . . . Woglinde*: direction in SSD.

20 *before *with a raw . . .* : **1876** Porges p. 8.

20   'Nicker': Jacob Grimm writes in *Teutonic Mythol-*
      ogy (see note 25, Introduction) that related forms
      nicerus, necker, nikker and even the English *old*
      Nick suggest 'monstrous' or 'evil' sea spirits who
      are related to the devil (p. 488). I have preferred the
      more neutral 'sprites'.

59 before   *He sneezes violently*: direction in SSD.

67 after 'here' *The sisters laugh*: direction in SSD.

82 *before *very fiercely . . .* : **1876** Mottl p. 15.

121   'Alb' / 'dwarf': to simplify two easily confused and
      indeed confusing categories, I prefer to translate
      'Alb' mostly as 'dwarf' and not 'elf'. See, e.g., Paul
      Battles's chapter 'Dwarfs in Germanic Literature'
      and Tom Shippey's '*Alias Oves Habeo*: The Elves as
      a Category Problem', in *The Shadow-Walkers* (note
      27, Introduction), pp. 29–82, 157–87.

141 before *flatteringly*: direction in SSD.

155 before *holding . . . arms*: direction in SSD; in SW *feurig /*
      with passion.

166 before *starting . . . arms*: direction in SSD; in SW *er-*
      schreckt auffahrend / starting up, shocked.

203 *before *With extreme ferocity*: **1876** Porges p. 30.

203 before *scarcely . . . himself*: direction in SSD.

204 *before *The Rhinedaughters' movements...*: **1876** Porges
      p. 30.

278 *before   *Showing no marked ...* : **1876** Porges p. 40; Mottl adds: *Here the Rhinedaughters have to remain completely still. / Hier müssen die Rheintöchter ganz ohne Bewegung bleiben.*

278–9   'versagt' / 'denies': authentic sources have either this or 'entsagt' / 'renounces' (the first printed score, WWV 86A Musik IX, has the latter and SW has both). In a 1914 essay 'Eine Erinnerung und eine Erklärung' [A Reminiscence and an Explanation], Wagner's assistant Hans von Wolzogen, the inventor of the famous leitmotif guides, reports that during the 1876 rehearsals it was decided that it had to be 'versagt' / 'denies' because the object of the sentence is 'Macht' / 'power', and not 'Minne' / 'love'. According to this argument, the more abstract verb 'versagen', meaning 'to deny' in the sense of not to serve or to accede to a force or duty, as opposed to the more personal 'entsagen', meaning 'to renounce' a feeling or belief, is the only logical choice. Hans von Wolzogen, *Wagner und seine Werke* (Regensburg, 1924), pp. 91–7.

308 *before   *brooding sinisterly*: **1876** Porges p. 45.

313 after   *in grausiger Hast / with macabre rapidity*: from direction in SSD; direction otherwise identical with SW.

320 before   *They ... recklessness*: direction in SSD; SW has only *lachend / laughing*.

321 *before   *with a terrifying ...* : **1876** Porges p. 47.

Scene 2

334 *before   *Not to be ...* : **1876** Porges p. 53.

343   'Achieved ... work': I see this line as an allusion to the final chorus of the second part of Haydn's *The Creation* – 'Vollendet ist das große Werk' / 'Achieved is the glorious work' [original English text] – a work that Wagner in his autobiography *My Life* (p. 328) says he knew well and conducted (see note 26, Introduction).

352 *after   *All the following ...* : **1876** Mottl p. 55.

370 *before   *the tempo the same ...* : **GLASENAPP** p. 56.

388 *before   *Very heartfelt ...* : **1876** Porges p. 57.

398 *before   *the following* . . . **1876** Porges p.58.

411 *before   *very violently*: **LEVI** p. 59.

417 before   *seriously*: direction in SSD.

456 *after   *Freia accompanies* . . . : **1876** Porges p. 63.

479 *before   *In a clipped* . . . : **1876** Porges p. 65.

486 *before   *With decisive* . . . : **1876** Porges p. 65.

492 *before   *The words* . . . : **1876** Porges p. 66.

495 *before   *From here* . . . : **1876** Porges p. 66.

498 before   *mockingly*: direction in SSD.

500 *before   *Fasolt begins* . . . : **1876** Porges p. 66.

512 *before   *somewhat hastily* . . . : **1876** Mottl and Porges p. 67.

514 *before   *holding back* . . . : **1876** Porges p. 67.

538 *before   *very forcefully*: **1876** Levi p. 69.

559 before   *aside*: direction in SSD.

579 *before   *with grand gestures* . . . : **1876** Porges p. 73.

581 *before   *more like* . . . : **1876** Porges p. 73.

594 *before   *Loge's utterances* . . . : **1876** Porges p. 74.

630 *before   *to be spoken* . . . : **1876** Porges p. 78.

646 *before   *with passionate expression*: **1876** Porges p. 79.

663 *before   *With a tone* . . . : **1876** Porges p. 80.

675 *before   *Fricka with*. . . **PORGES** 1 p. 81.

716 *before   *The gods look* . . . : **PORGES** 1 p. 85.

740 *after   *All react* . . . : **PORGES** 1 p. 88.

759 *before   *aside*: **LEVI** p. 90.

766 *before   *very clearly*: **LEVI** p. 90.

774 *before   *To be sung* . . . : **1876** Porges p. 91.

778 *before   *his passion* . . . : **1876** Porges p. 91.

803 after   **1876** p. 94 Porges notes the following: *The master explained the significance of the situation by saying that the gods until now haven't realized that besides themselves there is another power at work, namely that of the gold.* / *Die Bedeutsamkeit der Situation erläuterte der Meister durch den Ausspruch, wie die Götter bis dahin nicht gewußt hätten, daß es außer der ihren noch eine andere Macht gebe, nämlich die des Goldes.*

804 *before   *Loge is standing* . . . : **1876** Porges p. 94.

815 *before   *very forcefully*: **1876** Mottl p. 95; **MOTTL** p. 116: simply *Heftig* / *Forcefully.*

906 *before   *Expression has become* . . . : **1876** Porges p. 103.

911 *before   *to be stated* . . . : **MOTTL** p. 126.

912–16   In **1876** p. 103 Porges notes that Fricka should deliver these lines *In the grand manner of ancient times.* / *Im Charakter antiker Größe*; Mottl adds, citing Wagner: '*In the manner of an alla breve [i.e. a majestic two beats in a bar]! If I may say so, no dragging please.*' / '*Im Allabreve Charakter! Also keine Schlepperei, wenn ich bitten darf*'.

921 *before   *sounding glib again*: MOTTL p. 127.

Scene 3

943 *before   *Tense, forward-moving energy . . .* : 1876 Porges p. 111.

1006 after   I have retained the shorter direction in SW. The more elaborate one in SSD was perhaps no longer necessary, as the orchestral transition Wagner subsequently composed to lead into the entrance of Wotan and Loge now pungently and concisely expresses the visual and acoustical image it describes. But it is still worth reading: *The pillar of mist vanishes in the background: Alberich's blustering and scolding can still be heard receding into the distance; yelling and screaming answer him from the crevices down below, until at last they recede so far into the distance that they can no longer be heard. – Mime has slumped to the ground in pain: his groaning and whimpering are heard by Wotan and Loge, who lower themselves down out of a shaft above.* / *Die Nebelsäule verschwindet dem Hintergrunde zu: man hört in immer weiterer Ferne Alberichs Toben und Zanken; Geheul und Geschrei antwortet ihm aus den unteren Klüften, das sich endlich in immer weitere Ferne unhörbar verliert. – Mime ist vor Schmerz zusammengesunken: sein Stöhnen und Wimmern wird von Wotan und Loge gehört, die aus einer Schluft von oben her sich herablassen.*

1036 *before   *With somewhat . . .* : PORGES 1 p. 119.
1092 *after   '*You are certainly . . .* : 1876 Mottl p. 123.
1096 after   *embarrassed . . . closely*: direction in SSD.
1097 *before   *Mime becomes . . .* : 1876 Porges p. 124.
1101 after   The direction in SSD is worth noting: *The sound of Alberich's scolding and flogging comes closer*

again. / Alberichs Zanken und Züchtigen nähert
sich wieder.

1109	*after	*Everything . . .* : **1876** Porges p. 125.
1116	*before	*In a rush . . .* : **1876** Porges p. 125; Porges adds that this direction applies to Alberich's following lines as well.
1139	*after	*The dwarfs . . .* : **1876** Kniese p. 127.
1140	*before	*With a powerful voice*: **1876** Porges p. 127.
1145	*before	*controlling himself . . .* : **1876** Porges p. 131.
1223	*before	*With lascivious . . .* :**1876** Porges p. 136.
1335	before	*strong-fibred rope / Bastseile*, a paricularly resilient rope for binding with strong fibres made from the vascular tissue of certain plants.

Scene 4

1371	before	*brusquely*: direction in SSD.
1378	*after	*Somewhat . . .* : **1876** Mottl p. 157.
1443	*after	*Wotan takes . . .* : **1876** Porges p. 163.
1459	*before	*With piercing . . .* : **1876** Porges p. 165.
1537	*after	*Wotan is momentarily . . .* : **1876** Mottl p. 172.
1559	after	*in order to embrace her*: these words from SSD; otherwise direction is as in SW.
1560	*before	*to be sung . . .* : **1876** Porges p. 175.
1605	*before	*everything to continue . . .* : **1876** Mottl p. 180.
1607	before	*her . . . Freia*: direction in SSD.
1646	*after	*With sultry passion*: **1876** Porges p. 183.
1653	*before	*Fafner forces . . .* : **1876** Porges p. 184.
1658	*before	*always lively*: **MOTTL** p. 218.
1685	*before	*With the most unrelenting resolve*: **1876** Porges p. 186.
1686	after	*she is of noble stature . . . black hair*: from direction in SSD; direction otherwise as in SW.
1687	*before	*very slowly . . .* : **MOTTL** p. 222.
1687	*before	*to be conveyed . . .* : **1876** Porges p. 187.
1692	*before	*softly*: **MOTTL** p. 222.
1712	*before	*with expression . . .* : **1876** Porges p. 189.
1717	*after	*In a calm tone . . .* : **1876** Porges p. 189.
1732	*before	*In majestic strides . . .* : **1876** Porges p. 191.
1737	*before	*Fafner throws out . . .* : **1876** Porges p. 192.
1737	before	*throwing himself . . . way*: direction in SSD.
1764	*before	*Fafner mockingly . . .* : **PORGES** 1 p. 195.

1768 *before	*With a sharply . . .* : **1876** Porges p. 195.
1790 before	*Nebelschleier / a veil of fog*: taken from direction in SSD; SW has simply *Nebel / fog*.
1810	'Show the bridge': just as Donner has commanded the clouds, he now asks his brother first to show the way to Valhalla *not* to the gods themselves, as some translations have it, but to the rainbow bridge itself.
1810 after	*Fafner, who . . . on his back*: direction in SSD.
1828 *after	*Wotan takes . . .* : **1876** Porges p. 207.
1828 *after	*W[otan] points . . .* : **1876** Porges p. 207. See also *Cosima Wagner's Diaries* (30 May 1876) and **MOTTL** p. 246: *Before his departure Fafner threw away a nondescript sword belonging to the hoard in disgust. Wotan now catches sight of it and lifts it up towards the fortress as a symbol of his 'grand idea'. (The Master's specific instruction to the singer [Franz] Betz.) / Fafner hat vor seinem Abgange ein zum Horte gehörendes unscheinbares Schwert verächtlich vor sich hingeworfen. Jetzt erblickt es Wotan und hebt es als ein Symbol seines 'großen Gedankens' gegen die Burg. (Ausdrückliche Angabe des Meisters an den Sänger [Franz] Betz.)*
1881–2	'feig': in modern German this word means 'cowardly', but Wagner is using it in the older sense of describing something addicted to death, generally ill-fated and certainly damned.

THE VALKYRIE

Act I

1 before	*A short orchestral . . . scene*: direction in SSD.
1 before	*The trunk . . . stools in front*: direction in SSD; the pre-action scenic description in the first full score published with Wagner's authority (WWV 86B Musik XI) and reproduced in SW is much less detailed.
27 *after	*Sieglinde wants . . .* : **1876** Porges p. 11.
34 *after	*Sieglinde steps . . .* : **1876** Porges p. 12.
63 before	The direction in SSD is worth noting: *captivated by*

her response [Siegmund] turns round again: slowly and sombrely / von ihrem Rufe gefesselt, wendet sich [Siegmund] wieder: langsam und düster.

71 *after   *Sieglinde is . . .* : 1876 Porges p. 15

73 *after   *Now knocks . . .* : 1876 Porges p. 17.

77 *before   *curtly*: 1876 Porges p. 17.

78 *before   *not fast . . .* : 1876 Porges p. 17.

89 *before   *Not too . . .* : 1876 Porges p. 19.

116 *before   *somewhat . . .* : 1876 Porges p. 21.

120 *after   *in a painfully . . .* : 1876 Porges p. 21.

124 *before   *simply!*: 1876 Levi p. 21.

141 *before   *with a . . .* : 1876 Porges p. 22

179 *before   *More slowly . . .* : 1876 Porges and Mottl p. 24.

182   'und Frauen' / 'and women': above these words SW has *zögernd / faltering.*

201 *before   *Hunding looking . . .* : 1876 Porges p. 26.

205 *before   *with a tone . . .* : 1876 Porges p. 26.

210 *before   *The whole . . .* : 1876 Porges p. 27.

256 *before   *[And] goes . . .* : 1876 Porges p. 30.

263 *before   *stamping . . .* : 1876 Porges p. 31.

271 before   *Siegmund sets . . .* : 1876 p. 34. Porges supplements direction with: *Siegmund deep in agonized thought, which should not give the slightest hint of external movement. / Siegmund in tiefes Brüten versunken, das sich in keinerlei äußerer Aktion kundgeben darf.*

271 *before   *With hard . . .* : 1876 Porges p. 34.

281 *before   *With passionately . . .* : 1876 Porges p. 35.

342 *before   *has to be . . .* : 1876 Mottl p. 40.

375 *before   *with knowing expression*: 1876 Porges p. 42.

377 *before   *with intensifying . . .* : 1876 Porges p. 42.

421 before   For obvious reasons, considering Wagner's insistance that *The Ring* must be seen as transcending the old 'number' opera with its obligatory arias, ensembles and choruses, there was clearly concern that Siegmund's famous lyrical outpouring at this moment might come across as a traditional operatic set piece. (Richard Strauss once remarked that for all the intellectual demands Wagner placed on his audiences Siegmund's lovely song was proof that he never forgot the chambermaids sitting in the gallery.) In 1876 both Porges and Mottl, not

without miring themselves in Wagner's own contradictory attitude to gorgeous moments like these in *The Ring*, are clearly taking up the cudgels on his behalf: *Not in the manner of a lyrical concert piece, rather something that is to be presented not as an actual interruption in the flow of the dramatic action, but as an episode that makes it pause just a little; the tempo should therefore not actually be slow. / Nicht im Charakter eines lyrischen Konzertstückes, sondern als eine den dramatischen Verlauf nicht eigentlich unterbrechenden, sondern nur etwas aufhaltenden Episode vorzutragen; das Tempo also nicht eigentlich langsam* (Porges, p. 47). Mottl adds: *avoid any 'singing just for the sake of it'! Flowing! / Vor jedem 'Gesinge' hüten! Fliessend!*

422   'Wonnemond': it is impossible to convey the full resonance of this word in English in a short space. Among writers and poets and even sometimes officials up to the latter part of the eighteenth century it was regarded as synonymous with 'Wonnemonat', or the 'month of delight', i.e., the month of May. (As late as 1781 Goethe spontaneously dated one of his letters '1st Wonnemond' to mean '1st May'.) 'Wonne' was one of Wagner's favourite words, with a wide range of meaning from straightforward joy or delight (in the emergence of spring, say) to religious or sexual ecstasy. 'Month of joy', the most literal translation, sounds too bureaucratic to my ear. And anything too overtly sexual at this point would have spoilt the tension of the whole passage, during which the erotic implications of 'moon' and 'spring' are carefully calibrated to emerge fully only at the end. I therefore feel that the rather more low-key 'moon of joy' at the start is best.

480–81   'like . . . ear': 1876 p. 55 Mottl notes that: *'sound' and 'ear' had to be emphasized / 'Schall' und 'Ohr' mussten betont werden.*

537 *before   *Looking suddenly . . .* : 1876 Porges p. 62.
537 *after   *the following . . .* : 1876 Porges p. 62.
541 *before   *wistfully . . .* : 1876 Porges p. 62.

Act II

604 *before   *The dialogue* . . . : **1876** Porges p. 75.

649 *before   *In this entire* . . . : **1876** Porges p. 80; Mottl adds,
citing Wagner: '*Everything alla breve [two in a
bar]*'. / '*Alles Allabreve*'. In **MOTTL** p. 96: *This
dialogue must on no account be dragged out, but
must remain flowing all the time.* / *Dieser Dialog
darf nie geschleppt werden, sondern muß fließend
gehalten bleiben.*

654 *before   *stately* . . . : **1876** Porges p. 80.

684 *before   *Fr[icka] wants* . . . : **1876** Levi and Mottl p. 82.

711 *before   *with a fierce* . . . : **1876** Porges p. 84.

722 *before   *Really close* . . . : **1876** Mottl p. 84.

742 *after   *Fricka turns* . . . : **1876** Porges p. 86; Mottl adds:
Comes closer to him little by little. / *Kommt ihm
nach u[nd] nach näher.*

755 *after   *With great* . . . : **1876** Porges p. 87.

774 *before   *with momentous* . . . : **1876** Porges p. 88.

795–6   'win' / 'gewinnst': **1876** Porges p. 90: *An accent
must be placed on 'win'.* / *Auf 'gewinnst' Akzent zu
legen.*

839 *after   *Fricka remains* . . . : **1876** Levi p. 93.

841 *before   *terrifyingly* . . . : **1876** Porges p. 94.

842 *before   *trembling*: **1876** Porges p. 94.

846 *before   *Fricka continues* . . . : **1876** Porges p. 94.

855 *before   *very imperiously*: **1876** Porges p. 95.

865   'sacred honour': **1876** Porges p. 97: *With emphasis
/ Mit Emphase* ['heilige Ehre'].

875 *before   *his voice* . . . : **1876** Porges p. 98.

879 after   Alternative direction in SSD: *She climbs into her
chariot and drives off quickly into the rear.* / *Sie
besteigt den Wagen, und fährt schnell nach hinten
davon.*

999 *after   *the conclusion* . . . : **1876** Porges p. 107.

1073 *before   *looking Wotan* . . . : **1876** Porges p. 112.

1088 *after   *grimacing bitterly*: **1876** Porges p. 113.

1114 *before   *As if* . . . : **1876** Mottl p. 117.

1136 *before   *rushing towards* . . . : **1876** Porges p. 119.

1151 *before   *not yet too fiercely*: **1876** Mottl p. 120, with em-
phasis on *too* / *zu*.

1160 *before   *with passionate warmth*: **1876** Porges p. 121.
1165 *after   *Brünnhilde turns . . .* : **1876** Porges p. 122.
1166 *before   *in a terrible . . .* : **1876** Mottl p. 122.
1190 *before   *tries to . . .* : **1876** Porges p. 125.
1201 after   *She turns . . .* : **1876** p. 126 Porges supplements stage direction with: *Br[ünnhilde] exiting with faltering steps. / Br[ünnhilde] mit stockenden Schritten abgehend.*
1230 *after   *With an expression . . .* : **1876** Porges p. 131.
1235 *before   *with moving . . .* : **1876** Porges p. 131.
1241 *before   *accents of . . .* : **1876** Porges p. 132.
1246 *before   *with frighteningly . . .* : **1876** Porges p. 133.
1262 *before   *with implacable energy*: **1876** Porges p. 135.
1264 *after   *It is as if . . .* : **1876** Porges p. 135.
1278 after   *She stares . . .* : **1876** p. 136 Kniese, citing Wagner, supplements stage direction with: '*bursts out with demented laughter*' / '*lacht wie wahnsinnig auf*'.
1282 *after   *Sieglinde leaning . . .* : **1876** Porges p. 137; Levi adds: *Only here does she fix her eyes on S[iegmund]. / Hier erst heftet sie den Blick auf S[iegmund].*
1295 *before   *singing everything . . .* : **1876** Mottl p. 138.
1415 *after   '*The highest . . .* ': **1876** Porges p. 151.
1416 *before   *absolutely . . .* : **1876** Porges p. 151.
1463 *before   *with passionate . . .* : **1876** Porges p. 155.
1471 before   *Horn . . . distance*: direction in SSD; not in SW or first published full score (WWV 86B Musik XI), perhaps because Wagner decided to use trombones and tubas and not horns to create the sound of Hunding's approach. For the reader not necessarily listening to the score, however, line 1471 makes better sense if the direction is included.
1471 *before   *this episode . . .* : **1876** Porges p. 157.
1489 *before   *with the tenderest expression*: **GLASENAPP** p. 159.
1531 after   *For a moment . . . fighting*: direction in SSD.

Act III

1549 before   *On the right . . . full armour*: direction in SSD; shorter and without the list of the eight Valkyries' names in SW.
1549 *before   *Holding . . .* : **1876** Porges p. 172.

1557 *before   *'Sharply accentuated . . .* : **1876** Porges p. 174.

1603 *after   *All the Valkyries . . .* : **1876** Porges p. 181; Levi
                 adds: *and turn to face left / und wenden sich nach
                 links.*

1628–9   'dem braunen Wälsung': I am assuming that with
                 the adjective 'braun' / 'brown' Gerhilde is not ref-
                 erring to the colour of Siegmund's skin (!) – as
                 some translations have it – but comparing him to
                 Helmwige's stallion, the 'Brauner', her brown horse
                 or bay, whose unruly behaviour with Ortlinde's
                 mare has amused the sisters a few minutes before at
                 the opening of the scene (see lines 1560–75).

1660 *after   *Ortlinde going down*: **1876** Porges p. 189.

1764 *before   *'Each word . . .* : **1876** Porges p. 201.

1773 *after   *Oppressed by . . .* : **1876** Porges p. 201.

1776 *before   *but turns . . .* : **1876** Porges p. 201.

1779 *before   *the outburst . . .* : **1876** Porges p. 201.

1784 *after   *The words . . .* : **1876** Porges p. 202.

1784 *after   *This moment . . .* : **1876** Porges p. 202.

1804 *after   *Brünnhilde addressing . . .* : **1876** Porges p. 204.

1846   'O noblest of miracles': in **1876** Porges reports a
                 comment and an interesting warning from Wag-
                 ner about this important outpouring of emotion to
                 Brünnhilde by Sieglinde, the sentiment and music
                 of which is the mainstay of the *The Ring*'s ending:
                 *With the utmost fervour. The Master warns that at
                 such moments of lyrical ecstasy one should not sing
                 directly into the audience but stand in profile. / Mit
                 höchster Gluth. Warnung des Meisters sich auch bei
                 solchen Stellen lyrischer Ekstase nicht ins Publikum
                 hinein zu singen, sondern im Profil zu stehen* (p.
                 208).

1893 *before   *For all its warmth . . .* : **1876** Porges p. 217. From
                 this point until line 1917 and between lines 2013
                 and 2086 I have not treated the Valkyrie sisters'
                 words in their ensembles as two composite texts
                 of a few lines each (as is usual in the presentation
                 of Wagner's libretti) but presented the full extent
                 of what each is trying to express. Despite Wagner's
                 use of typical chorus language that goes back to the
                 wailing women's choruses in Act 3 of his early op-
                 era *Rienzi*, he clearly wanted to make the lines of

the eight sisters distinct with different orderings of the lines for each, and with some that others do not sing. Between lines 1909 and 1910 Waltraute is even given her own direction (*urgently*) that none of the others has, clearly suggesting that she is already emerging as the 'spokesperson' of the group that she becomes in Act 1 of *Twilight of the Gods*.

2165 *before	*to be uttered* . . . : **1876** Porges p. 241.
2207 *before	*in a tone* . . . : **1876** Porges p. 241.
2213 *before	*from here onwards* . . . : **1876** Porges p. 247.
2282 before	*softly . . . mystery*: **1876** p. 252 Porges supplements stage direction with: *With cryptic expression.* / *Mit geheimnisvollem Ausdruck.*
2286 *before	*with vehemence*: **1876** Porges p. 253.
2290 *before	*the sense* . . . : **1876** Porges p. 253.
2303 *after	*Utter despondency* . . . : **1876** Levi p. 254, adds citing Wagner: 'All in vain . . .' / 'Alles vergebens . . .'.
2338 *before	*Wringing her hands* . . . : **1876** Porges p. 256.
2346 *before	*with a passion* . . . : **1876** Porges p. 258.
2381 *before	*The fundamental tone* . . . : **1876** Porges p. 264.
2403 *before	*It must clearly* . . . : **1876** Porges p. 266.
2406 *before	*Wotan picks up* . . . : **1876** Levi p. 267.

SIEGFRIED

Act I

1 before	*The curtain . . . appliances*: direction in SSD; starkly reduced in SW.
11 *before	*Here Mime gently* . . . : **1876** Mottl p. 6.
32 *after	*makes an effort* . . . : **1876** Mottl p. 8.
33 *before	*then falls* . . . : **1876** Mottl p. 8.
49 before	*He . . . abandon*: direction in SSD; SW has only *lachend / laughing*.
83 after	*He . . . hand*: direction in SSD; SW has only *das Schwert prüfend / testing the sword*.
129 before	*feigning offence*: words from SSD.
133 *before	*Mime accompanies* . . . : **1876** Mottl p. 18.
182 *after	*Straight after* . . . : **1876** Porges p. 21.
186 *after	*and then* . . . : **1876** Porges p. 21.
205 *after	*Siegfried sits down*: **1876** Mottl p. 23.

208 before   *laughs*: direction in SSD.

217 *before   *as if giving . . .* : **1876** Mottl p. 24.

270 *before   *With exceptional. . .* :**1876** Porges p. 27.

276 *before   *looking straight . . .* : **1876** Mottl p. 27.

293 before   *evasively*: direction in SSD.

322 *after   *Mime looks . . .* : **1876** Mottl p. 31.

331 'She died' **1876** Levi and Mottl p. 32: *with an indifferent, al-*
               most derisive hand movement / mit einer gleichgül-
               tigen, fast verächtlichen Handbewegung.

355   'in Sorge': means both 'into care' and 'concerned'
               or 'anxious'. I have tried to capture both meanings.

369 *before   *with a vigorously . . .* : **1876** Porges p. 35.

370   'starling's song' / 'Starenlied': probably a reference
               to old troubadour songs in which the starling is pre-
               sented as – and as Siegfried thinks Mime is – an
               ugly, insincere messenger of feelings of love. In the
               estornel songs of the twelfth-century troubadour
               Marcabru the starling is a 'parodic, squawking'
               conduit, chosen by the poet because it had no song
               of its own and looked thin and scraggy into the bar-
               gain. In Marcabru's songs 'the starlings are aligned
               with the speaker's opponents, and are therefore set
               up as fools and losers in verbal and sexual com-
               petitions'. Simon Gaunt, Ruth Harvey and Linda
               Paterson, *Marcabru: A Critical Edition* (Cam-
               bridge, 2000), pp. 221–2.

381 *before   *with very . . .* : **1876** Mottl p. 36.

424 *middle   *runs after Siegfried . . .* : **1876** Porges p. 39.

473 *after   *Mime has become . . .* : **1876** Porges p. 44.

483 *after   *walks forwards . . .* : **1876** Porges p. 45.

492 *after   *[The Wanderer] strikes . . .* : **1876** Porges p. 45.

528 *after   *Mime 'the philologist . . .* : **PORGES** 2 p. 68.

550 *before   *as if infatuated . . .* : **1876** Porges p. 50.

581 after   Direction in SSD has: *He strikes the ground with*
               his spear with a seemingly arbitrary gesture; a quiet
               clap of thunder can be heard, to which Mime reacts
               in violent shock. / Er stößt wie unwillkürlich mit
               dem Speer auf den Boden; ein leiser Donner läßt
               sich vernehmen, wovon Mime heftig erschrickt

593 *after   *Mime is visibly . . .* : **1876** Porges p. 54.

604–7   'I've long forgone . . . womb': a reference to the
               song 'Scheiden und Meiden' (Farewell and Forgo)

among the folk songs and poems *Des Knaben Wunderhorn* (*The Boy's Magic Horn*) collected and edited by Achim von Arnim and Clemens Brentano and published in the early 1800s. I have adapted the standard English translation.

629 *before   *very lively*: **1876** Mottl p. 57.

633 *before   *raising . . .* : **1876** Porges p. 57.

650 after   Direction in SSD has: *forgetting his present situation more and more, and taking a lively interest in the subject / seine gegenwärtige Lage immer mehr vergessend, und von dem Gegenstande lebhaft angezogen.*

765 after   *gradually pulling . . .* : direction in SSD.

775 before   *grabbing . . .* : direction in SSD.

776   'What have you been polishing today?': in modern German the most common meaning of 'fegen' is 'to sweep'. One of its earlier meanings in German spoken in the Middle High Ages, however, was 'to polish, clean swords and weapons'.

844   'Neidhöhle': in modern German this would mean 'cave of envy'. But as elsewhere in *The Ring* the word 'Neid' is being used in its older and more aggressive feudal sense of doing someone real damage in battle. This applies to both the 'good' and the 'evil' characters: just as I have translated Siegfried's later description of his sword 'Neidliches Schwert' (line 931) as 'pitiless sword', I was tempted to translate the name of Fafner's nest as 'cave of pitilessness', as of course they will eventually both be determined to do remorseless damage to each other. But I thought better of it and decided to leave it in German.

905–7   'Now I'm as old . . . never seen': a reference to the changeling's words in the third part of the fairy tale *Von den Wichtelmännern* (*The Elves*), first brought to light by the Grimm brothers in 1812. I have adapted Jack Zipes' translation of their first edition (Princeton and Oxford, 2014).

929 *before   *Mime tells . . .* : **1876** Mottl p. 94.

1143 *after   *quickly*: **1876** Kniese p. 118.

Act II

1195 *before	*Stays in tempo* . . . : **1876** Porges p. 127.
1233	'Hella's armies': in Norse mythology Hella (or Hel) is the goddess presiding over the underworld, who with her armies of the dead will attack and destroy the world at *Ragnarök* or twilight of the gods.
1235 *after	*After these words* . . . : **1876** Porges p. 130.
1315 *before	*To be said* . . . : **1876** Porges p. 138.
1345 after	*sits opposite* . . . : direction in SSD.
1430 *before	*but sounding uninvolved*: **1876** Porges p. 148.
1499 after	*He ponders* . . . : direction in SSD.
1531 *after	*Siegfried leans* . . . : **PORGES** 2 p. 221.
1534 **after	*The body of the huge dragon* . . . : SW 12/ii, p. 134.
1558 after	*He moves* . . . : direction in SSD.
1570 **after	*During the fight* . . . : SW 12/ii, p. 150.
1593 *after	*the voice weakening* . . . : **PORGES** 1 p. 169.
1601 *before	*not to be* . . . : **1876** Porges p. 170.
1629 before	*Mime sidles* . . . : direction in SSD; version in SW less detailed.
1732 after	*He sticks* . . . : direction in SSD; version in SW less detailed.
1798 before	*He makes . . . feelings*: direction in SSD.
1830 before	*with a completely straight face*: direction in SSD.
1951-2	'Smiling in sorrow I sing of love': is the Forest Bird alluding to Ludwig Uhland's well-known poem 'Taillefer' (1816), in which William of Normandy thanks his minstrel Taillefer for singing to him 'in Lieb und in Leid' ('in love and in sorrow'), having helped him with his songs to defeat King Harold in the Battle of Hastings?

Act III

2074 *before	*'very eerily'*: **PORGES** 2 p. 307; **1876** Mottl p. 220. According to Porges and Mottl, Wagner's remark refers to the orchestral melody sounding in the orchestra 'recalling Brünnhilde' – *Die an Brünnhilde mahnende Melodie*.
2090 *before	*The extent* . . . : **1876** Porges p. 221.
2108 *before	*with extremely* . . . : **1876** Levi p. 223; Levi and Mottl add: *Erda covers her face with her hands. / Erda verhüllt ihr Gesicht mit den Händen.*

2202 *before   *The whole dialogue . . .* : **1876** Porges p. 234.

2336 before   *backing off*: direction in SSD.

2338 *after   *Wagner recited . . .* : **PORGES** 1 p. 246; **1876** p. 246 Mottl adds: *I vividly remember the [Wagner's] indescribable way of expressing this. / Ich entsinne mich genau des unbeschreiblichen Ausdruckes.*

2356 after   *He steps closer*: direction in SSD.

2369 *before   *without intensification . . .* : **1876** Levi p. 255.

2395 *before   *The following . . .* : **1876** Mottl p. 258.

2464 *before   *like a mother . . .* : **1876** Porges p. 269.

2470 *before   *with warmth*: **1876** Porges p. 269

2471 *before   *restoring her calm*: **PORGES** 1 p. 269.

2494 *after   *'Until now . . .* : **1876** Porges p. 272.

2571 *before   *with a tremulous voice . . .* : **PORGES** 2 p. 408.

2598 *before   *[Wagner] recited . . .* : **1876** Porges p. 283; Levi adds: *distraught / verzweifelt.*

2639 *before   *the following . . .* : **PORGES** 2 p. 417.

2723 after   **1876** Levi, citing Wagner, p. 295: *From here onwards both step away from each other. Not a love duet – 'a hymn to the gods' / Von hier treten Beide von einander. Kein Liebesduett – 'Hymnus an die Götter'/*; Mottl adds, also citing Wagner: *Completely uninhibited singing! 'Just like herdsmen and dairymaids exultantly yodelling into the mountains.' / Ganz herausgesungen! 'Wie die Senner und Sennerinnen ihre Jodler in die Berge hinein jubeln.'*

TWILIGHT OF THE GODS
Prologue

11 *before   *reading from the rope*: **1876** Kniese p. 4.

44 *before   *'She reads off . . .* : **PORGES** 1 p. 7 – valid for lines 44–59.

65 *before   *[IIIrd Norn] standing up . . .* : **PORGES** 1 p. 8 – valid for lines 65–80.

88 *after   *[Ist Norn] has cast a look . . .* : **PORGES** 1 p. 12, and adds as an alternative: *from which she garners news about the past / aus dem sie Kunde über die Vergangenheit sich erhalte.*

127 *before   *hastily as if becoming confused*: **PORGES** 1 p. 17 – valid for lines 127–35.

Act I

322 *before   *Gunther strides . . .* : **PORGES** 1 p. 55.
354 *before   *Hagen is the only one . . .* : **PORGES** 1 p. 59.
363 *after   *'The more movement . . .* : **PORGES** 1 p. 62.
460 *before   *'with a somewhat . . .* : **PORGES** 1 p. 76.
481 *before   *like empty words . . .* : **PORGES** 1 p. 79.
626 *before   *reeling back*: **1876** Porges p. 107.
718 *before   *Brünnhilde lets go . . .* : **1876** Porges p. 116.
737 *before   *constantly staring . . .* : **1876** Levi p. 118.
758 *before   *Waltraute is . . .* : **1876** Porges p. 121.
778 after   *Siegfried's horn-call . . . in joy*: direction in SSD.
800–801   'Hella's nocturnal army': see *Siegfried* line 1233.
830 *before   *raises herself . . .* : **1876** Porges p. 135.

Act II

938 *before   *walks with . . .* : **MOTTL** p. 65.
1000 *after   *The whole thing . . .* : **1876** Porges p. 159.
1024 and following   'Why the blaring horn?': **KNIESE** p. 164 re-
                  ports that every effort was made to fulfil Wagner's
                  demands for the many gradations between solo
                  voices and full chorus in the vassals' exchange with
                  Hagen, even down to naming the individual singers
                  chosen to stand out from the crowd. Levi reports in
                  1876, however, that the solos were eventually sung
                  by several / von Mehreren starting with three sing-
                  ers to a part, presumably for the sake of audibility. I
                  have detailed the exchange between the vassals and
                  Hagen in full to convey its conversational tone. It is
                  some time before the vassals realize that in calling
                  them to war Hagen is playing a massive joke on
                  them. He is in fact calling them to a pagan festi-
                  val and outwardly boisterous marriage procession.
                  This and the next two scenes are perhaps, with their
                  moments of bucolic fervour, the parts of *The Ring*
                  closest in spirit, at least on the surface, to the Greek
                  satyr-play (see Introduction).
1235 **before   *with these . . .* : SW 13/ii, pp. 148–9: the footnote
                  is placed and noted after each declamation of 'Be-
                  trug!' / 'Trickery!'

1248 *before　　[She] appears to be ... : 1876 Porges p. 201.

1260 *before　　Brünnhilde turns ... : 1876 Porges p. 204.

1391 *before　　Struggling for breath ... : MOTTL p. 235.

1429 *before　　Happy memories ... : 1876 Porges p. 228; MOT-
　　　　　　　　TL p. 239: Now she is softer. – Happy memories
　　　　　　　　come alive in her. / Nun wird sie weich. – Schöne
　　　　　　　　Erinnerungen erwachen in ihr.

1529　　　　　　'sacred vessel' / 'Eideshort': refers to the phenome-
　　　　　　　　non in Greek literature of the invocation of objects
　　　　　　　　rather than superhuman powers to witness an oath
　　　　　　　　statement (see Isabelle C. Torrance, '"Of Cabbages
　　　　　　　　and Kings": The Eideshort Phenomenon', in Oaths
　　　　　　　　and Swearing in Ancient Greece, ed. Alan H. Som-
　　　　　　　　merstein and Isabelle C. Torrance (Berlin and Bos-
　　　　　　　　ton, 2014), pp. 111–31). The concept can include
　　　　　　　　inanimate symbols of power or kings. Brünnhilde
　　　　　　　　and Gunther appeal to Wotan as sanctifying witness,
　　　　　　　　who as we have heard from Waltraute in the previ-
　　　　　　　　ous act is now with his broken spear in a state of
　　　　　　　　melancholic stasis. 'Eideshort' as distanced, object-
　　　　　　　　like, though still significant, witness of the oath
　　　　　　　　could therefore be seen as appropriate in this case.

1547 after　　　1876 p. 241 Kniese reports that in 1876 the wed-
　　　　　　　　ding procession already began to appear from be-
　　　　　　　　hind the wings in the closing moments of the pre-
　　　　　　　　ceding trio at five different entry points. It consisted
　　　　　　　　of the following: from entry point 1 on the right:
　　　　　　　　five boys, five girls with flowers on sticks, six horn
　　　　　　　　players, Siegfried carried by four vassals (chorus) on
　　　　　　　　a shield. From entry point 2 [presumably also on
　　　　　　　　the right]: Gutrune carried by four vassals (extras)
　　　　　　　　in a chair on poles, twelve women (chorus), vari-
　　　　　　　　ous weaponless vassals without shields, two vas-
　　　　　　　　sals with a shield onto which they can lift Gunther.
　　　　　　　　Above a male goat from entry point 5 – pushed by
　　　　　　　　two young men while being decked out with gar-
　　　　　　　　lands by two girls. [Above] a bull, entry point 4 +
　　　　　　　　the same. [Above] a ram, entry point 3 + the same.
　　　　　　　　/ aus der 1. Gasse rechts – 5 Knaben, 5 Mädchen
　　　　　　　　mit Blumenstäben, 6 Hornbläser, Siegfried von 4
　　　　　　　　Mannen (Chor) auf dem Schild getragen. [A]us der
　　　　　　　　2. Gasse – Gutrune von 4 Mannen (Statisten) auf

> *dem Tragstuhl getragen, 12 Frauen (Chor), sämt-*
> *liche Mannen ohne Schilde und Waffen, 2 Mannen*
> *mit Schild, Gunther darauf zu heben. Oben Bock,*
> *5. Gasse – 2 Mägde mit Girlanden schmücken, 2*
> *junge Männer schieben ihn heraus. [Oben] Stier, 4.*
> *Gasse – ebenso. [Oben] Widder, 3. Gasse – ebenso.*

Act III

1548 before   I have detailed the different horns and their differ-
ent distances that can be heard before the curtain
opens because they already vividly represent for the
audience the positions of the characters (Siegfried
ahead of Hagen and the main hunting party) before
they actually arrive on the scene.

1672 *before   *with a vigorously defiant . . .* : **1876** Porges p. 273;
Levi adds: *Siegfried crossly puts his shield aside /*
Siegfried stellt unmutig seinen Schild beiseite.

1680 *before   *dismissively, ironically*: **MOTTL** p. 287.

1760 *before   *Now all is calmer . . .* : **MOTTL** p. 304.

1760 *after   *The vassals react . . .* : **MOTTL** p. 305.

1879 *after   *Stormy reaction . . .* : **1876** Levi p. 306.

1884 *after   *Siegfried now stands up*: **1876** Mottl p. 307.

1901 after   *He calmly . . . in sympathy*: direction in SSD con-
tinues with: *A long silence of profound shock. With*
the appearance of the ravens dusk has already start-
ed to fall. / Lange Stille der tiefsten Erschütterung.
Dämmerung ist bereits mit der Erscheinung der
Raben eingebrochen.

1942 *before   *Everything Hagen says. . .*: **1876** Porges p. 322.

1960 *before   *It's no longer a funeral procession . . .* : **PORG-**
ES 1 p. 324; **MOTTL** p. 336, also citing Wagner,
has: *'It's not a funeral procession, but a procession*
of horror.' / 'Das ist kein Trauerzug, sondern ein
Schreckenszug.'

1982   'Beuterecht': an old legal concept referring to the
right (or rule) of capture originally enshrined in
early English law to secure the rights of persons
'capturing' natural resources for the first time. Ha-
gen blithely perverts the already problematical law
to include live beings as well, and not just the wild
boar he was supposed to be hunting, but the human
being he really wanted to kill.

1990 *before   '*It's the battle* . . . : **MOTTL** p. 341.

1993 and following   '*Silence* . . . ': **1876** Porges p. 329: *Throughout the whole scene, Brünnhilde must give the impression of a seeress of the old Germans. / Brünnhilde muß in der ganzen Szene den Eindruck einer Seherin der alten Deutschen machen.*

2008 *before   *Without bitterness* . . . : **MOTTL** p. 344.

2112 *before   '*She says* . . . : **1876** Porges p. 348.

2133 after   *The men and women . . . the curtain falls*: the final two paragraphs of the directions are mostly absent in SSD. As this text was published as late as 1872, this points to the remarkable fact that the scenic image of the destruction by fire of the gods and heroes in Valhalla only occurred to Wagner at the last minute. This is confirmed by the musical sketches which show that Wagner composed the ending originally without this image in mind as a scenic reality. (The sketches are transcribed and discussed in John Deathridge, *Wagner Beyond Good and Evil* (Berkeley, 2008), pp. 97–100.) What we can conclude from them is that Wagner probably originally wanted, as the text in SSD suggests, to leave the demise of Valhalla to the audience's visual imagination. In the end he expanded the sketch with Waltraute's music in Act 1 of *Twilight of the Gods*, where she describes the hapless gods and heroes languishing in Valhalla to Brünnhilde, and without her voice resolved to represent it scenically as well. It was the right decision. With the visual realism of the end of the gods introduced at the last minute and the more powerful music it inspired, the final moments of *The Ring* are now among the most memorable of the entire cycle.

Acknowledgements

First and foremost I would like to thank Stuart Proffitt for originally commissioning this project and Simon Winder, my indefatigable and imaginative editor at Penguin, for giving me the courage to complete it. Thanks are also due to Maria Bedford, Dinah Drazin, Anna Hervé and Sarah Hulbert, who provided invaluable help in the project's last stages.

Any translator of *The Ring* into English is inevitably grateful to the many people before him or her who have attempted the task. I have learned many things from the translations of William Mann (had he been reading too much Auden?), Lionel Salter, Stewart Spencer (a landmark translation informed by a truly Germanist scholarly spirit) and especially Andrew Porter, whom I met in New York when he was bravely translating *The Ring* for the now legendary Sadler's Wells performances in the 1970s conducted by Reginald Goodall. He was clearly devoting immense thought to the difficulties of creating a singing translation, and indeed states somewhat disconcertingly at the start of its printed version that it is 'not for reading'. The frank confession persuaded me from the beginning, the sheer elegance of Porter's translation notwithstanding, to consider the profound differences between a libretto translated to fit the musical inflections of its setting in its original language and its inevitably more accurate translation when one considers the rhythm of the text and its meaning independently of the score. There are opera directors who consider the simple reading through of a libretto before or during rehearsal as anathema to its communication via music. They may be right. And Wagner had his own troubles when the great singer Wilhelmine Schröder-Devrient flatly disagreed with him about his insistence that singers should give a sense of speech to his vocal lines as if they were part of a spoken play. The paradox remains, however, that especially in texts as complex as Wagner's, more is lost in translation if one remains faithful to the inflexions of the original musical setting than if one does not. My decision to translate *The Ring* in the way I have is directly contrary to Porter's. But I am grateful to his example for helping me to make it.

I also owe a debt of gratitude to students and colleagues in the universities of Cambridge, Princeton, Chicago, Vienna, and above all King's College London, who in many memorable courses and conversations about *The Ring* joined me enthusiastically in a detailed exploration of its fascinating universe and alerted me to the need for a new English translation. Valuable support came from Patrick Carnegy, my longstanding *confrère* in matters Wagnerian, as well as my former colleagues in the collected edition of Wagner's works in Munich, a now-finished project, who worked hard to provide the reliable scores of *The Ring* with proper critical reports that are now in general use by conductors the world over, and from which I have profited myself in editing the German text on which this translation is based. (Their names are mentioned in Sources for the German Text.) My warm thanks are especially due to Christa Jost, who generously provided me with the proofs of her edition of the sources for the 1876 Bayreuth rehearsals of *The Ring*, and to Rainer Mohrs of Schott Music in Mainz for permission to use excerpts from this edition in advance of his firm's publication schedule.

Thanks are due to friends who answered questions about grammar and the limits of colloquial translation, testings out of this phrase or that, the counting of lines (I am particularly grateful to Lawrence Wragg for helping me with this far from easy task), and even readings of long passages that probably tested their patience beyond the reasonable limits of friendship. Amanda Holden, whose vast experience and resourcefulness in translating opera libretti into English are well known, was very supportive and gave me permission to re-use the synopses of *The Ring* I wrote for her marvellous *Penguin Opera Guide*. Among the native German speakers I consulted, the opera director Annegret Ritzel (who speaks the language like an angel), Sarah Hegenbart, Andreas Dorschel, and Maria de Moraes Bonilha were especially kind in replying to queries, especially about Wagner's extraordinary inventiveness with German syntax and vocabulary. My greatest thanks are to my wife Victoria Cooper, without whose support the task of finishing this translation would have been much harder, and to whom I dedicate it with all my love.

PENGUIN CLASSICS

BEYOND GOOD AND EVIL
FRIEDRICH NIETZSCHE

'That which is done out of love always takes place beyond good and evil'

Beyond Good and Evil confirmed Nietzsche's position as the towering European philosopher of his age. The work dramatically rejects the tradition of Western thought with its notions of truth and God, good and evil. Nietzsche demonstrates that the Christian world is steeped in a false piety and infected with a 'slave morality'. With wit and energy, he turns from this critique to a philosophy that celebrates the present and demands that the individual imposes their own 'will to power' upon the world.

This edition includes a commentary on the text by the translator and an introduction by Michael Tanner, which explains some of the more abstract passages in *Beyond Good and Evil*.

'One of the greatest books of a very great thinker' Michael Tanner

Translated by R. J. Hollingdale with an introduction by Michael Tanner

PENGUIN CLASSICS

AGAINST NATURE (A REBOURS)
J. K. HUYSMANS

> 'He drank this liquid perfume from cups of that oriental porcelain
> known as egg-shell china, it is so delicate and diaphanous'

A wildly original *fin de siècle* novel, *Against Nature* contains only one character.
De Esseinte is a decadent, ailing aristocrat who retreats to an isolated villa where
he indulges his taste for luxury and excess. Veering between nervous excitability
and debilitating ennui he gluts his aesthetic appetites with classical literature and
art, exotic jewels (with which he fatally encrusts the shell of his tortoise), rich
perfumes and a kaleidoscope of sensual experiences. *Against Nature,* in the words
of the author, exploded 'like a grenade' and has a cult following to this day.

This revised edition of Robert Baldick's lucid translation features a new
introduction, a chronology and reproduces Huysmans's original 1903 preface as
well as a selection of reviews from writers including Mallarme, Zola and Wilde.

Translated by Robert Baldick and edited by Patrick McGuiness

PENGUIN CLASSICS

IDYLLS OF THE KING
ALFRED LORD TENNYSON

> 'There likewise I beheld Excalibur
> Before him at his crowning borne, the sword
> That rose from out the bosom of the lake'

Tennyson had a life-long interest in the legend of King Arthur and after the huge success of his poem 'Morte d'Arthur' he built on the theme with this series of twelve poems, written in two periods of intense creativity over nearly twenty years. *Idylls of the King* traces the story of Arthur's rule, from his first encounter with Guinevere and the quest for the Holy Grail to the adultery of his Queen with Launcelot and the King's death in a final battle that spells the ruin of his kingdom. Told with lyrical and dreamlike eloquence, Tennyson's depiction of the Round Table reflects a longing for a past age of valour and chivalry. And in his depiction of King Arthur he created a hero imbued with the values of the Victorian age – one who embodies the highest ideals of manhood and kingship.

This edition includes an introduction examining the publication history of the *Idylls*, a chronology, suggestions for further reading and explanatory notes.

Edited by J. M. Gray

PENGUIN CLASSICS

THE PROSE EDDA
SNORRI STURLSON

'What was the beginning, or how did things start? What was there before?'

The Prose Edda is the most renowned of all works of Scandinavian literature and our most extensive source for Norse mythology. Written in Iceland a century after the close of the Viking Age, it tells ancient stories of the Norse creation epic and recounts the battles that follow as gods, giants, dwarves and elves struggle for survival. It also preserves the oral memory of heroes, warrior kings and queens. In clear prose interspersed with powerful verse, the *Edda* provides unparalleled insight into the gods' tragic realization that the future holds one final cataclysmic battle, Ragnarok, when the world will be destroyed. These tales from the pagan era have proved to be among the most influential of all myths and legends, inspiring modern works as diverse as Wagner's *Ring* cycle and Tolkien's *The Lord of the Rings*.

This new translation by Jesse Byock captures the strength and subtlety of the original, while his introduction sets the tales fully in the context of Norse mythology. This edition includes also detailed notes and appendices.

Translated with an introduction, glossary and notes by Jesse Byock